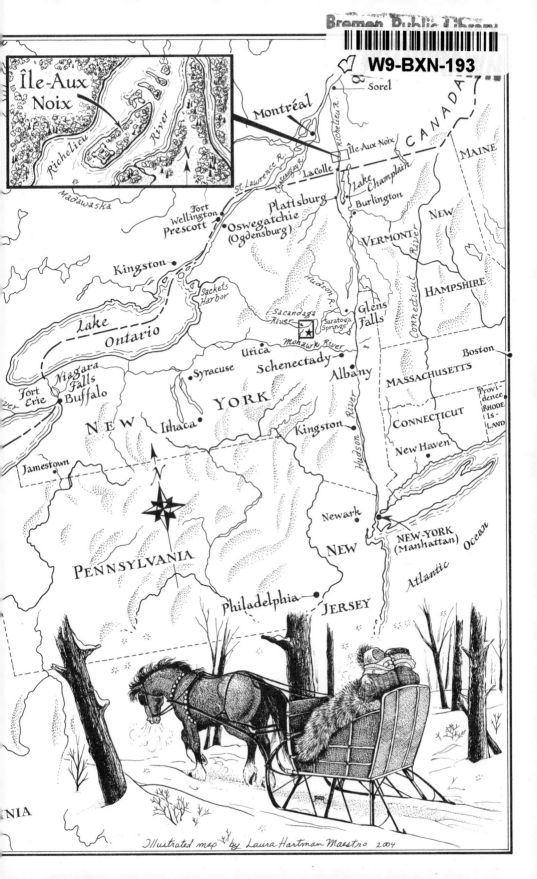

Île-Aux
Noix

Richelieu River

Madawaska

CANADA

Sorel

Montréal

Île-Aux Noix

LaColle

St. Lawrence R.

Plattsburg

Lake Champlain

Burlington

MAINE

NEW

Fort
Wellington
Prescott

Oswegatchie
(Ogdensburg)

VERMONT

HAMPSHIRE

Kingston

Sackets
Harbor

Lake
Ontario

Sacandaga
River

Saratoga
Springs

Glens
Falls

Connecticut River

Hudson R.

Boston

Niagara
Falls
Buffalo

Fort
Erie

Syracuse

Utica

Schenectady

Mohawk River

Albany

MASSACHUSETTS

Providence
RHODE
IS-
LAND

N E W

Ithaca

Y O R K

CONNECTICUT

Jamestown

Kingston

New Haven

Newark

NEW-YORK
(Manhattan)

Ocean

PENNSYLVANIA

NEW

Atlantic

Philadelphia

JERSEY

NIA

Illustrated map by Laura Hartman Maestro 2004

FIRE ALONG THE SKY

Also by Sara Donati

INTO THE WILDERNESS
DAWN ON A DISTANT SHORE
LAKE IN THE CLOUDS

FIRE ALONG
THE SKY

Sara Donati

BANTAM BOOKS

Dn15

FIRE ALONG THE SKY
A Bantam Book / September 2004

Published by Bantam Dell
a division of
Random House, Inc.
New York, New York

Book design by Lynn Newmark
Endpaper maps by Laura Hartman Maestro

Library of Congress Cataloging-in-Publication Data

Donati, Sara, 1956–
Fire along the sky / Sara Donati.
p. cm.
ISBN 0-553-80146-5
1. United States—History—War of 1812—Fiction. 2. Scottish Americans—Fiction.
3. Women immigrants—Fiction. I. Title.

PS3554.O46923F57 2004
813'.54—dc22
2004045095

Manufactured in the United States of America
Published simultaneously in Canada

10 9 8 7 6 5 4 3 2 1
BVG

For Penny and Suzanne

We've been through a lot together
And most of it was my fault

Primary Characters

In Paradise

Elizabeth Middleton Bonner, a schoolteacher

Nathaniel Bonner, a hunter and trapper; Elizabeth's husband

The Bonner children, in order of age:
- Luke Scott Bonner, Nathaniel's son by an early alliance, resident in Montreal. A merchant, importer, and fur trader; general manager of the Carryck holdings
- Hannah (also known as Walks-Ahead or Walking-Woman) Nathaniel's daughter by his first wife
- the twins Mathilde (or Lily) and Daniel
- Gabriel

Jennet Scott Huntar, a widow, sister of the Earl of Carryck and a distant cousin to the Bonners

Iona Fraser, Luke Bonner's maternal grandmother. Born in Scotland, resident in Montreal

Simon Ballentyne, originally of

Carryck, Luke Bonner's business partner, resident in Montreal

Many-Doves, a Mohawk woman who lives at Lake in the Clouds; she is Nathaniel's sister-in-law by his first marriage

Runs-from-Bears, of the Kahnyen'kehàka Turtle clan; the husband of Many-Doves; their children:
- Blue-Jay, their eldest son
- Annie (also called Kenenstasi), their youngest daughter
- Kateri, married and living in Canada
- Sawatis, their youngest son, living in Canada

Ethan Middleton, Elizabeth's nephew, Richard Todd's stepson and apprentice

Richard Todd, physician and landowner, widower

Cornelius Bump, a tinker

Curiosity Freeman, a freed slave, housekeeper for the Todds

Daisy Hench, Curiosity's adult daughter, a free woman of color

Joshua Hench, blacksmith, a freed slave; Daisy's husband; their children still resident in Paradise:
- Emmanuel, apprenticed to his father in the smithy
- Sally and Lucy Hench, servants in the Todds' household
- Leo, the youngest, Elizabeth's student

Jemima Southern Kuick, widow, resident at the mill house

Martha, Jemima's daughter

The Widow Kuick, Jemima's invalid mother-in-law

Charlie LeBlanc, miller, and his wife Becca Kaes LeBlanc; six sons by his first wife, five daughters by Becca

Jan Kaes, Becca's father, a widower; Michael, his adult son

Nicholas (Claes) Wilde, farmer and orchard keeper, and his wife Dolly, an invalid

Callie, their daughter

Cookie Fiddler, a freed slave and the Wildes' housekeeper and servant

Levi Fiddler, a freed slave, farm worker at the Wildes', and Cookie's son

Horace Greber, trapper, hunter, and his son Hardwork

Martin and Georgia Ratz, Martin's mother Addie, sons Jem, Henry, and Harry, Elizabeth's students. Adult daughter Lydia, unmarried

Jock and Laura Hindle; Jock's mother and father

Goody Cunningham and her grown son Praise-Be, his wife Jane (McGarrity), adult daughter Dora, unmarried

Missy (Margaret) Parker, unemployed housekeeper; her daughter Theodosia is married to Jonas Littlejohn, post rider

Anna and Jed McGarrity, owners of the trading post; Jed is also the constable

Peter Dubonnet, his wife Nettie, his widowed father Claude

Benjamin, Obediah, and Elijah Cameron

At Nut Island

Colonel Marcel Caudebec, commander of the garrison

Adam O'Neill, a Catholic priest

Major Christian Wyndham, King's Rangers

Major Percy Watson, Forty-ninth Regiment, Canadian Fencibles

Captain James MacDonald, Indian Department

Lieutenant Fitzwilliam Hughes, Thirty-ninth Foot, Lower Canadain Select Embodied Militia

Major Jacques-René Boucher de la Bruére, Second Battalion LCSEM

Captain David Le Couteur of the Canadian Chasseurs (Light Infantry), Fifth Battalion LCSEM

The voltigeurs: Kester MacLeod, Uz Brodie, Drew Clarke

Liam Kirby (called Red Crow by the Mohawk), gun captain on board the USS *Ferret*

Jim Booke, militia captain

FIRE ALONG THE SKY

Prologue: Jennet

Late Spring, 1812
Carryckcastle, Annandale, Scotland

Set free by the death of a husband she had not wanted nor ever learned to love, Jennet Scott Huntar of Carryckcastle left home for the new world on her twenty-eighth birthday.

Jennet told everyone that she had chosen Montreal for practical reasons, and she ticked them off on her fingers: the family's extensive holdings, the many friends and business associates to look after her, and the fact that Montreal was the closest city to the Bonner cousins in New-York State. These reasons, so rationally presented, fooled no one, not even herself: in a clan of men and women to whom reserve and restraint were as natural as breathing, Jennet was an oddity, unable to hide what she was feeling or even to try.

It was true that she was eager to see the cousins who lived deep in the wilderness of the endless forests in the state of New-York, but the first and most important truth was this: Jennet went to Montreal in pursuit of Luke Bonner, a distant cousin and the man she should have married instead of good-hearted, predictable Ewan Huntar.

It was true that Jennet had not seen Luke Bonner in ten years, but there was another truth, a more important one: in all those years he had never married. A handsome young man from a well-respected family, with a quick laugh and a considerable fortune, all of his own making; he could have married fifty times over, and yet he had not. It was both an invitation and a challenge that Jennet could not ignore.

For a month Jennet did what was expected of her as a widow, shutting herself away in her chamber not in sorrow but because she could not hide her relief. When she announced to her family that she would sail on the *Isis* it came as no great surprise; her mother only held her gaze for a long moment and then looked away, in resignation or perhaps, Jennet reasoned to herself, understanding.

As it turned out, Jennet got away at the last possible moment; the *Isis*—a merchantman in her brother's fleet—was barely out of the Solway Firth when they passed a packet on her way in with the unsettling news of a new war. The army of the fledgling and upstart United States had attempted and failed to invade British Canada near Fort Detroit. Jennet found herself headed for the very heart of the conflict. The packet captain waited while she scribbled her first letter to her family.

So was it meant to be, she wrote. And: *Send no one after me, for I have no intention of turning back. I can, I will look after myself.*

On that same afternoon she learned of the war that waited for her, Jennet met the other passengers.

At first report they seemed to be nothing out of the ordinary: a merchant who traveled with an eye on a hold filled with cognac and armagnac and exotic wines and spirits far too valuable to leave to the care of an agent or factor. He was more than fifty, with gray-blue eyes that slanted at the corners, an elaborate mustache that curled at the ends, and the striking Italian name Alfonso del Giglio. In addition to two old servants who seemed to be completely mute, Signore del Giglio had with him a small and very attentive dog who answered to the name Pip, and a wife, Camille Maria de Rojas Santiago del Giglio. At dinner the captain introduced the ladies.

Everything about the merchant's wife was as odd and beautiful as her name: she wore a silk gown the color of singed corn silk with tiny crystals sewn to the sleeves and hem; around her shoulders was a heavy silk shawl embroidered with symbols Jennet did not recognize. On a fine chain she wore her only jewelry: a dull red stone the size of an acorn, caught in a web of silver filigree.

From the beginning it seemed to Jennet that Camille del Giglio must be half-fey, just as one-half of her hair was a deep blue-black and the other shot with white, just as one side of her face seemed to be almost asleep while the other was always alive with motion. The del Giglios were seldom at rest in any way; they spoke to each other or to Pip as if they were alone in the room, slipping from Spanish to Italian to English to French in the same sentence. Jennet listened, at first confused and then, mustering those three of the four languages that she had studied, intrigued.

When they had finished dining, while captain and merchant talked of maps and winds and war, the merchant's wife leaned across the table and took Jennet's hand in her own. Her fingers were firm and cool and bare of rings, but a tattoo circled her wrist, as delicate as a spider's web. Jennet had never seen a woman with a tattoo, not even her cousin Hannah who was half-Mohawk, but she managed to restrain her curiosity and her gaze.

"You and I must talk," said Camille del Giglio in a voice like that of any other well-bred Continental lady who had learned English from a governess.

"Certainly," Jennet said, flustered and excited and barely able to control the trembling in her hand. "About what should we talk, madame?"

"About your destination. Tomorrow morning at ten, you will come to my cabin and we will begin."

Jennet blinked. "But my destination is Montreal."

"Tomorrow at ten," said Camille del Giglio. "That is soon enough."

Because the *Isis* belonged to Jennet's younger brother, the fourth Earl of Carryck, she had been given the Great Cabin for her sole use. Along with it came a whole squadron of cabin boys—some of them the same age as her brother the earl—to see to her needs. They wore flat caps with the name of the ship embroidered in scarlet along the rim and fearful expressions. Because, of course, they were all Annandale lads born and raised and they knew of her as she knew each of them, their mothers and fathers and their grandparents.

When she was finally alone in the suite of rooms, Jennet ignored the sleeping chamber with its carved bed and fine linen. Instead she curled up on the enclosed bench beneath the transom windows and pulled the heavy draperies closed to make a cave. It was too dark to see land but she imagined it there, slipping away moment by moment. She might never see Scotland again.

The ship groaned like a woman in travail. She had not been able to imagine the noise, the creaking and moaning and the scream of the wind. Sure that she would never be able to close her eyes, Jennet fell into a deep and satisfied sleep.

At ten o'clock, so nervous that her hands shook, Jennet found her way to the cabin just below her own. At her knock a cabin boy opened the door and jumped at the sight of her, coloring from the first pale hairs that peeked out from under his cap to the tight circle of the scarf knotted around his neck.

"Pardon, my lady." He ducked his head and shoulders, and slipped past her into the gloom of the passageway.

"Jamie," Jennet called after him and it seemed to her that for one moment he might pretend not to hear her. Then he turned.

"Aye, my lady?"

"It's nae sin tae smile, lad."

He bobbed his head again and ran off as if she had declared her intention to shoot him.

"Such a shy boy." Madame del Giglio's voice drifted to Jennet from the far corner of the stateroom, where she sat at a small table in an isle of morning sunlight. Against the backdrop of damask drapery the color of port wine she looked like a painting. One hand was spread flat on the table in front of her. With the other hand she was stroking Pip, who sat up at attention and wagged his fringed tail.

"Jamie comes from Carryckton." Jennet closed the door behind herself. "Where my brother is laird. And he's very young, no more than ten."

"And why should he be afraid to speak to me, then?"

The merchant's wife gestured to a chair opposite herself, and Jennet took it.

"I can think of two reasons," she said. "The simplest is just that the boy has no English and he's been forbidden to speak Scots to passengers."

"But you spoke Scots to him." Camille del Giglio had the darkest eyes Jennet had ever seen in a white woman; she found it hard to look away.

"Aye," Jennet said. "It is my mother tongue and the one I am most comfortable speaking, madame. When I was Jamie's age, I swore I'd never speak English."

"A vow you could not keep."

Jennet inclined her head. "In those days I never thought to live anywhere else. I could not have imagined leaving Annandale, much less Scotland."

"And now you cannot imagine going back again."

Jennet flushed with surprise and a fluttering of something she must call panic.

"Do you divine the future, madame?"

"No," said the merchant's wife. "But I have eyes in my head, and I have raised three daughters. You are very much like one of them, the eldest."

Sunlight rocked on the wall where Carryck's coat of arms hung: a white elk, a lion, a shield and crown. *In tenebris lux:* light in the darkness. Jennet swallowed and forced herself to look away.

"You were telling me about Jamie," the lady prompted.

Jennet said, "His mother and I were good friends when we were little. We disgraced ourselves by smuggling ginger nuts into kirk on a Sunday, and that was the least of it. To speak English with Jamie MacDuff would be as unnatural as addressing him in Greek. Or you in Scots, madame."

The lady smiled at that, her odd one-sided smile that made it seem as though she were at war with herself.

"And the second reason?"

Jennet folded her hands in her lap. "Why, he's afraid. He's never seen anyone quite like you."

Madame del Giglio murmured a word to Pip, who left her lap with a bounce and settled himself at her feet. In that same moment she produced a deck of cards—it seemed to Jennet out of thin air— and began to lay them out on the gleaming tabletop. In her surprise Jennet said nothing at all, but only watched.

"Do you play at cards?"

"A little," said Jennet, and felt the lady's evaluating gaze.

"Very good," she said finally.

"Madame?"

"You are either modest, or you have learned to keep your own council. Both are to be commended."

"The cards we play with look nothing like yours," Jennet said, and the lady laughed.

"And you know something of the art of misdirection. Excellent." Her hands stilled for a moment and then began to shift cards once more. They were worn at the edges and soft with handling; the figures were block printed, almost crude in execution, and the colors faded. She dealt three.

"This was my mother's deck," said Madame del Giglio. "And her mother's before her." She was quiet as she studied the cards she had laid out in a line, and then she touched them, one after the other, with a light finger.

"The two of cups, the star, the hanged man." She raised her face and gave Jennet her odd half-smile. "When I first saw you coming on board I suspected as much."

"A hanged man?" Jennet leaned forward to study the figure, who seemed so unconcerned about his fate that he had crossed one leg over the other. "Can that be a good card?"

Madame tapped the figure. "Very good indeed. This card promises an awakening."

"Awakening," Jennet echoed. She wondered at herself, that she should be so calm. A strange woman sat before her divining the future from cards. What she should do—what she was taught to do—was to walk away from such godlessness and spend the rest of the day on her knees saying a rosary for the lady's endangered soul.

And even as these thoughts went through her head Jennet saw that they were no secret from Madame del Giglio, who was waiting patiently for curiosity to win out over doctrine.

She is the spider; will you be the fly?

Jennet imagined her mother sitting between them, her brow creased in disapproval. She answered: *It is a way to pass the time, nothing more.*

"And that one, the two of cups. What does that tell you, madame?"

"A new friendship," said the lady. "One from which both parties will learn."

"I see." She paused. "And what can I learn from the cards?"

The lady tilted her head to one side. "You will learn to look inside yourself. Most of what you want to know is within you. The cards only open the door."

You see? Jennet said to her mother. *There is nothing of the devil in this.*

Her mother replied: *There shall not be found among you any one that maketh his son or his daughter to pass through the fire, or that useth divination, or an observer of times, or an enchanter, or a witch.* And then: *Ask her about Luke and see the temptations she spreads out before you.*

"There is a man," Jennet said, her voice coming hoarse and soft. "In Montreal."

Madame del Giglio touched the table. "There is still another card."

"The star, you called it? What does it tell you?"

"Montreal is only one stop on your journey, Lady Jennet. The first of many."

It was not what Jennet was expecting to hear, and it sent a small shock up her spine, a spark of something strange and familiar all at once. She felt perspiration gathering on her brow and in the hollow of her throat.

"My mother would not approve of this, madame. Are you—I think you must be Catholic?"

As I am. She did not add those words; the Carrycks might follow the church of Rome but they did so in strict secrecy. To admit such a thing in Protestant Scotland would bring repercussions that had been drummed into her since she was old enough to talk.

The dark eyes studied her for a moment. "My mother was the daughter and granddaughter of Catholic priests." She said this as she might have said, *I am the granddaughter of a carpenter* or, *My father was a lawyer.*

The three cards were gone, swept away.

"The door is open to you if you care to step through, Lady Jennet. That is a decision that only you can make. But I can tell you this: there is nothing evil in the cards of the tarot."

Awakening, friendship, a journey. But no word of Luke. Not yet.

"How do I begin?" she asked.

With a smooth movement Madame del Giglio spread the deck across the table in an arc: a rainbow, a bridge, the blade of a scythe.

She said, "We have already begun."

Prologue: Hannah
August 1812

In the gauzy high heat of late summer, a solitary woman walked a trail through the endless forests.

All around her the woods were alive with noise. A thrush sang overhead in the canopy of birch and maple, white pine and black ash, his long sweet melody caught up and cast out again by a mockingbird. Preacher birds scolded; a single crow called out to her. She raised her head and saw Hidden Wolf for the first time in ten years: the mountain where she had been born.

The sunlight brought tears to her eyes. She dropped her head and saw a footprint that she recognized as her father's. He must have been this way earlier in the day. For many years she had seen his face only indistinctly in her dreams, but she knew his footprint. Others were with him: her uncle, younger boys, and a man, tall and strong by his mark. Strangers to her, her blood relatives.

If she raised her voice to call they might hear her and come. This idea was a strange one—she had not used her voice in so long she wondered if it would even obey her—and it was frightening. She had wished for her father so often and so hard, and still she was not ready to look up and see him standing in front of her.

Sweat trickled between her breasts and soaked the small doeskin bag she wore on a piece of rawhide around her neck. Her overdress stuck to her, rank and worn thin as paper, a second skin she should have shed long ago. She walked faster, the swarming blackfly urging her on. At the point where the mountain's shoulder shoved itself up from the forest floor she turned onto a new trail, one that would take her to home by the way of the north face of the mountain. The climb was steep and winding and dangerous but it could take two hours off a journey that had lasted far too long.

The walking woman was thirstier with every step, but she forced herself onward through air grown so heavy and hot that it rested like another weight on the shoulders.

The sound of singing came and went, drifting on a teasing breeze, interrupted now and then with talk, too faint to make out clearly. A young girl, maybe six or seven years old by her sound, and playing alone on a part of the mountain where the woman herself was not allowed to play as a child.

The walking woman climbed for an hour. When she rounded an outcropping of rock the voice was suddenly clear. The child was talking to herself in lively imitation, the tone high and wavering and round with plummy sounds.

My dear Lady Isabel, may I pour you tea. How very kind, with sugar please.

The girl shifted from English to Mohawk, her tone scolding, as harsh as a jay's.

No sugar! No sugar! O'seronni poison, as bad as rum!

The girl was such a good mimic of her mother that the walking woman had to press a hand to her mouth to keep from laughing out loud. She paused to wonder at this oddity, that she was capable of laughter, and then the woman turned in the girl's direction.

She was a little below the trail, wading in one of the streams that ran down the mountain like wet hair down a woman's back. The water pooled between boulders before spilling down twenty steep and rocky feet.

The little girl had taken off her moccasins to set them neatly aside; blue-black braids were swinging at her waist as she hopped out of the water and in again in some game of her own design. For a moment the woman believed that it was a trick, that the mountain had conjured her own girl-self up out of stone and soil: a vision to answer the question she had asked herself with every step of this journey. An image to remind her that she was right to come. She belonged on this mountain where she was born, with her own people. With the living.

This thought was still in her mind when a fox stumbled out of the woods and slid down the incline toward the stream. Small and sleek, the red pelt dull with dust, and the worst of it: a grinning mouth that dripped white foam and crimson. It took an unsteady step toward the girl and snapped at the air, once and again, a sound like a dull blade against stone.

The girl stood perfectly still, one foot raised out of the water like a heron. So young for this particular lesson, but it had come to find her nonetheless; her silence was far too fragile to protect her.

Another lurching step and another, and a familiar smell came to the woman on a gust of wind. Madness in the blood.

Her bow came into her hands as if she had called it, the curved wooden shaft cool and smooth and familiar. She notched the arrow and felt the tickle of the hawk feather against her wrist

The boy's quick fingers tying the knot, the tip of his tongue caught between his teeth in concentration

and took aim. In that last moment of its life the fox raised its head to look directly at her. A look she knew very well.

"I bring you the death you seek," the woman said, and she let the arrow fly.

The little girl was her youngest cousin, born two full summers after the woman left home. She disliked her Mohawk girl-name and asked to be called Annie instead.

"My mother always calls me Kenenstasi," she added solemnly, watching out of the corner of her eye to see how well this fabled cousin would understand, or if she would have to be reminded of the way the world was divided into red and white.

"I will call you Annie," the woman promised.

The little girl managed a smile. For the rest of the walk home she was quiet except for a shuddering breath now and then, her mind still filled with the idea of death. Or maybe, the woman reasoned to herself, maybe the girl was quiet because all the questions she would ask had already been answered.

She asked, "Have they had word of me at Lake in the Clouds?"

The little girl let out a sound of surprise, someplace between a croak and a hiccup. She nodded. "A letter came a week ago. We've been waiting for you."

The walking woman did not ask who wrote the letter; she was only thankful that she would not have to tell her own story. More than anything else she feared having to look her father in the eye and confess her failures.

• • •

At the crest of the mountain where the sound of the falls was so loud that she must shout to be heard, Annie turned to the walking woman and cupped her hands around her mouth. Her face was shiny with heat and eagerness to be home.

"The fast trail or the slow?"

"You go ahead," the woman told her. "Tell them I'm coming."

She watched until the girl disappeared into the trees and then she sat down abruptly and wrapped her arms around herself to stop the trembling. Overhead an eagle coasted on a hot and rising wind. When it was clear that the eagle had no advice to give her, the walking woman got up and started on the last leg of her journey.

Standing in the forests above the glen tucked into the side of the mountain, she took in the changes all at once. At the far end, just before the cliffs fell away into the valley, where the sun shone hot and long enough for corn and squash and beans, the field lay fallow under a coat of coarse straw that shifted in the wind. That was a surprise in itself, but there was more.

The older cabin, the one built long ago by her grandfather, was as it had always been. The second, newer cabin was gone (*a fire*, she reminded herself; *they wrote to you about the fire*). In its place something else had been built, not a cabin in the Indian style or a house such as the whites who lived in villages built, but a combination of both. The walls were made of square-hewn logs, and like the older cabin it was long and el-shaped with chimneys at two ends, but this house had a second story. Shutters bracketed each of the glass windows, and above the front door someone had painted the symbol of the Wolf clan of the Kahnyen'kehàka.

On the porch of this strange cabin-house that she must now call her home, the woman's family was gathered, and they were looking at her, all of them, waiting for some sign that she was real; that she was the daughter they had been waiting for.

Her father stood straight and strong though the hair that fell over his shoulders was mostly gray; beside him was her stepmother, small and rounder with age, pale with worry. Her hair—still dark—curled around her face in the heat. Next to her, the walking woman's aunt Many-Doves stood, the living image of her own mother, long gone to dust. With her stood the walking woman's uncle Runs-from-

Bears and a man who must be Blue-Jay, his oldest son. Blue-Jay had been a boy when she went away, but now he stood taller even than his own father, the tallest man in a hundred miles. There was no sign of the other children of Many-Doves and Runs-from-Bears, not even of Kenenstasi-called-Annie, most certainly because she had been sent down to the village to spread the word.

The walking woman's own brothers and sister stood at the bottom of the steps. The twins, still children when she went away, were now eighteen years old, old enough to be gone, raising families of their own. Lily was small of stature but with a fierce and burning energy about her, at odds with her watchfulness. Daniel was so much like the grandfather they all had in common that the walking woman believed at first that time had taken to spinning backward.

Each of the twins had a hand on the shoulders of the boy.

The walking woman had never seen the boy before, and still she recognized the shape of his head and the set of his eyes, the way he held himself. Her father's son, her half brother, called Gabriel. From the few letters that found her in the west, always months out of date and rough with handling, she knew some of his story.

She was not surprised when he let out a high yipping cry, a trill from the back of his throat, and leapt forward so that the dogs twitching in their rabbit-dreams rose up in a fury of startled barks. They ran at his heels and with that the others began moving too. As if the boy had opened an invisible gate.

By the time she let her pack slide to the ground he was there, flinging his arms around her like a tether, a hangman's rope, a lifeline.

Her hands fluttered and then settled, one on his shoulder and the other on the curve of his skull, on dark, curly hair hot with the sun. She touched him as gently as spun sugar; as if the heat of her wanting might cause him to disappear. He was talking to her but the words swarmed around her head like blackfly, an irritation of no real importance. Beneath her hands she felt the strumming of his blood, the startling life force of this boy born within days of her own son.

"Finally," he was saying. "Finally you're here."

"Little brother." The English words tasted sour and coppery on her tongue, flecks of dried blood to be spat out. "How good it is to see you."

Prologue: Elizabeth

Luke Scott Bonner, Esq.
Forbes & Sons
rue Bonsecours
Montreal

Dear Luke,
Your sister Hannah is come home to Lake in the Clouds. She is alone, as your letter warned us she must be. While she is in good health, she has not spoken to us of the things that weigh heaviest on her heart and mind, except to confirm the worst: her son is dead.

The story of what happened to Strikes-the-Sky is less clear and very troubling. In the spring of last year he left their village on the Wabash on a scouting mission. Traveling with him was Manny Freeman. Neither of them was ever seen again, nor has there been any reliable report of them or their fate. Hannah does not speak of Strikes-the-Sky as alive or dead, or in any way at all. Her silence robs us of our own words.

Of your grandfather Hawkeye there is a little more news. Your sister saw him last in Indiana territory three years ago. He set off on foot in a southwesterly direction, taking nothing with him but his weapons and as many provisions as he could carry.

Your father sends his very warmest good wishes and this word: if your trade connections in the west have any news of your grandfather, we would be most thankful for any information they might provide.

Gabriel asks when you will come to visit. We have explained to him many times that it is neither easy nor safe to cross the border in times of war but this is something our youngest does not care to hear. Daniel would like to see you as well. I know that he hopes you will convince us, his most unreasonable parents, that he and Blue-Jay had best go join the fighting. They speak of little else, to our considerable disquiet.

Please give our best regards to your grandmother Iona. We think of you every day with love and gratitude for the kind services you have provided us in our worry for your sister. As Hannah continues to improve from her long journey—I dare not write of her *healing*—we hope to send you more and better news of her.

Your loving stepmother
Elizabeth Middleton Bonner

Chapter I

Early September 1812
Paradise, New-York State

Hot sun and abundant rain: Lily Bonner said a word of thanks for a good summer and the harvest it had given them, and in the same breath she wished her hoe to the devil and herself away.

But there was no chance of escape. Even Lily's mother, whose usual and acknowledged place was at her writing desk or in a classroom, had come to help; everyone must, this close to harvest. *The women must,* Lily corrected herself: the men were in the cool of the forests.

She glanced up and caught sight of her mother, all furious concentration as she moved along her row. She swung her hoe with the same easy rhythm as Many-Doves. They were an army of two marching through the tasseled rows, corn brushing shoulders and cheeks as if to thank the women for their care.

For all their lives the Mohawk women had spent the best part of every summer day in the fields tending the three sisters: corn, beans, squash. But Lily's mother had been raised in a great English manor house with servants, and she had not held a hoe in her hands—white skin, ink-stained fingers—until she was thirty. Elizabeth Middleton had come to New-York as a spinster, a teacher, a crusader; in just six months' time she had become someone very different.

Lily understood a simple truth: the day came for every woman when she must choose one kind of life or another or let someone else make the choice for her. For some the crucial moment came suddenly, without warning and when least expected; others saw it approaching, pushing up out of the ground like a weed.

It was an image that would not leave her mind, and so she had finally spoken about it to her mother, holding the idea out in open palms like the egg of an unfamiliar and exotic bird.

And how it had pleased her mother, this simple gift. She sat contemplating her folded hands for a moment, Quaker-gray eyes fixed on the horizon and a tilt to her head that meant her mind was far away, reliving some moment, recalling a phrase read last week or ten years ago. When she spoke, finally, it was not with the quotation Lily expected.

She said, "There are so many choices available to you, such riches for the taking. The very best advice I can give you is very simple. You have heard me say it in different ways, but I'll put it as simply as I can. When it comes time to choose, try to favor the rational over the subjective."

At that Lily had laughed out loud, in surprise and disappointment. Who else had a mother who would say such a thing, and in such a studiously odd way? Other people were satisfied with quoting the Bible and old wives' wisdoms, but Lily had a mother who preferred Kant to the Proverbs. Who made decisions with her head when she could, and was convinced that in doing so, her other needs would be satisfied.

Certainly she could point to even the most unconventional choices she had made in her life and argue that they were rational, and more than that: that she was happy with the choices she had made. As most of the other women Lily knew were happy with the lives they had.

Her cousin Kateri had chosen a husband from the Turtle clan at Good Pasture and gone with him to live among the Mohawk on the Canadian side of the St. Lawrence. It was too early yet to know how well she had chosen, or how badly. Other women misstepped and struggled mightily forever after; there were a few like that in Paradise, burning bright with the anger they must swallow day by day.

And then there was Hannah, her own sister, who had chosen to leave home and chosen well, in spite of the fact that the wars in the west had taken it all away from her. Now she was neither angry nor content but merely alive, as placid and blank as the clouds overhead and just as distant.

The war was coming closer all the time, and while they had not heard a single shot fired and none of the men had gone to join the fighting—*not yet,* Lily corrected herself—there were casualties. Lily counted herself among them.

Without the war she would have left two months ago for New-York City. The plan had taken a full year to finalize: she would live with her uncle and aunt Spencer in their fine house on Whitehall Street and study art with the teachers they had found for her. In time, when she had advanced far enough, she would travel with them to Europe where she could study the work of the great artists.

But all of that had come to a sudden end, because men must fight and to do that they started wars. Her own brother was infected with that need, her twin brother. The strangeness of it never faded.

Many-Doves was telling a story. Lily's mother laughed in response, a gentle hiccupping laughter that meant she was embarrassed. All these years living among the plain-speaking Kahnyen'kehàka women, but her mother still blushed and laughed like a proper young English lady when the talk turned to men and women and the things they were to each other.

This is the life my mother chose. Lily repeated this sentence to herself often, and every time she was overcome with admiration and resentment in equal measure.

When Many-Doves decided the time was right they put down the hoes to eat in the shade of the birch trees. Lily filled empty gourds with water from the stream and they unwrapped a parcel of corn-bread and boiled eggs and peppery radishes plucked this morning from the kitchen garden, still trailing clots of damp earth. Lily listened for a while as they talked about the coming harvest and the day's work.

When it was clear that today was not the day they would decide among themselves what was to be done to heal Hannah, Lily went off to wade in the lake, digging her toes into the mud and pulling her skirts up through her belt so that the duck grass tickled her bare calves. She wet her handkerchief and wiped her face and the back of her neck free of dust and grit, thankful for the cool and the breeze and the very colors of the sky. Lily felt her mother watching her, her love and pride and worry radiating as hot and true as the sun itself.

The sound of drumming hooves brought her out of her day-dream. The others heard it too, all of them turning in the direction of the village, their heads tilted at just the same angle, listening hard.

"Riders!" Her brother Gabriel exploded out of a clump of grass almost under Lily's nose, all pinwheeling arms and legs and spraying water. Annie, Many-Doves' daughter, was just behind him and they galloped toward the women, both of them sleekly wet and naked. Gabriel's skin was burned almost as dark as Annie's, so that his gray eyes worked silver.

"Five riders!" Annie shouted as if she must make herself heard on the top of the mountain.

"We hear." Many-Doves raised a hand to screen out the sun as she looked in the direction of the village.

"Your uncle Todd's letter said he hoped to be home today," Lily's mother said, wiping her neck with a kerchief. "But who does he have with him?" Her expression was a combination of worry and anticipation and excitement too.

"Whoever it is, they must be lost," Lily said, wishing herself wrong even as she said the words. "No stranger ever comes to Paradise on purpose."

The cornfield was on a little rise that gave them a good view of the village on the other side of the lake: the building that had once been the church but now was just a meetinghouse, as no minister seemed to want to stay in Paradise; the well; the dusty road that widened in front of the trading post and then narrowed again to disappear almost immediately into the woods; a few cabins; the smithy; here and there a curl of smoke from a chimney they could not see.

Every year Paradise was a little smaller, like an old woman hunching down into her bones. When a family gave up and moved on the cabin stayed empty and the garden around it lay fallow, simply because Uncle Todd could not be bothered to look for new tenants. At this moment the only sign of life was a cat asleep on the wall of the well, her fur gleaming in the sun. But folks would come soon enough: so many riders at once was almost as good as a fire for waking them up.

The sound of hooves on the road grew louder and louder still, and then the riders showed themselves. Five of them, as Annie had foretold. Uncle Todd and cousin Ethan among them—Lily made out that much and nothing about the others; she did not have her father's keen eyesight. Gabriel had it, though. Gabriel and Daniel and all her brothers; eyesight keen enough to count acorns on the highest branch. And now young Gabriel had caught sight of something that made every muscle quiver. He turned his head toward the women and his eyes were perfectly round with anticipation.

"Yes," Elizabeth said, answering the question he hadn't asked. "But put your breechclout on first. You too, Annie, you can't go greet people in such a state."

To Lily she said, "That will slow them down a little, at least. Come along, maybe we can get there first."

Without any discussion Many-Doves began to gather the hoes together.

"But there's six hours of sun left," Lily said as her mother moved off. She found herself as uneasy about the strangers as she had been eager to see them just a moment ago.

Many-Doves laughed and poked her shoulder with two fingers. "As if you could work now with your brother just come home."

All of the riders had dismounted but for one, a smaller figure—a lady by her bearing, Lily saw now. One of the men had a hand on the woman's saddle, his head canted up to talk to her—*argue with her,* Lily corrected herself, taking in the way he held himself—and in that moment she recognized him.

"Luke," she said.

Her brother Luke, come from Montreal without word or warning, and in time of war. Lily felt the shock of it in the tips of her fingers, shock and joy and a flash of fear.

Lily's mother had recognized him too, and picked up her skirts and her pace both. Gabriel and Annie streaked past, heels flashing.

"Who is that lady?" Lily asked out loud.

Many-Doves made an approving sound deep in her throat. "Maybe your brother has finally brought a wife home with him."

"They argue as though they were married," Lily agreed.

Luke turned away from the stranger and pulled his hat from his head in frustration. The lady turned her horse away and started up the path that led to Uncle Todd's place while Luke watched her, his fists at his sides.

Richard Todd was the most prominent man in Paradise, the richest in both land and money, and a trained medical doctor. His fine two-story house was the only brick building in a village of squared-log cabins. It had been the largest house until the Widow Kuick bought the mill and built her own fine house, but the Kuick place had fallen into disrepair these last years and sat hunched on the hillside overlooking the village, like a frowsy old woman without the wits to look after herself.

Richard Todd was rarely at home and the Kuick widows rarely stepped out of doors, but when Richard went off to Johnstown or Albany, his place in the world and the things he called his own—house, gardens, pastures, cornfields, barns and outbuildings, books and animals and plowshares—were cared for. A small kingdom beautifully kept, and the doctor had spent less than three weeks in residence in the last six months.

It was a situation that suited his housekeeper very well. At seventy-nine Curiosity Freeman still ran things, overseeing the house servants—her own granddaughters—and the farm workers like a benevolent general presiding over well-trained and adoring troops.

Together Curiosity and Elizabeth and Many-Doves looked after the medical needs of the village; they dosed children for worms, set broken bones, delivered babies, laid out the dead and comforted the living. Sometimes Curiosity went for days without giving the absent doctor a thought.

They were in the laboratory, the farthest of the outbuildings on the Todd property. Once this had been the heart of Richard's medical practice, and it had surprised Hannah to find that while she was gone it had been given over to a different kind of research. According to Curiosity, Joshua Hench had been conducting experiments with metals and blackpowder explosives, all with Richard's approval.

"Wouldn't do no good to tell you," Curiosity said in response to Hannah's questions. Her irritation was sharp and clear on her face. "You just have to wait and see for yourself. Unless you was wanting the laboratory for your own work?" She looked at Hannah hopefully. "Then Joshua will just have to clear out, go blow himself up someplace else where I don't got to hear it happen."

Hannah didn't want the laboratory; she hadn't come home to practice medicine, after all, and she said so.

"You've expressed your concerns to Richard, I take it."

At that Curiosity just snorted. "You wave a firecracker under a man's nose, he ain't going to pay no attention, no matter what kind of sense you be talking." Then she pushed out a sigh. "Ain't nothing to be done, but it do set my teeth on edge."

Hannah was relieved if Curiosity was willing to abandon the subject. She turned her attention to the stack of Richard's daybooks on the standing desk. Ledger after ledger in which he had logged his daily work: treatments, patients seen, raw materials ordered from Albany and New-York City and beyond, experiments he had undertaken and the results they had produced. All neat, well ordered and full of Richard's dry observations.

June 4 1808. Set right tibula on the youngest Ratz boy. Subject healthy if dull-witted ten-year-old; clean break; no tearing to the muscle or ligaments; prognosis good if he can be kept out of trees.

Curiosity had come along to keep Hannah company while she read. She sat near the door in the light from the single window, snapping beans in a bowl in her lap.

"Richard has been away a long time," Hannah noted; the last entry in the daybook was six months old.

"Wouldn't care if he never did come home," Curiosity said, her temper flaring again. "If it weren't for missing Ethan. I wish he'd leave the boy here with me. He won't ever make no doctor and everybody know it. Richard best of all."

"Ethan is hardly a boy anymore," Hannah pointed out. "He's nineteen."

"Of course he a boy." Curiosity poked into the bowl, fished an earwig out with two long fingers to crush it under her heel. "He tender at heart like a boy, our Ethan, and he always will be. I'm hoping that now that you come home they'll listen to reason, the two of them."

Hannah looked up from a copy of a letter Richard had written to a chemical warehouse in London, requesting a list of things that were unfamiliar to her. A strange prickling on the back of her neck: interest in things she thought she had left behind, curiosity, irritation that those impulses she thought dead could twitch to life without warning or bidding.

Curiosity was watching her, eyes narrowed. Hannah cleared her mind and closed the daybook.

She said, "Curiosity, what makes you think Richard will listen to me? He never did before."

For a good while there was no sound but the rapid-fire crack-crack-crack of bean pods while Hannah studied Curiosity and waited for an answer.

Of all the things Hannah had feared about coming home she had been most worried that she would find Curiosity gone. She should be, at almost eighty with a hard life behind her. But Curiosity was as steady and constant as the river itself, if bowed a little by the years. There were new sorrows etched into her face: she had lost her good husband to a stroke, a grandson to a brain fever, a daughter and granddaughter on the same day to a runaway horse and sleigh; and her only son was someplace in the west, fighting a battle that could not be won.

If he was alive at all.

But Curiosity's spirit was undaunted and her energy undiminished; the very nearness of her was a comfort.

Hannah had been home for weeks now, and while all the others were growing less and less able to keep their questions to themselves, Curiosity seemed content to wait until Hannah was ready to talk, if it took a year or ten years or never came at all.

Somewhere in the pines that ringed the clearing a kinglet was calling in a thin high *seet-seet-seet;* she heard kestrels and blackbirds and the soft, gentle song of a hermit thrush as sweet as the lullabies her grandmother Cora had sung to her as a child. In another month the birds would be gone south; they would pull the summer light along behind them like a bridal train. In two months the trees where they built their nests would be gravid with snow. Half-Moon Lake and the lake under the falls would freeze and beneath the ice, water without color would pulse and throb.

A sound bubbled up from deep in her throat and she swallowed it back down again.

How can you fear anything at all after the battle of Kettippecannunk?

In her mind Hannah could hear her husband's voice as clearly as the kestrel's. If she answered Strikes-the-Sky, if she reacted to his tone—calm and teasing all at once—he would be with her for the rest of the day. He would argue with her for hours and take great pleasure in it, if she let him. The only way to make him go was to ask him the one real question—the only question, the one she would not ask for fear of getting an answer.

She ignored him, but he was not willing to be ignored.

Walks-Ahead, you cannot hide within your silence.

Here was the most irritating thing of all: in this strange absence of his, gone but not gone, alive in some ways and dead in others, Strikes-the-Sky was always right, his arguments without flaw.

At Lake in the Clouds the women forbade talk of war in their hearing, but that changed nothing. It was all around and drawing closer every day. Twice a week the post rider brought the most recent news and the papers and the men gathered in the trading post to weigh it all out, bullet by bullet. Hannah turned her face away when her brother and cousin tried to tell her about it.

But she knew the truth of it: she could not protect herself from sorrows old or new. War was not *coming;* it had already pushed into their midst. It would not die of her neglect or be turned away by calm words.

More and more often Hannah had the urge to say these things to Curiosity, who was none of her blood but as close to her as her own grandmothers had been. Both those grandmothers—one a Scot and the other Mohawk—were long dead and content to remain silent in their graves, but Curiosity would speak for them and herself. Once Hannah gave her permission, Curiosity would ask questions that dug themselves beneath the skin like gunpowder.

"That's the thing about Richard," Curiosity said, and Hannah started out of her thoughts.

"What about him?"

Curiosity flicked her a concerned look. "I've known old mules beset with fly-bots less ornery. But I expect that don't much surprise you."

"He was never known for his brilliant personality," Hannah agreed. And then: "But there's something more, isn't there. Is he sick?"

"He is," Curiosity said, her tone subdued.

"How sick?" Hannah asked the question knowing she would not get an answer; the older woman could be deaf when she chose.

Curiosity had turned her head toward the door. She stood, clutching the bowl to her narrow chest.

"Speak of the devil."

Hannah heard the riders now, the drumming of hooves that seemed as loud as thunder. A flush of panic mounted her back to set its teeth in the tender curve of her neck.

Curiosity put the bowl of beans aside and crossed the room to Hannah in three steps. One hand, as lean and rough as leather, cupped her cheek. "There now," she said softly. "Rest easy."

Hannah blinked at her, swallowed hard and tried to speak.

"Hush." Curiosity made a comforting sound. "No need to explain, child. A rider don't necessarily mean bad news. Just settle yourself down again and I'll go see to it."

But Hannah could not stay away from the door. She followed Curiosity out into the sunlight just as a young woman pulled her horse to a quick stop and slid from the saddle to land lightly on her feet.

A woman, yes, but no taller than a boy with a pointed chin and sea-green eyes. Then Hannah saw the blond hair and the smile, and while her rational mind said it could not be so, her heart knew without hesitation or doubt. She felt herself moving forward, her arms open wide.

"Jennet." The word caught in her throat in a great rush of tears. "Jennet."

"Aye, it's me." She pulled the bonnet from her head with an impatient yank to show off a head of short-cropped curls as yellow as tow. "Hannah Bonner, why do you look so surprised? Have I not written a hundred times at least that I'd come one day?"

Others were running up now, Gabriel and Annie first and foremost with what seemed like half the village streaming behind them.

"And what great adventures we'll have," Hannah finished for her. "I've been waiting for you, cousin, and I didn't even realize it."

"I see you brought the doctor with you too," Curiosity said, coming forward now to catch Annie before she ran into the two women and knocked them over.

"And Luke." Jennet looked over her shoulder. "Here he comes now, with Simon Ballentyne. Hannah, you'll remember his great-granny, Gelleys the washerwoman."

"I remember a Thomas Ballentyne too," Hannah said. "It was on his horse I first came to Carryck."

"Simon's uncle, aye." Jennet laughed. "Everywhere I go I drag a wee bit of Scotland along. Like cockleburs."

"But how are we going to feed them all?" Annie wailed, and they were laughing still when Luke Bonner swung down from his saddle.

After Elizabeth greeted Luke and Jennet and the rest, she stepped back and watched, her hands pressed to her cheeks to keep herself from weeping. In the center of the crowd Hannah stood between Luke and Jennet, laughing and talking, touching one and then the other while Annie and Gabriel capered from person to person like puppies.

"Where are Richard and Ethan?" Elizabeth asked this question out loud and was surprised to get an answer from Lily, who had come up behind her.

"They went straight to the house."

"It looks like the whole village is on its way," Elizabeth said.

Lily made a sound in her throat that meant she would not take the trouble to correct her mother's exaggeration. Elizabeth glanced at her younger daughter in surprise and saw many things there: joy and disappointment at odds, and frustration. *Like a child left out of a party with no chance of gaining an invitation,* Elizabeth thought.

"I'll go fetch Da and the others." Lily turned away, flinging back the words over her shoulder. A challenge, and one Elizabeth must meet.

She had to run to catch Lily up, and then she walked beside her daughter in silence. Little by little the laughter and voices faded away behind them to be replaced by the sounds of water and wind moving through the corn and all the noise of the woods on a late summer day. Little by little Lily's pace slowed to something close to normal, and Elizabeth was glad of it; she found herself a little short of breath.

When they had got as far as the strawberry fields without talking Lily stopped suddenly, folded her arms across her waist and looked down the mountain toward Paradise.

"Da will be glad to have Luke home."

"Yes, he will."

"They'll go off with the men to talk about war and Hannah will go off with Jennet and I'll be left behind with the old women, as I always am."

Elizabeth bit back a smile. "They have a lot to talk about, it's true."

"Sister could have talked to me," Lily said, turning toward Elizabeth. Her face was flushed with color. "Why wouldn't she talk to me? I'm not a little girl anymore. She thinks of me as a child, you and Da think of me as a child. But I'm *not*. At my age Sally had two children."

It was a discussion they had had so many times in so many ways. From long experience Elizabeth knew that there was nothing she could say at this moment that would soothe this unhappy daughter, who had longed for one thing alone and now could not have it.

Elizabeth understood too well; she had lived all her own girlhood with a family whose loving concern had tied her down as surely as ropes. She had been the bookish cousin with too many opinions and too little income of her own, sometimes amusing in her own way but more often irritatingly informed and vocal. She had left that world behind and come to this one, as Lily wanted to leave here and find a place of her own and the life she wanted.

It is only a delay, Elizabeth promised her daughter silently. *Just until it is safe to let you go.* It was a sentence she repeated to herself whenever she looked at Lily, but one she tried not to say out loud, because an argument would follow as surely as thunder followed lightning. So she told herself what she could not say to her daughter: *Better unhappy than dead.*

After a moment they started walking again.

Lily said, "Did you know about Jennet and Luke?"

"Of course not," Elizabeth answered shortly. "I would not have kept it to myself if I had known they were coming."

"No," Lily said impatiently. "Did you know about *them?*"

Elizabeth pulled up in surprise. Her first inclination was to ask Lily to explain herself and then she saw the two of them again in her mind's eye: Jennet's eyes flashing down at Luke as he stood next to her horse. Something there beyond friendship, a tension as fine and strong as wire drawn out and out over the hottest of fires.

"I know of no connection between them," Elizabeth said, more slowly. "Jennet is recently widowed, and she hasn't seen Luke in such a long time. I don't think it's likely . . ."

She let her voice trail away because Lily was looking at her with one eyebrow raised, as she herself looked at children when they worked too hard to make reason out of fancy.

"Neither of them has ever written or said a word to me about a connection," Elizabeth said finally. "Nor has anyone else."

"Well, there's one there now," Lily said.

Elizabeth could not correct her but neither could she ask all the questions that came to mind, and so she was silent.

She found Nathaniel by himself rumbling through the baskets in the workroom. "Am I glad to see you, Boots." He thrust a bloody hand toward her. "I'm no good at bandages. Can you tie this up for me?"

"You're no good at stitches either," she said, catching his hand to look more closely at the gash that ran just below his knuckles from thumb to little finger. Blood trailed down and over the Kahnyen'kehàka tattoos that circled his wrist.

He put his head down next to hers to look at the wound more closely. "It's just a scratch. I already cleaned it out, so bind it up for me now and let me get back to work. We were in the middle of bringing down that dead oak on the other side of Squirrel Slough."

Elizabeth touched her forehead to his and looked him in the eye. "Nathaniel Bonner," she said. "I want you to listen to me very closely. You need stitches or this wound will not close properly, and you know it very well yourself. You must go to Hannah or Curiosity— that much you may choose." Then she pressed a piece of linen to the wound and began to wind it firmly.

He pushed out a frustrated sigh that rippled through the muscles in his shoulders and down his arms, giving in without more argument.

"And there's company coming," she added, tying off the linen and avoiding his gaze. "You'll want to be here."

A little spark of interest replaced the resignation in his expression. "Good company, I hope."

"The very best," Elizabeth promised, and kissed him on the forehead. He pulled her closer with his free arm around her waist and kissed her properly before he let her go. He smelled of honest sweat and pennyroyal ointment and pine tar and blood, and his mouth tasted of mint. Then he swung her around to pin her where she stood, his arms stemmed to either side of her head. It was one of Elizabeth's greatest pleasures in life, to have her husband catch her up against a wall to kiss her. He knew this very well, and he used it now to his advantage.

"Are you going to tell me or will I have to tease it out of you?"

"Promise me first that you'll let Hannah see to your hand straightaway."

He grinned at her, a flash of teeth that made him look half his age and up to no good, her wild backwoodsman of a husband, too clever by half.

"I promise you nothing but a good tickling, Boots, unless you speak up right this minute."

She put her hands against his chest, but she did not bother pushing; he would let her go when he had enough of this, and not before. "All right, a hint then. Who would you like to have here with us more than anyone else in the world?"

"Strikes-the-Sky," he said without hesitation, and the words jolted Elizabeth as surely as a slap.

"Oh," she said. "Of course. I wish it were Strikes-the-Sky, but I think you will be pleased nonetheless. Luke is come."

Nathaniel looked just as surprised as she was herself. "Luke? But he always sends word first."

She shrugged. "And he brought Jennet with him."

It was hard to shock Nathaniel, but she had managed it. He pushed her a little away from him to study her face, as if she would make up so outlandish a tale.

"Jennet Scott? Of Carryck?"

"Do you know another?"

"You're saying Luke brought that girl over the border in the middle of a war?"

"Yes, he did," Elizabeth said. "I expect they'll be here shortly, and I have to find places for them all to sleep. So if you'll promise me—"

He kissed her hard, the kind of kiss that meant he had more on his mind and meant her to know it too, though they both had work to do.

"I'll get Hannah to sew up my hand," he said. His disquiet and concern were giving way, slowly, to pleasure at the idea of seeing his son. "As soon as I've laid eyes on Luke and had an explanation."

There was a celebration to get ready on short notice, food for fifty people, wood to be gathered for the cook fires, and a hundred other tasks from the setting up of trestle tables to the tuning of Levi's fiddle. It seemed that Cookie's sons were known as far away as Albany for their musical talent.

The villagers came to the Todd place in a dribble and then in a steady stream, carrying kegs of ale and cider and squealing piglets that would find their way onto spits before the afternoon was much older. There were chickens to be plucked, a brace of trout and another of bass, baskets of plums and apples just off the trees, casks of bacon fat and butter, jars of honey and pickles, and loaves of bread. Curiosity directed the cooking, marching back and forth so that her skirts snapped smartly around her legs.

Jennet drew people to her without trying, and she met all of them with such openness and simple delight that Hannah found herself laughing at nothing. Then Curiosity put an end to it all.

"Get yourselves up to Lake in the Clouds," she said, putting one hand on Jennet's shoulder and one on Hannah's. "Get settled in, have a look around and meet the rest of the folks. Then chase everybody on down here. I expect it'll be two hours at least afore we're ready to start dishing up any food." She cast a glance across the field. "I'd tell you to take Luke and that Simon fellow with you but it look to me like Gabriel already got just about everybody who can hold a stick in the bagattaway game."

A group of men and boys had stripped to the waist and divided themselves into teams. Daniel and Gabriel and Luke stood together, the two older brothers with their heads bent down toward Gabriel in a protective posture that made Hannah's breath catch on memories too sweet and tender to deny, for once. She could feel Strikes-the-Sky and the boy both at her back, the solid warmth of them and their absence both.

"Ooh," said Jennet, craning her neck. "I've been wanting to watch—"

Curiosity gave her another gentle push. "No fear, Miss Jennet, that game won't be over soon. You can come back in plenty of time to watch them stomping on each other. Get on with you now."

They went on horseback, Hannah taking Luke's big gelding and leading the way. Now and then Jennet would ask a question, but for the most part she seemed so intent on taking in the details of the village and then the mountain trail that she fell silent. Hannah was glad of the time to think, though the thoughts that raced through her head were so many and quick that she could fix on none of them for very long, except this: her brother had come home and brought Jennet with him, and for no reason she could understand, Hannah felt as if she had just woken from a long and unnatural sleep.

Chapter 2

As soon as Luke's letter arrived with the news that Hannah was on her way home, Elizabeth had set about making one of the four chambers over for her; it was that, she told Nathaniel, or lose her mind with the wait and worry.

In a matter of days every fine thing in the house had found its way to the chamber: the best blankets, an embroidered pillow slip normally folded away in tissue, a heavy china washbasin and matching water jug sent all the way from England. A new standing desk had been placed between the windows and a worktable in the center of the room. A bright rag rug covered the plank floor and on a long shelf above the bed a dozen books stood between blocks of cherry wood sanded and polished to gleaming.

Everyone had come to leave some gift, large or small, for Hannah; clothing and soap and candles, a beaver pelt for the foot of the bed, a pretty rock. A panther skull, scrubbed clean, held down a pile of newspapers from Albany and Manhattan.

Daniel and Lily had argued for days about the right gift and finally decided on a bottle of ink, a dozen finely sharpened quills, and a new journal sewn from the best paper they could afford. Because, they reminded each other, Hannah always kept careful records of the patients she saw. In the old days her fingers had always been stained with ink.

In the week between the news of Hannah's coming and her arrival,

Lily had imagined the hours she would spend in this room with her sister, but she had found instead that the door was always closed. Now she stood in the middle of Hannah's chamber, and Lily saw what she had only suspected: since she had come home Hannah had not written a word; the quills and ink and paper were untouched. Nor was there any sign of her old journals, the ones she had taken west with her or the ones she must have written over the years. Whether they had been lost or stolen or destroyed only Hannah knew.

This was another kind of loss, one that Lily had not imagined, and it made her catch her breath and understand finally and clearly what she had been afraid to admit, even to herself: the sister she had missed so fiercely was not home and would never come home, because she did not exist anymore.

"Space will be very dear," Lily's mother said behind her. "I cannot put Luke and Simon Ballentyne in the same room with Daniel and Gabriel, and so I must make room for all the young women here. I trust you will not mind sharing with your sister and cousin. No doubt they will keep you awake all night with their talk."

Even an hour ago Lily would have been thrilled at this turn of events, but she was suddenly overcome with shame for her own selfishness. Her mother, occupied with the linen in her arms, seemed not to take any note at all.

Hannah's chamber had windows hung with white muslin curtains on two walls: one provided a view of the orchard and beyond that the cliffs; the other looked out over the whole glen and the mountains. Jennet Scott Huntar thought she had never seen a view so beautiful. Mountain upon mountain, fading away into a blue haze on the horizon where the sun made its way toward the other side of the world. The endless forests. Jennet had never been able to grasp the idea until she saw it for herself: a world overwhelmed with trees, and every one of them glowing in the sun and casting shadows like reaching hands.

"Hannah Bonner," she said finally. "I waited far too long to come. This is Paradise indeed."

"Yes, well," Hannah said, "it is not without its faults, this Paradise. But I'm glad you're here."

She sat on the edge of the bed with her hands folded in her lap, her expression calm and almost happy in the late afternoon light. They had been girls the last time they saw each other and they were women now. Both with tragedies behind them, or losses that were meant to be tragedies. Sometimes Jennet said it out loud: *I am a widow.* But it sounded strange and even silly to her own ears. Her widowhood seemed a plaything, of no real substance, while Hannah's losses had dug themselves deep into the bone.

Her cousin's face had set in its planes and curves, with faint creases on the brow and at the corners of her eyes. A line of black-fly bites arched across the high crest of her cheekbone like a new tattoo, and below that other scars shimmered faintly where furrows had been dug into the soft flesh and healed. She wore a small doe-skin bag on a string around her neck, one that she fingered when she was lost in her thoughts as she was now.

She has lost more than I ever imagined having, Jennet reminded herself, and came to sit across from Hannah on the single chair at the table.

"Look," she said, drawing a chain out of her bodice. "I've worn it since the day you left Carryck. My mother thought it was unlady-like to wear a bear's tooth next to my heart, but Ewan did not seem to mind."

Hannah said, "I'm glad you still have it." She looked away briefly. "I lost mine, some time ago."

Jennet hesitated. "Will you tell me about it?"

Hannah blinked at her. "I think I will," she said finally, and she managed a small smile. "Sometime I think I will. If you will talk to me about Luke."

"That's a promise then," said Jennet. "But let me ask you this: will you listen to what I have to say with an open mind, Hannah Bonner?"

Hannah had believed herself incapable of being surprised, but then she had not reckoned with Jennet, who reached into a pocket tied around her waist and took out a deck of cards wrapped in a rosary.

"This is called a tarot deck. It was given to me by a friend; I think someday you may well meet her." She unwrapped the rosary and laid it on the table very gently. "The beads are for my mother, to quiet her scolding." From the top of the deck she took a single card and turned it face up.

"This is the card I want to tell you about. It's called *Fuerza* in the Spanish tongue, that means 'strength' in English. You see that *Fuerza* is a woman in her full power. She holds a lion's mouth open with her bare hands." She looked Hannah directly in the eye. "This is what you may find hard to believe. The first time I saw this card I felt the bear's tooth growing warm against my skin." She paused and looked at Hannah very closely. "Shall I go on?"

Hannah was overcome by a rush of feelings she could not immediately sort out: unease and curiosity were foremost among them, but just beneath the surface there was a flickering of anger she could not explain.

"I'm listening."

"Very well. As soon as I arrived in Canada—as soon as Luke stopped his ranting long enough to answer a question—I asked for news of you, as I'd had no word or letter for more than a year. Luke told me what he knew, and that you were on the road home, and why.

"Well, of course I wanted to leave Montreal and come here straightaway but your brother would not hear of it. Every day there was news of another skirmish on the border, and he would not risk my neck, nor his own. But I could not stop thinking about you walking so far to get home to Paradise, and so every morning I laid out three cards thinking of you."

She paused. "Twice in a row *Fuerza* showed herself to me, but always in reverse, you see, like this. Now the lion has gained the advantage over the woman. On the third morning when I sat down I was almost afraid to turn the cards."

"If you are going to tell me that the woman was there again, I will have to ask you if you bothered to shuffle the cards." Hannah said this with a gentle smile, but Jennet was not to be distracted. She shook her head very firmly.

"I shuffled the cards," she said. "And I wish I could say *Fuerza* had shown herself again, but it was something very different. It's called the tower. Hannah, you may believe what you like, but when I saw the tower my heart leapt in my breast and I could draw no breath. It's a fearsome card, and it had never before showed itself to me since I began with this deck of my own. So I went straight to your brother and said that I must come here to see you, should I have to walk the whole way alone, and barefoot."

"I take it he gave in?"

"Not at first," Jennet said. "We argued for a long while. Then Granny Iona spoke up for me." Jennet's smile was so quick and overwhelming that Hannah found herself smiling in response.

"And I ask you, what mortal man can stand up to a runaway nun? Others may stand aside when the mighty Luke Bonner strides down the lane with his men trotting along behind, but not his granny Iona. To all his arguments she only flicked her fingers. I'll tell you this,

Hannah. It may be more than fifty years ago that Iona wore the veil, but she still has much of the nun about her when she's in a temper.

"And so Luke gave in, bit by bit, and we came to an agreement." She cleared her throat, and color rose on her cheeks as she let out an awkward little laugh. Her hands closed over the deck of cards in her lap thoughtfully.

Jennet had eyes the same green as Daniel's, rich and startling as new maple leaves, but the expression in them just now was solemn. Hannah was taken with the urge to stop her, but when she opened her mouth no sound came out.

"He believes—as you may believe, cousin—that the tarot cards are naught but bits of paper that tell me what I want to hear. I wanted to come to Paradise and so they told me I must. In the end we made a wager, Luke and I, witnessed by Granny Iona and Simon Ballentyne."

"Luke wants you to go home to Scotland," Hannah said.

"Aye. Should my worries prove unfounded, I promised to go home to Carryck without further argument and not to come back until the war is done."

"And if you are right? What must he give you?" Hannah leaned forward a little. "Will you have him marry you?"

Jennet flushed such a deep color that it looked as if she had been struck by a sudden fever. "Do you think I'd have him like that, on a wager?"

"I think you love him now as you loved him when he left Carryck," Hannah said. "I think you mean to have him."

Jennet did not seem to take offense, though a fine tremor fluttered in the muscles of her cheek.

"It's true that your brother will not admit he loves me, yet—"

"Yet," echoed Hannah with a smile.

"—but the day will come. Not even Luke Bonner can run from the truth forever, and after so many years I can wait a wee longer," Jennet said firmly. "I am his fate and he is mine, just as you and Strikes-the-Sky were fated for one another." She touched a finger to the hollow of her throat in a distracted way.

"It's all right," Hannah said. "I like to hear his name spoken."

"Oh, I'm glad," Jennet breathed. "For I'd like to hear your stories, and I will tell ye mine."

"First you must tell me what Luke wagered."

Jennet shrugged. "Just this: should I have the right of it, he will speak to me no more of going home to Carryck without him."

There was a longer silence.

"Say what's on your mind, cousin," Jennet said with a faint smile. "We must have honesty between us, you and I."

"All right, then. What if I tell you that I am well and that I am recovering from my losses. Will you really go home without an argument?"

Jennet's gaze was severe and unwavering. "I will say it again: you will have honesty from me in all things, and I ask you for the same. If you do not need me here you have only to say so. I will set off for home tomorrow."

"Oh, I need you here," Hannah said. Her throat was suddenly swollen with unshed tears. "I didn't know I needed you until I saw you, but I do."

Jennet's smile was bright and genuine and so welcome that Hannah had to pinch the web of flesh between thumb and finger to keep herself from weeping.

"You want me to stay?"

"Yes." She nodded. "I would like you to stay. But have you thought that Luke will be going back to Montreal without you?"

"Aye, he'll go," Jennet said. "And then he'll come back again, because he must. When he comes back to me of his own accord the time will be right."

"I can see that you believe that with your whole heart," Hannah said. "But has he spoken to you—"

"Of love?" Jennet's throat worked. "Once, long ago. The day he left Carryck to go home to Canada, just a week before I was to wed Ewan Huntar. He said, 'He's the husband your father wanted for you' and I—" She paused. "I called him a coward, and other things I dinnae like to remember, and all the while he stood there as uncaring as a stone in the rain. But then he kissed me."

"Not a brotherly kiss, then."

Jennet drew in a shuddering breath. "He kissed me as a man kisses a woman he loves."

"And still he left."

"Aye," Jennet said, rubbing her cheek with the back of her hand. "He left. The last thing he said to me was, 'I can't stay and you can't go, and what cannot be changed must be borne.'"

"So," Hannah said.

"So I married Ewan as my father wished and my mother insisted and I lived ten years with him and then he died, and I came to find Luke. And he was glad to see me, he couldna hide it for all he tried.

Now." Jennet jumped up and went back to the window. "It's time we went down to the village and joined the party. There's a great kettle of something."

"Beans and squash most probably," Hannah said.

"And there's Lily too, the poor wee thing. I've not had the chance to talk with her, but I think she has a secret or two to share. Perhaps we can make her smile again."

"Ask her to show you the meetinghouse," Hannah suggested, getting up from the cot. "And you'll have your answer, and her smile."

Elizabeth walked down to the village with Jennet, who was so full of questions and observations and plans that in a matter of minutes she found herself laughing. Jennet must know the names of the birds and trees, the smell of every flower; she asked about Hidden Wolf and then wondered out loud how long she would have to wait before she saw the wolves who gave the mountain its name. When they were close enough to the village to hear the bagattaway game her pace picked up, along with her questions.

While Elizabeth explained the game she watched Jennet's face: round of cheek and flushed with excitement under the wild tousled curls bleached almost white in the summer sun. She had been a lively child, quick of wit, and she had grown into a vibrant and curious woman. The question was not why she had left her home in Scotland, but how she had waited so long.

From the pasture where the game was under way a young male voice rose up in a wild yipping cry.

"Gabriel," said Elizabeth.

"You remind me of my mother when you talk about your sons," Jennet said. "Pride and fear always at war with each other. My mother always claims that boys are far easier to raise than girls, but she must be wrong about that."

"How do you come to that conclusion?"

Jennet shifted the basket she was carrying to her other arm. "Mothers and daughters must struggle, but it's out of understanding, in the end. A mother remembers what it's like to be a young woman, but a boy and the man he grows into—why, he must always be a mystery. And what we cannot understand we must fear."

Elizabeth smiled at her. "You may not have any children yet, Jennet, but you have observed a great deal."

"Och aye, my eyesight is keen," she agreed. "But no doubt I'll make the same mistakes my mother did and her mother before her. Seeing the truth of a thing is a far cry from making it your own."

Elizabeth was so taken aback that it took her a moment to gather her thoughts. Before she could even begin to reply, the sound of another rider coming into the village stopped her.

"More company," said Jennet. "And coming fast."

"The post rider," said Nathaniel, coming up behind them.

"You look as though you might be expecting bad news," Jennet said, looking between them.

"Any news of the war is bad news," Elizabeth said, picking up her pace.

Lily said, "And news of war is all he brings, these days."

She had been so silent for most of the walk that Jennet had almost forgotten that Lily was keeping pace behind them, and listening.

"Shall we go look at the lake then, instead?" She put her arm through Lily's and pulled her close, but her cousin only looked at her as if she made as much sense as a blue jay chattering.

"Of course we must go listen. Better to know than not to know."

"Are you sure of that?" Jennet asked, but Lily was already gone, the hem of her skirts kicking up in her rush toward more bad news.

The bagattaway game was abandoned; women left the cooking and wiped hands on aprons, and even the children put aside their games to gather around the post rider, their sun-browned faces furrowed with concentration. Missy Parker, a widow woman whose only daughter was married to the post rider and lived in Johnstown, pushed ahead importantly.

A hundred questions presented themselves to Jennet, but they must all be put aside; she could no more interrupt the post rider than a preacher speaking from the pulpit.

He was a middle-aged man with the great rosy-red nose of a dedicated drinker, beard stubble that reached nearly to his eyes, and a greasy old tricorne pulled down over the bushels of dark hair sprouting from his ears. But his reddened eyes were alight with excitement and the newspaper he held in his fist shook.

It was an expression Jennet had seen before, and not so long ago: when she passed through the port at Halifax it had been crowded with the British sailors celebrating their many victories over the

American navy. She had almost forgot about the war in the last week, mostly, she realized, because she had seen no evidence of it: Luke had led the way from Montreal to Paradise on back trails. She had seen more than one moose—a creature so outrageously odd that she would not bother to write home about it, for no one would believe her—mountain lions, hundreds of deer, and every other kind of animal the endless forests had to offer, but nothing of soldiers.

But here was the war, again, and in full cry. The post rider seemed to have memorized the newspaper report because he never looked at it while his voice boomed out over the crowd with the news: the *Constitution,* the gem of the struggling U.S. Navy, had captured the *Guerrière* and brought it into Boston Harbor. It was a full and resounding defeat of the British, a tremendous victory after months of nothing but one embarrassing defeat after another.

Questions were called out rapid fire: cannons and rounds fired; men injured or lost or taken prisoner; the prize money claimed.

"Jonas Littlejohn!" called out one of the younger men. "Tell us, man, is the *Constitution* still in Boston Harbor, or must we go to New-York to enlist?"

The post rider seemed to be waiting for just this question. He took a long draft from the tankard of ale that his mother-in-law passed up to him and withdrew a sheet of parchment from his coat with a flourish. Then he stood up in his stirrups and swiveled his great head to meet the gaze of each man present.

"Now's the time, boys," he began slowly. He shook the paper like a tambourine. "Now's the time for honor and glory, if you're men enough. If you're brave enough. It's time to try your fortune in service to God and country—high time, indeed, for everything that swims the seas must be a prize."

He was coming into his full voice, high and tremulous and still so compelling that Jennet could not look away.

"The British wolves are at the door again, boys, ready to bleed us dry if we don't put a stop to their thieving ways. Surely every man with an ounce of spirit must be ashamed to look away from such a challenge. Your country needs you. The navy needs you. And you—" He pointed suddenly. "You need the navy! Will you spend your life scraping hides for pennies? Why should you, when honor and fortune call? The navy will pay you, feed you, arm you, train you, and give you the opportunity to serve your country and relieve the English bastards of their goods and coin, all at once. I tell you, boys, it's the navy you're wanting. A company of men like yourselves, strangers to fear, American men. The lobsterbacks dare shake their fists at us again, the bloody sons of whores. We beat them once, we'll do it again, and this time by God they'll know they're beat for good."

He had worked himself up to such a foaming rant that Jennet, who had absorbed hatred of the English along with her mother's milk, must admire him at least a little for his fervor.

She caught Luke's eye, and in that moment all the trouble between them was simply gone. His thoughts were as plain to her as the color of his eyes: Luke would speak up now, because for all his silent ways, he could not keep the truth to himself when so much was at stake. She blinked her encouragement at him, and one corner of his mouth jerked up, as much acknowledgment as he could bring himself to give her.

"Littlejohn!"

The rider wiped his mouth with his sleeve and turned his great head toward Luke.

"Tell me this, how many of those navy ships in New-York Harbor are seaworthy?"

The crowd's happy murmuring died away as they took in this question; some of the young men—Daniel among them—looked irritated, but most turned back to Littlejohn with real concern.

"I don't recognize you, sir. Are you passing through?"

"I'm here visiting my family. Luke Bonner."

"You remember," called out Missy Parker. "The one that lives in Montreal."

"Aye, I remember, mother!" Littlejohn grunted in surprise and sought out Nathaniel with his eyes. "Your eldest boy? The Canadian?"

"Living in Canada don't make my brother a Canadian!" Daniel pushed forward.

Elizabeth was standing just in front of Jennet with her hands on Gabriel's shoulders; her fingers tensed so that Gabriel squirmed and sent her an injured look.

"My father doesn't speak for me." Luke barely raised his voice and he had the crowd's attention. "Nor does my brother, although he means well. Living in Canada doesn't make me a Canadian, but being born there does, I reckon."

Daniel's gaze—confusion and exasperation in equal measure—fixed on his brother, but he didn't interrupt.

"But it doesn't make me a British sympathizer either," Luke finished. "I'll take no sides in this war."

"I know what that means," shouted Littlejohn, shifting in the saddle. "You'll make your fortune off the backs of honest men who do the fighting for you."

"Jonas Littlejohn!" Nathaniel Bonner barely raised his voice but it stopped Daniel, who had begun to move toward the post rider.

Nathaniel stood beside his wife and youngest son with a fist curled casually around the upright barrel of his rifle. He looked like a man with no concerns in the world, Jennet thought, except for the fact that the muscle in his jaw had tensed into knots as big as a man's knuckles. He was a son of Carryck, after all, and his anger showed itself in a bristling silence that must make any man break into a sweat, just as the post rider had done.

Jonas Littlejohn opened his mouth and shut it again, wiped his face with a filthy sleeve, and never took his eyes off Nathaniel Bonner, as a rabbit never looks away from the wolf.

In an easy tone Nathaniel said, "If you're man enough to get down from that horse and repeat yourself, come on ahead. Otherwise I guess you'll want to be headed on out of here before I lose my temper and beat the stupid out of you."

After a long moment Littlejohn cleared his throat roughly.

"The post," he said, tossing a bundle tied with twine to a tall man at the back of the crowd. "See you in a fortnight."

"Littlejohn!" Nathaniel called, and the man stiffened.

"If any rumors about Canadians in Paradise start making the rounds, I'll know who to come looking for."

Jonas Littlejohn touched the brim of his tricorne and trotted off without a word.

When the cook fires had died down and the last of the food had been carried away, the fiddlers—one black man and a boy who might have been his son—climbed up on crates, and the music began. The men made a circle of light to dance by under the rising moon: a ring of torches on long pickets hammered into the ground, sending sparks up into the sky like errant stars.

The women moved through the dark calling to children who must be seen home to their beds, and for a moment Jennet thought how good it would be to be one of the little ones, bellies full of good food, tucked in next to wiggling brothers and sisters to fall asleep by the sound of fiddle music and laughter.

But it was her first night in Paradise and Jennet would not waste it on sleep. She watched as people who toiled so hard by day put aside their weariness. Elizabeth had met Jennet's surprise with a laugh.

"You mustn't confuse Yorkers with the pious Yankees of Massachusetts," she explained. "The people of Paradise will jump at any excuse for a party."

Now Jennet sat, weary but contented, on a long trestle in a row of other young women, with Lily on one side and Hannah on the other, all of them twitching with the fiddle music. The rhythm was lively and the girls were eager, but Jennet could see that most of them must be content to listen or dance with each other, because there would be little dancing tonight, and the reason was the post rider's news.

On the other side of the dancing circle most of the men and boys had gathered with the Bonner men at their center. Some of them cradled muskets like a sleeping child in folded arms, while others leaned on rifles that pointed sleek barrels up to the sky. Thus far Jennet had never seen a man without a weapon in his hands or on his person, a fact that said more about this place than any stories she had been told.

Jennet could not hear them but she did not need to; they had already read the newspaper into tatters, and the debate on whether or not to join the fighting was hot.

Not that Luke was saying very much. Even here with his family around him he did more listening than talking, his head canted at an angle that meant he was giving his brother Daniel all his attention.

"At least Simon Ballentyne isn't too busy talking to dance," Lily said, startling Jennet out of her thoughts.

Simon Ballentyne was indeed dancing, his plain, good-natured face flush with ale and music and the young woman he held by the hands—one of the Hench girls, according to Hannah. Jennet would have known Simon for a Ballentyne no matter where she came across him in the world: he had his father's dark eyes, black hair that grew as thick as a pelt on his head and chest, and the stolid Ballentyne temperament. He was only one of the men who had followed Luke to Canada to make his fortune, and he had done well for himself.

As Simon circled past them in the course of the dance his gaze met Jennet's and then Lily's. The expression that passed over his face like a flash of lightning was not lost on either of them.

Lily asked, "Is Simon Ballentyne angry at you, cousin?"

"Ooch, ne." Jennet wrapped her arms around herself. "The

Ballentyne men may be fierce of temper and stubborn as mules when it comes to business, but every last one of them is as meek as a lamb with the lasses. It wasn't me he was googling at, cousin, but you."

At that Lily laughed out loud. "You must be mistaken."

Jennet studied the younger woman's face to see if she really had no understanding of the looks that Simon Ballentyne was sending her way.

"Simon's had an eye on you since he came to Paradise last year with your brother," Jennet said. "And why should he not? A prettier lass would be hard to find, Lily, or a livelier one."

Lily flushed, in anger and something else, something that bordered on pleasure. "You must be imagining it."

"I am not. Luke told me. Have you taken no note, then?"

Lily spread her hands out over her skirt and then made fists of them. "No, I hadn't noticed. And he hasn't said anything, which is just as well."

"Then you've no interest in poor Simon." Jennet did her best to strike a light and teasing tone, but Lily did not hear that, or could not.

She said, "My only interest is going to Manhattan. But my parents keep reminding me that the city was held by the British for most of the last war. As if that mattered to me."

Jennet had little to say to this; after all, she herself had traveled much farther in time of war and it would be the worst kind of hypocrisy to preach caution to her cousin.

"You want to study painting, your sister tells me."

Lily cast her a relieved glance, as if she had expected Jennet to lecture her on the impossibility of her situation. "My uncle Spencer has already arranged for me to study with a Mr. Clarke—a landscape painter—and also with Monsieur Petit who is a master of color. When I have learned enough I will go to Europe with my aunt and uncle, to study the great artists." She stopped herself and composed her face. "Now it is your turn to tell me to stop dreaming."

At that Jennet laughed out loud. "You don't know me very well, cousin, if you think you'll hear such a thing from me."

Lily pressed her mouth together and her brow drew down so that for one moment Jennet was amazed at how much she looked like Elizabeth.

"They think I'm a child crying for the moon who will be distracted with a bit of maple sugar." Lily's gaze followed Simon as he moved through the dance. "But they are wrong. I won't be distracted."

"Of course you must study, as talented as you are," Jennet said.

"But you do realize that there are teachers in places other than New-York City? There might even be someone suitable in Johnstown, and that is not so far away."

Lily let out a sharp laugh. "By my mother's reckoning it is as far as the moon."

Across the dancing circle a young woman had marched up to the men gathered around the Bonners and begun to lecture them with her hands on her hips. They could not hear what she was saying over the fiddles, but from the embarrassed grins of the men it had something to do with their very bad manners.

"I see there's more than one lass in Paradise who kens what she wants," said Jennet.

"That's Lydia Ratz," Lily explained. "She's fond of dancing. And other things. Your Simon Ballentyne should dance with Lydia, she'll . . . distract him."

All the other single women had turned their attention in the same direction. Now that they had the opportunity they studied Luke cautiously, in the way of those who are taught to guard their good names and virtue if not their hearts. At Carryck, in Montreal, here in Paradise, and everywhere in between Jennet had seen it again and again. Young and old they fixed on Luke in a crowd, as they would fix on Daniel, as they had once fixed on Nathaniel. Granny Iona had told her the stories.

Two young girls no more than ten came to stand just at the edge of the dancing. One was dark of complexion and hair, while the other was freckled and had long plaits that flashed like polished copper in the firelight.

"The little one is Callie Wilde," Lily said, following Jennet's gaze. "The redheaded girl is Martha Kuick." She put her mouth directly to Jennet's ear. "I expect Hannah must have written to you about the Kuicks."

Jennet knew just enough of the girl's story to make her want to hear the rest, but before she could think how to ask, Elizabeth came to fetch her away to meet still more people: Nicholas Wilde, who owned apple orchards, and with him his housekeeper, a tiny woman as wizened and dark as a dried blackberry, and his hired man, who was, Jennet was told, though her eyes said such a thing was hardly possible, the housekeeper's son. He was as large as she was small, with a quick smile and even white teeth and hands like great leather mitts, in which he held his hat when he bowed his head and said a few words of greeting.

The housekeeper's name was Cookie and her son's, Levi, and they had taken the last name Fiddler upon gaining their manumission papers.

Cookie reminded Jennet of old MacQuiddy, who had run Carryckcastle for fifty years, and thinking of MacQuiddy put Jennet in mind of all the messages she had yet to deliver from Carryck. She went back to find Hannah, only to discover that her cousins were gone.

In their place sat Gabriel, who yawned widely enough to show her his tonsils, and passed on a message: Hannah had been called away to see Uncle Doctor Todd (a strange formulation, Jennet noted, but said nothing), and Lily had disappeared in the direction of home.

"Will you ride home with me and Mama to Lake in the Clouds?" he asked between yawns. "We'll show you the firefly meadow."

Jennet cast a glance back at the men, and saw that Luke was watching her. She felt his gaze at the base of her spine, as sharp and probing as a knife.

You'll come to me, this time.

It was a sentence she had repeated to herself every day since the *Isis* weighed anchor in Canada. The moment she saw Luke on the dock two things came to her clearly: she had been right to make the journey, and she must let him find his own way to her. She saw the truth of this every time she laid out the tarot cards, and with it came a calm understanding. He would come, in time. She knew it in her bones.

Elizabeth was walking toward them, an empty basket over her arm. Gabriel hopped down from the table. "Are you coming?"

"Aye," Jennet said. "I am."

Hannah knew the Todd house as well as her own, even in the dark. For a moment she stood in the kitchen taking in the familiar smells of tallow and toasting cornmeal, cinnamon and yeast and drying herbs, and when her eyesight had adjusted she made her way into the hall. Richard Todd stood in the open door of his study backlit by candlelight, waiting for her.

For a long moment she could find nothing to say. The doctor had always been a big man, broad and hard muscled, but quick of foot and graceful in his movements. He had lived among her mother's people, who gave him the name Cat-Eater for his ability to strike silently and for the fact that he shied at nothing, would do almost anything to reach a goal he had set for himself.

The man standing in front of her had lost as much as fifty pounds; the whites of his eyes were the color of poorly tanned doeskin.

"Hannah Bonner," he said, and she was relieved to hear that his voice had not withered away with the rest of him. "I hear that your husband ran off and left you and never came back. You did right to come home."

Then he turned and went back into the study, moving as if every step rattled the marrow in his bones.

Hannah took a deep breath and followed him.

Ethan was sitting at the desk, with a sheaf of papers before him and a quill in his hand: another boy turned into a man while she was gone, but something was different about Ethan that had nothing to do with the passing years. Another story to hear, more loss or loneliness or frustration.

Suddenly Hannah was overcome with weariness; she would have liked to simply walk away, but she could not, not when she saw the way Richard held himself. Pain had a posture of its own; it sat in the spine and across the slope of the shoulders and bowed bone.

"I wondered if you would come without being summoned," he said. "But I see the party was too much for you to resist."

She had not seen him in ten years, but he had lost none of his sharp tongue.

"Ethan." Hannah nodded in his direction and ignored Richard completely. "It is very good to see you."

"What, no word of greeting for your old teacher?" Richard had turned his back to her to pour himself a glass of port. "I am cut to the quick."

Hannah came forward into the light. "Curiosity told me you had not improved in the niceties. She also said that you are ill."

He glanced at her over his shoulder. "I expect you want to talk about your dead son and missing husband as much as I want to talk about my health."

"The dead cannot be helped," Hannah said, hearing the irritation in her own voice but not trying to hide it. "The sick are another matter."

From the desk Ethan said, "He wants you to diagnose him from twenty paces, cousin. It's a test he puts to every doctor he comes across."

"And how do his colleagues meet that challenge?"

"Poorly, for the most part," Richard Todd said, turning to face her. He held up his glass in a toast. "But then they were not trained by me. What do you see, my girl?"

"It is your liver," Hannah said in as neutral a tone as she could manage. "I expect there's at least one palpable tumor, most probably more, in your abdomen and chest as well. You're taking laudanum for the pain, I can smell it. You need quite a lot of it."

He grunted in satisfaction. "You see how well I trained her, Ethan? She not only sees in the dark, she sees through skin and bone. Not to say anything of that sense of smell." He raised a glass in her direction.

From the darkened hallway came the sound of Curiosity's sharp laugh, the one she reserved for people who might deserve some sympathy but who would do best without it. "You didn't train her all by yourself, Richard, and you sure as sugar cain't take any credit for her nose."

He squinted in Curiosity's direction and waved his free hand dismissively. "After I'm dead you can take all the credit, Curiosity, and there will be nobody left to correct you. Well done, Doctor Bonner. Well done indeed."

Hannah was surprised at the satisfaction his approval brought to her, the thrill of the words from a man who had not often thought to praise.

She said, "Shall we talk about treatment? My first advice would be to empty that bottle into the pig trough."

"Advice he has heard before," Ethan said dryly. The expression in his eyes, something between resignation and sorrow, told Hannah more than anything that had been said thus far.

"Advice I will continue to ignore." The doctor's voice lifted and wavered just short of breaking. He fell into a chair so heavily that the glass rattled in the windowpanes.

When he spoke again he had regained control of his voice. "You came just in time. Tomorrow you'll go on rounds with me, and then I wash my hands of this godforsaken place, once and for all."

"And where will you go?" Hannah asked. "Back to Johnstown? You prefer the medical treatment you get there?"

"The only journey I have left to make is to my grave," Richard Todd said, taking a last swallow from the glass and wiping his mouth on his cuff. "Hopefully before the last of the laudanum runs out."

Chapter 3

In the rising heat of a new day, Nathaniel Bonner sat on the edge of his bed and thought of waking his wife. She would come to him happily if he reached for her, but for the rest of the day there would be shadows underneath her eyes and a slowness to her speech.

A curl of hair lifted in the breeze from the open window and swept across the curve of her cheek. There was little gray in her hair, but age had touched her in other ways. The faint lines between her brows had become a crease, and the flesh at her jaw was softer, just as all of her was a little rounder and softer and prettier.

He could wake her just to tell her all this—as he had told her many times before—because it gave him pleasure to see her blush. She would hush him and grumble and point out that it was the height of silliness for a woman of her years to make any claims on beauty. But it would please her nonetheless, and she would come to him flushed with embarrassment.

It was more than twenty years since Elizabeth had left England but many of the ideas she had been raised with still trailed along behind her like ragged tail feathers. That women did not age into beauty was one of her ideas; that children could be kept safe from the world was another. Even the losses they had suffered had not convinced her to let go of that second idea.

This particular day ahead of them would be a hard one. All of the children were home at once, which pleased him more than he knew how to put into words. But each of them carried their own bundle of problems, some he had never imagined.

Luke, for one. Luke and Jennet. Elizabeth had pulled that idea out of thin air and put it down in front of him, trouble wrapped up in a pretty ribbon. Nathaniel had lived too long among sharp-eyed women to discredit out of hand what his wife had to say, especially in matters of the heart. So he watched for himself and saw the truth, like words springing to life on the page when a candle is lit in the dusk.

There was a connection between the two of them, but it had nothing to do with new love. Instead of the shy smiles and questioning glances, Luke and Jennet circled each other warily and sparked like steel on flint. It was an old love, a knotty one with deep roots, one that had survived Jennet's marriage and long years of separation, and it explained why Luke had never brought home a bride. What Nathaniel didn't understand was why his oldest son was holding back from the inevitable. Because he wanted Jennet, of that much Nathaniel was sure.

He would have to raise the subject, and soon. But maybe not today.

The bigger problem, the one that couldn't wait, was Daniel.

Elizabeth was fond of saying that if Nathaniel had his way, he would build a wall around Paradise and burn every newspaper at the gates, and she wasn't far from right. The boys were wild at the idea of a war and they couldn't be held back for much longer.

The old way, the way of all the tribes and the way Nathaniel himself had been brought up, was to send a young man off to his first battle under the wing of a father or uncle or older brother. But Elizabeth would not hear of it, and truth be told Nathaniel had trouble remembering why he had ever been eager to go to war.

It was Luke who had presented them with the first glimmer of a real solution, one they could all live with. Late last night he laid it out to Runs-from-Bears and Nathaniel: Daniel and Blue-Jay would leave here with him and head northwest. Luke knew where to find a man called Jim Booke, a Yorker born and raised, with a small band of militiamen under him, loosely attached to Benjamin Forsyth's company of riflemen. Booke and his men moved back and forth along the river, keeping track of the British on the other side, who liked to send raiding parties into New-York. If the boys were the marksmen that Luke claimed they were, Jim Booke had declared himself willing to take them on for a provisional nine-month commitment.

With any luck the war would be over by then. Luke said this last part without looking the men in the eye.

"They'll be far safer with Jim Booke and his men than they would be in that sorry excuse for a navy," he added. "There's no man who knows the river better."

"A smuggler, was he, before the war?" Nathaniel had asked, and Luke grinned at him.

"And will be after, unless they call off the embargo."

That had satisfied Nathaniel and Runs-from-Bears both, and Elizabeth as well.

"Nine months," she echoed when Nathaniel told her all this. And then: "He'll be home in the spring."

Now Nathaniel watched his wife sleep, at peace in the world of her own imagining, where she had only to speak the words to end a war and bring her son home.

He touched his forehead to hers to breathe in the scent of her and left the room without a sound.

Runs-from-Bears was already climbing up out of the lake under the falls, shaking himself so that the water flew off him in sheets. Then he waited in the sun while Nathaniel swam the length of the lake and came to join him on the broad expanse of rock where they met every morning to discuss the coming day. They had been doing this since Many-Doves took Runs-from-Bears as her husband and he came to live on Hidden Wolf. When they were both on the mountain they met here, no matter what the weather.

"We must let them go." Runs-from-Bears started the conversation in mid-thought. He spoke Mohawk, as they always did when they had important matters to discuss. "They must test themselves as we were tested at their age."

There was no blood tie between the two men but they had fought side by side as young men and brought up their families the same way. Over the years friendship had grown into partnership, one with no name but just as strong a bond as brotherhood.

"Elizabeth is reconciled," Nathaniel said. "At least she thinks she is."

Bears let out a soft sound, an acknowledgment.

Nathaniel said, "Many-Doves has given her permission?"

He shrugged a shoulder. "She knows she cannot stop them. And even she has heard of Jim Booke."

"We survived our share of battles," Nathaniel said, mostly to himself. "And they will watch each other's backs."

In the light of the new morning he studied Bears, still lean and heavily muscled and as quick as the son he was about to send off to fight yet another white man's war, this one even stupider than the last. On one thigh Runs-from-Bears bore the pucker of a healed bullet wound; a scar as wide as a man's finger and shiny pink arched across the expanse of his chest like a ribbon. There were a dozen more scars, each with its own story. Nathaniel rarely bothered with mirrors, but he knew that he looked much the same.

"I've been trying to remember what it was like at that age," Nathaniel said. "Wanting to go to join the fighting that bad."

"Like an ache in the balls," Runs-from-Bears said, and Nathaniel snorted in agreement.

Bears said, "They are waiting to hear our decision."

"They will have to wait a little longer," Nathaniel said. "There's somebody else I have to talk to first."

"Lily."

"Aye." Nathaniel ran a hand over his face.

Runs-from-Bears was looking at him with an expression that Nathaniel knew very well, one that said he had advice to offer but knew it would not be welcome.

"Go ahead, say it."

"You know she'll find a way to get what she wants," Bears said.

Nathaniel got up with a groan. "That's exactly what I'm afraid of."

Hannah woke when she heard her father leaving the cabin for his morning swim under the falls, and then she lay perfectly still, listening. Jennet slept deeply, her back turned to Hannah. Lily was watching her. Hannah felt the blue of her eyes like a cool hand.

"Little sister," she whispered across the room. "Do you hear the mockingbird calling?"

It was the question she had used to wake Lily as a child, and now it brought a smile to the beloved face, true and sweet. When Hannah closed her eyes she could call forth the picture of Lily in her first minute of life, wide-eyed and curious, bloody fists waving. Even then she had been at odds with the world. Her Mohawk girl-name had been Sparrows, for her size and quickness and the way she must argue, even with her own kind.

For the moment, though, she was at peace, this little sister who had grown into a woman while Hannah was in the west.

"Many-Doves will be looking for me," Lily said. "It's already time to go down to the cornfields."

There was a watchfulness about her as she said this, a waiting. Hannah recognized it for what it was.

"Not this morning," she said. "This morning you and I must show Jennet the mountain and the village too."

"I thought you had to go visit patients with Uncle Todd," Lily said.

"I do, but that won't take long. You can come along, both of you. And then you can show her the meetinghouse."

"What about Many-Doves?" Lily asked, hardly able to contain her smile.

"I will tell her," Hannah said. "And we'll all go to the cornfield this afternoon to help."

Jennet sat up suddenly, clutching a blanket to her breast like a child. She blinked in the morning light and then a smile transformed her face.

"I feared it was all a dream," she said, leaning over to hug Hannah. "And that I would wake with Ewan snoring next to me."

She colored even as she said it, a sudden blush that reached even her earlobes. "Och, I'm as wicked a lass as was eer born, Lily. Pay no mind to the things I say. I must say a rosary for Ewan's soul, puir wee mannie as he was."

"Did you not love your husband then?" Lily asked and she sat up and slung her arms around her knees.

Jennet's mouth puckered. "He was a good man, and harmless enough." Her Scots was already giving way to English, like sleep that could be rubbed from her eyes. "I wish I could say that I loved him. My father promised me on his deathbed that I would learn to do just that. But I never did."

"I would never marry on my father's command," Lily said firmly, though she cast an apologetic glance at her cousin.

"Who will you marry then?" Jennet asked playfully. "You've already said you won't have Simon Ballentyne."

"When she was little she intended to marry Blue-Jay." Hannah was hoping that Lily might flush a little at such teasing and take pleasure in it, but instead she went very still.

"Blue-Jay has a woman at Good Pasture." There was nothing of disappointment in Lily's face or tone. "You know her, sister. Long-Hair's youngest daughter. They are well suited."

"Are they? Why has no one told me?"

Lily shrugged. "You haven't asked a lot of questions since you came home."

"Och weel, we'll make up for that now." Jennet laughed and hugged her knees to her chin. "Does your twin have a woman at Good Pasture as well?"

Lily wrinkled her nose. "Daniel? What sane girl would want him? All he thinks about is going to war." She flung herself up out of bed, her fingers working to loosen her plait. "Enough talk of marriage. Maybe I'll sail the seas, instead. Like your old friend the Pirate."

Jennet let out a laugh. "Perhaps we should go looking for Mac Stoker. What an adventure that would be, the three of us. We could call on Giselle and take her along with us. A ship of pirate women, not to be trifled with."

Hannah threw back the blanket and got out of bed. "There's adventure enough in Paradise today." She yawned and stretched and then yanked the blankets from her little sister's bed with a grin.

Richard Todd was waiting for Hannah in his study. The draperies had been drawn against the sun and the air was thick with tobacco smoke, brandy fumes, and the sticky sweet smell of laudanum. He looked over Hannah's shoulder to Jennet and Lily and managed an elaborate but not very sincere frown.

"I see you've brought your ladies-in-waiting."

Ethan sent them an apologetic look from the desk. "He means to say good morning."

"Do I?" Richard snorted.

"Aren't you coming with us today?" Lily asked Ethan.

"No, he isn't," answered the doctor for him. "There's work enough right here for him. He prefers a quill to a lancet anyway, don't you, Ethan my dear?"

When they were outdoors Hannah said, "You are fortunate he loves you so, or he would not put up for so long with such treatment."

Richard Todd sent her a sidelong glance. In the sunlight the yellowish cast to his skin and eyes was more pronounced, the pain lines around his mouth deeply carved. "Put up with me?" He stopped to look around himself at the farmstead and pastures and the forests that he called his own. "When I'm dead he'll have a fortune in land and every penny I've put aside. Not that he wants it. He'll hand it over to you as soon as I'm gone and close himself up with his books." He cleared his throat noisily. "He has nothing to complain about."

Hannah gave up the argument for the moment, long enough to stop and talk with Curiosity, who pressed a napkin folded around three hot biscuits into her hand.

Curiosity said, "You going to come back and sit with me when you done with the calls today?"

Richard sent the two of them an impatient look. "If we ever get to the calls in the first place—"

But she cut him off with a hard look and a flick of her fingers. "I wasn't talking to you," she said firmly. She took Hannah's elbow and steered her away. "Come on back now, you hear me? And bring the girls with you. I got a pie in the oven."

In the end Hannah and Richard started off alone, as Lily and Jennet had disappeared back into the house. They would catch up, and Hannah had things she wanted to say to Richard out of their hearing.

He used a cane now, and leaned heavily into it with each step. When they had gone a few steps he said, "Spit it out, girl, before it chokes you."

"I didn't come back here to take over your medical practice."

"No?" He raised a brow at her. "Why did you come home then?"

Hannah ignored the question. "Curiosity will manage very well, when you decide to step aside."

Richard glared down at her. "Well, first off, missy, Curiosity isn't so young anymore either, in case you haven't took note. Second of all, there are two patients in this village she can't do much for. They'll be your responsibility, unless you decide to run off. Again."

He had given her the choice of a number of arguments. Hannah picked the easier one. "I hope you're not talking about the Widow Kuick," she said.

"I am." Richard grinned at her, all of his old combative spirit rising up so that blotches of color stained his pale cheeks.

Hannah looked away, afraid that she would not be able to keep hold of her temper if she met his eye. "Jemima isn't about to let me treat her mother-in-law, and you know it."

He laughed hoarsely. "I'll admit she won't like it much."

"The Widow will spit in my face and die," Hannah said.

"Then you'd be doing her a favor. She should be dead the last three years at least. I expect it's all that venom running through her veins that keeps her going."

"Oh, something to look forward to."

He was untouched by her tone. "Venomous though she may be, you won't hear her complain. She hasn't spoken a word since that night in the meetinghouse. When I saved you from hanging, let me remind you."

Lily and Jennet were coming along the path now, swinging a basket between them. Jennet was ten years Lily's senior but at this moment, with the summer sun bright on her head of cropped blond curls and her cheeks flushed with running, she looked no more than seventeen. Hannah took a deep breath and then another.

"All right then," she said finally. "I will offer my services." And then: "And who's the other patient you're worried about?"

Richard lost his smile. "Dolly Wilde."

It would have come as no surprise if Hannah had been thinking like the doctor she was trained to be. Since she had come home Hannah had seen Dolly only once, and at first she had not recognized her.

They had grown up together, sat next to each other in Elizabeth's classroom, picked berries together, and on the rare occasion that Dolly was free to play, they had spent that time together too. But the Dolly she had known held no resemblance to the woman who went by that name now.

Hannah tended to think that the things she had experienced during the wars to the west had robbed her of the ability to be surprised, but Dolly had proved her wrong. Hannah had crossed her path at twilight, a woman wandering through the village like a lost spirit. Her unbound hair was streaked with white and it floated around a face blank of all expression. And in her eyes Hannah saw something she had hoped never to see again: Dolly reminded her of men left to die of their wounds on a battlefield where they had fallen. The stunned, placid look of the almost-dead.

"You're thinking there's no treatment for dementia," Richard said.

Hannah might have corrected him, but Lily and Jennet were close enough to hear. They came running up, full of laughter and good spirits.

"Sister," Hannah said. "Maybe you had best take Jennet to see the meetinghouse instead of coming with us."

Lily's glance darted from Richard to Hannah and back again. "You're going to see Dolly."

"And the Widow Kuick," added Richard.

The small mouth twitched. "All right then." She touched Jennet on the arm. "We'd only be in the way. Come, there are better things to see."

On the way to the Wildes', walking through the orchards so lovingly tended, Richard told Hannah the little there was to say about Dolly's history and condition. There was nothing surprising in the story: a difficult pregnancy, a hard birth followed by prolonged melancholia and a general decline into senselessness.

"The worst is her tendency to wander away," Richard finished. "Once it took a day and a night to find her. Since then Nicholas has been locking her in her room at night."

"Not all the time. I saw her in the village at dusk, not three weeks ago."

The air was filled with the hum of wasps feasting on fallen fruit, and from somewhere on the far side of the orchard the sound of men singing.

On the day Cookie and her two grown sons had received their manumission papers they had all come to work for Nicholas. In the village folks liked to joke that Nicholas Wilde would pay Levi and Zeke any wage they asked, just as long as the three of them could sing together while they worked. *Like a heavenly chorus come down to earth,* Anna McGarrity had told her, and now Hannah heard it for herself.

The cabin was visible now, small and well kept, with shutters closed against the sun. Dolly sat in a rocker on the porch, her hands folded in her lap and her daughter at her feet. The girl's eyes, sharp and bright, watched them as they came closer. She took after her mother, dark-haired and round of face, but instead of having her mother's sweet temperament she seemed to bristle.

"There's a child who never learned to smile," said Richard while they were still out of earshot.

It surprised Hannah to hear him say such a thing. Richard looked at the human body as he would at a mechanical clock that needed repair. In her experience he put little importance in a patient's state of mind.

She said, "Smiles won't get her through the world she was born into."

Richard grunted his agreement.

•   •   •

The little chamber that was Dolly's alone was crowded with people: Cookie, who stood nearby with her arms crossed at her waist; Callie, who sat next to her mother and held her hand; Nicholas, his hat crumpled in his hands and his work clothes wet with sweat. All of them were watching Hannah as if she had some magic that would fix the woman who sat silently on the bed, staring at a pebble she held in her hand.

Richard stood back and said nothing while Hannah examined Dolly. She seemed content to be touched, smiling vaguely when Hannah said her name or asked her to turn, like a friendly stranger from another land, without the language or any understanding of the customs of the place where she found herself.

Physically Hannah could find nothing seriously wrong with Dolly: she was thin, and her muscle tone was poor, but her heart was strong and steady and her lungs and eyes were clear. While Hannah gently probed her liver and spleen and abdomen Dolly turned her face away.

Cookie was watching closely, and now she spoke up.

"She ain't in any pain, if that's what you looking for."

Hannah turned to her. "How do you know?"

Callie was stroking her mother's hand. "She cries when something hurts."

Very evenly Hannah said, "Does she ever try to harm herself?"

Nicholas cleared his throat and studied his shoes before he raised his head to meet her gaze. "I don't think she means to cause herself harm . . ." His voice trailed off.

"She likes to swallow pebbles," Callie said. "She knows she's not supposed to, but she still does. And sometimes she eats dirt, if we don't watch her."

Hannah glanced up in surprise and caught Nicholas's expression: worry and sorrow, desperation and disgust, all fighting for the upper hand. And he was ashamed and angry, at his wife and at himself. That he could not cure her; that she had retreated away from him and the world to a point out of reach but not quite gone.

There was little to offer him in the way of hope or relief, and so Hannah turned back to the patient. She touched her on the cheek and tipped her head up to look directly in her eyes.

"Dolly," she said firmly. "You have a beautiful daughter. Can you tell me her name?"

Dolly blinked at her, opened her mouth and closed it again. A flicker of consciousness chased across her face and was extinguished as quickly as it had come.

"Callie," Hannah said. "Does your mother ever seem to wake up and take note of you when you are sitting with her?"

The girl glanced at Cookie and then at her father, as if there were more than one answer to this question and she was afraid of choosing the wrong one.

"No," she whispered finally. "Never."

"She could live to be eighty just as she is," Hannah said much later, when she and Richard were alone again.

"Or she'll choke to death on a stone tomorrow. And it would be a blessing."

Richard's complexion was very bad, and in spite of the fact that they were walking slowly and in the cool shade of the forest his face was wet with perspiration. He stopped to pass his handkerchief over his brow, and then he lowered himself to sit on the stump of an old oak that shifted and groaned beneath him. His breathing was labored as he took out a small flask of dark glass from his coat pocket and uncorked it. The smell was unmistakable.

Hannah watched his throat work as he swallowed enough laudanum to kill a smaller man. How long had he been dosing himself like this, to have built up such a need? It was a question she did not bother to ask, because he would take pleasure in refusing to answer. His mind was still with his patient, and he would discuss nothing else.

"I've never heard of this compulsion to eat rocks and dirt before," he wheezed. "Have you ever seen the like?"

She shook her head and leaned against a tree. "I have seen many things, but nothing like this."

He squinted up at her, and for the first time since Hannah had come home, she saw the worst of his old self: the acid mockery that he spat up now and then like an excess of bile he must share with whoever stood next to him. "What have you seen, little Hannah Bonner? Men's battle wounds, women's sorrows."

It had been so long since Hannah let herself feel anger, true anger, that she did not recognize it at first: the rush of blood to her face and hands, the way the nerves in her fingertips tingled. A force like water falling, unstoppable. The words leapt from her just like that.

"You haven't asked me about my uncle," she said sharply. "Why haven't you?"

Richard's gaze flickered just enough to show his surprise and he shrugged. "I heard through Nathaniel that Otter—"

"Strong-Words," Hannah corrected him sharply. "Otter was his boy-name."

He inclined his head. "That Strong-Words fell at the battle at Tippecanoe. If you were expecting my condolences for a man who took every opportunity to shoot at me—"

All the old history between Richard Todd and Hannah's family rose up like a battalion of ghosts as distinct and undeniable as the moving shadows cast by the trees. For a moment there was silence, and then Richard found the good grace to look away and clear his throat.

"Over the years I've come to regret the part I played in what happened at Barktown. I would have told Strong-Words so had I ever had the chance."

"I'm sure that would have meant a great deal to him," Hannah said, her tone as bitter as the words themselves.

Richard sighed and ran a hand over the bristle on his chin. "I'm not asking your forgiveness, girl, but I'll give you my condolences. Your uncle was a brave man from what I've heard, and he died honorably."

"Honorably," Hannah echoed, the word like gall on her tongue. "He died in a battle that was lost before it even began. They brought me his body in a pile with ten others, two of them his sons. Do not presume to speak to me of women's sorrow, Richard Todd. Do not dare."

For a long moment there was no sound but the birds: the chittering of the wrens, crows bickering, a solitary blue jay at odds with the world. Hannah's own heartbeat seemed as loud in her ears. Finally Richard got up with a sigh and started off again in the direction of the village.

Over his shoulder he said, "Come along then, woman. I don't have all day to listen to your tales of woe."

It was then that Hannah saw that he had laid a trap, one that she had walked into without hesitation. No amount of questioning could have made her talk about the last few years, but he had turned her anger into a tool for his own use and got what he wanted anyway. He had opened the door, and now she would find it hard to close.

For a moment Hannah watched Richard Todd walk away and she was filled with reluctant admiration. She took note of his thinning frame, the way he stooped in pain, the set of his shoulders. That his death was not far off Hannah could not deny, but she knew something else just as unsettling: he would try to get her stories to take with him; he would work to dig them out of her one by one, using whatever tools necessary.

From the outside, Jennet could see nothing particularly interesting about the abandoned meetinghouse. A wood-frame building in a village of buildings built of square-hewed logs, all in the middle of a remarkable world crowded with trees. It sagged at the door and windows but the floor was solid underfoot and the door hinges had been recently oiled. When Lily opened the shutters, the emptied room filled with light.

"Holy Mary," Jennet whispered reverently. "Lily, what have you done?"

She turned in a circle, trying to take it all in at once. Everywhere she looked, every inch of wall space was covered. Paper had been tacked up from floor to ceiling, and every paper was filled with Lily's work, drawing after drawing in lead or charcoal or ink. Her whole world was here: everyday items from buckets and shoes to chairs and doors, studies of trees and leaves and animals. A whole sea of human figures rolled across one wall, waves of hands and feet, eyes and noses and ears, floating aimlessly.

But it was the portraits that drew Jennet to them. Hundreds of portraits: Daniel running, holding a chicken under his arm, firing a musket, scowling, sleeping, laughing. Up the wall and down again Jennet could follow him through the years. They were all here, all the Bonners, and most of the villagers, a history drawn in quick and knowing strokes. Sometimes the drawing could not be contained by the paper and seeped out over the rough whitewashed walls: a forest in chalk, full of life and wind.

She stopped in front of a study of Luke, his hair tousled and his eyes half-cast, and she knew without a doubt that Lily had caught him as he got out of his bed, before he had had anything to eat. She reached out a finger to touch his chin, sure that she must feel the stubble there, and stopped herself. Instead she wrapped her arms around herself and turned.

In the very middle of the empty building was a single table with a chair beside it and a stool tucked beneath it. It was piled high with books and stacks of paper, cracked pottery cups filled with bits of charcoal, ink pots and quills, a small pile of stones, an empty bird's nest, a piece of broken glass. Jennet fell into the chair and spread out her arms.

"Cousin," she said softly. "This work of yours will outlive us all."

Lily opened her mouth as if to thank her and then shut it again, so sharply that Jennet heard the click of her teeth. When she had quieted herself she said, "Thank you, Jennet. That is the best compliment anyone has ever paid me."

"And she had to come all the way from Scotland for you to hear it."

Nathaniel Bonner was standing at the open door, his large frame filling the square of light. "I've had that thought many times, but I've never said it. For that I apologize, daughter."

Lily's expression shifted from surprise to uneasiness to uneasy pleasure. "Da, what are you doing here?"

"It's too long since I came to visit."

There was a small and tender silence. Jennet felt the warmth of it like the sunlight on her face.

Finally Lily said, "There's something wrong, isn't there."

Nathaniel ducked his head to clear the low doorway and came into the middle of the empty meetinghouse. He hesitated, lifted his face into the light and then lowered it again to look at his daughter. This man called himself Bonner, but Jennet could not look at him without seeing Carryck in every bone. Just at this moment he reminded her so strongly of her own father that her eyes filled with warm tears.

In Nathaniel's expression she saw regret for pain about to be inflicted, and she knew what he had come to say.

Lily knew too. She had backed up until she was half sitting on the worktable, as if she must have this support to keep herself upright. Very calmly she said, "You're letting him go, aren't you? You're letting Daniel go to war."

"At least you're consistent," said Richard Todd, letting himself down into the straight chair beside the Widow Kuick's sickbed. "You'll neither pay me for my time nor will you follow my prescriptions."

Richard's words hung in the air along with the hissing hitch and sigh of the old woman's breathing. The chamber was hardly big enough for the narrow bed and a chair; the shutters on the single window held in the early morning heat and the stench of old flesh gone soft, human waste, and sweat. Hannah knew that if she were to raise the woman on the bed she would find open sores the size of eggs on her back and buttocks and legs.

In the doorway stood Jemima Southern Kuick. She looked no different than she had when Hannah last saw her ten years ago. She was a sturdy woman, with plain, strong features and a mouth as curved and sharp as a sickle, and yet there was something different. She was angry; Hannah had never known Jemima to be anything but angry, but now weariness had the upper hand, or maybe—and this idea unsettled Hannah—it was not so much weariness as a resignation so complete that it went beyond despair.

Her daughter stood next to her and slightly behind, a slender girl who kept her eyes on the ground but even so hummed with curiosity.

Jemima said, "There's work in the kitchen, Martha." Her tone was unmarked by affection or even concern; all her attention was on Hannah.

Martha Kuick's gaze flickered over the bed. The Widow—the woman she believed to be her grandmother—lay as peaceful and unmoving as a bundle of kindling loosely bound. The girl looked as if she meant to say something to the doctor, to ask a question or make a promise, but her courage failed her.

"The kitchen," Jemima said again. "Now."

When the girl was gone Richard said, "If you won't take proper care of this woman then hire somebody to do it."

"I feed her," Jemima said. "I wipe her shitty arse. I bathe her. Maybe not enough for your tastes, but then fine folks don't have to haul their own water, do they."

She was talking to Richard and looking at Hannah. Her smile was meant to frighten, and still Hannah could find nothing inside herself but pity for the women in this house. It would make Jemima howl to know that, and so she kept her expression blank.

Richard said, "She's lost more weight."

Jemima shrugged. "She eats as good as I do."

For a moment Hannah thought the doctor might rouse himself into one of his old tempers, but then the tension in his face seeped away.

"I'm going to examine her now," he said wearily. "And then I'll relieve her." For the last week the Widow had been unable to let down her own urine; once a day someone had to help her with it by means of a probe as thin as a reed. Sooner or later an infection would set in and finish off the old woman, and it would be a blessing. In spite of the nastiness and ill will the Widow had spewed over the years, Hannah thought she had suffered enough; her rest would be well earned.

"I suppose you're going to be coming in his place," Jemima said to Hannah. The corner of her mouth jerked as if the idea of such an arrangement amused her.

"When necessary," Hannah said.

"Unless you want to do this yourself." Richard looked up from the instruments he was laying out.

"Oh no, I wouldn't rob anyone of the pleasure," Jemima said, laughing. "Especially not her." There was some satisfaction in her voice, a mealy pleasure that made Hannah's stomach lurch. Such a quiet hate was far more frightening than any threats screamed in passion.

All through the examination, while Richard palpated the slack abdomen and put his ear to the dirty camisole and counted respirations, Jemima watched. The Widow offered no resistance, but her eyes, filmy with cataracts, flicked from side to side like a deer under the gun.

"She's nervous," Jemima said. "She probably thinks you're here to poison her." She said this as if she might have offered tea or asked about the weather. "She still thinks you killed her Isaiah."

Hannah met Jemima's expression. "And what do you think?"

Jemima's mouth contorted. "Your sins are many, Hannah Bonner, but that is one death you are not responsible for."

Richard was swabbing an open sore on the Widow's shoulder, but he raised his head to look Jemima directly in the eye.

"If there's any poisoning to be done here, I'll keep that pleasure for myself," he said. "I should poison her and put her out of the misery you've made of her sorry life."

The woman in the bed made a whining sound, like air let out of a bladder.

Jemima's face blanched of all color. "She's laughing at you. You made her laugh."

"Is she?" Richard said softly. "Is it me she's laughing at?"

• • •

Hannah left the sickroom before Richard, made her way through the dark hallway and the kitchen to find young Martha in the dooryard. She was scrubbing out a cooking pot with sand, singing softly to herself. She had a clear, true voice and in that moment Hannah remembered how much Jemima had loved to sing as a girl.

She had her mother's voice, yes. But in the bright summer morning the girl's skin was as translucent as parchment and her hair alive with light. Not Isaiah Kuick's daughter but Liam Kirby's, without a doubt; anyone who had known the two men could see that truth no matter what lies Jemima told.

Most probably Martha didn't know that Isaiah Kuick wasn't her father; Isaiah had died when Jemima was pregnant, and Liam Kirby had never laid eyes on this daughter he could not claim. How Jemima had managed to get Isaiah to marry her because she was pregnant by Kirby was a question that would probably never be answered.

No doubt the Widow Kuick knew, and she would have taken delight in disowning the child to her face, had she not lost the power of speech and the ability to hold a quill. A strange blessing on the girl, but it was not the only one. Along with the color of his hair, Liam had given his daughter a sweet temperament and a forgiving spirit.

Hannah did not know where Liam Kirby was or if he was even alive.

The girl caught sight of Hannah's shadow and looked up, the long plait moving like a quicksilver snake over the thin back. Her expression was guarded, but hopeful; she said nothing, because, Hannah knew, any child raised in this household would not speak unless spoken to.

"We saw your friend Callie earlier today."

Martha smiled shyly, ducked her head in acknowledgment. "Are you going to heal her ma?"

"I will try to help her," Hannah said.

The girl chewed her lip nervously, glanced at the kitchen door and back again. "Can you make her better? Do you have the right magic to do it?"

"Ah." Hannah looked out over the neat garden: cabbage, kale, potatoes. The kind of garden where flowers were as unwelcome as weeds. She said, "I'm sure you've heard things about me, but the truth is, there is no magic in medicine. Faith, yes, and science. But no magic."

"You can't fix her then." The girl went back to her scrubbing, her movements slow and deliberate. "Callie will be sad." After a moment she cast Hannah an uneasy glance.

"I don't mean to be rude, Miz Bonner—"

"Your mother doesn't want you to talk to me," Hannah finished for her. "Will you tell the doctor that I've gone ahead, and I'll wait for him on the bridge? I'd much appreciate it."

Chapter 4

Later, Curiosity wanted to hear every detail about both visits; she asked questions about the examinations and listened closely to the answers. When Hannah had finished the older woman sat down wearily in the rocker next to the hearth and shook her head.

"Poor Dolly's in a sad state and the Widow even worse, but it's that girl that worries me. Such a tender little thing being brought up by Jemima Southern. Jemima Kuick," she corrected herself.

"She looks well fed," Hannah said, offering that small comfort.

Curiosity snorted. "Don't talk to me about food," she said. "The girl need a kind word now and then as much as she need food." She paused and then said: "Tell me now, don't Martha remind you of her daddy? Not just the color of her hair, but the way she go at the world. He had an affectionate heart as a boy, a forgiving nature if there ever was one."

She was talking about Liam Kirby, but neither of them said the name out loud. Hannah said, "Let's hope she got his stamina too, because she is going to need it."

"He surely was tough as old leather, even as a boy." Curiosity laughed softly. "Wouldn't have lived through the beatings Billy dished out otherwise. My, those was hard days."

Now that the subject had been raised, Hannah decided she would not turn away from it. "Do you ever get news of Liam?"

Curiosity raised her apron to wipe her face. "Not a word in all the years." She sent Hannah a probing look. "You relieved, or dis-appointed?"

Hannah sat down on a stool opposite Curiosity. "I hardly know. Numb, I suppose would be the right word. I hadn't thought of him in such a long time until I saw the girl. His daughter. If he is alive he should know about her."

There was a longer silence while each of them sorted through memories too obvious or painful to share. Curiosity seemed to come to some conclusion because she straightened and looked Hannah directly in the eye.

"Did you notice anything unusual about Jemima?"

The question took Hannah by surprise. She considered carefully. "It seems to me that some of the fight has gone out of her."

Curiosity snorted a soft laugh. "I suppose it might look that way, but truth be told, she got me worried. That girl has got something cooking, you wait and see."

She set the rocker moving with a twitch of her foot.

"I hope you're wrong," Hannah said. "But you could always smell trouble on the wind."

"And there's more, while we're at it," Curiosity said. "While you was out with the doctor your daddy came looking for Lily with some news she didn't like much."

"Ah. About Daniel, and Blue-Jay. They're going with Luke." Hannah stopped herself before she could say anything more; it would do no good, and the words couldn't be taken back.

"We all knew the day was coming, but Lily just didn't want to see it." Curiosity spread out her hands on her lap. "You know they quarrel something awful, those two—"

"They always have," Hannah agreed.

"That's most usually the case with twins when they get to a par-ticular age. But Lily and Daniel ain't never been apart for long, not really. She don't know what to do with the idea of him going off to war without her."

"How angry is she?" Hannah asked. "Should I go find her?"

"Won't do no good," Curiosity said. "She went up the mountain and hid herself. I expect we won't see her again for a good while."

With more energy Curiosity said, "I'm going to make some cake to send along with those boys. It ain't much, but I got to do something."

She pushed herself out of the rocker so hard that it thumped back and forth and sent the cat running for a safer corner.

"What is it?" Hannah asked, though she knew very well.

Curiosity gave her a grim smile. "I am mad enough to spit nails, and there ain't no use in pretending otherwise. What is the Almighty thinking, letting me live long enough to see more boys go off to war? I don't know as I can stand it, Hannah. The waiting and wondering and imagining. Sending off letters that never get where they supposed to be. Waiting for word that won't come no matter how hard I bargain with the Lord. I'm likely to turn into a bitter old woman if anything should happen to either of those boys, and that's one thing I promised myself I would never be. I'd rather die. Sometimes I'm just weary of it all."

With her fury drained away Curiosity seemed almost to wilt and collapse inward. She sat down again, heavily.

Hannah let out the breath she had been holding. Now was the time to say things that were meant to be a comfort, to recite the facts they both knew to be true: Daniel and Blue-Jay would make the best of warriors; they were both excellent marksmen and woodsmen; they would look out for each other as no one else could. But truths like these were too fragile to bear the weight of fear.

Instead of talking, Hannah did something else, something harder for her. She knelt in front of Curiosity and put her arms around the woman's thin shoulders.

"We'll bear it because we have to," she said.

Curiosity pulled away with a sigh and wiped her face with the back of her hand.

"Did my father say when—"

"Tomorrow, at first light."

"Then we know when Lily will be back," Hannah said. "She won't let Daniel go without trying to talk him out of it again. What I'm less sure about is Jennet, and how she'll react."

Curiosity was rattling cake pans with a vengeance, but she paused to look at Hannah over her shoulder.

"She ain't going back to Montreal?"

"She says not," Hannah said. "But I expect Luke could change her mind."

Curiosity snorted softly. "Those two put me in mind of porcupines in mating season. They don't exactly mean to hurt each other but they don't seem to know how to get the business done without some bloodshed neither."

It was an image that made Hannah laugh out loud, and one that stayed with her for the rest of the day while she looked, without success, for her sister and her cousin.

•   •   •

"You should have waited." Elizabeth looked up from the quill she was sharpening; she could not hide her irritation or her worry, and neither did she care to. "It might have gone better if you had come to fetch me, Nathaniel."

Her husband sat on a low stool leaning forward with his elbows propped on his knees and his hands dangling. He looked up at her with his head cocked, an expression that meant he was calculating how much of an argument he wanted just at this moment. He could say what they both knew to be true, that the conversation with Lily might have been worse too, especially if Elizabeth hadn't been able to hold her tongue. But Nathaniel had never been cruel, and he was worried about his wife almost as much as he was worried about their troubled daughter.

"I made a promise to her, Boots. I kept it."

The penknife slipped and she put her thumb to her mouth to still the welling blood.

"I been thinking about your aunt Merriweather a lot lately," Nathaniel said. "We never gave her much credit for telling the future, but she was mighty good at it. She promised you that Lily would give us a run for the money, didn't she?"

Elizabeth blew out an exasperated breath. "Her exact words were 'she'll lead you a merry chase,' I believe. But I do not think I was quite so much trouble to my aunt and uncle . . ."

Her voice trailed off suddenly and was replaced by a reluctant half-smile, one that Nathaniel was relieved to see.

"You needn't give me that look," she said dryly, winding her handkerchief around her thumb. "I take your point. In spite of all the concern I was to them at Lily's age, their concerns were unfounded. Things did turn out in the end, though not exactly as Aunt Merriweather had hoped at first. Nathaniel Bonner," she said, her tone sharpening suddenly. "Do you ever tire of being so irritatingly clever?"

"It ain't cleverness, Boots." He got up and brushed one hand over her hair while he reached for his rifle with the other. "I don't suppose there's much either of us could say or do anymore—good or bad—that would surprise the other one."

"Is that true?" Elizabeth frowned. "I'm not sure I like being so predictable."

Nathaniel laughed. "Wait until we get the youngsters sorted out before you hatch any plans about surprising me. We got our hands full as it is."

Elizabeth's smile faded away, and she looked out the window toward the falls. "You really think I shouldn't go look for her?"

Nathaniel said, "Right now she wants to be left alone," he said. "And then she'll need to talk to Daniel. In the meantime I need to have a word with Luke."

"It's a complicated business, this raising of children," Elizabeth said. "It's almost a relief, knowing there won't be any more of them to bring up and worry about."

"You sure of that, are you?" He raised a brow at her, and she blushed in spite of her resolution not to. "Reasonably sure," she said, and blushed again. He laughed at her over his shoulder on his way out the door.

"Don't feel obliged to prove me wrong!" she called after him, but he did not hear her, or chose not to.

Nathaniel found Luke sitting alone in the spray of the falls, his hair still dark with water and his expression unreadable. A strange thing, that his firstborn should be the most mysterious of his children, but Nathaniel had never seen or known about the boy until he was already on the brink of manhood.

He had a good memory, and he prided himself on the fact that where many men seemed unable to tell their children one from the other he could summon pictures of all of his own as newborns, both the ones still living and ones who had not lived long enough to get to really know. Red-faced and screaming or wrinkled and curious about the world, each of them had come into the world showing signs of the person they would grow into.

Over the years three women had borne him eleven children, and five of those had survived. Of those, four were grown and ready to start families of their own. Gabriel, the youngest one, was the sweetest of them all but wild at heart; Gabriel would keep them hopping into old age. Sometimes Nathaniel woke in the deep of the night sure that he could hear the beat of the boy's blood through walls and floors. He knew the four younger children well, but Nathaniel could read Gabriel's mind just by looking at him sideways.

For Luke, for his firstborn, he had no such talent. He told himself it was because he had got to know him too late. They itched at him, all those missing memories, like a wasp sting in a hand left behind on a battlefield.

Now Luke was watching Nathaniel, as Nathaniel had watched his own father for all his life, reading mood and thought and intention from the set of Hawkeye's jaw or the flickering of an eyelid. No doubt he was as big a mystery to the boy as the boy was to him, but somehow that was little comfort.

"Tomorrow," Luke said when Nathaniel was close enough. "We'll set out tomorrow."

"And here I was thinking we didn't know each other well enough." Nathaniel sat down close enough to talk without shouting over the noise of the falls but not close enough to make the boy uncomfortable. He rested the butt of his rifle on a convenient rock and leaned into it.

"Or maybe you read everybody's mind that easy."

Luke snorted. "That would be a useful talent, but it's one I can't claim for myself."

"You're too modest," Nathaniel said. He brushed the wet from the falls out of his eyes. "I bet if you concentrated real hard you'll guess my next question."

Luke gave him a sharp look, one edged with curiosity and irritation both. "If it's Jennet you're worried about there's no need. I'm planning to talk to her tonight and settle some things."

Nathaniel raised a brow. "Reading minds again."

Luke shrugged. "More Elizabeth than you. She watches me when Jennet's nearby."

"That's true, she does. And I did come to talk to you about that very thing, but I can't claim I was especially worried about Jennet. She's got what she wants."

Luke squinted at him. "And that would be?"

"You. Tied up nice and neat, just waiting to tire yourself out struggling. You might as well give it up now, son."

Another man might have taken offense, but Luke was too much like his grandfather. Hawkeye hadn't been a man to expend energy on a battle he couldn't win, and neither was Luke.

"I always meant to marry her when she was free," he said after a while. "But I couldn't admit that while she was married to a man her father picked out for her. It got to be a habit, I guess, keeping it to myself."

"Time to break the habit," Nathaniel said. "She'll be a good wife to you, though I expect you'll tangle more than most."

Luke didn't bother trying to hide his grin. "I'm counting on it."

Gabriel came out of the house on the far side of the lake and stood on the porch. He had made himself a toy rifle out of a branch and he had a crow in his imaginary sights. Nathaniel watched the boy stalk his prey. Next summer he would be big enough for a rifle of his own, and the thought struck Nathaniel that this would be the last child he would teach to track and shoot until some grandchildren came along, or he managed to prove Elizabeth wrong about the size of their family.

He said as much to Luke, who began to get dressed by pulling his shirt over his head.

"Well, then I guess I better get busy and give you some grandchildren," Luke said.

"You don't much like the idea?"

"It's not that, not exactly." Luke ran a hand through his hair to get it out of his face. "It's got more to do with where to bring them up once I've got them."

This surprised Nathaniel, but he managed to keep his tone even. "I thought you were settled in Canada."

Luke hesitated. " 'Settled' is a strange word, but maybe it fits. I've got a house, I've got land and a business and friends. I was born and raised there. But I don't feel like I need to stay there, and I don't call myself a Canadian." He rubbed the bridge of his nose with a knuckle. "Don't know if I want my children to either."

Nathaniel said, "That's the first I heard of this. What do you call yourself, if not a Canadian? A Scot, like your grandmother?"

Luke shrugged. "She brought me up not to think of myself as anything. Not Canadian, not a Scot, not French, not American."

"Not an Englishman either," Nathaniel said. "Not if I know Wee Iona."

"Not an Englishman," Luke agreed. "Never that."

He did in fact have an English grandfather, but Wee Iona would not speak his name, had not spoken it even on the day she learned of his death.

"I never did hear the story how it was that Iona Fraser ever let Pink George get a child on her without slitting his throat," Nathaniel said. "I always thought Robbie MacLachlan would tell me before he died, but I missed that chance."

"I'm guessing that's a story she'll take to her grave," said Luke.

"You don't think your mother knows?"

Luke's mouth jerked at the corner. "I'll ask her, the next time I see her."

Giselle was a topic they rarely discussed; Luke, out of loyalty, and Nathaniel because he knew her so little.

"So what do you call yourself?" Nathaniel asked. "If not Canadian?"

"Iona always said I could choose my own place and name when I was old enough. She thought it was a gift she was giving me, and I thought so too, at first."

He looked at Nathaniel straight on, something he rarely did. "You don't call yourself American."

"No," Nathaniel said. "I don't think of myself as an American."

"But you pay taxes to the American government."

"I pick my battles," Nathaniel said. "And my wars too. Is that what this is about, the new war?"

Luke nodded. "I put the question out of my mind for a long time, but a war makes a man take sides. The only conclusion I can come to is that I won't do anything to help the British."

"Will you do anything to hurt them?"

He got a shrug for his answer. "Haven't got that far yet in my thinking. What I do know is, I'm a fortunate man but it'll take a lot more than good luck if I want to hold on to what I've got."

"And Jennet is one of those things."

Luke took a deep breath. "She's the most important of them."

Chapter 5

When they were younger, the boys had built a fort in the woods, an elaborate construction of rocks and cast-off boards and interwoven branches that they were always improving. In the winter it fell prey to the snows, to bears and foxes and wolves. Every spring they repaired it.

In their day Daniel and Blue-Jay and Ethan never allowed Lily or any of the girl cousins into the fort. But now Gabriel and Annie had claimed it for their own and made up new rules. They liked Lily, who drew them funny pictures and sometimes brought them apples or maple sugar, and so she could come and sit with them in the fort and listen to their stories.

She walked the mountain for most of the afternoon before she went to the fort where the children were waiting for her. It was where Daniel would come looking, and because she could not avoid him forever she sat down to wait for him. Lily felt the chill of the approaching storm on the nape of her neck, and in the lengthening shadows she saw the coming of an early dusk.

Annie caught sight of Daniel first. She flung herself out of the fort and ran at him, climbed him like a tree to take a seat on his shoulder where she held on to his head and balanced precariously. As Lily had once done with Runs-from-Bears; that memory came to her now bittersweet.

Gabriel stood too, but kept his distance. "Is it true you're going off to war tomorrow?"

Daniel nodded. "It is."

"And my brother too," Annie said, thumping Daniel companionably on the head. "So you can keep each other out of trouble."

"That's the way of it," Daniel agreed. His gaze had never left Lily's face. She felt it like a touch.

"Sister's pretty mad," Gabriel said, as if Lily were not there at all. "I don't know if you can talk her out of it this time, brother."

"He's got to try," Annie said. She swung down from Daniel's shoulder and landed with a thump.

She produced a hopeful smile and turned it on Daniel full force. "Can we stay and listen?"

He looked out over the valley and the bowl of the sky brimming with storm clouds. Heat lightning flickered in the distance. "Better get home before the rain comes," he said.

And when the threat of rain did little to move them Daniel said, "There's a prize for whoever gets back to Lake in the Clouds first."

They were gone in a flash. Daniel stood right where he was for a full minute and then another.

Finally he said, "I don't know why you have to make this so hard, sister."

His expression was almost comical: outrage and righteous indignation and confusion. If he were closer she might slap him. Her throat cramped closed.

"I'd like your blessing."

As if he were hungry and she were refusing to feed him. Lily blinked back tears.

"You can't have it," she said.

"I'm going anyway," he said. "I've got to go."

"No, you don't." She kept her voice as quiet and calm as she could; it was the only way to make him listen. "You're going because you want to. It makes no sense to put yourself in harm's way like this."

"Not to you, maybe." He looked away, the muscles in his throat working. "Just the way you do things that don't make sense to me. But I ain't ever tried to stop you."

Words like cold water, like diving into the lake under the falls at first light: a revelation. She opened her mouth to say something, anything, and what came out shamed her.

"I don't know what you mean."

The hardest thing, the one thing she had not counted on: her brother's sympathy and understanding.

"It's only a matter of time before somebody else figures it out, Lily. I think Ma half suspects now."

"I don't know what you mean." Her voice creaked like an old lady's.

"You're headed for heartbreak," he said.

"And you're headed for an early grave." The words choked her but they did their work: he jerked as if she had reached across the ten feet that separated them and struck him. They looked at each other like that for three heartbeats.

"I have to go, sister. I wish I could make you understand."

"So do I," she said, and turned away.

I may never see you again. The unspoken words trailed behind her like smoke.

Lily ran, her skirts kilted up through her belt; she ran until her breath came ragged and her lungs were on fire, and then she pushed, dug herself into the pain and ran harder. The rain came first in stuttering waves and then it steadied and in a matter of seconds she was soaked to the skin.

There were two ways into the village without a boat: she could take the long way around the lake through the marsh or she could go over the bridge.

It's just a matter of time before somebody else figures it out.

She hesitated for a moment, her face turned up to the storm.

What did it matter anymore? She went the quicker route, still running until she came to the bridge where she stopped. Beneath her feet the wood thrummed with the running river, a living thing that would take her away from here if she let it.

She stood under the pulsing sky, arms outstretched, and then she began to make her way across the village by the way of back lanes. At the edge of the Wildes' orchards she paused to watch the trees, leaves snapping and fluttering in the wind. Apples thumped to the ground with each gust. The darkening storm had taken all the color out of the world but the lightning brought it back in quick bright pulses.

Then a double fork of lightning lit the sky with a million candles and showed her everything: the neat rows of trees, the cabin at the far end of the orchard, its windows shuttered against the storm. Smoke drifted up from the chimney to be caught by the wind and scattered.

The barn door stood open just wide enough to show her the man standing there, his arms at his sides. When the light was gone Lily closed her eyes and saw him still, burned into her flesh.

She wrapped her arms around herself and walked on, the sweet smells of wet grass and bruised apples rising up like a cloak. At the barn door she stepped into cool darkness, gooseflesh pebbling her wet skin.

Nicholas was waiting for her. The lightning showed him white and blue and white again: more ghost than man, until he came forward and stopped, close enough to touch her if he wanted. If he dared. She imagined she could hear his heartbeat, slow and steady. Such a strange thing, that a heart could keep on without faltering for so many years, undeterred by loss. Lily put her hand on her own chest.

Light flickered on his face: planes and circles and intersecting lines drawn on the fragrant dark. Simple geometry that arranged itself into something extraordinary. When she was still a girl, long before they had stumbled upon each other in the way of man and woman, she had put down his likeness on paper many times.

On the day he married Dolly Smythe she had drawn them together. He had still been in mourning for his sister but his expression had been clear and full of hope. And why not? Dolly was the kindest young woman in all of Paradise, sweet and hardworking both, and she had been in love enough for both of them. And a farmer needed a wife.

Then for a long time Lily had given Nicholas Wilde little thought, until Callie had come into the world and her mother had left it, in her own quiet way.

Dolly lost on the mountain, the second or third or fourth time; they had stopped keeping count. Anyone who could hold a lantern and call her name went looking. The searchers came to Lake in the Clouds for coffee, soup, an hour's sleep, news. Lily was there alone half-asleep in front of the hearth when Nicholas came with Dolly cradled in his arms like a child. He had put her on the cot by the fire so gently, stroked her damp hair from her face, watched while Lily lifted his wife's head and fed her broth. When she was asleep Nicholas went out on the porch and wept.

He had frightened Lily so with the terrible power of his weeping, beyond anything she had ever imagined. She was standing behind him, uncertain and afraid, when he turned and pressed his face into her skirts and wound his arms around her legs.

For an hour or more she had held him while he talked and wept and told her things she had no right to know and did not understand, not really. Then he had raised his head to look at her and all her doubts and worries fled. She had comforted him, somehow, with the simple fact of her presence. They had been friends, at first. Nothing more.

"My brother and Blue-Jay are going to join the fighting," she told him now. "With Luke."

His expression softened. "Your parents?"

"They gave their consent."

"You knew it would happen, sooner or later. He will not be satisfied until he goes."

"But you won't." Poking at him with words as sharp as a nail because she did not want to touch him, could not allow herself to touch him. "You won't go."

"No. You know that I couldn't even if I wanted to."

The long list of things that could not be done, yes. Lily knew them well. She often went to sleep reciting them to herself: he could not leave his orchards, his wife, his daughter; Dolly could not be cured nor could she die.

Thirteen years and innumerable laws of both God and man separated them. They never pretended otherwise to each other; they made no promises or plans. They had exchanged nothing beyond the occasional awkward and lingering kiss. They could not be together, and so finally Lily had made plans to go to the city, and he had averted his face when he might have asked her to stay.

Such a good man, people said of him. Clever, a hard worker, always ready to help a neighbor, with a calm smile in spite of the burdens he bore.

"Look," he said, putting his hands on her shoulders to turn her.

A rain-soaked orchard alive with the churning wind, shadows that shivered and jumped. She waited for the lightning and then saw what he meant her to see. The bear stood on her hind legs swiping at the ripe apples. Her fur was beaded with light and her eyes shone red in the lightning.

The men in the village shook their heads over Nicholas Wilde, a man who wouldn't shoot the bears who raided his orchard. If they knew, as Lily did, that Nicholas named his bears as a farmer named his cows, they would conclude that he was just as mad as his wife.

"Which one is that?" Lily asked.

"Maria," he said. "I call her Maria. She likes the Seek-No-Further best of all."

A terrible sadness came over Lily, a sense of loss so strong that her body could not contain it. It was something she could not hide from him, nor even try.

"Lily," he said softly. "Tell me the rest of it. What are you planning?"

"I don't know yet. Something. Anything."

"Montreal?"

In the flashing light she saw his face and wished she had not. How was it he saw the very things she meant most to hide?

"If Luke agrees."

He grunted softly. "Even if he doesn't."

She reached out toward him in the dark. "Will you kiss me goodbye?"

"Ah, Christ. Lily."

She was turning away when he reached out and pulled her into his arms. Where they pressed together from hip to shoulder he was quickly as wet as she; Lily felt him shudder with cold or longing or both. His mouth on the curve of her neck, at her ear, his breath soft and warm.

"You know I would marry you if I could." It was something he had never said to her before and Lily was surprised to find that those words she had imagined so often could sound so hollow.

He kissed her mouth gently, his fingers on her face. The kiss of a friend. She took his head in her hands and pulled him to her and took the kiss she wanted.

Then she looked at his face as if to memorize it, and she left him for the waning storm.

By the time Lily had got home the sun had come out again to simmer on the edge of a sky washed clean of clouds.

Gabriel came bolting out of the house to tell her the news: Jennet was to stay with them at Lake in the Clouds when Daniel and Blue-Jay went to join the fighting. It was good news, of course. It meant company for Hannah and distraction for Lily's mother. These thoughts she kept to herself, for the time being, while anger had the upper hand.

"You're not surprised," Gabriel said, deeply affronted that his news should garner so little response.

"There are surprises and surprises," Lily said. "And more to come."

She had meant to speak up during the going-away supper, but the conversation at the crowded table was quick and lively and full of laughter and Lily could not find it in herself to put an end to it. Instead she kept busy passing plates and refilling bowls, laughing with the others when laughter was called for.

Finally Many-Doves simply took a bowl out of her hands and pushed her back to her place at the table, where she had no choice but to let herself be studied.

They were all watching her when they thought she would not notice. Her parents, Daniel, Many-Doves, even Gabriel, each of them concerned, not all of them able or willing to hide it. Simon Ballentyne sat across from her and he watched too, silently. His admiration should have pleased her, she knew, but instead Lily felt only irritation: yet another man who was willing to keep his distance.

There was apple grunt for dessert and then Gabriel wanted to hear the old story of the gaol break at the Montreal garrison the winter that the twins were born. Just at that moment Lily realized that if she did not speak up now she must scream. She stood suddenly and the room went silent.

"I have something to say."

Nathaniel had been waiting for this, but it seemed to take Elizabeth by surprise. Or maybe, he corrected himself in the small silence that followed Lily's announcement, maybe it was not so much surprise as simple fear.

Daniel put down his fork and folded his hands in front of himself. "Go ahead then, sister."

He was expecting a lecture at best, but there was something else coming. Nathaniel could smell it in the air. He said, "We're listening."

Lily pulled herself up to her full height, ready to do battle. Sometimes when she held herself like this Nathaniel saw his own mother in the line of her back and the set of her jaw. Which was both a comfort and a curse; he loved his mother and he missed her still every day, but Cora Bonner had been a force to reckon with when she made up her mind.

Nathaniel watched his daughter gather her courage together. "I'm leaving tomorrow too. If I can't go to New-York City, then I'll go to Montreal, with Luke. If he'll take me."

It wasn't a question, and nobody mistook it for one. Elizabeth looked almost stunned, but she held her peace for the moment. Sometimes dealing with Lily was like finding a bear rummaging around in the larder. It could end in laughter or bloodshed, and it usually wasn't the bear who made the decision on how it would go.

Luke looked his half sister right in the eye, his expression doubtful. "What is it you want to do in Montreal?"

"She wants to study painting," Gabriel offered. He was looking uncertainly between Lily and Luke.

Nathaniel smiled at the boy and then leaned over to him. "Let your sister speak for herself, son."

"What she wants," Daniel said, matching his sister's tone, "is to get away from Paradise."

Lily's whole body jerked with that, but before she could turn on her twin Elizabeth spoke up. She was angry now, but not at Lily.

"Daniel," she said calmly. "Do not put words in your sister's mouth."

Lily's throat and face were flecked with bright color, as if a sudden fever had come over her. "That's exactly right. The decision is mine and mine alone."

"There's a war on," Nathaniel said. He said it because if he didn't, Daniel would, and that would be the start of another kind of battle, where words would cut as true as any knife.

"I'm aware of that," Lily said. "My brother is going to join the fighting, after all."

With a voice that wavered only slightly Elizabeth said, "If we are unwilling to send you to New-York City in time of war, daughter, what makes you think that we would let you go to Canada, of all places?"

Hannah made a sound, not quite a laugh or a cry but a little of both. "She's not asking for permission, Elizabeth."

"That's right," Lily said. She gripped the edge of the table so hard that her knuckles went the color of milk. "I'm not asking for permission, just as you didn't ask for permission when you left England. Just as Jennet didn't ask for permission when she left Scotland, or Hannah when she went west. I will go to Montreal and live under my brother's roof, and I will study art there, and someday when I am ready, I may come home again."

It might have ended just there, for the moment at least, but Luke wasn't happy and he wouldn't keep it to himself, no matter what warning looks Nathaniel sent his way.

Luke said, "Maybe you ain't asking Da for permission, but what about me?"

"Ah," said Lily. Her face had gone very still. "I see. You'll take their side in this. In that case I will find a way to go on my own."

From anybody else this would have been an empty threat, but Nathaniel knew his daughter. Daniel was going and she would go too, unless they tied her down. She had the money she had inherited from Elizabeth's aunt Merriweather, after all, and she would use it to get what she wanted.

Daniel sat perfectly still and said nothing at all, though his gaze was fixed on Lily. He knew her better than anybody, and he was too clever by far to jump into a fight he knew he couldn't win.

Luke, on the other hand, hadn't spent enough time with Lily to read the signs. He reached for the bowl of beans and made a sound deep in his throat. "This is between you and your folks," he said. "I won't go against them."

"I will," said Simon Ballentyne.

Ballentyne was the kind of man who never spoke up unless he had something to say, and Nathaniel had almost forgot that he was sitting at the table until he heard his voice.

Everyone was looking at Simon. Luke irritated, Daniel uneasy, Jennet intrigued. Nathaniel couldn't read Hannah's expression, but he saw that Elizabeth was ill at ease and confused, both.

"Mr. Ballentyne," Elizabeth began in her most polite tone, "I'm sure you mean well—"

Lily held up a palm to interrupt her mother. "You will what, Mr. Ballentyne?"

"I'll see you to Montreal, and make sure that you're settled there."

For the most part Nathaniel liked Ballentyne, a competent man, hardworking and quick, a little dour in the Scots way but not without a sense of humor when it was called for; he could laugh at a joke at his own expense. But this conversation was taking an unexpected turn, and Nathaniel wasn't easy with it. Neither was Elizabeth, who had gone very pale.

For her part Lily looked just as surprised as Nathaniel felt, which was some kind of relief: at least she hadn't planned this.

"Ballentyne," Luke said. "This is none of your business, man."

Lily turned on her eldest brother furiously. "This is none of *your* business," she snapped. "And I'll thank you to stay out of it."

"Lily!" Elizabeth could barely contain her embarrassment or horror.

"I'm sorry, Ma," Lily said in a calmer voice. "But this is between Mr. Ballentyne and me."

"As is any marriage proposal," Jennet volunteered. And then, in response to the shocked silence around the table: "What did you think he was offering? The use of a horse?"

Daniel was on his feet suddenly, all his pretense at calm gone. "Are you offering for my sister's hand, Ballentyne?"

Lily picked up her plate and banged it down on the table so hard that the cutlery jumped. "And if he is, what business is it of yours, Daniel Bonner!"

"Da!" Daniel turned to Nathaniel. "Stop this nonsense!"

They were all looking to him now. Elizabeth and Daniel demanding that he take charge and put an end to the discussion, Hannah and Jennet and Many-Doves suspended between surprise and curiosity, the children hopping with excitement. Runs-from-Bears and Blue-Jay were amused, and Lily was plain mad. Only Simon Ballentyne was oddly calm. A man not easily riled, then; something in his favor.

Nathaniel said, "I'd like to hear what Many-Doves has to say about this."

Many-Doves had once been his sister-in-law, but over the years Nathaniel found himself turning to her more often as he would have turned to a clan mother, for her insight and good sense. She had been listening to the whole conversation with interest, but her expression gave away nothing. Now that she had been asked, though, she stood and looked around the table.

"A brother may hunt for a sister who has no husband to bring her meat," she said. "But he does not make decisions for her. This is a matter for the women to settle among themselves."

"But Mr. Ballentyne never even asked for her to marry him." Annie's voice trembled with energy. "Maybe he *was* just offering her the use of a horse." She sent Jennet an apologetic look, and ducked her head.

Lily, still standing, turned to the man who sat across from her. "Are you asking for my hand, Mr. Ballentyne?"

Runs-from-Bears grunted softly. "He is now if he wasn't before."

It took everything Nathaniel had in him to hold back a smile, but Jennet wouldn't be silenced. "Will you no speak up, man?"

Ballentyne hadn't taken his eyes off Lily. Now he said, "It's no how I meant to go about it, but aye, I'm offering for your hand, Lily Bonner. Should you care to have me." He glanced at Nathaniel and then at Elizabeth. "I would have come to you first, had there been time."

Luke pushed back his chair so abruptly that it squealed. For Nathaniel to see him standing over the table, his temper barely in check, was to see himself at seventeen, the year he had left home against his mother's wishes and his father's advice. The winter Nathaniel had gone to Montreal and met Giselle Somerville; the winter Luke had been conceived.

He might never know this son the way he knew the ones he had raised himself, but at times flashes of understanding came to Nathaniel as pure as rain. Luke did not want the responsibility that would come with taking his sister north, just as he was anxious about taking a wife. Because he was afraid he couldn't keep them safe; because he knew what it would mean, that double yoke, given the life he must lead.

Luke's gaze was fixed on Jennet, who had her chin pushed out at an angle that could bode no good.

"I want to speak to you right now," he said. "Outside."

Then he strode to the door, opened it, and waited there. For the first time, Nathaniel saw indecision and something like guilt on Jennet's face. Finally she got up gracefully.

"If you'll pardon me," she said. "I apologize for the rude interruption. My lady mother and his took pains to teach him manners, truly they did." She walked to the door without hurry, nodded to Luke as a queen might nod to a lesser being, and went out onto the porch.

Luke said, "I'll be back. Don't make any decisions without me." And he shut the door behind him.

Jennet walked fast, but she couldn't say exactly why. It wasn't as if she had anything to fear from Luke Bonner; she was no longer a schoolgirl to be scolded, after all. He was just a few steps behind her when she rounded on him suddenly to say just that, but he took her elbow and kept her moving.

"Wait," he said.

"For what?" she asked sharply. "If you're planning to beat me, Luke Bonner, I assure you they'll hear my screams on the Solway Firth."

It was not a good sign that he had nothing to say to that, and in fact Jennet had rarely seen Luke so angry. His whole body trembled with it, but while the look he gave her would have made most men reach for a weapon, Jennet found herself oddly at peace. How many weeks now had she been waiting for him to show his feelings? If it must come out in a temper, so be it.

She let herself be propelled across the clearing to a corner of the fallow cornfield that smelled vaguely of fish. There they were out of sight of the cabins, and there he let her go, abruptly.

"What in God's name were you thinking?" he thundered, thrusting his face toward her. "Putting Ballentyne up to such foolishness!"

At that she had no choice but to laugh. "First of all, there's no need to shout at me like a banshee. And second, I put Simon up to nothing at all. Do you think I cast a spell and made him fall in love with your sister?"

Luke ran a hand through his hair, turned away in frustration and back again. "You read his fortune in those damn cards of yours," he said in a voice that was only a little calmer. "You said he was lonely!"

"And so he is!" Jennet said, drawing herself up. "Something you could see for yourself, if ever you thought to look. And if I did, what then?" She poked him in the chest so that he took a step backward. "You said yourself that the cards are naught but foolishness."

"You put the idea in his head," Luke said, but some of his bluster had gone.

"Ach, ye great gomerel. Did you not tell me yourself Simon was in love with your sister? And had you not said a word it would make no difference. Anybody with eyes can see for himself the way Simon looks at Lily. Much in the same way you look at me, Luke Bonner, try as you like to deny it."

He went very still then, his jaw working hard. There was a faint buzzing in her ears because she saw something new in his expression: reluctant agreement.

Finally he said, "You have to talk her out of it."

Jennet shook her head to clear it. "Talk Lily out of what? Out of going away from here? A fine bit of hypocrisy that would be, and should it be possible."

"Talk her out of marrying Simon Ballentyne," Luke said, his

voice dropping to a whisper, one that was meant to intimidate and in fact would intimidate almost anyone else.

Jennet met his gaze directly and matched his tone. "And why shouldn't she marry him? He's a good man, is he no?"

"Jennet Scott," Luke said slowly. "You of all people know what it means to marry where there's no love."

She slapped him then, in her surprise and anger and frustration. Before her hand had left his face he had grabbed her by the wrist to keep her from running away, and though she might twist and yank she would be going nowhere until Luke decided to let her go. Neither would he bring her close enough to really touch.

"How dare you." Her voice was trembling but she couldn't help it. "How dare you throw that up to me."

"In battle a man uses the weapons to hand," he said. "And in this case the truth is all I've got. You can talk her out of this foolishness, Jennet. She doesn't know Simon Ballentyne."

"Is he a murderer then, a thief, an abuser of women?" She looked pointedly at her wrist caught up in the manacle he made of his hand.

"Don't be ridiculous."

"Then she must make up her own mind."

He pulled her closer. "Christ, girl, do you have any idea what you're asking?"

She stilled and for a moment there was just the heated silence while they struggled, each of them, to calm their breathing.

"If you don't want her to marry, then you must agree to take her to Montreal," Jennet said finally. "It's only because you took it upon yourself to make that decision for her that she's in there, right this very moment, considering taking Simon as husband."

He let her go suddenly but he didn't step back. "You did plan this."

"You're just angry because you can't have your way. Admit it, man, and be done with it. You can't force your sister to do your will, and you can't control me, and no more can you wish away the way you feel about me."

And because he was so close, and because she was so angry, Jennet slung her arms around his neck and kissed him with all the fury in her. For a moment his hands were on her waist and he was holding her and he kissed her back, really kissed her and she tasted it on his mouth, the rightness of it.

"Jennet," he said wearily.

She pressed her face to his chest and then raised her head to look at him. "Why do you fight it so?"

There was a tenderness in his expression that she had only seen once before, on the day he left Scotland. It made everything inside her clench with hope and fear at once. Jennet touched his face lightly, traced the high sweep of his brow and the curve of his cheekbone and the hard line of his jaw, rough with beard. She touched him as she would touch a half-tame cat, for the pleasure of it and because there was the chance that this time he might allow it.

He caught her hand in his own and turned it, kissed her palm and let it go. "What I want doesn't matter, not right now," he said. "What matters is your safety."

"Tell me then if there's someone else," Jennet said. It was the question that sat like a rock in her throat, one that she must cough up or choke on. "If you tell me that, I'll leave you be."

"There's someone else," he said, and before she could take even one more breath he kissed her, a sharp, hard kiss.

"Jennet," he said. "There's a war. She's as jealous as any woman, this war, and greedier by far. I could be dead tomorrow."

"But you aren't a soldier," Jennet said, mystified and frightened too. "You aren't planning on joining the fighting, you've said so again and again."

He shook his head at her, his gaze steady. "There's more than one way to fight in a war, girl. Not everybody wears a uniform."

She stepped back from him and pressed a hand to her mouth. He was looking at her steadily, and Jennet realized that he had been holding back this information for weeks, and he was glad to be free of it.

"Does your father know?"

"No. Not exactly, at any rate. You're the only one I've told."

She turned and walked away from him to sink down onto a boulder. Dusk had seeped into night; on the edge of the world a new moon was rising, a sliver of old bone pressed into the bruising flesh of the sky. Owls called, one and then another, and somewhere far off a wolf raised her voice in offering.

Jennet wanted to ask what government he was spying for, how he had been drawn in, what he meant by taking sides when he said he could not, would not. She wanted to know these things and she was afraid to know them. And she was excited, too, and trembling with it because they had come, finally, to the place where he would deny her no longer.

He was standing next to her, close but not touching.

"That's why I don't want to take Lily back to Montreal," he said. "That's why it's better that you stay here."

"So that if they catch you and hang you we won't be there to watch," Jennet said numbly.

He gave a low laugh that was meant to comfort. "Ach, and what lobsterback is quick enough to catch a Scott of Carryck?"

"Ah," Jennet said, for he had answered one question, at least: he was not working for the English Crown.

"Will you do what you can to keep my sister here?" he asked.

The anger came back to her in a rush, and she stood to face him. "No," she said. "I won't do that because it can't be done, and because to have her there is the best guarantee that you'll be careful. For her sake, if not for mine. If not for your own."

In the near dark his expression was hard to read, but Jennet knew suddenly that she must leave him or embarrass herself with tears. He reached out to stop her but she shook him off.

"There are things I need to say to you," he called after her. "Things we need to have clear between us before I go."

"You made me wait ten years, Luke Bonner," she called back over her shoulder. "Now it's your turn. See how you like it."

In Carryckcastle where she had been born and lived all her life Jennet could have hid for days at a time. As a child she had perfected the art of slipping from chamber to chamber as silently as a shadow, but there was no such escape at Lake in the Clouds. She was not so rash as to go out into the forests after dark, and so she must settle for the barn. There was an empty stall between the two horses and she made herself at home. She had been there no more than an hour when Hannah found her.

"The mosquitoes will eat you alive if you don't come in," she said at the door.

"Too late." Jennet slapped at her neck. And then: "What was decided about Lily?"

Hannah said, "She's going."

"Of course she's going. But what about Simon?"

"Simon was politely refused," Hannah said. "And Luke has agreed to take Lily under his wing."

"There's no telling when she'll come home again." Jennet said out loud the thing they were both thinking. Wars were unpredictable; this one might bleed out in three months or stagger on for years. Her own homeland was never at peace, not really.

"Elizabeth?" Jennet asked.

"She's putting on a brave face."

"Daniel will be furious."

Hannah said, "He's young. He thinks he can keep her safe if he ties her down."

Jennet let out a harsh laugh. "The men of Carryck all think like that. It's bred into them, I fear."

There was a small silence interrupted by a nightjar's call.

"Luke asked me to find you," Hannah said after a minute. "He says you must finish your conversation."

"Did he now. And here am I, too tired for talk. I'll sleep here, I think."

Hannah hesitated only for a moment. Then she went to a shelf on the wall and pulled down a pile of blankets, which she tossed to Jennet. They were worn soft with age, and smelled of hay and horse and sunshine.

"Sleep well," Hannah said softly, and disappeared back into the dark.

Chapter 6

The surprising thing was, Jennet did fall asleep and quite quickly, once she had stripped down to her chemise and underskirt and arranged the blankets to her satisfaction. One moment she was studying the stars through a crack in the timbers and then she was dreaming of home, of the fairy tree where she had spent so many hours as a girl. In her dream the branches were filled with tiny dancing lights, the fairies like stars that had fallen down from the sky to be caught up in the branches.

She woke suddenly and with a gasp: someone had slapped her.

Luke was sitting next to her. He had brought a lantern with him that cast his shadow on the wall; a moth fluttered around his head.

"Mosquitoes on your face," he said calmly, showing her the bloody smear on his palm. "Three of them at once, feasting."

Jennet touched her own cheek and felt the swelling bumps. A quick pass over her face found too many more to count.

"If you want to sleep out here you'll need this." He was holding out a jar, already uncorked. "Pennyroyal ointment."

She put an arm over her face to hide the fact that she was close to tears, for no reason she wanted to contemplate.

"Jennet."

"What?"

"Pennyroyal ointment." He thrust it toward her again, and when she refused to take it, he swore softly under his breath and reached out for her arm.

She knew she should stop him, but he had already dipped two fingers into the pot and was busy rubbing the ointment into her skin. It was cool and his touch was gentle, and so Jennet sat glumly and let him have his way, waking up little by little as he worked up one arm and then the other, stopping at the shoulder where her chemise started.

By the time he had finished both arms she was very much awake, awake enough to wonder at herself, that she should sit here half-naked beside Luke. Outwardly she might be calm, but her body was responding in a way that she could not hide; he must see her flush and feel it in the racing of her pulse.

"Hold up your face," he said, and she heard a gruff note in his voice that was new to her but immediately recognizable.

He was so close that she had no choice but to study him. He looked tired, his eyes red rimmed, his hair tousled, cheeks hollow and shadowed with beard stubble. There were faint shadows of pox scars on his cheekbones. It was the scars that scoured what might have been prettiness out of his face and gave him a hard look, but he was beautiful to her and could be no less. He was looking at her with cool blue-gray eyes as if he knew that, and more.

Luke touched the rising bumps on her forehead and cheeks and chin with the ointment and then, very gently, he smoothed it out with his thumbs, lingering over her cheekbones. His mouth was set in a line.

"What am I going to do with you?" His breath touched her face and woke all the nerves in her body.

"You might kiss me," she said. "That's one place to start."

He snorted softly at that but he smiled too, and took her chin between two fingers. Quickly, lightly, he brushed his lips across hers and then turned her head hard to the side. He went to work on her neck, both hands massaging the ointment in gently.

Her voice trembled, though she willed it not to. "Do you mean to throttle me?"

His mouth jerked at one corner. "Tempting, but no."

He stopped at the hollow at the base of her throat where the ribbons tied her chemise closed. Her breasts pushed against the thin fabric, and she saw the muscles in his jaw knot and flex and then he swallowed.

He sat back abruptly. "Your legs," he said.

"I beg your pardon." She must feign shock, at least.

"Your feet and legs." And he pulled the blanket to one side to expose the tangle of her skirt.

How very improper. She should say: *You mustn't,* but she did not. Instead when he took a foot in his hands she put back her head and tried not to sigh out loud. His hands were strong and very clever and they worked their way up over her ankle and to the knee.

He tugged the muslin free of its tangles and his hands were on her thigh; such big hands, rough and gentle too. She could not catch her breath. Then his hands were gone and he was reaching for the other foot, and with that Jennet collapsed backward onto the blanket and closed her eyes.

"You've been bit pretty bad."

She jerked in his hands. "Unto death," she agreed.

Then he was done and he let go of her. He was waiting, she knew that, waiting for her to say something. *Come to me,* or *Leave me be,* or *Tell me that you love me.*

She touched her own mouth and said, "You missed a bump." She felt like a girl of sixteen and not a woman almost thirty, a widow who had shared her bed with a lawful husband for ten years full. A husband who had been tender when the need was on him, but who had never made her feel like this, as if her body were no longer her own to govern.

Luke leaned over her and looked, very seriously, at her mouth. "Ah. So I did. But you don't want pennyroyal ointment on your lip, girl. It tastes terrible."

So he kissed her, because she wanted him to and he wanted to and they both were tired of not kissing for all the long years they had been apart and the weeks since she had come to him. He kissed her softly and then not so softly at all and Jennet sighed into his mouth and closed her eyes.

Then his fingers wandered down and down to work the ties on her chemise and his tongue touched hers, hesitantly at first and finally with purpose: to claim her, once and for all.

"More bumps," he said, and slipped away from her to press his face to her breasts and then to suckle them, his mouth greedy now, pulling sounds from her that no lady would make. Sounds that she had never imagined she had inside her.

It went on and on, the kissing and touching and peeling away of clothing, so that Jennet slipped deeper and deeper into such terror and joy that she shivered with it. Luke soothed her with his smile and voice, words whispered against her ear, *hush,* and *hush,* and *come now.*

But even his touch could not stop the things that were flashing through her mind, odd, disjointed images and words, bright and brighter still until her mouth opened and they spilled out.

"Why?" she whispered to him. "Why now?"

She could feel his flesh all along her own, his wanting just as immediate as the ache in her own body, but the question had come out of her mouth and he heard it and he stopped and seemed to wake up.

For a moment he looked at her blankly and then he pushed out a sigh and he rolled over on his back and slapped at a mosquito on his neck and another on his shoulder. Finally he came up on an elbow to look in her face.

"I was going to come to Scotland," he said. "When I got word that Ewan had died, I was going to come to claim you."

This admission took her by surprise, filled her with a stunning happiness and confused her all at once. He wiped her cheek with his thumb and she realized that her face was wet with tears.

He said, "Then the war started."

When it was clear he wasn't going to say anything else, Jennet pushed herself up on one elbow. "But I came to you," she said. "I came to you and you acted as if you didn't want me."

He flipped her onto her back with such sudden force that she hiccupped in surprise. Above her Luke's face was contorted with frustration and anger.

"Of course I want you," he said. "I always have. When I saw you on that dock—" He stopped and his mouth tightened.

Jennet said, "When you saw me on the dock you looked as though you wanted to beat me. I could barely breathe for the joy of seeing you but you turned and walked away." Her voice caught, remembering the terrible disappointment of that moment and the taste of it, bile and blood.

He pushed out a heavy breath. "I was angry, yes, but beating wasn't what went through my mind at that moment."

Very quietly she said, "You might have made me feel welcome."

"Jennet," he said, pulling her face to his and looking at her with such intensity that she must believe him. "Listen to me now. When I saw you standing there, my heart leapt in my chest."

"You don't have to sound so very put out about it," she said. "If you care for somebody, if you . . ." Her voice trailed away, because she could not say what she was thinking, not even now.

He said, "No matter what I felt, no matter what I feel, I can't ignore the fact that there's a war, and I'm stuck in the middle of it, and your welfare is my responsibility."

She put a hand on his chest to feel the beat of his heart against her palm. "So you pushed me away."

"You call this pushing you away?" He drew back a little to frown into her face and with one hand he pulled her to him, lifted her leg over his hip, and poised there at the quick of her, he paused.

She swallowed the sound that wanted to come out of her throat.

"You were going to come to Scotland to marry me, were you no?"

His face tightened ever so slightly, but he nodded. Jennet wondered if he had ever used those particular words to himself when he was thinking of making the journey and claiming her, and decided that he had not.

"And the war stopped you, aye, I can see it. Then I came to you, but you still haven't spoke to me of marriage. In spite of . . ." She hesitated. "This bump business. So what am I to understand? You do want to marry me? You don't want to marry me, but you'd still like to—"

"Don't say it," he said roughly. "Don't even think it."

"Then explain it to me," she said, a little breathlessly because he was rubbing against her in a way that distracted her from even this most interesting of subjects.

Luke was built like his father, long boned and lean, but muscular in the way of men who must be quick as well as strong. *Wicht and braw and bonnie,* the Carryck girls had called him. *Look at the hands on him,* they had said knowingly, when Jennet was too young to really understand. *Look at the breadth of his wrist.* He had spent time with some of them, but never enough so that any lass could lay claim. How they had all mourned when he went away without a wife.

Jennet roused herself suddenly.

"Luke."

He collapsed onto his back. "Yes. I wanted to marry you. I still want to marry you, but for the war. Or I'll say it this way: I'll want to marry you the day the war is over."

She wanted to ask him about all the lost years, and if he regretted the decision he had made when he left Scotland without her, but now she realized that the question must wait. It would lead to nothing but more arguments, while the issue at hand might go in a very different direction. And there was the matter of his hands and wrists and fingers so strong and clever . . . she swallowed again and turned her hips away.

"Married men don't go to war?"

He put back his head and groaned. "I won't marry and go to war."

"Because you might die."

He nodded. "Among other things."

"But tomorrow a tree might fall on your hard head, Luke Bonner, and kill you just as dead as a hangman's noose. I'll admit it would have to be a bloody great tree to do the job, but in theory at least it is possible." She wound a hand in his hair and tugged until he brought his face to hers, and then she nipped his lower lip. "And still you won't marry and go to war."

"Jennet." His breath on her skin, and suddenly all of him cradled between her legs, but he was talking and she must listen.

"Think for a minute. Remember that I live in Canada. If a common soldier falls in battle his widow and family get a pension from the king, or they should. If things go badly for me—" He paused, moved his hips experimentally and grinned when she could not hold back a gasp.

"They'd hang you for a spy and traitor." She tried to close her knees and he turned expertly to stop her, raised his own knee and lodged it against the heat of her.

With his mouth touching hers he said, "And all my holdings would be forfeit to the king, and should I have a wife she'd be penniless and—people would not be kind. Now can we finish what we've started, girl?"

He gave her a hard look and for a moment she was reminded, uncomfortably, of the days long ago when he had tutored her in Latin and French and philosophy. He had been a demanding teacher, uncompromising and infuriating. How often had she wished him and his mulish ways to the devil.

"But," Jennet said.

His knee nudged more insistently; his belly touched hers and she felt herself start to melt away.

"But what?"

She forced herself to say it. "I don't understand why you've got to run off and spy, like a boy who can't stand to be left out of a game."

At that his face tightened just enough to let her know that she had gone too far.

"You wouldn't understand."

"Of course I wouldna," she said, twisting away from him suddenly. She pulled the blanket up to cover herself. "I'm naucht but daftie, a jaud, a wee lass wha doesna ken her place."

"You wouldn't understand," he said very deliberately, but he didn't put his hands on her again.

"Och, I see," Jennet said bitterly. "Politics. What wad I ken o sic things, coming up as I did a papist in Protestant Scotland."

"You're being dense," he said in his severest schoolmaster voice. "It doesn't suit you."

Her temper flared so quickly that she could not stop herself from raising a hand, which he caught neatly.

He said, "You can slap me a thousand times, Jennet Scott, you can wish me to the devil in a hundred languages. But I will not marry you until this war is over."

She forced her breathing to a calmer place, uncomfortably aware of his arousal and her own. "And if I will not lay with you until you do?"

"Then we'll both suffer for it," he said with a flash of anger as bright as her own. "For you want me as much as I want you. Or will you deny it?"

He pulled the blanket down and pressed her against him, his hand spanning the small of her back. And he wanted her, oh yes, and she wanted him so fiercely that for a moment she simply forgot how to draw breath. Then he pulled her beneath him and pinned her hands with his own and kissed her so thoroughly that everything else was driven from her mind but the taste and feel of him.

"Deny it," he demanded, and kissed her again before she could say even a single word.

"Deny it," he said again, more fiercely. Luke in a temper, and because he wanted her; it was more than she had let herself hope for, so soon.

"I canna." She shook her head feebly from side to side. "I cannot deny that I want you, Luke Bonner. Can you deny that you love me?"

He smiled against her mouth, turned his hip with the grace of a dancing master and then in one strong thrust he locked himself inside her.

"Finally," he said hoarsely, spreading one hand beneath her to lift her hips. She opened her mouth to welcome him but he kissed her and closed the circle, belly to belly and mouth to mouth.

• • •

Later, when the fury had passed, Luke picked her up. They were both naked and slick with sweat, speckled with straw.

"Take the lantern," he said, crouching down so she could snatch it by the handle, and then he carried her out of the barn toward the rushing of the waterfall.

"Somebody will see," she said against his neck. She knew she should be concerned but could not find it in herself. Everything in her throbbed, every nerve, and what else was there to know?

"We're just soaking your bumps." He was grinning in the way of a man who has got what he wanted, which both infuriated her and made her want to give him more.

With the lantern set on a plane of stone they slid into water so blessedly cool in the slick heat of the night air that anything she might have wanted to say was lost in a sigh of contentment.

For a long while they did nothing but float together in the water, paddling quietly or clinging to the mossy rocks to exchange kisses. Then Jennet remembered the question she had asked, but that he had not bothered to answer.

"You never did say," she scolded him. She had to raise her voice to be heard over the waterfall, and he was ever a man to take advantage of such things.

"What?" He put his head back to wet his hair again and then shook himself like a dog. "What did you want me to say?"

She began to swim away but he caught her up and then he subdued her while she struggled, and when she was exhausted and could do no more than let him hold her he said it, against her ear. "I love you, Jennet Scott, and well you know it. I've loved you since you were a girl with dirt on your face, I loved you the day I left Scotland and every day since."

"And?"

"And?" he asked in mock outrage. "Is that not enough? Don't be greedy, girl."

"And?" she said, pinching him mercilessly until he yelped and snatched at her flying hands.

"And on the day the war ends I'll marry you. You harpy."

"The war could go on for years and years," she said into his ear, so he would hear her and the rest of the sleeping world would not; what she was about to say was hard, even for the brazen wanton she had just proved herself to be.

He went very still. "It could."

"So I have an idea."

He nodded, though Jennet felt the muscles in his arms tense. "Go on."

"Handfasting. You know the old custom, for a year and a day."

Luke was very quiet. "And? What happens in a year and a day?"

Jennet heard her voice going very rough. It was irritating to have her own voice betray her, but she pushed on. "In a year and a day we meet, right here."

"Just like this?" His hand slid over her bum and slipped between her thighs.

She pinched him again and he caught her hand and bit it, lightly. "And then, what happens in a year and a day when we meet here?"

"If you have changed your mind, or if I have changed my mind, then we part peacefully from one another."

"I've waited ten years for you, Jennet. I can wait ten more, if I must."

"Then you're far more patient than I," she said testily. "For I'll not pace away what's left of my youth counting out empty days and wondering. Hear me weel, Luke. I'll not wait more than a year and a day."

He frowned at her. "And if neither of us have changed our minds in a year and a day?"

"We marry."

"And if I don't come on that day?"

"Then the assumption is you've released me from my promise and I'm free to bestow my favors elsewhere."

"Ah." A shadow passed over his face. "And would you?"

She bit back a smile. "Finally."

He frowned at her, inclined his head, and his arms tightened around her. "Finally? Finally what?"

"I'm thinking of Thunder," she said, leaning back in his arms to study his expression.

"My horse."

"Aye, your horse. All the care and grooming and worry for a great bloody beast, and when Dugal Montgomerie offered you three times what any animal is worth—"

The muscles in his cheek jumped. "What's mine is mine."

"Aye. And here am I, the happiest of women because you value me as highly as your horse."

The corner of his mouth twitched. "All this by way of promising that you won't go off with Dugal Montgomerie."

"Or anyone else," Jennet said. "Should you keep the terms of the handfasting, of course. Luke Bonner. Or Luke Fraser or Scott or whichever name you've settled on. What is it to be, may I ask? So I can have my initials sewn into my linen." She tried to look serious, and failed.

"I'm using Bonner for the time being," he said, studying her face. "If that suits you."

"Very well," she said. "I'll take it, in a year and a day."

He brushed her wet hair back from her face. "This feels like a trap."

Jennet studied his expression by the light of the lantern reflected on the water. There was some worry there, but more resignation.

"Och, nae. It's just the opposite."

"It feels like a trap," he said again. He studied her face as she studied his. "But if you're in need of a promise, Jennet, then fine and good."

"You'll marry me in a year and a day whether or not the war is over?"

He was looking at her intently. "In a year and a day I'll come back here and we'll settle it then. That's as much of a promise as I can give you. Will you be satisfied with that?"

It was very late and the moon was long gone, but Jennet had never felt more awake in her life. He was leaving tomorrow and she would not see him for a very long time, perhaps all of the winter and spring and through the summer, but he would come back to her. And he would marry her then, she would see to it.

"Aye," she said. "I will."

Then he was towing her toward the falls and through the rush of water to the cavern behind, cool and dark. The lantern light wavered thinly through the curtain of the falls so that she could make out his face, but she had to shout to be heard.

"What are we doing here?"

"Sealing the bargain," he shouted back. There was a little ledge of rock and he pulled himself up on it and held out his hand for her.

She paddled away and treaded water. She could not deny that she wanted to go to him, but more than that Jennet needed simply to look. With the light flickering on his wet skin he was like an illustration out of the great book of myths in her father's library, a grinning messenger of the gods come to teach her a lesson or play a trick on her.

She said, "You'll be very tired on the morrow, and you've got a long way to travel."

"Come to me now," he said, curling his fingers at her. "Come, hen."

It made her laugh out loud to hear him call her hen, as if they were old dears married thirty years. She came closer and closer still, but not quite close enough.

She said, "There's only room for one to sit there."

Quick as a snake he leaned forward, snatched her wrist and lifted her out of the water as if she weighed no more than any other fish that might swim into his net.

"What are you doing?" A stupid question if ever there was one, but he grinned at her, this new grin she had already come to recognize and appreciate.

"Why, Jennet Scott," he said, pulling her into a straddle over his lap so that they were face to face. "What else would I be doing but once again proving you wrong?"

Chapter 7

Late September, Paradise

In the cool hour before dawn Elizabeth woke with a start and realized two things: her husband was gone, and a white owl was perched in the jack pine outside her chamber window like a lost child huddled into a blanket.

A bird and nothing more, she told herself. Feathers, beak, eyes that shone like lanterns. She would not entertain dramatic notions or talk of omens; this was her home, not a theater or one of the novels that her cousin sent her from the city.

Nathaniel was gone to hunt or check his traps or both. She would see him before long, coming into the glen with a brace of grouse or a turkey or with a doe draped around his shoulders and he would smile and hold up a hand in greeting when she came out on the porch.

Her husband was gone and so were Daniel and Lily, but Nathaniel would be back in a few hours and they would not; not today or tomorrow or even next week. Lily was in Montreal living a life Elizabeth could imagine with little trouble. She led a day-to-day existence something like the one she herself had led at the same age, when she still lived at Oakmere with her aunt and uncle Merriweather. Elizabeth had been an orphaned cousin of little means or beauty but great ambitions and imagination, but Lily was far richer in every way.

There had been one letter from Lily, if it could be called a letter at all. When the string was cut a whole sheaf of drawings had unfolded in Elizabeth's lap, each with words scribbled along the margins. Houses and shops and lanes, a market square crowded with people, a butcher's errand boy clutching a piglet while he argued with a soldier three times his own size, Wee Iona asleep in front of the hearth with her knitting in her lap, Luke bent over his ledgers. By piecing the drawings together it was just possible to extract the story of Lily's first days in Montreal.

But there was no word thus far from Daniel and Blue-Jay, who had disappeared into the war, doing things Elizabeth would not, could not, let herself think about.

She made herself look out the window only to find that the owl was gone. Some of the tension ran away from her like water wrung from a cloth; she was relieved and irritated at herself too. Elizabeth had started to think that perhaps superstition crept into a woman's mind as she got older and could no more be willed away than the lines that dug themselves into the corners of the eyes and mouth.

She sat up in bed and was thankful for the common things: the crackle of the mattress, the feel of linen against her skin, the smell of wood smoke and pinesap and her own body. The ache in her belly that only food would quiet; the fact that her fingernails needed trimming and her hair washing. Things to anchor her to this world, the one in which she must live and move no matter where her children might be.

Enough light had seeped into the dark that she could see Nathaniel's imprint in the bed beside her, the long fact of him, his weight and shape. He had left a single hair behind, a long dark hair on his pillow like a line of writing in a strange language.

Autumn had settled down over the world and the evidence was everywhere to be seen. Every day another wash of color in the forests, each more insistent than the last; the first geese vaulting themselves into the sky in the shape of a giant wing; the first squash and pumpkins ready for harvest. But even without those things Nathaniel's absence said the same thing to her, and said it more loudly.

Now that the hunting and trapping season had started she would wake every morning alone, because they were no different, really, than the beaver or the squirrels or any of the animals in the forest who must make themselves ready for the snows. Every year it was the same and every year she must struggle anew and struggle harder not to be resentful of the work that took him away from her while she slept.

Overhead Elizabeth heard stirring followed by a good thump and the sound of Jennet's laughter. She had fallen out of the bed again, as she did most mornings, dreaming herself back to her wide bed at Carryckcastle. While Elizabeth dressed she listened to the sounds of talking, too muted to really make out what Jennet and Hannah were saying, but musical and pleasing as the singing of thrushes.

They were women well versed in the sorrows of the world, but together they worked some kind of magic on each other. In this house they were become girls again. Jennet and Hannah and Gabriel and Annie; Elizabeth thought of them as four children, brimming with surprises and promise and distraction. When Hannah and Jennet had more serious things to discuss, something that Elizabeth knew must happen, they did that out of her hearing. Whether out of concern for her state of mind or simply for privacy she did not know, but Elizabeth was thankful for the wall they built between herself and melancholy.

Today when her part of the housework and fieldwork was done she would sit down at her desk. First she would finish the essay she was writing for the editor of the *New-York Spectator,* which must go with the next post to the city. In six or eight weeks it would come back again in smeared newsprint. When that obligation was met she would write a letter to Lily, and one to Daniel.

Elizabeth finished with her hair and went out to start breakfast. At the door she paused to look back at the bed, and for a moment she wished she had left it unmade, at least until Nathaniel was home again.

When Luke went back to Canada and left Jennet behind she had two things to sustain her: his promise, and her own natural curiosity.

Every day Hannah must wonder at her cousin, at her enthusiasm and a courage that often bordered on the reckless. At home in Scotland she had roamed far and long, and no threats or punishments had ever been able to curb her curiosity or her determination to see it satisfied. Age had not tamed her, and loss had only taught her to be bold in seeking out what she wanted for herself.

When Hannah pointed this out to her Jennet had an answer, as she did for most things.

"Because I have no bairns," she decided after some thought. "It's the raising of bairns that teaches a woman the meaning of fear."

They were sitting on Eagle Rock after an afternoon of helping with the corn, both of them sweaty and in want of a swim but still unwilling to move out of the breeze. Beneath their bare feet the rock was warm and all around the forest was a sea of burning color, almost too bright to look at.

Jennet said, "You've never asked me why it is I bore Ewan no heir. In Carryck the old women decided long ago that I'm barren."

"And do you think you're barren?" Hannah asked.

Jennet lay back suddenly and put an arm over her face. "I wished them away, the bairns. I told them to stay away, that I couldna be a mother when I didna ken how to be a wife."

One part of Hannah, the woman who had trained with Richard Todd and studied O'seronni medicine, that part of herself did not believe that it was possible to wish unwanted children away. In the months she had worked in the poorhouse in the city she had seen too many women hollowed out with children they did not want and could ill afford, women not thirty years who looked fifty or more, who greeted the birth of a fifth or sixth or seventh child with cold indifference or plain fury.

"You think I'm daft," Jennet said.

"No," said Hannah. "I was thinking about the time I spent working in the sick wards at the poorhouse."

"Tell me about it," Jennet said, settling in for the story.

So Hannah told her something she had rarely told anyone at all, about the dissections she had watched, what she had learned from those women who had died heavy with child or in childbirth or of fever soon afterward. Women whose bodies were claimed not by families but by doctors ravenous always to know more, men who stood around in bloodied shirtsleeves, their heads bent together over flawed wombs, the smell of pipe smoke intertwined with blood and decay while they pointed and prodded and argued. Misshapen wombs, withered or lopsided or torn, diseased in ways she would not tell Jennet or any woman for the dreams those words would conjure.

When Hannah had finished talking about what she knew and what she could not know, no one could know, about the bearing of children, Jennet said nothing for a long while. One of her hands lay lightly on her stomach, fingers curled. There was a blister on Jennet's thumb, perfectly round and pulsing with rich blood. Hannah was taken with such deep affection and sorrow that her throat swelled with tears. But instead of weeping she forced herself to go on.

"But this is only one kind of medicine," she said. "And it comes from men who only know how to look in one way, with a knife. My Kahnyen'kehàka grandmother and great-grandmother and aunts would laugh at such blindness.

"They taught me that it is possible to will away a child, to keep it waiting in the shadow lands. They taught me the songs to sing to keep a man's seed from taking root. They showed me how to make the tea that washes the child away before it is a child at all."

Jennet was studying her, but Hannah did not let her ask the question. "Yes," she said. "I have drunk the tea, three times."

"But you loved your husband," Jennet said quietly.

"Oh yes, I did. I do still."

"Then why?"

Hannah pulled her knees up under her chin and wrapped her arms around her legs.

"After our son was born, Tecumseh called on Strikes-the-Sky to travel with him," she said. The familiar names had a strange taste on her tongue, but she went on. "I followed the men as they went from village to village, recruiting warriors from all the tribes to join the battle to hold the land. With my son on my back I followed them. Everywhere people were desperate for food, for clothes, for weapons to defend themselves, for hope. The things I saw—the things my son saw when he was still a baby—they were worse than the poorhouse could ever be."

She paused to sort through her thoughts, and in the silence she counted the birds in the sky.

"Go on," said Jennet. "Please."

"Late one summer the army burned all the crops, and so when the winter came many of them starved, youngest and oldest first, as it always is. Their empty bellies swelled and then they died. All my medicines, the things I had spent so much time learning—none of that meant anything at all."

Hannah forced herself to take a deep breath and hold it for three heartbeats.

"That winter was the first time I drank the tea that sends a child back to the shadow lands."

And later, Hannah might have said, *later when the fighting started in earnest I wanted no other child. Foolish woman that I was.*

Jennet drew in a shuddering breath. "And is there a tea to do the opposite, when a woman wants a child?"

Hannah sent her a sidelong glance. "There are medicines to encourage a child, yes, and songs to summon one. You will ask me when you are ready, and together Many-Doves and I and you will prove the old women in Carryck wrong."

At that Jennet smiled, and leaned forward, and pressed her forehead to her cousin's cheek, damp with perspiration and tears and hope.

"I'm ready now," she said. "If only your stubborn brother would come back for me."

Jennet was determined to learn everything she could about living in the wilderness, so that when Luke did come back he would find her a worthy wife. No one was safe from her quest; she sought out strangers to ask questions with such complete sincerity and interest that no one ever thought to deny her. Whatever resentment there may have been in the village—and there were some young women who were not happy to learn that this interloper from Scotland had snatched Luke Bonner for her own—it disappeared in the face of Jennet's resolute goodwill and generosity. Jennet was in love and the world was not strong enough to resist her; it must love her back.

She had her favorites: Curiosity was one of them, Joshua Hench, Curiosity's son-in-law and a blacksmith, was another. She made fast friends with the children, who competed for the honor of teaching her the things they knew and showing her their secret places.

In short time she had learned how to make biscuits, how to forge a nail, how to grind corn into the finest meal by hand, how to distinguish between the tracks of raccoons, fox, dog, cats of different kinds; she had thrown herself into the harvest without hesitation and laughed when Hannah insisted on treating the scratches and blisters that resulted. She knew where the children went to search for arrowheads and she took lessons in skinning rabbits, loading a rifle, and walking a trail with the quiet watchfulness that was the true sign of an accomplished woodswoman.

On a Sunday in the late afternoon Hannah and Jennet set out together for the village, the tarot cards tucked safely into the basket Jennet carried with her everywhere. Almost everyone had asked for a reading, once it was understood that she asked nothing in return except answers to her endless questions. When she came back to Lake in the Clouds it would be full of the things she had gathered, from pinecones to mushrooms to spent bullets, but at the moment it was empty and light enough to swing.

When they left the glen Jennet raised her head and sniffed the air, her nose wrinkling.

"A frost tonight," she said, pulling her shawl around her shoulders. Jennet's eyesight was only average, but her sense of smell surprised and impressed everyone.

Gabriel had made a game of testing her by covering her eyes and passing ever stranger items under her nose: a rusty nail, an apple stem, corn husks, a piece of cherry wood, a scrap of fur from the old pelt the dogs slept on. Only rarely would she be unable to put the right name to a scent, and thus far Hannah had never known her to mistake a change in the weather.

For her own part, Jennet seemed to take this talent of hers for granted. She made announcements and then moved on.

"You did say we could go by way of the marsh?"

"A half hour more won't make a difference," Hannah agreed. In truth she was just as happy not to go by the bridge under the millhouse, as Jemima Kuick would no doubt be keeping watch, as she did most evenings. Her biweekly visits to the widow were bad enough as it was. Jemima stayed in the shadows but she hovered like a spider over a web.

"Good," said Jennet. "I haven't been to see the beaver today."

She had taken a huge interest in the dam that crossed the narrowest point of the marsh on the west end of the lake. It was the biggest beaver dam that Hannah knew of, and more than that, it was a rare collaboration between man and beast. The dam was wide enough for two people to walk abreast without disturbing the animals who lived inside and worked so hard to maintain it. Jennet called it a miracle of natural engineering and one that would have delighted her father.

She spent many evenings long past dusk sitting near the dam with Gabriel and Annie, who could identify each of the beavers and answered all of Jennet's questions.

Jennet had early sought out Runs-from-Bears, who told her the story of the Kahnyen'kehàka who lived on the lake before the whites came, and how they had made a pact: Brother Beaver would maintain the bridge across the marsh and his Mohawk brothers would do what they could to protect him from the wolf.

The men in the village had a different take on things, which they also shared with Jennet. The beaver dam was a bridge that cost them neither time nor money to maintain, and more than that: it gave them some level of protection against spring floods.

"To make hats out of such wondrous creatures." Jennet always ended her visits with this muttered condemnation.

This Sunday evening as they crossed the beaver bridge the dusk was already on them and a light rain had begun to fall. The high keen smells—mud and rot and fish—made Hannah think of Elizabeth, who could not keep her nose from wrinkling even after so many years.

But Jennet did not mind the stink; she had grown up in circumstances far richer and grander than even Elizabeth's, but she had spent all of her girlhood running wild in the Lowland hills, and she was more likely to investigate the cause of a stink than to turn away from it.

Underfoot the dam was solid and thick with many new layers of dried mud patted into place. It made crossing the marsh quick and clean and still Hannah was bothered.

A hard winter was coming by all the signs, and the thought of it made her break out in gooseflesh where the cold rain had not.

To Jennet she said, "You will need furs to wear too, in the winter. We must talk to Many-Doves about your clothes."

"But not beaver." Jennet cast a last glance at a large form moving placidly through the deeper water on the lake side of the dam. And then, more thoughtfully: "Runs-from-Bears says the winter will be cold, with more snow than usual. As bad as the winter the twins were born. I remember you telling me about that when first you came to Carryck."

"It was a very bad winter, yes. The river froze solid, which it seldom does."

Jennet said, "I have so little experience of snow, real snow, I am almost looking forward to it."

Hannah made a sound she hoped would be sufficient to end the conversation. But Jennet was not so easily discouraged.

"Gabriel says he'll teach me about snowshoes."

In the tall grasses that framed the footpath rabbits were playing in the last of the light, and they scattered as the women passed by.

"You'll have little choice," Hannah said. "Unless you spend the entire winter by the hearth."

Jennet looked genuinely shocked at the idea. "Why would I want to do that?"

"Because it's warm and safe," Hannah said.

Her cousin let out a soft laugh. "Aye, and boring, forbye. Do you skate on the lake in winter?"

The question took Hannah by surprise. She felt herself flushing with it, all the way up her spine to the ends of her fingers.

"No," she said, and heard her own voice cracking. "The ice is too rough and uncertain."

"But if the winter is as bad as you say," Jennet insisted. And then, more thoughtfully: "Maybe I could ask Mr. Hench to make me a pair of blades."

They were silent for the rest of the walk to the Todds'. Hannah wondered at herself, that she could be wounded so easily and without any warning at all by something so simple as a discussion of the coming winter.

Tell her, Strikes-the-Sky said behind her. For a single moment Hannah knew with absolute certainty that if she turned around she would find him there, looking down at her, his expression impatient.

Tell her and free yourself, he said again.

Jennet was sniffing the air once more as they came closer to the Todds' place. "They've been making soap. Do you remember the Sunday we spent with my granny and old Gelleys the washerwoman?"

"It's been a long time since I've thought about that," said Hannah. She cleared her throat and when she spoke her voice had transformed itself, taken on the comfortable creak of breathy old age. " 'Thirty year was I heid washerwoman, wi' three guid maids under me. Six days a week did we wash and press.' "

"I miss my granny." Jennet's tone had softened and Hannah knew that she, too, was hearing a voice long gone.

"I remember many things from that afternoon," Hannah said. "I remember the vicar coming to call. What ever became of him?"

Jennet's face lit up. "Och, did I never write to you about Willie Fisher? And such a lovely story it is too. He inherited some money from an uncle and he went to sea and became a pirate."

Hannah stopped where she was and sent Jennet her severest expression, to which her cousin held up both hands.

"I swear on my good name, it's aye true. He bought a ship and named her *Salvation* and went off to the Spice Islands."

"Jennet," Hannah said with a smile. "How does that add up to piracy? It sounds to me as though he's gone off to be a missionary."

The corner of Jennet's mouth twitched. "Aye, and are they not one and the same thing? Stealing souls from someone else's God to give to your own. Sometimes it seems to me that a war must soon break out in heaven itself, with such shameless poaching as goes on among the deities."

Without realizing that she had intended to, Hannah hugged her cousin.

"And what did I do to deserve that?" Jennet asked, pleased.

"You made me laugh," Hannah said. "It's a rare talent you've got, cousin."

Jennet looked embarrassed, but pleased. "I hope I can be of more help to you than that," she said. "Let's go see what work the doctor has for us."

Richard said, "You'll need an assistant, but Ethan is gone to Johnstown and Curiosity to a birthing." He sent Jennet a severe look from under a lowered brow, but the Earl of Carryck's youngest daughter had been fed a steady diet of such looks from men even more imposing than Richard Todd. She gave him a grin in return.

"Are you up to the job, Lady Jennet?"

Richard was the only person in Paradise who still called Jennet by her rightful title, and not out of respect but only to goad her. He was bedridden with nausea and in a great deal of pain today, but Hannah had the idea that he was enjoying himself.

Jennet said, "Och aye, dinna worry yer heid."

To Richard Todd, Jennet always spoke Scots. The only reason for this, as far as Hannah could see, was to pay him back in aggravation. For his part Richard seemed determined to deny her that pleasure by steadfastly refusing to make any comment, no matter what language she used with him. And if she suddenly addressed him in Greek, Hannah thought, he would not raise a brow.

Now he just grunted, but his mouth jerked at the corner. Hannah bit back her own smile.

She said, "I could stop by the trading post and ask Anna to assist. Then Jennet could stay here and keep you company."

For her troubles she got sharp looks from both of them: from Jennet because Richard Todd was one of the very few people in the village she would not spend time with unless compelled, and from Richard because he would resent being challenged until he was laid in his grave.

He grunted. "If I wanted company I would get a dog."

" 'Gin ye could find one wha'd hae ye," said Jennet clearly, looking him directly in the eye.

He pointed with his chin to the door before he lost the battle completely and gave in to smiling. "You're dismissed, the two of you. God protect me from the Bonner women."

"What exactly will I have to do?" Jennet asked as they made their way to the Grebers' cabin. She was carrying the lantern in one hand and her basket over the other.

"Hand me things when I ask for them," Hannah said. "Stay calm. Distract the patient. Don't faint."

At that Jennet looked truly insulted. "I've never fainted in my life, and weel you know it, Hannah Bonner."

"I beg your pardon," Hannah said. "I don't know what I was thinking."

But Jennet was not so easily appeased. "What's a bit of blood, after all? Have I not seen many a bloody man dragged into the courtyard at Carryck?"

"Good," Hannah said, being careful not to show her concern. "Because it's likely to be unpleasant."

For the rest of the walk Hannah explained to Jennet exactly what she would have to do. A horse had stepped on Horace Greber's foot while he was in Johnstown. The infection had spread fast, and the surgeon there—a disreputable sort who barbered and let blood and did the odd surgery that came his way, all with the same scalpel—had taken the leg off above the knee to stop it. Then he had sent Horace home to Paradise in the back of a wagon driven by his frightened nine-year-old son while he raved with fever.

"His boy, the one with the strange name—"

"Hardwork," Hannah had supplied.

"He came by to fetch me," Richard had reported. "From his description it sounds like it's infection but no gangrene, not yet, at any rate. No doubt it'll need abrading, maybe cauterizing. Take a bottle of brandy with you. For a few swallows of good brandy Horace Greber will let you take off his other leg as well."

In its construction the cabin was no different from any of the others in the village, but it was in such bad repair that it seemed at first that it must be deserted. Shutters hung lopsided or were altogether missing, and the porch was hidden behind a high wall of weeds and nettles. The hunting dogs tied to the rail gave them a sullen look, and then one of them lunged suddenly at a chicken that ventured too close, his jaws snapping. The chicken flew off with a startled squawk.

"Mr. Greber lives alone?" Jennet asked.

"With his son," Hannah said. "His wife left him and went home to her family in Schenectady. She took the girls with her, most of them grown enough to go into service already."

"Och," said Jennet. "A scandal. It's just at times like these that I miss Lily the most. She would have told me all about it long ago. I must remember to ask Curiosity."

"There's nothing much to tell," said Hannah. "Mariah couldn't face another winter in the wilderness. He didn't want to go and she did and so she left. It happens all the time. It could happen to anyone, and usually does."

Jennet was about to argue that point when the door opened and Hardwork Greber came out on the porch. The boy was tall for his age, and Jennet could count every one of his ribs in the light of the lump of tallow he carried on a piece of broken crockery. The dogs were better fed than the boy, but then the dogs were good trackers and could be sold for hard cash, whereas the boy was too young yet to bring in a real wage.

"Pa's been waiting," the boy said, trying not to stare at Jennet, whose face floated like a heavenly apparition in the pure light of the lantern. "I'm afraid he's mighty drunk. We might have to tie him down and his language—" A short glance at Jennet and his color rose in a flash.

"You might want to wait out here, miss."

Jennet flicked her fingers at him. "And what Scotswoman worth her salt is put off by a man in his cups? Just bring along the rope, lad, and let us get to work."

Horace was lying on a bare mattress stiff with sweat and blood and other things that did not bear naming. He snored softly, his head tilted back to expose a neck thick with graying beard stubble, his mouth open wide. A slug of white-coated tongue flickered against fever-blistered lips with every snore. Jennet found it hard to look away from a sight so resolutely disgusting.

As was the whole cabin, heaped with refuse and filthy clothes and tools and traps and hides. In the dim light of a single tallow candle and the lantern Jennet could only make out some of it, and she was glad of the shadows. The stink could not be avoided, nor could she identify the worst of it. Human waste and sweat and spoiled food, mold and hides half-tanned, wood smoke and sour clothes, those things were all to be expected; but there was something more, something that set itself high in the nose and clung to the soft passages of the throat.

"You brought the leg home with you?" Hannah said quietly, looking around herself until her gaze settled on a package lying in the corner. It was wrapped in bloody paper and muslin and tied with string, and the whole was crawling with flies. Jennet swallowed very hard and looked away until she could compose her face.

"Pa wouldn't leave it behind," Hardwork said in an apologetic tone. "If we put it outside to get rid of the stink the dogs will be after it."

Horace had come awake at the sound of their voices.

"If things go bad, the boy knows to bury it with me," he said. His voice was hoarse with fever. "Don't want to be stomping around heaven on a peg leg."

"Hmmmm." Hannah made a sound deep in her throat. "Let's see to the leg you've got left first."

Jennet forced herself to watch as Hannah unwrapped the stump, which was, she would admit to no one but herself, far worse than she had imagined. Hannah used a scissors from her basket to cut away the filthy bandages, stiff with blood and pus.

"A surgeon did that?" Jennet asked the question though she meant not to.

Hannah snorted softly. "He calls himself a surgeon, yes. I would guess he learned his trade in a butcher shop."

"He charged good money," said the boy behind them. "Money we meant to spend on supplies."

Horace's face contorted as Hannah tugged at the bandages, and to Jennet he looked like one of the faces in her father's illustrated *Paradise Lost*, peering up from the bowels of hell.

"This won't be pleasant," Hannah said. "There's a leather strap in my bag if you need something to bite into."

The man's head fell back against the mattress and he burped and farted at once. Perhaps not Milton, after all, but more of Robert Burns, thought Jennet dryly.

"Just go away," he said. "I ain't got a red penny to pay you."

"Hardwork," said Hannah, ignoring this direct order. "I am going to need a lot of water. Bring me a basinful and then set more to heating." She pulled a length of clean cloth from her basket and spread it out on the only unoccupied corner of a table piled high with dirty dishes and cutlery. In quick movements she began to lay out her instruments on the cloth.

"A full bucket's worth, do you understand? Make sure the kettle is clean before you put the water to boil, scour it with sand if you have to," Hannah said, looking up to make sure the boy was listening. Her tone was short and a little sharp but not unkind. "And make sure you stoke the fire well, I need it very hot."

Hardwork was studying his bare feet, his mouth pressed into a thin line. "Ma took the kettle with her." He almost whispered it, but it was enough to rouse Horace, who had fallen back into a stupor.

He looked right at Jennet with such a strange mixture of pain and fury that she must lean forward when he beckoned with one finger.

"I'll die, and then she'll be sorry she took that kettle." He hiccupped softly. His breath was so heavy with alcohol that Jennet felt momentarily dizzy.

Hannah made a dismissive sound. "You won't die today, Horace Greber, though you may want to before I'm done. Hardwork, listen now. I need that basin of water to start with, and then you can go borrow a kettle and some soap and some clean linen too. And hurry or you'll miss the start of Jennet's story."

"What story is that?" said Hardwork, looking more interested now and not quite so desperate.

"Hurry back or you'll never know," said Jennet. "And won't you be the poorer for it?"

In the short time Jennet had spent in Paradise her stories had already become legend, for she was filled with them and they must spill out, often at the oddest times. Stories of her clansmen and battles fought for freedom from tyranny; villains and heroes and those who were a little of each; the well-loved stories of the Pirate Stoker and how she and Hannah had outfoxed him as girls, or tried to; stories of treasure lost and never found; stories about her home and her childhood and her family; stories about her journey and a little dog named Pip who could do the most amazing tricks and understood three languages.

She read the tarot cards for anyone who showed an interest in them. Each time was the same: she would lay them down in a pattern, study each with a great seriousness, consult her notes, and then launch into a reading that was a combination of anecdotes, observations, suggestions, and gentle admonitions. Curiosity was especially interested in the cards and she and Jennet sat down with them whenever Hannah came to see Richard or work in the laboratory.

Now Horace Greber peered up at her from the depths of his drunkenness, his face wet with perspiration, and asked for something he would have never allowed himself under other circumstances.

"Will you read the cards for me?"

What Horace was looking for, Hannah knew without a doubt, was a promise that he would not die today or tomorrow or next week. This was clear to Jennet too. She would refuse his request, Hannah knew, but first she was deciding what story she would tell to appease him. Just as she herself must think long and hard about what medicines would serve the problem at hand most effectively, Jennet chose her tales carefully. Many-Doves called Jennet Moon-Spinner, and it fit her well: she could cast stars up into the sky with her words alone.

"Not the cards," said Jennet. "Not today. Today I think you'll want to hear about old MacQuiddy, and why it was he never took a wife."

At that Hannah could not hold back a smile. Jennet's supply of stories about MacQuiddy were each of them more outrageous than the last, and stories about him were a favorite among the villagers.

Under a layer of grime and sweat Horace had gone very pale as Hannah began her work, but he was determined to ignore her. He grunted his approval at Jennet.

"A clever man, MacQuiddy."

"Was he, do you think?" asked Jennet. "You'll have to listen and decide for yourself."

"First," Jennet began when Hardwork had taken a stool on his father's far side, "you must recall that MacQuiddy was steward to my father the earl and his father before him. For fifty years MacQuiddy was the best of servants, and the sourest of men.

"Now you might ask, what was it that filled Colin MacQuiddy with such gall? He could not open his gob to shovel in a spoonful of porridge but that sour words must fall out first, no matter how fast he ate. Perhaps it was the heavy responsibility on his shoulders. Perhaps his teeth were a misery to him, or a bunion on his big toe, or worry for a brither who went to sea as a boy. But the truth is far stranger, and it starts with a simple fact. MacQuiddy had no wife and no bairns of his own to order about, you see, and so he must make do with the servants and other innocent wee lasses as chanced to come across him unawares."

Horace grunted in pain and then cleared his throat in embarrassment. Without interrupting her story Jennet fed him a spoonful of the medicine Hannah had prepared, strong smelling and dark.

"The truth of it was, MacQuiddy should have found a wife without doing so much as flicking a finger. He was aye bonnie as a young man, from a good Carryckton family, and he served the earl himself in a position of trust. He should have had a wife, and he could have had a wife, except—"

At the other end of the bed Hannah had opened a vial and a smell filled the room, slightly bitter and still sweet. Horace tensed and tried to sit up, but Jennet put a hand on his shoulder and pushed him back down again.

Beneath the grime his skin was milky white. "Except?" he croaked.

"There's always an except," Hannah volunteered in the calmest of voices.

"Aye, that's true." Jennet spread her hands out on her lap. "You see, in the days when he was young, before he came to serve at Carryckcastle and long before he began his life's work of making wee lasses miserable, it fell to MacQuiddy to drive the cows in from the field to the milkmaids. Now one summer as he was coming along with the cows at gloaming, he chanced to spy a wee creature all clad in green, and with long yellow hair like gold, coming toward him."

Hardwork's expression was blank with wonder. "A fairy?"

"Aye, a fairy, a bonnie fairy no bigger than a lass of three years— but still a woman grown, in her body and face. Fair beautiful she was, but with something wild in her eye, something fierce that was hard to look at. MacQuiddy couldna describe it with words, try as he might.

"I havena told you yet that in his youth MacQuiddy was far and wide the tallest of all the lads and men alike, long and thin as a stick bug, so very tall that the wee fairy reached only to his knee. She had to put her head back to look him in the face. And she raised up her voice, high and unearthly it was, and she looked MacQuiddy right in the eye and she called up to him as from the bottom of a well. 'Colin MacQuiddy! I'm looking for Colin MacQuiddy!'

"Now, everybody knows that the polite thing to do when a body calls your name is to stop and greet them, fairy or no. But MacQuiddy lost his nerve and he ran away, right into the milking barn and shut the door behind himself with a crash.

"He could hardly speak for trembling, but when he finally found the words to tell the tale, the milkmaids laughed at him. It was young Gelleys Ballentyne who told him. 'Why, Colin MacQuiddy,' said she with a wink and a smile, 'that's a wife come for you this night. You must go and take her hand.'

" 'A wife!' cried MacQuiddy. 'May the good Lord keep me from such a wee wife as that!' And he told everyone later that he was in such a fear that the hairs stood up on the back of his neck like the bristles on a hog. All the time he stood there trembling the fairy was outside calling him by name, you understand, for she had set her eyes on MacQuiddy for a husband. He waited and waited for her to go, and when he could wait no longer the fairy followed him back home and then—believe it or not—Colin MacQuiddy closed the door in her face."

Jennet looked sternly first at Horace and then at Hardwork. Horace was sweating openly, his face tight with pain, so it fell to Hardwork to ask the question.

"Is it wrong to close the door on a fairy?"

At that Jennet straightened her back and put a hand to her breast. "I can see you've no had the pleasure," she said. "Listen then and I'll tell you what happened. The wee folk are proud creatures and sly too, and spiteful when they've been slighted."

The boy leaned forward, but Horace had closed his eyes, and the muscles in his neck and jaw convulsed alarmingly.

Jennet said, "MacQuiddy never found a wife who would have him. Can you imagine it? No lass would have the MacQuiddy."

"For fear of the fairy?" asked Hardwork.

"Do you think? Perhaps, for fairies are aye jealous creatures. But if that was the revenge she took on him, it wasna enough to satisfy her hurt pride. It was a year or more before anybody took note, but starting on the day MacQuiddy turned away his fairy bride, he began to get smaller. Just a wee bit every year," she added quickly, holding up her fingers to show them. "But nothing he did would stop it. Nothing he ate or drank, no prayers he might say, no teas or cures or charms, year in and year out he grew a wee bit shorter.

"When I was a girl he was a small man, and when I was a young woman I could look him in the eye. On the day I married I could look down on his bald head and count the freckles there."

She looked Hardwork directly in the eye. "One hundred and three there were, exactly. And the smaller MacQuiddy grew, the worse his temper. Gelleys the washerwoman was the only one wha would speak the truth to him. She would raise her finger—to MacQuiddy!—and tell him what he didna want to hear.

" 'You called it doon on your own sorry heid,' she told him. 'The night you shut the door on your bride.' And what a temper would be on him then, enough to make the moon hide in the sky.

"Weel. In his later years MacQuiddy took to dragging a stool wherever he went, and he'd climb up on it so as to look a person in the eye when he had a word to say. And sometimes he'd hop from foot to foot so that the stool rocked and wiggled. And woe to him— or her—who laughed. As wee a man as he was, MacQuiddy had a fist on him like a giant and a tongue as sharp as a new-stropped razor."

"How big was he when he died?" asked Hardwork.

"And have I ever said a word about MacQuiddy dying?" asked Jennet, wiping Horace's face with the freshly dampened linen.

"He's still living?" Horace's voice was hoarse with strain, and he didn't open his eyes.

"That I canna say." Jennet tilted her head as if to consider whether or not to tell the rest of the story.

"But this much I can tell for certain. One day at sunrise when MacQuiddy didna come into the kitchens, the cook went to look for him. She must start her day with a good battle of wills, you see, so if MacQuiddy didna come to her she must go to him. But his bed was empty, and neither was he anywhere in the castle nor on the grounds. The men went out to look for him and the children too, and they looked under every bush and peeked in every hidey-hole and picked up every rock. There was no help for it, MacQuiddy was gone."

Hardwork let out a sigh. "He was never seen again."

Jennet gave him a reproachful look. "I wouldna go so far as that. You see, were you to go to Carryckton and pay the milkmaids a visit in the gloaming you might see what they see, most summer evenings just as the last of the light goes from the sky. A couple walking across the fields arm in arm, neither of them any bigger than a child of three years. One of them with long hair the color of gold, and the other as bald as a peeled egg."

Hardwork turned to his father to see whether or not he dared believe something so strange and wonderful. Then his face fell.

"Look," he said, disappointed. "Pa's fallen asleep right at the best part of the story."

"Hmmm." Jennet knew a faint when she saw one, but she saw no reason to further upset the boy. She said, "You'll have to tell him how it ends when he's had his rest."

At the far end of the bed Hannah was looking very flushed. Her hairline was damp with perspiration but she managed a small smile. "Well, it wasn't pretty, but it isn't as bad as it looked either."

Hardwork looked at Jennet with relief and a new respect. "You're done, and we didn't even have to tie him down. Miss Jennet," he said solemnly, "your stories are better than ropes."

"Och, I canna take all the credit," she said easily. She began to help Hannah gather her things. "A man's pride will tie him doon as sure as any rope ever made. Or story told."

Hannah allowed herself to smile. "I think the stump will heal now as long as he keeps it clean and drained. And he must drink a weak tea made of this—" She handed Hardwork a brown paper packet tied with string. "Every four hours. A full cup, mind."

When they left the cabin Jennet was surprised to find that night had fallen. Less of a surprise was Nathaniel, who was waiting for them with the horses so that they wouldn't have to walk back to Lake in the Clouds in the full dark. He saw them mounted and then he trotted off to scout the path ahead of them, his rifle resting easy in his hands.

Because, Jennet reminded herself, there were wild beasts about, and for all its appearance of peace this village had seen a great deal of treachery over the years. Indian raids, schoolhouses burnt to the ground, murder. The Bonners did not share these stories with many, but Jennet was a cousin and would be more once Luke came back for her.

The day after the matter was finally settled Gabriel and Annie had shown her the secrets of the mountain: the caves under the falls, the cavern on the north side of the mountain where the Tory gold had been hidden away for so long, the silver mine that had given up the last of that precious metal some ten years ago. Paradise could be a dangerous place for so many reasons. The miracle of it all was that the idea should excite her more than it frightened her. She liked to think of herself as brave, though she knew her mother would call her foolish; her father would have had stronger words still.

"Your menfolk are as protective of you as any of mine are of me," Jennet said now to Hannah, deeply satisfied that it should be so. As they had not yet started up the mountain proper the horses could still walk side by side and she turned to look at her cousin's profile.

Hannah was often in a subdued and sometimes melancholy mood when she finished with a patient. Now she looked up at the sound of Jennet's voice with a start, as if she had forgotten where she was altogether. In the swaying light of the pierced tin lamp she carried, the bones of her face cast shadows that made her look more spirit than breathing flesh and blood.

Jennet was afraid for her suddenly and did not know why, or if there was any comfort she might offer.

Then Hannah said, "I didn't mean to practice medicine again. Ever again."

Jennet considered all the things she might say or questions she might ask, and she discarded them one by one. They went on in the soft warm night, through a world of sounds: night birds and creatures that hunted in the dark, the wind in the trees and leaves fluttering to earth. In time the horses began to climb, muscular sides clenching, sure of foot and eager to be home.

A half hour passed and then another and then the sound of the falls at Lake in the Clouds came to them. Once in a while Jennet caught sight of Nathaniel just ahead of her on the path, but she had the unsettling notion that if she were to turn around she'd find that Hannah was gone, hiding herself until she had sorted through memories she had locked away but could not always govern.

But she was there still, and she spoke when they were in view of the cabins. "Thank you, Jennet," she said.

"You've no cause to thank me," Jennet said, relieved and shaken too, though she could not say just why. "I was happy to be what help I can."

"No. Thank you for not telling me how I should feel. Have I told you about the village the whites called Prophet's Town?"

The question was so unexpected that Jennet drew up and turned to her cousin. "You know that you haven't," she said. "But I'd like to hear about it. Did you live there?"

Hannah made a sound in her throat. "From the day it was founded until the day it was burned to the ground," she said. And then, before Jennet could think of what to ask: "It was a dream, and it did not last."

• • •

They stayed a few minutes in the common room talking with Elizabeth and eating. Usually Jennet loved this quiet time in the evening when the whole family sat together. Elizabeth would read aloud from a book or play or newspaper, and they talked about the strangest combinations of things, *King Lear* and the squash harvest, political intrigues in Washington and London and how much more wood the men needed to put up for the coming winter.

Tonight Jennet was impatient with the talk and unable to concentrate on anything but the promise of hearing at least some of Hannah's story. She was afraid that the mood would have left her by the time Elizabeth put out the lamp and they all went to their beds.

On the stairs Hannah stopped and looked over her shoulder at her father and stepmother. "The night air is cool," she said. "Leave your window open."

It was such a strange request that no one could think of what to say, but as soon as Jennet closed the door of the chamber she shared with Hannah behind her, she understood.

Hannah went to sit by the open window with her back to the room, and Jennet.

"In the old days the village was called Ket-tip-pe-can-nunk," she began in a clear voice that must travel on the night air. The tone was familiar to Jennet and strange too, filled with anger and sorrow in equal measures.

"It was a beautiful place, on the river the whites call Wabash. Tecumseh and his brother chose it to build a new town where all the Indian tribes would come together."

"Tecumseh?" Jennet asked, the strange name sounding light on her tongue.

"A Shawnee warrior," Hannah said patiently. "A great warrior. His name means Panther-in-the-Sky." When Jennet had no more questions, she went on. "Our son was four years old when my uncle Strong-Words and Strikes-the-Sky both swore allegiance to Tecumseh and we went to join him on the Wabash."

She was silent for so long that Jennet felt herself sliding toward sleep, only to be startled awake when Hannah took up her story again.

"Tecumseh's brother had a vision of a place where all the People lived in the old way, free of influence of the white man, free of alcohol. It was hard work to convince other tribes but by the winter of eighteen ten there were more than five hundred warriors in training. Many of them brought their families. Sometimes I would hear five languages in five minutes walking from one place to another, and not understand any of them. The village was crowded and food was a problem. It was not always peaceful, but those were good years."

Hannah made a sound that might have been a laugh; it made the flesh rise all along Jennet's back. Jennet said, "As when the clans came together against the English. They can put aside old grudges and rivalries for only so long."

"Yes," Hannah said. "It was like that."

"You were the only doctor?" Jennet ventured.

"Oh no. There were healers who came to us from many tribes, but never enough, just as we never had enough medicines or even corn husks for bandages. I was busy all day with the sick, and Strikes-the-Sky was busy with the young warriors or with Tecumseh, in the middle of discussions and negotiations.

"But we were content. I was doing what I wanted to do, working among my own people and learning everything I could about medicine from any healer who came to the village. I vaccinated hundreds against the smallpox.

"We stayed because my uncle and my husband had real hope in Tecumseh."

Hannah's voice had taken on a new rhythm, as if by telling this story she found herself talking to the people she was describing, lost to her now. She recited bits from Tecumseh's speeches and again Jennet could not help but think of Scotland, where men had fought for hundreds of years to loosen the hold of the English, all for naught. Something had always gone wrong, and most usually the flaw was to be found in men of lesser understanding or courage.

Hannah would tell that part of the story too; Jennet could feel her nearing it and she was weary, suddenly, of such stories. She would have turned away from this one if it weren't for the fact that it was Hannah telling it.

"In the fall of eighteen eleven Tecumseh and some of the warriors left to visit villages and I stayed behind with my son. There were many new people in the village who needed to be vaccinated, that was the excuse I gave. It was the first time Strikes-the-Sky and I were ever really apart since we were married."

She was pointing with her chin out the window. "Right here, at Lake in the Clouds. There, on that spot."

For a long time there was silence and Jennet thought of her own wedding, something she rarely did. The images came to her as dull as tarnished copper: Ewan's blameless face, twitching with anxiousness; her mother pale in her mourning clothes, summoning a trembling smile whenever Jennet caught her eye. The clansmen like a wall all around her, impenetrable. Even her brother had been subdued.

Hannah's voice dropped to an almost-whisper. "I kept my son with me, and the men rode off at dawn in the rain. That was the last time I saw my husband."

In her surprise Jennet found it hard to keep her silence. "I thought he died in battle, the one your father told me about—"

"The whites call it the Battle of Tippecanoe. But no, Strikes-the-Sky wasn't there. I wish he had been. If Tecumseh hadn't been away and taken the best minds with him, things might have turned out differently when the whites decided to attack the village."

"What went wrong?" Jennet asked.

"Tecumseh's brother." Her voice had soured. A shivering moved Hannah's shoulders, like a woman taken suddenly in a fever.

"He was no warrior, but he believed himself to be equal to the decisions that had to be made, and no one had the courage to challenge him. When it was all over close to four hundred warriors were dead, my uncle and his eldest sons and so many others, young men and old. I knew them, every one."

Jennet couldn't really imagine what Hannah was telling her, and she didn't really want to. But her cousin went on, as if she could simply not stop the flow of the story.

"Harrison's men burned the village to the ground and all our hopes with it. We ran," Hannah said. "We ran for our lives and we dragged the wounded and the children behind us. And that is as much of the story as I can tell you, for now at least."

She got up from the chair and shut the window firmly. Then she went to her bed, where she laid herself down fully dressed and crossed an arm over her face.

Jennet wanted to know so many things: where Strikes-the-Sky had died, and how, if not at the battle of Tippecanoe; what exactly had gone wrong, and what had become of the man people called the Prophet. And the most important question, the one that might never be answered at all: what had happened to Hannah's son, the boy whose name she never said aloud? Had he died in the battle, or its aftermath?

Instead she said, "Cousin, what happened tonight to make you need to tell that story?"

It seemed at first as if Hannah would not answer. Then she said,

"When they brought my uncle Strong-Words' body home, he was missing both of his arms. They had been chopped off at the shoulder, very deliberately. The next day we all went to the battlefield: his wife and daughter, my son and me. To find his arms so we could bury him properly. But we failed. Some white man carried my uncle's arms away with him."

In the dark Jennet found she could hardly swallow, so rough and swollen was her throat.

"Sometimes," Hannah said, and her voice crackled like spring ice. "Sometimes in my dreams I see my uncle swimming in the lake in the clouds, armless and sleek, like an otter. That was his boy-name, you know. Otter. In my dream he puts his head up out of the water and even sleeping I can smell the battle on him. There is such terrible sadness and disappointment in his face. I carry it like a stone around my neck."

Hannah turned her face to the wall. Just when Jennet thought that she had gone to sleep, Hannah sat up and began to rock in the bed, her arms around her knees.

"I was happy," she said. "I want you to know how happy I was. I want you to know about Strikes-the-Sky, what kind of husband he is, what kind of father he was to our son. He is a good man."

"I know that already," Jennet said, shocked above all things that Hannah spoke of her husband as if he might still be alive.

Satisfied, Hannah lay down again. "If I can find the words to make him real again," she said. "Then I will tell you his stories."

It was not her uncle that came to Hannah in her dreams that night, nor her husband or even her son, though the boy was most likely to show himself when she was unsettled by memories. Instead a white man came to find her. She had never learned his name, though he died under her scalpel while she fought to save his life.

An Ottawa chief called Sabaqua had taken the soldier as a prisoner early in the fighting. Though wounded himself, Sabaqua and another warrior called Shabbona had brought the prisoner in on horseback just past dawn. Sabaqua claimed the soldier for his own; he would bring him to his wife to take the place of the son who had fallen in the battle.

But Hannah took one look and knew that Sabaqua could not have this white soldier for a son. He was a young man in his prime, strong and straight, but there was a wound in his side that pierced his liver and one leg was crushed; there was nothing any healer could do for him.

And still she tried. She packed the wound in his side and dug deep into the flesh of his leg to stop the bleeding, and while she worked the man alternated between screaming and talking. It was so long since she had spoken English it was possible, at first, simply not to understand him. But then the words had begun to order themselves in her mind and she could not ignore them anymore.

He told her about his home in the Indiana territory and his sister and his father, talking to her as if she were an old friend, someone he had grown up with, and not an Indian woman covered with great gouts of his blood. There was an urgency in him as he entrusted her with his memories as they faded out of his mind and heart.

And all the while he talked there were more wounded coming in: men of her own tribe, her own family, her husband's. Men she knew well, whose children she had helped into the world, whose sons had played with her son. Warriors who had a chance of surviving their wounds and perhaps living to fight another day. If she would only turn away from this dying man with skin darkened by the sun to a shade that would be always and forever nothing less than white.

Many of the men she had failed to save came to her in the dark of night; some to talk to her about matters of no importance, others to say nothing at all. In this dream the white man without a name smiled at her, reached out a bloody hand and touched her cheek with one finger. His wounds had shifted from his leg and side to his chest, where a single bullet had carved out a hole over his heart.

The white man opened his mouth and spoke to her not in his own voice, but with her husband's.

Take care of the boy, Strikes-the-Sky said through the dead white man. *Save the boy. My brothers will raise him to be a warrior.*

I failed, she told him. *I tried to save him but I failed. He's in the shadow lands. He is yours to look after, now.*

Look after the boy, Strikes-the-Sky said again. *You must save the boy.*

Chapter 8

Montreal

In an attic room on the top floor of her brother's home, Lily Bonner worked in the last light of December afternoon. Her breath hovered damp and white around her head, and her skin was flushed with cold. The woolen cloak she wore to start with lay forgotten in the sawdust and wood shavings.

She carved, her movements sure and quick, quicker with the waning light. With all her concentration fixed on the block of cherry wood on the worktable, Lily coaxed the lines of a flowering tree into revealing themselves.

Now and then Lily paused in her work to study the branch propped up as a model on the deep windowsill. On the low table beneath the window there was a neat row of woodcarver's tools: chisels and knives and blades, gifts from her brother, who made such things appear before she could even think to ask. Each tool was wrapped in a rag, tucked and folded in precise angles, damp with oil.

She had started work with the rising of the sun, moving from one task to another: three hours with one teacher, two hours with another, the rest of the time at an easel or drawing table or in the attic with the wood. After dinner she had taken her daily walk through the city.

Every day she understood a little more of the French spoken all around her by farmers and tinsmiths, shop clerks and milkmaids. Often Lily thought of her mother's classroom and wished that she had been less impatient with the things she had been given to learn, French among them.

Today she had found the courage to try her luck when she bought a penny bun from an older woman with kind eyes, her red cheeks roughened by pox scars. To her surprise Lily found that she could answer when the old woman asked after Luke and Iona, something that pleased her very much, even if it was strange to be reminded that even in this great city everyone must know her face and name and her family history. Long before she came to stay here people had been telling stories about her father and grandfather— breathless ones, sometimes funny, always exciting, and so far as Lily could tell, they were all true, at least in spirit.

As a little girl she had listened to the stories and wished for her own adventures. Then Gabriel Oak began to teach her how to draw and those wishes had been replaced by very different ones. For so long she had wanted just what she had been given: teachers and tools and time to work. Freedom from the endless, mindless jobs: spinning, grinding corn, wiping dishes. No children to plague her with questions and stories and excursions into the forests. At home much of November would be taken up with spinning tow for wicks and candle dipping, Lily's least favorite of all the endless household work. No doubt they were dipping candles in Montreal too, but it had nothing to do with her, not here. This is what she wanted, Lily told herself. Everything she asked for.

It was almost four; time to change and go down to the dinner table, where food and drink appeared magically, carried up the stairs from the basement kitchen. There would be company, as there always was; her brother was known throughout Canada for his conversation and the generous table he set. There were stories about him too, though they were not told in his hearing. Lily heard snatches wherever she went, and gathered those bits and pieces to take back to Luke. When they sat together on Sundays she would bring them out and quiz him: *Is it true that?* and, *How did you come to?* and, *Where was it you came across?*

But at the dinner table she kept her questions to herself in front of company. His friends or business acquaintances were many and always welcome, and some of them had got into the habit of bringing wives and daughters and most especially marriageable sons along to meet Lily. All of Montreal was curious about her, this girl raised in the wilderness who came to study art. Nathaniel Bonner's daughter, with paint stains on her fingers.

She did not mind keeping silent and watching. In these weeks Lily had learned a great deal about her brother during his dinners. He was clever and quick and opinionated; he was never directly cruel, though he did not suffer fools. Most of all, he liked a good argument.

Wee Iona sat at the head of the table and said very little; she never volunteered an opinion and seldom gave one, even when asked directly. Lily had come to like Iona, though she was still shy of her and unwilling to ask questions, even when they were alone. From the first day she had known that Iona would be her only ally in this household, the person who would stand up for her when Luke overstepped, as he was wont to do.

The younger men who came to Luke's table watched Lily closely when they thought she didn't notice, and sometimes when they knew that she did. They talked to her of art and Montreal and things she must see, people she must meet. They loved the city and wanted her to love it as well.

Lily knew she should be pleased with all this attention, but she found it unsettling. She wanted to do what was expected of her— what she expected of herself—to fall in love with Montreal: the shops and lanes and hidden corners, the odd houses with their tin roofs, the beauty of the fields and hills and the people. It was a city of artists, of painters and miniaturists and engravers and wood-carvers and goldsmiths. Many of them had fled France during the Terror and settled here; all of them were eager for any student, even a female student, as long as the tuition was paid promptly.

This is everything you wished for, she told herself sternly as she put away her tools. She sucked at a cut on her thumb and tasted her own blood, as salty as tears.

At night she often dreamed of home, of her mother and her father and the lake under the falls. The dreams were bright and quick, gone when she woke no matter how determined she was to hold on to them. She dreamed of her brother, her twin, sleeping in snow with his rifle cradled in his arms as he had once cradled a pet raccoon. She dreamed of Nicholas, the look on his face when she turned away from him that last day when she was in such a hurry to be gone to this new life.

She dreamed of her sister Hannah. Hannah sitting by the banks of the lake under the falls. Hannah frozen in place with eyes like marble.

•   •   •

"You will ruin your eyes working in the half-light," Iona told Lily when she came down to the dinner table. Iona's own eyes were filmy with age, and still she seemed to see everything and understand more. When Lily passed the old woman reached up and stroked her cheek with such kindness that she drew a sharp breath.

Just that simply she realized that no one had touched her since she came here. Her hands, yes. Men held her elbow on an icy street, or took her gloved hand while she climbed into a sleigh. French women kissed her cheek fleetingly, a touch of breath and perfumed skin. Luke never touched her at all.

She missed her mother's cool hand on the back of her neck; Gabriel's weight in her lap; Annie's fingers in her hair. Many-Doves' habit of pressing her shoulder whenever she was nearby. The brush of Daniel's arm, of Blue-Jay's, her father's hug. Nicholas Wilde's breath on her skin, the taste of him.

> When I happen to see Nicholas in the village he is very drawn and pale, though he greets me politely and asks after you and your brother both. Yesterday when your father took your newest drawings into the trading post to show, Nicholas spent a long time looking at them.

Lily kept this most recent letter from her mother folded and tucked inside her bodice. Because Nicholas could not write to her and she could not write to him, her mother's letter was the only evidence that he was still in the world. With a wife whose health seemed to be improving.

From her spot at the head of the table Iona was watching her, and for one moment Lily had the uneasy feeling that the old woman was reading her mind.

"She's lost in her thoughts," Luke said to his grandmother. "I don't think she heard you."

Lily said, "Of course I heard her. You're right, I must take better care of my eyes."

"I'll have more candles sent up for you." Luke sent a pointed look to the woman who was circling the table with a platter of meat and repeated himself in French.

Jeanne, Lily reminded herself. Her name was Jeanne or maybe Jeannette; none of the servants spoke English, and she hadn't tried very hard to talk to any of them except Ghislaine, who was her own age and friendly.

It was hard to know how to talk to the servants, as she had never had any before. Now she was in her brother's household, and he never hesitated to say the words that sent them running for whatever he thought she might need. He was never cruel or even thoughtless, and they adored him, every one.

This was the way Lily's mother grew up, in a household where young ladies were waited upon, their needs anticipated, their wants indulged—within reason. Lily had imagined that life with wonder and longing.

What a contrary creature you are. She could hear her mother's voice, ripe with frustration. Lily was coming to see the truth of it.

The table was crowded, and her brother's attention had already moved on to another discussion. Mostly the guests were men he did business with, French and Scots and Irish. A few of them were English born, and now called themselves Canadian.

They talked of the war as men of business must: prices going up and profit with them, the difficulty of moving merchandise, how hard it had become to get the products people wanted most and needed least. The streets were full of soldiers and sailors and officers in uniforms as gaudy as peacocks, but none of them were at this table to join in the discussion, and never would be; Iona would not allow it. Lily was thinking of excusing herself when Simon Ballentyne caught her eye.

"Would you care to take a walk?" he said to her in a clear voice, meant to be heard by all. "There's a full moon rising this evening." This deep in winter the night came quick and left reluctantly: they could get up from the dinner table and go out into the dark.

The men around the table went silent. Luke was waiting for her response with an unreadable expression, but Iona would have none of his brotherly bluster.

"Och, aye. Go on. The fresh air will do you good, child. Your complexion will suffer with you sitting inside all day." After so many years in Canada Iona's English was still full of the Gaelic, softly rounded and sibilant.

They were looking at Lily expectantly, each and every one of them. Some of them calculating out the benefits of the match, others thinking of their own sons. Her father might be a backwoodsman but her brother was one of the richest men in Montreal, and he would see to it—how could he not?—that his sister had a fat dowry. The only thing that held some of them back, Iona had explained to Lily, was the confusion about her religion. Was she

Catholic, or Protestant, or did she worship trees like the Indians she had grown up with?

Ghislaine had told her about this topic of conversation, not to give offense, but to make Lily laugh. She said, "Tell them I was raised as a rationalist." It pleased Ghislaine, the odd English word, and she carried it off in her pocket like a sweetmeat.

Now Lily wanted to go to her chamber, but more than that she needed to confound her brother. To Simon Ballentyne she said, "I'll get my wraps."

They walked for half an hour in the cold, talking of nothing in particular: the new snow, the moon, the news from New-York. She recited what she could remember of her letter from home and Simon grunted low in his throat and said nothing that might reveal his thoughts or tell her what she wanted to hear: her brother was safe.

"You miss your people," he said, as he might say *you're fevered* or *you've cut yourself.*

"I didn't think I would," she admitted, almost relieved to have the idea out of her head and in the world. "Don't you miss your family?"

The question surprised him, she could see that. He said, "I've no wish to see Scotland ever again."

There was a story here, of course; one he would tell her, if she were to ask. If she didn't, he would keep his peace. Simon Ballentyne was a rare man, one who was neither put off nor unmanned by a refusal and able to bide his time.

At the banks of the St. Lawrence they stopped to watch the rising of a wafer-thin moon, bruised with shadow. The river was normally crowded with ships and boats of every kind, some of which were the property of her cousin the earl far away in Scotland. The few that remained were iced in and the rest were gone now to warmer seas: the world was such a large place, almost too big to fit inside her imagination. Lily shivered thinking about it.

"You're cold," said Simon. "We should turn back." From his voice she could hear that he did not really want to go back, just yet.

"I'm not so very cold." Lily wrapped her cloak more tightly around herself. "It's beautiful here."

"Aye," he said gruffly. And then: "Are you thinking of the sweetheart you left behind?"

A bold question, but Lily couldn't find it in herself to be offended. Her mother would rebuke such impertinence with a few well-chosen words, but the truth was, Lily was weary of deception and she had the idea that she could talk to Simon Ballentyne. He was strong and quiet and competent, and young women turned their heads when he went by and blushed prettily.

The silence drew out between them. Lily thought of telling him the truth. *I love a man who has a wife.* To say those words out loud was such a strange thought that she might have laughed.

"What makes you think I left a sweetheart behind?"

"It's plain to see you're heartsick, and fair green with it."

A flush crawled up her neck, irritation but mostly panic; the impulse to share her secret with him left her just as suddenly as it had come.

"I left no sweetheart behind." When he said nothing she looked at him and saw things in his face she couldn't quite read. Anger, or disappointment.

She said, "You don't believe me."

"You don't believe yourself."

"Very well," Lily said, hugging herself and rocking back and forth on her heels. "Believe what you like." Then her anger got the best of her anyway.

"And what of you? I suppose you left some unhappy girl back in Carryckton."

"Aye," said Simon Ballentyne. "That I did. Brokenhearted and miserable unto death."

"You want to talk about her?"

"Christ, no," said Simon. "I'd rather cut out my tongue than talk about it." He paused and looked down at her with eyes that seemed almost black in the night. His expression was severe, as if she were the sinner and he the confessor.

Lily turned away and he stopped her with a hand on her shoulder. Even through the layers of wool she imagined she was feeling the heat of him.

He said, "Her name is Ellen Cruikshank, and she's the wife of the man who lives across the lane from my mother. I last saw her ten years ago, when I left home."

Panic filled Lily's gut and rose into her throat and made her fingers go numb. In his face she saw an understanding that should not have been there.

"I left because otherwise I would have shamed her and myself and my family, and we needed no more of that. I left my home for the same reason that you left yours."

Lily forced herself to breathe deeply, drawing in the cold air and holding it until her lungs screamed in protest. She wanted to slap him and run away; she wanted to tell him that wherever he got this idea about her, he was wrong; she wanted to weep.

But when she opened her mouth something very different came out. She said, "Do you still love your Ellen?"

"No," Simon said very calmly. "Love needs to be fed, and mine starved long ago." He blew out a noisy breath and drew in another one. "So I'll ask you again, lass. Did you leave a sweetheart behind?"

Lily said, "I left no one behind who would claim me as his sweetheart." The truth and a lie all at once. Nicholas would claim her, if he could.

"Ah, then," said Simon. "Then maybe it's time you had one."

He kissed her without further discussion or question or excuse. His beard prickled; his mouth was cold and warm, soft and knowing all at once. He was no stranger to kissing; it had been ten years since he saw his Ellen, but he had not been without the company of women, that much was clear.

"Stop thinking of Ellen," he said, and kissed her again, more purposefully this time.

That was the first surprise and the second one was this: she liked his touch. He was not Nicholas; she should not be moved by him, but she was.

Walking away from the river Simon said, "I'll come fetch you Sunday and we'll go for a sleigh ride."

"My brother won't like it."

He had a way of shrugging that said more than words. "It's not your brother I'm inviting."

Which was, of course, just the right thing to say. Lily thought carefully before she responded.

"If I go for a sleigh ride with you, you mustn't think of yourself as my sweetheart."

At that he gave her a good strong smile. "I'm a patient man," he said. "All in good time."

At the door she said, "How did you know? Did you follow me, when you were at Lake in the Clouds?"

He looked at her with kindness and maybe with a little irritation as well. "You could have anyone you wanted, Lily Bonner. It must be a man who isn't free to love you back."

Her anger took her by surprise. "He loves me," she said, and then flushed hot to have said the words, and hotter still to see Simon's expression: understanding, and pity.

For two days she thought about Simon Ballentyne constantly and when she woke on Sunday morning to the sound of church bells she knew that if he came to the door in his sleigh, she would go with him.

The bells reminded Lily, day in and day out, that Montreal was Catholic in its very bones. Most of the city was on their way to mass, dressed in the clothes they kept for that purpose alone. The servants in this house went too, drifting down the stairs silently as ghosts so as not to disturb their mistress, who always kept to her chamber on a Sunday. Wee Iona, who once wore the veil and called herself a bride of Christ, never showed her face on the Sabbath. It was one of the great mysteries that she trailed along behind her, along with the question of how it was she had come to bear a daughter, so many years ago, to George Somerville, Lord Bainbridge.

As a young girl Lily had sometimes gone to Paradise with her mother to listen to Mr. Witherspoon's sermons on Sunday mornings. Then he moved away and instead of services her mother would read from the Bible on Sunday evenings, enough church for anybody, Daniel used to say and Lily agreed with him. In time her uncle Todd had said she might as well use the meetinghouse for her work, and now she had somehow lost all interest in sermons.

As they were, Sunday mornings were the time Lily liked best. It seemed as though she and Luke had not just the house but the whole city to themselves. Her brother spent this time in his little study, writing letters and catching up on his bookkeeping, and Lily had soon got into the habit of sitting nearby with a book in her lap, though she did not read very much.

The room was well lit and there was always a good fire in the hearth. While snow brushed the windows they would talk, of the week that had passed or the week to come. If the mood was on him Luke would tell her stories about his boyhood here in the city, or Lily would talk of Lake in the Clouds and most of all of her brother. It was the only time she allowed herself to speak of Daniel, and she looked forward to it all week, as she imagined Catholics looked forward to confession and being relieved of their sins.

This morning when she came into his study Luke sent her one long look and said, "If you're going to let Simon Ballentyne court you, there are things you should know."

In her surprise and irritation Lily thought of turning on her heel and leaving, but the challenge in her brother's face was such that she could not.

"He's not courting me."

Luke tapped his finger on the desk, once and twice and three times. "He thinks he is."

Lily shrugged. "I made myself clear."

"And you accomplished that by kissing him under a full moon," her brother said calmly.

She felt her temper ignite like paper put to candle. "Who I kiss is my own business, brother, and none of yours. You can call off your spies."

"I don't need spies," Luke said gruffly. "Not in this city. The news comes to me unbidden."

For a long moment Lily thought about that, a truth that it would do no good to challenge or even rage against.

Luke said, "I won't stop you—"

"No," Lily interrupted him. "You won't. Because I won't let you. I did not leave one kind of prison behind for another."

When he was angry Luke looked most like the father they shared. Their coloring was so different that the connection might be missed, until Luke frowned and the furrow appeared between his brows. Disapproval rose off his skin like body heat; it was all too familiar.

"I can't stop you," Luke said pointedly, as if she hadn't interrupted. "But you should know—"

"About Ellen Cruikshank. Yes, he told me."

Surprise flickered across Luke's face. "He told you about Ellen Cruikshank. And did he tell you about his family too?"

Lily raised her eyes to Luke. "His family is no concern of mine, but go on then, if you must."

He said, "Before she married, Fiona Ballentyne was Fiona Moncrieff. She had two brothers. One was a Jesuit who took the name Contrecoeur, and the other was—"

"Angus Moncrieff," she finished for him.

Luke was watching her closely, hoping for something particular: shock or dismay or anger. Lily could find none of those things within herself.

She said, "Simon is Angus Moncrieff's nephew."

"He is."

"Angus Moncrieff, who betrayed our family and kidnapped Daniel and me when we were babies. And why would you bring Angus Moncrieff's nephew to Lake in the Clouds?"

Luke's calm expression faltered, and a muscle in his cheek twitched. "I judge a man on the way he lives his own life, not on his family."

"And how does Simon live his life?"

Luke cleared his throat. "He's clever and hardworking and trustworthy. In business matters I trust him completely, and he has never given me cause to do otherwise."

"I congratulate you on your rational philosophy," Lily said, pointedly picking up her book. "I think I will take it for my own."

"You are your mother's daughter," Luke said gruffly.

"I will take that as a compliment."

His mouth twitched. "It was meant as one." He turned back to his books, and Lily to hers.

Chapter 9

Dearest Daughter Lily,

The calendar tells me that it is not so very long since you left us, and so we were especially surprised and delighted to receive a second packet from Montreal just yesterday. Twenty-five drawings—your little brother counted them straightaway—and in addition to such riches, letters and gifts for all of us. There was much celebration here during the unpacking. Had you been able to see the look on Annie's face when your letter was put into her hands, you would understand how much joy your thoughtfulness brought to us all. Even your aunt Many-Doves had tears in her eyes.

Each of your drawings is studied at great length and discussed, for we find so much to wonder about. You father was surprised to see that Luke chose to give you Giselle's old bedchamber for your own. It is a beautiful room, of course, and you must be very comfortable there. And still your father is not satisfied; he says that he must write to your brother and require that the secret stairway that leads out into the gardens be bricked up so as not to tempt you into running about the city at night. You see that neither his fatherly concern nor his rather odd sense of humor are improved or made milder by the long distance between us.

Gabriel took one look at the likeness of Monsieur Picot—if I have understood correctly, the gentleman who tutors you in the painting of landscapes—and gave him the nickname Catfish for his bristling mustache and puffy mouth. He was admonished for such discourtesy but I fear it was all for naught, as your father laughed out loud in agreement.

Between your drawings and notes and Luke's very informative letter we have come to understand that you are flourishing; the neighborhood is delighted with you, your teachers praise you for your powers of concentration, excellent sense of proportion and line, and for your hard work, and Iona looks after you as if you were her own granddaughter. That you are making so much of this opportunity does not surprise us, but your father and I are nonetheless pleased and gratified. You make us all very proud.

Your aunt Many-Doves asks me to report to you that the harvest is done and she is well pleased. The three sisters are here in abundance: the rafters groan under their happy burden of corn and squash and beans. We have ten full bushels of apples this year. The last of the geese have passed over and the first snow fell yesterday, no more than a dusting, but in the morning there was a half-inch of ice on the water bucket.

The winter is come; Jennet holds up her head and sniffs the sky and tells us so, and we have learned that when it comes to predicting the weather her sense of smell is without peer. All the signs point to a hard winter, but I fear she does not rightly understand what that means in the endless forests; she looks forward to it now, but by December I fear she will long for Scotland's milder weather.

Right now your cousin sits across from me scribbling furiously on her own letter to your brother, in response to the one she received from him. She has folded the silk shawl he sent around her shoulders and there is bright color in her cheeks. His letter first made her scowl and then laugh out loud. I trust her response will provide him with the same joy.

Jennet has made herself indispensable to all of us. We have had more visitors from the village in the last few weeks than we had all year, people coming with messages that could wait or to ask questions that require no answer, and who only stay for any length of time if Jennet is about. They come to hear her stories or simply to talk to her, as a man who has been chilled to the bone will be drawn to a well-laid fire. She is our own Scheherazade, and I think of her as your counterpart: she tells the tales that you would draw if you were here with us at dusk, gathered around the hearth, each of us busy with some work but all listening attentively.

By day Jennet is always occupied with whatever work presents itself, most usually as Hannah's assistant when she goes to see patients in the village. Hannah tells me that Jennet is a quick learner and an excellent assistant, not only for her powers of distracting the sick but also because she understands what is required of her with few words and has an excellent memory.

In truth it is fortunate that Jennet is willing and able to assist Hannah. Your uncle Todd's health continues to decline and Curiosity is more and more consumed with his care. He is often in considerable pain and very short of temper but even he seems to gentle when Hannah and Jennet come to sit with him. Hannah has brought him paints and paper, in the hope he will take up his old hobby of painting landscapes, while Jennet lays out her tarot cards for him. Uncle Todd scoffs and grumbles and tries not to smile in delight at her more outlandish predictions: he will travel to India and be crowned a prince, or a messenger with green eyes and a broken front tooth is on his way to bring news of a long-lost friend.

Because Hannah and Jennet have taken on responsibility for the sick in the village, cousin Ethan is free to pursue his own studies. He now takes my place as teacher four days of the week, a task which pleases him well and, I must admit, has provided me considerable relief. I had thought to use the extra time to see to household chores but your aunt Many-Doves will not hear of it, and neither will your father: I am to write as much as I like. Yesterday I sent off three essays to Mr. Howe of the *New-York Spectator*. In his last letter he reported to me that the writings of E. M. Bonner have been well received by the readership and he looks forward to more submissions.

Your sister is writing a letter to you, but as I did promise you regular reports on her health and state of mind I send you my observations. Every day she seems a little improved. Jennet, I think, must be given a good part of the credit. She understands Hannah in a way I cannot, though I have spent much time in thought on how to best serve her needs. Jennet knows when to speak, when to admonish, when to cajole, and most importantly when to listen quietly and ask no questions. I will confess to you alone that sometimes I envy their closeness, but then I am ashamed of my selfish thoughts.

Hannah has begun to teach Gabriel and Annie how to use the bow and arrow, and she is a patient if exacting teacher. When she does not need to go to the village to see patients she is happy to take up whatever household chores present themselves, and it seems to me that she dislikes being out of doors, an idea so truly outlandish that it seems strange to put it down in words. And yet the impression persists.

Every day Hannah visits with Dolly Wilde and brings her teas to drink. In fact it seems as though cautious optimism is not out of place, as Dolly sometimes seems to recognize the people around her now. Whether this is Hannah's treatment or the natural course of her condition no one can say. And still when I happen to see Nicholas in the village he is very drawn and pale, though he greets me politely and asks after you and your brother both. Yesterday when your father took your newest drawings into the trading post to show, Nicholas spent a long time looking at them.

We have had only one short note from your twin, written on poor paper with poorer ink but in his true hand. I will copy it out at the end of this letter for you to read. Your father tells me that there is nothing in its cautious language to cause us concern. In this, as in so many things having to do with men's wars, I must depend on your father's interpretation and be directed by him. If only my imagination and dreams were so easily constrained.

I do hope this bundle of our thoughts and good wishes reaches you by means of your brother's mysterious trade connections, and that it brings you some relief from your homesickness. We think of you every day with great affection and pride.

Your loving mother
Elizabeth Middleton Bonner
October 30, 1812

To my dear family, mother and father,
A courier leaves at dawn headed for Canajoharee and so I burn my last candle in order to send you our news. Please know that Blue-Jay and I are both well in body and spirit. The worst injury

we have between us thus far is an infected blackfly bite on my arm which I cleaned out and cauterized with the tip of my knife, as Sister would approve.

The war here on the St. Lawrence is a strange affair. We drill in full view of the British on the other side of the river and they do the same. All real business takes place under cover of night. Blue-Jay has made himself especially useful as he moves like an owl in the dark, and thus has he won Jim Booke's admiration. We all call our captain by his family name, for he thinks very little of the American army and will not use any of the titles that he might claim for himself. He has begrudging admiration for one officer only, Jacob Brown, who commands all the regulars and militia from Oswego to Oswegatchie, where he has set up headquarters.

We are not much loved here by the Yorkers, who had been selling their beef on the hoof to the British army at tremendous profit and now must pretend at least to obey the law. On the street I heard one farmer say to another that he found it damned hard to call any man an enemy who offered him such a good price for his cattle. In general the farmers and tradesmen alike are unwilling to support Mr. Madison's war, as they call it, though they shout loud enough for us to protect them when the British come raiding, and steal what they might have otherwise paid good coin for.

The only regulars General Brown has under him are a unit of riflemen in smart green uniforms. They are excellent shots, every one of them, but Booke dislikes the captain who leads them, called Benjamin Forsyth. He is a spectacular rifleman in his own right, but his bravado outstrips his common sense too often, or so claims Jim Booke.

Be content to know that we are honing every skill a soldier needs to stay alive and do his duty, and we are learning from the best. Booke may dislike the American army and distrust the government that gave it birth, but he truly hates the British Crown and is single-minded in his goal to chase them off once and for all. He is a hard taskmaster but an honest and fair one, and we count ourselves fortunate to be under his command. I hope one day that you will make his acquaintance, but as he is shy of crowds and any settled place, I fear that day may never come.

My love to all the family, to Curiosity and Uncle Todd and especially cousin Ethan, and anyone else who might ask after me.

To my beloved sister and brother in Montreal, when you next write
to them, my most affectionate greetings and hopes that Lily has
forgiven me my trespasses.

Your son
Daniel Bonner of
Jim Booke's militia
7 September in the year 1812

Dear Sister Lily and Brother Luke,
Cousin Jennet puts down my words for me because the quill
behaves in her hand as it will not in mine and she need not bother
our mother to ask how to write every word. Mother would do this
service but first she would change around what I say in order to
suit her ear and Jennet has promised to put down all my words as I
say them. You see it's true for our brother Luke sends a letter that
doesn't sound like him, and yet our mother is proud and says what
a good writer he is become. I asked her then, for what reason do we
write letters but to hear each other's voices? And she said I would
understand better when I had studied more, though she did look
thoughtful and was quiet for a good while after.

The only news I can think to tell that no one else will bother to
write is what happened last week when Many-Doves declared that
the corn was dry enough to start the milling. Everyone put down
their work and loaded oxcarts and wagons to line up at the scales,
but *then* it was discovered that Charlie LeBlanc had taken down the
sluice gate to mend and couldn't recall where he left it. Then when
the boys found it finally under a pile of empty sacks, it turned out
that he had never repaired it at all. Anybody determined to make a
study of cursing would have learned a great deal that day, most
especially from old Missus Hindle who can be wonderful angry in
five languages. Among other things that dare not be writ down she
called Charlie a rot-riddled pumpkin head.

Thank you very kindly for the drawings and the tin of chocolate
for drinking and the sweets and the carved horses. The tin is already
empty, a true mystery says our father, and our mother says I am
not to ask for more, for it would be greedy and ill-mannered. She
says I may have the empty tin to save my treasures in. I must share
it with Annie who has no tin of her own unless you were to send
another one. Empty or filled, it is most certainly up to you.

Yesterday the dogs chased a possum up the pine tree with the broken top. I tried to hit it with my bow and arrow and missed, but Sister did not. We had stew for our dinner. She says I have a keen eye and will make a good marksman, which of course I do and will, as I am the son of Nathaniel Bonner and grandson of Daniel Bonner who is still called Hawkeye by all who knew him. This letter has grown too long for the paper and soon cousin Jennet will have a cramp in her hand so I will stop.

Your best loved brother
Gabriel Bonner

Our dearest girl Lily,
There's a rider headed up Montreal way and timely, too, for I have just finished a pair of good stockings to send to you, of lamb's wool bought from Mrs. Ratz that young Annie helped me card and comb and spin. Good heavy stockings, and warm. Mind me now: Canada cold a wily cold, damp and slick. Before you know it that wind will weasel way deep into your lights to start you coughing. So you put on your warmest underclothes and woolen skirts and thickest stockings, every day. Cold feet will be the undoing of you, child, and if you take sick up there your mama or your daddy or your sister or the Lord knows the whole clan will set off to come rescue you from your own folly. I love your people like my own but can't nobody deny, the Bonners run off cockeyed at any chance to get themselves in a fix. I fear it is bred in the bone. So keep warm, child, and for the Lord's sake don't take no advice from them Frenchified doctors and don't let them get near you with those lancets they so fond of. I'm too old to be marching off to Canada to keep you all out of trouble.

Along with the stockings I send you a half-dozen of my best candles, fine bayberry beeswax, just dipped with good strong wicks spun by Many-Doves' Annie in my kitchen. She is a clever child, is Annie. Mind you use these candles, for if you don't look out for your pretty eyes why then they won't look out for you when you need them most.

In your letter you wrote that you have taken up what you call sculpture and to me sound more like carving or working wood, as my husband Galileo may the Lord bless his everlasting good soul was so fond of. If it turn out you got a feel for wood it wouldn't surprise me none, coming up as you did surrounded by trees. What I mean to say, though the words don't seem to want to order themselves on the page, is this: you make good use of whatever they got to teach you up there, so when you come home again you ready to stay put. The truth is plain and won't be hushed. You belong here, Lily Bonner, on the mountain where you came into the world. Montreal may be a big city but it's too small a place for a soul like yours.

writ by her own poor hand your friend good and true
Curiosity Freeman

Dear Lily,
This is the first time in more than a year that I have taken up quill and ink. It comes to me with difficulty, but I could not let another packet be sent off to you without at least a few words.

We miss you here at Lake in the Clouds, as you are missed in the village. Wherever I go on my rounds people ask of you and your studies and your life in Montreal. They tell stories of you and bring out the many drawings you have made and given over the years, as they might take out a letter from the president himself, with great respect and admiration.

Most of all I miss talking to you late into the night and waking to find you just across the room. I tell myself that this separation will not be forever, and I tell you the same. When you are come home we will have much to tell each other.

Your loving and devoted sister
Hannah Bonner, also called Walks-Ahead by her mother's people or Walking-Woman by her husband's.

Chapter 10

The morning was half gone when the sky came over dark and Nathaniel first tasted new snow on the wind. He wiped his sweaty face on his sleeve and in one practiced motion slung the doe he had tracked for more than a mile across his shoulders. She was young and there wasn't a lot of fat on her, but fresh venison would be a welcome change from salt cod and dried bear meat stew.

Game was thin this winter. The last few nights he had dreamed of bear and deer and moose on the run, side by side, in a hurry to be gone to the west, looking for a place less honeycombed with the trails made by white men. In his dreams the animals would sometimes bear the faces of the people who were gone from him: his first wife, old friends, the children they had buried. His grandfather Chingachgook, his father, who had walked away ten years ago to find some peace in the west.

He couldn't say for sure if Hawkeye was alive or dead. With every passing year it was a little more likely, of course. And still Nathaniel couldn't make himself believe that his father could be gone for good; he would come back to die here, where his people were buried. Nathaniel told himself this now and then, because he didn't want to think of Hawkeye in a shallow grave on the Great Plains someplace, with no mountains in sight. He might die alone or among strangers, but either way there would be no one there to sing him his death song in his own language.

On the morning Hawkeye left there had been no time or energy to feel much at all, not regret or fear or loneliness. Even at the time Nathaniel had known that those things would come later. His Hannah was about to leave home too, and the fact that Hawkeye was with her almost made up for the fact that his daughter was old enough to have chosen a husband.

The snow came fast and thick in a rising wind that was busy scouring away his tracks and all trace of the creatures that moved over the face of the mountain. He had thought to run across Runs-from-Bears, who should have come this way to walk the trap lines. No doubt Bears had started back to Lake in the Clouds a good while ago. He had more sense than Nathaniel when it came to the weather, but then most people did. Most years it didn't matter much.

None of them could remember a winter with so much snow so early, not even Curiosity Freeman, who had a memory for such things and was the oldest woman in Paradise. He was thinking about Curiosity when he came to a sudden stop.

A wounded animal makes a track all its own in deep snow, one any good backwoodsman could read with greater ease than words on a page, and Nathaniel didn't like what he saw in front of him. No sick wolf or moose, but a woman dragging her skirts along and fumbling through the drifts. That was bad enough—a woman on the mountain—but even worse was the fact that the snow was stained pink with blood.

His first thought was of his own womenfolk, but none of them would be so foolish. Just as soon as he had put that idea away he realized that Dolly Wilde had run off again, and from the tracks at least, nobody had caught up with her yet.

Nathaniel dropped the doe where he stood, an unwilling offering to the wolves who had given the mountain its name, and turned into the woods. With an impatient hand he pushed his hood back to make sure he would hear when the shouting started, as it must. The men from the village would be on their way up here with their dogs unless the storm turned into a whiteout. This time, though, Nathaniel doubted that they'd be able to find her in time. The north face of the mountain was treacherous in good weather, and that's the way she was headed.

Just past Squirrel Slough he came across a shred of shawl caught up in a hawthorn bush, proof at least that she hadn't wandered off in nothing but a night rail. With every minute he was surprised not to come across her. Nathaniel picked up his pace and his breath rose up into the swirling snow.

He skirted a windfall and then a hibernating bear jutting up from a hollow like a gently trembling hillock. Dolly's tracks went around the bear, and he was glad to see that even in her extremity she hadn't lost all her common sense, which meant that if she had got as far as the top of Hidden Wolf she wouldn't just walk off a cliff. If she was still walking at all.

In time Nathaniel began to wonder if maybe nobody realized she was gone, down at the Wilde place, because it seemed to him he was the only living thing moving on the mountain. He was considering that when he came across Dolly, sitting up against a young alder bent low with snow. She sat there as if it were summer and she had sought out the tree for its shade, as if there were no better spot to watch the world go by.

Her gaze flickered toward Nathaniel as he squatted down next to her. He took a hitching breath and tried to make sense of what he was seeing.

Dolly was dressed warm, at least, which was both a good thing and a surprise. The question was, how had a woman as sick as this one managed to put on so many skirts and shawls and then walk away from the cabin without drawing attention to herself?

"Dolly?"

She looked at him from the corner of her eye. Wary, like a deer that had never seen a man before, or maybe, Nathaniel corrected himself, more like a hungry dog with a bone. Suspicious, not exactly afraid, willing to fight for what was hers.

The tip of her nose and the ears that peeked out from the tangle of her hair were the color of milky ice. Worse than that, the right side of her face and her right hand were jerking and trembling, as if to make up for the silent rest of her. The blood that speckled the snow around her came from the cuts and scratches that covered her hands.

"Dolly." He said it louder this time and in response she closed her eyes. Her cheek muscles jumped and shivered as though she had tucked a frog up there for safekeeping. Then she rocked forward and cradled her right side with her left arm and let out a low moan.

She resisted at first, but Nathaniel picked her up. Even through the layers of wool and linen he could feel the heat of her.

All the way down the mountain she lay across his shoulder as heavy and inert as the doe he had abandoned on the trail behind him. Every now and then she tensed and began to shudder and tremble and flex like a fish on the line.

Nathaniel began to sing under his breath, a death song he had first learned from his Mahican grandfather as a boy and had sung too many times to count. In case she passed over to the shadow lands before he could get her back to Lake in the Clouds.

It was a full two days before the blizzard blew itself out and Nathaniel could start down the mountain to tell people what they must know already: there was no need to come in search of Dolly Wilde, because she was dead. She had lived for a few hours on a cot in front of the hearth while Elizabeth and Many-Doves worked to bring down her fever, but in the end she had died in a convulsion so extreme that her spine arched into a bow.

He went by back trails so as to avoid meeting anybody before he had a chance to talk to Nicholas Wilde directly. The man had a right to know first, to break the news to his little girl in his own way and time. But when he came out of the trees into the Wildes' orchard he saw straight off that something wasn't right. There was no smoke coming from the chimney though the temperature was well below freezing. The empty feeling in his gut was replaced by something much more solid, a foreboding that coated his mouth with the taste of bile.

The snowdrifts reached up to the window shutters and blocked the doors to the cabin and barn both. Nathaniel called, and called again.

It took him a good while to clear the door, and all the while he was at it he was listening, too, for any sound that would explain all this strangeness away. In the end he braced himself for the worst and knocked once and then again. Unlatched, the door swung open.

Nathaniel left it open for the light and walked through all four rooms, his footsteps echoing. Little by little he began to believe what he was seeing, which was nothing at all. No blood had been shed here, there had been no struggle. He opened shutters to see better and walked through the rooms again.

The common room, the workroom crowded with loom and spinning wheels, and both small chambers were clean and well ordered in the winter light. Bright counterpanes were spread neatly over feather beds. Someone had arranged dried maple leaves in a blue bowl that sat centered on the scrubbed plank table. In the cold hearth where motes danced in the slanted sunlight cooking trivets and pots hung, polished to gleaming. Cookie's sewing basket was in its place next to her rocker, and the pipe Nicholas sometimes smoked in the evening sat on the mantelpiece next to a school primer with a warped spine. There were four books, two of which, a volume of poetry and *Macbeth,* had been presents from his own wife to Dolly, presented at the end of each year she spent in Elizabeth's classroom.

In the chamber where Dolly and Nicholas had slept— Nathaniel knew it by the wooden dowels that had been nailed across the window casement to keep Dolly from climbing out and wandering away—he could find no sign of trouble. Dolly's clothes still hung on the wall pegs, along with the one good suit of clothes Nicholas owned.

Back in the common room Nathaniel stomped his feet to keep his blood moving and took another look around. Now he saw that some things were gone: no mantles or coats hung on the wall pegs, and the mat next to the hearth where boots must stand as a matter of course was empty, as was the gun rack over the door.

It didn't take quite so long to dig his way into the barn, but whether he was working faster out of dread or simple curiosity, Nathaniel couldn't say. What was behind this door would either solve the mystery in the worst possible way—he kept thinking of the empty gun rack—or make it all the more complicated.

The doors opened silently on well-oiled hinges and showed him what he had hoped for: the horses were gone, and the sleigh too. Not a tool or bucket or bushel out of place. The only thing wrong, as far as he could see, was the fact that the Wildes kept a cow, and the stall where she normally stood was empty.

He found the cow in the pasture, frozen in place where she had died on her knees, the snowdrifts behind her gory with evidence of a burst udder. Her eyes were gone, plucked out by ravens who had retreated at the sound of Nathaniel's approach and stood waiting, impatiently, for him to go and leave them to their meal.

Nathaniel turned toward the village and tried to order all the things he had seen in his mind. He would have to give an accounting to Jed McGarrity, who was the constable and would have no choice but to listen.

In all the years Elizabeth had lived on Hidden Wolf, she had never quite been able to talk herself out of the fanciful notion that each winter storm had a personality and a voice all its own. The storm that had come down while they tended to Dolly and watched her die was malicious, clamping a great cold hand down on the face of the earth to trap each living thing just where it stood. Like a witless and mean-spirited child who caught up beetles in a jar for the pleasure of watching them scramble themselves to death.

The storm had gone, leaving a world of blinding white, and Elizabeth found herself alone, something that happened very rarely. Gabriel and Annie were staying in the other cabin with Many-Doves and Runs-from-Bears, Nathaniel was gone to bring Dolly's family the sad news, and Hannah and Jennet had been stranded in the village by the storm. No doubt they had spent the whole time reading tarot cards with Curiosity and laughing over Jennet's stories.

One part of Elizabeth, the part that was a mother first and always, was glad that the girls were spared Dolly's terrible last hours, but the rest of her was impatient for the company of women. Dolly must be laid out; her body must be washed and dressed and wrapped in a shroud. Then the men would carry her out to the shed where she would stay like so much firewood until the spring thaw, when her grave could be dug.

Most especially Elizabeth wanted Cookie to be here, as Cookie had been with Dolly through all the years of her marriage, through childbirth and illness. Aside from Dolly's own daughter, there was no woman in the world who was more attached to her.

To anyone who did not know their history, it must seem a strange arrangement. Mild, sweet Dolly, who could not raise her voice to save her own life and Cookie, a dry husk of a woman, taciturn in word and deed, rubbed raw by loss and anger and fifty years of slavery to a woman with a heart like cold steel. On the day that Cookie and her sons had been given their manumission papers and found themselves on the brink of a world full of uncertainties, Dolly had offered Cookie a home and work for a fair wage, apologizing that she and Nicholas, newly wed and already in debt, could not offer as much to Cookie's grown sons. A few years later, when their hard work had begun to return a profit, they had sent to Johnstown. Levi had made a life for himself there, but Zeke came back to Paradise to work the orchards with Nicholas.

Cookie must come to tend to Dolly; she would come, if it was in her power. This last thought made Elizabeth get up and poke nervously at the fire, because it raised the question she had been avoiding now for days: who was responsible for this sad business?

Elizabeth glanced at the still form folded into a blanket at the shadowy end of the common room, and then she sat down again and took up her sewing, smoothing the linen that would serve as Dolly's shroud with the palm of her hand.

She had just finished the last seam when the door opened and Hannah and Jennet came in, shuddering snow with every step and laughing like schoolgirls. They stopped where they were when they saw the work in Elizabeth's hands.

"Who?" asked Hannah.

"None of us," said Elizabeth quickly. "Dolly Smythe. Dolly Wilde, I should say."

The girls exchanged a look that told Elizabeth the worst of it: no one knew that she was missing; and therefore, no one knew that she was dead.

"You mean to say that no one is looking for her?" Many-Doves asked. It was a question already asked and answered, but even Many-Doves, the very soul of calm, was shaken.

"There was no alarm raised while we were in the village," Hannah said. "Before the storm or after. And no word from the Wildes that anything was amiss, not since Missy Parker has been going up to help with the widow. In fact, I've seen no sign of them for a week, at least."

"Blessed Mary." Jennet's breathing hitched once and then again. "The poor wee thing."

"This is very disturbing," Elizabeth said again. "But there is nothing to be done except wait for your father to come home and explain. Hopefully he will bring Nicholas and Cookie with him."

They were standing around the trestle table with their heads bowed in the glow of candle and firelight. On the table was Dolly Wilde's body, not so much a human form but a poorly made wax effigy.

Hannah said, "It does sound as though she had a brain fever, from what you've told me. But I'd have to do an autopsy to be sure."

Elizabeth's face contorted in horror even as Hannah was speaking. Her mouth opened and then closed with a sharp sound.

"Don't worry," Hannah said. "I have no intention of cutting her open. I haven't attended an autopsy in years, and I don't have the right instruments."

Or any at all, she might have said. Once she had carried a full set of surgeon's tools with her wherever she went, beautifully crafted blades and probes that had been a gift from a teacher she had not heard from in years. Now she borrowed Richard's things when she could not do without.

"I see no evidence of violence done," Hannah finished. "The cuts on her hands and face are mostly from pushing her way through brambles, I think. She must have lost her gloves or never had any; you see that all her fingers were badly frostbitten."

Jennet had leaned in very close to study Dolly's hands, which were covered with cuts and scratches, some long healed and others still bright red. "She kept cats," Jennet said, and smoothed a gentle hand over Dolly's hair. "A gentle-hearted woman, then."

"She was, yes," Elizabeth agreed, and the sorrow she had been keeping at bay for so long welled up fiercely.

"And she said nothing while she lived?" It was more a statement than a question, but Elizabeth answered anyway.

"No. She was convulsing for much of the time."

"Then what of the inquiry?" Jennet asked. "When will it be?"

"Inquiry?" Hannah said, as if she had never heard the word before.

Jennet shot her a look that was surprise and irritation both. "Why, of course," she said. "Someone is responsible for this. Justice must be done."

Elizabeth wondered if she had seemed so superior and condescending when she first came here as a young woman, just Jennet's age and just as sure of the proper ordering of the world. By the look on Many-Doves' face, she thought she must have been.

She said, "Here on the frontier justice wears a very different face. As does compassion."

"Compassion?" Jennet almost sputtered the word, and hot color shot into her cheeks. "Are you suggesting that they sent her out into the cold to die? Purposely? But that's, that's—"

"Barbaric," Hannah supplied evenly. "You want to say it would be barbaric."

"Well, yes." Jennet drew up a little, less certain of herself now. She glanced uneasily at Many-Doves, who returned her gaze without blinking. More softly she said, "Do you think they might really have done such a thing? I know that she was a burden to them, but—"

"No one has suggested that her people turned her out," said Elizabeth. "And to speculate is only to invite trouble."

"Then there must be an inquiry, and I will attend it," Jennet said, more calmly now.

"Certainly," Elizabeth said wearily. "No one would try to keep you away." She wiped the perspiration from her forehead and pressed her handkerchief to her nose, inhaling lavender water deeply. Outside Runs-from-Bears had begun to cut firewood and it seemed to Elizabeth that she felt each fall of the axe echoed in her own pulse.

Just then the faint sound of the village bell came to them through the clear winter air, and each of them turned toward the door. The sound of the axe had stopped; Runs-from-Bears would be counting, as each of the women counted to herself. Five tolls of the bell for a missing child.

A missing child.

Before any of them could think what to say, the chiming started up again. This time the bell tolled four times, then another four, then—Elizabeth would have thought she was imagining it if it weren't for the faces of the other women around her—three tolls and three again.

"But what does it mean?" Jennet asked, a wild note breaking in her voice.

"Two women missing, two men, one child." Elizabeth heard Hannah answer from far away.

"The whole family?" asked Jennet, unbelieving. "The whole family is missing, and the servants with them?"

"Possibly," said Elizabeth. "Or perhaps it is unrelated, other people have got lost in the storm."

Even as she said the words she knew, somehow, that this was not the case. As they all knew.

"We had best look after her then," Many-Doves said, drawing the sheet up around Dolly's shoulders. "It sounds as though there won't be anybody else coming to do it."

Chapter 11

December, Montreal

The courier's knocking woke Lily at first light to a chamber so cold that the wool blanket tented over her face crackled, frozen stiff by her own moist breath.

Even huddled beneath blankets and comforters on a thick feather bed, there was no avoiding the clatter of Lucille's pattens as the old lady grumbled her way along the tiled corridor to answer the knock. She began her scolding litany even before she opened the door. The courier—either a very brave man or a foolish one— barked out a surprised laugh. For this he earned not the bowl of coffee and milk he must have been hoping for, but a curtly closed door.

Post at sunrise. It shouldn't surprise Lily anymore, really. Couriers came to her brother's door with astounding regularity, even with the port closed for the winter. At Lake in the Clouds they might get mail once every fortnight if the roads were good; in a muddy spring it could be much longer between deliveries. Here in Montreal it seemed that letters and packages and whole sledges came for Luke every day.

If Lily waited just a little longer Ghislaine, the youngest and friendliest of the servants, would come to wake her. Ghislaine would bring coffee and gossip and serve them both in generous portions while she opened the shutters and coaxed the embers in the hearth into new life. Ghislaine spoke a rustic English full of odd turns of phrase that she had learned from her American grandfather, a

Vermont farmer, and they had come to an agreement: in the mornings they spoke English, in the afternoons, French.

It was a friendship based on mutual admiration but also, they were both very much aware, need. Ghislaine was Lily's only source for certain kinds of information about what was happening in the house and the town; in return Lily knew some old stories, shocking enough not to be told around a crowded hearth, that Ghislaine had never been able to prod out of any of the older servants. Lily knew these stories of the Somerville family and Wee Iona, because her father and grandfather and brother had had a part in them.

This grand house that belonged to Luke had once belonged to George Somerville, Lord Bainbridge, lieutenant governor of Lower Canada, a man no one had liked or mourned, dead of an apoplexy long ago. Lily told Ghislaine about the night that the Bonner men had escaped from the Montreal prison only to be caught up again here, in the secret stairway that, Lily and Ghislaine were both very sad to discover for themselves, Luke had indeed bricked closed when the house came into his possession.

Ghislaine longed to see Giselle Somerville, now more properly called Giselle Lacoeur for she had finally settled on a husband, late in her life. Lily would have liked to meet her half brother's mother as well, but Giselle had found a climate more suited to her temperament in Saint Domingue, and Iona was sure that she would never see her daughter in Montreal again. Not in the winter, at least, Luke had agreed. He knew his mother well.

Why Montreal cold should be so very harsh, that was a question Lily had been considering for some time. Over the weeks she had come to realize that it must have something to do with sleeping alone. In the winter nobody at Lake in the Clouds slept by themselves. Lily shared her bed with Annie and sometimes Gabriel, too, if Daniel happened to be away. They huddled together under the covers like kittens, their smells mingling together: milky sweet breath, sharp soap and wood smoke, pine sap.

She missed them, for all their pinches and giggling and pulling of the blankets and sneaking away of pillows. The truth was, even in the heat of summer Lily did not much like sleeping alone in a bed, and she did not have to: she could go with her blanket to lie under the stars or sleep under the falls, if the notion took her.

Before homesickness could dig in, Lily tried to remember what it was she had to do this morning. Was it Monsieur Picot, who clicked his nails against the easel and clucked his tongue when she displeased him, or Monsieur Duhaut, who was teaching her how to grind and mix her own pigments? Monsieur Duhaut was a strange man, morose one day and more morose the next; when his mood lifted a little he would stand too close while Lily worked and breathe onto her neck. She had spoken to Iona about him, and at their next lesson he had greeted her with such a studiously wounded expression that Lily was reminded of a dog caught stealing eggs; sorry not for the transgression, but for his clumsiness in being found out.

Suddenly Lily realized how quiet the lane outside her window was and she remembered that it was a holiday of some sort. What holiday she couldn't really say—the Catholics seemed to have so many of them—but soon the bells would begin to ring the mass. And, she remembered, more awake now, she had promised to go out with Simon to an all-day sleighing party. That made her heart beat faster, as a lesson with Monsieur Duhaut never could, though she was loath to admit it to herself. She had come to Montreal to study art, after all.

The virtuous thing to do would be to spend the day in front of her easel. But of course, she had promised.

"Wake up, sleepyhead," Ghislaine called at the door even as it swung inward. She stood there with a tray held high, the steam rising up to make the hair at her temples curl. Ghislaine was a pretty girl and always seemed to be in motion; the whirlwind, Iona called her, but affectionately.

"Yesterday," Ghislaine began straightaway. "Yesterday the youngest daughter of Pierre-Amable Dézéry dit Latour—Amélie, she is called—agreed to marry Gérard Berthelet, in the rue de l'Hôpital. Such a scandal, you cannot imagine. A daughter of the surveyor to the governor engaged to an apprentice joiner who suffers from—" Ghislaine stopped to search for an English word, her small mouth pressed together in concentration. "Early balditude."

Ghislaine was vain about her own beautiful hair, and expected no less of others. When Lily pointed her lack of charity out to her, Ghislaine only flicked her fingers. "Pffft. Do not preach to me, Miss American Who Knows All. I haven't seen you spending time with the hairless. In fact, your sweetheart has so much hair that his head cannot contain it. It sprouts from his collar and cuffs."

At that Lily could not help but laugh, though what she wanted to do was to correct Ghislaine: Simon Ballentyne was not her sweetheart. But it would not do to rise to the bait. Instead she swallowed her coffee, very strong and laced with sweet fresh milk, and with it the protests that would only start Ghislaine off on a tangent.

"I see you do not disagree," Ghislaine said with a satisfied sniff.

"No," Lily said, finally throwing back the covers. "I simply do not argue."

At breakfast Luke watched her. Lily could almost see the questions pooling in his mouth, puffing out his cheeks, ready to spill: *What is it Simon Ballentyne wants from you?* and, *Have you written to our father or must I?*

Lily applied herself to her porridge and refused to meet her brother's steady gaze. Iona gave her less room.

"Simon's a good man," she said to Lily when Luke had excused himself from the table and gone off to see to the post. "But he's just a man, after all, lass. You mustn't forget that men are all weak willed when it comes down to it. It's the woman who must bear the burden, in the end."

Down to what? Lily might have asked, but this would be the worst kind of deception. She knew what Luke and Iona were worried about: that she would allow Simon too many liberties and end up with child, which would mean, in turn, that she would have to marry him and make a life here in Montreal. Or go home carrying her shame before her and admit to everyone that she had not been equal to the freedom she was given. As had been the case with Iona herself, and with Giselle too, both women having borne their children without the benefit of a husband. No wonder they were worried.

At this moment Lily understood, and she could promise Iona that she would be sensible. She could say the words, and mean them. The problem was Simon; could she say the same to him? When he put his hands on her face so gently and kissed her with such skill that the muscles in her belly fluttered with it, could she remember what was expected of her, or even more to the point: what she expected of herself?

The best thing, of course, would be to stay at home today. Just as Lily was forming this resolution in her mind she heard the jangle of harness bells flying past the door. The first sleighs on their way out of the city, on their way to Mount Royal or Lachine.

She went to Iona and leaned over her shoulder. The old woman smelled of herbs and tallow candles this morning, as she often did; there were fresh ink stains on her fingers that said she had been writing. But what? And why? She never sent a letter out with the courier. Iona did not speak of the things that kept her busy behind the closed door of her chamber, and Lily had never had the courage to ask.

She kissed Iona's soft cheek. "I will be sensible," she said. "I am my mother's daughter, after all."

"And your father's!" Iona called after her.

A suitable warning, of course, as Lily's father had spent a winter here when he was younger than she was now, and fathered a son on Giselle Somerville.

But Lily only raised a hand in acknowledgment and wouldn't turn back, not now, not with the sound of bells filling the lanes.

When Simon stopped the sleigh at the door Lily was ready in her layers of wool, wrapped in a hooded cape lined with fur. It was impossible to walk normally when she was bundled up like this, but then she only had to negotiate the few steps to the cariole.

It was a small affair, just big enough for two, and painted a bright red with green trim. The bridles were woven with ribbons to match, altogether too fine for the team of country horses: tough little beasts, shaggy coated, narrow of chest and half-wild but able to run for hours in the cold and then stand for even longer. They were spanned not side by side but nose to tail so that they could pull the cariole through the narrow lanes. For all their rough appearance they were clever things, and affectionate: once out of their traces they would follow Simon around like dogs and push their damp velvet noses into his pockets looking for maple sugar lumps and dried apple.

The sleigh came to a halt just as she heard Luke call her. He was holding a letter out as he came forward. "From your mother," he said. "It was in among the others."

Lily was thinking of leaving it for reading in the evening when Luke grinned at her, a teasing brother at this moment rather than a worried one. "Take it along," he said. "Best to have Elizabeth along with you in that sleigh, in spirit at least."

But he was looking beyond her when he said it. At Simon, Lily thought, and then she turned and saw the scarlet uniform coats. The sight of soldiers always seemed to take her brother by surprise, though the city was full of them.

When she turned back again, Luke's expression had changed, from playfulness to concern.

The reason she liked these rides so much, Lily told herself as she settled in, was that nothing was required of her in the way of conversation. Simon was busy with the horses; Lily's only job was to stay warm in the piles of buffalo hides and bear pelts and to enjoy the ride and the view. They rushed over the countryside toward the hill that all Montreal liked to think of as a mountain. Mount Royal, they called it, six miles away and a good place to go for a view of the city.

The sky was a clear, hard blue, cloudless, serene, the sun so bright on the snow and ice that Lily must squint. *The trouble with blue eyes,* her father would remind her, smiling to take the edge off the truth, *they let too much in.*

A letter from her mother was tucked up Lily's sleeve but it was her father who came along on these sleigh rides. In all of the stories he told, Nathaniel Bonner never spoke of the winter he spent here; and still Lily could imagine him sleigh racing, wild to be off, to be moving. As he must run, sometimes, for the beat and rhythm and rush of wind on his face. Wolf-Running-Fast he was called by the Kahnyen'kehàka, or Between-Two-Worlds. The first name always seemed to Lily the better one.

There were ten sleighs altogether now: bright green, blue, yellow, red. Most of the party were known to Lily, friends of Simon's and her brother's, all younger men, all of them come out with a girl tucked in beside them. In the city young women vied for these invitations, Ghislaine had told Lily, as if she weren't properly appreciating the honor bestowed upon her by Simon Ballentyne, who could fill the spot beside him twenty times over.

Lily had asked about Luke, if he never went out with a sleigh and a girl beside him, and with that earned a surprised laugh from Ghislaine. Luke Bonner, it seemed, was above such things, too much a gentleman, far too seriously busy with all his many concerns.

And had this superior godlike brother of hers never had a sweetheart? Lily wanted to hear, unless of course Ghislaine simply didn't *know.* This brought a long recitation of the names and connections of those young ladies who had set their sights on Luke without success. Some had wondered if Luke was the kind of man who preferred the company of other men, but then of course Mademoiselle

Jennet had come from Scotland and all was made clear. Ghislaine was looking forward to having Mademoiselle Jennet as a mistress; she *laughed,* and she made Monsieur Luke laugh too, a rare skill indeed.

The citizens of Montreal put a great deal of value on good humor, Lily had noticed that right away, and these sleigh parties were the very best example of their lighthearted playfulness.

The sleighs had been brought to a halt while the men made plans about the route and the women called out in English and French to each other, good-natured challenges and outrageous boasts calculated for laughter. The horses nickered and tossed their heads too, holding their own conversations.

Simon sent Lily a sidelong glance, his dark eyes alive with the challenge, as excited as a boy with his first bagattaway stick. He flicked the reins and they were off, caught up in the scream of the wind. Lily heard herself cry out with it.

All around them the countryside rose and fell like the wings of a great bird, snowy fields crisscrossed by lanes beaten down smooth. But the colors were the thing. *White snow, blue sky,* Daniel would tease her when she talked of such things. *What more is there to see?*

This. She wished her brother were here so she could make him understand what white could be. Trees tangled together against the horizon, a web thrown up to hold up the sky and still its color seeped away and into the landscape itself: blue in layers upon layers, melding into shadows purple and copper that faded to rosy golds. The winter sun, too heavy for the sky, moving down and down like a sleepy child, radiating colors that defied pigment and palette and brush, putting every artist who had ever lived to shame.

This, she would tell Daniel. *See this.*

He would look, out of brotherly love, out of curiosity, but he would not see. It was not in him; it was not in most, it seemed. Daniel had many gifts that she did not, of course: even as a very little boy his talent with animals had been undeniable, a fellow feeling, her father had called it, that allowed him to pick up birds and call wolves to him to stand, watchful, a few feet away. As if he only had to choose between one family and another.

He was a creature of the woods, her brother, alive to them in the way that few could be, but in his world color was just another piece of a larger understanding.

Gabriel Oak, who had been Lily's first drawing teacher, had told her that it would be so, that there would be many who loved her but could not understand this gift she had been given, the seeing. She had been a little girl and not taken his meaning, and just as well; it saddened her now to think of it, that the people she loved best could not share what she valued most.

Nicholas would see. Nicholas had the eye. If he were here with her they would sit and watch and never say anything at all until much later, when they tried to find words to make it last between them, this wonder, this fiery brilliant cold world. He understood why she had come so far, to another city in another country to live among strangers.

Simon turned and cupped Lily's head in one gloved hand, pulled her close and kissed her and she tasted the color there: hot and bright, his joy in the day as plain as salt on the tongue. She kissed him back, in gratitude, at first, and then more.

Nicholas was at home in Paradise, tending to his apple trees and his bears and his sad daughter and sadder wife, and Simon was here. The letter in her sleeve crackled and whispered, but the beat of her heart was louder.

The noise was tremendous, everyone talking and shouting and laughing as they recounted the morning's races, each of them with their own story that must be heard above all others as they tumbled out of the carioles.

They stopped for dinner at a farmhouse that belonged to Paul Lehane's aunt or maybe it was Jamie MacDonald's brother, the whole crowd of them moving into the warmth where they shed coats and furs like snakes frantic to be free of old skin. As soon as hands emerged from mitts a servant with one brown eye, as bright as a sparrow's, pressed a pewter cup of hot cider against chilled fingers.

In a far corner someone was tuning a fiddle. The house was full of comforting smells: lamb stew and new bread and beans cooking in molasses over a fire of apple wood and aged oak, coffee and hot milk and cider and too many people. The tiny windows dripped with steam and rattled with noise. Someone upset a basket of kittens and they scattered with tiny red mouths open in alarm.

Lily picked up a gray kitten with a tail as long as its body and found a spot on the bench that ran around the great tiled oven, as tall as a man. Then she pulled out her letter and broke the seal.

"Dearest Lily," her mother had written in her strong, slanted hand.

"Ho," cried a girl Lily had not yet met, the flush on her cheeks having less to do with cold and more with brandy, by the smell of her. "Are we here for a school lesson then?"

She tried to snatch Lily's letter away, would have snatched it had Simon not caught her hand and swung her around with a laugh.

"You need something more to drink, Meggie," he said, and winked at Lily over his shoulder. "Coffee, I think, and lots of it."

Lily pushed herself harder against the warm tile and bent her head over the lines her mother had put down on the paper.

> I write to you today with news that is both tragic and strange, because you will want and need to know the particulars, but also simply because to put them down on paper requries careful thought and ordering of the facts, a process which, I hope, will resolve some of my own confusion.

"From home?"

Lily started, losing the sound of her mother's voice just as easily as she had found it in the words on the page. Daniel Fontaine, a man with her brother's name and none of his understanding, stood before her. He came from a wealthy family, Lily remembered. *More money than sense,* Simon had said of him. *But good with horses.* Simon was on the other side of the room, pouring coffee for Meggie while she leaned in toward him, her face turned up like a calf wondering at the moon.

"Yes," she said, turning the paper away from his curious gaze.

"Good news or bad?"

Lily gave him a pointed look. "I won't know until I've read it," she said and he turned away, affronted but trying not to show it.

Within a few sentences the shock of what her mother had to report had settled deep in Lily's bones: Dolly Wilde was dead, and had been—Lily struggled to count the days—for more than a month.

> . . . at first we believed them all, mother, father, and child as well as both the Fiddlers, to have been the victims of some unthinkable and inexplicable act of robbery or retribution or kidnapping, but I must put your mind at ease straightaway: Nicholas had gone to Johnstown some days before the incident, in order to take care of some business with the county, and he took with him Callie and Zeke. Dolly's condition made travel impossible, and so Cookie stayed behind with her.

Just when we were almost resigned to the idea that all five of them were dead, the three travelers returned. In truth, we were very relieved to see them, not only because we feared the worst, but also because the suspicion entertained by some—though most assuredly not by me—that Nicholas or Zeke might have been responsible for Dolly's death could be set aside.

There was an inquiry in the trading post in which the known facts were laid out for all to hear. They are few and insufficient, so that no reasonable person can draw even a preliminary conclusion. Two days before your father found Dolly half-frozen on Hidden Wolf, Cookie came to the trading post for a pound of lard and a half pound of salt, and with her came Dolly. Anna McGarrity, who served them at the counter, reported that Dolly seemed fevered and started easily, but that has been the case with her for so long that Anna took no special note. Cookie said nothing of the trip to Johnstown, but again that fact was not alarming in itself. You will remember that Cookie is not a talkative person, and rarely volunteers information if not asked directly.

Constable McGarrity is in the unfortunate position of having neither clues, nor hope of any, though speculation is rife in the village. Some believe that Dolly finally lost the last of her reason and attacked Cookie and then wandered away in confusion or fear or both. The proponents of this theory believe that Cookie's body won't be discovered until the warmer weather comes and with it the thaw. Others of lesser understanding suppose that Cookie led a troublesome mistress onto the mountain to abandon her there and lost her way home in a storm called up by a vengeful and quick Almighty; still others that a stranger—for what man among us would do such a thing?—came upon them and took advantage of two women without means of protecting themselves.

Not one of these possibilities—for they must at least be taken into consideration, no matter how unlikely they may seem—has any basis in observable fact. Only Zeke entertains any real hope that his mother might still be found alive, and in fact he came to me just last week to ask if I would write down an advertisement to be placed in the Johnstown and Albany papers, in his own words, which I give you here:

Good woman gone missing. Mrs. Cookie Fiddler, a free woman of color, resident in Paradise on the Sacandaga. About sixty years, medium complexion the color of milky coffee. Last seen she was wearing a brown blanket coat, a yellow head wrap sprigged with greenery, and sturdy boots. Reward for information on her whereabouts or the fate that took her from us. God keep and protect my mother. Send word to Zeke Fiddler, care of McGarrity's Trading Post in Paradise.

For my part, I must think that some third party was involved, but to what end, that I cannot imagine. For now Constable McGarrity has written his official report of death by misadventure.

In the two weeks since this sad affair, I have seen Nicholas Wilde twice: once when he came to claim his wife's mortal remains, and once in the village. He was and is as distressed as any loving and attentive husband must be by a good wife's unhappy and violent end.

The neighbors have taken it upon themselves to help Nicholas in whatever way they might, bringing him a few birds or a measure of milk or a pie. I am told that Jemima Kuick comes to the orchard house every second day to clean and cook. Callie has not spoken a word, it is said, since she saw her mother's poor body, and she spends all of her time with Martha Kuick and will not be separated from her. An invitation from Curiosity to spend the rest of the winter at the Todds', and a similar invitation from us to come to Lake in the Clouds, were politely refused. My heart goes out to poor Callie, for I know what it is to lose a mother at such a tender age.

The words blurred on the page, and still Lily did not realize that she was weeping until she felt Simon's hand on her arm. She looked up into his face and saw concern there, and curiosity too, though he would never give it voice. Around the room the others had gone silent.

"A friend," she said, her voice breaking with the effort to be as calm as she wanted to be. "At home a friend of mine has died. She was lost in a storm."

A burst of laughter tried to force itself up into her throat from deep in her belly. *How very inappropriate,* her mother would say and at that Lily really did let out a hiccup of a laugh, one that might have been taken for a sob, had been taken for a sob by Simon, who settled down next to her and put an arm around her shoulder.

As if she were his to comfort.

The neighbors have taken it upon themselves to help Nicholas in whatever way they might.

Lily stood up suddenly. "I need fresh air," she said, holding the letter against her breast. Simon was looking at her, but she would not meet his eye. "Just a few minutes of fresh air, alone."

Chapter 12
December, Paradise

One of the mysteries of the young United States that Jennet could not sort out to her own satisfaction was the matter of holidays. It seemed that Americans worked every day but the Sabbath, and were loath to give up that habit, even to celebrate, no matter what the reason.

"Why, that's not entirely true," Elizabeth said when Jennet presented her observations. "You saw that we celebrate Thanksgiving, did you not? And in the summer Independence Day is very important. Then there are the celebrations around Christmas."

This took Jennet by surprise. "You celebrate Christmas?"

Elizabeth seemed a little embarrassed to admit such a thing. "Really, it is more a matter of going along with the Dutch," she said. "There are so many of them here, you realize, and they have particular ways of celebrating. Hannah can tell you about it, or better yet, ask Gabriel and Annie."

Soon after, on a snowy afternoon when Annie and Gabriel and Leo Hench were playing with Blue's new puppies before the hearth, Jennet raised the subject again.

"You mean Saint Claas?" Leo asked, his brow creased with excitement. "Why, he's a Dutch saint, come over on a ship, I suppose, just like the others." To this he added, very thoughtfully: "Nobody ever has told me what a saint is, not so as I understand it."

Annie gave him a look that was evenly divided between tolerance and irritation.

"The important part," she said with a superior air, "is that Claas comes to Paradise on the sixtieth of December, every year."

"The sixth of December," Gabriel corrected Annie, giggling as a puppy clambered up his arm to lick his face. "There's no sixty days in December."

"He's a tall man with dark eyes," Leo went on, ignoring the smoldering argument.

"And a wild beard," Annie said. "The grown-ups take special note of his beard, 'cause it grows all over his face. Like a dog, except yellow as corn silk."

Elizabeth was at the far end of the room sorting through some clothing, but Jennet heard her muffle a surprised laugh. The children were too wound up in their story—and puppies—to take note.

Gabriel pursed his mouth in disgust. "What's important is, Claas carries good things in his pocket."

"Only in one pocket," Annie corrected in turn. "In the other pocket he's got a bundle of birch rods as thick as my father's thumb. For the children who don't deserve sweets."

At this she sent a pointed look at both Leo and Gabriel, who were stacking puppies like wood chips, one atop the next.

"And he comes to the door?" Jennet asked Gabriel.

"Oh no," he said. "Well, at least not when children are about. He comes in the night, you see. The Dutch children in the village hang their stockings up, and old Claas, he comes by and fills those stockings up while they're all asleep."

"Ah," Jennet said. "And what about your stockings? Does he fill them too?"

Annie laughed out loud. "We ain't Dutch," she said. "You know that."

"But he comes to call anyway," said Gabriel. "While we're sleeping. We don't hang up stockings but he leaves the sugar cakes on the table. Last year we got an orange too, each of us."

Leo nodded eagerly. "Juice sweet as sin," he said, and again a muffled laugh came from Elizabeth.

The rest of the conversation had to do with what Claas might bring this year, and if any of them had earned a birch rod instead of an orange.

But in the end all the anticipation was for naught: a three-day blizzard kept Jed McGarrity from making his scheduled trip to get supplies from Johnstown, and coincidentally, Saint Claas stayed away from Paradise. The children were disappointed, but stoic. On the sixth of December they went off to bed consoling each other and trying to calculate how long the snow would keep the old Dutch saint away.

The wind and snow scoured the walls of the cabin, but in front of the hearth it was warm and Jennet had to keep herself from yawning.

"It seems rather hard," she said. "That the children should look forward to this all year and be let down."

Nathaniel winked at her. "Have a little faith," he said. "The snow might have slowed Claas down, but he'll get here in the end. One year he didn't come till January, as I remember it."

Hannah was bent over some sewing, working by the light of a pine knot. She said, "For the Todds' sake I hope the weather clears before that."

At this they all went quiet. After a while Hannah looked up, her expression blank. "What?"

"Are you saying that Richard is waiting to die until after Saint Claas comes to call?" Elizabeth asked.

"No," said Hannah with a grim smile. "But he will have his Christmas celebration first, and his firecrackers and all the rest of it. He has told me as much."

Nathaniel shrugged one shoulder, running a hand over his face. "Stubborn unto death," he said.

"Did you expect anything else?" Elizabeth asked.

She began to put her knitting away, a deep frown between her brows.

"Is that possible?" Jennet asked. "To just will yourself alive when your body is ready to die?"

"In Richard's case I wouldn't doubt it," said Nathaniel.

To Jennet it was clear that there were stories here that she had yet to hear, and also that this was not the time to ask. Instead she said, "As soon as the storm breaks I'll go down to spend a few days with Curiosity and help with the nursing."

This earned her a brilliant smile from Elizabeth and a thankful one from Hannah. Nathaniel put his hand on Jennet's shoulder as he passed, and squeezed.

•   •   •

"Claas will have to come on Christmas Eve," Anna McGarrity told Jennet when she stopped in at the trading post on the way to the Todds' place two days later.

"Fearful late," said Jed, who was fishing among the pickled eggs in a large jar. "But better than no visit at all. And we can get all the foolery done with at once."

"Foolery?" Jennet asked, looking from Anna to Jed, who was nailing a new hand-painted sign among the great variety of them on the wall: *No More Cone Shugar.* "Do you mean the firecrackers?"

"And the rest of it," said Anna. "Firecrackers and a turkey shoot, that's something we do every year. Wait and see if it don't cheer even the saddest folks right up."

Anna was thinking of the Wilde family, no doubt, and Jennet must think of them, too, for the half hour it took for her to walk from the trading post to the Todd place. Certainly anything they could do to help the Wildes must be undertaken. Indeed, all of Paradise needed something to take its mind off the mystery that still surrounded Dolly's death and Cookie's disappearance.

When she turned on the path that led up through tall stands of evergreens to the Todd property she saw Joshua Hench coming toward her. The blacksmith was driving a small bobsled, standing on a board set over one end. His son Emmanuel sat behind him, holding on by means of a leather strap nailed to the floorboards.

Joshua drew the horse to a stop and touched the brim of his hat. Emmanuel jumped up like a puppet and they both smiled at her, identical strong, wide smiles that no one could withstand for their honesty and simple goodwill.

"Why, Miz Jennet," Joshua said. "I was just thinking about you today. The Lake in the Clouds folks all come through the blizzard?"

"Everyone healthy and accounted for," Jennet assured him. "And you are all well?"

"Daisy got a catarrh," Joshua said. "I was hoping Hannah might have time to come see. Don't want to bother Curiosity about such a little thing right now."

"Yes," Jennet said. "Curiosity is very busy with Dr. Todd."

"That's true," Emmanuel said. "He sure do keep everybody jumping, my grandma most especially."

Joshua sent his son a quiet look that made the boy drop his head and study his own shoes.

"Emmanuel been helping me get the firecrackers ready for the

Christmas Eve party," Joshua said evenly. "He's got a good steady hand, but his mouth do get away from him, time to time."

"Why, I have that very same problem," Jennet said. "I sympathize with young Emmanuel. But let me ask you—just out of curiosity—I suppose all these preparations mean that you haven't had time to work on my skate blades."

"Now, I wouldn't go that far." Joshua rubbed a spot on his chin. "Why don't you stop by the smithy tomorrow, see what I got for you." And with that he spoke a few soft words to the horse and they were off again.

"I'll ask Hannah to stop by to look at Daisy's throat when she comes down later today!" Jennet called after him, and he raised a hand.

She found Curiosity and both her granddaughters in the kitchen. Lucy was up to her elbows in soap and water, scrubbing the plank table that dominated the middle of the room, while Sally tended a pot of beans and bacon hanging from a trivet over the fire. The smells of lye soap and cooking were strongest, but just underneath was the sweet-sharp smell of the herbs that went into the tisanes and teas that Curiosity cooked, day and night, for Dr. Todd. Just below those smells were the more usual ones: wax candles, hot milk, wet wool, and wood smoke, always and forever. If she went back to Scotland tomorrow and never came to this country again, Jennet knew that wood smoke would immediately bring Paradise to mind.

Curiosity herself was sitting in front of the hearth in her rocker, asleep with her knitting in her lap. In repose, her bright eyes closed to the world, she looked her age and more, and bone weary. Sally held a finger to her lips and Jennet nodded, slipping off her pattens to walk in her stocking feet across the room.

"Child, you think you can hide from me in my own kitchen?"

All three of them jumped, Jennet most of all.

"I can try," Jennet said. "Hope lives eternal, as they say."

Curiosity let out her low chuckle and raised her arms over her head to stretch. "I know every creak of these boards," she said on a yawn.

"Grandmama was up all night with the doctor," said Lucy. "We was hoping she'd get a few hours at least this afternoon."

"Catch as catch can," said Curiosity. She held out an arm toward

Jennet, palm up, and curled her long fingers. "Come on over here, girl, and give me news from the mountain."

Jennet settled on a three-cornered stool just in front of Curiosity, whose eyes were bloodshot but sharp as ever. For five minutes she told everything she could think to say, from what books Elizabeth had been reading to them in the evenings to this morning's visit to the trading post and the plans to delay the visit of Saint Claas until later in the month.

Curiosity smiled at that. "Those children will be hopping out of they skin with waiting."

"Yes, they already are. But it's not so very long."

After a moment of looking into the fire Curiosity said, "I should get back upstairs and see to Richard. Ethan been with him since sunrise." And then, with a quick look at Jennet: "Is Hannah on her way down here too?"

Hannah had been so distracted lately, so withdrawn, that Jennet hesitated to say with any certainty at all what she might do. "She is supposed to look in on the widow, tomorrow at the latest."

Curiosity was looking at her sharply, but after a moment her gaze flickered away. As if she realized the questions she wanted to ask had no good or satisfying answers.

Jennet said, "How is the doctor?"

Curiosity shrugged. "No better. Some worse, I suppose. He passed a tolerable night and this morning he asked for tea. I expect he'll hold on a while longer."

"Hannah thinks he is waiting to see the Christmas firecrackers before he dies."

Too late Jennet saw Lucy's expression of alarm and warning; the words were spoke, and she might have pinched Curiosity for the reaction she got. The old lady's face contorted, and a bright blaze of anger came into her eyes.

"Don't talk to me about no firecrackers," she said. "I'd like to throw every one of them in the lake, and Richard Todd right after. Burning up Lord knows what just to hear the bang and watch the sizzle. As if we ain't had enough fire in Paradise."

She set the chair to rocking hard and the old tomcat moved away in alarm.

"Grandmama," said Lucy in a consoling tone.

"Don't you grandmama *me*," Curiosity snapped in her direction. "You know I'm right. Wasn't you standing right there two years ago when Ben Cameron blew his fool thumb right off?"

"He was drunk," offered Sally.

"Yes, he was. Stupid with it. Stupid without it too. Pouring salt-peter and Lord knows what else in a newspaper cone and setting fire to it."

"I take it this is an old argument," Jennet said.

"That's so," said Curiosity. "Every year the doctor gets it into his head to try something bigger and more dangerous, and do any of the menfolk say, hold on a minute? Do anybody say, now is that a good idea, pouring all those chemicals and whatnot together? Your daddy just as bad as the doctor," she said, jabbing a finger first at Sally and then at Lucy. "He go right along with the whole thing. And what good a blacksmith with all his fingers blowed off, may I ask you that?"

She sat back suddenly, her anger spent. A great expanse of hand-kerchief appeared out of her cuff, and Curiosity wiped her face with it. When she raised her head again she looked a little sheepish.

"You'll have to excuse a crankit old lady," she said. "That blizzard got on my nerves. But I am glad to see you, child. Your face light up the room, it surely do."

"I've come to help with the nursing," Jennet said.

Curiosity reached out to press Jennet's hand with her own. "Good thing too. Let Ethan get some rest. The boy wore down to a shadow."

There was a tentative knock at the kitchen door, so soft that Jennet mistook it at first for a log falling in on itself in the hearth. Then Sally got up and went to the back door.

"Why, Miz Callie. Miz Martha. Come on in before you freeze right—" She stopped herself. "Come on in, children."

The two little girls blinked and nodded and came in.

"Now look here," Curiosity said, a real smile breaking over her face. "Now ain't this a treat. Come over here by the fire, take off your wraps. Lucy, give the children some tea, they must be chilled clear through."

Martha looked at Jennet and then at Curiosity. Finally she cleared her throat and said, "Thank you kindly, but we can't set. My ma sent us to say, the widow died in her sleep last night and can you get word up to Lake in the Clouds that there's no call for Hannah Bonner to come by anymore."

The words tumbled out in a rush, punctuated by sharp indrawn breaths. Callie said nothing at all but only studied her shoes. As far as Jennet knew she hadn't spoken to anybody since her mother's death.

Curiosity pushed herself up out of the rocker and made her way across the kitchen, hobbling a little, Jennet saw, and favoring her right leg. She was barely taller than the girls, but she stretched out her arms and drew them to her, and they went willingly.

"Why now, that's sad news," she said softly, rubbing thin shoulders through blanket coats still crusted with snow. "It surely is. You come in now and take off these cold wraps and drink something warm, and then you tell me all about it."

Martha's expression softened and her eyelids fluttered, as if she might fall asleep right where she stood. Even Callie seemed to take some comfort from Curiosity, but when Jennet caught her eye, she turned her face away.

"Sometime the best thing is to just say a thing out loud." Curiosity pulled her head back to look Martha in the eye. "Just let the whole story out. You'll feel better for it, child. You surely will."

The little girls exchanged a look full of shadows and worries. Martha shook her head. "Thank you kindly, but we've got to go on now, my ma wouldn't like it if we made her wait."

In the late afternoon, when Hannah knew she could no longer put off the trip to the village, Charlie LeBlanc came to Lake in the Clouds with news of the widow's death. The first thing Hannah felt was relief, that she would not have to leave home today after all. She was so relieved that she could think of no questions to ask, which turned out not to matter anyway: Charlie told what he knew without prompting.

Elizabeth's questions were all about Martha, who had found her grandmother, stiff and cold, her eyes open wide.

"Like she saw a ghost," offered Charlie. A very Charlie-like embellishment, one that none of them challenged. Nor did they ask any real questions; confronted with one, Charlie LeBlanc could always think up an answer. He had never been one to be slowed down by facts.

He said, "Lots of graves to be dug this spring. Folks say the doctor will be next."

"How is Richard?" asked Elizabeth. "Do you have word of him?"

"Oh, he's about the same. On the decline." Charlie's jaw worked as he tried to settle his false teeth more comfortably. Then he seemed to remember something and he turned to look directly at Hannah.

"I almost forgot to say. Curiosity sends word—" He coughed twice into his mittened hand.

"Becca is after me to give up tobacco," he said when he got his voice back. There were tears in his eyes. "Don't know if she's more interested in saving the money or my lungs."

"That's not a tobacco cough," Hannah said. "You've got a catarrh coming on."

"Well, jumping Jesus," Charlie said. "That too."

"What was it Curiosity wanted you to say?" Elizabeth asked, with something less than her usual patience.

Charlie blinked at her. "Curiosity?"

"You said 'Curiosity sends word,'" Elizabeth prompted.

"Oh, so I did. She sends word Richard had a good night and there ain't much going on to worry about just now."

"Ah," said Hannah, and realized that she had been holding her breath. "Then there's no need for me to come down to the village."

"I suppose not," said Charlie, but he looked at her thoughtfully. "Not if you got reason to stay away."

"I'll come down in a few days," said Hannah.

"I'll let her know," Charlie said.

Late that night, awake in her bed and without hope of rest, Hannah got up and went to the window. There was no moon and little light, but she had grown up in these woods and she knew how to keep still until her eyes could adjust. In time the starlight showed her familiar shapes, places she had walked as a girl, trees on a ridge silhouetted against the sky that she knew one by one. Even in the night this place held no secrets, waves of dark on dark and gauzy grays but familiar to her and comforting.

Below, at the foot of the mountain in the narrow river valley, the village was asleep. Hannah felt it there, a quiet hive humming to itself in the cold dark. She closed her eyes and tried to see it but all that came to her mind's eye was the lake, bow shaped, moon shaped, ice encased. Unyielding, dead to the eye, but pulsing with life deep below the surface. Like a great expanse of belly thrumming full of life. In the spring the sun would stroke that smooth surface until it weakened and cracked and life could push its way back up into the light and air.

In the spring the lake would come to life, and the earth would soften and in the village they would dig graves for the dead.

Behind her she heard Gabriel stir and shift and sigh to himself in his dreams. Since the twins had gone away he slept in Lily's bed, a restless sleeper always at odds with covers, always struggling with his dreams.

She went to sit on the edge of the bed. In the dark he was just a little boy, any little boy. Hannah lay down next to him and went to sleep.

Curiosity ran an orderly household, one that rolled along smoothly without any discussion or argument, so different from the kitchen at Carryckcastle that Jennet sometimes wondered if the women went behind closed doors to bicker.

One day passed and then another. Most of the chores that Jennet took on were easy enough, at least the ones outside the sickroom; more than that, she liked talking to Sally and Lucy and Curiosity and most especially to Ethan, who was a quiet soul but a thoughtful one, full of odd observations and willing to tell stories, when he was asked.

The sickroom was the hardest part, not because Richard was a demanding or difficult patient. An argument would have been far preferable to watching the man struggle with pain. The illness had got the upper hand now, and while Richard Todd seemed unwilling to die quite yet, he had forfeited his temper and moods, good and bad. For the most part he slept with the help of opium, and it was during those long periods that Jennet sat beside his bed, watching his breathing and counting his pulse, as Ethan had taught her to do.

She did not like to touch him. She didn't like the hot dry skin stretched tight over heavy bones, skin that had gone such a deep shade of yellow that Jennet must think of egg yolks congealed and rotting. She didn't like the fact that any touch at all—her own light fingers, the sheet pulled up over his swollen abdomen, the cup held so gently to his mouth for him to sip—any touch at all caused him to moan in pain. She didn't like these things but she did her best to hide her own feelings.

"You make a good nurse," Ethan told her one evening when they sat together at the supper table. Soon he must go and relieve Curiosity, who was sitting with Richard, but for now he seemed relaxed and even content. Jennet studied him closely but could find no glimmer of resentment or unhappiness in his expression.

"You have remarkable calm for a man of just twenty years," Jennet said. "Where does it come from?"

Ethan lifted a shoulder as if to disavow the compliment. "I have had good teachers. Curiosity and Galileo and Nathaniel and Elizabeth."

He said nothing of Dr. Todd, and Jennet did not make a point of the omission. She said, "What will you do, when—"

"I haven't thought much about that," Ethan answered before she could finish. For the first time Jennet had the certain sense that Ethan was lying to her. He thought, she was quite sure, of nothing else except what he would do with himself. When this vigil had finally taken its end.

When going down to the village could be avoided no longer, Hannah offered to take the children along with her. For the exercise, she said; but in truth because she needed the company and the distraction. But Many-Doves needed Annie with her for the day, and so Gabriel had Hannah to himself, as he put it.

And he was a distraction of the first order, moving first faster and then slower than she wanted to, stopping to study tracks in the snow or gather up treasures, disappearing and reappearing without warning. He knew no fear, and that in itself made Hannah fear for him, as she had once feared for Daniel, and for her own son. Sometimes it seemed that time had folded back on itself and merged this youngest brother with the older one, they were so much alike in their physical beings, in their curiosity about the world and the way they moved in the woods.

Once in the village Gabriel ran ahead to the trading post, shedding his snowshoes and disappearing through the door before Hannah could think of an excuse to call him back. On her own she would have forgone the pleasures of Anna McGarrity's curious company and plodded on, but now she couldn't avoid at least a short visit without giving offense. She followed her brother, taking more time than she needed with the unbuckling of her snowshoes.

After a blizzard the trading post was always busy. People came for supplies and news and simple companionship outside their own walls. Men settled in front of the hearth or the Franklin stove to play drafts or skittles or to whittle while they talked; children studied the jars of peppermints and malt drops with their hands folded decorously behind their backs; women nursed babies and traded advice and weaving patterns and gossip.

When Hannah came in every head turned in her direction, took stock of her health, or lack of it, the mantle she was wearing, the color in her cheeks, her expression. Some called out a few words, others only nodded. A few ignored her studiously. Coming into the crowded trading post always reminded Hannah of running a gauntlet, though it would have shocked and offended the people of Paradise if she were ever to say such a thing. They might overlook the fact that she was red-skinned—the ones who had known her since she was a child, at least—but their tolerance would not extend to such a comparison.

One small blessing presented itself in the form of old Mrs. Hindle, who was taking all of Anna McGarrity's attention to settle a debt. The widow Hindle took a coin from a pile of tarnished pennies she had poured out in front of herself, examined it front and back, and then pushed it across the counter to Anna with one swollen red finger.

"Seventy-four," Anna said patiently, and winked at Hannah.

"You heard the news about the Widow Kuick?" called Jed from a far corner. He was stacking boxes and dust whirled around him like a storm cloud.

"That's old news," said Charlie from his spot by the hearth. "I went up there a week ago to tell them."

Hannah agreed that he had indeed brought them the news, looking not at Charlie but for her brother, whom she finally found where he had inserted himself into the crowd around the stove. Gabriel had all their attention, because—Hannah realized now, and with some disquiet—he was giving them the best news he had to offer, the things he could remember about the letter from Luke that had come just before the storm.

And he had their attention. Jan Kaes, the oldest man in the village now, had hunched his shoulders over and turned his good ear to Gabriel. Horace Greber and the Cameron brothers were listening with their mouths hanging open. Martin Ratz and Praise-Be Cunningham had crossed their arms on their chests, affronted by what they were hearing.

Hannah heard it too: *my sister Lily* and *my brother* and *Simon Ballentyne* and then she walked forward as quickly as she could.

"Gabriel Bonner," she said in her severest tone.

He looked up at her, big-eyed. "It's only news from Montreal," he said. "They want to hear about how Lily's an artist and all."

"Sounds like she's doing more husband hunting than studying," said Missy Parker, who was not sitting with the men, but examining a keg of nails nearby.

Obediah Cameron grunted. He was forty and single and had bad eyes but was still hopeful of a wife; his brother had got one, after all. He squinted up at Hannah. "You think your Lily will marry up there and we'll never see her again?"

"Well, what else did you expect," Hannah said, trying for playful and not quite making it. "With Charlie LeBlanc married off, was she supposed to sit around and pine?"

They laughed uneasily and exchanged glances she was not meant to see or understand.

"The boy did right to come tell his news," said Horace Greber. "Don't you scold him now." He scratched at the stump of his leg with the stem of his pipe.

"I hope she does find a husband up there in Canada," said Lizzie Cameron, looking up from the baby at her breast. "There's not enough men to go around as it is, God knows. Didn't Margit Hindle have to go all the way to Albany to find herself a husband?"

Her brother-in-law made faces at that, but Lizzie wasn't bothered.

"Not enough of anything to go around here," added Charlie.

"If and when Lily marries, you will hear about it, I'm sure," Hannah said in a calmer tone. "But right now there is no such news."

Gabriel's eyes blazed defiance. "That's not what Luke says!"

She shot him a warning glance. "Enough, little brother."

"But—"

She stopped him by reaching over and grabbing him by the ear. Gabriel howled once and hopped until she let him go.

"I was only being neighborly." He rubbed his ear and scowled up at her, red faced.

Hannah took him by the elbow and turned him toward the door.

Nicholas Wilde stood there, his face as white as milk. Snow covered his bare head and shoulders.

"Why, Nicholas," said Anna from the counter. "You look plain sick. Set down before you keel over, man."

He managed a small, tight smile. "It's just coming in from the cold," he said. "I'll be all right in a minute. It's just the shock of the cold."

Curiosity looked up from the butter churn when they came through the door and Hannah could almost see the worry that had sat heavy on her shoulders lift and float away. The kitchen smelled of gingerbread and yeast and roasting pork and, underneath it all, the sickly sweet smell of laudanum.

"I'm sorry it took me so long," she said. What she should say, what she wanted to say, was so much more complicated that Hannah had no words. But it didn't matter, Curiosity was glad to see her.

"Why, child," she said, catching Gabriel as he launched himself at her. "No need to apologize. Here you are, and ain't the two of you a sight for sore eyes. Don't know who I'd rather see at my door on the shortest day of the year." She was looking at Gabriel, but talking to Hannah.

"I should have—" Hannah started, and Curiosity held up a palm to stop her.

"Never mind that. You here now. Richard been asking for you."

"And what about me?" asked Gabriel, tugging on Curiosity's arm. "Did he ask for me?"

"Why don't you set here for a minute and catch your breath before you start with your everlasting questions," Curiosity said, steering him toward the bench by the hearth.

"I'm not out of breath," Gabriel said, drawing himself up. "I'm never out of breath."

"Lord bless you, boy." Curiosity laughed. "Then let me catch my breath. Set there. Churn some, if you got so much energy needs using up. In a little bit the gingerbread will be coming out of the oven and you can see if I did it right this time."

"Gingerbread for the Christmas party?" Gabriel drew up, such hopeful expectation in his face that both Hannah and Curiosity laughed out loud.

"Yessir," Curiosity said. "Yes, indeed, for the party. But I can spare you a taste, I reckon. Just now, though, I got things to talk to your sister about."

"He can't hold on much longer," Curiosity said once they were in the hall with the door closed behind them. "Don't hardly know how he made it this far."

Hannah said, "Opium."

"It's the only thing that helps at all," Curiosity said. "The only thing he can keep down, anyway." She straightened her shoulders with an effort. "He'll hold on for those fireworkds he sets such store by and then he'll let go. The damn fool."

"In the trading post I heard that the lawyer was here. Mr. Bennett?"

Curiosity nodded. "Come in yesterday midday and sat with Richard for an hour. Come out with his hands full of papers and went straight back to Johnstown, didn't even stop to take dinner. Next thing Richard say, he want to talk to you and Ethan together. You might as well go right in, get it over with."

"Where's Jennet?" Hannah asked.

"I sent her over to the Wildes' place with some tea for Callie."

Jennet was out tending to the sick, then, while Hannah had been sitting at Lake in the Clouds mending socks and reading newspapers. She blinked away this image, but not before Curiosity read it off her face.

"Go on now, see Richard. He's waiting on you, girl."

Richard lay in the exact middle of the feather bed, covered by only a sheet. Ethan sat on a chair, a closed book on his knees.

Ethan said, "I just gave him a full dose. In a minute or two he'll be able to talk to us."

Richard's eyes, red rimmed and watering, were alive with pain as sharp as broken glass. He blinked at her and blinked again, and every breath was followed by a shallow gasp.

Across the bed Ethan met her gaze, but they said nothing. There was nothing he could tell her that she could not see for herself.

The part of Hannah that was still a doctor and always must be noted that Richard's neck and arms were withered to almost nothing, but his abdomen was swollen, barrel shaped and ripe as a nine-month pregnancy. In his prime he had been a big man with fair skin and a head of thick red-gold hair, mostly gone now. His skin was the color of singed parchment, such a deep yellow that it was almost brown. Everything about him was yellow: the whites of his eyes, the palms of his hands, even the beds of his fingernails.

Hannah pulled the second chair up beside him and sat, folded her hands in her lap and waited.

The clock on the mantelpiece had stopped. The only sound was the fire hissing and rumbling to itself, the wind in the trees outside the windows, and Richard's breathing, in and in and out, hitching and uneven. Hannah could almost feel him coming alive as the opium pushed the pain back and back. There was a clicking sound in his throat. Ethan offered him water and he sipped from the cup.

"Well, then," he said. "Let's get this over with."

He spoke in stops and starts, his voice hoarse but purposeful, punctuated with wheezing gasps. "I want you to hear this from me before the will's read out. I'm leaving my medical practice to Hannah and the house and farm to Curiosity."

Hannah was surprised, but Ethan was struck dumb. He opened his mouth and then closed it again, looked at Hannah for help, but got none.

"You're surprised," Richard said. His voice was as thin and weak as old thread but there was considerable satisfaction in it.

"I don't need the house," Hannah said. "And I don't want the practice."

Richard's eyes narrowed. "Then burn it all down," he said, his fingers fluttering on the coverlet.

Hannah bit back the things she might have said.

"I don't mind, Hannah." Ethan's concern was for her, which both touched and aggravated Hannah. And Richard too, by the expression on his face.

Richard grunted. "You'll get all the rest of the land, here and in Albany. And most of the money. There's a lot of it." His voice left him and he swallowed convulsively.

There was a small silence, broken by the sudden trill of Gabriel's laughter from far away.

"No more tenants. When the leases expire don't renew them. Let this place fade away. God knows it was a mistake to settle here in the first place."

Then Richard managed a smile, just one side of his mouth drawing up to show bloody gums.

Ethan glanced at Hannah again.

"Don't look at her," Richard said. "She can't tell you what I'm thinking."

He coughed, just once; a cough that could have been muffled in a lady's handkerchief but must have felt to him like a hot blade. Hannah watched him swallow the pain, and she remembered that he had lived among her mother's people for much of his boyhood. The lessons he had learned there were still with him, even now. Especially now.

His gaze flickered to Hannah and fixed. He said, "A long time ago your father promised to bury me at Lake in the Clouds, next to Sarah."

Hannah was more surprised at this than she had been at the gift of the house, but she managed to keep it from her face.

"I've changed my mind," Richard said. "I want to be buried next to Kitty. I owe her that much."

Ethan turned his face away but not before Hannah caught a flicker of satisfaction in his eyes. This request at least had pleased him, though Richard did not seem to care what any of them thought.

"One last thing," he said, his voice worn down by exhaustion to a whisper. "A question for you." He was looking at Hannah. "And I want an answer."

She wanted to walk away, to turn around and close the door behind herself and never come back into this room until Richard Todd was beyond asking questions. Until she was safe from him and his need to understand things she could never explain to anyone. He wanted to know about her son and Strikes-the-Sky; for all these months he had been worrying at her, determined to extract an answer, like a splinter dug into muscle. Now he would have his answer, because he was dying; because she could not deny him. She wondered briefly if he had decided to leave the house and practice to her just so he could call her here to ask questions.

He said, "What did your mother tell you about me when you were a girl?"

The words would not order themselves in Hannah's brain; they made no sense, though she worked through them once and twice and three times. "My mother?"

"Your mother. Sarah. Sings-from-Books. What did she tell you about me?"

He was looking at her intently, his breath coming fast and shallow. If she were to put her hand out and touch him she would feel his pulse shiver and jump.

Once Richard had tried to claim her as his own daughter. Her grandmother Falling-Day had told her the stories, because, Hannah realized now, she had known this moment would come. Sooner or later, Falling-Day had said, Richard would try to take her away from Nathaniel. All these years he had been waiting for this chance, this dying man, who wanted to claim her as his own blood.

She could feel pity and compasion but she could not lie, not about something so important.

Hannah said, "She never spoke to me about you as anything but a friend and neighbor."

After a moment he nodded, and turned his head away.

Curiosity came then and Hannah went out into the hall without another word. At the top of the stairs all her strength ran away, leached from muscle and bone like water from a wrung cloth, flowed down and away so she staggered and would have fallen, if not for Ethan.

They sat side by side on the step, neither of them able to talk at first. It was cold in the hall, so cold that their breath mingled white and damp in front of them. Looking straight ahead Hannah could see out the hall window, a perfect rectangle of cold sunlight, and into the colder world beyond.

"He isn't my father, you know. No matter how much he wants that to be true."

Ethan took her hand in both his own and simply held it. It was a kind gesture and a brotherly one.

He was weary and sad and quiet. Not quite twenty years, but right at this moment Hannah could see the old man he would be someday. Just as she could close her eyes and see him as a newborn, ruddy faced and wide-eyed and so small that they had feared for his life. Ethan was quiet and solitary and lonely to the quick; his mother had been like that, unable to settle on happiness, unable to take nourishment from the best things around her.

Hannah was glad of his hand, of its warmth and firm grip and the things it meant, the comfort he was offering and asking for, all at once. The truth was, Ethan was smarter than his mother had been, and there was a generosity to him that was all his own. People talked to Ethan Middleton, opened up their secrets to him without thought or concern, because he knew how to listen, and when to talk.

Born to another family he might have made a Catholic priest, Hannah thought to herself wearily. A man who heard confessions and passed out forgiveness like sweets to a repentant child.

She said, "I thought he was going to ask me about my son. About what happened to Makes-a-Fist."

But Ethan had nothing to say, even to this: her son's name, spoken out loud for the first time since— She stopped herself then, unwilling to pursue the memory. When she looked at Ethan his expression was so completely calm, so empty of curiosity or calculation, that she had the urge to pinch him, just to hear him make a sound.

The clock in the downstairs hall chimed four, and Hannah was surprised to realize that they had been sitting like this for more than an hour. In the snowfields outside she imagined the shadows stretching out and out, seeping into the forests, like ink poured across paper. The shortest day of the year, Curiosity had said. The darkest, the coldest. And yet there was something comforting about the still fields and the dark, something promising. A snowfield was like a bed, white and smooth and inviting: come and lay your head. Lay your head and sleep. A glittering soft death, a sliding away without noise or pain.

She said, "My son drowned. It was a day a lot like this one, in the winter dark. He fell through the ice and drowned."

Ethan's breath came in a short, sharp burst. He squeezed her hand, and waited.

Headed back to the Todds' place in the late afternoon with only Ethan's dog Big for company and protection, Jennet decided that she liked the world like this. The cold had loosened its grip for the moment at least, overhead stars burned bright in a clear sky, and at night the snow was beautiful. Right at this moment she was happy, and why should she not be, Jennet reasoned to herself; next to her skin she carried the five letters that had come from Luke since he went away, and all the people she loved best in the world were healthy and accounted for.

With the last post there had been letters from Scotland, from Montreal, and from Daniel and Blue-Jay, who were not, as Elizabeth had fretted, sleeping in snow caves every night but in farmhouses and cabins as they made themselves available. Lily was applying herself to her studies and enjoying the winter season, though it seemed from Luke's own letter that perhaps she spent as much time being courted by Simon Ballentyne as she did at her work.

This news bothered Nathaniel more than it did Elizabeth, who was glad to know that her daughter was taking advantage of the things the city had to offer. Jennet, who knew a little about Montreal and more about Simon Ballentyne, kept her thoughts to herself and did not offer to read Luke's latest letter out loud. To her he had written more explicitly about Lily's behavior. Jennet had the idea that he wanted her to pass on information he scrupled to write directly, but in this she would not comply, no matter how slyly he maneuvered for her to take up this unpleasant task.

As Jennet saw things, the real concern was not Lily, or even Daniel or Blue-Jay, who were in true mortal danger, but Hannah. And she seemed to be the only one who was worried.

Outwardly Hannah seemed well enough: she did what was expected of her and more, but every day she seemed to be a little more removed from the world, a little more inward turned and unreachable. Jennet had talked to Elizabeth and Nathaniel and Many-Doves about this, trying to put her worries into words and failing. With Curiosity she had had only a little more success.

"The winter sets hard on her," Curiosity had said when Jennet finished with her awkward recitation of her concerns.

"Yes," Jennet said. "Harder than it should, I think."

At that Curiosity had looked thoughtful. After a long moment she said, "She lost a child."

She did not say, *You can't understand,* but Jennet flushed with color anyway, as if Curiosity had reached over and slapped her hand. "I know that. I know she lost her son."

The older woman looked up from the work in her hands and there was something in her expression, some kindness that lessened the sting. "You know and you cain't know. Not really. And I pray to the good Lord that you never do. She lost her boy and her man both, and it will be a long time before she find her way back again."

Jennet had wrapped her arms around herself to contain her frustration and anger. "But she's not on her way back, Curiosity. She's headed away from us. Every day a little further away. I see it happening. I feel it happening."

At that Curiosity had looked at her hard, the kind of piercing look that came over her when she was examining a child with fever or belly pain. After a moment she nodded. "All right, yes. I'll see what I can do."

All week Jennet had been watching for Hannah, who must surely come down to the village but never did. She thought of going up to Lake in the Clouds to fetch her, but there was always more work than Curiosity could handle and Jennet would not leave her in such circumstances. Nor was there any reason to send someone else up the mountain, at least not any reason she could put into words.

On the twenty-fourth of the month, when it seemed that

Richard could not last even a single day more, Jennet had begun to wonder if Hannah would ever come to the village or if she might spend the rest of her life hiding on Hidden Wolf.

Jennet was contemplating this possibility when she came up around the final bend to the house and Big let out a single sharp bark. Two shadows rose up from the porch and came running. The three dogs met in a rearing dance, tails wagging fiercely and jaws open wide in greeting. And why not, Jennet thought, they were litter brothers, after all. She herself felt a great rush of happiness and relief, because if Mac and Blue were here that meant people were here from Lake in the Clouds.

Jennet picked up her skirts and pace and the dogs trotted along beside her.

Chapter 13

Christmas Eve there was no help for it, and so Nathaniel and Elizabeth went down to the Todds' to pay their respects and take their leave of Richard.

They found a house crowded with whispering people, neighbors and friends and acquaintances who had come to keep watch and wait. Every chair in the parlor and dining room was taken and the hall was filled too, and so they went into the kitchen, more crowded still, but these faces were all black and most of them were at some kind of work.

Zeke Fiddler, in from Johnstown to visit his brother, was sitting on the bench near the fire with Levi when Nathaniel and Elizabeth came in. Elizabeth took the spot Zeke offered and the men went off to a corner to talk in low voices about nothing in particular. Then Curiosity came in and caught sight of them together.

"It's about time to go down to the lake for the firecracker show," she said. "I got my hands full with Richard so I'm counting on you three to see that those fools don't blow themselves and everybody else up."

Nathaniel might have reminded Curiosity that her son-in-law was a responsible man and not given to drink, but he knew it would do nothing to calm her, and might accomplish just the opposite.

Elizabeth said, "Come rest for a moment, Curiosity. Sit here with me."

The only balm that Elizabeth had to offer was distraction, and so she drew Curiosity into a discussion of the saddle of venison that she would roast for Christmas dinner, of puddings and pickled oysters that had been put by because Richard insisted on them, and of the work to be done.

Nathaniel heard the first of the visitors begin to slip away, the front door opening and closing and the fire in the hearth jumping in response. There was a lot of movement overhead: Hannah, most probably, or Jennet or Ethan, all of them busy with the dying man. If he concentrated Nathaniel thought he could hear Richard himself, the hoarse rhythmic grunting of a pain sunk so deep that nothing could quiet it but death itself.

He spoke to Levi and Zeke about the weather and the firecracker show to come and the news of the war, but all the while Nathaniel's mind was with Richard Todd. In a few minutes he would have to go up there and say something to sum up all the years of out-and-out war and then even more years of uneasy truce.

Nathaniel was listening to Levi talk about the latest battle—so many killed, wounded, captured—and thinking about Richard Todd when Ethan came into the kitchen looking flushed.

"He wants to go down to the lake for the firecrackers," he said.

There was a small silence while they all thought the same things: that it could not be done, should not be attempted, could not be denied, this strange and difficult last request.

Lucy said, "I'll look after things here while you go on ahead." She was talking to Curiosity, who stood in the middle of the kitchen, still and watchful and already in mourning.

Zeke said, "We'll fetch the sleigh around."

"Fetch both of them," said Curiosity.

Nathaniel went to help them.

It was a strange procession they made: two sleighs hung with lanterns, the harnesses strung with bells in honor of the holiday, and in the middle of a pile of bear furs, a dying man. Zeke Fiddler drove the sleigh that carried Curiosity and Ethan and Jennet and Richard. They had not allowed Hannah to join them. She shared the smaller sleigh with Nathaniel and Elizabeth, still and quiet in her wraps, her face painted in shadows and bright patches of light by the swinging lantern.

Levi sat on the box with his back to them. The horses huffed and tossed their heads and blew great clouds of moist breath. Off in the woods wolves howled, just the right sound, Nathaniel thought, for this particular ride. Beside him Elizabeth was silent but agitated; he felt that, even through layers of wool and fur and cold. Her worry was not so much for Richard—they were all past that now—but for Curiosity and Hannah and Ethan and even for Jennet, for anybody but herself.

He put an arm around her and pulled her closer to him, tucked her into his side. Across from them Hannah had closed her eyes, but she did not sleep. As a child she had never been able to fool him about such things, and that much had not changed. Elizabeth was less hesitant than he.

She said, "Hannah, are you unwell?"

She did not open her eyes, but a muscle jerked in her cheek. "I'm only tired," she said, and there it was, a lie. Why she was lying and how he knew she was lying Nathaniel could not say. But of all his children he understood this one best, knew the way she thought and how she hurt and most of all how she struggled to hide pain she did not want to own. Elizabeth began to speak again and he squeezed her hand to stop her.

The whole village had turned out at the lake for the party. The light of the torches and bonfires reflected pearly white and blue on the low clouds that hung over the lake, so that it seemed as if the village were caught between two layers of ice. The liquor was flowing freely and had been for a good while, by the signs: high laughter and muskets fired into the clouds for the noise of it, off-key singing and shouted challenges. Children shrieking as they ran and mothers calling out warnings.

Nathaniel listened hard for Gabriel and knew Elizabeth had caught sound of him first when she tensed and sat up straighter, her expression shifting from thoughtfulness and worry to expectation. Her love for this youngest of their children was something that she could never hide, though she remained convinced in herself that the world must see her as a woman ruled by reason, equally bound to each of her children.

The lake came into view and Levi clucked softly to the horses, who were uneasy with the noise and the gunfire and perhaps most of all with the eerie light of the fires reflected in clouds overhead and ice underfoot.

The villagers had been feeding the bonfires that followed the shore of the lake since noon. They were ferocious, living things with voices of their own, worthy of fear, demanding a respectful distance. On this part of the lake the ice was a good three feet thick and so they had built another, smaller bonfire right on it. Children skated around it chased by their own dancing shadows. Gabriel was out there among them, and Annie too, on blades Joshua Hench had made for them.

Joshua was there too, surrounded by boxes and barrels. On a makeshift table he had laid out rows of heavy layered paper twisted into long capsules. Each of the twists held more capsules, each filled with some particular chemical, Nathaniel knew, carefully weighed out and poured according to Richard's written instructions. Every year the two of them spent months considering new combinations and materials, some of which came from as far away as England. Both of the men—blacksmith and doctor—took such pleasure in the collaboration and its fruits that Nathaniel wondered if it could go on once Richard was gone.

Joshua sat on a crate, head bent over a small object in utter concentration. There seemed to be an invisible circle around him, a silent oval of cold space and air where no one was allowed to set foot. This was Richard Todd's precaution, set out in no uncertain terms when Ben Cameron had played loose with the rules and lost a thumb for his trouble. Now even the drunkest stayed clear, whether out of concern for their own hands or fear of Richard's temper, that was a debate that always flared back into life at this time of year.

The sleighs came to a halt and Hannah opened her eyes. Nathaniel saw that they were full of many things and wet with unshed tears, but most of all he saw that she would not welcome his questions or even his comfort, at this moment. He helped Elizabeth out of the sleigh and went to lend a hand with Richard.

Elizabeth found Many-Doves and Runs-from-Bears by one of the bonfires, and then Gabriel and Annie came running from the lake, shedding skate blades with impatient kicks.

Gabriel launched himself into his mother's arms and she found herself sitting on a snowbank, her breath knocked out of her. He was so full of news about Saint Claas—who had come by earlier in the evening, she heard, and given him a pocketful of hard candy— that he didn't even notice.

"You know," Gabriel said in a low and conspiratorial tone. "I think it wasn't really Claas after all. I think Charlie LeBlanc pasted on a fake beard and pulled his cap down and pretended to be Claas."

"What makes you think that?" Elizabeth asked, trying very hard to keep a sober expression.

"Because his false teeth kept slipping, the way they always do," Gabriel said. "I think Claas couldn't get here because of the weather and Charlie didn't want us all to be disappointed."

"Most probably you're right," Elizabeth agreed, and took the arm Many-Doves offered to lever herself out of the snow.

"Bump is come," said Runs-from-Bears behind Elizabeth, and she turned.

"Where?"

Runs-from-Bears pointed with his chin and Elizabeth saw the little man, wrapped so elaborately against the cold that he looked like a small tree stump on the move. Nathaniel was helping him climb into the sleigh next to Richard.

Cornelius Bump was an old friend and a cherished one, a traveling man who came through Paradise only at this time of year, but that was as dependable as the phases of the moon.

"I didn't even think," Elizabeth said. "I completely forgot, with all the concern about—" And then it occurred to her, the truth of it.

She said, "Richard was waiting for Bump."

Beside her Bears made a sound deep in his throat, the sound that meant she had overlooked the obvious.

In the sleigh she could make out Curiosity's narrow face turned toward the visitor, the sway of her head as she spoke, the set of her shoulders. More relaxed now, Elizabeth thought, but wondered if she imagined this.

Richard wanted Bump with him when he died. It made a kind of sense, knowing Richard, who must plan everything to the last detail. Why Bump in particular, what connection there was between them, that she would probably never understand unless Bump told her himself, and that was unlikely: Bump was a keeper of secrets.

Gabriel saw none of this. He knew only that his mother was distracted and he wanted her attention. He hopped from one foot to the other and back again and talked and argued with Annie and raced to the lake and back again, reporting on the blacksmith's progress and guessing how long it must be before the first firecracker was lit.

But Annie saw. She had stilled beside her mother, her face solemn in the firelight, her gaze fixed on the sleigh. Annie looked at Elizabeth.

"He's dying now."

"Yes," Elizabeth said.

Many-Doves was watching too, humming a death song under her breath.

The first of the firecrackers sputtered and then exploded, throwing up fistfuls of light: first gold and copper, then yellow and apple red, then sulfur yellow and summer green. Joshua had disappeared behind billows of smoke. The smell of gunpowder was heavy in the air and tickled the back of the throat.

Daniel, Elizabeth thought, gripped by sudden and irrational fear. Daniel lived with this taste in his mouth day after day. Her son was gone from her, gone from here, and would not be back. For a moment fear held her tight, and then the next volley sputtered and fizzled and exploded against the sky and she shook herself free of black thoughts. She thought of Lily in Montreal, how Lily had loved these firecrackers, and hoped that she had something just as fine and colorful and full of wonder to watch tonight.

Another volley and the whole village sighed in delight, heads turned up at an angle to watch the fading colors: more greens this year, bilious greens and grass greens and the green of aging copper. She must ask Richard what chemicals he had used this time to get such an effect.

Richard. Elizabeth looked back at the sleigh, and saw that things had changed; Richard had gone with the noise and color and light, slipped away with his eyes fixed on the clouds and Bump holding his hand.

Many-Doves said, "It is done, then."

Elizabeth nodded, and started in the direction of the sleigh.

He was perched on high like a king on a throne of furs. Curiosity sat to one side and Bump to the other; Ethan knelt on the floor of the sleigh. Across from them Hannah and Jennet sat shoulder to shoulder, like children who have been hushed by a stern father and called to accounting.

On the lake the firecrackers had begun in earnest. Elizabeth saw the reflected colors in Richard's eyes, still open. His expression shifted and seemed to move with the next barrage of sound and light and color. Gone, and not quite gone; still watchful, still curious.

Nathaniel stood just behind Elizabeth, his arm across her shoulders. She leaned into him and turned, put her arms around him to contain his trembling. They were standing just like this, waiting for the noise and light to fade away for good, when they heard a little girl scream.

Hannah's ears were ringing with the noise of the firecrackers, nothing like a battlefield at all and yet she jumped with each new barrage. And behind that, a high keen whining that went on and on. Then she saw Curiosity's face and Ethan's and Jennet's and Bump's, all of them alive with fear. The firecrackers had stopped, she realized; and a child was screaming.

Jennet stood in the sled and put out a gloved hand to steady herself. "Did someone get burned?"

"No," said Curiosity. "That's a different kind of scream. Nathaniel—" she began, but it wasn't necessary. He and Ethan and Bump had already started off at a trot toward the lake where the last of the smoke hung like a tattered curtain over the heads of the crowd, Bump moving fast for a man his size, almost rolling, it seemed, his short legs pumping.

Jed McGarrity's voice boomed and echoed and some of the men turned back to stop the women and children coming forward. Many-Doves had Gabriel and Annie by the hands and was leading them away.

The men made a circle on the ice, shoulder to shoulder, torches held overhead. Jed had knelt down and put his arms around two smaller shapes: young girls.

"Martha." Elizabeth's voice hitched and broke. "Martha Kuick and Callie Wilde."

A nighthawk wheeled above the lake. Hannah raised her face to watch it circle once, twice, three times, and then disappear toward the forests.

In the lantern light Elizabeth saw Hannah's face stripped to the bone, the face of a woman in the grip of a walking dream: not asleep and not awake, her eyes glittering with icy tears. And a thought struck Elizabeth as forcibly as a fist, an irrational thought but still true, in the way that the hardest things are true: this was the Hannah who had been hiding from them all these months. This was the real Hannah.

This strange thought was still in her head when Hannah stood and made a graceful leap to the ground, her wraps flapping around her like wings. Elizabeth understood then what was happening at this moment and what was about to happen. She understood that she couldn't stop it, but she reached a hand out anyway, as she would reach for a child walking toward the edge of a cliff.

She said, "Wait—"

But Hannah was out of the lantern light already and moving fast. Beside Elizabeth Jennet said, "I'll go with her. Shall I go with her?"

And Curiosity stood, fists pressed to her breast. "Yes," she said. "You go ahead with her, be quick about it."

Jennet ran off, and Curiosity sat down next to Elizabeth. Beside them Richard was still and still and still.

Jennet was winded by the time she caught up with Hannah, winded and unable to speak, but she silenced the men who would stop her with a look and followed Hannah, through the milling crowd and to the circle of ice where Jed was still kneeling with his arms around Callie and Martha.

He was whispering something low and comforting, words with no meaning really but calculated to calm. Hannah came to a stop just behind them and Jennet would have run into her if Nathaniel hadn't put out a hand and caught her up short.

The little group of people were looking into the ice as if it were a window. Ice like glass, shot through with cracks but still clear, and pressed up against it two palms, fingers stretched out and between them a small dark face, its mouth open to a perfect round.

Levi was kneeling there and beside him Zeke, two grown men kneeling on the ice with their faces almost touching over the ice.

Hannah's voice came clear and hard, but in a language that Jennet didn't understand. Nathaniel understood it; Jennet felt him jerk in surprise. He said some words to his daughter in the same language and took her by the arm, drew her away.

Jennet followed them and listened as they talked, voices reasonable and steady, as if they might be discussing how best to get home or whether it would snow before daybreak. Nathaniel caught Jennet's eye and shook his head sharply, as if she had tried to join the conversation.

Curiosity was at the shoreline and Elizabeth with her, the two of them watching and listening and trying to hide their fear, and failing.

Nathaniel and Hannah passed them as if they weren't there at all, but Jennet stopped.

"It's Cookie," she said. "Under the ice."

"Cookie?" Elizabeth echoed, watching Nathaniel and Hannah disappear into the dark. And then, with the confused air of a woman waking from a long sleep: "Are you sure?"

Curiosity said, "It's Cookie all right. Just look at Levi and Zeke."

Both of them were down on their knees, looking through the ice as they would stare into a mirror.

Jennet touched Elizabeth's sleeve. "Did you hear Hannah? What was she saying? What was she talking about?"

Elizabeth brushed her mittened hands across her face, and said nothing at all.

Christmas morning, and Jennet woke with the sense that the world had slipped on its axis.

Nothing looked out of the ordinary in the little chamber Curiosity had given her for her own while she stayed in the village. The same pictures hung on the walls, the counterpane still glowed turkey red, and her clothes hung on the pegs where she had left them. It was true that there was a good inch of frost on the window, and it was also true that it was still snowing. But that, Jennet had come to understand, was the way of things. It would snow in this part of the world, snow again and forever. The snow fell without reason or mercy, without sound.

The house was too quiet, so quiet that her own breathing seemed the loudest thing in the world.

Dr. Todd was dead.

It came to her then, and with it the rest of the strange night: the doctor dying in the arms of the man called Bump, smiling up at him as though he were an angel and not a little man with a humped back. Firecrackers and ice skates and young girls weeping. Cookie in the lake like a stillborn child in the womb. Men shouting in the night, torches held high, as they went to fetch Nicholas Wilde and Jemima Southern and found them both gone. The accusations, the shouting.

And Hannah. Hannah was the worst of it.

As a little girl, Jennet had seen a cottage burn to the ground, the fire so hot and fast that nothing could be done to save the family sleeping inside it. More horrible than the fire itself was the old woman who stood too close, so quiet and still, her face turned up to the heat. Embers settled on her shoulders and raised blisters on her scalp and still she fought the men who carried her away, keening to the gods in the old tongue, a sound that filled up the world. It was her daughter and her daughter's children in the cottage, and she demanded the right to join them.

Jennet had been very young, but she had seen something in that old woman's face that she recognized, the very essence of pain. It was the same quality she saw in her own mother's face when she stood beside the earl's deathbed. Last night she had seen it again, in Hannah. Whatever she had been holding back all these months had been let loose last night, and Jennet would have to hear about it. Today sometime the story would come to her, through Elizabeth or Curiosity or Hannah herself.

Except she didn't want to know, didn't want to hear about this particular burden. She didn't know if she was strong enough or wise enough to face it.

She could sleep, instead. Turn her face to the pillow and burrow into the feather bed, and let sleep take her away from here, back to happier times and memories.

Then Curiosity was at the door, looking as though she hadn't slept at all, had never slept a peaceful moment in her life.

"What is it?" Jennet asked, struggling up out of the covers. "What?" Her voice rising sharp and breaking.

"Hush," Curiosity said, raising a hand. "Hush, it ain't nothing. I just come to see if you was ready for breakfast. It's past ten, child." She managed a faltering smile. "Dinner be on the table before you get out of bed."

Remorse chased all thought of sleep away. Jennet was out of bed in a flash, apologies tumbling from her mouth as she reached for her clothes. There was so much work to be done, mourners would be coming later today, dinner to cook, chores to be done, what was she thinking, lying abed?

Curiosity came into the room and put her arms around Jennet.

"Never mind," she said, her voice rough and low. "It's all right, girl. Never mind."

Jennet said, "How is she? Hannah, I mean. How is she?"

Curiosity's smile was stronger this time. "She's got her folks with her. High time she let it all out, whatever it is that she been sick with all this time. She'll come through, don't you worry."

"And you? How are you?"

That got a low laugh. Curiosity picked up the skirt that Jennet had dropped and shook it. "I'm weary, is how I am. Weary to the bone. Don't look so guilty, it ain't housework that's got me down, girl. My old heart is 'bout filled to the brim with sorrow, and it won't take no more. Those little girls wept themselves to sleep last night in one room while Ethan was doing the same down the hall." She paused and shook her head. "It seem to me sometime that the Lord has got a mean streak, it surely do."

The sound of harness bells came to them, and Curiosity went to the window.

"Jed McGarrity," she said on a sigh. "More trouble."

"I need to go up the mountain, to see Hannah."

Curiosity's mouth drew itself into a tight circle. "I know you do. But let's see first what the man got on his mind."

Chapter 14

It happened like this.

Harrison's troops, edgy with their victory, well rested, fed, and full of ale set to work in the abandoned village on the Wabash. First they stole what they wanted: kettles and blankets and baskets of wampum beads ready to be strung, and then they trampled what was left. When they tired of that, Harrison called for torches.

They burned the longhouses and council house and stores: corn and beans to feed five hundred through the winter, gone in mid-November. The smell of burnt corn would linger in the air like a taunt for days.

But before they left for good, fresh scalps swinging from the barrels of their rifles, they dug up every grave, old and new, and scattered the remains to rot in the sun.

The women and old men and the men not yet recovered from battle wounds came back while the dust and smoke still hung in the air. They came back to rebury their dead and build shelters among the ashes and ghosts.

They spoke of leaving. Before the white settlers came to finish what Harrison's men had started; before the snows. Before the real starving began.

It had been the Prophet's responsibility to keep the peace; now he sat aside, silent and disgraced, huddled under a bearskin and waiting for his brother to come home and see what he had wrought. Tecumseh was still some-

where in the south, recruiting warriors for the Ket-tip-pe-can-nunk that was no more.

The women prepared for leaving. At night, by their family fires, the eldest boys argued, but their words could not produce food where there was none. The warriors who healed left to find new battles, and some of the boys went with them. Walking-Woman's son, eight winters old, was too young. One thing to be thankful for.

They wandered away in small groups, women and children and the very old. Some went north to live among the English in Canada. The rest, Kickapoos, Dakotas, Sacs, Mingos, and the others, simply scattered with the winds.

Walking-Woman allied herself to Late-Harvest, a young Wyandot whose Mingo husband had been among the sixty-six killed by Harrison's men. Walking-Woman and her son would travel with Late-Harvest and her group and then, when the time was right, they would strike northeast for Mohawk lands. She would take the boy home to Lake in the Clouds. She would take him to her father and uncle, who would raise him to be the kind of man Strikes-the-Sky wanted him to be.

Makes-a-Fist disappeared in the night before they were to start. She found him sitting in a tree, his bow cradled in his arms. New snow made a cap on his dark head that flew around him when he shook it. He said, I will not go, *and* my father would not want me to run *and* you are a coward *and* I do not want to live among your white people. *These were strong words, words like a shovel digging a grave; words to break bone. Every one of them true.*

They were six women and thirteen children, the youngest still in cradle-boards, the eldest twin boys on the brink of manhood. There were two old men, Little-Mouth and Red-Hoof, uncles of Late-Harvest's dead husband. They had a single precious sack of corn from the Kickapoos' hidden stores, a musket with no powder or balls, some knives, four bows, and enough arrows if they were cautious.

Makes-a-Fist would not tolerate his mother's voice or touch or nearness. Instead he attached himself to the twins, Light-Crow and Dark-Crow. The three hunting boys ranged ahead of the women. Grouse, squirrel, rabbits: never enough. The boy brought in his share, and more, and still it was never enough.

They walked hungry. They walked trails the white men had forgotten or never known about; fading back into the woods when they heard horses or people.

At the Ohio they found an old Shawnee with a raft. He was willing to take them over the river to the beginning of Miami territory for three skinny rabbits and the news they had to share.

He poled them through drifts of ice, singing under his breath. Then Red-Hoof lost his footing on the wet log, and the river took him away, his gray hair floating for a moment in an eddy of maple leaves the color of fire. It was too cold to stop and so they sang the story of his life as they walked.

For the first time in her adult life, Walking-Woman stopped thinking of herself as a healer. All her medicines, all her tools, the surgical instruments, all her journals and notes and the records she had kept so faithfully, everything was gone, burned or trampled or stolen. She had nothing to offer these people; she could not fill their stomachs or quiet their fears.

They died, as she knew they must, the oldest and youngest first. A four-month infant of a fever, the second old uncle in his sleep, the mother of the twin boys because her kidneys stopped doing their work. By the time they came to the rolling hills of the Shawnee territory they were five women and nine children.

Makes-a-Fist spoke of his father more with every day of walking. He told stories about Strikes-the-Sky in his mother's hearing, so that Walking-Woman could neither ignore his anger nor put aside her own memories. When her son's fury was hottest, she closed her eyes and saw Strikes-the-Sky dead in a hundred different ways: convulsed with fever, swollen with snake-bite, drowned in a fast river overhung with weeping trees. She imagined him on battlefields, or ambushed, or lying on a pallet among the Osage, unable to ask for water or tell them his name. She saw him shot in the heart, his throat cut, his spine severed, flayed so his skin could be carried away and tanned, an artery in his stomach pumping blood. She blinked, and saw her son beside her husband, dead on the battlefield.

Strikes-the-Sky spoke to her often. He stood just behind her, calmed by death and, it seemed to her, amused by it too. Sometimes he spoke to her of nothing important at all; he reminded her of things they had done, the day he had first seen her, the day they had started the long walk west to join his people. He always ended his visit with the same stern words.

Keep the boy safe.

Makes-a-Fist had been born with a caul. Walking-Woman had watched him appear between her thighs with eyes open wide behind the thin, pearly-white skin of the birth sack. A ghost of a child, she had thought and then he howled, a sound like a panther screaming, and she was so relieved that she might have swooned, if not for the strong hands that held her own: her sister-in-law, gone now too, killed by a soldier when she ran back to the village to get the cooking pot. Walking-Woman remembered the arc of the soldier's sword, so swift and somehow casual, like a man out for a walk, lopping the heads off nettles.

In the newborn's clenched fists they had found more of the birth sack, something that set the women to conjecturing among themselves. This one will run into battle, her uncle's wife had said with great pleasure and pride. This one will be a great hunter.

Good fortune seemed to find them on the day they came to a lake that one tribe called Goose Neck and another, Hollow Waters. It sat among the wooded hills, ringed with a marsh like the stubble on a white man's chin and frozen solid, early and quick, in a series of deep and furious frosts. The weather was clear and the sky bright overhead, with a moon like a fat berry bumping along the horizon to cast pink shadows on the snow.

Late-Harvest found a cave she remembered from her girlhood and in it, waiting for them, a small bear in its winter sleep. Light-Crow killed it with an arrow through the eye and that night every one of them ate their fill. Makes-a-Fist ate until his belly rounded, but in his face his mother saw disappointment. He could not claim any part in the kill, and so the meat was not exactly to his taste.

The food and the warm shelter put them all in good spirits and for once the women spoke among themselves with more animation. Late-Harvest told stories of her girlhood here and of her village, just a few days' walk away. She spoke of her family, who sometimes made winter camp on the shores of this lake. From the mouth of the cave they could see it, glimmering under the moon. Here her father and uncles and brothers and cousins had played bagattaway, as many as fifty of them at a time. Here they hunted and fished and celebrated midwinter.

That night Walking-Woman dreamed of a village put to the torch, the air filled with the reek of burning flesh. She woke with a start to find that her son had put his pallet down next to her for the first time since they had left Ket-tip-pe-can-nunk. His hair had fallen over his face and fluttered with every breath. Walking-Woman touched his skin to feel its warmth. She put her face next to his and slept.

They spent a second day in the cave, rendering bear fat and cooking: food enough to take them to Late-Harvest's village and to offer as a gift to the sachem. The twins went out and brought back more game: two turkeys, a brace of rabbits, a porcupine. Almost more than the women could manage, but they were so pleased and the hunting boys so proud that nothing was said to discourage them.

Walking-Woman woke the next morning with the first scream of the blizzard. She was warm and her belly was full and the snow could not find its way into the cave, and still. She sat up in the near dark and looked hard into the coals in the fire pit, irregular red hearts pulsing and pulsing, close to death now and needing to be fed.

She made herself turn her head, knowing what she would see: the boy's pallet was empty. His bow and quiver were gone and his knife and a small axe; he had taken one of the four pairs of snowshoes they had among them.

Gone to prove the words spoken over him at his birth: this one will be a great hunter.

She would have started out after him but they held her back while the blizzard screamed, all through the day. Walking-Woman did the work they put in her hands, cut strips of meat and turned them on the fire, poured fat into lengths of knotted intestine, took a little girl into her lap and rubbed snow on sore gums where a new tooth was coming. Through all of that she was casting her thoughts out into the world. She spoke to Strikes-the-Sky and he did not answer her.

Too busy looking for the boy, she thought and then: now he will turn away from me too. Now they are both angry at me.

The storm died late in the afternoon, but the wind stayed behind. It blew hard, moving snow across the lake in gusts and then back again, sending eddies swirling up into the trees. The sun showed itself, cold and serene, and played on the ice that weighed down branches, scattering rainbows for the wind to hurry away.

They went out to find her boy, the twins and two of the other women and Walking-Woman, who first searched all around the hillside looking for places where he might have taken shelter.

Then she heard the twins calling her, and in that moment something caught up in her throat. Something as hard as a bullet, something with the wet-penny taste of blood. She walked toward the sound of their voices, opened her mouth to call back and found she could not.

They were standing on the lake in the last of the light, two brown faces as alike as chestnuts. They had cleared away a dimpled spot in the new snow that blanketed the lake to find, first, a single snowshoe, then the axe and finally the truth.

Makes-a-First had chopped a hole in the ice in the shape of a moon not quite full. Just big enough to drop a fishing net; big enough to swallow a young boy blinded by a snowstorm. It was frozen over again, the new ice thinner and clearer, and caught up in it, like a fly in a piece of amber: the heron feather that Makes-a-Fist plaited into his hair.

• • •

In the end they went on without her. Walking-Woman had some clothes and furs, and they left her what they could: enough meat and bear fat to last a few weeks, a bow and some arrows, a knife and axe and whetstone, a pair of snowshoes, a few flints, some string, a little salt. Late-Harvest promised to send one of her uncles or brothers back with more supplies.

Walking-Woman stood at the mouth of the cave and watched them disappear over the next hill.

In the day she walked the lake, stopping now and then to scrape away the snow, more than three feet deep in some places and nowhere less than two, and stare into the ice and talk to the spirit of the lake, who never answered her.

When the food was gone she made herself a slingshot and began to set snares. Sometimes she found herself without a fire because she had simply forgotten to gather wood and on those nights she went to sleep wondering if she would wake up again.

The Hunger Moon came and went and Walking-Woman learned the shape of the lake by heart. The cold dug in, the kind of cold she remembered from winters in the endless forests: cold leached of color, cold that would not allow snow to fall. And still she went out every day to walk the lake. The snow had grown a crust as hard as glass, but not so fragile: she used the axe to clear a spot when she wanted to study the ice.

Toward the end of the next moon Walking-Woman realized two things: there had been no snow for eight weeks, and her ribs had pushed out against her skin so that she could trace the shape of each of them with the tip of a finger.

It was then that Strikes-the-Sky came back and began to talk to her again as if he had never stopped. At first he only pointed out practical things that she had overlooked: fallen branches for the taking, a good place for a snare. Then, when she had been in the cave for three full moons and the cold had begun to loosen its grip, she found a doe at the mouth of the cave with crows sitting on its head. They looked at her with their sharp black eyes.

Behind her Strikes-the-Sky said, Now you will eat. *Walking-Woman chased the crows away and that night she slept deeply with the taste of fat bright on her tongue.*

Another moon waxed and waned. On a morning warmer than the ones before it, a morning with the first smell of spring in the air, the lake spirit took Walking-Woman. She was moving across its center, following her own tracks, when the layers of snow and ice under her feet let out a sound like a tree falling and then simply opened. One moment she was standing in the sunshine and the next she was tumbling, loose-limbed, hard snow in her mouth, waiting for the bite of the water to snap her in two.

She thought, Now I will see him, my son, *and,* How bright it is in the shadow lands, *and then she found herself standing, breathless and dry, on the bottom of an empty lake.*

It was the sound of her own harsh breathing that made her understand that she was not drowning, could not drown because the lake water had drained away over the long dry moons. Overhead the roof of ice and snow creaked and sighed like a living thing, flexing in the sun. Walking-Woman stood and listened to the ice talking while her eyes adjusted to the odd shadowy lake-cave.

She took a step, cautiously, and stumbled on a catfish frozen into the rutted lake bottom. A few more steps took her out of the light from the hole she had broken in the ice, further into the shadows. She walked until she could no longer stand, and then she crawled in the dark, over bones and fish and other things she could not name and did not like to imagine.

When she came to the first grasses she used the axe and struck at the ice, bowed her head while it fell in great chunks that would leave bruises on her shoulders and back. Then she stood up in the sunlight, ice clinging to her bearskin coat, and saw that she had walked most of the way to the shore.

For three days she searched the empty lake, carrying a torch before her where she could stand, or pushing it before her when she must crouch. The fish lined the lake bottom like Dutch tiles, the scales catching the firelight in flashing colors. She found rusted blades and fishing spears, the hull of a canoe and, inside of it, a cage of ribs. The bottom of the lake was littered with bones enough to build a city of the dead.

On the third day, when the sun was hot overhead and the ice roof groaned like a woman in travail, Walking-Woman dropped down into the lake and saw that the crows had followed her. There were a dozen of them, prying fish from the icy mud, and they paid her no attention. Enough for them all.

Late that day Walking-Woman found a snowshoe, a bow, a scattering of arrows. And then the boy. Curled like an infant on the floor of the lake, he looked like a child carved out of wax. She took him in her arms and cradled him, and thanked the spirit of the lake for returning her son to her.

When she woke the next morning the rain had come again and the lake was already filling. She had nothing with which to dig a grave in the frozen ground and so she climbed the tallest pine tree she could find and wedged the boy there among the branches.

The same day she started out for Lake in the Clouds.

Chapter 15

Dear Cousin Lily,

Your mother and father bid me write down for you the events of the last weeks. It is a task I take on out of concern for them and you, but it is neither an easy nor a pleasant one. Nor am I your mother's equal in matters of the pen, but I hope my poor efforts will serve.

On Christmas Eve, while Blacksmith Hench was busy lighting firecrackers, Cookie Fiddler's remains were discovered floating beneath the ice on the lake. And more shocking still, it was Callie Wilde and Martha Kuick who first came upon this gruesome sight.

You will remember that Mrs. Fiddler has been missing since the day late in November when Dolly Wilde was found near death on this mountain. Foul play was feared, and indeed it seems as if foul play has been done. Our first worry was for Callie, as you can well imagine. It is a very hard burden indeed for such a young lass, to lose the two women she loved best in the world in such a violent way. Martha was just as distraught as Callie herself, and the two of them clung together and wept so pitifully that it took all of Curiosity's and your mother's efforts to see them to an uneasy sleep in Curiosity's own bed, where she could watch over them in the night.

While we were busy with the lasses, Constable McGarrity and Mrs. Fiddler's sons and some of the other men had managed to retrieve her remains from the lake. I did no see her myself but Mrs. McGarrity tells me, and I have no cause to doubt her, that there was a great gash to the back of her head, it is believed made by a blunt object such as a piece of firewood.

It was midnight before the constable made his announcement. It was only by accident that I was in the trading post to hear him, where I had been sent by your mother in the hope that I might find your father. (Which I did no, for he was at that time already back at Lake in the Clouds with your sister who was, I think it is fair to say, in a state of shock. But that is another story that is best told by your mother.)

Never have I seen the trading post so crowded. The constable stood on a box with Mrs. Fiddler's two sons standing to either side of him, and all of them looking like the wrath of God. Constable McGarrity announced that he would rule Mrs. Fiddler's death (these were his words, most exactly) as "murder, by person or persons yet unknown."

Just as he was saying this, Charlie LeBlanc came in, who had been sent to fetch Nicholas Wilde but came back instead with another story, this one as aye strange and disturbing as the rest of what had passed that night: Nicholas Wilde was nowhere to be found. There was no sign of him at hame nor in the barn nor anywhere in the orchards, and his horses and sleigh were gone, and some other things from the house that made Charlie think he had left Paradise.

You who grew up in this wee village can well imagine what kind of talk began then, some arguing that Nicholas must have killed his poor guidwife and housekeeper both, and now had run rather than wait to be hanged, leaving poor Callie behind to make her own orphaned way in the world. Others thought there must be a murderer among us who had struck again, making Mr. Wilde the newest victim. Still others claimed that it was Dolly herself had attacked Mrs. Fiddler in a fit and then wandered off to die on the mountain. Mrs. McGarrity put a stop to the worst of the talk by promising to thrash the next man who spoke of hanging in her hearing—and no doubt she would have, too, for she waved a stout stick about her head as she said as much.

Then Mr. Hench took off his wooden leg and pounded with it on the wall to get everyone's attention and asked had anyone thought to go to the millhouse? For it turns out, or so he claims, that Claes Wilde had been courting Jemima Kuick for some weeks at least. A wild and, aye, almost violent argument followed, most of the women saying that if there was any courting being done, it was Jemima who was behind it for hadn't she been husband hunting since the day she buried her first and lost all his fortune? At that some of the men blushed and hung their heads and studied their shoes, for it turns out that Mrs. Kuick had indeed been looking for a new husband and had cast a wide and well-baited net, all without return.

And in the end the whole party marched together from the trading post to the millhouse, waving torches overhead. Their aim, they said, was to call Jemima Kuick to an accounting and perhaps more, though those words were not spoke aloud. I must admit that I went along out of naught but morbid curiosity for I would never sleep without knowing what was to happen next.

I'm sure you can imagine the crowd's disappointment and—the only word that comes to mind—delight when they found the millhouse deserted and Mrs. Kuick gone. And now the talk began in earnest, a wild conjecturing that lasted for an hour or more in the cold millhouse kitchen, until Constable McGarrity shouted loud enough to be heard and said they could talk all night without getting anywhere, or they could wait until morning when the wee lasses might be able to tell what they knew.

In the moment of quiet that followed, one of the Fiddler brothers—I believe it was Zeke but it may have been Levi, I could not see very well from where I stood—said while they all stood around wondering who Jemima Southern was bedding and where, his mother lay murdered and he'd have justice or revenge or both, and he wouldn't be fussy about which came first.

He spoke in a voice that made the gooseflesh rise on my neck, low and calm and as serious as the grave, and some of the men looked at each other and shifted on their feet the way men will when they disapprove but must bide their time to say so. And then Jed said in his gentle way, justice will be done, I vow it, and then all the energy was gone from the room and people began to drift away to their beds though it was only a few hours to sunrise.

And in all this I had forgot my errand, to find your father and sister, but it was too late and truth be told I was too weary, and so I went back to the Todds' place and found a bed and went to sleep and did not wake until well into the morning.

I found your mother in the kitchen with Constable McGarrity, and she looked very relieved to see me. The constable had come to talk to Martha and Callie and wanted another witness present, for Curiosity had gone to Lake in the Clouds to see about Hannah and Ethan was sitting with his stepfather's remains and receiving visitors who called to leave their condolences. And this you must imagine: Ethan in the parlor with such a solemn purpose and in the kitchen the constable and Elizabeth and I, and two young lasses as still and white as ghosts.

They answered the questions Constable McGarrity put to them, but always first looking one at the other. Aye, Callie's father and Martha's mother were away, aye they had left together, no, they had no said why but they would be back today or tomorrow. They had left enough firewood and food for the girls, who were to do their chores and milk the cow and goats—at this they looked at each other in great alarm, until the constable assured them that the livestock had been cared for—and not speak to anyone in the village about family business.

At that both girls began to weep again, quietly, holding hands in such a touching way that I should have liked to weep myself.

Then the constable asked about Mrs. Fiddler and Martha broke out in great racking sobs that shook her shoulders and would not cease even though Elizabeth rocked her and spoke calm words. And this was strange, of course, because it is Callie who suffered the greater loss, but she sat still-faced and like an old woman who has seen so much in a hard life that she has no more tears left to shed.

No matter how the question was put to them, by Elizabeth or the constable, neither of them had even a word to say that shed any light on the circumstances of Mrs. Fiddler's death, and indeed it seemed to me that with every passing minute they were more and more distant. This troubled Mr. McGarrity and indeed I, too, had the idea that they knew more or suspected more than they cared to say. Later I had a moment alone with your mother and I asked her what he might be thinking, but she only shook her head and begged not to be asked, as she could not say such terrible things aloud without evidence. Which proves once again what an unusual and thoughtful woman your mother is, for no one else in the village (except, of course, Mr. McGarrity himself) scrupled to say exactly what they thought, and that in a loud voice.

All day long men were gathered in the trading post, suggesting more and more outlandish scenarios and murder plots, which stopped only because the Ratz boys came in to say that Mr. Wilde's sleigh was just coming into the village and seemed to be headed for the millhouse.

And as it turns out, the younger widow Kuick *was* with him, but she had come back to Paradise as Mrs. Wilde, for they had been married the day before in Johnstown in front of the magistrate, and had the marriage lines as proof. I suppose this would have been a gey great scandal even without the discovery of Mrs. Fiddler's murder—

the women in the village hold a verra low opinion of Jemima's manner of getting husbands, I'm told—but taken together you might have thought Benedict Arnold had come to Paradise, such outrage was there among the villagers.

Someone had set the meetinghouse bell to ringing and everyone came running, the men gathering around the sleigh. And that is how I saw them first, the bright red sleigh in the middle of a crowd. There was a great shouting of questions and threats and promises of damnation.

Mrs. Kuick—Mrs. Wilde, now—looked curiously untouched by it all, and even pleased, like a cat let out after being closed up in the buttery all night. She sat in the sleigh with her hands crossed in her lap and looked over the faces turned up to her as she might have looked at a field full of crows. As if the questions they were asking— the accusations they threw in her face—were irritations only, and not to be taken seriously. To my mind this makes her either smug in her innocence, or arrogant and the worst kind of heartless wretch, who could do murder and shrug it off so easily.

Her new husband was far less composed. The news of Mrs. Fiddler's death shook him so that I thought at first he might faint. But then the constable claimed both of them and took them into the trading post. As there is room in the jail for only one, Nicholas is being held there while Jemima is locked up in the cabin where your old teacher Mr. Oak once lived, with a guard at the door and the shutters nailed closed. She would have been allowed visitors, but none went to her, not even her own daughter.

The Wildes were charged with two counts of murder, and now the whole village waits impatiently for the judge to come through on his circuit. It is his job to decide whether they must both be tried, or, as most in the village have decided, Jemima alone is guilty of these terrible crimes. Mrs. McGarrity explained it to me thus: Jemima wanted what she wanted, and the two women who stood in the way—both of whom she hated for years—are both dead.

And indeed it seems that Mr. Wilde cannot have had a hand in either death, for even Mrs. Fiddler's sons say openly that Nicholas and his daughter were in Johnstown at the time of their mother's disappearance.

In all of this it seems that the wee lasses suffer the greatest injury. The women in the village ask each other again and again what is to become of them, too young still to go into service or fend for the family holdings, and without means or family to take them in.

Perhaps the one good thing to come of all of this sad business has to do with your sister, who seemed determined never to leave Lake in the Clouds again. The only time she came to the village was to examine Mrs. Fiddler's remains and write a report, for she is the only trained physician in the village now. Otherwise she stayed at home and cared to hear nothing about the turmoil. Then, a few days ago while Curiosity and Ethan were with us for dinner, the subject of the lasses and what would become of them was raised and for the first time Hannah seemed to be paying attention.

And she said, quite calmly and in a tone that was almost normal, but the girls must come to live in the doctor's house, don't you think, Curiosity?

The surprise in the room was almost comical, and if the subject matter had not been so very serious someone might have laughed. I was certainly in danger of it.

Ethan recovered first and said what a fine idea, it would do them all no end of good to fill up the empty house with little girls. Of course we have not yet had the reading of the doctor's will, and your father seems to fear that there might be some trick there that would make a shambles of such plans.

For my part I will stay at Lake in the Clouds with your parents, whom I have come to love and respect as my own. When your brother comes back to make a bride of me he will find me here, as we agreed.

This is a very long letter and one I know must cause you great pain and distress. I hardly know how to end it, for anything I might put down now must sound trite. The village waits impatiently for Mr. O'Brien, a strange thing, I am told, for while he is the circuit judge he is also the tax collector and most go out of their way to avoid him. When he is come and the matter is settled, I will write to you again with whatever news there may be.

In the meantime, I beg you to turn to your brother for comfort. He is sometimes too strict (I have written him a stern letter reminding him that you are not a child, and your private business is none of his concern). He is also overly fond of teasing, but in times of trouble you will find out now how truly devoted he is to you and how very much he cares for your well-being and happiness.

I do pledge that I will do my best—with your little brother's help—to keep your good parents in high spirits.

Your cousin and friend and soon-to-be sister,
Jennet Scott, once of Carryck

Chapter 16

In the first of the new year the talk in the village revolved around two separate but equally interesting events. The first was the reading of Dr. Todd's last will and testament. The second, even more exciting to the imagination, was the coming of the circuit judge who would—as common wisdom decreed—listen to the evidence and then order Jemima to be strung up for the murder of Cookie Fiddler and Dolly Wilde.

Then Mr. Bennett, who had done them such good service over the years, did yet another by announcing straight off that only concerned parties would be invited to the reading of the doctor's will. Nathaniel was glad of it, first and foremost for Hannah's sake; she was unsteady still, sleepy and inward turned. She reminded him of a woman who has given birth for the first time: astounded that life should go on just as it always had, when everything of real importance had shifted so absolutely.

Nathaniel had lost children of his own, but there had been others nearby to share that burden. His mother, the first and second times, and then Elizabeth. Hannah had been alone in every way. He hated to think of it, not so much for the loss of the boy—a grandson he had never seen and could hardly imagine—but because he had gone about his business unthinking, unknowing, day by day, while his daughter had suffered.

But there she was, well fed and healthy in body if still wounded in heart and soul. There was work for her to do, work she thought she didn't want, but Nathaniel knew her better; it was the practice of medicine that would help her put the shadow lands behind her. Richard Todd had seen that, too, and acted on it, and Nathaniel knew that no matter what harm Todd had done in his life, he must forgive him everything for this last act of understanding and generosity and healing.

Unless, of course, there was something else in the will they weren't expecting. A tingling at the base of his neck gave Nathaniel the feeling that Richard Todd wasn't done with them yet. Leave it to the man to figure out how to make people dance to his tune from the grave itself.

On the way down the mountain Nathaniel said as much to his wife, who bit back a surprised smile and then clucked at him, as she did at a child who made much of a small scratch. Any other time she would have taken the chance to argue with him about this, but these days Elizabeth was short-spoken and distant, and the reason was no mystery: they hadn't had word from Daniel or Blue-Jay in a month.

That was no time at all, of course. A man living rough in the bush might not have a chance to put pen to paper for weeks or months, even if there was a way to send a letter once it got written. He had told Elizabeth as much at the very beginning; she had nodded and smiled and refused to consider the possibility that her son would be so far away, unreachable, unknowable. That he might die without her permission or knowledge or tears.

Right now there was nothing they could do for Daniel or Blue-Jay, but Hannah was here. The urge to stay clear of the reading of Richard Todd's will wasn't near as strong as the need to be close by if his daughter needed him.

The afternoon was already sliding toward dusk when they were finally settled in the doctor's parlor with the door closed. Bump was sitting near the windows and Nathaniel perched on a stool next to him, where he could keep track of Elizabeth and Hannah and still watch for anybody who might approach the house from the front.

"You expecting an ambush?" Bump said, pulling Nathaniel out of his thoughts. "Richard's good and gone, never fear."

And he was right: some part of Nathaniel was having trouble believing that Richard was dead. It would be easy enough to convince himself. He could go out to the woodshed and look at the body in its fine carved coffin, brought all the way from Johnstown some months ago, another dying-man's fancy. The body would be frozen solid as deer hung in a tree, sunken in on itself with no more personality than any cut of meat. But Nathaniel would recognize Richard Todd by the bones in his face and by his hands, broad across the knuckles, splayed thumbs, the deeply scarred palm that Nathaniel was responsible for. That summer day in the endless forests when they had shed each other's blood. For Elizabeth, for land, for everything important in the world.

Nathaniel looked at his own hands where they rested on his knees and saw the years in them: a certain looseness in the skin, the knuckle joints a little swollen with the cold and work and time flowing by.

"It won't be long," Bump said. As if it were the hour spent here that worried him rather than the weight of days he felt on his shoulders.

Mr. Bennett cleared his throat and began to speak in his quiet, steady voice as he explained the ways of the law and what the government had to say about death and land and money, once again sticking its nose in where it was neither needed nor wanted.

Ethan, it turned out to nobody's surprise, was Richard's executor, which meant that he had the say of how things were to be done after the lawyer packed his bags and went back to Johnstown. A sensible decision on Richard's part, as Ethan was as sober minded a young man as could be found anywhere, and unimpressed by money.

Because, Nathaniel reminded himself as he looked around the comfortable parlor with its brocade and silk and velvet, polished silver and brass, glass and crystal and oil paintings on the wall—some of them Richard's own work from long ago, in the years he had tried to make himself into somebody he could never be—Ethan Middleton had never been without money and would never know what it was like to be hungry.

And still Elizabeth had worried about the boy every day of his life. Last night, before she fell asleep she said, "It is not good for him to be so much alone with his books." She shifted a little, embarrassed and rightly so, for as a young woman her family had said just the same thing of her.

Nathaniel was so wound up in his thoughts that he missed much of the first part of the will, but one phrase caught his attention, for in it he heard Richard's voice as clearly as if he had taken over the elderly lawyer's portly body to speak his mind one last time.

. . . my soul into the hands of the Almighty that he might do with it as He deems fit, and may He have mercy on an Unrepentant and Enthusiastic Sinner. Second, my ruin of a body sore abused I leave to Dr.

Hannah Bonner, Physician, that it might prove some use to the science of anatomy and autopsy.

Curiosity shifted uneasily at this bit of godlessness but Hannah herself seemed unmoved, and maybe, Nathaniel thought, studying his daughter closely, a little amused. The next paragraph took the half-smile from her face.

> *. . . unto said physician, my student, Hannah Bonner, my medical tools, books, supplies, and research materials of all kinds, and with them I pass into her able hands my medical practice in the village of Paradise. Further to Hannah Bonner I bequeath my laboratory and the parcel of land on which it stands.*

They knew about this already, from Richard's own mouth, and still Nathaniel's pulse ratcheted up a notch to hear it put out there for the world to know. It was good and right and generous and still some part of Nathaniel wished it undone. In death Todd had found a way to tie the girl to him, something that he had wanted since the day she was born.

The next part of the will was like listening to Elizabeth read from one of Swift's stories, odd ideas and pictures all woven together to present a new view of the world.

To Curiosity—a freed black woman—Todd had left the house and farm and enough money to maintain them and herself in thin years. It was a bequest that might not hold up in a court of law if challenged, but it would not be, not by anyone in this room. To Curiosity's surviving daughter and granddaughters he left all of Kitty's clothes and shoes and trinkets, and to Joshua Hench and his son, whatever chemicals and materials they wanted from the laboratory, along with an annual stipend of twenty dollars to purchase what they needed to make firecrackers. If the boy showed an interest, there was money for him to go study at the African Free School in New-York City. At this Curiosity sat up very straight and still; he had managed to surprise even her.

Mr. Bennett paused to clear his throat and shuffle, a little nervously, through the papers before him. The whole room sat forward a little, curious and unsettled, but most of all intrigued.

" 'To Elizabeth Middleton Bonner,' " he read, his voice hoarse now. " 'I hereby bequeath any books from my library that she might like to have, my mule Horace (for they are well suited to each other in temperament), and the sum of five hundred dollars with which to have a schoolhouse built, and further with it a parcel of land of her choosing so long as it is in the village proper. Also to Mrs. Bonner I bequeath an annual sum of one hundred dollars for the maintenance and running of the school and for monies to hire a teacher, for the day she decides she has had enough of teaching. These bequests I make in thanks for the kindnesses she showed my dear departed wife, and in everlasting gratitude for the fact that Mrs. Bonner once broke her promise to marry me.' "

There was a sniffling in the room and a muffled laugh, from Curiosity and then Elizabeth herself. Even Hannah was smiling, truly smiling, which Nathaniel supposed must be a good thing.

Richard Todd had left Elizabeth the one thing she really needed and wanted—freedom and means to do as she wished without depriving the village of a school—but in such terms that it would pain her to accept them.

Mr. Bennett was studying them over the edge of his papers, his clear brown eyes troubled.

"If you will bear with me," he said. "Please let me read this next section before you make any comments—" He cleared his throat. "You will understand soon enough."

" 'To my mother's brother, my beloved uncle Cornelius Bump,' " Mr. Bennett read, and then stopped to look around the room, as if he expected everyone to rise up in one voice after this strange announcement.

For it was strange, the strangest thing to be said so far today. Cornelius Bump was Richard Todd's uncle. Richard might have claimed to be the president or the king of England with less reaction, for Nathaniel had known Todd all of his life and Bump for almost as long, and the connection had never even occurred to him.

The shock rocked through the room even as the lawyer read on, steady as a plough in well-turned earth. The thoughts going through Nathaniel's mind were too varied and quick to be pinned down, but one part of him noted two things: Bump seemed completely unworried by this revelation, while Curiosity looked embarrassed. As well she should, Nathaniel thought. For keeping this to herself for so many years. He remembered just then that Falling-Day, who had been his mother-in-law, had given Curiosity a Kahnyen'kehàka name many years ago: She-Who-Keeps-Silent.

Mr. Bennett pushed on, reading out the rest of it. To Cornelius Bump, Richard had left a thousand acres of virgin timberland, for him to do with as he wished, another five thousand dollars for his own use, and finally a request: that he take the same amount of money with him and find Richard's brother, who had lived all his life among the Mohawk. If he was not able to find that brother or any of his family, he was free to do with the bequest as he saw fit.

The rest was done in short order, for it was simple enough: what remained of Richard's money and land—a fortune larger than anyone in the village had ever imagined—was now Ethan's.

Except, of course, that there was a condition.

Now, thought Nathaniel, settling forward and planting his elbows on his knees. Now we come to it.

The lawyer explained it straight-out: Richard had made his stepson a rich man, but only so long as he left Paradise to take up residence in any city of his choosing and did not return for two full years. He could have a month to ready himself for the journey, but not a day more.

The room was very quiet when Bennett finally put down the papers. He looked like a man who had put an unavoidable and disagreeable task behind him and now must wait for the repercussions. His blue eyes seemed very large behind the small round lenses of his spectacles, moving from face to face and assessing the things he found: surprise, disquiet, anger. The last from Elizabeth, who would chafe against this bit of mischief until she was rubbed raw with it.

Curiosity was the first to speak. "Now look at this," she said, pushing out a low laugh. "The good doctor still tying everybody in knots just for the plain pleasure of it. Bless his surly old soul, I'ma miss him, but not as much as I'll miss you, child."

All eyes turned to Ethan, whose expression was very calm, almost blank.

"You don't have to go, if you don't want to," Elizabeth said, her voice clear and sharp. "Your mother left you enough that you can do as you please, Ethan. Mr. Bennett," she said, turning to the lawyer. "What becomes of the bequest if Ethan doesn't comply with the terms?"

"By law?" The lawyer ran a hand over his bright pink pate and patted it gently. "It would go to the doctor's next of kin. His brother, if he is alive and can be found. His uncle, otherwise."

It was then that Nathaniel realized that Bump was no longer next to him. He had slipped out of the room without a sound, and was not to be found anywhere in the house.

•　　•　　•

The news of what was in Richard's will would explode in the village like a volley of forty-pounders, but Nathaniel wanted no part of the talk and neither did Elizabeth, it seemed, for she left with him willingly enough and kept her thoughts to herself on the way home. Which meant that a different kind of battle was to come, one he couldn't avoid.

Not once did she add her own thoughts while Nathaniel told Many-Doves and Runs-from-Bears about Todd's will, another bad sign.

When supper was over she sent Gabriel over to the other cabin to spend the night and even then she said nothing. While she wiped dishes and put them up, measured out beans and put them to soak, rubbed bear grease into moccasins and trimmed candlewicks, looked through schoolbooks and marked pages for the next day's lessons, through all of that she was so uncharacteristically quiet that Nathaniel could hardly sit still.

Elizabeth in a fury was something he knew how to deal with; he could ride that storm until it wore itself out and she was ready to pull reason back around her shoulders like a warm blanket. Until then he would keep his opinions to himself.

But this was something rarer, this quiet white anger that pinned her down and gagged her. What end it would take, even Nathaniel couldn't predict. He watched her from his spot near the hearth while he cleaned his rifle and then sharpened his knives, poured lead into bullet molds, refilled his powder horn. These were things he had done every day of his life, the movements as natural to him as breathing, and he could do them in a quiet cabin or with a battle raging around his ears. What he couldn't do, what he couldn't imagine, was what she might say when the power of speech came back to her.

It wasn't until they had banked the fire and gone to bed that the last of his patience was spent. Lying next to Elizabeth in their marriage bed, he studied the back of her head for a while and then he said the first thing that came to mind.

"You could go put a bullet in the man, Boots. It wouldn't do him any harm and it might make you feel better."

A tremor ran through her and then another and another, a tide that she was determined to hold back. And still it took her as easily as a dog took a rabbit, shook her playfully until she was limp and couldn't protect herself or run. Nathaniel let her weep, one hand on her shoulder, and tried to remember the last time he had seen her like this.

It took him back a long way, to the summer they were first married. Trouble with Todd had driven them into the endless forests, the summer she had fought for his life and her own, fought Richard and Jack Lingo, that old devil, fought the bush and the weather and terror and her own weakness. She had faced all of that down and the strain of it had carved a hollow in her.

Nathaniel thought of those days, oddly as clear and bright in his mind as the things he had done this very morning, and then found out she had followed him back through the years to the very same place.

"I should have done it back then," she said. "I should have killed him in the bush and left him to rot. Think of all the heartache it would have saved."

The weeping came over her again, harsh as a scouring snow. When the worst of it was over he pressed himself up against her back, draped his arm around her shoulder. He cradled her against him and stroked her hair until she slept.

He slept too, and woke in the dead of night to find her sitting, her arms looped around her knees and her hair flowing around her shoulders like some witchy woman from one of Jennet's stories.

She said, "I won't let Ethan go away. He is my only brother's boy, and he should be here near us, where we can keep an eye on him."

There were things he could say, rational things that she would not try to deny in the light of day: that Ethan was a man grown, with a mind and will of his own. That this day had been coming for a long time and they had all known it, even if they never spoke of it.

The truth was, Ethan wanted to leave Paradise and had not known how to do that. Richard had only given his stepson what he could not bring himself to ask for. Ethan would go off to study at some college in New-York City or Boston or Philadelphia, and in two years' time, if Richard had his way, he wouldn't remember why he had ever hesitated to leave Paradise, or why he might want to come back.

Nathaniel could say all those things that Elizabeth knew anyway, or he could leave it all and say something even truer: this had less to do with Ethan moving away than it did with their own Daniel, gone now for more weeks than either of them wanted to count, and no word for the last month.

It was something they lived with minute by minute, each of them, and did not discuss: what it might mean, if the worst had come to pass.

In the faint light from the window he saw her expression harden, as if he had spoken those words, and more.

"Damn you, Nathaniel Bonner." Her voice trembled, close to breaking. "Damn you, you're going to let Richard win. You'll see Ethan off and build the schoolhouse and let your daughter take over his practice. You're giving Richard Todd everything he ever wanted." Her eyes flashed at him, tear-filled and furious.

He had been holding his anger tight and small and close to him, but now it began to run like sand from a clenched fist. He swallowed hard and met her eye, saw the challenge there.

"He never got you, did he? He never got you or Hannah, and by God, Boots, what the hell do I care for the rest of it, so long as I kept hold of what matters most?"

She trembled and then broke like a branch in a high wind, falling toward him, back bowed, and he caught her as he always had and always would as long as he lived. He caught her up against him and rocked her, whispered soft things against her hair and touched her gently, his fingers tracing her jaw and the line of her lip and the widow's peak that carved her face into a heart.

"He'll come home in the end," Nathaniel said. "He will come home safe."

That was what she needed to hear and so he gave it to her, against his better judgment. She did not press him for names, for times and days, as she would have done as a younger woman. She was satisfied, right now, with *in the end*.

In thanks and need she pressed against him until they began to move together with subtle, quick, knowing touches, the old questions so often asked and answered. Finally she was naked in his arms, her pale skin soaking up the little bit of moonlight until it glowed, her breath rising damp and harsh in the cold room.

He felt her thinking mind pushing its way up, trying to intrude itself between them. She made a sound, a *wait* sound, but he held her close and closer, held her down and kissed her until she gave up, gave in, dropped all the worries long enough to admit again what Nathaniel could never let her forget: that she belonged here with him and nowhere else, that no matter what trouble came to them they would face it together.

•   •   •

In the morning Elizabeth woke to the sound of a long "halloo" echoing off the cliff walls; Nathaniel's side of the bed was empty, and Gabriel stood at the door, his cheeks red with the cold, snow in his hair: her beautiful boy. She held out her arms and he ran to her, bounced on the bed like the child he was, pushed his face into her neck and hugged her. A boy as rough as a bear cub and just as irresistible and dangerous too. She said a silent thanks that he was too young for this newest war.

"Who's come to call this early?" she asked him, running her fingers through his hair and thinking vaguely of her brushes on the dresser; he would be gone before she could reach for them.

"Bump." The boy bounced away from her and off the bed, landing on his feet like a cat. "And he's brought the post, Mama. The rider came in late last night."

"Is there a letter from your brother? From Daniel?"

"Maybe." Gabriel grinned as if the idea had not occurred to him; as if he did not know how worried she had been. "Come and see." And he ran away, shutting the door behind himself.

She could go out just as she was, in her nightclothes, but she forced herself to dress, slowly, methodically, carefully, listening as she did to the men's voices from the other room. Runs-from-Bears said something and Bump laughed, a high, hopping laugh that would make his oversized head wobble on a spindly neck. Nathaniel had gone silent and when Elizabeth opened the door she understood why: he sat by the hearth, bent over an open letter, reading.

Then he looked up at her and smiled. "All's well, Boots. Both the boys safe and sound and in good spirits."

Elizabeth took a deep breath. "Mr. Bump," she said, "how kind of you to bring the post. I will make tea, shall I?"

In the end she sent Gabriel down to the village to tell all her students that school was canceled for the day. Not so much because of the letter, though Elizabeth would gladly have read it again and again, but because of the other news that Bump brought. He was on his way to Canada to fulfill the last request Richard Todd had made of him.

Nathaniel and Runs-from-Bears exchanged glances at this revelation.

"It's been a while since I heard any word of Throws-Far," said Runs-from-Bears. "But then he was making winter camp on the lakes." He volunteered this information before Bump could ask, and Nathaniel carried on in the same way.

"You should talk to our Hannah, she would know more."

"I did just that, and she gave me a name," Bump said. "Somebody to talk to, an old Mohawk woman near Montreal. Since I'm headed that way, I thought I might as well call on Lily. Curiosity is already busy putting together a parcel. Is there anything you'd like me to take your daughter, Mrs. Bonner?"

"Now you've done it," Nathaniel said, grinning. "These women will load you down like a draft horse."

Later, Annie came to find Elizabeth while she packed things into baskets: more socks, a woolen underskirt, a beautiful pair of winter moccasins that Many-Doves had worked on for a month, a package of dates and another of dried apricots, a jug of the last of the maple syrup, a bundle of newspapers and magazines, a small pile of books.

The little girl watched and helped where she could, and it was some while before Elizabeth noted the expression on her face.

"What is it?" she asked. "Come, talk to me while I work."

Annie cast a sidelong glance in her aunt's direction. "It's about Jemima Kuick," Annie said.

"She is Mrs. Wilde, now," Elizabeth reminded her.

"Mrs. Wilde," the girl echoed, and there was a long wait while she gathered her thoughts.

"What about her?"

"People say that when Baldy O'Brien comes—" Annie paused.

"Judge O'Brien," Elizabeth said quietly. "Or Mr. O'Brien."

"Mr. O'Brien," Annie echoed again, and then said nothing more. Instead her teeth worked the soft flesh of her lower lip.

Elizabeth closed the lid of the basket and made firm knots in the rawhide strings meant to hold it shut. She studied Annie while she did this, and saw that the girl's worry went deep.

"Start at the beginning," she said. "What people, and what do they say?"

Nathaniel had come to the door and stood listening, his arms folded. Annie glanced at her favorite uncle and lost her train of thought; a scattered child, at times, but a bright one.

She said, "Jem Ratz says we will all have to watch when they hang Nicholas and Jemima. It's the law that everybody watches. Is it true? Will we all go down to see them hang?"

Elizabeth sat down heavily on the edge of the bed and drew the little girl closer to her. She said, "Jem Ratz may be a dab hand with a slingshot, but I despair of ever putting the empty space between his ears to good use. No, it is not true."

"Boots—" Nathaniel began, and she cut him off with an upraised hand.

"If anyone should be condemned to hang—and I do not see that anyone will, if the rule of law is followed—no one will be compelled to watch. In fact, you will not be *allowed* to watch. No child will, if I have my way."

"Not even Martha and Callie?" Annie asked, in a surer voice.

Elizabeth blanched visibly, and then the color rushed back into her face in uneven blotches. "Most especially not. Neither Martha nor Callie," she said. "I will have a talk with Jem Ratz and make the matter clear to him too."

Nathaniel said, "Woe unto Jem Ratz."

"The very idea," Elizabeth said. "I can hardly imagine what silliness people will begin with next."

"Oh, I can tell you that," said Annie, completely at ease now. "They're saying that Jemima is a witch and that if they don't hang her they should burn her. And," she hurried on, eager to tell all of it, "they say that Jemima spins all day, tow enough for a thousand candlewicks, but that nobody will buy any from her for she weaves a spell in with every twist of the spindle, a curse on all of us in Paradise."

And with that she turned and skipped away, a child who had unburdened herself to those she loved and trusted.

With considerable disquiet of his own Nathaniel saw Elizabeth's expression and recognized it too well. His wife gearing up for yet another battle. One he feared she could not win, not if she took it into her head to protect Jemima Wilde from the entire village of Paradise.

Chapter 17

January 1813, Montreal

Luke was gone to Québec on business, and the house on the rue Bonsecours had grown larger without him in it. Lily thought it would be good to be free of her brother for a little while, but before two days had passed she missed him, despite his moods or maybe, she realized, because of them. Luke gave her something to think about that wasn't Nicholas Wilde, and the letter that would not come.

The noisy dinners around a crowded table had stopped when Luke left, and Lily was at first surprised and then hurt and then a little embarrassed to realize that the company who had joined them was less dependent on her than she had imagined. It was odd to eat alone at the big table with Iona, who did not need to fill the emptiness with talk. It was not that she was unsympathetic to Lily's loneliness, she realized, but that Iona was not one to talk unless she had something to say. Much like Lily's Kahnyen'kehàka cousins, but here in Montreal it did not suit.

And she suspected that Iona would have even less patience with Lily's confused heart than Lily had for herself. It all sounded too silly to her own ears. The Catholics, she learned from Ghislaine, believed that a person could be possessed by the devil or an evil spirit, a belief the church of Rome had in common with the Kahnyen'kehàka. To be possessed by the idea of a living man was not much different, and Lily thought sometimes of finding a priest to ask about how to be free of her thoughts.

She thought of going home, but how would she explain herself? *I have studied enough,* she might say. *I was homesick.* Her mother would look at her face and know the truth. Lily wished she could sleep through the rest of the winter like a bear.

Ghislaine, keen and clever enough to guess at least part of the problem, suggested that Lily go visit a black woman from the Sugar Islands who lived on the outskirts of the city. This woman could give her potions to make her forget about Nicholas Wilde and Simon Ballentyne both.

Lily had sent Simon away, and he had gone. Without the strong words she expected. Without argument. Another thing to wonder about, what it might mean; why it was such an irritation to her to have him do what she asked him to do. Contrary creature that she was, Lily missed him, or perhaps, she admitted to herself, the things Simon had given her: sleigh rides and snow picnics and outings with people her own age.

And kisses. She had liked kissing him, liked it so much that she felt guilty later, thinking about it. It was best that he was gone, and if she needed someone to talk to, there were her teachers, and Ghislaine, and the old lady in the bakery who was always glad to see her. And there was her work, which was distraction enough, in the daylight.

At night she thought of Nicholas Wilde and Simon Ballentyne and suffered sharp dreams that woke her to find that she had sweated through her nightclothes.

On a Saturday when Luke had been gone for a week and would be gone for another, Lily and Iona sat down to another solitary dinner just as someone knocked at the door. The gust of cold air came from down the hall, sharp and sweet with snow, to announce the visitor. Lily would have got up to see for herself who it was out of simple curiosity and boredom, but Lucille came straight in to announce the company.

"A visitor for you, Miss Lily," she said, not so grumpy as she usually was, with a flush of something that might even be curiosity.

"Who is it?" Iona said patiently.

"A strange little man, called Mump or was it Bump, who," she added in a disapproving tone, "has no French." Lucille had very little English, and was proud of that fact.

Lily was up and flying down the hall before Lucille finished, and there he stood: Cornelius Bump, as true as life. No taller than she was herself and humped of back, with a face as creased and folded as an apple forgotten in a dark corner of a winter cellar. His head, the shape of a lopsided egg, was covered with a thick pelt of hair that stuck out from under his cap as straight as straw, the color of yams heavily peppered with gray. His long earlobes were fire red with cold, in contrast to the blue of his eyes, endlessly old and wise and sweet, her old Bump, her friend. Lily's face was wet with tears as she hugged him.

"There now, girl, there, Lily my sweet. No call for tears, none at all."

She did not trust her voice at first and so she hugged him again. He had always been small and light of bone as a bird. As a child she had often asked him if he was a pixie, a question he had never answered with anything but a smile.

"I've been wishing to see somebody from home," Lily said. "I've been wishing and wishing. And here you are. Did you come from Paradise? Did they send you? Do you have news? You must be hungry."

He laughed at her good-naturedly, the odd little man who had been such a friend to her when she was a girl. While she tugged his coat from him and his cap and his mittens he answered her questions: he had indeed come from Paradise with news enough to tell and he would welcome a bit of dinner, milk would be much appreciated if there was any to be had, and would Lily remember her manners please, they weren't alone in the house after all.

She took him by the arm and led him into the dining room, only to find out that there was no need of introductions; Bump was no stranger to Wee Iona.

Iona, as settled and unflappable an old woman as Lily had ever known, was so happy to see Bump that there was a glittering in her eyes when she took his hands in her own.

"Weel, and look at you now, Cornelius. Look at you. How long has it been? And are you well?"

"Too many years, Iona my dear. Old bones and growing older, but old friends too, to ease the ache."

"And so they do," Iona said, and without warning she leaned forward to kiss the old man on a bristled cheek.

Standing back, Lily watched and listened and saw things: Iona and Bump were much of a size, so that for once she herself seemed to be the tall one, without Luke here to prove her wrong. The servants saw how Iona had greeted the stranger and they began to flit around him, offering food and drink and the comforts of the house.

Bump said, "First things first." He began to undo the letter case he wore around his middle, his fingers working the buckle and the ties and more ties until it was free in his lap. He unfolded the leather flaps and a whole great stack of letters appeared. Most of them he put on the table. "For Luke."

On the top of the pile Lily recognized a letter in Jennet's small, angled handwriting, but then Bump was holding out more letters, to Lily. A smaller packet tied with string. Lily could barely keep her hands from trembling, and the urge to get up and run from the room was so strong that for a moment she feared the others must see her agitation and ask questions she couldn't answer. This was the first post she'd had from home since the news about Dolly's death.

"There are packages for you in the sleigh," Bump said. "But I expect the letters are what you want first."

She nodded because she did not trust herself to speak.

"Now," Bump said with a smile that showed off a row of small white teeth. "Is that soup I smell?"

Lily's hunger had disappeared, but she ate nonetheless from the bowls and platters that Jeannette and Lucille put on the table: stew thick with potatoes and bacon and beans and cabbage, fresh brown bread still warm from the oven. A steaming bread pudding studded with cherries and apples and currants, with a jug of cream to pour over it.

She had so many questions to ask but then so did Iona. Lily must wait, though she could not keep herself from jittering while they spoke of the war and of old friends and of the things that Bump had seen and heard as far away as Washington and Baltimore and Philadelphia. The letters in her lap seemed almost to hum at her, as impatient to be read as she was to read them.

"I didn't know you came so far north in your travels," Lily said when it seemed that Iona had had her fill of Bump's answers.

"Not often," Bump admitted. "Only when there's special reason."

"Don't you ever tire of traveling?" Lily asked him, because it had already occurred to her that it would be a fine thing, indeed, if Bump should decide to stay in Montreal for the winter.

At that Iona snorted softly. "You might as well ask your brother if he never tires of work. It's in the blood, is it not, Cornelius? Your mother's people were tinkers in the old country."

At that Bump only gave them his small smile, the one that meant he would keep his thoughts to himself.

"Have you really been as far as Washington?" Lily asked the question more out of politeness than real interest, and because she imagined her mother had asked the same question. Her mother was always interested in what was happening in Washington.

"I have," Bump said. "Though the credit must go to my good little horse. She does all the heavy work. Now you tell me, Lily, where is this Simon Ballentyne I've heard so much about? Is he gone to Québec with your brother, or will he come by this evening so I can see him? I did promise your father I would pass on a message to him."

A silence fell around the table. Even Lucille, who had been gathering up bowls, stopped to watch Lily, who felt herself flushing with embarrassment and anger, white and strong.

"What—" she began in a voice that wavered and broke, though she meant it not to. "What do you mean? What have you heard?"

Bump's smile trembled and faded, and Lily's fear grew all the brighter, and on its heels came a keen cold anger. "Did my brother write home—" She stopped and tried to think how to say the awful things in her head. "What did he say? What have you heard?"

Bump's expression was solemn now, his quick blue eyes adding things together and taking things away. He said, "You're not set to marry, I take it."

"I am not," Lily said tightly. "I never have been. I never have been," she repeated. "Not to Simon Ballentyne or anyone else."

"I'm sure Luke never wrote of you marrying," Iona said calmly. But she looked uncomfortable and ill at ease and that was all the proof Lily needed.

Iona said, "I'll write to your father straightaway, Lily, and make the truth known."

"Please do," Lily said. "Tell him I haven't seen Simon Ballentyne in a month and have no plans to see him." She was trembling and so she folded her hands in her lap tightly and tried to smile.

Bump said, "I've handled this badly."

"No," Lily said quickly. "Not at all. It's not your fault, but my brother's." She glanced at the letters in her lap and all her joy was gone, replaced by worry about what might be in them.

"I have more news," Bump said. "And I promised your mother I would tell you myself. She didn't want you to read it in a letter."

Lily's heart was beating so fast and loud in her throat that she couldn't speak, even to ask for the reassurance she wanted.

"Your uncle Todd is gone, Lily," Bump said. "It was the cancer that took him, in the end."

Lily nodded, because she couldn't say the things that were in her head. *Not my brother,* was what came to mind. *Not my father or mother, nor any of my people, thank God. Thank God.*

But of course Uncle Todd was one of her people, she reminded herself, and she should feel sorrow. Uncle Toad, they had called him as children, and laughed behind their hands for their cleverness.

Uncle Todd who had been married to Kitty, who had first been married to Lily's uncle Julian. Family and not family; no blood kin but a man she had seen almost every day of her life before she came away to Canada.

For a moment Lily was unable to call his face to mind. Nor could she recall the last time she had thought about him.

As a little girl she had been afraid of Uncle Todd, afraid of his gruff manner and his sharp judgment and most of all afraid that he would try to hurt her father or mother again. She had heard the stories, and while there seemed to be an uneasy peace between the two families she sometimes dreamed at night of Uncle Todd with bloody hands.

Bump had put an end to those nightmares, when he came back to live in Paradise. Bump had known Richard as a very little boy and he had stories to tell, funny stories that he told right in front of the doctor, who turned an astonishing shade of red but never denied the truth of it. Bump had cured her of her fear of her uncle, but Lily had been grown before she learned to see past his curt manner, to the sharp wit and sense of humor.

Her uncle had never spoken to her of her drawing, but he sometimes brought her paper when he came back from one of his journeys, and once a set of pencils that came all the way from France.

It was Bump who had cured her of her fear of Uncle Todd and now he had come to tell her that he was dead.

"Did you come just to tell me that?" she asked, and blushed to hear how raw the question sounded, how childlike.

"Not just that," Bump said. "But that's the worst news I have, and I wanted to get it out of the way."

Lily felt herself nodding, felt some of the fear and worry leaving her at this. Then she thought of her uncle again and she wondered about her father, how he had taken the news and if he had been happy or sad. In the spring they would dig his grave in the small graveyard behind his house where Aunt Kitty was buried with the babies she had tried to bring into the world. Her cousin Ethan was alone now, in a way Lily could hardly imagine.

She said, "I must write to Ethan."

Bump smiled at her. "That would mean a great deal to him, I'm sure."

.   .   .

In her chamber Lily closed the door and drew her shawl tight around her shoulders though the room was quite warm. She sat on the edge of the bed under the embroidered silk canopy that had been Giselle Somerville's when she was a young woman. On the lace counterpane worked by nuns Lily put down her letters and studied them for a moment.

One thick letter from her mother; another one, even thicker, from Jennet; the last, a single sheet, from Curiosity. Nothing from Nicholas Wilde.

Disappointment had a taste, sharp and salty. She chided herself for her foolishness, for her hope, for her faith in a man who had never been able to claim her and never would.

Or maybe, Lily reasoned to herself, maybe it was just too soon for him to write. It was a small comfort, but a comfort nonetheless.

She tucked her legs up under herself, took the letter her mother had written and held it against her cheek and inhaled, hoping for some vague scent of her. Right now she would give almost anything to have her mother here, but there was only the letter, and that would have to be enough.

The wax seal cracked under her thumb. Lily spread out the sheets and counted them. Eight in all, closely written: the essence of her mother, her thoughts and words in strong even lines, straight and clear.

She began to read. The story began without preamble or niceties or polite inquiries or reassurances, and that in itself set Lily to worrying. And here it was, finally: Hannah's story, the one they had waited for and despaired of ever hearing.

Her mother had written it in clear sentences, in logical order, and yet Lily could hardly make sense of any of it. She stopped and went back and read through again, and again, until her mind opened itself to the ideas and images, and then she put down the pages and wept for a while, her hands pressed to her face.

All this her sister had been carrying around with her, while Lily's worst problem was a love letter that would not come. She flushed with shame and sorrow for Hannah and the need to do something, anything that might help.

Finally she picked up the letter again.

> . . . I might have started this letter—perhaps I should have started
> this letter—with very different, far more cheerful news of your brother
> and cousin. We have had a letter from Daniel and Blue-Jay, written

in tandem, it seems, passing a quill filled with bullet lead back and forth. They are well, they tell us, and seem to be relishing the soldier's life. Gabriel is just across from me at the table, copying out your brother's letter to include with this one, so that you may read the news for yourself. Your little brother takes this job very seriously and I fear in his concentration he may bite through the tip of his tongue and never notice until blood spots the page, already much mishandled and smeared. In itself the letter is a true portrait of Gabriel, one you will appreciate, I think, for its own self.

Of your uncle Todd's death I find myself strangely unable to write at any length, but Mrs. Freeman assures me that she will do this and indeed you may have read that letter first, and of course Mr. Bump will have passed along our messages. It must suffice to say that he suffered greatly in the last weeks and is now at rest, for which we must be thankful.

Finally there is news in the village, news of such a shocking nature that I find myself again unable to even begin any reasonable accounting. That story I leave to your cousin Jennet, who is not so very attached to the persons involved and will, in this matter at least, be more capable than I of putting the story into words. I have specifically requested that Mr. Bump not speak to you of this matter, so that you have the whole directly from Jennet, who experienced much of it personally. Once you have finished reading you may wish to interview him, and indeed I believe he will have much to say, and his own perspective to add.

Having piqued your curiosity, I will close this already very long letter with the assurance that we here at Lake in the Clouds are in good health. As to your sister Hannah, I can say only that there is a blessing to be found in those sad events of Christmas Eve. For so many months she carried a terrible burden hidden inside her that is now open to the healing power of light and air and reason, and will mend, we trust and pray, in the fullness of time.

I have not written anything here about you or the news in your last letter, I realize now, but you mustn't believe, even for a moment, that I do not think of you. You are in my thoughts constantly. Some might believe that by now I should have become accustomed to your absence, but every morning it is a surprise to me to see your bed without you in it.

You must remember that whatever foolishness the men might discuss among themselves, I know you to be an intelligent and sensible young woman, capable of making decisions for yourself.

They may not always be the decisions I would make. They most probably will not be the decisions Luke will try to make for you, in his brotherly concern and overly protective way. They may even be wrong decisions, at times, but they will be *your* decisions. And yet I am still your mother and so I will ask you (as you have been waiting for me to do, no doubt) to strive to favor the rational over the subjective as you select one course of action among those available to you.

I will admit that I hope you will not settle too far from us when the time comes (if, indeed, it does come; you may decide to travel from one teacher to another for the next ten years, and in that, too, I would support you, for how could I not support a curious daughter who longs to see the world?).

Your loving mother,
Elizabeth Middleton Bonner
January 3, 1813

It was an hour before Lily could bring herself to open Jennet's letter. She sat with it in her lap, and thought of throwing it in the fire. In it was a story so upsetting that her mother had not been able to write of it.

Lily felt in her bones that it must have something to do with Nicholas. This story, whatever it was, would explain why there was no word from him.

The very worst news, of course, would be that Nicholas had died. She imagined what Jennet might have written: of fire, of runaway horses or fever or a hunting accident. A strange thought came to her, one that sat heavy in her throat and would not be swallowed: *If he is dead, then the worst has happened. If he is dead, I am free of him.*

She was shocked at herself, so shocked that she looked around the empty room, sure someone must have heard her, for how could such wickedness be kept quiet?

Lily opened the second letter and began to read.

Later, she fell into a weary sleep with Jennet's letter pressed to her breast; she slept so long and so deeply that when she woke at sunset she was disoriented and even frightened, forgetting for that moment where she was in the world, thinking first of her mother, until she saw the canopy covered with embroidered flowers over her head. Her cheeks were tight with dried tears, but why?

The crackle of paper under her cheek brought it all back, every word and image. Lily sat up and looked at the letters, her mother's words and her cousin's. Curiosity's letter was still unopened.

There was a hollow feeling deep inside, as if someone had stolen something from her while she slept. Lily got up and walked to the hearth, stood for a moment looking into the flames and then dropped all the closely written pages in Jennet's hand into the heat. She could destroy the words on the page, at least. They caught one by one, glowed briefly, curled along the edges and became nothing more than drifting ash.

She washed her face and hands at the blue and white basin, pouring water that was close to freezing from the ewer and scrubbing her skin until it burned. Then she straightened her hair and went out into the hall and down the stairs.

The house was quiet and dim. Standing in the front hall Lily listened very hard and heard nothing but the wind in the shutters and the faraway voices of the women working in the basement kitchen. There was no sign of Bump, and for a moment she wondered if she had imagined the whole thing. Then she saw the smear of ash on her hand and she had one thought only: to get away.

Lily dressed carefully, slowly, and then she opened the door and went out into the near dark. She took one of the lanterns that hung in the entryway out of the wind and began her walk across the city.

It was a cold night but not especially windy, and the snow seemed to hover in the air, not quite ready to fall. She passed the bakery where she visited most mornings, a milliner who had a fur-lined cap she had long admired, the butcher, other shops, all closed up for the day with shutters firmly latched. Her boots were hobnailed and she moved quickly and surely, throwing little divots of hard-packed snow up with every step. A soldier passed her and touched the brim of his hat; Lily averted her eyes and dropped her chin, walked a little faster until she was sure that he had gone on.

It was full dark by the time she came to the rue St. Paul, but she found the door without trouble. Between a bookshop and a tailor, she had heard him say, and here it was. The two small windows were shuttered like all the others but light leaked out from around the edges, like the halos that the saints all wore in the stained-glass windows of the churches.

Lily had visited Ghislaine's family in a house just like this one, and she knew what she should find here: a ground floor that served as a stall, home to one or two cows and goats and perhaps a pig, while the family slept and lived overhead. Lily was frontier raised and it took a lot to affront her sensibilities, and still it surprised her to find Simon Ballentyne living here. The man she knew took great pains with his clothes and his speech and had ambitions, or so she had thought.

She contemplated the knocker for a long moment and then used it: once, twice, three times, firmly. There were voices, one female, and for the first time Lily felt a rush of doubt. She would have turned right then and run away but the door opened. The woman who stood there was old, but straight of back and unflinching, her red hands folded below a substantial bosom.

"Mademoiselle?" she asked, her expression a little surprised but not unkind.

Lily opened her mouth to ask, and found she had lost all her French, every word of it gone.

She said, "I'm looking for Mr. Ballentyne. Simon Ballentyne."

Then he was there. It seemed he was twice the size of the servant woman, and his face was in shadow.

"Simon," said Lily, trying to smile and not quite succeeding. But it was enough. For him, it seemed, her almost-smile was enough.

Simon Ballentyne kept no animals, after all. The cobbled floor was scrubbed to gleaming, covered here and there with thick rugs. A hearth and scullery took up the far end of the long room. Near the door there was an oven tiled in the Dutch fashion, a table, a settle, and some other furniture she could not make out in the shadows. A screen as tall as she was kept the draft from the door out of the rest of the room, and Lily saw, with some surprise, that it was finely carved and painted with an elaborate hunting scene. On the opposite wall three paintings hung in simple frames, all landscapes. One of them, Lily saw immediately and with some surprise, was her own work: a small oil she had done after one of the sleighing parties. She had made a gift of it to Monsieur Picot when he admired it.

Behind her Simon Ballentyne said, "I bought it from your teacher."

"Ah," she said, a little affronted at Monsieur for selling her gift and, at the same time, pleased that Simon Ballentyne should have bought it and said nothing to her. It was a true compliment, and she meant to repay it in kind but found she could not. She said, "I should have thought to give you one of my paintings. I didn't realize you were interested."

And turned her face away, because it was a lie and they both knew it. Simon showed as much interest in her studies and work as Luke did. More, sometimes, and she had never had the feeling that his questions were simple courtesy.

The old woman served them soup and bread and they ate in silence at the table. The little house was spartan, but comfortable; well ordered and clean. Every once in a while Lily thought of the letters—one unopened, one tucked into her bodice, the last burned—and that image shook her out of her daze.

Simon Ballentyne didn't notice, or perhaps he chose not to. He spoke to her as if this visit were nothing out of the ordinary, an unmarried young woman of good family calling on a single man, alone. She answered him in the same way. They spoke of the weather, of her brother's trip and when he might be back, of the business he hoped to accomplish in Québec. Simon told her what he had read in the day's papers of the war, and to this she listened a little closer for names of places that were close to home, and hearing none, relaxed again.

When they had finished eating the old woman cleared the table and then put on her mantle and her clogs and went to the door. Simon followed her and said a few words, put something in her hand and waited for her nod.

He said, "Genevieve will send her grandson to Iona to say where you are, that she's not to worry and that I'll bring you home this evening."

There didn't seem to be any words left inside her, and so Lily said nothing. She straightened the saltcellar on the table and brushed away some crumbs and studied the wood grain.

Finally when she understood that he would not make it any easier for her she said, "You have a very comfortable home."

"And so do you," he said with a hint of a smile. "But here you sit. I'm mindful of the honor, lass, but—" He spread out his hands.

Lily said, "Does one friend need a reason to visit another?" It sounded silly and false to her own ears, but Simon was kind—she must credit him with that—and he spared her the sharp words she had earned.

Instead he blinked at her and a knot of muscle flexed in his jaw; even under his beard she could see it. He said, "You asked me to stay away, Lily. I take it you've changed your mind?"

She stood abruptly and moved to the other side of the room. A desk and bookcase stood in a shadowy corner and she put her back to the wall between them, crossed her arms.

"I shouldn't have come," she said.

"Perhaps not," agreed Simon Ballentyne from his chair.

He seemed content to leave the work of it all to her. Irritated now and close to tears Lily said, "You might at least try to make me feel welcome."

At that he gave a short, surprised laugh and got up. When he was so close that she must raise her head to look him in the eye, he put a hand on the wall next to her head and leaned in. She felt his breath on her forehead, warm and soft.

"What is it you want from me, Lily? What's happened that brought you to my door? Word from your lover? Has your brother been wounded?"

"No," she said sharply. "My brother is well."

Daniel's letter, she thought then. *I never even read the copy of his letter that Gabriel made.* And: *What is the matter with me?*

"But news, then. A letter from your mother?"

She raised her chin to glare at him and saw that he was not laughing at her, and in fact that he was angry. It was in his eyes, the way he narrowed them at her, and in the flush on his cheeks, and the lines that bracketed his mouth. He was angry and trying not to be.

"And if I had a letter from home, what of it?" she said, angry too, but at herself. "I was foolish to come here, and I'll go now."

He stepped back suddenly, released her from the cage he had made with his body.

"I'll see you home."

Then the tears did come, great hot tears streaming down her face that could not be denied or hidden and still she turned away, pressed her face to the rough wall and shuddered.

Simon Ballentyne put a hand on her shoulder and pulled her to his chest and there was no hope for her then. The sobs came in great breaking waves, and through all of it he held her gently and stroked her head and spoke, slow kind words, words he might have used to comfort a grieving child, a beloved sister, a friend, and that made the tears come all the harder so that she shook with them.

When the worst had passed he led her to the bench against the tile oven and sat down with her there in the soothing warmth.

"Tell me," he said.

She told him all of it, in words that first came slow and halting and then in a great rush. She told about the terrible things her sister had lived through, the story of the hollow lake and the nephew she had never even seen, and then she told him about Nicholas, winding her fingers in the fabric of her skirt as the story pushed its way out.

He interrupted her only once, to ask was this the same Jemima who had caused such trouble for her sister Hannah over the years? And when Lily told him yes, exactly, Nicholas Wilde who would have married her but for his invalid wife—dead now only two months—had instead married *that* Jemima Southern.

And I worried he might be dead. Lily said those words and stopped short, distraught but not distraught enough to say the terrible thing that came to mind next: *Would that he were. Better to know him dead.*

As he might be, of course. Perhaps they had hanged him already. Though she could not imagine him doing Cookie or anyone else real harm, a judge might see things differently. He could be hanging from the gallows at this very moment, and Jemima beside him.

The weeping began again, this time springing up from a different place: horror and shame at herself, that some part of her should like that idea.

Simon produced a handkerchief and she took it thankfully, pressed it to her face and bent forward to press her forehead to her knees, cursing herself and still unable to stop.

She felt his hand on her back, his touch light and without demand; nothing there but comfort. She straightened suddenly and spoke to him, her face turned away.

"I shouldn't have burdened you with my problems," she said. "I'd like to go home now."

"Would you?" he asked, and she heard something else in his voice now, surprise or even amusement.

A ripple of irritation moved up her spine. "Yes. I want to go home."

"Look me in the eye and say that."

"No." She shook her head. "I won't. I can't."

"And why not?" Simon Ballentyne asked.

"Because my face is swollen and red and—"

He laughed out loud then, and the anger came over her as suddenly and forcefully as the tears had come earlier. She stood, and he took her hand and pulled her down again.

"Ach, Lily," he said, rubbing his forehead against her cheek. "You'll be the death of me, but I'll die with a smile on my face."

She tried to pull away and found that she didn't really want to; in the back of her mind she heard not her mother but Curiosity: *Don't rise to the man's bait, girl, unless you got a mind to play the game out.* But it was such a relief, to have said it all out loud, to have somebody hear the words that rang like great bells in her head and now might be quiet long enough for her to sleep through the night.

"What have I done to you?" she asked, combative and liking the feel of that.

"You come to my door in the dead of night—"

"It's hardly six of the evening!"

"—and weep on my chest about a faithless lover—"

"And my sister!"

"And your sister," he agreed, more seriously now. "And no one would begrudge you those tears, for it's the saddest tale I've heard in a very long time. But it seems to me that all these tears are less for your poor sister than that ignorant fool Wilde—"

She drew away in her outrage, or tried to, sputtering and fumbling for something to say that would make sense and put him in his place all at once. "I am so sorry to have inconvenienced you with my little problems—"

"—and now you want to run off before I've said my piece."

"Oh." She stopped struggling. "What is it you wanted to say?"

He straightened and sat away and looked at her, as though she were a horse he might buy, if the price were right. That thought made Lily want to stand up again and run away, but he pressed her hand with his own and she settled, uneasily.

"He's a fool, is your Nicholas Wilde—"

She started to pull away but his grip was firm on her, unrelenting, distinctly comforting.

"—for he might have come here to claim you and take you home and instead he let himself be seduced by this harridan Jemima Southern."

"Jemima Kuick," Lily said sullenly.

"Jemima Wilde," he corrected her in turn.

Lily flared up at him. "You don't know him. You can't know him—"

And neither do I, for he married Jemima Kuick. The thought robbed her of the urge to defend Nicholas and, oddly enough, made her even angrier at Simon.

"I know a man by his actions, and so do you," he said, undaunted. "You are your father's daughter, after all."

She could not deny this truth, and so she ducked her head and swallowed the words that came to mind, the stories she might have told of Nicholas Wilde's kindness and generosity and tenderness. His intelligence, his dreams for the future, the love and skill that made his apple trees flourish and produce such wonderful fruit.

The man who married Jemima Kuick.

"So you were mistaken in him. And so what I have to say is this: it's a good thing he married another, for you deserve better, Lily Bonner."

"Like you, you mean."

"Aye," said Simon Ballentyne, meeting her gaze without flinching. "I'd be a far better husband to you than Nicholas Wilde ever could be."

Lily was suddenly very weary, her head aching with it. "You know that for a fact," she said bitterly.

"And so do you, lass, if you'd only admit it to yourself. For where did you turn in your time of need, but to me?"

She could not meet his eyes, but he solved this problem by catching her chin in his fingers and raising her face to his.

"Where did you turn, Lily Bonner?"

Her mouth worked, but nothing came out.

"I can see ye need some reminding."

He kissed her, his mouth trailing along her tear-swollen cheek to her mouth. And this was why she had come, of course. Because she wanted Simon Ballentyne to put his arms around her and comfort her and kiss her as he was kissing her now, with such purpose and warmth and sincerity.

When he broke the kiss he was breathing hard. Gooseflesh had run down her back and arms and all over her body, leaving little pools of warmth.

"Where did you come?" he whispered and then kissed her again, openmouthed and warm and deep, before she could even think of answering. He pulled her into his lap and cradled her there and kissed her until Lily thought her skin must surely be on fire, and then when he lifted his head she nodded, weakly.

"To you," she said.

"Aye," said Simon. "And why is that?"

The question took her by surprise, and this time she really didn't have an answer, at least not a clear one. "Because you're—" She hesitated.

"Aye?"

"My friend."

He drew in a breath then and put his forehead against hers. "And that's all there is to it?"

"No," said Lily. "I came because I thought you might—I hoped you might—" And her courage failed her after all.

"What? What do you want of me?" His arms were tense around her, and she realized with some part of her mind that he was frightened; Simon Ballentyne was frightened of what she might say.

"I want you to take me home." And then, quickly: "To Paradise. Home to Lake in the Clouds."

He held her away from him. She could see the thoughts rushing behind his eyes as he calculated and came to some conclusion.

"You want me to take you home. Why not your friend Mr. Bump?"

Lily shifted uncomfortably on his lap. "I don't like to ask him—"

"Because he would say no."

She shrugged. "He came to Canada to find someone, and he won't leave until he's done that."

"And you won't wait for your brother to come back from Québec because he'd say no too. What makes you think I'll do what Luke will not?"

Now the whole thing sounded so very childish that she was embarrassed and ashamed, and more than that, she saw in Simon's face that she had offended him.

She said, "I hoped you might understand."

He studied her for the length of a dozen heartbeats and then he tipped her off his lap and back onto the bench, stood abruptly, pushed his hands through his hair and walked away from her, across the room in a few strides, to turn and glare.

"Have you no idea how I feel about you, Lily? Are you so cruel?"

Lily felt herself flush, but she made herself hold his gaze. "I know how you feel about me."

A look passed over his face, comprehension and disappointment. He rubbed it away with his palm. "You still love the idiot with the apple trees." He said it matter-of-factly, as he might have told her that she had dropped a glove.

"And what does it matter if I do?" she said dully. "Most likely they hanged him already."

Simon let out a surprised grunt. "Do you think him guilty of the murder, then?"

"No!" Lily's head came up sharply. "He wouldn't. He isn't capable of something like that."

"Men are capable of anything," Simon said. "But in this case I tend to think you may be right. He's a coward, is your Nicholas Wilde, love him as you may."

Lily turned her face away, for what was there to say to that? Simon Ballentyne loved her and wanted her to love him back. It was there in his eyes and the set of his shoulders and the way his hands were fisted at his sides: he was jealous. And with cause.

"Alive or dead, Nicholas is lost to me," she said. "I know that."

"No," said Simon Ballentyne. "You don't know it, not really. You want me to take you back home so you can see for yourself that he lied to you. And you hope he didn't."

She hadn't admitted that much to herself, but once the words were said there was no way she could deny them, to herself or to Simon.

He crossed the room to her with such a furious look on his face that she drew back in fear. But he took her by the arms and raised her up to him and kissed her once, hard.

"I'll take you home," he said. "But I've a condition of my own. Once you've seen your precious Nicholas Wilde and learned the truth about him, you'll marry me."

Lily studied his face for a moment, the fierce purpose there and the anger he held in check. It was a dare, and one she might well lose. She could agree to this and find herself bound to Simon Ballentyne for the rest of her life. The idea felt so odd that she wasn't sure what to do with it.

"But what of your family . . . connections? What about Angus Moncrieff?"

He made a face at that, and she saw doubt flicker across his face. He was thinking of Luke, who had made his concerns known, and of her own father, whose reaction he could not predict. Nathaniel Bonner might feel as strongly, or more strongly, than Luke did about such a connection.

"Were this Scotland, then aye, that would be a problem. But your father is a fair man, is he no?"

"Yes," Lily said. "But he has a long memory too, and the things Moncrieff did—"

"Are unforgivable," Simon finished for her. "But I hardly knew the man, and I'm nothing like him. Your brother can attest to that. I'll do what must be done to convince your father that I'm worthy of you. Do you doubt that I'm able?"

"No," Lily said, quite honestly. "I don't doubt that you could convince him, though it might take some time."

"Well then, I'm waiting for your answer, Lily Bonner. And let me say this: I'll no ask again."

"Yes," she said, and started to hear her own voice so firm and unwavering.

He looked at her hard. "You'll marry me, then?"

"If . . . if things are as they seem at home. And if my father and my mother agree. Yes."

In her relief to have this settled—to know that she was going home—Lily relaxed against Simon and felt him tremble, his body responding to hers in a way that was unmistakable, and anything but unpleasant. For a moment they stayed just that way, eye to eye.

"I must take you back to Iona," he said, and set her down on the bench with a thump. Then he sat next to her, breathing as hard as a man who has run a mile uphill.

Unable to meet his eye, she examined her own hands. "But there are details to discuss."

That earned her a sharp and suspicious look. "Details," he echoed.

"Well, yes," she said. "When we'll leave and the rest of it . . ." Her voice trailed away, because he was grinning at her. Defiance was the only weapon she had to hand, and so she used it. "And it's really very early, still."

"Ah," said Simon Ballentyne, and pulled her back into his lap as if she weighed no more than a feather pillow. "It's talk you want? Are you sure of that?"

She struggled a little, and in response he held her tighter. "Must you be so . . . so . . ."

"Honest?"

And he kissed her before she could find the words to admit he was right.

Later, when they were both so heated that they could hardly breathe, when Lily's bodice was off her shoulders and loosened to her waist and her breasts so sensitive to his touch that she thought she must scream, Simon pulled away from her.

"What?" she said, her voice rough.

We must stop, he would tell her now, and he was right.

Lily thought of Iona, waiting for her. She thought of her mother and the words she had written. *I know you to be an intelligent and sensible young woman.*

Simon Ballentyne said, " 'Gin I dinnae take ye hame, lass, then I mun take ye tae ma bed. Tell me noo, which shall it be?"

"You're speaking Scots." She pressed her mouth against his throat. It thrilled her to feel him shudder.

"Aye," he said. "And ye havena answered ma question."

His hand was on her breast, callused fingertips exploring in light circles. A sound escaped her, a harsh sound that he caught up in his mouth, tongue against tongue. Sometime later he cupped her through layers of skirt to rock her on the heel of his hand. Behind closed eyes colors flashed, and she arched against him.

"Shall I take ye hame?"

"Please," she said. "Don't."

He picked her up and carried her up the stairs. In the dark she could just make out a bed, a single chair, a shelf. He put her down on the coverlet, made a sound that meant she should wait, and left her for a moment. The air was cold enough to show her breath, coming too fast; her skin erupted in gooseflesh and she pulled the coverlet over herself.

Then he was in the doorway with the candle painting his face in flickering golds and shadows. He looked at her for a moment and Lily thought, *He's going to change his mind, he's going to take me home,* and, *I should go,* and, *God help me, I want this.*

Simon put the candle on the wall shelf where it threw a circle of light onto the very middle of the bed, and then he sat down next to her, close but not touching.

"Lily Bonner," he said roughly. "Have ye heard the expression 'all's fair in love and war'?"

She nodded. "I have heard it."

"Let me tell you then what it means to me. I'll do what I can to make you my wife, and that means I'll spend every minute in this bed doing my best to get a bairn on you. Now will you be sensible and let me take you back, or will you stay?"

She was shaking, in fear and arousal and a little anger too, that he should put it before her like this, should rob her of the lovely fog they had spun between them. And he meant it; she could see it in his face. She wanted him, she wanted this, but the *why* of it slid away from her when she tried to make sense of it all. *Nicholas,* she thought, *Nicholas and Jemima Southern,* and then, *Is that the only reason?*

No, it wasn't, truly. But was what she felt right now, what she felt when Simon Ballentyne put his arms around her, was that reason enough to risk the rest of her life?

He was a good man and a kind one, a man who loved her, and made her laugh, and would take good care of her. A man who had hung a painting on the wall because it was her work, and never mentioned it to her. A man who seemed to understand her body better than she did herself, and who might do just as he threatened and start a child inside her, if she would not be sensible.

When she got up from this bed again, she could be pregnant. A shocking thought, but she made herself contemplate it, thinking of the way women talked together, when no men were nearby.

Once Lily's courses had started they had allowed her to stay and listen, and it had been a revelation to her. Women who would not speak in front of their husbands, who cast their eyes down rather than reveal what they were thinking, those women put their heads together and laughed, talking boldly of things Lily had only dimly imagined. Her own mother, while she said little, smiled into her lap and blushed in the way of a woman who is satisfied with her lot.

Lily thought of girls who stood up to say their wedding vows with rounded bellies; she thought of others who had not married at all, but raised a child without a father. Such things happened often enough for Lily to know that she was not the first woman to find herself in this situation.

She thought of the women who came to Curiosity or Many-Doves for medicine that would start a child, or keep one from coming. There were no simple answers, but some things seemed constant: there was a rhythm to a woman's month, good times and bad ones, depending on what she wanted.

"Not every coupling starts a child," she said, remembering the most important point suddenly, and with some satisfaction. Then she saw Simon's face. "And don't you dare *laugh* at me. It's true. I grew up in a household with books and I was encouraged to read and ask questions. I know a little bit about these things. One coupling doesn't mean a child."

"Ah, but lass," he said, running a finger down her arm so that she shuddered. "What makes ye think that either of us wad be satisfied with just once?"

At that she could say nothing. She opened her mouth to chide him for such arrogance and then shut it again, because he knew more of this business than she did, and it was a point she could not argue.

"Will ye stay?" he said again, calm now, so calm that she could barely contain her anger. Could not contain it. She leaned forward and cuffed him, hard, once and again, until he caught the offending hand and then flipped her over onto her back, held her there with the whole long length of himself.

Against her mouth he said, "Will ye stay or shall I take ye back to Iona?"

"For God's sake—"

"Ye'll no draw the Almighty intae this, ye wee heathen. Bide or gang?"

It took all her power, but she quieted herself, pulled in deep, even breaths, and made herself go calm.

And he waited, studying her as she studied him: the dark eyes under heavy brows, the shadow of his beard, the shock of dark straight hair shorn short, so different from the men of her family. Her father and grandfather and brother went to great length to keep themselves clean shaven; they wove their long hair into plaits.

Simon Ballentyne wore the hair on his head short, for ease, he told her, and cleanliness, as did the Roman soldiers of old. More than that, he was proud of his beard. She had noticed that early on.

Lily said, "There are two things you must know. First, even if I do have a child, my mother and father might not approve this match—and without their approval I will not marry. The second thing is a condition."

He was looking at her very solemnly, all his attention on what she would say. Lily made herself breathe deeply, not knowing what she was hoping for: he might laugh and see her home, or give her what she asked for.

She said, "If you will shave your beard, I will stay. And *if*—mind, I said *if*—we are to . . . make a life together, then you must stay clean shaven."

Maybe he had read her mind, for he showed no surprise at all. Instead he rolled away to stare at the rafters. "You must do it for me then," he said, in English now. "And you must do it straightaway, before I lose my nerve."

They lit all the candles and the lamp that hung over the table, stoked the hearth and heated water, sharpened the straight razor and scissors, found a pannikin of soft soap and beat it into a lather, and finally Simon Ballentyne sat bare-chested on a chair with a piece of toweling around his neck and his hands fisted on his knees.

"You have a pelt like a bear," she said in a conversational tone, trying not to look too hard at his chest, well muscled and broad, the way his shoulders sloped away from a strong neck. His body hair was fine and straight, and it feathered across his chest and stomach and arms too, though there was none on his back, she was relieved to see. She said, "The Kahnyen'kehàka would call you Dog-Face."

"I've been called worse," he said. "And for less reason. Get on with it, lass, or I'll bolt."

Lily went about the task as she did all her work: quickly, neatly, with no wasted motions, exchanging scissors for soap for razor, standing back to study her work and sometimes adjusting a candle for the light. After a while she began to hum a little.

"You needn't enjoy it so," Simon grumbled openly, and she stopped, razor poised, to look at him.

"And am I not worth a little hair, Simon Ballentyne?"

He reached out for her but she danced away, moving around the chair to work on his other cheek, the razor making rough scraping sounds as it revealed stripe after stripe of pale skin, such a contrast to the sun-darkened forehead and cheeks that she realized now how strange he would look, at first.

Standing in front of him she said, "Sit forward, I have to be here to do your throat properly."

At that he raised an eyebrow, but he did as she asked and she stood between his open knees and tipped his head back to expose the long stretch of his neck, the prominent Adam's apple bobbing nervously beneath the shorn beard.

"Don't swallow," she warned him and instead he broke into a sweat.

"There," she said finally. "As smooth as a—"

She hiccupped her surprise when his hands closed around her wrists. The razor clattered to the floor and the chair thumped. He lifted her bodily and settled her astride his lap.

"But you've upset the bowl," she scolded. "You've spilled the water."

"Damn the bowl," said Simon, rubbing his freshly shaven cheek against hers, "and damn the water too."

He kissed her for a long time, his fingers busy on her ties and buttons until her bodice was loose once more, cold air on her skin and a warm mouth. A sound came up from deep inside her, from the knot of wanting that was centered low in her belly. She was frightened, mortified, and aroused beyond all imagination.

She touched the hair on his chest and said, "Wait, wait . . ."

"Will you keep the bargain we struck?" he asked her, all seriousness.

She bit her lip and nodded, and at that he laughed, a full laugh from deep in his belly, and pressed her against his chest until Lily began to wonder if perhaps chest hair was not such a bad thing after all. He grinned at her as his hands worked her clothes and his own.

"Simon Ballentyne," she said, trying to slow things down at least a little. "You have dimples."

He paused then, raised a hand to a cheek and looked first surprised and then—oddly, sweetly—abashed.

"Great deep dimples," she added, tracing one. He grabbed her hand and held it away.

She laughed. "You can't have forgot about your own dimples. That's why you grew a beard, isn't it? To hide the dimples because they make you look—"

"What?" His hands moved to her back, hands so big that they covered her from nape to the small of her back, warm and sure, moving lightly, fingers curving around her ribs, thumbs stroking. "What do they make me look?"

His grin returned and with it his intention, for he caught her mouth before she could have thought what to say.

When next he let her catch her breath she said, "The bed?"

"Damn the bed, most of all." His hands moved under the tumult of her skirts to cup her bare buttocks. She started, and then settled.

"Here?" Lily asked, feeling a little faint and wide awake, all at once.

"Right here," said Simon. "To start."

Later she hobbled up the stairs—refusing to let him carry her, out of embarrassment and confusion and so many other feelings she did not want to examine closely—and collapsed on the bed. It was then that Lily saw a different and entirely unexpected look on Simon Ballentyne's face.

He drew back the blankets and the comforters and settled her into the feather bed, tucked her in and clucked softly, kissed her on the cheek and studied her as though she were burning with fever.

"You never said you were a virgin." There was regret in his tone, and accusation too.

Lily said, "I thought you realized."

He frowned at her. "You and Wilde—"

"No," she said shortly. "We did not. He was married."

He is married, to Jemima Southern. Is it like this for them when they come together? The questions presented themselves and she pushed them away.

Simon let out a great sigh and lay down next to her, his hands crossed on his chest. "On a chair," he said, shaking his head. "What a bloody great idiot am I."

"Simon Ballentyne," Lily said, turning on her side to face him. "If you're an idiot, what does that make me? Have you heard me complain?"

He sent her a sidelong glance. "Ye squealed like a grumfie."

Tears sprang to her eyes and she brushed at them angrily. "What a disappointment I must have been, to make noise like a *grumfie*. Whatever that might be."

He sat up so suddenly the bed rocked. "Listen to me now, Lily Bonner," he said, every word pronounced very carefully. "It's myself I blame. You did nothing wrong."

"And nothing right, either, it seems. You don't seem to have enjoyed it very much." She was fishing not so much for praise but simple encouragement. Because, she admitted to herself, she wanted to ask him questions about this whole mystifying business.

"Och, I enjoyed it," he said, smiling. "You just took me by surprise. I'm an aye fortunate man, Lily Bonner, to have been your first, but I regret the pain I caused you. I would have been more gentle, had I known."

"Enough of that," Lily said, irritated now and strangely heated, too, by the conversation. She said, "Do you always speak Scots when you're . . . you're . . ."

" 'Aroused' is the word I think you want."

"Aroused." She cursed herself for blushing.

He thought for a minute.

"I suppose Scots is what comes to me first when I'm in extremity of one kind or another. Surely when I'm angry, for English is far too weak a tongue when a man has a true temper on him. As far as this goes—" He ran a hand over her hip and rocked her a little. "That's a question you'll have to answer for yourself."

"So no one has ever mentioned it to you before," she said, a question of course and an impertinent one that he would not answer, she was sure. And yet she was curious.

He was looking at her, his brow creased. "Do you want to have that conversation, Lily? It's your right, though you might not like it, in the end."

She pushed herself up on an elbow and the comforter fell away. Cold air made the flesh on her back rise into goose bumps.

"Sometime," she said. "Not now."

"But there is something you want to ask, is there no? I can see it on your face." His hands had begun to explore beneath the bed-clothes, light touches on the inside of her thigh that made her catch her breath and tense.

She struggled to make her tone casual. "It won't always hurt, will it?"

At that he loomed over her and showed her the dimples he had kept a secret for so long.

"No if we do it right." And he lifted the blankets to crawl beneath them.

"Wait," Lily said, breathless already. "First I want to know . . . what's a grumfie?"

He hid a smile against her breast; she could feel it, as surely as the warmth of his breath and the words he spoke against her skin.

"Shall we stop now and have a Scots lesson?"

And then he did her a real kindness: Simon Ballentyne pulled her down into the cave he had made for the two of them, and spared her from the embarrassment of an answer.

Chapter 18

Inquest regarding the Death of Cookie Fiddler,
Manumitted Slave and Servant

Officials present:
Circuit Judge Baldwin O'Brien
for the Northern District of Hamilton County
in the State of New-York
Constable Jedadiah McGarrity
Ethan Middleton, Esq., Recording Clerk

15th Day of January 1813
Paradise, New-York

Statement of Mrs. Anna McGarrity,
Constable's Wife

Claes Wilde may be a pure idiot for taking up with Jemima
Kuick, but stupid ain't ever been a hanging offense and were
it, why, none of you men would be sitting here in judgment
on him for you'd all have gone to the gallows yourself long
ago. It's the curse you bear, you men, being led around by—
well, I don't suppose I need to say it plain. Claes has done

himself a mischief, but he didn't raise a finger to hurt Cookie and I'd bet my good name on that.

It's Jemima you want to be asking about, for Jemima was here in Paradise and Nicholas was gone away to Johnstown, and that I know for a fact as he brought post back with him and the newspapers too, and a whole box of Elixir of Life, a favor to me, you see, for I do depend upon it as my husband there can tell you. Nicholas Wilde was gone and Jemima Kuick was here, and when he came back he found he was a widower without a housekeeper nor anybody to cook for him or look after his Callie. And just shortly after that it was, that Jemima started taking covered dishes over to the orchard house, she who never lifts a finger for a neighbor unless it's to scold. You listen to me, Baldy O'Brien, you had best let Nicholas Wilde go and look a little harder at his bride, for it was Jemima who profited from those deaths, and no one else. Motive and opportunity is what you're after, as I understand it. My husband there explained it to me. Motive and opportunity, and I ask you, who else but Jemima had them both in abundance?

Statement of Mr. Jan Kaes, Trapper & Veteran

I'm here to speak for my daughter Becca LeBlanc, who's in childbed still and can't come herself to say what she knows of Jemima Southern. Mima made plenty trouble up by the millhouse, back in the days when they were in service there together, she and my Becca. You may call it hearsay if you like, Baldy O'Brien, but young Ethan there will put it down just the same on paper and that's all I care about. So listen. Jemima be mean as a kicked dog, just like her pa before her. Bitter to the bone, that's what I'm saying. Now that be a shame, but as far as I understand it, the legislature down in Albany ain't made a sin of meanness, yet, by God, and wouldn't it put them all out of business if they did? And the other thing I got to say is this: Jemima couldn't have struck Cookie on the head and dumped her in the lake, and I'll tell you why. For all her years Cookie was quick of eye and limb, and Jemima moves like sap in January.

Statement of Mrs. Margaret Parker, Widow &
Unemployed Housekeeper

While you high-and-mighty men are trying to figure out about Dolly Wilde and Cookie and whether it was Nicholas Wilde or Jemima who worked such evil deeds, let me remind you that the first Widow Kuick died not too long ago, and that needs looking into. You had best call Hannah Bonner here to speak for she might know something about that, and while you're at it, ask her to tell what she knows of how Isaiah Kuick died too, for that sorry business weren't never settled. Jemima stood in this very meetinghouse and swore Hannah had killed Isaiah Kuick but she shut up right smart when Becca Kaes—for this all happened before she went and married that no-good Charlie LeBlanc—when Becca told about that letter that went missing. I for one think Hannah Bonner must have it, and you need to see it to make sure justice is done. She's a blight upon the name of good women everywhere—it's Jemima I'm talking about here, Curiosity Freeman, not your precious Hannah, so there's no need for you to make such eyes at me. Jemima Southern Kuick Wilde is a blight upon the nation, and who will stop her, if not you, Judge O'Brien?

Statement of Mr. Horace Greber, Farmer & Veteran

I come here to say, I never had nothing to do with Jemima no matter what Missy Parker might be whispering behind her hand. Writing it down don't make it true. I could say that black's white and white's black and Ethan there would write it down, but it would still be a lie. Just as the things been said about me and Jemima are all lies. Lies up and down and sideways, pure and simple. I can't deny that my wife left me and took our girls with her to Johnstown, but the why and how of it, that's between her and me and nobody else, not even Missy Know-It-All Parker. And if I talked to Jemima now and then about getting her cow serviced, why then that's no more than the normal intercourse between neighbors, and was done out of Christian concern for a widow woman. It shows her good sense that she seeks out the opinion of men who by nature know the business best, don't it?

Statement of Mr. Nathaniel Bonner, Hunter & Trapper

I came across Dolly Wilde on Hidden Wolf when I was hunting. She was near froze and burning up with fever, so I took her home to Lake in the Clouds where my wife and sister-in-law did their best to nurse her. She died soon after. She never spoke in all that time, and that's all I know of the sad business. You can badger me all you like, O'Brien, but you'll get no more from me except this: my daughter Hannah sent along this letter Missy Parker was talking about and you asked for. It's been sitting up at Lake in the Clouds ever since Isaiah Kuick died, in a bundle of papers our Hannah left behind when she married and went west. So you've got the letter, along with the statements she gave Ethan there about the two dead women. If that ain't enough, you'll just have to call Mrs. Freeman to the stand and question her, like you should have done to start with.

Letter Submitted into Evidence
Dated 24 April 1802
Sealed and Witnessed

I, Isaiah Simple Kuick, being in good health and in full possession of my faculties, write this Statement in my own hand with Miss Rebecca Kaes nearby to Witness the seal and signature. My purpose is, first, to clarify the circumstances around the death of Reuben, a young slave boy who has been part of the Kaes household since his birth and who was laid to eternal rest today. I make this confession in order to stop this business here, to forestall retribution where it is unearned, and in fear of further bloodshed. In case of my death, I will leave this document in the care of a person who can be trusted to deliver it to the appropriate authorities when and if that becomes necessary.

Item the first. Reuben died as the result of burns that were inflicted—not accidentally, but certainly without premeditation—by our overseer, Ambrose Dye. I was present when this happened, and I consider myself guilty of not acting quickly enough to stay Mr. Dye's hand. He acted in anger and intemperance, and should by rights be tried for this crime. And yet I have not informed the authorities of this, and in fact, I have concealed it in order to protect Mr. Dye, to whom I am bound by ties too complex to name. I have made it impossible for justice to work its normal course and so I put this confession down here. Further, I do this in the full knowledge that unless he is dead or has left this area, Ambrose Dye must now be tried for murder. I cannot protect him at the cost of more lives, or something as insubstantial as my own comfort and reputation.

Item the second. In the spirit of full confession, I make known here that while my marriage to Jemima Southern was legal, it was entered into under duress. My wife threatened to reveal the nature of my attachment to Mr. Dye to my mother and to the entire village. To protect him and myself I entered into this marriage of convenience. I write this knowing full well that it will cause my mother severe pain and the utmost mortification. While I take full responsibility for my actions, I make no apologies to her or to anyone else. What sins I have committed and what punishment may be mine is a matter between myself and God alone.

Item the third. Our marriage was never consummated. I have never, at any time, lain with my legal wife or had intimate congress with her. The child she carries is not mine. Who may be the father, I do not know with any certainty, for I have never asked and have no wish to know.

Item the fourth. Though the child is not mine, I have no wish to cause it harm, and I am content to know it will bear my name and live its life out as my legal issue, for there will be no other and I am the last of my line. While it will fall hard on her, I require that my mother acquiesce to my wishes in this matter.

May the Lord have mercy on my soul. I, Isaiah Simple Kuick, sound of mind and diminished body, do hereby swear by the Almighty God and all that is Holy that what I have put down on these pages is true. Witness to my signature: Rebecca Kaes, of Paradise on this 24 day of April 1802.

> *Light hath no tongue, but is all eye;*
> *If it could speak as well as spy,*
> *This were the worst, that it could say,*
> *That being well, I fain would stay,*
> *And that I loved my heart and honour so,*
> *That I would not from him, that had them, go.*

Supplemental Statement of Mrs. Margaret Parker, Widow & Unemployed Housekeeper

And didn't I say so all along? Didn't I? You put it down there on paper, Ethan Middleton, for everybody to see plain as day. Missy Parker said from the beginning that there was evil doings up at the millhouse, and she was right.

Statement Submitted into Evidence
Signed by Hannah Bonner, Physician
Witnessed by Mrs. Elizabeth Bonner
and Ethan Middleton, Esq.

On the 20 day of November I examined the body of Mrs. Dolly Wilde in the presence of Mrs. Bonner and Mrs. Freeman of this village, as Dr. Todd was too ill to leave his bed. The subject was a woman of thirty years, of medium height, with dark hair gone mostly white, and of pale complexion. In her life she was well nourished and her person cared for. I found no wounds as might have been made by a bullet or knife or any weapon. The few scars on her person are in keeping with the life of a farmer's wife, with the exception of a healed bite mark on her right hand. In addition, her hands and arms were heavily scratched and torn from having pushed through bush for some time.

From the evidence available to me, and without performing an autopsy, it is my opinion that the subject died of a severe infection, most probably of the brain but possibly also of the lungs. I saw no evidence of violence done to her.

This statement dictated to and taken down by Ethan Middleton and signed by my own hand and sworn to be true to the best of my knowledge and ability. Hannah Bonner, also known as Walks-Ahead by the Kahnyen'kehàka of the Wolf Longhouse at Good Pasture and as Walking-Woman by her husband's people, the Seneca, this first day of January, 1813.

Statement Submitted into Evidence
Signed by Hannah Bonner, Physician
Witnessed by Mrs. Elizabeth Bonner
and Ethan Middleton, Esq.

On the 26 day of December I examined the remains of Mrs. Cookie Fiddler in the presence of Mrs. Bonner and Mrs. Freeman of this village, as Dr. Todd is recently deceased and there is no other with the training to perform this last service.

The subject was a Mulatto Negro woman of about sixty years, very small and slight of stature but well nourished and without obvious external signs of illness. Both her ears were pierced. The body bore numerous scars, primarily of whippings to the back and legs. The right fibula was once broken and set crookedly.

First observations indicated that the subject died by drowning when the water was at or very near freezing, for her remains were well preserved. On autopsy it was determined that her lungs were in fact filled with water, which indicates that she was alive when she fell into the lake. All other internal organs appeared unremarkable for a healthy woman of her years.

The only wound on her person was on the back of her head, an indentation about a half-inch deep, three fingers wide, and a half foot long, regular in shape, as might have been made by a blow with a wood stave or by falling and striking the head on a wood structure such as the handrail or edge of a bridge. The blow was severe enough to slice the scalp to the skull, cleave the skull itself, and render the subject insensible. There were no other signs of struggle, that is, no broken fingernails or wounds as might have been received in a struggle for her life. In addition, there were a few grains of sand clutched in her hand and found in the folds of her clothing. Thus is it my opinion that Cookie Fiddler's death may have been an accident or a murder, but it is not in my power to declare which on the basis of the evidence I had before me. I surmise that she received a blow to the head and fell unconscious into the lake, where she drowned.

This statement dictated to and taken down by Ethan Middleton and signed by my own hand and sworn to be true to the best of my knowledge and ability. Hannah Bonner, also known as Walks-Ahead by the Kahnyen'kehàka of the Wolf Longhouse at Good Pasture and as Walking-Woman by her husband's people, the Seneca, this first day of January, 1813.

Interview of Levi Fiddler, Man of All Work,
Freed Negro
By Judge Baldwin O'Brien, Esq.

Q: State your name and occupation for the record.

A: Levi Fiddler. Mostly I hire out as a farmhand, but now and then folks fetch me to play the fiddle for a party. Since the new year I been working for Mr. Middleton, there, who's writing all the words down.

Q: And before that?

A: I worked for Mr. Wilde. In his apple orchards, ever since I got my manumission papers. Before that I was a slave at the millhouse, belonged to the Kuicks from the day I was born.

Q: You bought your freedom from Mrs. Kuick?

A: Not me myself, sir. It was Mr. Gathercole, who was minister when this meetinghouse was still the Paradise church.

Q: Yes, I've heard that story. And the deceased was?

A: My mother.

Q: And she also worked for the accused, Mr. Wilde?

A: Yes, sir, we started work there on the same day. She took care of the house and looked after Miz Dolly and the baby, once she come along.

Q: What kind of employer was Mr. Wilde?

A: Fair. Even handed. A God-fearing man.

Q: Your mother was happy in his employ.

A: For the first time in her life, yes, sir.

Q: Mr. Wilde stands accused of your mother's murder. What is your opinion on that?

A: Pardon my language, sir, but that's damn nonsense. He couldn't have had nothing to do with it. He was in Johnstown, him and Miz Callie and me, the three of us. The two of them stayed with Mr. Wilde's cousin, you could ask him, Mr. James Guthrie, a cobbler. When we drove off from here Mama was standing in the door, waving. That's the last we saw her breathing. He couldn't have had nothing to do with it, and it wasn't in him neither.

Q: So I'm told by everyone I've interviewed. And what is your opinion of the new Mrs. Wilde?

A: I wouldn't take her name in my mouth, no, sir.

Q: You think she may have been involved in the death of your mother?

A: I don't want to say nothing about that. Best you ask the other white folks.

Q: Now Levi, before the first Mrs. Wilde died, did you ever witness any special connection between Mr. Wilde and the younger Widow Kuick?

A: No, sir. He never paid her no mind, as far as I could see. She never come to the orchard house, you can be sure of that. Missus Kuick never could abide Miz Dolly, and my ma would have chased her off, anyhow.

Q: Yet Mr. Wilde married her, not a month ago. How do you explain that?

A: Loneliness, I suppose, and the other thing.

Q: Other thing?

A: I don't like to talk that way in front of ladies, sir. The thing that men wants from women.

Q: I see. Now what of the first Mrs. Wilde, Levi? Other witnesses have testified that she was out of her mind. You saw her every day. Would you agree?

A: No, sir, not exactly. Seem to me she was all tangled up in her mind, like she was a prisoner inside herself.

Q: Do you think she was capable of violence? Might she have hurt your mother, maybe in a fit of some kind?

A: Why, no. It just don't seem possible. I seen Miz Dolly weeping over a dead bird more than one time, sir. Stroking it and talking to it, like maybe a kind word would be enough. No, sir, Mrs. Wilde—the first Mrs. Wilde that was—she couldn't have hurt Mama. I'd swear on it.

Interview with Mr. Nicholas Wilde

Q: Mr. Wilde, all charges against you in connection with the death of Cookie Fiddler have been dropped for lack of evidence. But we would like to ask you some questions about this sad business before we discharge you.

A: I've got nothing to say except, may God bless Cookie Fiddler and keep her. She was a good woman.

Q: Well, then. Let's start with your wife. Your first wife. Dolly Smythe, I believe was her name before you married. Your wife was unwell for the last few years?

A: Since the birth of our daughter, yes.

Q: And can you describe that illness?

A: No.

Q: You can't or you won't?

A: Both. I didn't understand it then and I don't now. Dr. Todd didn't know what was wrong with her and neither did Curiosity Freeman or any of the others who tried to help her, and nor more do I.

Q: Was your wife ever violent?

A: No. Never.

Q: She never struck you or anyone else, to your knowledge?

A: Never.

Q: No fits or apoplexies?

A: None. I would never have left her alone with Cookie if there had been any danger to either of them. Haven't you had testimony about this from Curiosity Freeman?

Q: I'll ask the questions here, Mr. Wilde. But no, Curiosity Freeman has not testified and will not testify before me. If your wife was so docile why didn't you take her to Johnstown with you?

A: She was easily upset, most especially by loud noise. And her condition had been worse of late.

Q: In what way?

A: In every way. She was in a decline.

Q: Her mania was worse?

A: I— Yes.

Q: You hesitate, sir. What is it you meant to say?

A: She was worse, I cannot deny it.

Q: Well, then, to the subject of your recent marriage to the Widow Kuick.

A: Ask her to leave the room, first.

Q: This is a public hearing, sir, and the accused has a right to be present. You will answer the questions put to you about Mrs. Wilde, or go back to gaol.

A: Then send me back to gaol, for I've nothing to say except this: I'll be filing for divorce with the court in Johnstown as soon as I can get there.

Q: Quiet! Quiet! I'll have quiet or see the lot of you out into the weather. Constable McGarrity, can you do nothing with this rabble? Now, Mr. Wilde, you say you intend to divorce your wife of a few weeks. Has the marriage been consummated?

A: That's none of your business.

Q: Quiet, or I will put you all in gaol if I have to drag you to Johnstown to do it! Now, Mr. Wilde, you must have grounds for divorce.

A: She lied to me.

Q: Your wife lied to you. Are you referring to the letter written by her first husband and submitted into evidence in this hearing?

A: That and other things.

Q: I doubt the court will be swayed, if that is all you have to offer when pleading a divorce.

A: I won't live with her as her husband, no matter what the courts have to say.

Q: Did this change of heart have to do with the death of your wife, or of Cookie Fiddler?

A: It has to do with many things.

Q: Well, then, do you think Mrs. Wilde had something to do with those deaths? Mr. Wilde?

A: I don't know.

Q: But you think her capable of violence?

A: I don't know.

Q: Mr. Wilde, your wife's name has been raised in connection with a number of deaths. The elder Widow Kuick, your first wife, and Cookie Fiddler. Do you know her to be guilty of any of these crimes?

A: I don't know anything about her, and it seems I never did. You'll have to talk to her if you want to know what happened. Not that you should expect to hear the truth.

Chapter 19

For once, Elizabeth would have welcomed a good hard January blizzard, but the weather would not cooperate. She saw that when she went out on the porch to put on her snowshoes. Overhead the skies were crystalline blue and uncaring of her dilemma.

"You don't have to go," Nathaniel said next to her. He finished buckling her shoes and unfolded himself, looking down at her with a disapproving frown that reminded her, for just a passing moment, of Daniel.

"I promised Curiosity that I would be there," Elizabeth said, squinting at the glare of sun on the snow. "To speak up for her, if need be."

At that Nathaniel made a deep sound of disapproval. His dislike for Baldy O'Brien, always a substantial one, had been nourished by the things he had seen and heard in the first day of the hearings. Sitting next to her husband in the meetinghouse, Elizabeth had felt his irritation taking firmer hold of him with every new witness or statement.

"He shouldn't have read Isaiah's letter out loud," Elizabeth said now, as if Nathaniel had complained. "For the sake of the girl, he could have kept that much quiet, at least."

"There's a lot he could have left unsaid. No doubt there will be a lot more of it to listen to today."

With that they set off into the clear morning, and for a long time they didn't speak at all. Nathaniel was listening to the world, to the rustlings and calls and whispers that gave him a clear picture of the woods beyond what Elizabeth could see or even imagine. It was his way, and she could not find fault with it, no matter how much she would have liked to carry on the discussion.

The evening before, on the way home, she had found it very hard to keep her silence until they reached Lake in the Clouds. They had barely closed the door behind them when she said, "That did not go very well."

"Goddamn Baldy O'Brien for a pompous fool," Nathaniel had answered. "By Christ, I'd like to know how he holds on to these appointments of his. He's got a headlock on somebody in Albany, that much is sure."

"What would you have him do?" Elizabeth had asked, a little taken aback at the degree of her husband's anger. "He must question the witnesses." And thus found herself in the odd position of defending a man she did not respect or trust.

"Well, Christ, Boots. Ain't it obvious? Curiosity could have done what six of the others did, in no more than a quarter hour, clearer and cleaner too—" He broke off and sent her a sidelong frown. "I'm surprised you ain't more put out about it yourself, him not letting Curiosity testify."

"I am put out," Elizabeth said. "But I know when my energy is wasted, Nathaniel Bonner. As do you. What is really bothering you?"

Elizabeth was at the window, pulling the curtains shut. A white owl swooped suddenly out of a spruce, almost invisible against the snow. It was gone just as suddenly, a limp form caught in its hooked beak.

Behind her Nathaniel said, "I'm disappointed in Nicholas Wilde. But I'm madder at myself for not seeing the weakness in him. I had just about decided that he was the right kind of husband for Lily, when he goes and proves what a damn fool he is."

Elizabeth turned and opened her mouth but nothing came out but a squeak of distress, much like the one the owl had caused just a moment ago.

Nathaniel managed a grim smile. "Did you think I didn't know?"

"Know? Know what? There was nothing to know," Elizabeth said, moving to the other window. "They both showed a great deal of good common sense and reason."

"Now that's a first," Nathaniel said. "I've never heard it described that way before when a married man takes up with a young girl. And tell me why is it you never told me about this, if you knew?"

"First of all," Elizabeth said, struggling to contain her voice, "there was no taking-up. They might have been in love—"

Nathaniel grunted.

"Don't you growl at me, Nathaniel Bonner. They were in love, yes, that much must be supposed, but nothing—inappropriate happened."

"You know that for a fact? She tell you that?"

"No," Elizabeth said, more quietly. "I could never think of a way to broach the subject. But I know she would have come to me, had things advanced that far. I *know* it."

"Rest easy, Boots. You're right, it didn't go beyond a few kisses. That's bad enough, but it ain't a hanging offense."

Over the years he had surprised her many times, but now Elizabeth found herself almost short of breath. "And how do you know that much? And if it's true, why didn't *you* tell *me*?"

"I know because I talked to Wilde, that's how. The day Lily told us she wanted to go to Montreal. I wanted to make sure she was going for the right reasons."

Elizabeth said, "And those were . . ."

"To suit herself," said Nathaniel. "And not him."

At that Elizabeth said nothing, could think of nothing to say, because she was embarrassed to have been so silly. Of course Nathaniel had known about the flirtation, and of course he had acted.

"And so his foolishness, as you call it, was what?"

Now it was Nathaniel's turn to look at his wife in surprise. "He could have written to her, asked her to come home from Montreal."

"Now you are being dense," Elizabeth said. "What do you think she would have said if he had asked her to give up her art and teachers and all the rest of it?"

"I don't know for sure," Nathaniel said. "But one way or the other she would have figured it out, finally. What she wanted more, Nicholas Wilde or the life she's made for herself in the city."

Elizabeth pushed out a great breath. "Yes, all right. I concede that point. And you're angry at him because—"

"He was too much of a coward to write the letter," Nathaniel said. "And he went down in front of Jemima Southern like deadfall in a high wind."

Then Gabriel had come to fetch them to the supper Many-Doves had made for them, and there had been no more opportunity to talk with the children present.

Now, on their way back to the village for the second day of the hearing, Elizabeth thought of Nicholas Wilde as he had been yesterday. Straight of back in the witness chair, his complexion pale under a few days' growth of beard. Older, suddenly, with lines bracketing his mouth. Grimmer, and with good reason. For all his foolishness—and Elizabeth must agree that he had been foolish—it seemed he was being punished very harshly. After almost ten years of marriage to a woman who could not be a wife, he was now bound to Jemima Southern and would not be her husband. His pride had been injured, not so much by the trumpeting of her sins, but by the fact that he seemed to be the only one in the village who had not heard the rumors over the years.

Beyond that, he had lost his daughter. Callie had left the orchard house to live at the doctor's place with Curiosity and Hannah, and she showed no interest in going home again. He could make her, of course; the law was with him, if he wanted to force her. But after yesterday, Elizabeth doubted he would do such a thing. She wondered if he would even stay in Paradise.

They had come as far as the bridge, iced over once again and slick. Nathaniel took a shovel from the sand barrel and cast it out in a smooth arc, and then he took her arm anyway as they crossed.

On the other side he stopped at the second sand barrel and cast another shovelful, and then he looked up at the millhouse and his mouth contorted. The millhouse was one of the newest buildings in the village, but looked to be the oldest. Broken shutters hung here and there like loose teeth, and many of the fine glass windows the first Widow Kuick had been so proud of were boarded over. The house looked deserted, Elizabeth thought and then corrected herself: it looked unhappy. It was a silly idea and yet it stuck with her—the millhouse collapsing in on itself in mourning.

"What do you think will happen to it?" she asked.

"I heard Charlie and Becca were going to try to buy it. They could use the space since the twins come along."

"Oh, yes, that would be just the thing for Becca," Elizabeth said. "But Jemima will hate it."

Nathaniel took firmer hold of her arm. "She might not be around to see it happen."

The meetinghouse was crowded so that to get from one side to the other they had to wind their way around benches and stools and settles, all dragged here by people who wanted to be entertained in comfort. Baldy O'Brien sat at the very front at a table with Jed McGarrity and Ethan, and directly before them was the witness chair.

Elizabeth studied Jemima, something she had not been able to do for a very long time. She didn't show her years, even with the trouble at hand; instead she radiated . . . what? An angry heat, a fierce purpose, a conviction of sorts, and it came to Elizabeth that for all her faults, Jemima was one of the bravest women she had ever known. She faced the crowd and the law with courage that bordered on religious fervor; were they to burn her at the stake, Jemima would use her last breath to spit on them.

Across from Jemima sat Nicholas Wilde. Elizabeth had thought that after his testimony yesterday he might have gone off to hide and nurse his sorely wounded pride, but he sat with the Fiddler brothers. The three of them were silent and untouched by the loud and almost cheerful crowd that surrounded them.

"Scoot on over," Curiosity said, coming up beside Elizabeth with Jennet. "Baldy's about to get started."

The voices died away as O'Brien began to talk. He had to shout to be heard anyway, over the noise of a rising wind, the scuffling of feet and sneezing and coughing and whining of children. It was inevitable that everyone be here, Elizabeth knew, but she wished again for the blizzard that would send them home in a hurry and leave this sad business to the injured parties.

Jemima's voice brought her up out of her thoughts, and Elizabeth realized that she had missed the first question.

"Yes," Jemima answered in a clear, almost impatient voice, the same voice she used to answer all his questions. She understood the charges against her, she understood the nature of the hearing, she understood that she could be bound over for trial in Johnstown.

Baldy O'Brien had a sharp manner, but it was no match for Jemima, who met him straight on and without apology. Like a dog up against a bear, Elizabeth thought.

O'Brien was studying the papers before him. "What do you say to these charges, Mrs. Wilde?"

Jemima looked over the crowd, her expression imperious. "Damn you all to burn in everlasting hell."

A ripple ran through the room, part disapproval but mostly, Elizabeth knew, excitement. They had come to this hearing as they had come to see the firecrackers on the lake, wanting the noise and the shock, and Jemima would not disappoint them.

Dryly O'Brien said, "I take it you are pleading innocent to the charges."

"I am. I do. I never laid a hand on Cookie nor on Dolly."

That brought her a sharp look from O'Brien, shot up through the tangle of eyebrows. "You never struck Cookie Fiddler?"

"I didn't kill her. I didn't hit her in the head or throw her in the lake."

"Answer the question, Mrs. Wilde."

Jemima shrugged a shoulder. "When she was a slave at the mill-house I hit her, and more than once. Is that a crime, taking a hand to a slave with a smart mouth?"

Elizabeth's gaze shifted to Levi and Zeke, who sat straight backed and never flinched, even while O'Brien led Jemima through a list of questions about her relationship with their mother.

"So it's fair to say you hated Cookie Fiddler," O'Brien concluded.

"Fair enough," Jemima said, looking directly at Levi. "As much as I hate snakes. But I wouldn't go out of my way to step on one."

"Mrs. Wilde, it sounds to me as if you had a motive to want Cookie Fiddler dead."

At that Jemima looked directly surprised. "You mean, so I could get Nicholas to marry me? You think Cookie could stop that?" She snorted softly. "She didn't stop me marrying Isaiah, did she?"

There were sharply indrawn breaths all around the room, and whisperings that were meant to be heard.

"Oh, listen to them," Jemima said. "As if they ain't had their heads together talking about that very thing since you read Isaiah's letter out loud yesterday."

"Mrs. Wilde," O'Brien said. "You'll restrict your comments to answering questions put to you. You heard Mr. Wilde's testimony yesterday, and his statement that he would petition for divorce on the grounds that you lied to him."

Jemima's mouth twitched. "I heard him. You want to know if I lied?" She looked up, and seemed for a moment seriously amused. "Of course I lied to him. I lied and I let him into my bed. If that's a trick, then it's an old one and I'm not the only woman here who used it to advantage."

"That's all very informative," said O'Brien gruffly. "But it has nothing to do with my line of questioning—"

"Oh, but it's what they want to hear. Look at them, like crows ready to peck out a lamb's eyes. They want the dirty details. They want to know what I had to do to get Nicholas Wilde to marry me. Now see how he goes pale, my dear husband, to hear the truth told. Did you think I'd keep still, Claes, and let you go free so easy?"

The room had begun to shift and quake like a ship in high winds, voices rising. O'Brien's face flushed a good deep shade of red and he pounded with his fist on the table so his papers jumped.

"Quiet! Quiet! Quiet, or I'll have the lot of you put out, I swear it!"

From the back of the room Missy Parker called, "Mr. O'Brien, don't cut her off just when she gets going!"

O'Brien began to sputter, but Jemima cut him off with a wave of her hand. "If you'll just hold your trap long enough, I'll tell you what you want to know."

"I'll hold you in contempt, missus, if you dare speak to me like that again."

Jemima laughed out loud. "You do that, if you like. Won't matter much to me if I hang a few days sooner. Now do you want to hear this story or not?"

It took another ten minutes of negotiations between O'Brien, Jed McGarrity, and the crowd before Jemima was allowed to go on. By that time Elizabeth found that she was perspiring so heavily out of dread and unease that her handkerchief was already damp through. Nathaniel sent her a sharp and questioning look, which she ignored.

"So then," Jemima said, almost primly. She turned her head to catch the constable's gaze. "Jed, you'd best see Nicholas out before he pukes on his shoes."

"I'm not going anywhere," said Nicholas Wilde.

Jemima shrugged. "Be it on your head."

"I'll remind you once more, Mrs. Wilde," Baldy O'Brien said in his most imperious tones. "I run this hearing, not you."

"Aren't you so high-and-mighty, Baldy O'Brien, and need I remind you how I paid my taxes last time you came knocking on my door?"

This time it took fifteen minutes until the room was settled enough for Jemima to go on. O'Brien's complexion was flushed bright with indignation and, Elizabeth noted to herself, guilt.

Nathaniel leaned over and whispered, "I got a feeling she might be bringing Lily's name into this," he said. "If she does, you sit tight and let me handle it."

Elizabeth was so taken aback at this suggestion that for a moment she sat staring at her husband.

"I won't shoot her," he said, as if to assure her. "At least, not right here and now."

". . . you think you know everything," Jemima was saying. "About poor Nicholas Wilde. What a good husband he was to his sick wife, what a fine father. How he mourned his Dolly. Fools, all of you. It was Lily Bonner he was mourning all the winter, and if you doubt me, look at his face, he's gone the color of paste."

"You bitch." Nicholas strained forward.

"Call me what you like," Jemima said. "I've been called worse."

"Lily Bonner went to Montreal," said Charlie LeBlanc, standing up suddenly. He pointed at the drawings that still hung on the walls. "To be a painter."

"She went to Montreal before the truth came out and her reputation was ruined once and for all," Jemima shot back. And: "Why are you looking at her father? Do you think he'd admit the truth about one of his own?"

They were looking, Elizabeth could not deny that, but more out of confusion than curiosity. Nathaniel met everybody's eye with his usual calm, almost weary now, as if Jemima were a ranting toddler who must eventually scream herself into a trembling quiet.

At the table where he was recording the proceedings, Ethan took the opportunity to trim his quill, and Elizabeth wished she had even a tenth of his calm spirit.

Jed McGarrity cleared his throat. "Get on with it, Mima. Even if that's true—and I ain't saying it is—it don't have anything to do with Cookie."

"But it does," Jemima said. She straightened her shoulders. "If you're smart enough to hear what I'm saying. So there was Claes Wilde, taking care of his imbecile of a wife and pining for Lily Bonner. Then Dolly did him a favor and died, and Cookie disappeared. Now who profited from that, I ask you, but Nicholas himself?"

Anna McGarrity called out. "If things are the way you say, Jemima, why didn't he send for Lily to come back from Canada?"

"Oh, he would have," Jemima agreed. "Except that letter came from her brother, the one saying she had gone and got married."

The noise in the room was such that Elizabeth couldn't hear Jennet and Curiosity, who had their heads bent together to talk. O'Brien was on his feet, pounding on the table, and even Jed's deep voice made no difference; the crowd must have its say. Then Nicholas stood up and turned, his eyes moving through the crowd until they settled on Nathaniel.

He said, "She lied to me about Lily being married. I didn't find out the truth until we got back from Johnstown."

"Of course I lied," Jemima said. "Your precious Lily was gone away and I was here, with a girl of my own to raise and never knowing if I'd be able to feed her the next day or the day after that. I needed a man to support us and put food on the table. I did what needed doing, and you never complained when you were lying on top of me, now did you?"

Zeke and Levi were big men and strong, but it took a lot for them to hold Nicholas Wilde back.

Jed said, "I don't want to take you out of here, Claes, but I will if you don't settle down."

Jemima went on, her voice cold and hard now. "I would be cooking your supper this minute if whoever killed Cookie hadn't done such a piss-poor job of it. Now hang me if it will make you feel better about yourselves. That would suit Nicholas just fine too. It would save him the trouble of divorcing me so he can court Lily Bonner in the open instead of sneaking around barns in the dark of night."

"I never touched her that way," Nicholas shouted. "Never."

"No, of course you wouldn't." Jemima's expression had lost all of its fury, and she looked like nothing more than a weary young woman, beaten down and used up. She said, "You saved that for the likes of me, didn't you? When you couldn't stand it anymore you came to me to get your itch scratched, and now you've gone and married me for it. Fool that you are."

The meetinghouse had gone very quiet.

Jemima blinked, finally. It looked as though she had been in the grip of a fever that had suddenly broken, for her neckerchief was sweated through and the muscles in her jaw were fluttering.

She said, "The day Cookie went missing and Dolly died I was home doing mending. My daughter can testify to that if you care to fetch her here and ask her before you hang me."

It was Jed McGarrity himself who came to collect Martha, and with him Curiosity, to speak calm words to the girl and comfort her on the way back to the meetinghouse. When they were away, Hannah saw that something must be done to distract Callie Wilde, and so she set about teaching her to brew a fever tea.

Callie was by nature a quick student and a willing one, but today she was distracted and even clumsy. When she came close to scalding herself for the second time Hannah took the kettle from her and set it back on its trivet. Then she put her hands on the girl's shoulders.

"It might be best to say what is on your mind."

Callie couldn't meet her eye, which worried Hannah even more. The girl said, "I should be at the meetinghouse with Martha."

Hannah kept her peace, neither agreeing nor arguing, and settled the girl in one rocker while she took the other. One of Curiosity's cats immediately jumped into the girl's lap and began to purr loudly.

The kitchen was warm and quiet and smelled of new bread and baking apples. Apples that had come from the orchards that Callie's father had planted and tended so carefully. The orchard that he could return to now, to take up his life. Except of course he couldn't, not after the things that had been said yesterday in front of the whole village. Hannah had read Ethan's transcript, and knew the whole of it.

Callie and Martha had only heard those things that the women thought must be said and that the girls could bear to hear. They still had not decided how or when to tell Martha about the revelations in Isaiah Kuick's letter, though that must clearly be done. If they did not tell her, someone else in the village would, and in a way that did not bear long thought. Children used words like cudgels and delighted in drawing blood.

In the evening, the girls had sought Ethan to ask more questions. He had told them a little more, enough to keep both the girls awake most of the night, whispering together.

In the morning Callie came to Hannah and Curiosity with Martha at her side.

"My father isn't going to gaol," she said. "And I'm glad. But I don't want to go back to the orchard house."

"You can stay here as long as you like," Hannah had answered her, and that had seemed to be enough for both the girls. Neither of them had thought of the law, or what a child might be compelled to do against her wishes. But Hannah was not so worried about that; she had the idea that Nicholas Wilde would not argue. He was at war with his new wife, and when men turned their minds to battle they put children out of their minds and hearts. To survive; to come home to them, when the fighting was done.

Chapter 20

Statement of Mrs. Elizabeth Bonner,
Schoolteacher

I had thought to keep my silence during these proceedings, but find now that I cannot, in good conscience. What I have to say has nothing to do with the death of Mrs. Fiddler or even of the first Mrs. Wilde, but with the well-being of a young girl who faces an uncertain future. In just a few minutes she will come into this meetinghouse and answer questions put to her about her mother.

You all know Martha Kuick to be a good-hearted child, friendly and kind and helpful. Mrs. Ratz, I have seen Martha carrying firewood for you. Mrs. Parker, I know that you have called on her more than once to card wool and churn butter for you and found her to be a hard and dependable worker, as young as she is. Though she often came to my classroom hungry I have never heard a word of complaint from her, and I would guess that no one in this room has ever had a cross word out of Martha's mouth, though she may have had cause.

Judge O'Brien found it necessary to read a letter that reveals some facts that are exceedingly personal in nature, and none of our concern. Now we know what we only suspected about Martha's parentage, but I stand here today to ask you to keep the contents of that letter to yourselves until I or someone else close to Martha may have the chance to talk to her privately. I do not ask for secrecy, for I know that is simply beyond the bounds of human nature. Instead I ask for compassion, for charity, and most of all for each of you to think before you cause more pain for a young girl who has suffered much and may suffer more, depending on the outcome of this hearing. No matter what she might say here under questioning, I beg you to remember that she is only a young girl.

Interview with Miss Martha Kuick, Aged 8 1/2 years
Conducted by Constable McGarrity

Q: Martha, we have just a few questions for you now and we can all go home to our dinners. Is that your mother sitting there?

A: Yes, sir. You know her yourself, Jed. I mean, Constable McGarrity.

Q: Jed'll do just fine. Now, tell me this, do you remember the day the blizzard started that Mrs. Wilde got lost in?

A: I do. It was a Monday. I know because we was just getting ready to start the washing when the wind come up smart. That was about mid-morning. So we couldn't wash after all, nor go out neither though we was short of firewood.

Q: And what time did your mother wake you that day?

A: Why, she didn't. It was me who woke her, like always. At sunrise I did the milking, and when that was done, I went to shake her awake. And she got out of bed and made the porridge.

Q: Was there any time that day, that first day of the blizzard, when you didn't know where your mother was?

A: No, sir. In the morning she was busy with mending stockings and then the blizzard came up. It was a hard blizzard. Nobody went nowhere for two whole days, except early to bed to save the firewood and the candles.

Q: Now, Martha, tell me this. You understand about telling the truth, about right and wrong?

A: Yes, sir, I understand.

Q: And you swear here today that you were with your mother

that whole day that Mrs. Wilde went missing. That she never left the house from dawn when you woke her, not that whole day nor the next.

A: Yes, sir, that's right. I swear it.

Q: You know that your mother has been charged with the murder of Cookie Fiddler?

A: Yes, sir.

Q: Do you think your ma did Cookie some harm that day, Martha?

A: No, sir, I don't.

Q: So your testimony is that you were with your mother the whole day in question, and that you never saw Cookie Fiddler or Mrs. Wilde, and know nothing about what happened to either of them.

A: I can't say that. Not exactly.

Q: Well, what can you say exactly then?

A: I saw Mrs. Wilde. She was walking upmountain through the woods behind the mill. I saw her from the porch when I went out to fetch water.

[Recorder's note: The questioning of this witness was interrupted for the half hour it took to calm her, quiet the room, and remove some of the spectators.]

Q: Martha, are you telling us that you saw Mrs. Wilde that morning she disappeared? Walking in the woods behind the millhouse?

A: Yes, I did. She was headed upmountain.

Q: And what time was that?

A: Mid-morning, sir, I'd guess. Ma sold the mantel clock so I couldn't say exactly.

Q: But before the blizzard started?

A: A little while before. The sky was already lowering, and the wind was up.

Q: And she was alone?

A: Yes, sir, nobody anywhere near. Not even Cookie, which was odd, I remember thinking it right off.

Q: How was she dressed?

A: Why, normal. A cloak and boots and a hat, and mittens.

Q: You knew, didn't you, that Mrs. Wilde was ill? That she wasn't to be left unsupervised?

A: Yes, sir. I knew that. I saw how much trouble they took to keep her from wandering. Callie told me about it, and everybody talked about it in the village too.

Q: Martha, you're a brave girl. Don't look at your mother now, just at me. Do I understand right? A blizzard was coming on and you saw Mrs. Wilde walking up the mountain by herself, and you didn't call an alarm? Didn't go after her to help her find her way back home?

A: No, sir.

Q: Why on earth not?

[Recorder's note: Judge O'Brien directed the witness to answer the question put to her.]

A: Because Mama said I was to mind my own business. She came to the window and looked and said, never you mind, Martha Kuick, that's her trouble and none of ours.

Callie got up to put more wood on the fire, spilling the cat, who arched her back and then went back to her kittens in their basket. There was the sound of pattens at the back step, the scraping of snowy heels and a hand on the door.

"Curiosity's come home," Callie said, blanching. "The hearing must be done."

"It is," Curiosity said as she came into the kitchen. "Done once and for all, I hope."

And at that moment it occurred to Hannah, looking from Callie's frightened expression to Curiosity's sober one, that something had happened in the meetinghouse when Martha was called to testify, something that Callie had known might come to pass.

Curiosity unwound her shawl and managed a small smile.

"Set down again, child," she said mildly. "I got some things to say."

When Curiosity had finished telling them the whole of it in her calm way, her hands folded in her lap, Callie was silent for a long moment and then she looked up, her face drained of color.

"They aren't taking Jemima to Johnstown?" she asked for the second time. "She won't be hanged?"

"No," Curiosity said. "Not after what Martha had to say. Baldy

O'Brien was surely disappointed, but without more evidence he cain't bind Jemima over for trial. What she done might be a sin in the eyes of God, but there ain't no law that say she got to raise a hand to help a woman in need."

Callie held herself very still. She reminded Hannah of a child who knows that even the slightest movement might bring on a beating.

"Callie," Hannah said calmly. "You knew, didn't you? Martha told you what happened that day that your mother disappeared on the mountain."

The girl raised her head to look at them, shadowed and far older than her years, and nodded. "Yes. Martha told me."

"You were afraid to speak up," Curiosity prompted gently.

Callie nodded again, and for a while Hannah thought that she would have nothing more to say. Then a tremor moved through her and a single tear ran down her face. She said, "We talked it through, me and Martha. We talked it through and it seemed to us that if we told, they'd take Jemima away and hang her. We thought it would be better if at least one of us had a ma, even if—" She broke off to swallow and wipe her face with a trembling hand. "Then my pa started up with her and we didn't know what to do. I wanted to tell him, but I couldn't think how."

"That's a heavy burden for a young girl to be dragging around for so long." Curiosity reached out as if to touch Callie, but the girl pulled back, almost alarmed.

She said, "We didn't mean harm. And we didn't lie either. We made a promise that if anybody asked the question straight-out that we'd tell the truth. But nobody did ask, not until today. Oh, poor Martha. I should have been there."

It was a terrible thing to see her weep tears so long held at bay, tears far older than her years.

"Sometimes a hurt is so bad and so deep that tears is the only thing to wash it away," Curiosity said. "You go on and let it out, child. We know what it is to weep."

Jed McGarrity and Jennet brought Martha back not an hour later. The girl was pale and shaking as if she had taken a fever. Hannah put a hand on her brow, cool and damp, fed her a bowl of soup, and then sent her to bed with Callie to sit beside her.

"Let them work it out between them," Curiosity said. "They come this far together, they'll come a little farther."

Curiosity made tea and they sat around the table, Jed with his big hands wrapped around the cup and resting on his long silky brown beard. He said, "I seen and heard some things in my day, but what happened in that meetinghouse—that beats all."

"It was aye shocking," Jennet agreed. "To have let the poor woman wander off into a storm like that."

"What do you think will happen now?" Hannah asked, and Jed shot her a surprised look.

"Why, cain't you guess? As soon as O'Brien set Jemima free Nicholas set out lickety-split for Johnstown. Looking for a lawyer to plead him a divorce. Not that it'll do him much good, I fear." He cast a sidelong glance at Jennet and cleared his throat.

"Jemima claims to be with child," Jennet explained, looking over her shoulder to be sure the girls were not within hearing. "She called it out to Nicholas when he left the meetinghouse. Everybody heard it."

They were silent for a moment, thinking of that. Jemima had bound Nicholas Wilde to her with a child. She was not the first woman to take such a step, nor would she be the last. More ammunition in this new war she must fight to claim her place as Nicholas Wilde's wife.

"Come on then, and tell us the rest," Curiosity said, thumping her cup a little. "Spit it out."

"There's naught to tell," said Jennet. "Jemima marched off like a soldier, straight of back. Gave nobody any quarter. Were it not for the wicked things she's done I should almost have to admire her for it."

At that Curiosity laughed out loud. "I suppose it might look that way to you. You ain't knowed her long enough, is all."

"Do you think she'll come here to fetch Martha?" Hannah asked.

"No chance of that," Jed said. "I warned her away."

"But will she pay you any mind?" Jennet asked. "That's the question."

Jed grunted. "Oh, she'll mind. It's not Martha she's worried about, anyway. It's keeping her place at the orchard house."

"If Claes throws her out she'll just go back to the mill," Curiosity said. "Unless there's something else you got to tell. I can see it on your face as plain as pimples."

"She sold the house," Jennet and Jed said together.

Curiosity looked as if someone had stuck her with a pin. "What?"

"Charlie LeBlanc offered her fifty dollars for the millhouse, and she took it," Jed explained.

Even Hannah laughed at that. "And where would Charlie LeBlanc get fifty dollars?"

It was a reasonable question, for even with his wife's good sense and calm guidance, Charlie barely managed to make a profit from the millworks. Without the free labor that came with six sons, he would have been bankrupt long ago. Charlie was more likely to grow horns than he was to save fifty dollars all together.

Curiosity said all this and more, while Jed studied the bottom of his teacup.

"Aye," said Jennet. "So the story goes. But the good men of Paradise decided to take action." She explained how they had started a collection on the spot to get the fifty dollars together. It was all in chits, which were handed over to Charlie for credit on the next summer's milling.

"The idea," Jennet said, looking almost embarrassed to admit such a thing, "was that Jemima would be so glad of the fifty dollars that she would go away to Johnstown to live."

Curiosity snorted. "What a fool plan," she said, and Jed flushed a deep red that mottled his neck and cheeks and made him look, just for that moment, like a boy who has helped himself to more maple sugar than was his due.

"Aye," said Jennet. "The ladies said as much. And loudly, forbye. But Jemima took what was offered her, and Ethan drew up the agreement and she signed it."

"Go on," said Curiosity. "I can guess what happened next, but you might as well say it. She ain't going nowhere. She'll set right there at the orchard house and wait till she's collected on those chits."

"You can imagine how put out Missy Parker is," Jennet said, barely containing a smile. "For she was right and the men were wrong, but were she to say that, she should also have to admit Jemima had won out, yet again."

Through all of the telling, Jed had pressed his mouth into a thin line with increasing embarrassment, but now he looked up finally and shrugged.

"It was a good plan," he said. "We thought she'd go, if she only had the means."

Curiosity set her rocker moving with a push of her foot. "When Nicholas comes back from Johnstown he'll find her settled in."

"Not if the court gives him his divorce," Jed said. "Though I suppose that's unlikely, with Jemima in a family way."

"Ain't this a fine pickle," Curiosity said. "Jemima has got herself a husband who's bound by law to provide for her, hate her though he might. It's a hard punishment he's earned for his foolishness."

"I must write to Lily," Jennet said with a deep sigh. "I promised her I would, when there was news to tell. But of course I didn't know of the connection then . . ." Her voice trailed off. "Did it really come as a surprise to you, Curiosity?"

The older woman was looking into the fire with an expression that was hard to read: regret and sadness and maybe irritation, whether with herself or Lily it was impossible to know. She said, "I suppose I knew she admired the man. She always did, since she was a little girl—do you remember, Hannah?"

"She tried to convince me that I should marry him, once," Hannah said. "That seems very long ago."

"Well, it hurts my pride to admit it, but I didn't have no idea at all." Curiosity's fingers drummed on the arms of the rocker. "Didn't know it had gone over to something so serious that she would run off to avoid getting herself in trouble. And maybe it ain't so. Don't know as we can believe Jemima's version of things."

"I'd say we cain't," Jed said gruffly. "I for one don't believe that Lily and Claes Wilde—" He cleared his throat. "I just don't believe it."

"I hope for Lily's sake that you're right," Jennet said, her expression very sober now, almost sorrowful. "For if she did think he loves her, it will be hard news indeed to find out that he's bound to Jemima Southern."

Curiosity rocked herself harder. "That's just what we're all worrying about, child. One thing you cain't deny about Miss Lily, she got a temper, and it do run off with her at the worst times."

The talk ebbed away, and they sat together in silence, each of them thinking of Lily, and the things she might do.

Chapter 21

Lily wondered, sometimes, that two people who liked each other—for she did like Simon Ballentyne, when she could think of him from a distance—could find so much to fight about. It seemed that all they could do when they were face to face was to argue. The first and biggest battle was this: Lily wanted to leave for home immediately, and Simon simply refused.

"I won't run off like a thief in the night." He said those words so often that Lily began to understand something: he truly believed he was taking something away from Luke, some possession that he valued and would not hand over easily or gladly. When she pointed this out to Iona, the old lady looked at her with something close to surprise.

"But of course men think of their women like that," she said. "And no bemoaning the fact will change it. One day you might even find there's advantages in it, child."

It was not what she wanted to hear, but even Lily understood that to lecture Wee Iona on the rights of women and the writings of Mrs. Wollstonecraft would be a waste of time. Instead she waited for Simon's next visit and pointed out to him, straightaway, she was not a prisoner in her brother's home, that she might leave when she pleased. To that she added—before he could do it for her—that Luke had made a home for her here and deserved the courtesy of an explanation.

One more battle lost; she must face her brother, and defend her choices.

"Your brother is no dragon," Iona said. "Anything he has to say to you will be just, though probably not pleasant."

That was just what Lily feared. That Luke would tell her that she was being foolish to run home like this in the dead of winter, in time of war, with a man who might not be welcome at Lake in the Clouds, once the whole truth was revealed. She could not tell Luke all of it, for that would only make her look the bigger fool: using one man to go to another who did not want her.

Even Ghislaine, who should have been her natural ally, had little of comfort to say. "Your brother will make noises like a bull, but in the end, what can he do? You have already settled the matter between you."

Lily had hoped she could keep the nature of her attachment to Simon a secret, but Ghislaine made short work of that conceit. On the morning after the deal was struck she had brought Lily her morning coffee and stood at the foot of the bed with a small smile, a little sad.

"So," she said. "Now you know."

She knew, yes. She knew Simon Ballentyne in every way a woman could know a man, and oddly enough, she felt that she hardly knew him at all. He was, simply, the most frustrating human being she had ever come across.

They argued about everything, from how much she could pack to take back to Lake in the Clouds, to whether or not they should tell people of their engagement, to Lily's eating habits. When they were together they argued, or rather, Simon made an announcement, which caused Lily's temper to flare. She explained herself at length while Simon listened, stone-faced and unbending, or laughed out loud, or cooed at her and called her hen and lovey until she must laugh herself, or box his ears.

Iona watched it all with a half-smile, not the least worried, it seemed to Lily, which must be a good sign; surely Luke could have no real objection, if his grandmother did not.

Then Luke came home on a sledge piled high with boxes and barrels and bundles, filthy as a trapper after a winter in the bush, his skin burnished by snow and sun and wind. One look at him and Lily's courage failed her; she was glad, for once, to stand back and let someone else do the talking.

It was Simon who told him, standing in the hall. He said what must be said clearly and cleanly and without apology, and Luke listened, his head bowed a little, looking at Lily from under the shelf of his brow with an expression she couldn't quite name. She tried to meet his gaze evenly, and almost succeeded.

When Simon was finished Luke thought for a moment, his mouth pursed. To Lily he said, "Are you with child?"

"No!" She jumped as if he had made to strike her, and felt the color flashing up from her chest, over her neck to her face. Because, of course, it was too early to really know the answer to that question. She might be, of course. Though she had resisted the temptation to go back to Simon's bed since that first night—and temptation was the only word for the sleepless hours she spent thinking of doing just that—she must admit to herself that it might already be too late.

Every morning she felt Ghislaine looking at her and thinking just the same thing. Ghislaine knew the rhythm of her month just as well as Lily did, and would not let her pretend to forget. This was the other reason Lily wanted to leave Montreal straightaway, before the day came when she must bleed, or know herself caught, well and truly, in Simon Ballentyne's web. Somehow it would be easier to cope with that particular question if she was far away from here, and Iona's knowing eyes.

"Then there's no hurry," Luke said. "You can wait until it's safe to travel."

"We leave tomorrow," Simon said. His voice even and calm, and he would brook no disagreement. "I know the safe ways into New-York as well as you."

Luke seemed to be weighing that for a moment, and then he nodded.

"Why not marry before you leave?"

This was the question Lily had feared most, but Simon was ready for it.

"We could," Simon said. "But Lily wants to be married at home, with her mother and father's blessing."

"Ah," said Luke, and he ran a hand over his hair. "That will be the trick, now won't it?"

Just that easily it was settled, which both relieved Lily and upset her, contrary as she was. She went off to her chamber to finish packing, waiting for a knock at the door and hearing none. Finally it was Ghislaine who came to her, with a letter and a bundle.

"To take to Lady Jennet," she said. "He's writing another letter to your father."

Lily took the letter and tossed it on the bed, piled high with things to be folded away into her trunk. Then she burst into tears and was glad of Ghislaine, who put her arms around her and rocked her as a sister would, whispering soft words that were no comfort at all.

Luke gave her two presents, just before they set off: a thin, sharp knife in a beautiful beaded sheath, and a gun. In the confusion of leaving she had little time to look at it nor could she, really: her eyes were filled with tears that threatened to fall, no matter how she might forbid them.

"If the time comes to use them, don't hesitate," Luke said, touching her cheek with one finger. "Though I doubt it will. Ballentyne will look after you as well as I could." It was the only compliment Simon cared to hear, or needed, and for his sake Lily was glad, and pleased with her brother.

Then they were off, the sleigh moving silently through the familiar lanes and then they were passing the garrisons, crawling with soldiers and militiamen whose job it was to protect the city from American invasion.

That was something people were truly worried about, though they had very little regard for the Americans in general and certainly none at all for American military prowess. On this matter at least Luke agreed with the rest of Montreal. Whenever the subject came up he snorted and said that an army so poorly organized and run as the American army was more likely to be invading the Plattsburgh taverns than Lower Canada. And still the threat hung in the air: Lily counted three different groups drilling, but they were too far away for her to make out any familiar faces.

On the ice road the horses whinnied to each other in the winter sun, touched noses and broke into a fast trot while Lily looked back over her shoulder at Montreal, numb not so much from the cold as from confusion.

Now that she was on her way home she couldn't remember, quite, why she had been in such a hurry to leave. She thought of Ghislaine and the other servants in the steamy kitchen, of Monsieur Picot, who had thundered at her when she told him she was leaving, and Monsieur Duhaut, who had wept a little and pressed a present into her hands: a miniature of herself, so beautifully done that Lily had felt immediately guilty.

How often do we find love in the world, that it should be set aside so thoughtlessly?

The thought came from her in her mother's voice, and for a

moment Lily regretted that she had not been kinder to Monsieur Duhaut, who was far from home, as she was, but with no way to go home, as she was doing now.

People had come from all over to wish her a good journey and well in her marriage, words that made her jump and twitch, which people took for a bride's shy manner because they could not see the truth of it. Lily would have preferred to keep the whole thing quiet for she was not sure, yet, that she would marry Simon; that was something she dared not say aloud, but it was still the truth, no matter how foolish: she was not ready, not yet, to concede that Nicholas was lost to her.

But in this matter Luke and Simon agreed: the engagement must be announced. Otherwise the gossips would claim that Luke's sister had eloped with his business partner, and both men were too proud to have such things said about themselves, or her.

"He is thinking ahead," said Ghislaine when Lily complained about the fuss her brother was making over this engagement. "You may want to come back to Montreal and make a home here, one day."

And that was the problem exactly, Lily realized as Montreal disappeared from view. She did like the city; she liked everything about it, the people and the noise and even the smells, though in the summer, she was warned, she would change her mind. She liked Montreal and she missed her home, and she felt herself caught between them. If by some miracle Nicholas Wilde might still marry her—and it would be a miracle, she understood that—she would never see this place again. For as long as she could remember she had wanted Nicholas to claim her; she wanted it still, she reminded herself, but the cost was higher now.

The one thought she could hold on to was this: she must know, once and for all. Had Simon Ballentyne not agreed to take her back to her mother, she would have soon been desperate enough to have done something truly foolish.

Like pledging yourself to a man you hardly know.

She pushed the voice away and settled back in the furs, taking the chance to study Simon, or the little bit she could see of him that was not well covered. All of Montreal believed that she was about to marry him. *Lucky you,* the baker's daughter had said, hardly hiding her disappointment. *Lucky you.*

Simon sent her a sidelong glance, a smiling one from the way his eyes creased at the corner, and spoke a few firm words to the horses.

Lily was warm and comfortable, which was a good thing, indeed, for she would be spending a great deal of time just like this, sitting beside Simon Ballentyne on her way home to her mother and father and her own bed under the eaves, to her brother and cousins and friends. To Nicholas Wilde.

In time the rhythm of hooves on the ice lulled her away into sleep, where she stayed until late in the afternoon when the sleigh came to a stop in front of a cabin deep in the woods. A trapper's cabin like a hundred others, with nothing to distinguish it except that it seemed deserted, no smoke coming from the chimney or snowshoes on the porch.

"A good six hours without an argument, but then you slept for most of it so I suppose it won't count." One of the horses, the one called Pete, turned its head to nudge Simon and he laughed out loud and clapped a hand on its neck, as he would a friendly dog.

Lily sat up, confused and sputtering, but Simon was already gone, leading the horses off to brush and feed them in the lean-to stable. She sat for a moment and watched him, and then she fought her way out of the furs and the sleigh, holding her wraps around her as she waded through snow to the tiny front porch and then stumbled through the door into the dark cabin.

Lily found the flint box on the mantel and enough kindling to start a fire, her fingers stiff at first and then warming quickly to the familiar task. If Simon Ballentyne thought she was helpless he would have to think again, for she had been brought up on the New-York frontier and knew more of this kind of life than he could begin to imagine. For months she had lived in a house with servants, but it would take far longer than that for Nathaniel Bonner's daughter to forget how to take care of herself in a cabin in the woods.

The fledgling fire showed her the rest of the little room: one window with shutters nailed in place for the season, two cots with threadbare blankets over sagging corn-shuck mattresses, a rough table and stools, a few tin dishes and cups, a box of candles almost empty. Somewhere nearby there would be a well or a stream or a rain barrel, but that job would require an axe, too, to get through the ice and she was content to leave that to Simon. Instead she put her cloak back on and made trips back into the dusk: for her satchel, for provisions, for three armloads of firewood from under the tarpaulin against the north side of the cabin. She was full awake now and hungry and glad of the work.

When Simon came in from looking after the horses and the rig he found the fire blazing, the beds made with furs from the sleigh, and the table set for supper. Without a word Lily handed him the water bucket and he backed out again, smiling at her but saying not a word. Later while she set water to boil he cleaned his guns and then they sat down to a simple meal of bread and cold meat and tea.

And still he said nothing at all, which was at first as Lily wanted it and then, slowly, not what she wanted at all. She was aware of the cots behind her, the shadows that the fire threw against the wall, and Simon's hands. She watched the turn of his wrist as he cut meat and lifted his cup and rubbed the beard stubble on his cheek and with every bite she swallowed down things she might have said.

Finally he cleared his throat and met her eye directly.

"You haven't asked, but I'll tell you anyway," he said in an easy, reasonable tone. "We stopped early today because the next cabin like this, one that we can use safely, is a good day's journey away."

Then he got up from the table and went to the cot farthest from the fire, where he lay down and, just that simply, went to sleep.

For three days it went just like that: a long day in the sleigh, a few hours in a strange cabin, and then they went to their separate beds. When they did speak—of food or firewood or other matters that could not be ignored—the tone was pleasant and unremarkable. On the second night Simon examined the pistol that Luke had given Lily. It was only twelve inches long, and it fit her hand neatly.

"An officer's pistol," she said. "From all the engraving and scroll-work."

"Your brother thinks a great deal of your marksmanship," Simon said. "For you'll have to aim true to do any damage with this. But I'll keep it primed and loaded, nonetheless."

"It's true I'm not as good a shot as my father or brother, but I had good teachers," Lily said. She heard the defensive note in her own voice, and wished it away.

"It was the pistol I was doubting," said Simon. "Not you, lass." He leaned over and kissed her, a quick stamp of the mouth that was over before she could register surprise.

Lily could not call herself dissatisfied or unhappy, not exactly. Simon was everything he should be—everything her brother would want him to be—thoughtful and helpful and polite above all. It was precisely because they had run out of things to argue about, Lily reasoned to herself, that she was sleeping so much.

She slept on strange cots, deeply and without dreams; she slept the days away in the sleigh. She could not think how to start a conversation, and so she slept. Sometimes the reasonable part of herself wondered why she was acting as she was, what exactly she meant to prove by holding back this way, but she was too sleepy to pursue such complicated questions and so she didn't; she pulled the furs over her head and let herself drift away again.

For Simon's part, he seemed vaguely amused by everything, not in an ill humor or any humor at all.

Then on the third day, as she made yet another strange cabin comfortable for the night, it came to Lily that Simon Ballentyne was a great deal like her father, in at least one way. He had the gift of *patience,* a word far too simple to really convey the quality. It was the thing that made the difference between a man who learned to hunt and one born to hunt. Her father had it and her grandfather and brothers and her uncle Runs-from-Bears and his sons. Men who could wait with utter calm because they understood their prey as it did not understand itself, knew what it was thinking and feeling and what it needed, most of all.

Simon Ballentyne was like her father in this one, crucial way, and Nicholas Wilde was not, and never could be.

It was that thought that woke Lily out of her long sleep, once and for all, on the night that the blizzard started. On the heels of that thought came another one: her courses were late. Just two days late, but late nonetheless when she could never remember, even once, when her bleeding had failed to start with the full moon.

They were sitting at supper when this realization came to her. Lily looked at Simon, who had already started the evening ritual of looking after his weapons. Today he had shot a turkey and they had eaten fresh meat for the first time since Montreal.

Lily looked at him and saw that a perfect line of three pin feathers had settled along one straight black brow and it struck Lily fast and hard: it was the funniest thing she had ever seen.

At first it was just a hiccup of laughter, coming up from her belly, but soon she could hardly contain herself; she leaned forward to put her forehead on the table and her shoulders shook and shook with the force of it. She laughed until the tears came and laughed more, raised her head to try to explain and saw the feathers buckle and dance as he drew his brows together, fixed as surely as quills sewn to leather. She pointed, weak with laughter.

Simon touched a finger to his brow, pulled away the pin feathers and looked at them with a blank expression while Lily laughed on and on and tears ran down her face to plop onto the table, great fat drops like rain. Then Simon was up and pulling her up too, holding her against his chest while she laughed and cried and tried to talk, all at once. He held her very close, his arms around her so that she could let herself go limp and not be afraid of falling, and Lily remembered suddenly and without warning her mother bent over Gabriel when he was just a few days old, Gabriel bawling like a calf, red faced and furious, his toothless mouth open to tell the world that he did not like the order of things, not one bit. And Lily's mother talking to him, calmly, reasonably, while she folded a blanket up and across and across again and then flipped him neatly, binding him toe to head, so firmly that he couldn't kick or wave his arms or fight, and just that simply he stopped, closed his mouth with an audible click and looked up at her, his mother, their mother, and all was right with his world because he was caught, well and truly in the web she had made for him, and the comfort of that was absolute.

Against her ear Simon Ballentyne said, "Ach, Lily my love. You've got the heart of a lion, lass, but you must learn to bend or you will break."

They stood like that for a long time until her breathing had righted itself, the shuddering lessening until she could hear the beat of her own heart and his, the fire whispering to itself, the wind in the trees around them, purposeful and growing louder.

Lily let herself be led to the single cot, she let Simon tuck her in and kiss her cheek. She watched him wipe the table and heat water and get out his razor and set about shaving, something he hadn't done since they left Montreal. He scraped the bristle from his cheeks and chin and throat carefully, working without a mirror, using his fingertips to tell him what he needed to know.

Then he came to her and sat on the floor on the furs and blankets he had put down for himself. That way he could look at her directly, his face so close that she could smell the soap still on his skin.

"Sleep," he told her. "Go to sleep now, lass, and I'll keep watch."

•   •   •

When she woke, finally, thirsty beyond memory, the skin of her face tight with dried tears, it was to the howling of the blizzard. The only light in the world came from the banked fire, a few pulsing coals. Lily sat up and tried to remember where the water bucket might be.

"I'll fetch you a cup," Simon said in the darkness beside her, and she started at the sound of his voice, so close, and then settled back and waited while he stirred the fire and moved through the near dark. Then he pressed the cup into her hands and she drank greedily, icy clear water that was the best thing she could ever remember tasting.

"What time is it?" she asked finally, pressing the cup to her cheek.

"Past dawn," he said. "But you needn't rouse yourself. We can't travel in this storm." He sent her a glance over his shoulder. "I'll go see to the horses."

It was his way of giving her some privacy, and Lily was glad of it. When he was gone she drew out a cracked chamber pot from its spot beneath the cot and laughed out loud to find that it had been painted, not with flowers or vines, but with the likeness of old King George.

The mad king had no good news for her: her courses had not started, and now she was too awake to put that thought conveniently out of mind. While she washed in the last of the water and shook out her clothes and brushed her hair, she thought of that simple lack of blood and tried to reconcile herself to what it most probably meant, until Simon came in and suggested a game of cards.

They played through the morning, talking a little of unimportant things and drinking cup after cup of strong tea laced with sugar, a going-away gift from Ghislaine, who had been worried about the lack of comforts during such a long and difficult journey. When they tired of cards Simon lit a candle and Lily read to him, first from *Poor Richard's Almanac,* a little book she had taken with her to Canada out of sentimentality, and finally from one of the newspapers her mother had sent, not from the essays or war reports but the advertisements.

"Oh, look," Lily said. "Poor Mr. Mather, his wife has run off again."

Simon sat straight up and looked at her. "You know this Mather?"

"Not really," Lily said. "Except through the advertisements he puts in the paper, just about every year at this time." She read: "'Hereby be it known that Margaret Mather, lawful wife of the subscriber, has eloped from a faithful and good husband. She took with her a half-dozen silver spoons as well as the subscriber's best coat with pewter buttons. A reward will be paid for return of the silver and coat, but a husband so oft maligned is glad to be free. This time he will not allow the wanton back into his home. He will pay no debts of her contracting. Jonah Mather, Butcher. Boston Post Road.'"

Simon frowned at Lily as though she had made the whole thing up. "You mean to say this isn't the first time the man has put such a thing in the paper?"

"I'm afraid not," Lily said. "She seems to leave him at least once a year, and he always claims he will not take her back again. But it looks as though she does come back, and he does take her in, and then in the deep of winter, she goes again."

Simon grunted. "The more fool him, to put up with it. Has the man no pride?"

"What he has, I suppose, is hope." Lily put down the paper. "What would you have him do when she comes back? Turn her out to starve?"

"I wouldn't be waiting for her," Simon said, putting both hands flat on the table and leaning toward her a little, as if he were speaking a language she only understood imperfectly. "She would come back to find me gone, for I'll let no one make a fool of me twice."

There was a moment's silence between them, awkward and uneasy, filled with the howling of the storm.

"My mother says that love makes a fool of everyone."

If Lily could have reached out and caught up those words out of the air, she would have done it. But they were said, and they had done their mischief. Across the table from her Simon Ballentyne's expression had gone very still, but his eyes were sharp with anger. He got up so suddenly that the table rocked on its legs.

"I'm off to look after the horses." In a moment he was gone, the door shutting firmly behind him.

She had hurt his feelings, or his pride. Or both, Lily told herself, because of course she had reminded him of what might be ahead. She was not his, not really; she might never be. Most of the time he kept his uncertainty and hopes to himself, but they were there, just under the surface. Like a careless child with a stick, she had poked too hard and exposed what he was determined to keep to himself.

• • •

For their supper they ate turkey stew with the last of the bread and some cheese. The silence was heavier now, fraught with things that Lily wanted to say, but could not. How could she apologize for the truth? And yet she wanted to, because she did not like to see him unhappy. An odd pair they made, the two of them, each with tender secrets that could not stay hidden for long. Lily turned her face away from him when these thoughts came, lest he should see for himself what she would not say.

Simon did not tuck her in or kiss her cheek, and Lily was first surprised and then hurt and then angry at herself; she could not have things both ways after all. If she wanted . . . what? What was it she wanted from him? She turned over and tried again to sleep, without success.

It was the noise of her own thoughts that kept her awake, louder than the storm and just as relentless. On the floor beside the cot Simon was a great mountain of furs, absolutely still. In the dim she watched for the telltale white of his breath in the chill room, and decided in the end that he must have turned his face downward. Surely that was it; if she watched long enough he would shift in his sleep and then she could see that he was breathing. He was a healthy man in his prime, after all. He could not simply leave her here alone, no matter how angry he was at her.

She coughed into her fist to relieve the tickle in her throat, once and then again. Leaned over the mountain that must be Simon and coughed again.

He sat up so suddenly that their heads knocked, hard, and Lily fell from the cot, all flailing arms and legs, keening with surprise and embarrassment and pain too.

"What!" Simon half shouted. "What!"

He grabbed her by the shoulders and peered at her face and Lily realized first, that he was not completely awake nor was he asleep, and second, that she had put herself in a terrible position, for how was she ever to explain this?

Simon blinked at her and touched his own forehead where a bump must surely rise, and fell back into the confusion of furs.

"Christ, Lily," he said, his voice hoarse. "You'll be the death of me. What do you mean by barking at me like that?"

"You weren't breathing," she said. To her own ears she sounded more silly than defiant, and to his, too, for he sat up again and glared at her, his face painted red by the glow of coals from the hearth.

"I wasn't breathing?"

"You—you didn't seem to be." She tried to get up and was defeated by the tangle of covers. Yanked at them furiously, near tears and angry with herself and mortified beyond all experience.

"I was worried," she said, and then she dared to cast a glance at him, only to find that he was smiling.

"Lily Bonner," he said. "Every night I've waited for you to ask me to share your bed. A simple word would have been enough. No need to bang me in the head first."

By the time he had finished she was sputtering in anger, unable to find a curse hard enough to throw in his face. She would have cuffed him instead, if she had been able to find her hands, and so she settled for howling, putting back her head and howling to the rafters, which only made him laugh harder.

He reached to help her and she elbowed him as hard as she could, not hard enough to stop him laughing or even to stop his clever hands, moving fast and sure, and then she was free, her hair swirling around her head.

For just a moment she drew in breath, her chest heaving, and then she reached down deep to summon the memory of her mother in a temper, that look of hers that made the world tremble. Lily gave that very look to Simon Ballentyne.

Who grinned at her, and brushed the hair away from her face.

"Come, hen," he said, catching her hand to bring her closer. "Come lay your head."

"I will not," she said. "I was not—not—"

"Of course not. It was gey wicked of me to say such a thing." He crooned to her, soft and softer still. "I'm sorry I laughed, truly I am. Come, catch your breath. Breathe easy, love."

"You—" she began. "You're—"

"Hopeless, aye, it's true." Somehow she was lying beside him and he was bent over her, supporting himself on his arm. "A witless man. A fool in love."

He kissed her then, softly and sweetly and with devastating effectiveness. His beard had already begun again and his cheeks were rough to the touch and cool, and in response something small and warm ignited deep in Lily's belly, something strange and oddly familiar at the same time.

"Will ye gang back tae your bed?" He was whispering against her neck, his mouth moving against the tender skin below her ear so that her flesh rose and shivered.

"Or will ye bide?" That damnable question she had hoped never to have to answer again. So she turned her head to touch his mouth with her own: an invitation, a demand, a plea for rescue from the decision he was pressing on her.

He pulled back to look at her. "Lily."

"What?" She pushed out a great sigh. "What do you want me to say?" And bit her lip until it hurt, for she already knew what he wanted but now she must listen to him tell her.

He pursed his mouth in mock thoughtfulness and then rolled over to lie on his back, his hands behind his head.

"Repeat after me," he began.

"Oh, no." Lily pressed her face into the covers.

" 'Simon, please let me bide here with you, for I have no wish to go back to my lonely bed.' "

Lily summoned all the self-control she had. "I will not say that."

"Good night, then."

She sat up. "You are infuriating."

"You only need say what you want, lass."

"I don't know what I want."

He blinked at her and said nothing.

Lily turned her face away. "I'm afraid."

He put a hand over hers, ran it up her arm. "Afraid of me, Lily?"

"No. No, I'm not afraid of you. I'm afraid of—"

Too many things to name, but the images were bright in her mind; blinding in their clarity.

"Getting with child," he supplied for her and those words hit her as surely as a fist. When she opened her eyes he was looking at her with surprise, and unease, and dawning understanding.

"It's like that, is it?" he said softly, his hand closing more firmly around hers.

She turned her head away, or tried to, but he would have none of that. He caught her chin and studied her face, his expression keen and sharp, as if he were looking at something he had never seen before, and Lily supposed that that much was true: she was carrying his child, after all. She drew in a hiccupping breath.

"Ach, Lily." He drew her down until her head was nested on his shoulder and closed his arms around her.

After a while he said, "You may not care to believe me, but I would not have had it happen so quick."

She did believe him, and it did help, but she could not make herself say that out loud.

"And still, there's one thing to be thankful for," Simon said more softly, his fingers tracing a pattern on the skin of her throat.

He was thinking of her father, no doubt, that he would not object to the marriage if she was carrying Ballentyne's child. Lily was just about to explain that her father might very well object when the warmth of Simon's breath distracted her.

He had shifted a little so that they were face to face. "If you've fallen pregnant already, why, the deed is done. We needn't worry about it happening, lass, for it already has."

She found herself almost smiling, which would not do, not at all. "Trust a man to see it that way."

One brow peaked, and on its heels a flash of the dimples he had hidden for so long. "You mean to sleep alone, then?"

Lily barked a sharp laugh. "You mean to make me ask, don't you?"

"Ach, aye." Simon pressed her against him, so she would understand how serious his purpose, and how intent he was on getting the answer from her that she wanted to give him.

"Unless it's just a few kisses you're after," he said, almost innocently. "Those I'll give you without asking. To start with. You tell me when you've had enough."

Lily put her arms around his neck, suddenly at peace, ready to capitulate the battle, if not the war. It felt good to let Simon Ballentyne hold her.

Chapter 22

"Now this," said Jennet, "this is curious."

She tapped a finger on the table and sent Martha and Callie a questioning look. "What do you make of it?"

The girls leaned toward the two cards that lay face up and crossed one over the other.

Callie pressed a knuckle to her upper lip. "The empress?"

"And the wheel of fortune," added Martha.

"The empress *crossed* by the wheel of fortune." Jennet sat back and held out her hands, palms up, and wiggled her fingers. "We laid out this cross for Hannah. What is she to learn from it?"

"Change is coming." Callie lifted her face and looked directly at Hannah, who sat across the table with her daybook open before her. "You must be diligent."

On the other side of the kitchen Curiosity let out a gruff laugh as she took the lid off the lye barrel and dumped in a hopper full of ash. "Now maybe that's what those cards want to tell us," she said. "But that ain't no news. We know the sun going to set, too, and come up again."

Martha flushed a little. "But this means great change, doesn't it? Something *big*."

Curiosity met Hannah's gaze, a smile jerking at the corner of her mouth. It was good to see that Martha was able to get up at least a little temper; the girl was too timid by far.

"It does," Jennet said. "Something that calls for considerable caution and care."

"I suppose there could be news of the war," Lucy said from her spot at the big loom.

"The post rider is due tomorrow, and he's always got news," added Sally.

"Och, you mustn't waste your time guessing," Jennet said, gathering up cards from different piles to square them neatly. "Whatever it is will come soon enough. Now I understand the two of you have schoolwork, is that no the case?"

"Just once more, please," said Martha. "Just one more cross for Hannah, maybe it will make things clearer."

Jennet rolled her eyes and smiled, too, in case the girls understood her sigh for what it really was, no more than a bit of playfulness. In her hands the shuffling cards flapped like wings as they flew from hand to hand. Then she flipped one onto the table and laid another across it.

"The seven and the knight of swords." Her smile faltered and then flickered back. "Silly me," she said, scooping them up. "It's only the face cards you're meant to use when laying out a cross."

The deck disappeared into her apron pocket as she got up. "Off with you now, the two of you, or you won't have your lessons ready and then Elizabeth will come looking for me, and what would I say in my defense? And I did promise Ethan that I would help him with his packing this afternoon . . ." Her voice trailed away, unconvinced and unconvincing.

But the girls did as they were told, still far too unsettled in this new home to even contemplate disobedience, though Martha cast a glance back from the door.

"The knight of swords, that card has to do with soldiering, don't it?"

Then she left without waiting for an answer, and the women in the kitchen were quiet together while they listened to the sound of the girls settling down to their work in the parlor.

"They are so serious, those two," Jennet said finally.

"Cain't recall the last time I heard them laugh," agreed Sally.

"Don't you change the subject," Curiosity said, coming to the table to sit across from Jennet. "That knight of swords has got you worried, don't it?"

Hannah caught a questioning glance from her cousin and returned it with a smile. "Don't hold back on my account," she said, and tried to mean it; she hadn't decided, yet, how she felt about Jennet's fortune-telling. For the most part she listened and kept her thoughts to herself.

"Well," Jennet said. "It does, aye. The knight of swords crossed by the seven is worrisome. A dangerous trip over water for a military man."

"Is that so."

Curiosity kept her thoughts to herself while her granddaughters made the looms clack and thump, thump and clack. "Just as well you ain't got no menfolk in the navy, then, Hannah."

"Just as well," Hannah echoed. She smiled at Jennet to ease the concern she saw there in her face. "Why did you send the girls away?"

Jennet pulled a bowl of soaking beans toward her and began to sort through them. "Martha worries so about the war, surely you've noticed?"

"Better to worry about something far off that don't feel quite real than to be thinking about her mama all the time," said Curiosity. And in mock outrage: "Why, are you laughing at me, missy?"

"Oh, no," said Hannah. "I'm just wondering if I'll ever be as quick as you are. What a clan mother you would have been."

That earned her a crooked smile and a sniff.

Jennet said, "She is a clan mother, look about you. A house full of girls and women and all of us happy to jump at her word. Those girls would do anything for you, Curiosity, but even you cannot keep them safe in their dreams. Martha is still screaming in the night?"

"She'll settle down in good time," Curiosity said. And then they were silent again, because for once Curiosity was reluctant to say the whole truth out loud: it would take more than time to cure what ailed Martha Kuick, who ran a gauntlet every time they went into the village or to the schoolhouse. Just yesterday the Ratz boys had waited for her and Callie after school—well out of Elizabeth's sight or hearing—to ask was it true that Martha's mother had put a hex on Callie's?

The girls had walked away, stiff backed and blank of face, until they came into Curiosity's kitchen, where they wept openly.

"We cain't lock those girls up," Curiosity said now, reading Hannah's thoughts as easily as words on a page. "Not even to keep them safe. Now I know Elizabeth has talked to the boys, but look to me like they need another kind of convincing. And your daddy is just the man to have a little set-down with those nasty-minded boys, show them the way of things. Yessir, Nathaniel will stop the talking." She looked like she relished the idea. Then she lifted her head sharply toward the door, for the dogs had begun to bark in the way that meant that someone they knew and liked was coming to the door.

"That will be him now," Curiosity said with some satisfaction. "He said he would stop by late afternoon."

But it was Jed McGarrity, and his news was not good. When he had made sure the girls were out of hearing he laid it out plain.

"Jemima's got a gash on her head that needs stitching," he explained, clutching his snowy cap to his middle. "She says she won't let herself be sewed up, but if she bleeds to death then I'll have to charge Nicholas Wilde with murder, and that's one thing I'd like to avoid."

"Did he beat her?" Jennet asked, concerned but not surprised at the idea. In the village they talked constantly of the things that went on at the cabin in the orchard since Nicholas Wilde had come home from Johnstown without his divorce.

"Jemima says so, Claes says not." Jed scratched at his head with his thumb. "I ain't sure what happened, to tell the truth, except when I come up to the cabin—I was stopping by like I do every couple days or so, given all the trouble—and I saw Mima standing on the porch. Bloody-headed and pitching plates against the wall and howling like one of them banshees you told us about, Miss Jennet. I thought it was best if I came to fetch you, Hannah, as she's in a family way. Will you come?"

Jed was not a coward, but Hannah had rarely seen a man look more relieved than he was when she told him she would go to the orchards on her own.

Lately she had so little chance to spend any real time alone, first and foremost because somebody seemed to come by at least once a day who needed medical attention, and second because her own people were so worried about her that they hovered. She didn't dislike either circumstance, exactly, but she needed this too, a world empty of people who wanted something from her or for her.

The air was cold on her skin, the snow such a deep and pure white that her eyes leaked tears that would have frozen on her cheeks if not for the good wool scarf that Curiosity had wrapped around her, clucking all the while. Hannah followed elk tracks through the woods to the orchards, and then she stood there, a little winded, and gathered her thoughts.

The last time Hannah had come to the orchard cabin was to see Dolly in the fall. They had sat together on the porch and listened to the workings of the cider mill, a great creaking that reminded Hannah of the noise of a ship at full sail, except it was not wind that moved the cider works but mules. Cookie had been stirring a big iron pot of apple butter and singing to herself, an old ballad well suited to her husky deep voice. The whole world had smelled of apples, and that afternoon, at least, Dolly had seemed a little better.

Those few months ago and so much had changed. When Cookie Fiddler had had the care of this place it had been comfortable, well ordered, and clean inside and out: the porch swept, the kitchen garden weeded and fenced from the attentions of a dozen fat and sassy hens.

Now the snow had wiped most of that away, and the drifts around the porch were littered with broken dishware, the remains of a shattered stool, and a spattering of blood. The cabin itself was quiet, so quiet that a shiver of unease ran up Hannah's back. She waited for a moment, listening to the sound of the wind in the bare branches of the apple trees. At the first step she hesitated and considered the evidence of mayhem at her feet: pottery shards covered with a pattern of twining roses, the handle of a jug, a dented tin cup.

She looked up to see Nicholas Wilde on the porch. He ran a hand over his face and blinked at her, as if he were trying to remember her name.

"Come in," he said evenly. "Come in and see what there is to be done."

"This must make you happy," Jemima said. She was sitting, back straight, on a stool by the hearth. She met Hannah's gaze straight on and composed while blood dribbled over her cheek and neck from a deep gash just over her ear. "What a treat for you. You'll be writing to your sister about this, no doubt. To pass on the good news."

"I'll need more light, Nicholas, please," Hannah said as she took what she needed from her bag. And: "Could you open the shutters? Jemima, I'll have to cut some hair away from the wound to clean it out."

"And what distress it will cause you," Jemima said.

Nicholas brought the things she asked for while Hannah started her work, and through it all Jemima talked, her hands clenched tightly in her lap.

"They'll want all the details in the village too," she said. "So let me tell you what happened. My good husband tried to throw me out of the house. He doesn't want me to wife, you understand, but the law won't oblige him. So he threw me out the door and I fell down the stairs and cracked my head. No doubt he was hoping I'd lose the child, but I'm not bleeding. Do you hear that, Claes? I'm still with child, and with child I'll stay until I bring it into this world, a son, if there's any justice, to carry on your sorry name. And I'll be sure to tell him, as soon as he's old enough to understand, that his father tried to do away with the both of us. He wants to divorce me, you see, and take up again with your sister Lily. I'll make that especially clear to the boy, that the Bonners were behind all of it. We'll sit right there at that table every day and I'll remind him what kind of man his father is, who would throw a pregnant wife off a porch."

Nicholas said, "I'll fetch more water."

"Jed wanted to know if I would press charges." Jemima laughed. "Stupid man. As if I would deprive myself of my husband's loving care and company."

Hannah cleaned the wound and drew it together, working as quickly and gently as she could and still, she knew, it must cause considerable pain. But Jemima gave no sign of it, not even when the needle pierced her scalp, though she shuddered like a woman in a deep fever.

"Of course, Jed will be back," Jemima said, her voice cracking with effort. "Tomorrow or the day after when my good husband loses his temper again. Maybe next time he'll kill me. That's what he'd like to do, you understand. I'm sure he lays awake at night thinking of it, wherever it is that he sleeps. Just to be clear, now that I have such an honorable and respected witness, let me say this: if you find me dead, you'll know it was my husband who did it."

Nicholas Wilde said, "If there's nothing else you need, I'll wait on the porch."

"He doesn't talk to me, you're meant to understand," Jemima said tightly. "Hasn't said a word to me since he got back from Johnstown. He'll talk to you. He talks to his horse and to the apple trees and to the clouds in the sky, but he won't say a word to me. He does his best to ignore me, does my good husband, but sooner or later he'll understand that I won't be ignored."

"One more stitch," Hannah said.

"You're cut of the same cloth, aren't you. Think you can stand there and ignore me, high-and-mighty Hannah Bonner."

Hannah said, "Once I amputated a leg on the bare ground. The smoke was so thick in the air that I could hardly see the scalpel in my hand. There were horses screaming and men too, and the fighting was so close that my ears rang for a week afterward with gunshot. And that was the least of it. So maybe you'll understand, Jemima, that your whining doesn't slow me down at all."

With that she tied off the last stitch and stood back.

Jemima's complexion had drained of all color. Her hands twisted convulsively in her lap and a shudder ran through her whole body, but she never turned her head toward Hannah.

"Get out," she whispered. "Get out of my house and never come back. I'll bleed to death before I let you touch me again."

"Do you want me to take a message to your daughter?"

Jemima looked at her then, a look so blankly hostile that a knot of fear rose up from Hannah's gut to lodge in her throat.

"I had a daughter once," Jemima said. "But she's dead to me. All I've got now is this child I'm carrying and a husband who doesn't want me."

"And a roof over your head," Hannah said. "And a full belly. You've thrown everything else away, but maybe you can hold on to that much."

On the porch she stood for a moment with Nicholas. There were things to say, but she couldn't think, just for this moment, where to begin, or how; all she could see before her was her sister Lily as a young girl, running down the orchard on a summer day, her wild hair trailing behind her like a banner and the air full of her laughter. How she loved this place.

"I wanted to say—" he began.

"Wait," Hannah said. "You've got a bump on your head the size of a turkey egg. A snow compress will help a bit. If she starts to run a fever, you must come fetch me."

Snow had begun to fall in gentle waves of large, wet flakes, and Hannah turned her face up to the sky, glad of the clean cold air on her skin.

Nicholas said, "Two things I want to say. First, thank you for the kindnesses you've shown my Callie. She's better off with you just now. Nobody should have to live like this."

He swallowed hard, his voice catching. Hannah waited, her gaze focused on the orchard.

"The other thing is, I never touched Jemima. Not once. It's what she wants, but I won't be pushed to that. She did fall down the steps, but it wasn't my doing."

"Good," Hannah said, picking up her bag. She hesitated, and looked at him over her shoulder. "You could leave here," she said. "Take your daughter and start new somewhere else."

She saw the color spread up his neck, the fury and embarrassment and sorrow at work in the clenching of his jaw. He said, "I can't leave my orchard."

"Is that it?" Hannah asked. "Is that really what you can't leave?"

He said, "The child she's carrying is mine. I won't pretend otherwise."

For that much at least Hannah must respect this man, who had caused himself and others so much pain. "And Lily?" Hannah asked, although she had meant to keep her thoughts to herself. "What of Lily?"

He blinked at her. "Lily is lost to me," he said. "I know that."

"Good," Hannah said again, and left him there on his porch.

It was Elizabeth's experience that the middle of winter was the time when she was most likely to make real progress with her students, especially when the cold was deep and dry and unforgiving, as it was now. Even the most difficult of her charges—boys who hated anything that kept them indoors—would settle, twitching but resigned, with their primers and slates, glad of the hearth a little too large for this small cabin.

Of course, there was a price to be paid. In the good heat, with shutters and doors closed tight, it became clear, as it did every year, that many of Elizabeth's students would not bathe until ice-out. Some, it seemed, were sewn into their underclothes, a custom Elizabeth had heard about but could never quite explain to herself; the mechanics of it baffled and revolted her in equal measures. The end result was, the schoolhouse stank and would continue to stink, every day a little worse.

She thought idly of the new schoolhouse she was to build, and the possibility of a closet where students might wash, stocked with soap and towels and a tin hip bath. They would laugh her out of the village, of course, but she had been laughed at before. If she was to have a schoolhouse built—if she was to be compelled to do such a thing by Richard Todd, of all people—she would see it done to her own vision, exactly.

With some effort Elizabeth forced her attention back to her youngest students, who were in the middle of a recitation of the times tables. Maggie Cameron was mumbling and studying her shoes; later, Elizabeth would have to take her aside and see what was keeping Maggie from her studies. Leo Hench belched softly and the smell of pickled cabbage wafted through the little room.

Elizabeth pressed her handkerchief to her face, both to blunt the smell and to hide her grimace. There was no other way to cope with the thick miasma of wet wool permeated with body sweat, among other things.

Every year she set herself the task of solving the problem of the winter stink, as the children called it, and every year she failed. It had become a joke in the village. Her schoolboys, frontier raised and not easily offended, wagered on the day she could no longer keep her handkerchief in her sleeve. This year it had come out much earlier than usual.

"Teacher," called out Jem Ratz from the last bench that he shared with his two younger brothers. "Can we have a turn near the hearth next?"

If Elizabeth really were to give up teaching—something she was not sure that she wanted to do, just yet—it might well be the Ratz boys behind that decision. But the three of them were the youngest of their tribe and with any luck, she consoled herself, they would be the last.

Jem was looking at her with that particular blank stare of his that was meant to hide some new scheme coming laboriously to life behind dun-brown eyes. At almost thirteen Jem Ratz was as big as most full-grown men, broad of hulking shoulder, with a heavy, square head topped by a spiking of blond hair. A rash of pimples covered his forehead and cheeks and bracketed a full mouth filled with a jumble of strong white teeth.

Harry, a year younger, was almost as big and it was generally believed in the village that he would outstrip Jem by the end of the year. Henry, Harry's twin, was the smallest of the three, a boy as stout as a plug with hands and feet like great battered shovels.

Without Jem to lead them, Elizabeth knew, the twins would be mostly harmless. Studying them now, she wondered what kind of men they would grow into. Harry, called slow by his indulgent mother and witless by his impatient father, was picking his nose with great concentration while Henry studied the freckles on his hand.

"Teacher?" Jem said.

"In due time. When the recitation is over." She made herself turn back to the youngest students, who were watching her with that combination of awe and fear that she worked so hard to dispel. Frightened children could not attend to their work, she had always believed. Looking at the Ratz boys, she wondered if she had perhaps gone too far with this particular policy.

At the end of the next schoolday, Elizabeth called Callie Wilde and Martha Kuick to her and asked them to help her carry some baskets: she would walk them home, today, as she had business at the doctor's place.

From the corner of her eye she saw Jem Ratz freeze at this news, his brow coming down low and hard in displeasure. Once again the teacher was interfering with his plans, and he did not like it.

She smiled at him pleasantly. "Is something wrong, Jem? Harry? Henry?" And got in response only mumbled goodbyes and dark glances.

Later Martha said, "You can't walk us home every day, Miz Elizabeth."

Callie pressed a little closer to Elizabeth's other side so that their snowshoes touched. "But it would be nice if you could."

This was new. Until now the girls had denied any trouble; all the reports about the games the Ratz boys had been playing with these two came from the other children or from Curiosity. Elizabeth saw Callie and Martha exchanging glances and she held her tongue. It was the right thing to do, for after a few minutes that were filled only with the sound of their snowshoes and breathing, Callie hiccupped.

She said, "Is it true that witches are born with a mark on their bodies?"

Oh, for a whip when I next see those boys, Elizabeth thought, and: *Nathaniel was right, I cannot manage this on my own.*

She took a deep breath and forced her voice to its normal tone. "I have never read or heard of or seen any evidence that leads me to believe that there is any such thing as a witch. I think 'witch' is a label people use when they are frightened, and nothing more than that."

"But if there were witches?" Callie went on. "How would you know? Would there be a marking?"

At that Elizabeth stopped and looked first Callie and then Martha directly in the face. "Let me say this clearly. There are no witches in Paradise, or anywhere else, as far as I know. As there are no witches, talk of marks upon the body is without merit or sense."

There was a moment's silence, and then Martha said, "But I have one. I have a mark on my shoulder. A red moon, on my shoulder."

"Do you?" Elizabeth said, flushed with sudden anger. "A red moon on your shoulder? Well then, if we are to talk of marks on the body, what about this?"

And just like that she began to pull at her cloak, her fingers working fast at buttons and ties until she had bared a bit of her chest just below her throat. "You have a moon and I have a star. Does that make us witches together, or perhaps astronomers?"

It was madness, of course, in this weather, but the look on the girls' faces made it worthwhile. First wide-eyed with horror, then melting quickly toward surprise, and finally wobbling, fast and faster, into laughter.

Martha started it, a low, reluctant giggle that blossomed into something larger. Then Callie joined her, her mittens clamped to her mouth so that all that came out was a muffled squeaking. Then they were all laughing, great raucous laughter that echoed through the snowy woods and sent small animals scuttling. They laughed and laughed while Elizabeth righted her clothes, and then they went down to the village together, giggling softly to themselves all the way.

Of course, Elizabeth thought to herself when she was calm again, the Ratz boys could easily undo all the good work of that laughter, and they would, at their first chance. She was thinking about this and what could be done when they came over the bridge into the village and she saw Nathaniel standing outside the trading post, deep in conversation with Jed McGarrity and Martin Ratz. There was a heap of bloody carcasses on the ground before them. A sheep, Elizabeth saw as they came closer, and a wolf too. The deep snow had driven the pack from the mountain down to the village, where pickings were easier. They were hungry enough to take the risk, but this one had run out of luck.

Then Elizabeth caught a glimpse of the Ratz boys slinking around the far corner of the porch, and wondered what new devilment they had in mind.

"Boots," Nathaniel called to her when they were in earshot. "We were going to come look for you."

"That is a coincidence," Elizabeth said. She greeted the men and took a minute to send the girls into the trading post, where they could get warm by the hearth and be safely out of earshot.

"Mr. Ratz," she said finally. "I'm glad to see you here as well. Would you be so kind as to call your youngest three to come here? I think they are listening from just over there."

Martin Ratz was a tough little man, curt of manner but fair, for the most part; Hannah had done his family good service when the scarlet fever had come to Paradise, and saved all but one of his children. He would listen to her, at least, before disregarding what she had to say. Especially with Jed McGarrity and Nathaniel standing by.

For all their size the Ratz boys were clearly afraid of their smaller father, for they came when he called without hesitation or delay. All of them studied their feet while Elizabeth talked.

She said, "Apparently your sons have been busy studying up on witchcraft."

Martin Ratz squinted at her so that his face folded into wrinkles from eyelid to mouth. "What about witchcraft?"

"Pa—" Jem began.

His father cuffed the back of the boy's head so smartly that his cap flew off. "Hold your trap. Nobody was talking to you."

"They are convinced that you can tell a witch by a mark on her body," Elizabeth continued.

Nathaniel's mouth twitched, but he kept quiet. Jed was looking less amused, his arms crossed hard on his chest.

Ratz said, "Well, ain't that true? I always heard it was. Lots of folks believe it, anyway."

"People believe many things that are not true, Mr. Ratz. In any case, would you say that it is appropriate to ask little girls to disrobe in order to see if they have any such marks?"

"Disrobe?" Ratz scratched his chin, and then his eyes widened with understanding. "You mean, strip down?"

"I do."

"Strip down," he repeated thoughtfully, looking sideways at the three boys who were inching away from him.

"To the skin," Elizabeth said. "In this weather."

"Now, Marty," began Jed, seeing the way things were moving.

"Strip down to the skin," said Ratz, his voice rising and wobbling. "You three tried to get those girls to strip down to the skin."

"Pa—" began Harry, who was cuffed in turn by Jem.

Ratz narrowed his eyes thoughtfully. "Well, then, what's good for the goose is good for the gander, ain't that the way it goes?"

Nathaniel sent Elizabeth a grim look, one that said this matter was already out of hand and would get worse, if she did not keep her peace.

"It is," said Elizabeth. "But—"

"Well, then," Ratz interrupted. "You boys go on then, peel."

"Pa!" Jem began, stepping backward as his father advanced.

"Don't you *Pa* me," said Ratz. "Get on with it. Strip."

"We wouldn't have made those girls do anything," wailed Harry. "We just wanted to see if they're really witches."

"Strip down now," said their father, his color and voice rising apace, "or I'll do it for you."

Elizabeth would have appealed to Jed McGarrity to put a stop to such insanity, but he had retreated up the steps to the trading post porch where he stood with Callie and Martha. Martha looked alarmed and Callie satisfied at this turn of events.

"Those boys been looking for a beating for a good while now," Jed called to her. "This won't hurt as much."

The three boys were still backing away from their advancing father. Then they stopped, looked at each other, looked at him, and for a moment Elizabeth thought they had decided to get it over with.

At the last moment, Jem looked at the trading post porch, where a half-dozen of his classmates had appeared, all wearing wide grins.

Without a word the three boys broke and ran. Martin was after them in the same second, and on his heels a stream of children poured off the porch and out of the trading post. Only Callie and Martha stayed behind, blinking in the sunlight.

Elizabeth joined them on the porch where the view was better. They watched the chase through the village, the boys winding through frozen gardens and jumping woodpiles, dragging a long and bedraggled tail of children behind them. The noise was loud enough to rouse the rest of the village: old Missus Hindle came to her door with a baby on her hip and waved a spoon over her head to urge them all on.

Nathaniel said, "I don't think you girls will have any more trouble from the Ratz boys. And if you do, a word to Martin should set them straight in no time."

Callie and Martha, their eyes fixed on the chase, could only nod.

• • •

Later, Elizabeth and the girls told the story to an appreciative audience at Curiosity's hearth. Callie and Martha fell to giggling again when Elizabeth got to the part where Jem Ratz had skidded into a steaming manure pile.

"Did their pa ever get their clothes off them?" Sally asked.

"He did," said Elizabeth. "The last we saw of them, the boys were running down the river in nothing but their boots. They were as white as geese, from foot to neck."

"As long as they don't come down with lung fever," Curiosity said, who wanted to laugh but wasn't sure she quite approved. "Otherwise they'll be dragging our Hannah out to tend to those fool boys in the middle of the night."

"I don't think there is much chance of that," Elizabeth said. "They were only a minute from home. I'm sure their mother wrapped them up and got some tea into them."

At that Curiosity snorted; she thought very little of Martin Ratz, who simply refused to pay any midwife's fee for the birth of a daughter, and even less of Georgia, who was a slovenly housekeeper and could not control her own children.

"Where is Hannah?" said Jennet. "She's missed the telling of the story."

"Out in the barn," said Sally. "With her da."

"I'll go see her there," Elizabeth said.

"Don't be too long," Curiosity said. "I'll have supper on the table in a half hour, and I don't want this food to go to waste."

Elizabeth found Nathaniel in the barn, but no Hannah, who had gone down to the village to look at a trapper with some frostbitten toes that might need amputation.

"But I haven't had a chance to talk to her yet," Elizabeth said, disappointed and oddly put out that Hannah should evade her so neatly.

"She'll be back shortly," Nathaniel said. He had been examining the hoof of Curiosity's horse, which he dropped as he straightened. Then he grinned at her in a way that made her step back, and draw in a breath.

"Ain't it neighborly of you to come out here to keep me company," he said, advancing.

"Nathaniel." Trying to sound firm.

"Boots. That was a good piece of work you did today."

She stepped back again, and found herself up against a wall. "It didn't go as I expected it to. All I wanted—"

He stopped in front of her. "Was to get those boys to behave. You did that."

"There were less . . . disruptive ways to accomplish the same thing."

"But what fun would that have been?" He tilted his head, stemmed one arm against the wall behind her, and kissed her briefly. "I for one don't have anything against a little excitement in the middle of winter." His free hand strayed to her waist and then to the small of her back.

"What is it about this barn that always gets you started?" Elizabeth asked, her hands on his chest. "I have never understood it."

He cocked an eyebrow at her. "Are you telling me you ain't in a romantic frame of mind?"

"I'm asking a question," Elizabeth said, slipping out from between him and the barrels. "And we're too old for such foolishness in the middle of the afternoon."

"Speak for yourself." Nathaniel walked over to the tackle shelf and the bench underneath it, where he sat with his hands on his knees. "Come set over here next to me, Boots."

She did it against her better judgment, and realized immediately what he was about.

"Oh," she said. "You're thinking of the night—"

"You asked me to marry you."

She swallowed down her irritation. "Yes, I suppose that's the way you'd remember it. It was right here."

At that he laughed out loud and slipped an arm around her waist, put his face to the crook of her neck. With one hand he worked the ties of her cloak while he pressed a kiss just under her ear.

"Nathaniel."

"Boots."

"Really, Nathaniel, you can't—"

"Watch me."

She made an effort to pull away, halfhearted, wanting to be held down, wanting to be convinced. And he knew it, of course. That was the miracle.

On an indrawn breath she said, "What kind of example are we for the children?"

He paused to think about that, though his hands continued to stroke her back.

"The best kind of example, seems to me. We like each other real well even after all these years and the troubles we been through. I ain't in the habit of beating you and you don't throw dishes at my head when you're feeling out of sorts. A man who likes to touch his wife, and a woman who likes it that he does—I don't know there's anything to be ashamed of in that. Most men I know would call us damn fortunate. Most women too, I'd wager."

Elizabeth grasped his hands in both of hers and kissed one callused palm. "Drat you, Nathaniel, I had a whole list of excellent arguments and I can't think of a single one. You disarm me every time."

He turned her to him then and kissed her soundly. "You go ahead, Boots," he said, smiling against her mouth. "When those arguments come to you, I'll be right here. Listening."

"Supper on the table," she muttered. "It'll be cold."

"You won't," he said, and drew her down to the hay.

Chapter 23

By the fourth morning of the journey, Lily had begun to suspect that they were the only people not just in the endless forests, but the world. Every other kind of living thing seemed to show itself: moose, elk, deer, wolves, panthers—at that, the team nearly bolted, but for Simon's quick handling. He never had to go very far or long to bring them a steady diet of meat: partridge, turkey, grouse, and the occasional rabbit. Lily was at first amused and then put out when Simon took it upon himself to point out tracks, as if she had not taken note, or did not know what they were. Then she realized that while he had been in this country for a long time, the bounty of the woods still surprised and delighted him.

She remembered nothing of her short time in Scotland; she had been no more than a baby. But the stories were fresh in her mind and she asked him about the bare Scots hillsides and the fairy tree that figured so largely in Jennet's girlhood stories.

Jennet. She would give a great deal to have Jennet along on this journey, or Hannah, or any woman, really.

Lily was just thinking about her sudden and very intense yearning to be among other women, when Simon cleared his throat in a way she recognized: he had something important to tell her.

"It's the next day or two that are the most dangerous," he said in his calmest, most disturbing voice. "For we're near the border and only a few miles from the Sorel. The woods are full of every manner of man who ever put on a uniform. Revenue agents, mostly, looking for smugglers."

"And militia," Lily suggested.

"Aye, militia and regulars both."

"But you must know every man in uniform, in this part of Canada, at least."

"I know a good many of them," he said. "But generally it's best to keep clear of revenue agents, for they're known to be aye humorless. One with a grudge could decide to make things difficult for us. Your brother isn't without enemies, you know that."

Of course. No one could come as far as Luke and Simon had in the world of trade without making trouble for himself. Something occurred to Lily, a question she had never thought to ask.

"Do they have cause to suspect that you're breaking the law?"

He sent her a sidelong glance. "That depends," he said finally. "On which laws you mean."

"Why, Canadian, I suppose," Lily said. "At least on this side of the border. What laws concern you?"

"Your brother's," said Simon with a grin. "And nobody else's."

"That's a very Scottish thing to say, as if he were a laird in the old country."

He shrugged. "Old country or new, not much changes."

That made her think for a good while. Smuggling was an age-old problem on the border, one that had got worse with the war and the embargo; whole family fortunes had been built on it, and the greatest rivalries all seemed to come down to who traded what, and where. None of that was a secret. And still it seemed to her that there was something Simon hadn't told her, some worry that had made him go to such lengths to get them over the border without the knowledge of the authorities on either side.

"Are you spying?" she asked, and got for her trouble the harshest look he had to offer.

"Don't ever say that word," he said. "Or even think it."

It took some effort for him to compose his face. "I shouldn't have snapped at you, and I apologize. But that's a subject we can't discuss."

"Maybe not right now," Lily said, putting him on notice.

They were up to something, Simon and her brother. Lily knew that she ought to be afraid, but she could not find it in herself. They were, after all, not carrying any contraband; they were not smugglers, and whatever the men were up to, there would be no evidence of it in this sleigh; Simon was not in uniform and had never been. The border between New-York State and Canada might be a bit tricky just now, but she was Nathaniel Bonner's daughter and Hawkeye's granddaughter and allied to the Mohawk; no man who had spent any time in the endless forests would dare raise a hand to her.

Simon interrupted this conversation she was having with herself. "Recall, Lily: you must promise to let me handle the questions, should we be stopped."

Lily bit her lip rather than say something smart that would start another argument. She was in the mood for a quarrel, but she was also enough of a woodswoman to hold her tongue in the woods.

A ruffled grouse exploded up from its cover and sent a cloud of snow into the air. Lily jumped.

"You're more nervous than you let on," Simon said. He patted a lump in the furs that was her knee. "All will be well, lass. Hold steady."

His words were still hanging in the air when men's voices came to them like the low rumbling of an avalanche in the distance.

"Hold steady," Simon said again, just as the men came into sight on an old trail, a half mile to the west and headed toward them. Lily, whose eyes were as good as any sharpshooter's, studied the line for a moment: soldiers, yes, but all of them experienced backwoodsmen first.

"Voltigeurs," she said.

"Aye," said Simon, visibly relieved. "And Kester MacLeod has the command."

When she was younger, Lily had dreamed of adventures like the ones her mother and grandmother had had. The stories she grew up with were brightly colored and exciting beyond words: her grandmother Cora caught up in the battle at Fort Edward, her mother running through these very woods with the terrible Jack Lingo on her heels.

And here now was her own adventure: a patrol of rough men like all the men she had grown up with. They were consummate woodsmen and good shots, and they made effective if not very obedient militiamen. They were in uniforms, of a sort: their own clothing, with bright blue sashes and regulation blanket coats, and the hats, of course, the silliest part of the whole, in her eyes.

Uniforms or not, they farted and scratched themselves without apology while their sergeant asked Simon if he had any spare to-bacco, and what news was there to share from Montreal?

The platoon, it turned out, had been stationed at the Chateauguay River and was now on its way to Lacolle. The details were a little cloudy, which, of course, was intentional; they liked Simon, but would not say too much to a man out of uniform, one who was clearly headed for the border.

"And then with any luck to Nut Island," said Lieutenant MacLeod. Behind him his men grinned.

"The garrison at Nut Island is well provisioned," the lieutenant explained with a wink and a nudge. As if Lily wouldn't know that he was talking about women, or what these men wanted with them. She studied her mittens and hoped she looked disinterested and un-informed.

"Where are you headed tonight?" asked MacLeod. "You're not planning to bivouac with the young lady, are you?" He flashed his rotten teeth at her in such a boyish and charming way that she smiled back and regretted her surliness.

Simon had been rumbling through boxes. Now he hauled a small sack out of the back of the sleigh and offered it to Lieutenant MacLeod, who took it with a crow of delight.

"Sorry Tom's cabin is not a mile off," he said. "We'll spend the night there."

Even as he was saying the words, a knot of dread pulled tight deep in Lily's belly, and with good reason.

"Sorry Tom!" MacLeod put back his head and laughed, exposing rings of dirt on a neck much like a tree trunk. "I haven't thought of Sorry Tom in many a year, the old thief. By the Christ—sorry, Miss Bonner, but we've been sleeping raw for two weeks."

Simon might have simply warned them off, but instead he looked at Lily and cocked his head. And wasn't it like him, Lily thought, to leave the hard decisions to her. She could allow them to follow along and spend an uncomfortable night, or suffer the knowledge that could have provided some comfort, and had acted selfishly.

"It's just a cabin," she said. "But you can put your blankets on the floor and squeeze together."

When they had started off again Simon put his arm around her and drew her close. "You've a soft heart, Lily Bonner," he said. "And a generous one."

She wanted to be irritated, but could not; that was Simon's spe-cial talent, to disarm her with the truth when she wanted to be difficult. She couldn't be angry at him when he flashed his dimples at her, all admiration and approval, and underneath that, not very far, the thing that kept drawing them back together. Tonight, of course, they would have chaperones. Twenty-one of them. Lily should have felt relief, she knew, but she did not.

The voltigeurs were men who had never cared much for the ways of civilized folk, but they were jovial and friendly and willing to do almost anything to entertain Lily; one of them had a fiddle, and he offered to play, later, if she would like it; another dug a chunk of maple sugar out of his pack, brushed it off on his mantle, and offered it to her.

They knew who she was, of course, and asked after her father's health and what kind of season he was having. No one asked about her brother, and whether he had joined the fighting. Maybe because they knew the answer; maybe because they didn't really want to know.

After those first few awkward moments, there was nothing for Lily to do except watch them fetch wood and water and arrange the room so that she might have some privacy. They ran a rope across one corner of the room and from that they hung blankets that were pungent, but effective in screening off the one bed from the rest of the cabin. Lily disappeared behind the makeshift curtain as soon as it was up and lay down to stare at the ceiling and listen to the men as they sorted through their packs and shaved and began to cook. They spoke English and French rolled together with words from other languages—some clearly Indian—in that strange but oddly effective manner of the Canadian woodsman. It was rough and musical and Lily liked the sound of it. Someone put meat to roast over the hearth and the smell made Lily realize how hungry she was. Then Simon came in and they greeted him with such warmth that Lily was pleased for him.

After a while her attention drifted to the wall where a picture had been nailed, a drawing of a severe man with a chin beard. Next to him was a much younger woman, round cheeked with a dimpled chin, who was smiling shyly. Lily wondered if this was Sorry Tom, and how he had earned such a name, for in this picture he did not look sorry in the least, but grim and disapproving. Then, intrigued, she got up on her knees and studied the drawing more closely.

Something hard and sweet clicked in her throat, as it would if she had come unexpectedly around a corner to find her mother or father there. She touched the paper carefully with a fingertip and leaned forward to smell it, with the silly thought that there might be some scent left of the man who had done the work. Because she recognized it, now that she looked closely. Gabriel Oak had drawn this likeness; Gabriel Oak had been in these woods some many years ago and had sat in front of the hearth and drawn for his supper and a warm place to sleep. In a corner he had placed his mark, but she would have recognized his work without it.

Gabriel Oak, who had been her first teacher and her most beloved. Hot tears pushed up into her eyes and fell without warning, a great waterfall not so much of sadness, for he was dead these many years, but of thankfulness for the gift he had given her: a knowledge of herself.

Lily thought of the box in the sleigh she had packed so carefully. Her most cherished possessions: the old book that Gabriel had left her, filled with his drawings and notes, the letters her mother had written, her good pencils and a block of paper, things she had meant to use to make a record of this journey. Not once had she opened it, but that would change. She cleared her throat so the voltigeurs would know that she was about to make an appearance, and went out to take their likenesses.

Backwoodsmen, usually solitary by nature, were generally argumentative when herded together, and these men were no different. A fistfight might have broken out over who was to sit for Lily, and in what order, had not Lieutenant MacLeod intervened. The lucky ones were sent out to scrub their faces in the snow, and someone produced a wooden comb out of a haversack and passed it around, though from what Lily could see it would do little good.

For all their grime and coarse talk, they were strong men in their prime, and she found the truth of them in letting her pencil move over the paper.

Her third subject was a man with the remarkable name of Uz Brodie, who was eager to tell her the history of the war farther to the west. That caught Lily's attention.

"You've been as far as the lakes?" she asked.

"I spent three months on the St. Lawrence," he said, not without pride. "But they sent us home for the Yule, and after I thought I'd be better off under Salaberry, so I joined up with the voltigeurs."

"He'd had enough of Red George and his clergymen," called a voice from the other side of the cabin. "A priest six and a half foot tall."

"A magical priest, for he grows a few inches with each telling," added another voice.

MacLeod raised his voice to be heard. "Uz tells us the priest goes into battle with a great crucifix that he uses like a pike."

"A Jesuit, no doubt," Simon said in his dry way. That set the room off again; Catholics, Lily noticed, liked a joke at the expense of their priests, if they did not skirt too close to the truth. Simon especially liked such jokes, perhaps, she reminded herself, because he had an uncle who was a Jesuit.

"Uz Brodie, chased off by a priest," hooted a small man on the other side of the room.

The reaction was immediate, for Brodie flushed a mottled red and thrust out his chest like an affronted turkey. Indeed, he looked a great deal like a turkey, Lily thought, with a wattle of red skin on his neck and a nose blue with cold and sharp as a beak and quick black eyes.

"You laugh, Clarke, laugh on. But there's no place for priests among fighting men."

"And why not? I've nothing against priests," said the small man, who, Lily noticed now, was missing all the teeth on one side of his mouth and, as if to compensate, had a thick red scar where the opposite eyebrow should be.

"You wouldn't like these priests, that I promise you."

Drew Clarke said, "I was hoping there'd be a priest or two at the garrison. My Jeanne, she has got marriage on the mind, and she'll want a priest to do the job."

An unfortunate turn of phrase, but it was said and Clarke must wait out the laughter. Then MacLeod unfolded himself from his spot on the floor and raised both hands in the air in a gesture that managed to be both forceful and easy.

"Brodie," he said. "Tell the whole story, now. Wasn't there a parson too?"

Simon's head came up suddenly. "I've heard of this. A Mr. Brown, who's got the habit of moving laggards into battle by thumping them with his Bible."

This time the laughter went on for so long that Lily gave up her work for a moment until the worst had passed. Her subject on his stool before her ducked his head but could not hide his embarrassment. He grinned at Lily, sheepishly.

"I take it you had dealings with this Mr. Brown," she said, going back to her drawing.

"Well, yes," he said, subdued. "I did. But it was an accident, him falling into the river, I swear it."

"Bible and all," said MacLeod. "A sorry accident indeed."

"And Forsyth? Did you ever get a look at him?" Lily asked, and felt Simon stiffen beside her, as if she had given too much away about her own interests and loyalties.

But none of the men seemed to be unsettled by her question, and instead launched into piecing together what news they had of the campaigns along the St. Lawrence, where raids moved back and forth with regularity and the smugglers had grown bold. Lily listened, but heard nothing of Jim Booke's riflemen or her brother or Blue-Jay, and after a while the conversation turned in other directions.

She had done drawings of most of the men when weariness overtook her and she excused herself, leaving Simon to talk to the men while she retired behind her blanket.

"A fine wife you've found yourself," she heard MacLeod say to Simon, who made a deep sound in his throat, the one that a Scot made when he was deeply satisfied, but didn't care to say so plainly.

She thought of calling out that she wasn't his wife yet, and that she did not care to be handed off so easily, when another voice spoke up.

"Her brother approves the match?"

"And if he didn't, it's not the brother I'm marrying," said Simon.

"You're still partners, you and Luke."

Lily reminded herself that these men were trappers, and would go back to trading furs when the war was done; they weren't so much interested in her marriage as they were in Luke's business affairs, and by extension, Simon's.

"Aye," said Simon sharply.

"I was just asking, man. No need to bristle."

"Well, you're talking about his wife's family," said Uz Brodie. "A man's got a right to be prickly about something like that. Especially a man married to Luke Bonner's sister."

"I heard tell she was pretty," said another voice, one Lily couldn't put a face to. "But she's all hair and eyes. You'd have to shake the bed sheets to find her. I like more meat on the bone, moi."

There was an ominous silence, and Lily imagined that Simon had fixed the speaker with his most displeased look, for the man muttered an apology.

"No offense," he said.

"Not if you keep a civil tongue in your head," Simon answered.

Fully awake now, Lily listened closely but heard nothing more about herself. Gradually she drifted off to sleep, only to wake and find Simon sitting on the edge of the bed.

"Am I too thin?" she asked him.

In the near dark she could not see if he was smiling, but his voice told her that he was.

"Slender," he said. "And finely proportioned."

"You've got no complaints, then." She was angling for compliments, of course; too late she remembered that such tactics never worked with Simon Ballentyne and in fact took her just where she would rather not go.

"One," he said. "I'm cold, and tired."

She had meant to make him sleep on the other side of the blanket with the soldiers, but that would shame him, she understood that. And what difference did it make, really. She would never see these men again, and they believed her already married. She made room for him on the narrow bed and discovered that he had stripped down to his shirt.

"You cheeky—" She started, and stopped, too much involved with removing Simon's hand from her breast to talk just then. Finally she whispered, "You cannot be serious."

"If you can be quiet, I can be aye serious," he answered, his hands roaming.

She caught them up in her own and held them away from her. "We are in the same room with twenty-one strange men," she hissed.

"There's a blanket." He tried to kiss her but she turned her head away and felt his mouth on her cheek, as hot as a branding iron.

"Simon. A blanket is not a wall."

"For a lass who grew up on the frontier you're aye particular, Lily Bonner. How do you think men and women who live in one-room cabins ever get bairns?"

That question silenced her for a moment, because of course it was something she had thought about quite often when she was younger and had first started contemplating the things that men and women did together in the dark. In her own home her parents had a chamber to themselves, but most cabins in Paradise had only one room where everyone slept together. Much like this.

A few feet away a man coughed softly and cursed to himself.

Then came the distinct sound of piss hitting the walls of a metal pot in a forceful stream.

The ridiculousness of the situation struck Lily then, and her shoulders began to shake with laughter.

"Ah, that's more like it," Simon said. "Laughing Lily, come to me, lass."

"I will not," she said, fighting off his hands, but with less conviction now. When he caught her up against him and kissed her, the last of her resistance faded away.

"I'll make too much noise," she said. "I can't help it."

"That's true," he said, pressing her down into the thin mattress, his hands to either side of her face. "You are a noisy wee thing when I've got you beneath me. And you wiggle too."

"You are—" she said, and bit back a gasp.

"Just where I want to be," he said against her mouth, and caught up every bit of noise she could make in his kiss.

In the morning she waited until the voltigeurs had left the cabin before she came out from behind the blanket to wash and dress in the warmth from the hearth. Simon had gone out some time ago to see to the horses and hitch them to the sleigh. Outside she could hear the voltigeurs, getting ready to be on their way. Lily raised her chin high to face the twenty-one men who had listened to the muffled sounds that came from the other side of the blanket.

If any one of them grinned at her, she would simply pull out the gun that Luke had given her, and shoot.

With this happy thought in her head she stepped out into the bitter morning cold. And found that their number had grown: the clearing around the cabin was crowded with soldiers—proper soldiers, in uniform and standing in formation—with no sign of Simon anywhere.

Lily was too surprised to be frightened until she saw Lieutenant MacLeod's expression, and understood there was some good reason for concern.

Then she saw a band of Mohawk warriors at the edge of the clearing. Among them was a familiar face, and she stepped off the porch in that direction without thinking.

"Miss," said a very English voice behind her. "If you would be so good—"

"Sawatis!" Lily called, waving. And then, aloud in her surprise and pleasure: "That is my cousin Sawatis. Oh, and see my uncle Spotted-Fox with him." She was so excited to see those two familiar faces that she forgot again that there was reason to be concerned, and she turned to the man who had addressed her with a great smile.

It would be much later before Lily came to realize how well timed her smile had been; at first, she only saw that the man she aimed it at was blinking in surprise. Then, slowly, he returned her smile with one of his own, albeit small and awkward. The effort made his cheeks jerk, as muscles seldom used will twitch when pressed into sudden service.

As distracted as she was, Lily could not help but note that the smile suited him; it turned a fine-looking man into a strikingly handsome one. Severe, yes, but with an intense quality in his eyes that must draw women to him.

She noted all of this with one part of her mind while the rest of it dealt with the jumble of questions that had no answers: Where was Simon? Who were these soldiers, wearing colors she did not recognize? And oddest of all, it seemed that her cousin and uncle had joined the fighting, on the side of the British Canadians, when Sawatis' brother Blue-Jay was somewhere on the St. Lawrence fighting for the American side.

Then Sawatis and Spotted-Fox were close enough and Lily went forward, quickly, her hands extended, and greeted them both in their own language, the familiar sounds gushing out like water from a crumbling dam. Tears in her eyes, and she dashed them away, impatient with herself.

To each of their children who lived to reach a certain age, Many-Doves and Runs-from-Bears had presented a choice: they could stay at Lake in the Clouds, or leave to make a life among the Kahnyen'kehàka. Blue-Jay had stayed and so would Annie, no doubt, both of them preferring English names and a red and white world to one that was, in Annie's eyes at least, monotone; Kateri and Sawatis had gone.

Kateri had taken a husband from the Turtle clan at Good Pasture, a serious young man called Broken-Blade, who might have also joined the fighting, for all Lily knew. With a pang she realized that she had given these matters—these life-and-death matters—little thought in the face of her own problems. But Good Pasture was a good twenty miles to the east of here, on land that the Canadians called their own, something that the Kahnyen'kehàka studiously overlooked.

Sawatis had wanted to be trained as a warrior, and so he was sent to the Wolf longhouse at Good Pasture, where his mother had been born. To Spotted-Fox, who would take on his training and see to it he learned what was necessary. Spotted-Fox had lost his own children to typhoid and measles, and was glad to accept the responsibility.

But here he was, the boy Lily had grown up with. She had played with him and wiped his face, and now his scalp was plucked and he wore stripes of paint on his cheekbones. He had chipped an eyetooth, but otherwise his smile was unchanged, and his hands on her shoulders made her realize how tall he had grown, and how strong.

He said, "Satahonhsata!" *Listen*. "Do not turn around to look at the officer behind you, he is already suspicious. Smile at me and listen."

In the same language she said, "What of—" She hesitated to say the name. "The man who brought me this far?"

"He is being held on the other side of the cabin," said Spotted-Fox.

"Held?" Lily echoed. "But why?"

Gooseflesh had risen all along her back but she smiled as she had been told, and wondered if her muscles might freeze just as they were.

"You must tread carefully, cousin," said Sawatis. "And gather your courage to you. The officer is no fool, and he will question you closely."

Of all the things Lily might have asked, one idea presented itself: it could be no coincidence that she had come across family just here and now. She said, "Why are you two here? What has happened?"

Sawatis stepped forward to put his arms around her; it looked like an embrace between cousins, but when he spoke at her ear it was nothing she wanted to hear. "The soldiers are on their way to Nut Island. We will go with them, now that you are here to carry our message back to Lake in the Clouds."

She tried to speak but he quieted her with his expression, and the press of his hands. "My brother and yours have been taken prisoner," he said. "They are being held in the garrison stockade on the island."

"Miss Bonner," said the officer, so close behind her now that Lily bumped into him when she tried to step backward. Then she pivoted awkwardly, lost her balance, and fell at his feet.

He bent down immediately, this man who had appeared without warning and changed everything in the world. The officer leaned in closer. Even in her duress she could not overlook that he was, in a word, beautiful. His face was square of jaw and perfectly proportioned, with eyes as blue as the sky overhead. As blue as her own, but cold.

"I startled you," he said. "My apologies. Have you injured yourself?"

"My ankle," Lily said, and then she did something she had never done before. Out of agitation, out of fear for herself and her brother, for Blue-Jay and Simon, out of anger and pain and shock, she burst into tears in front of this strange man, and gave him an advantage over herself.

Anyone who lived in Montreal knew of the King's Rangers, three hundred professional soldiers of the first stripe, Canadians and Englishmen. And in command of the corps a Major Christian Wyndham, born in Canada but schooled in England. The details came to Lily by way of the company surgeon, who was called immediately to look at her ankle as soon as she had been carried into the cabin.

Mr. Theriot was a French Canadian, a small, round man who stank of stale tobacco, mutton fat, and rum. Lily remembered Curiosity's dislike of Canadian doctors; she would give a great deal just now for Curiosity, who would deal with Theriot and Wyndham too, in short order. Lily felt a bubble of frantic laughter try to push itself out of her throat, and bit her lip.

The surgeon did not take long to examine her ankle, and he never took a lancet from the box of instruments he had propped open—with a panther's skull, Lily saw—at his side.

She said, "I have a skull like that, at home." And wondered how it was that such a thing could come out of her mouth at a time like this. The doctor didn't seem to notice, or care. He sat back on his heels and gave her moderately good news.

"The ankle is not broken," he said. "But the sprain is serious. You have injured it before, I think?"

She agreed that, indeed, she had sprained it once as a girl, and quite badly. The same summer of the panther's skull; she almost said that too, but stopped herself by biting her tongue.

"A weak spot then. You will not be walking on it for a week at least, mademoiselle. I will bind it for you."

The watery brown eyes considered her from underneath a tangle of eyebrows. "The major is waiting to question you, you realize." He jerked his head over his shoulder. The blanket had been hung again, hastily, to provide her with some privacy.

"I can put him off while you rest for a few hours, if you prefer."

Lily thought of Simon being held in the stable, under guard. She thought of Sawatis and Spotted-Fox and their news. For a moment she thought she might faint, but then she pinched the skin between thumb and first finger until her vision cleared.

"I am quite happy to speak to the major," she said, conjuring up a smile from some spot inside her that she hadn't known existed.

Simon had been very specific: if they fell into unfriendly hands, she was to let him do the talking. But now he was somewhere else, and in his place was this man called Wyndham, with his cold smile and colder eyes.

He waited until a junior officer had helped her to the only stool in the cabin, set before the hearth. Then the same man went to a small table he had set up in the corner, where he bent over paper and picked up a quill.

This was an official inquiry, then. Lily did not know what to make of that, but she managed to keep her curiosity to herself and not ask any of the many questions that came to her, most of them highly unsuited to the occasion.

The major stood before her with his hands crossed on his back; Lily thought of reminding this English-schooled gentleman that it was rude to stare. Instead she counted the silver buttons that marched from the scarlet sash around his waist up the dark green coat to disappear in a ruffle of silver lace that spilled over a black velvet collar and lapels. His epaulettes were silver too. Altogether this Major Christian Wyndham was a splendid example of his kind, and now Lily remembered something: her teacher Monsieur Duhaut had been engaged to paint this man's portrait as soon as he returned to Montreal from an assignment to the west. No doubt she herself had prepared the very canvas where his likeness would be preserved, in green and black and silver. Lily thought of telling him that he had chosen the right unit—a scarlet coat would not have suited his complexion half so well. Instead she gave him a narrow and impatient smile.

The major did not like her smile, it seemed; he turned his back on her.

"Where are you going, Miss Bonner, in the middle of winter, and why?"

In a situation such as this, Luke and Simon had told her, the truth is the only defense. And what else? She struggled to remember. It came to her then: *Say as little as possible, and volunteer nothing at all.*

"Mr. Ballentyne is taking me home to my mother and father," she said. She meant her voice to sound as it would when she spoke to any well-bred gentleman she might have met in her brother's parlor. She feared it did not, but then hoped that her fall and injury would explain any agitation.

"In the middle of winter, by such a backwoods route?"

"It is the fastest way to travel, in a sleigh. Or so I understand it."

"And what is the hurry?"

She could not read his thoughts from the straight back or the set of his shoulders, but his tone gave her the idea that he did not believe anything she said.

Lily said, "That is a very personal question, sir."

"One that requires an answer nonetheless, Miss Bonner." He stood at the window, looking at his troops. The shutters had been pried away and lay about his feet in splinters.

Lily took a very deep breath. She said, "I wanted to be married at home, with my parents' blessing."

"Ah," said the major. "The infamous Nathaniel Bonner."

To that Lily could say nothing. Of course her father's reputation would be known to this man. He had caused the British army enough trouble over the years.

Major Wyndham said, "I know your mother, or I knew her."

Lily tried to look politely disinterested. "In England?"

"Yes, in England. You are familiar with the Spencers of Manhattan?"

Uneasy, Lily shifted and remembered her ankle, too late; it began to throb more insistently. "I have an uncle Spencer—"

"Once Viscount Durbeyfield," said the major. "A traitor, I am sorry to say, to king and country. This continent seems to breed them."

"Sir," Lily said. "Whatever quarrel you have with my uncle, it has nothing to do with me."

He shot her a sharp look. "You are not in Canada at your uncle's request?"

Lily wondered if she looked as surprised as she felt. "I came to Montreal to study painting."

"That is the story people tell, yes." He studied her as though she were some odd insect, and Lily did not like it.

She said, "I am not a spy, I never have been." She thought to say that she had not seen her uncle Spencer in two years. Then she remembered that she was not to volunteer anything.

It struck her suddenly as almost funny, that this man should really believe she might be a spy. She might have laughed, but for the way he was contemplating her; but for her brother and Blue-Jay.

"And your brother?"

She started to have her thoughts plucked from her head and presented in words, but the major didn't notice. He was gesturing to the ensign who stood at attention at the door. He was so young that Lily doubted he had to worry about a beard. The boy was well trained, at any rate; he brought the major the papers he wanted without even glancing at Lily.

What Wyndham held in his hand, Lily saw now, were her own papers. The letters from home in her mother's handwriting, her sister's, Curiosity's. She closed her eyes and fought her temper, concentrating on the throb in her head and ankle, on the vision of her brother in chains.

"Your brother serves in the American militia." It was not a question, and so she did not answer it. He did not seem to know that Daniel had been taken prisoner, and she couldn't think what that might mean: was it good news, or bad?

After a while he said, "You have nothing more to say in your own defense?"

"If you are accusing me of spying, then I say very firmly that I am not, and have never been, a spy."

"You speak Mohawk," he said.

Lily pulled up in surprise. "I do, yes."

"Fluently."

"I learned it as a child."

"And the Mohawk seem to consider you family."

"We are family, by marriage."

His gaze narrowed. "I should not pronounce such a thing so proudly, if I were you."

"But of course," Lily said, her anger pushing up again, harder to govern with every passing moment. "*You* would not. But I am proud of all my family."

That earned her a sharp look. "Even the ones who fight for England?"

She said, "Even them. They have their own reasons."

"You would be an asset to Montgomery's efforts here, Miss Bonner. I am tempted to take you with me."

Her mouth snapped shut with a sound. She started to speak and then stopped herself. After a moment, during which he waited with something like curiosity in his expression, she said, "You would interfere with the business of a private citizen?"

He inclined his head, as if he might actually consider this line of reasoning. "In time of war, yes. Of course. Does that surprise you?"

"Sir, you are a stranger to me. How could anything you do surprise me?"

At that he laughed. A sharp, barking sound but a laugh nonetheless. Turning back to the window he rocked on his heels, his chin bedded on his chest while he thought.

"It is tempting," he said finally. "But no. I don't care to bring the wrath of Carryck down on my head. There are more important things to attend to just now."

Lily forced herself to take a deep breath, once and then again. She felt his eyes on her.

"You may go," he said. "You and Mr. Ballentyne."

She said, "I want my things returned to me. My letters, and whatever else you have taken from the sleigh."

He tilted his head at her. "But of course, Miss Bonner. I am at your command."

She saw him hesitate. A little color had come into his face now, and Lily realized that they were not done, after all.

He said, "I wish you a safe journey, Miss Bonner. It is a dangerous one, certainly."

"I grew up in these forests," Lily told him. "They do not frighten me."

"It is not trees that you need fear," said Major Wyndham. "But men."

Once Simon had assured himself that Lily was well, and she had done the same, they set out. Neither of them was in the mood for talk, once the basic information had been exchanged, and so they traveled in silence. Lily, so agitated that she could have run the rest of the way to Lake in the Clouds, found herself pushing with her feet against the floorboards.

Mile by mile, Simon retreated behind a mask she could not quite read: fury, certainly, but also something of damaged pride. There was nothing to say to that; no matter how undeserved the guilt he was feeling—and Lily was not sure, to be honest, that he hadn't mis-judged—anything she might say would only make it worse. Men did not like to be comforted in times like this, even if she had had any comfort to offer.

In the first fading light of the afternoon Lily looked up and saw that they had ended where they began, at Sorry Tom's cabin. The King's Rangers were gone; if not for the trampled snow and the leavings of the officers' horses, Lily thought, there would be no sign of them having been here at all.

Simon brought the sleigh to a standstill and sat for a moment, contemplating the reins in his hands.

She said, "Why? Why are we here? I have to get home, my fa-ther must be told—"

"Wait," Simon said. He put a hand under her elbow and urged her out of the sleigh. "Go inside, I'll be as quick as I can."

He had found a branch to serve as a crutch. With it propped un-der her arm Lily hopped, awkwardly, into the cabin while he pulled the team and sleigh around to the stable.

Inside she closed the door behind herself and was glad of the cold dark, for that moment when she did not know if she could keep herself from screaming. In time she found her way to the stool that still stood before the hearth, cold now, and sat. The room smelled of the quail they had roasted for their supper and the men who had slept here last night, crowded shoulder to shoulder, laughing and telling their jokes by the glow of the banked coals.

When the door opened to frame a bloody dusk-red sky it was Sawatis who stood there, with Spotted-Fox and Simon just behind him.

Stripped of mantles and furs and weapons, Sawatis was much more the boy she had grown up with. He crouched before the fire and poked at it, and Lily saw the scar on his arm and remembered how he had come by it falling out of the boys' fort, one summer when he had been four or five. Her brother and his had brought him back to Lake in the Clouds where Many-Doves had stanched the bleeding with yarrow leaves and tied the wound shut with corn husks and then sent him out to play again.

Lily said, "Tell me."

It was quickly done, as they did not know very many of the details. The news came to them as all news did: a Mohawk who scouted for the British at Nut Island had seen Blue-Jay and Daniel among a group of prisoners brought to the fort just five days ago. He told another Mohawk, who carried the news to the next, who took it with him to Good Pasture and delivered it to the longhouse of the Wolf, where Blue-Jay's brother lived with the rest of the clan.

The news arrived at Good Pasture at an awkward time. For days the war council had been sitting in deliberation on where they would fight in this new war, or if they would fight at all. Some of the men, not many, wanted to travel over the border to fight for the Americans; most thought that fighting for the British would serve them better. Some of the older men, Spotted-Fox among them, were not interested in yet another white man's war.

The news from Nut Island had taken Sawatis and Spotted-Fox away from the council fire. Together they set out immediately for the garrison on Nut Island, to see what might be done. Spotted-Fox had connections to the militia and he was respected by the British, who wanted all the Mohawk support they could muster; it was even possible that Blue-Jay would be released to him. Together with Red-Wing and Three-Horns, Mohawks who had been fighting for the British since the war broke out, Spotted-Fox had gone to make an appeal to the commander. And come away empty-handed.

He did not say so, but Lily saw that this single fact disturbed Spotted-Fox a great deal. She knew, too, that questions would do no good; he would not reveal what he meant to keep to himself.

"But did you see them?" Lily asked, knowing how rude it was to interrupt the flow of the story as it needed to be told, and still unable to control her anxiety and worry.

Spotted-Fox blinked at her. She ducked her head in apology and asked the question again.

"We have seen my brother," answered Sawatis. "But not yours."

"But why not?" Lily demanded. "Is he so badly injured? Have they locked him away by himself?"

"We have seen Blue-Jay, but we could not speak to him or ask questions," said Spotted-Fox. "What we know of your brother we know from Red-Wing and the women in the followers' camp."

Lily folded her hands together in her lap and forced herself to think it through, step by step. "I don't understand. They were supposed to be on the St. Lawrence. They wrote from Oswegatchie not six weeks ago."

They had been speaking English for Simon's sake, and now he joined the conversation for the first time.

"Jim Booke wouldn't like the kind of hair-pulling MacLeod was telling us about last night," Simon said. "Raids back and forth, like ill-tempered boys arguing over playthings. I'm not surprised to hear he moved his men."

"What of Jim Booke?" Lily asked. "Is he there too, in the stockade?"

He was not in the stockade, Spotted-Fox assured her, but not far off either.

"His sign is all around, but we didn't have time to go looking for him."

"Those garrison stockades are full of disease," Lily said, mostly to herself. "A healthy man is in danger, and Daniel is wounded."

Simon drew in a breath, and she rounded on him as if he had struck her.

"We can't leave them there," she said. "We have to get them out. My father would get them out. My *mother* would get them out. How can I do any less?"

"This is Nut Island we're talking about," Simon said. "The fortifications alone—"

She would have said things to him then that she could never have made right, but Spotted-Fox stopped her with a raised hand. He said, "He is right. No one man could get them out, not even your father. It would take an army."

Lily felt the panic rise up from her belly into her throat, but she forced herself to swallow it.

"What then?" she said. "You must have a plan. You were traveling with the King's Rangers and on your way there. Can you get close to them? Can you get me close to them? I could join the camp, you said there are women—"

Her voice spiraled up and broke, and for a moment there was only the sound of harsh breathing and the hiss of the fire. She was proposing to join the ranks of the camp followers, the ones who washed for the soldiers and gave them the other things they required of women, in exchange for food and a place to sleep in a tent. In exchange for the chance to save her brother, Lily would have done that and more.

But Simon was looking at her, his expression guarded. He would never allow her to do such a thing, even if Sawatis and Spotted-Fox could be convinced. In that moment she hated this man she had bound herself to, for standing between herself and her twin.

Sawatis said, "We can be close enough to see that they get extra food and blankets. But there is something more important for you to do."

"You want me to go home," Lily said dully. "And tell my father, what? To raise an army?"

"No," said Spotted-Fox. "There is something your people can do. Something your sister Walks-Ahead can do."

On the back of her neck Lily's skin prickled, and a wave of nausea rose into her throat. The men took no note, and Spotted-Fox went on.

"There are only two doctors in the garrison, and they have no time for American prisoners. Walks-Ahead is a Kahnyen'kehàka healer, and she has experience on the battlefield. The British will be glad of her help as long as they don't know who her people are."

"A well-thought-out plan," Lily said, and Simon threw her a sharp look.

Sawatis said, "One of us would have gone to Lake in the Clouds to fetch her, if we hadn't come across you."

"One of you will still go fetch her, if you must," Lily said. "I'm not leaving Canada until my brother and Blue-Jay are free."

She was being childish and selfish and eventually she must give in; Lily knew that, and still she turned her face away when Simon tried to talk to her.

They were back in the narrow bed behind the blanket, in the cold dark. Lying on her back with her hands crossed over her stomach Lily tried to make out Gabriel Oak's drawing on the wall and could not. She was so determined not to listen to any more arguments that it was a moment before she realized the latest thing Simon had said.

He was so close that she could feel his breath on her cheek, but she would not look at him.

"Did you hear me?" he asked.

"I did."

"And?"

"You would do that. You would go on to Lake in the Clouds without me."

"Aye, if you will promise to stay with Sawatis and Spotted-Fox and not do anything foolish."

"And you would bring my sister back."

Maybe it was her tone that warned him, for he turned away to stare at his own bit of the ceiling. After a moment he said, "Do you have another plan?"

"You mean, there is nothing for me to do here. You mean that I will only be in the way and cannot help my brother."

"I said none of that." Simon's tone was edgy now; it was late in the night, and the day had been long and difficult and maybe, Lily thought, maybe she had finally found the limits of his patience.

"And yet it's true. Daniel needs Hannah but he doesn't need me."

She heard herself, full of self-pity and bitterness; her mother would be ashamed. She was ashamed. It should have been enough to stop her, but Lily found she was no longer master of her own tongue.

"It's nothing new," she continued. "I've heard it my whole life, you know."

Simon said, "Your brother has need of your sister, aye. And your mother will have need of you. Or had ye no thought of that?"

Before Lily could turn to bury her face in the bedding a moan escaped her, and on its heels came the tears she had been holding back.

Simon got up from the bed and disappeared behind the blanket, into the darkness. For a moment Lily was satisfied: it had taken a great deal of work, but finally she had driven him away.

He was back before she could turn her head on the folded blanket that served as a pillow. His weight pulled down the edge of the bed and she shifted toward him against her will.

"Sit up," he said in a firm voice.

She gave him no answer, and did not move. After a moment he leaned over her and took her by the shoulders, pulled her up until she was sitting, and then she felt his fingers in her hair.

"What are you doing?"

He worked her plait until her hair hung free to the waist and then Lily felt the brush at the crown of her head; it caught and held and began the long journey down and down, pulling nerves to life as it went. In the dark Simon brushed her hair from scalp to waist: ten strokes, fifty, a hundred. Her hair, too curly, too thick, too everything for fashion, resisted. He pressed on.

As her father brushed her mother's hair, every night. Lily tried to remember if she had ever told Simon about that, but she was so weary that her memories slid away. A shudder ran through her, and then another. Her head felt too heavy to hold up and still the brush continued on and on.

When he stopped, finally, she lay down. Her face was wet with tears, but she fell asleep before she could wipe them away.

In the morning Lily found that her courses had begun, after all. The evidence was impossible to deny, or hide. She wondered if she had been mistaken altogether, or if this was another loss to mourn.

Simon's expression was carefully blank. He asked what he could do for her and what she might need; if they should stay another day here in the cabin. He said this as if it were a possibility; as if there were endless fodder in the little stable; as if there were no reason to hurry.

All the anger had drained out of Lily; she pressed his hand and thanked him and saw how relieved he was to be released.

Simon went out to see to the horses and the sleigh. Lily wondered what he was thinking, really; if he was sad, as she found herself to be. Oddly sad and relieved at the same time. He had never used the child as an argument for her to go home, an act of generosity, it seemed to her now, and kindness.

It seemed a strange dream she had had, the idea of rescuing her brother. She would go home with Simon, to her mother and father and the rest of her people, and she would stay there with them until there was word of Daniel and Blue-Jay.

While she made ready Sawatis gave her news from Good Pasture to carry back to Lake in the Clouds, and she committed it all to memory. It was something to think about, and she was thankful.

At the door her cousin took her free hand in both his own and looked at her face. He looked so much like his father that for a moment Lily found it impossible to speak. Many-Doves and Runs-from-Bears did not know about their eldest son; it would be up to her to give them the news. Better news than she had for her own parents.

She said, "Do what you can for them. I will send my sister."

His lips were cold where he pressed them to her forehead. Spotted-Fox blinked his eyes, not in disapproval this time but because the sun on the snow was so bright that even his eyes must tear. They helped her to the sleigh and saw her settled.

Lily turned to wave goodbye but they had already disappeared into the forests.

Chapter 24

"Ain't no music in the world so fine as little girls laughing," said Curiosity.

Ethan looked up from the box of books he was packing. "They are having a high time. Elizabeth, take this copy of Cicero, there are two."

Elizabeth accepted the small leather-bound book from her nephew and looked at it more closely. "He never even cut the pages."

At that Curiosity made a gruff sound in her throat. "Unless it was something about medicine, Richard didn't care much about books. He bought them because he thought a fine gentleman should have them on his shelf."

Ethan's face clouded, and it was not lost on Curiosity. "You think I'm speaking bad of him, but I ain't. What I'm saying is, the man spent his whole life trying to be something he wasn't, and didn't really want anyway. Don't you make the same mistake, you hear me?"

Elizabeth hissed softly. "As if he were even in danger of such a thing." It earned her a sharp glance from Curiosity and an amused one from Ethan.

He said, "I appreciate your faith in me, Aunt Bonner—"

"Then say nothing more on the subject," she interrupted him. "The only promise I care to hear from you is that you will make the most of your travels, and then, when you are ready, that you will come home to us again."

With a very pointed look, Curiosity stopped Elizabeth before she could say more. She said, "Don't matter that they never got read before," she said. "These books sure will look fine in the new schoolhouse."

"If you insist on changing the subject," Elizabeth said, "please change it in another direction."

"You are reluctant to talk about the new schoolhouse, Aunt." Ethan put another small pile of books in her lap. "But I saw you yesterday, inspecting the lumber."

It was true that she had selected a spot for the new school, and it was also true that she had paid Peter Dubonnet to cut and haul the lumber that must wait until spring before building could begin. But still she chafed at the whole business, and could not even tell why except in terms that she did not like to admit. The whole venture seemed to her somehow a challenge to fate, and fate was too nebulous and irrational a concept for her comfort.

It had to do with the war, of course. With the fact that her children were away, and that she couldn't see to their welfare; it had to do with getting older. It had to do most of all with the fact that she had hoped that Ethan would take over the school, and that now he could not. Because Richard had willed it so.

Curiosity said, "Now look, here's old Mr. Shakespeare who went missing some weeks ago right while we was in the middle of reading about that foolish child Juliet and her Romeo, just as bad. I'll ask Jennet to read some more to us tonight, though I expect it'll take a bad end, the whole sorry business. Don't know what the girl's folks was thinking, letting things get out of hand the way they did."

Elizabeth and Ethan exchanged smiles.

"Don't you be laughing, you two. You know I'm right."

"Curiosity," Ethan said. "You know that these stories are pure invention but you always talk as if the characters might show up at your door for advice."

The older woman put both hands on her head kerchief to right it. "If only they would," she said. "I'd send that Romeo into the bush with Joshua. Let him chop a few trees, raise a few blisters. You tire a boy out good, he won't get such foolish ideas in his head. Climbing up walls in the middle of the night." She sniffed.

"No doubt you're right," Elizabeth said. "Though I doubt Shakespeare would have come up with such a novel solution."

"He don't like happy endings, ain't no secret in that," Curiosity agreed. "But the words sound pretty, the way he wrote them down. If you got the right person reading, that is."

"I imagine that Jennet must read these characters very well," Elizabeth said. "She has just the right dramatic flair."

At that the door flew open so abruptly that it cracked against the wall. Callie and Martha burst into the room, pursued by Jennet. All three of them were flushed with high color and almost breathless with laughter and running.

Callie had one arm extended up over her head, and in her fist, a sheet of paper. Jennet lunged, and Callie hopped backward just out of her reach. Together the two younger girls backed around a wing chair while Jennet advanced.

"Now!" Curiosity said. "What is all this thundering and shouting?"

They spared her not a glance.

"You said we might!" Martha squeaked. "You said we could!"

"I'll pluck ye bald, ye wee de'ils," Jennet crooned in a sweet voice. "And use your hair tae stuff ma pillow." Her fingers wiggled before her.

"You did say so!" Callie echoed, as Jennet snatched and the girls jumped.

"Och, I said nae sic thing." Jennet circled to the other side and the girls pivoted with her. "I said I'd share the tale wi' ye, but no the letter! That's for ma brither."

Curiosity marched forward and inserted herself between Jennet and her prey. She held out her hand, palm up. "You two girls know better than to go reading somebody else's private mail. What are you thinking?"

Callie looked at Martha and Martha at Callie. With a bob of the head, the stolen letter was put into Curiosity's hand.

"But it's a new story she's writing down for Alasdair, and she said she'd share it!" Callie's bright eyes blazed defiance, first at Jennet and then, subdued, at Curiosity.

"What I said was that I would tell ye the tale. When I was finished with it. Which I am not." Jennet drew herself up to her full height, which was not so very tall, and raised her chin. What she could not do, Elizabeth saw, was hide her smile.

"But it's taking so long," Martha said, wheedling now. "We can't wait."

"Och, but ye will wait. When I'm finished working it out you'll hear it. Or perhaps not." She sniffed. "It will take some wooing to get me back in the mood to tell tales."

"Tea?" said Callie, brightly.

Jennet pursed her mouth. "And some of the little cakes Sally baked this morning too, I think."

At that the girls laughed out loud and ran out of the parlor, followed closely by Jennet. She stopped and turned, and saw that Curiosity was holding out the stolen letter at arm's length, her eyes narrowed to read the small hand.

Jennet snatched it away. "Et tu, Brute?" Then she laughed and, tucking the rumpled paper away, she left for the kitchen.

"My Lord, what I wouldn't give for a half of that girl's energy," Curiosity said.

"I'd settle for a quarter of it," Elizabeth said. "In any case, it is certainly doing those girls some good."

"I will miss Jennet's stories," Ethan said. "By the time I come back here I suppose she will be married and settled in Montreal."

That silenced both women, who exchanged sober looks over the boxes of books.

"Montreal ain't so far off," Curiosity said finally. "I suppose folks have traveled that far to hear a good story. Once folks got full bellies and warm feet, a story's what they like best." And then, looking out the window: "Here come Nathaniel now, and by the look on him he got a story of his own to tell."

Elizabeth turned to look out the window. Then she put the book she had in her hands down and left the room.

"What is it?" Ethan said, still sitting on the floor before the hearth.

"Your cousin Lily is come home," said Curiosity from the window.

"Is Luke with her?" asked Ethan as he got to his feet.

"No," said Curiosity. "But that Simon Ballentyne surely is, and all the rest of the Hidden Wolf folk. Something's up, for sure."

Hannah, dragged against her will and wishes back into the practice of medicine, found that of all the small tasks she was called on to do, midwifery was the thing she liked the best.

Or had been, until she was called to Dora Cunningham in travail, and found herself in the middle of a scandal the village had been talking about for months. Now she wished she had paid more attention.

The woman on the narrow cot was thirty-five years old, unmarried, and about to bring her fourth child into the world. Only one of the others had survived beyond its fifth birthday, and that boy sat playing with blocks in the corner, his too-small head wobbling atop a spindly neck. He was called Joseph, and while he had little language he was sweet and biddable, content to sit by himself or work at the small tasks he had been taught to take on.

"I want to push now," Dora said, grabbing for the ropes tied to the foot of the bed.

"Not yet," said Hannah. "But soon."

"You listen to her now, Dora, or you'll tear up your fundament worse than last time." Goody Cunningham had a single tooth left in her head, but somehow she managed to speak clearly enough that Missy Parker heard her from her spot at the door. Hannah knew she had heard by the sharply indrawn breath that was louder even than Dora's moan.

Dora's face was contorted, her eyes near popping out of her skull, as she lifted herself up on her elbows.

"Listen to your mother," Hannah said. "She's right, you'll tear, and badly."

Hannah said it calmly, and with little hope that Dora would listen. Curiosity had warned her that Dora Cunningham, normally an even-tempered woman, could turn into a hellion when the misery was at its worst. And still she would find herself in this situation again, no doubt; every village had a woman or two whose generosity or need for affection outstripped good sense. In Paradise, that woman was Dora Cunningham. It was enough of a scandal that her brother Praise-Be had taken his wife and children and moved to another cabin, leaving his mother and sister without male protection.

"I want it OUT!" Dora bellowed. "Get it OUT!"

Hannah had come to the conclusion long ago that no man could really know the woman he called his wife unless he had seen her in travail. The man who had fathered this child had no idea what his few minutes of pleasure had wrought. Not that he would care; men were endlessly philosophical about the agony of childbirth. This one, at any case, might never even know he had a child. Not unless Dora gave up his name and demanded the little bit of support the law promised her.

And that explained Missy Parker standing at the door of the cabin with her hands folded primly in front of herself. Since Paradise had lost its last man of the cloth, Missy Parker had taken many of those responsibilities on herself.

"It's coming," Dora said. "It's coming now."

Dora Cunningham was a big woman, well built and comely, strong in body and mind, if not especially bright. If she got it in her head, Hannah thought to herself, she could probably expel her own internal organs. Her first push was evidence of just that, for it brought the child's head to crowning. The next pushed it into the world, but only as far as the neck.

Hannah, all her concentration on the proper rotation of the baby's shoulders, had not noticed Missy Parker moving. From the other side of the bed she leaned over and said, "Now is the time you must ask the question."

"Ask it yourself," Hannah answered.

"Oooooooh!" Dora wailed.

Missy Parker leaned in closer. "Dora Cunningham, in accordance with the laws of God and man, I ask you, who is the father of your child?"

Dora opened her mouth and wailed again and shook her head, this time covering her inquisitor with a shower of sweat and spit. Thus it happened that as Dora delivered her fourth child, a girl, Missy Parker was howling as loud as mother and child.

"The name of the father!" Missy thundered, using her immaculate apron to wipe her cheeks. "Tell me now, is Horace Greber the father of this child?"

Dora fell back against the bed and howled one last time. Then her gaze focused on Missy Parker, and something sour came into her expression.

When she had caught her breath she said, "You want the truth?"

"Of course," said the older woman, unable to hide her eagerness. Three other times she had carried out this ritual with Dora, and three times she had gone away disappointed.

A deep sense of unease came over Hannah, but she forced herself to concentrate on the task at hand. While she examined the child and cut the cord, she listened.

"Then here it is," Dora said, her hoarse voice raised above the cries of her daughter. "As you're so eager to know. You remember last May, when the letter come from Johnstown saying Mrs. Greber had run off from her husband and wasn't coming back?"

In Missy Parker's round, full face her eyes darted from side to side. One corner of her mouth jerked.

"Yes. Yes, I remember. Mr. Littlejohn brought the letter and Mr. Greber asked Mrs. Bonner to read it for him, right there at the trading post. And all those people right nearby."

She seemed to relish the memory.

"I need another push," Hannah interrupted. "Not too hard. For the afterbirth."

Dora's face knotted while she gave Hannah what she had asked for. When it cleared again, she blinked the sweat from her eyes and looked at Missy Parker.

"You remember it was Jonas Littlejohn who rode post that day."

Missy drew back. "Well, of course. Yes. What does he have to do with Mrs. Greber and her letter?"

"Listen and I'll tell you. Jonas Littlejohn left more than bad news behind him when he rode off the next morning. Say hello to his daughter."

Missy Parker clutched fists to her bosom, her mouth working wordlessly. A great rash of color had broken out on her face and neck. "You're *lying.*" She turned on her heel and marched to the door, where she fumbled with the latch, and then out into the cold.

The fire in the hearth roused at the sudden draft and then settled again. In the quiet the new mother and grandmother giggled softly.

"You gave her a shock," Hannah said, handing the swaddled newborn to her mother. "But what does Mrs. Parker have against Jonas Littlejohn?"

"He's married to Missy's youngest, her Thea," said Goody.

"Oh, dear," said Hannah. "I fear you'll have a hard time getting any help out of Mr. Littlejohn, then."

"Never thought I would," said Dora. "Never would have said his name, except—" Her chin trembled and she let out a squawk of laughter, rocking the mewling baby to her breast. "It was worth it though, wasn't it? Here she was hoping to get a new club to hit Horace Greber over the head with, and instead— Wasn't it worth it, to see the look on her face?"

On the way home, smiling to herself at nothing in particular, a series of sudden and unsettling realizations stopped Hannah in the snowy woods.

On her way home. She had a place that she thought of as home. Not her father's house or her grandmother's longhouse or her husband's village, but the house that was as much her home as Curiosity's. People had called it the doctor's place while Richard was alive and they called it that still, except that now she was the doctor. They gave her that title, some of them at least. In a village of whites, she was the doctor. She lived in a brick house with ten rooms, and fine furniture, and china, and beeswax candles. A library. A dispensary, filled with all the instruments a doctor might need. A laboratory, to experiment with whatever interested her by way of new herbs or medicines. A microscope.

Paradise had accepted her, because Richard Todd had made it clear that he found her worthy.

Hannah shook herself, and thought it through again.

The people of Paradise accepted her because they had known her all her life, as a girl and then as a young woman, at first carrying a basket for her grandmother or Curiosity, and later to bind their wounds and treat their fevers and to comfort their dying children. Nowhere else in the white world would such a thing be possible.

And then this idea, more surprising still: she was comfortable here, against all hope and expectation, and with that comfort came a new peacefulness and a quickening of the mind.

Sometimes when Hannah was looking at a sore ear or a gash or a listless child that needed worming, she thought of her journals and notes with regret, an emotion she had almost forgotten. Now and then she took down one of the books she had been left, an anatomy or a treatise on fevers, and found herself drawn in by the formal language of medicine. She understood that her native curiosity was coming back to life. The part of her that was a doctor approved; the rest of her, when occupied too long with these thoughts, began to hum with panic.

At times she saw glimpses of what life might be, here. With family around her, and girls to look after who were of an age to be her own daughters. She could live out her life like this or she could force herself back, all the way back, and live a woman's life.

Well nourished, her body had woken at a pace with her mind. At the last moon she had bled again, though it had been a year or more. To remind her: she could bear more children of her own, and raise them in the fine brick house. She could marry again; as strange as the idea might be, it had presented itself. In theory, she could marry again.

Or she could follow Dora Cunningham's example, and take pleasure and release where and when she pleased. It would be easier than finding the right husband in this white world.

There were trappers and backwoodsmen who would be glad of her, men who cared little what others might think of them. Such men often took Indian wives. Some of them helped themselves to more than one such woman at once.

It would shock her stepmother to hear such a thing said, but some part of Hannah did not dislike the idea. Such a husband would leave her with most of her freedom. He would spend a few weeks with her in the fall and spring; he would satisfy himself and her too, if she was lucky or demanding enough, and give her a child every year. Children three-quarters white, who would be accepted here in Paradise, begrudgingly, because they were Nathaniel Bonner's grandchildren.

She felt Strikes-the-Sky nearby. He had started coming to see her again, though not often. She wondered if he would go away for good, if she were to take another man. The laws of her people allowed her this, of course; she could have put him aside even while he lived. He had teased her about it now and then, when she was angry with him.

Look, he said. *Look at Kicking Bird. Would he be a better husband, do you think? Such a small thin man as Kicking Bird, surely he is not so selfish and thoughtless as to eat the last of the red corn soup.*

He said that with his arms wrapped around her waist and his mouth at her ear, tickling her with his breath while she struggled, saying ridiculous things until her anger slipped away from her. Then he would take her down to the furs and cover her until she forgot that she had come back to their hearth after working all day among the sick, to find that he had emptied the cooking pot.

Strikes-the-Sky, her husband. Gone now more than two years and still her tongue remembered and craved the taste of him.

As meat craves salt. She said those words aloud and watched them drift off in the white cloud of her breath. In that substance she could see his shape, far off at the edge of the forest. His voice was much closer.

There are other kinds of food in the world, he said to her. *Food without salt still fills the belly.*

It was true. There were worthwhile things in the world, and many of them were already in her hands. A home, a family, work, people who needed her help. Good things that held her here as surely as a pinned fly. Life here would be safe, and comfortable, and sterile.

Hannah wondered how long she could manage such a delicate balance, and where she might land when she lost it.

That thought was in her head when she stepped out of the woods a hundred feet from her door, candle lit in the dusk, and saw the snowshoe tracks leading up to the door. Many people, come at once, and with them, she knew somehow, the answers to some of the questions that haunted her.

• • •

At first, the shock of what Lily and Simon had to tell them took all the air from the world. In Curiosity's crowded kitchen they sat, each of them, robbed of the ability even to breathe.

It reminded Jennet of the day her father died. At the time it had been a revelation to her, that words, insubstantial words that could not be held or touched, could have silenced a whole village. *The laird is dead.* Four words that first struck the world dumb and then drew a cry from it that must be heard in the heavens.

Hannah said, "Of course I will go to them."

"I'll take her," said Nathaniel, and with that the turmoil began. Nathaniel would go; Elizabeth would not have it, nor would Curiosity. Nathaniel had promised his wife never to set foot in Canada again, and she would hold him to that promise.

"And if it means hog-tying you," Curiosity added with grim conviction.

Elizabeth said, "I will not lose both of you at once."

And Lily: "He is not dead. No one said that my brother was *dead.*" That word, spoken for the first time, brought forth weeping: from Elizabeth and Lily and young Gabriel, who sat beside his father as still as stone while the tears ran down his face.

"I will go," said Runs-from-Bears. His tone was steady and low and in response Elizabeth's tears welled again; in thankfulness, Jennet thought, and shame.

It was Simon Ballentyne who brought some quiet and calm back into the room. When he stood they turned their attention to him, and Jennet saw how much he was like his grandfather. The Ballentyne, they called him, capable and strong and clear-sighted in the face of disaster; her father's right hand for so many years.

Simon said, "The men who know the situation best are your son Sawatis"—he nodded to Many-Doves and Runs-from-Bears. "And the sachem Spotted-Fox. They know the island and many of the soldiers. Their faces are familiar but not suspect. They will do everything they can to see that your sons come home again hale. They have asked for Hannah, and she has agreed. Runs-from-Bears knows the territory better than I do, but I know it well. Will you let us take her to them?"

Jennet saw the words do their work. Elizabeth's face, cold and pale, Nathaniel's, alive with frustration and anger. Many-Doves, un-readable as ever to Jennet, and Runs-from-Bears, who stood behind his wife, unable or unwilling to sit.

Then Elizabeth turned to Lily. She said, "What do you think, daughter?"

Lily's hands were knotted in her lap. She studied them for a moment, and when she raised her head Jennet saw how much these months away had changed her. Lily said, "Simon is right."

"I will travel on my own and leave first," Runs-from-Bears said to Simon directly. "When will you follow?"

"Tomorrow," he said. "If you can be ready, Hannah?"

Hannah stood and smoothed her skirts with her hands. Then she managed a smile, a small one but a smile nevertheless. "There is a great deal to do, but yes, I think I can be ready." And here was the surprise: it had taken such catastrophic news to finally wake Hannah fully out of her long sleep of loss and sorrow. For the first time since she had come home, they saw in her the girl and daughter and sister they had been missing. Because she had been called back to the war she dreaded, to care for young soldiers who needed her.

Nathaniel made a sound, a clicking like a death beetle in the wall, perceptible to nobody but the two of them. She closed her eyes, and summoned the image of her son to her mind's eye.

They worked late into the night to make things ready. Hannah was in the middle of it all. She moved from room to room, giving direction and answering questions. She examined all the surgical instruments and sent most of them to the smithy for Joshua to sharpen, as Richard Todd had trained him to do. She sorted through baskets of linen and set the little girls to tearing what she needed into serviceable pieces. She sent Gabriel and Annie out to borrow every mortar and pestle in Paradise, and then under Many-Doves' watchful eye, dried herbs and roots were ground and mixed and carefully wrapped in greased paper.

Blankets were stacked, along with all the warm clothing that could be spared. Ethan insisted that his new mantle be added to the pile, and the woolen stockings that Curiosity had made for him to take on his journey. Curiosity emptied her stores of everything sweet, sugars white and brown and maple, hard candy and gingerbread, dried apples and pears and cherries. Word had spread through the village and neighbors came with loaves of bread and dried meat and crocks of honey.

Sometime, very late, Curiosity took the little girls off to bed in spite of their protests. Gabriel disappeared and would not show himself until Curiosity gave up the idea of doing the same for him. Lily was glad to have the boy nearby; of all the family, Gabriel's pleasure at her sudden homecoming was unconditional, without un-spoken questions or doubts.

Lily, working beside her mother, said very little. She did not trust her own voice; tears were a luxury that would have to wait until the work was done and the travelers were gone north.

Simon was going. Of course. She hadn't thought of it, and now there was nothing she could do to change that or even to delay it until they could speak to her parents of the arrangements between them. Not that there was any hurry, now. She felt faint at times, thinking of the things she would have to say, if only to her mother.

She would say them because she understood that to keep this to herself would build a wall that would always stand between them. She was frightened and ashamed to reveal the secrets she had kept, but they must be said.

For the first time since they came across Sawatis, Lily allowed herself to think of Nicholas Wilde and wondered what news there was; if he was even alive. Once or twice she felt Curiosity's sharp gaze on her, brimming with questions and worry. Lily forced herself to smile, and pinched her cheeks to give herself color, and turned her mind back to the work at hand.

In spite of everything she was thankful to be here, where she could reach out and touch her mother and talk to her about simple things. When he passed her Gabriel always stopped to wrap his arms around her waist and Lily swayed into his wiry embrace. Once he said, "Will Simon come back, sister?"

Before Lily could think how to answer, her mother spoke in her calm, even way. "I would suppose not," she said. "His home is in Montreal."

Jennet, who was near enough to hear this, cast Lily a questioning glance. Lily fixed her eyes on the chopping board and the knife, and refused to speak.

It was unfair to Simon, yes. She should speak up now and say: *he will come back, because I have asked him to. He will come back, because there is unfinished business between us.* But Lily needed time to think. *Coward,* she whispered to herself. *Coward.*

Yet another knock at the kitchen door, and then standing there in the firelight reflected off copper and brass, Nicholas Wilde. He was carrying two stout brown jugs, and he looked a hundred years old.

Next to Lily her mother stopped what she was doing, as did

Curiosity and Many-Doves and Jennet and Hannah. No doubt the mice in the walls had gone still too.

He was not dead, nor was he in prison; here was proof, but of what? His innocence, his duplicity, his poor judgment, his good luck. Lily realized two things: he was looking at her in a way that asked certain questions, and their connection was no secret to anyone in this room. How that had come to pass, she could only guess; she would rather cut out her tongue than ask, just now.

"I've brought cider," he said, his voice low and familiar and vaguely trembling. "I hope it might be some help." And he touched his brow and backed out of the kitchen, never quite there to start with. Before the door closed he caught Lily's eye directly and without apology.

"Welcome home," he said, and closed the door.

Hannah said, "You never got my letter about the hearing, did you? Your paths must have crossed, yours and the messenger."

"No," Lily said with a forced smile. "I didn't get it. But there's no time for village gossip just now."

What a poor liar she was, and they all saw it on her face. But they were good women and none of them meant to shame her, and so they turned back to their work.

Lily felt her mother's gaze on her, warm and concerned and disappointed, in her mild way. If she looked up she would see the same thing in Curiosity's face. Lily would have preferred anger and shouted insults to disappointment. She blinked the tears from her eyes and made careful examination of an imaginary nick on her paring knife.

It was midnight before the women were finished, and then they sat, wrung dry and giddy with exhaustion, around the hearth.

"Where are the men?" said Jennet, as if she had just remembered that such creatures existed in the world.

"In the parlor," said Sally.

Curiosity grunted. "No doubt with their dirty feet up on the good cushions."

In his mother's lap Gabriel yawned. "They sent me away." Too tired to show them the full measure of his resentment.

Elizabeth's long neck arched as she put her head back and blew a sigh at the rafters. "I cannot rouse myself to go ask questions, though I should."

Many-Doves said, "Let them think they can plan what will come, if it comforts them."

Jennet stretched a little and then looked around the circle. "I'm sorry to be so selfish," she said, two spots of new color on her cheekbones. "But I canna wait any longer. What word do you bring from your brother Luke?"

Hannah saw Lily start up out of a near sleep, and blink in surprise. "Oh, my," she said. "I meant to give it to you right away. I did promise him." To Gabriel she said, "Would you get the parcel I left in the front hall?"

Suddenly they were all awake, roused by the promise of one of Luke's packages. When the boy came again, Jennet touched the bulky parcel and closed her eyes.

"It ain't going to open itself," Curiosity said, a little impatiently. "Go on, girl. We could use something to smile about just now."

There were two letters, first of all. One Jennet handed to Elizabeth and the other she put carefully aside. Then a lumpy object wrapped in paper proved to be two brightly painted tops; those went to Elizabeth too, though Gabriel followed them with his eyes. Then came beautifully embroidered handkerchiefs, a small muslin bag of oddly smooth nuts, a box of nutmegs and curls of cinnamon bark, a large tin of cocoa that brought exclamations from Gabriel, a length of silk in a deep bright crimson and one of figured damask in blue-green, packets of tea, and at the bottom of the box, two soft packages wrapped in many layers of silk paper. Jennet took the first one in her lap.

"Oh, my," said Sally as the paper fell away. A length of lace spilled over Jennet's lap to the floor.

"Lace," said Curiosity, with a crackling satisfaction. "Fit for a bride."

"Valenciennes lace," added Elizabeth, catching one end in careful fingers to examine it more closely. "What workmanship, and look at the pattern. I have never seen the like."

"The color suits your complexion just right," Curiosity said. "That's a thoughtful man you got yourself, Jennet."

"What's in the next one?" Sally asked.

"Some silk, maybe," Curiosity said, as excited as a bride herself.

They all leaned forward as the paper was unwound and another length of lace came to light.

"It's not for me," said Jennet, reading a piece of paper that had fallen into her lap. "It's for Lily. 'A wedding gift,' it says."

In the silence that followed they heard the men's voices in the hall. Lily, who had gone very pale, looked no one in the face. She said, "It is complicated."

"I suppose it must be," said Curiosity. "But we ain't slow, child. You tell us, and we'll ask questions when we get confused. Or maybe we should call in Simon. He's right good at putting things in words, I'll bet he can explain it."

Gabriel, invigorated by the news, stood up as the hall door opened. "Da," he called with all the energy of a boy bent on bringing down the roof. "Our Lily's getting married!"

In the doorway Nathaniel pulled up short, and then came into the kitchen slowly. Behind him were Runs-from-Bears and Ethan.

Lily touched the lace in her lap: a pattern of swirled petals and delicate leaves in a pale rose color. When she looked up she saw her father's face and her mother's, both of them slack with weariness and worry and yet watchful, as if a strange creature had walked into the room and they were not sure, quite yet, what to make of it.

Then Simon was there too, his expression so sober. Lily wanted him to smile, to make light of it all. To take away this question that hung in the air, almost visible: more than she could bear, now.

He said, "It is a matter that should wait, I think, until I come back from Nut Island."

"From Montreal," said Jennet. "When you come back from Montreal."

All eyes turned to Jennet. Lily was so thankful to her cousin that she might have wept.

Jennet said, "It has been months since I've seen Luke. I would like to go to Montreal, just for a short visit. Since you are going that way anyway, Simon Ballentyne, you'll not refuse me, will you?"

Chapter 25

Luke Scott Bonner, Director
Forbes & Sons
Rue Bonsecours
Montreal

Dearest,
If you are the wise and thoughtful man I believe you to be, you will not
strike out at the messenger who brings you this letter. Simon Ballentyne
has done only as I compelled him to do. If he has taken my advice, you
are reading this alone, and he will absent himself until you have had time
to remember that if you must be angry, it should be at me, and me alone.

I am in Canada, with your sister Hannah. We are well; we have
adequate shelter and food and are in no danger of our lives or persons.
We are, as you will have guessed, on the Île aux Noix, or Nut Island. I
will use the English, as the French name is far too exotic for such a
rough jumble of blockhouses and barracks and parade grounds and boat
works.

Sawatis and Runs-from-Bears are here, just returned from their short
visit with you. Thus you know what brought us here, so let me give you
the most important news straightaway: your brother and cousin are
alive, if in some danger. It is for them we came, but it is only today that
we are assured of the possibility of caring for them.

After three days of waiting, your sister was finally admitted to an audience with the garrison commander, a Colonel Caudebec, originally of Québec, a man unknown to Simon and thus I would guess to you as well. The colonel was at first affronted by your sister's temerity and then too harried to resist her persistent logic; he has granted us permission to come inside the garrison from sunrise to sunset every day, if we restrict ourselves to the stockade.

There are only two surgeons here, and they see to the needs of hundreds of the soldiers and sailors and militiamen who come through daily. And had they time, I doubt they would find their way into the stockade for fear of the smallpox, which has taken many lives in the past weeks.

Now I ask you to remember that I was vaccinated against the smallpox at the same time you were, by Hakim Ibrahim. Likewise are the rest of your family safe, for your sister saw to their vaccinations long ago, the summer that she interned at the Kine-Pox Institute in Manhattan.

Here is what we know thus far of the conditions in the stockade after Hannah's first brief visit there today:

There are some fifty prisoners in a room designed for thirty, at the most. A month ago there were still more of them, but illness has reduced their number by a full third. Many have dysentery. Others have wounds that are poorly healed and require surgery, and perhaps amputation. They exist on a diet of poor gruel and bread. The food we brought with us, which seemed so much, is already gone. Hannah's medicines will last a little longer.

Blue-Jay has lost two toes to frostbite and may lose more. He took a bullet to his right leg, which was dug out for him by one of his compatriots. What infection resulted is mostly healed. Like many of the prisoners he has had typhoid, but unlike the majority of those unfortunates, he has survived and is recovering. He is thin, but in relative good health.

News of Daniel is more complex. His injuries are as follows: he took a bullet in his left side. Hannah bids me tell you that if the bullet had done irreparable harm, he would not have survived this long. Whether or not she will have to remove it surgically remains to be seen.

All the other injuries follow from the fact that he was in a tree when he was shot, and fell from a considerable height. He suffered a blow to his left shoulder and arm, and a number of ribs were cracked or broken.

Somehow he was spared typhoid, which would most certainly have killed him in his diminished condition.

Hannah had only a few minutes with him today, but she bids me assure you (and by extension, your parents) that with proper care, medicines, and food, he will recover. We are here to see that he gets all those things, and more.

The best indication of Daniel's condition I can send you is this: when Hannah came to him he was asleep, but woke and seeing her asked if she had brought any maple sugar from the first tapping. His second question was about his sister Lily, and his third, about his mother. Then he fell asleep again with maple sugar on his tongue.

You may not believe me, but I did not plan this turn of events. I truly meant to come straight to you, and to stay as long as you would allow me. But given the conditions here, what choice is there left? I could not, I simply could not leave Hannah here alone while I went on to feather beds and hot baths and amusements in Montreal.

You will argue, I can hear you across the miles, that she is not alone. But while these good men look out for *our* safety, they cannot go into the stockade to care for those whose need is far greater.

For what assurance it might provide, let me tell you of our lodgings in the followers' camp. We have paid for the privilege of putting down our pallets in a hut that belongs to an Abenaki woman who does laundry for some of the officers. In exchange for tobacco and coin she has given us much information and advice and a place at her smoky fire. It is of course the coarsest of housing, but we are only there while Sawatis builds a shack for our use, and in any case, we are there only to sleep.

You will want to come here, to take me away. I ask you to reconsider. If you must come, bring food and warm blankets and money to bribe the soldiers who guard the stockade, on whose goodwill and whim we must depend. Bring your support, your understanding, your patience. If you cannot, please stay away, but send us Simon with the things we need, and I will write to you as often as time permits.

Of course we must count on you to relay this information to your father and stepmother. It is your decision whether or not you will pass on all the details. And yet I must remind you that your stepmother is a strong woman and will not thank you for keeping the whole truth from her.

Finally, you should know that neither of us have ever used your name, nor shall we. The commander does not know of our connection to you, to Carryck, to Daniel, or to any family in New-York State. Here I am known as the Widow Huntar.

I will come to you, I promise, as soon as I can do so in good conscience.

Your loving bride,
Jennet
6th day of March, 1813

Chapter 26

When they had been on the island for not quite a fortnight, the thaw came upon them and forced a concession from Jennet, who had only scoffed at the stories: Canadian mud was not just water and earth, but a force unto itself, and a bloody-minded one, at that.

It all happened very suddenly. One night it snowed, the next day snow turned to rain, and within hours the island, overpopulated with pigs and dogs, mules and horses and men, had been churned into a great sticky pudding that sucked boots from feet and brought sleighs to a standstill. There were still frosts at night, and deep ones, but every day the weather was a little warmer, and the mud deeper.

"Sugaring days come around late this year," one of the prisoners told her in the same wistful tone he spoke about his wife and children. "But the sap's running now, I can smell it in the air."

So many of the prisoners were farmers and backwoodsmen; they talked very little about the war, but never tired of talking of the weather. Most of all they seemed to get pleasure in arguing: about the best way to tap a sugar maple or neuter new lambs or set a trap for a raccoon that wouldn't stay out of the corn. The muddy floor of the stockade was easier to forget, Jennet realized, when they set their minds on blackfly in July or harvesting flax.

At night when she and Hannah went back to their little shack, they found dried mud in their belly buttons and the creases behind their knees and under their arms. The hems of their dresses and stockings were caked with it; there was mud in their hair and eyebrows and in the baskets they used to carry supplies into the stockade. The only respite from the mud was the ice-clogged, swollen river, crowded with every vessel the British navy could commandeer.

Within days Jennet had forgotten completely what it meant to be warm and dry and clean. It was only the work that distracted her from chilblains and blood blisters and the growling of her own stomach. There was little food, or time to eat it; certainly she would waste no time on vanity.

Except that today she must rouse herself to notice such things and more. Shivering still from her sponge bath, Jennet took a gown from her traveling box. It should have been suitable for her meeting with Colonel Caudebec, except that the damp had found it first and the damask was sprinkled liberally with mold, and wrinkled beyond repair. Even to her desensitized nose it stank.

"I suppose the smell might get his attention," she said in a conversational tone. "Perhaps he'll give us the braziers just to get rid of me."

Hannah, her mouth full of cornbread, held out another gown. This one, never pretty, had seen hard use in its life; it was stained at hem and cuffs and a burn on the skirt had been patched with a fabric that matched neither in color or pattern. And still it was the best they had between them.

"I'll have to kittle up the skirt with my belt," Jennet said, reaching for it. Water ran from her hair over her arm and hissed into the fire.

Hannah said, "Come and let me comb through your hair again, and then we must be gone. It's almost light."

Jennet did as she was bid, pulling the cocoon of blankets more closely around her shoulders.

"Tell it again," Hannah said.

Jennet said, "Braziers, firewood, rations, Sergeant Jones."

"But not in that order," Hannah prompted.

"Not in that order. Jones first, or nothing else will do any good."

Behind her Hannah hesitated. "It's a fine line you'll have to walk."

"Och, that you leave to me," Jennet said. "I'm a daughter of Carryck, you mustn't forget. Did my father the earl not declare I could charm blood from a stone?"

"We don't need any more blood," Hannah said.

Jennet's mouth tightened. "We'll be rid of the wee Welsh cockerel before the day is out, or I'm no my father's daughter."

•   •   •

Just before sunrise they took their leave from Runs-from-Bears and joined the queue of women waiting at the garrison gates, all of them with blankets wrapped around their heads against the cold rain, all of them ankle deep in the muck and mud. Most were bent low by the weight of baskets filled with laundry or mending. A few of the youngest, still supple or pretty enough, carried nothing and wore little under their blanket coats.

Most of the women greeted Hannah, but to Jennet they gave only shy nods. Jennet might dress rough as they did and her hands might be as blistered with work; she could speak Scots and plain English and a common French, but the cap of damp curls under her hood was the yellow of corn silk, and her skin was as translucent as milk after all the cream has been skimmed from it. A white woman among the camp followers was odd enough, but one as young and fine-born as Jennet Huntar who was here to nurse prisoners of war—she must be a mystery and a danger.

The gates swung open and the crowd pushed forward.

"Do not put yourself in danger," Hannah said as they went forward. In response came only her cousin's grin and a fluttering of fingers.

"What is there to fear, with Sergeant Brodie to escort me?"

Waiting for Jennet just inside the gates, Uz Brodie heard this, exactly as Jennet meant him to. His cheeks had been scrubbed clean, resulting in two very red and shiny spots to either side of a blue-veined nose. On that hard-worn face a schoolboy's blush was both comical and touching.

In the followers' camp Jennet was an object of suspicion and some jealousy, but inside the garrison a pretty young Scots widow with a friendly word for everyone was highly thought of, and sought out. Doors opened quickly when she approached, and jackets and hats were put to rights. There were a dozen men who took every opportunity to cross paths with her, and then always found some topic to keep her talking for a minute or two.

In the first days the men had hesitated to ask questions. Then one of them had got up the courage and wondered out loud what it was that brought a young woman of good family to Nut Island. Jennet, ready for the question, had cocked her head to one side like a little bird and returned curiosity with wonder and Bible verses. And, she added, innocently enough, wouldn't any of the brave men of His Majesty's forces want and deserve a nurse like herself should he ever find himself, Lord preserve, on the other side of the border, in such a place as this? Among themselves the men decided that Mrs. Huntar was a war widow, a rumor that she did nothing to correct.

When asked about her connection to the Mohawk medicine woman called Walks-Ahead, Jennet would change the subject so neatly and sweetly that no one noticed, at least until it was too late, that she had provided no information at all. Jennet had the gift for pleasing and appeasing with a few bright words. It worked to their advantage and solved many of their problems, but not all.

Standing in front of the stockade was the problem that had sent Jennet to the colonel: one of the few men who had resisted her charms. Approaching him with mud sucking at her heels, Hannah kept her expression studiously blank.

"Sergeant Jones," she said. "Good morning."

He was a small man, soft of jowl and gut but with a jaw carved out of twisted gristle. The frizzled hair that showed under his hat had once been red, but had faded to a rusted iron gray. Wiry twists of the same color exploded from his ears and nostrils and cascaded over his pinkish eyes. When he opened his mouth he showed bloody gums studded with teeth like bits of weathered wood.

The muscles in his jaw popped and worked. Then he leaned forward and spat so that the gob of tobacco and spit landed just short of Hannah's toe. One of his better moods, then.

"Where's the princess?" he said.

"Mrs. Huntar had an errand this morning," said Hannah. "She will be here soon."

He considered her for a moment and then stepped aside just enough to let her walk by, though not without brushing against him. He smelled of sweat and stale tobacco and ale, and other things she did not want to contemplate.

As she passed he said, "I hear there's a pig upriver can speak French. But we got our own wonders, a redskin what talks like you."

"For what do I live and breathe," said Hannah, "but to amuse you, sir?"

There was no better way to rile Sergeant Jones than to speak above his understanding, something that was amazingly easy to do. For a moment Hannah thought that she had gone too far, but she watched him compose himself—he had not lasted so long in the dragoons without some measure of self-preservation. Hannah cursed her own short temper; she would have to be especially watchful today.

"I'll look forward to seeing her," the sergeant said as Hannah walked away. "Coming here all alone, like."

It was an empty threat. He might be prodigiously dim, as Jennet liked to put it, but Sergeant Jones was cunning enough to save his games for the prisoners who were least able to protect themselves. Sometimes, when she saw him from afar, Hannah was reminded of the fox she had killed so long ago on the mountain, and she wished for her bow, and a good straight arrow.

The armed guard at the double doors that opened into the stockade paid her less attention. Whether out of disinterest or fear of their sergeant, Hannah had never been sure. They went through her baskets, as they always did, and then the doors swung open.

The stockade was far better guarded than it was built. A building much like a stable, slung together as an afterthought. It had a few narrow windows that leaked cold through their shutters, a plank floor with mud oozing up between the cracks, and rows of narrow wooden bunks. On each bunk was a thin pallet of muslin ticking stuffed with straw, and on each pallet two men were meant to take their rest with the comfort of one or, if they were very fortunate, two blankets. The only heat came from an ancient and inefficient stove in the very middle of the room.

In her first interview with the colonel, Hannah had been informed that there was no space even for the most desperately sick prisoners in the regular infirmary, nor was there money or inclination to build a separate hospital for them. If the Mohawk medicine woman called Walks-Ahead was insistent on tending to the injured or ill in the stockade, then she must make do with a few tables, a pierced tin lamp, and however much firewood and water the prisoners were willing to haul for her. He said this with no malice or any emotion at all, and Hannah was thankful for his honesty, if not his lack of generosity.

As she stood at the door, fifty pairs of eyes turned to her, and she saw there what she saw every morning: surprise that she had not fled in the night, and varying degrees of relief and resentment.

One corner of the room she had taken over as her sick ward, but before she could go there and see her brother, she must spend the few minutes she had with the healthiest of the prisoners, who were assembling for work duty. One of them caught her attention immediately.

"Josiah," she said. "They've put you on the work detail? How is your wrist?"

The young man bobbed his head and would not meet her eye. "It'll do, miz." In the interest of their own safety and hers, the men knew her as Walks-Ahead. Some of them, the ones who were uncomfortable with her presence here, never called her anything at all, although they were polite enough, and tolerated her attention when they required it. She would have liked to think it was out of respect for her, but Hannah knew it had more to do with Blue-Jay, whose reputation as a swift dispenser of justice was well established.

She took a quick look at the young man's wrist, which had been badly broken and was still not completely healed. Certainly if he was asked to dig, the damage would be substantial. Hannah could go to the guards and ask for a favor, or to the sergeant and ask for a dispensation, or even to the garrison commander, if she felt strongly enough. But today Jennet was pleading a more important case in front of the colonel, and they must all tread very lightly.

She said, "If the wrist begins to swell, ask to be transferred to some other kind of work."

Something flashed in the young man's eyes, and she knew that she had both amused and affronted him. Of course Josiah Adams would do no such thing. He was a hotheaded son of Vermont, and he would cut off his hand before he asked quarter of a redcoat.

Quickly she walked down the line, looking for signs of fever and asking questions. Most of the men were not well enough fed for the kind of work that they would be asked to do: hauling wood or water or digging latrines or building fortifications. None of them would complain.

Blue-Jay was at the end of the line, as always. Compared to most of the others he was in excellent health, and his mother would have wept to see him.

She said, "Let me look at your tongue."

He shook his head, impatient, amused; boy and man she knew him, and expected little else. He said, "Daniel's fever was so high last night I almost sent for you."

"I will have to take the bullet out." Hannah said it aloud for the first time, and in response he blinked at her.

"Will you have the help you need?"

"Jennet will be here soon," Hannah said. She spoke Kahnyen'kehàka, because it drew a wall around them in this place without privacy. "And there was a package from Montreal yesterday. I have the medicines I need."

He might have had questions, but the queue was moving forward and the guards were quick to strike out at laggards. Hannah waited until the doors had closed and then began to pick her way across the room, crowded even now with half the men gone. From outside came a short scream and an explosion of laughter. Sergeant Jones, doing what he did best.

Hannah swallowed down her frustration and stopped to look at a man who had lost the sight in one eye. Every day he asked her when he would be healed.

The truth could not come as a surprise to him, but Hannah saw no need to rob him of hope, just yet. Instead she went to her little sick ward where her brother lay in this, his newest fever.

The prisoners were an odd mix of militiamen, army regulars, rangers, scouts. They were white and red, young and old, back-woodsmen, fishermen, and farmers from Vermont and New-York State and from as far away as Maine. The newest of them had been brought to the stockade just a week ago after a week's march. Of those fifteen men, six had already died, three were here among the hopeless, and the rest had been sent out to work.

She started, as she always did, with the worst wounded, the ones no one could help. John Trotter, once a butcher, was in the last stages of the smallpox; an Abenaki who called himself St. John had suffered a blow to the back that had rendered his kidneys incapable of their work; Olivier Theriot, a pig farmer from the Vermont–Canada border, had pneumonia in both lungs and a rage against the Tories that kept him alive far longer than Hannah would have predicted.

And there was the boy. They did not know his name and never would, for the bullet that had destroyed his jaw and burrowed into his head had plunged him into a coma so deep that no pain could rouse him. He lived only because the other prisoners had carried him here, dribbling water and gruel into his mouth. Out of respect for his bravery, they told her, but Hannah knew that it went far deeper: they nursed him for his youth and his beauty and for other reasons none of them could put to words.

The boy was no more than fifteen, slender and sleek, with a perfect face as blank as a doll's. Every day his eyes sank a little deeper in his skull, and soon he would slip beyond their reach and be buried in a pit under a blanket of quicklime.

Hannah spent a few minutes with each of these men, wiping sweaty faces and giving them teas she had brewed not to cure them, but to give them relief from pain, and rest.

While she was busy with them Mr. Whistler brought two more buckets of snow and set them to warm near the oven. He was one of the older prisoners, his freckled skull fringed with hair as stiff and straight as straw. Because he had been an apothecary's assistant in Boston, Mr. Whistler had appointed himself Hannah's majordomo, and had quickly got into the habit of reading her mind, or trying to. Most of the time he was close to right.

He was a strange little man but willing to do the most disagreeable jobs, and cheerfully; he didn't care that Hannah was Indian, or that she wasn't a man. He cared only that she had proper doctor's instruments and a surgeon's kit and medicines, and most of all, that she could name all the bones of the body with their Latin designation.

"A doctor without Latin ain't no doctor at all," he explained to the men who needed her help, to make sure they understood their good fortune.

"The food's come," he said to her, first thing.

Under direction from the guards two of the men were carrying in the great cook pot, its contents sloshing.

"Then take this," Hannah said, pushing one of her baskets toward him and pulling back a rag to show him the day's treasure.

"Eggs!" he said, his eyes flashing surprise and delight. "There must be three dozen of them!" He picked up one of the bigger ones, no bigger around than a silver dollar, but far more precious.

"It's hardly worth the work of cracking them," Hannah said. "They are so small. But I thought you could stir them into the gruel."

"Crack them?" Mr. Whistler echoed, looking at the egg in his palm. "Why, we'll swallow 'em whole. Where'd you get eggs?"

"A delivery came from Montreal late yesterday," she said. "From our good friend."

She never mentioned Luke's name, and neither did Mr. Whistler ask. But he was looking at her down the curved slope of his long nose.

"Did he send the medicine you wanted?"

"Some of it," Hannah said. "Enough."

"You'll do the operation, then?"

Hannah glanced at her brother. "Yes," she said. "As soon as Mrs. Huntar comes."

With a grunt of satisfaction Mr. Whistler gathered up the bundle of eggs and trotted over to the men who were gathered around the gruel.

Hannah went to her brother and crouched beside his pallet. He was asleep, a rare thing given the pain he must deal with, day and night. Later he would need all the strength he could muster, and so she did not wake him. Instead she did as she had been trained to do: she observed him.

At twelve Daniel had already been taller than every female in the family, and now his lower legs extended well beyond the end of the bunk. All the bones in his face shone through his skin. Even a full month's beard, dark brown and curly, could not disguise the way his mouth was bracketed with pain lines. His lips were cracked and bloody with fever.

If he had learned only one thing in his brief time as a soldier, it was the meaning of pain. On top of that he was wound up tight in a heavy wool blanket.

No matter how patiently or firmly she explained that a fever was not a fire that could be suffocated, Mr. Whistler could do nothing less than swaddle a fevered man like a newborn. Usually Blue-Jay was able to stop Mr. Whistler by simply making sure that there were no blankets to spare, but this morning Daniel was wrapped as Hannah had swaddled him the day he was born in the middle of a February blizzard.

Without any effort at all she remembered the smell of him, the rosy slick skin, how hot he had felt in her arms, how he had quieted when she held him and spoke to him. How he had opened his eyes and looked at her, eyes green from the start under a mass of damp dark curls. Eyes as green as the sea.

When he was still an infant she had sometimes unwrapped him just to study the shape of his knees or wrists, the curve of his shoulders, the folds of skin at his neck. Her father's son, her brother.

Now if she were to unwrap him she would find the evidence of the lost battle that had brought him here. She had heard the story many times already, and no doubt would hear it again. Every time she had to contain her temper and impatience and listen as if she could never have enough of such things: messengers gone wrong, poorly marked trails, troops waylaid, ammunition lost in whitewater, failed maneuvers, flawed strategies, bullets spent and graves dug.

And the result: her brother's body, a map of the war. Bruises from hip to neck, still dark over the broken ribs but otherwise faded to the yellow-green of a storm sky. Nicks and scratches and the bullet wound, raw and seeping.

The bullet in his side was what concerned her at the moment, but it was not what worried her most. She had dealt with wounds like this one so many times that she had a feel for them, and this one would not get the better of her. She would not allow it.

She could not say as much for his arm. Crouched beside him Hannah studied the curve of his neck where it met his shoulder. A year ago she would have been hard-pressed to remember the names even of the major muscles, but now it seemed she could simply look through cloth and skin and past bone to the heart of the damage caused when he had fallen unconscious from the tree. He had asked her, and she had given him the details he wanted: the brachial plexus, a braid of nerves bedded in the shoulder, protected by bone and muscle, the names of the five trunks that moved down into the arm to branch and branch again. More names he did not need to know and would not recall: radial, ulnar, median, musculocutaneous.

It had taken all her strength to hide her unease when she had first examined his arm and seen how little control he had over elbow and wrist and fingers. The fact that he was not able to lie to her about the pain was just as alarming: this brother, who had once sat still while she stitched a long gash on his leg without uttering a sound.

She made a sling for his arm and told him to keep it still. She used her firmest and most threatening voice, her older-sister voice. As if it were her bossy nature and not the injury that kept him from walking around the room on his hands.

Then he had used his good hand to stop her, catching the fabric of her overdress in his fingers.

"Will you have to take it off?"

The first amputation she had ever done on her own had been of an arm, and somehow Hannah had the sense that he was remembering that, and how it ended.

"There is no sign of gangrene," she said. Something she had said before, but he must hear it again. "There is sufficient blood flow to your fingers. You see, the color is good and they are warm to the touch."

"Will you have to take it off?" His gaze never wavered, nor his voice.

"No," she said. "No, I will not."

"Will I have the use of it again?"

Another man might have asked when the pain would stop. Hannah wished he had asked that question.

"I don't know," she said, meeting his gaze. And then, in a firmer voice: "Maybe."

He had closed his eyes and turned his face away, but not before she saw that he was weeping.

At night, sometimes, Hannah lay awake and wished for the Hakim, who had been her teacher for a while. While the men prayed aloud to Jesus and his mother and the saints, she conjured forth her many teachers out of her memories: her grandmothers Falling-Day and Cora Munro, Curiosity, Richard Todd, Valentine Simon. They came at her bidding and each of them told her what she knew already. There was nothing she could do for her brother; no medicine or knife existed that could mend damaged nerves. They would recover and he would have the use of his arm, or they would not.

She put a palm to Daniel's cheek, and he roused himself to her touch.

He was thirsty. She helped him to water, and then to the gruel. Two of the larger eggs had been put aside for him. He wrinkled his nose at the idea of eating them raw and swallowed them whole, as most of the others did. When he had eaten she helped him lie down again, and then set about unwrapping him.

"There was a package late yesterday, from Luke."

She studied his face while she worked. From the set of his eyes and mouth she could read how fierce the pain was.

"He sent the medicines you asked for?"

"Yes. Dragon's blood and willow bark and laudanum, and the rest of it. New needles too."

"Simon?"

"Yes," Hannah said, not bothering to hide her smile. "If you're in a mood to argue about Simon Ballentyne you must be feeling strong today."

At that he pushed an impatient breath out through his nose. "My business with Simon Ballentyne is my business," he said.

"Spoken like a protective brother," Hannah said.

His mouth twitched, but Daniel did not take up the challenge.

She said, "I think it must be today, Daniel. The bullet."

Wherever his thoughts had been, he turned his attention back to her.

"I thought you said it would work its way out."

"I hoped that it would," she said. "But the infection is worse, and I can't take the chance of leaving it any longer."

"Today?"

She paused. "Yes. As soon as Jennet is here."

His gaze flickered toward her and along with it came a faint smile. "You've sent her to see Caudebec."

"I would not put it like that," Hannah said. "Jennet can no more be sent on an errand than a cat. She decided what must be done, and she is doing it. I only hope she hasn't lost her touch."

That made Daniel laugh, at least. A low, deep chuckle that turned into a shallow cough. Hannah did not like the sound of it, but she was a healer before she was a sister, and she kept the full force of her alarm hidden away.

Jennet had only seen Colonel Caudebec from afar once or twice: a man of medium height and build, with nothing out of the ordinary to recommend him except that it was within his power to make the prisoners miserable. Stepping into his quarters, she learned something else: the colonel was a man who appreciated art and beautiful things and the comforts of civilization, and not even war was enough to make him give such things up.

He had taken over the entire upper level of one of the blockhouses for his office and quarters, and filled it with fine things: china and glass and a beautiful India rug. A servant asked her for her muddy boots before she had come more than two steps into the room, and then made them disappear where they would do no damage. A large crucifix dominated one wall, and in a corner was a statue of the Virgin, cast in bronze. Next to that was an ornate chair, carved and cushioned with red velvet, and in the chair sat the tallest priest she had ever seen. Even without an introduction she would have known him from the stories the soldiers told.

The colonel almost simpered, so proud was he of his visitor. "Father O'Neill, may I present Mrs. Huntar, who works among our prisoners."

He unfolded himself from the chair, a man six and a half feet tall, with a head of black hair going gray at the widow's peak and sharp blue eyes and a smile that spoke more of the ways of the world than those of heaven.

"Mrs. Huntar," he said, not quite meeting her eye. "Please, sit. I have questions for you."

"Questions," she echoed, and wondered if she looked as dim as she sounded.

"About your work here. You must be a very unusual and courageous lady indeed."

"Ah," said Jennet. "Weel."

He was examining her face closely. "Not many have the fortitude or courage to take up missionary work, especially not in time of war."

Jennet's first assessment of the priest was shifting rapidly. In part because she couldn't place his accent—it was not Irish, not English, not American, but some odd combination of all those with a strong undercurrent of French. Beyond that first and distracting question, there was a crumble of bread at the corner of his mouth, tucked into a crease. And whoever had shaved the priest this morning had been distracted enough to leave a patch of bristle in the thumb-sized indentation under his lower lip. Jennet simply could not look away, though she knew that she must.

If the priest minded he was good at hiding his discomfort. He went on making observations and assumptions and drawing the most incredible conclusions without any encouragement. One part of Jennet's mind wondered where he might end up if he went on like this.

"—known to me."

She blinked. "I'm sorry, sir. I'm a wee muddleheided the morn."

And now Scots. It had the habit of pouring out of her at the oddest moments.

"You are a widow, as I understand it? I was asking what brought you to this part of the world."

Jennet had always been particularly good at making up stories on the spot, and she had polished and refined the gift over the years. A gift that might fail her now; she felt herself blanching.

"I meant to cause you no distress," the priest said. He put a hand on her wrist where it rested on the arm of the chair, and Jennet started at that: the heat of him, and his closeness, and something else she could hardly name.

She remembered then why she was making this visit, and the men in the stockade, whose well-being depended on what she could accomplish here.

Jennet withdrew her hand. "I am a widow woman, aye. My husband was a vicar, ye see. We were on our way here as missionaries when he took ill. He wanted me to carry on without him, and so I try, poor woman that I am."

The priest's blue eyes considered her, calculating openly, adding things together and taking others away. Jennet had the strangest sense that she had met the man before, and realized then that he reminded her of her own father: someone with the gift of seeing the truth no matter how well hidden it might be, and using it to his own advantage.

She must rise to that challenge, for her own sake and for the sake of the men who were counting on her.

He said, "Would you object, then, to my visiting the Catholic prisoners?"

She didn't like the idea at all, of course, but Jennet could do nothing but smile and assure him that his company would be welcome.

"I would like to have the chance to talk to you a bit about my mission," said the priest. "I think my work will interest you. I have a sister who took orders with Grey Nuns in Montreal. You remind me of her."

Jennet pressed her hands together in her lap. "But of course, Father O'Neill. I would be pleased. In the meantime there are a few matters I must discuss with the colonel."

The priest's gaze never left her face. "Ah, yes. You've come to ask for favors for the prisoners, have I guessed it? I'm sure that Colonel Caudebec would be happy to see that your needs are met, is that not so, Colonel?"

Jennet thought of Sergeant Jones, and wondered if trading that problem for the one in front of her was such a very good idea. But the colonel was looking at her, his expression all eagerness. She took a deep breath, and presented her case.

"I'll tell you aye true," Jennet told Hannah much later. "I came close to wetting my drawers when I saw him sitting there. As big as a house, and hawk-eyed, forbye."

"You know this priest?" Hannah whispered, pulling Jennet farther into the corner where they had gone to talk. Next to them the boy slept on with his eyes open and fixed on nothing in particular. The regular slow hiss of his breath was the only sign that he still lived.

"I know of Adam O'Neill, aye," Jennet whispered. "And so do you. The priest wha thumped Uz Brodie on the head with his crucifix. You recall, he told us the tale when we were here no two days, when he was on guard duty."

Hannah said, "You're speaking Scots. You must be worried."

"A wee bit, aye." Jennet pursed her mouth. "I've known many priests in my time, but none like this Father O'Neill."

"You knew that before," Hannah said. "From the stories."

"Och, I don't mean the fighting. There are stories enough about soldier-priests. I canna tell ye what it is exactly that bothers me. Nor can I tell ye what the man's doing here, beyond the fact that he's got some connection to Caudebec. It's no like I could ask, you'll agree."

"All right," Hannah said, forcing herself to breathe deeply. "Could he be some kind of spy?"

"I thought of that," Jennet said. "I suppose it's possible, but what could he want to learn from this poor lot?"

She cast a quick look over their patients. Mr. Whistler, watching them closely while he tended to the brazier, nodded at her and she raised a hand in greeting. Then she sent Hannah a sharp look.

"I've been thinking, perhaps it would be best if I let the colonel know whose daughter I am."

Hannah saw a particular look in her cousin's eye that made her nervous indeed. She pitched her voice a tone lower. "Jennet. We've discussed all this. If they know *that,* then they know that you're connected to Luke. And there's good reason to keep Luke out of all this, you'll remember that much."

She pushed out a breath and the curls that fell over her forehead stirred irritably.

"Out of what? I'm here against Luke's wishes, am I no? You read the letter." She flushed a little, remembering the single closely written page delivered by Simon Ballentyne. The only thing that had made it bearable was the fact that along with the letter came all the things she had asked him for: food and blankets and medicines. The gift of a good friend, an anonymous donor. The man she was supposed to marry. If she did not drive him away, first.

"Jennet," Hannah said sharply. "Don't forget why we're here. As soon as Daniel is well enough to travel we'll be away. Runs-from-Bears and Sawatis will find a way. And how would it look, once we're gone? Then Luke would be connected to the escape, and maybe to worse."

She didn't say the word, the one word that could bring disaster down on all of them. The Tories made short work of anyone they suspected of spying. It was one of the reasons that both of them were careful never to talk to any of the guards or soldiers about things even vaguely military.

The small red mouth contorted. "Aye. Aye, aye, aye. I see that, I do. But I just thought—"

Hannah waited.

"Had ye thought," Jennet began again, "how much I could do for these prisoners, were the officers to know who I am? Jennet Huntar brings them a handful of eggs. But there's verra little they could refuse Lady Jennet of Carryck. And aye, it's far too great a risk. I'll bide my time, you have my promise."

There was a small silence. Hannah smoothed her cousin's hair away from her face and managed a smile.

"What about the rest of it? Were you able to present our case to Caudebec? You do remember? Braziers, firewood, rations, *Jones.*"

"Och, aye. Of course I remembered." Jennet was looking over Hannah's shoulder.

"And?"

Jennet pointed with her chin. "Yon's your answer on one point, at least."

Sergeant Jones had appeared at the doors. His face was contorted with anger, white and red and trembling. Jennet and Hannah stood just as they were, unflinching.

For a moment Hannah thought the sergeant would speak, but then he turned on his heel and left. The doors closed behind him.

"That's the end of Jones," said Jennet. "He's been reassigned to Halifax, I think the colonel said."

It took a moment for Hannah to understand. "Caudebec has sent him away?"

"Aye. Father O'Neill said Caudebec should, and so he did. And then he promised braziers and wood and better food, forbye—and all in front of the priest. What Father O'Neill said was, to tell it all, that if the British army was living off American pork smuggled over the border, American prisoners should get no less."

"Did he?" Hannah bit back a smile. "He sounds like a good friend to have, this priest of yours."

"It does seem that way. To tell you true, I had the sense that the priest could talk the colonel into sending us all home, if he got that in his head."

A flush of color moved over her neck, and she dropped her head to study her shoes.

"And what did all of that cost?" Hannah crossed her arms at her waist. "What did you have to give him?"

"Och, no so verra much," Jennet said.

"Let me guess. You said he could come preach, here. Among the prisoners."

Jennet's mouth twitched. "As if he needed my leave, or yours. He'll come, no doubt. And we canna stop him, even if we cared to."

"What then? I know you well enough, Jennet. There's something you're up to."

Her cousin was smiling now. This was Jennet with a hand of cards she liked: whether to bluff with, or to take the pot, Hannah was not sure.

"I think he wants to win me over for the church, and I intend to let him."

For once Hannah felt herself completely at a loss. "Win you over . . . baptize you into the Catholic church?"

"Aye."

"Jennet. You are Catholic."

Her cousin smiled up at her prettily. "Aye, I am. But there are so few of us in Scotland these days—and Father O'Neill doesn't need to know I'm one of them, does he? He wants to tell me about his sister the nun."

For a moment Hannah studied her cousin. There were faint lines at the corners of her eyes that told not so much her age as her temperament. For all her laughing ways, Jennet was sharp-witted and keen-eyed, and there was something about this priest she was not saying, and did not want to say. Out of fear, or the idea that she must protect others before she thought of her own welfare.

I cannot manage her on my own, Hannah thought. *I should send her to Luke. As soon as Daniel is well enough to travel, I must send her to Luke.*

Instead she said, "You mustn't take unreasonable risks, Jennet. Promise me."

Jennet closed her eyes and opened them again. "I promise. But it's no so bad as you imagine. Caudebec wants to please the priest. Why, I canna say. There's something afoot there. But so long as the priest is here, Caudebec is far more likely to be generous. And if it makes yon bloody great Irish priest happy to poach a soul for Rome, why then he shall have his convert. Who will it hurt, I ask you?"

Hannah could not help herself: she burst into laughter.

The men turned from their pallets to look at her, pleased at her laughter and a little wistful, that there should be something to laugh about that excluded them, hungry for diversion as they were.

When Hannah had calmed herself Jennet said, all business now: "Shouldn't we start with Daniel while we still have the light?"

Hannah said, "Yes, I suppose we should."

And then she followed her cousin to her brother's bedside, and set about making him ready.

It was not hard to assemble the things she would need: the single brown bottle of laudanum, dressings newly washed and folded, the herbs she had ground into a salve this morning, tincture of winterbloom, willow bark, and meadowsweet. Jennet went to the guard to request Hannah's surgeon's kit, kept under lock and key in the sergeant's office. She would come back with the box and two armed guards, who would not leave again until the operation was done and they could take the instruments away with them. As if sick men armed with scalpels might overpower the garrison. Mr. Whistler ranted at the idea, but it pleased him, too, that the redcoats should fear such a motley collection of underfed farmers and trappers.

There was a moment, while Jennet was out of sight and Daniel lay on the table before her, pale and sweating, that Hannah imagined the worst: Sergeant Jones had taken her surgeon's kit with him. She was wishing that she had thought of this possibility before Jennet went to see Caudebec, when her cousin appeared with the box in her arms and two great guards behind her, their scarlet coats like beacons in the dim barracks.

And that, of course, was what had taken so long: Jennet had needed the time to convince them that they wanted nothing more in the world than to bring every candle they could find.

Mr. Whistler said, "She was born with the touch, was our Miz Jennet."

From deep inside his laudanum haze, Daniel laughed.

"A swallow more?" Mr. Whistler asked her, and then lifted up Daniel's head to slip the spoon between slackened lips.

Hannah, convinced not so long ago that she would never again pick up a probe or scalpel, had found that she hadn't forgotten anything at all. The instruments came to her hand as easily as a quill came to her stepmother's, and obeyed her in the same way. In her first day she amputated four frostbitten fingers and six toes, sutured and cauterized and abraided wounds, moving from one man to the next.

She was reminded, to her surprise, that there was a pleasure to be had in the work. When things went well she brought relief. Some of the men had lived with severe pain for so long that its sudden absence rendered them as helpless as infants, who must weep themselves to sleep. Even if she had to take a foot or an arm to save a life there was some satisfaction in doing it well and cleanly. A farmer without a leg might still tend his crops and raise his children and give a wife comfort.

The first thing was to forget who the man tied to the table was. He was not her brother or anyone she had ever met or hoped to know. What she had before her was simply a body, a long plane of abdomen, winter pale. There was so little fat on him that she could see each of the muscle groups clearly defined, and the beat of his pulse, too, between breaths.

The wound itself, a dark red dimple in the plane of the oblique muscle, had made a bed for itself as angry and threatening as a wasp's nest. One she must disturb.

In the light of the candles Hannah traced the bed of infection first with her eyes and then, gently probing, with her fingers.

Sleepily Daniel said, "Don't you be a coward, sister, and neither will I."

Across from Hannah Jennet said nothing, but she was pale and sweat had broken out on her forehead.

With a quick, neat movement, she made a curved incision. A thick river of pus and blood welled up in the track of the scalpel. There was a tensing in the muscles, and Daniel made a small sound: relief more than pain.

All through the room men had gone very quiet. Cards and dominoes and dice were forgotten, arguments faded away as Hannah worked.

"Christ, what a stench," said one of the redcoats. Then he turned away and vomited onto his boots. The smell of porridge and ale joined the miasma that hung around the table: laudanum, sweat, blood, infection.

"Just a little put–ri–fi–cation," sang Mr. Whistler, rolling each syllable. "Just a spot of corruption to be washed away."

Hannah heard her own voice clear and sharp and far away, asking for the things she needed. When it came time to dig into the muscle, Jennet handed her the probe with a hand that shook only a little.

"Shall I give him more laudanum?" asked Mr. Whistler, and got a negative grunt from Daniel in reply. In the minute it took Hannah to find the bullet and extract it, that was the only sound he made.

"Well, look there," Mr. Whistler said in a conversational tone. "There it is, the devil. I suppose that was a bullet once, but it don't look like much now at all."

Hannah was pulling something from the wound: thin and ragged and bloody, it unwound itself endlessly from its cave, and then fell with a wet plop to the table.

"Christ above," said Mr. Whistler. "What *is* that?"

"A piece of shirting," said Hannah.

"Well, no wonder then," Jennet said, gently scolding. "You're meant to wear clothes on the outside, man."

Soft laughter echoed through the room. From Daniel there was nothing at all, for he had finally fainted.

"It took him long enough," said Mr. Whistler, and even Hannah must smile at that.

"Now you've done it," Jennet said quietly. "Now you've gone and saved your brother's life. You'll never hear the end of it, my dear."

Chapter 27

Dear family,

Simon Ballentyne has stopped here on his way back to Paradise and must be soon away. I write in my own hand so you will see and understand the full truth of my words. Runs-from-Bears sends his own message to my aunt and cousins with news of Blue-Jay, and so here I will write only of Daniel.

Just today I removed a bullet from my brother's side. It was bedded deep in the muscle and did not come out willingly, but the wound is clean now and drains as it should.

The damage to his left arm is more troubling, and about it I can say only that there was some unknown injury to muscles and nerves in the shoulder. He is in some considerable pain, but he bears it without complaint. Please tell my aunt Many-Doves and Curiosity that he drinks the tea they sent every day, as they would approve.

Jennet and I are very busy caring for the prisoners, but we are well. Outside the garrison my uncle and cousin look after our needs, and inside the garrison we have the colonel's promise of safe-passage. For Simon's good help we are especially thankful.

In all haste,
Your loving daughter
Hannah, also called Walks-Ahead by the Kahnyen'kehàka, her mother's people, and Walking-Woman by her husband's. Written in her own hand the first day of March 1813.

Chapter 28

With the news of the misfortune that had befallen Daniel and Blue-Jay, the gossiping quieted for as much as a full day, and then flared back to life with a roar: Lily Bonner had come home, after all, to find her lover married. Whatever disappointment the villagers might have felt about the loss of Jennet and her stories was offset by the idea that sooner or later Lily would have to speak up and put an end to all the rumors.

Given her choice, Lily would have pretended that she had never been away, had never seen or heard of the city of Montreal, and most certainly had never known anyone who went by the name of Nicholas Wilde or Simon Ballentyne.

During the day she kept busy enough with the sugaring, which had always been one of her favorite things. She spent her days with Gabriel and Annie, checking the sap buckets and pouring them into the cauldron Many-Doves watched over. It was work Gabriel disliked but he knew better than to complain to his aunt or father, who would have scolded him or, worse, laughed at him. He satisfied himself with saving his complaints for Lily and Annie.

"I don't hear you complaining in the morning when my mother turns out the cakes," Annie pointed out to him now and then, and he had the good grace to duck his head and grin. Like the rest of the men at Lake in the Clouds, Gabriel had a weakness for maple sugar in all its forms.

The nights were harder. Sometimes, alone in the chamber she had last shared with her sister and cousin, Lily lay awake and wondered what was worse about going into the village: the questions about Simon, or the stories about Nicholas and his new wife. Stories so awful that she did not want to believe them, no matter how many times she was told.

Everyone had their own ideas about Jemima and Nicholas, and everyone was sure that Lily must share their conclusions, if only they could try to explain it one more time.

Curiosity's report was all that Lily had needed or wanted, and that she had got straightaway, and without embellishment. Jemima had acted as Jemima had always and would always act: with her own interest and survival first and foremost. She had let Dolly Wilde wander off to her death, and then she had taken advantage of a lonely man in mourning. And now she was pregnant by Nicholas, who had become the brunt of the joke.

"He was ripe for the picking," Curiosity had told Lily. "All she had to do was shake the tree a little." And then Curiosity had put her long, cool hands on Lily's face and said the rest of it.

"He did a foolish thing, child. But he ain't the first good man to be towed down the road to perdition by his privates, and he won't be the last. No call to go red in the face, now. I'm speaking plain, woman to woman. No call to hate the man either. Lord knows he's reaping a fool's bounty."

Lily said, "I don't hate him. I couldn't hate him."

"Good," Curiosity said. "Now the next thing is, you got to put him out of your mind."

That would be harder, of course. First, because unless she avoided the village completely, she must come across Nicholas or Jemima with some regularity; and second, because everyone in Paradise knew that there had been some connection between them. Some illicit connection, the nature of which required grave and nonstop discussion, if not direct questions.

In the trading post to buy some salt a few days after she came home, Lily came face to face with Missy Parker, who studied her waistline openly. According to Martha and Callie, who were willing to share all the village gossip that her own mother and Curiosity had held back, Missy Parker was convinced in her soul that Lily had been sent to Montreal to bring Nicholas Wilde's bastard into the world. Now, confronted with the fact of Lily's waist—narrower now than when she left—even Missy Parker must concede that point.

"You must be very disappointed," Lily said.

Missy Parker sniffed, the tic in her right eye fluttering. She had no idea what Lily was talking about, and no time for such nonsense either.

Lily would have been satisifed to leave it at that, but Anna could not. To the men playing skittles in front of the stove and the girls examining hair ribbons and Nettie Dubonnet who nursed her youngest in the corner, she announced her opinion in a loud and clear voice: Lily Bonner was a fine girl of upstanding moral character and a friend to many folks, young and old, men and women, rich and poor, and if some folks had got the idea that she was anything but Christian and charitable, why then they should bring those claims directly to her, Anna Metzler Hauptmann McGarrity, so that she could set them back on the straight and narrow. And by the way, shouldn't those folks who professed themselves to be scholars of the good book remember that part about motes and beams and minding your own business?

This story Lily took to her mother, hoping to make her laugh. There was very little laughter at Lake in the Clouds since she had come home, or more upsetting still, very little talk at all. But Elizabeth had only listened in silence and then thought for a while, in her quiet way. Then she said, "In a week or so they will find something else to occupy them. You must be patient."

Lily had been expecting something very different from her mother: a long talk about rights and responsibilities and appropriate behaviors. Elizabeth Middleton Bonner would approach the problem of a daughter's compromised reputation from a number of directions at once, and leave books on her bed with passages marked for her to read: Locke on education and potential, Paine on liberty and the rights of man, and most certainly her mother's favorite, the staid old German philosopher Kant, with his eternal chasing after truth on the wings of categorical imperative.

Lily admitted with some reluctance that she had missed such discussions with her mother, and had been looking forward to them again, even if it were her own behavior and poor choices that were to be taken apart and examined with the help of Mr. Kant. And it would have happened, if not for Daniel. The truth was, they were all too worried about what was happening in the stockade at Nut Island to talk philosophy or to pay any attention to the gossips, even when it came to the mess that Lily had got herself into.

It wasn't fair, and there was nothing to be done about it. Curiosity seemed to be the only one who took note, but the comfort that she had to offer was laced with bitter truths.

"One of the worst things about being a woman," Curiosity had said to her, "is the waiting. Seem like you always waiting for something. Just now your mama plain out of her head with worry about your brother, and you got to wait until she come up for air and see you standing there. It don't seem fair, I know. It ain't fair, I suppose. But she ain't forgot about you."

In the evening they sat together and her mother read aloud as she always had, except that now sometimes her voice trailed away to nothing. Then they would all sit in silence looking into the fire and thinking of Daniel and Blue-Jay and Jennet and Hannah, thrown back into the maw of the war she had never even wanted to talk about. Even Gabriel was withdrawn and difficult to reach. In the night sometimes he cried out.

It was a relief to have him to comfort. Lily sat with him, his head bedded on her lap while she stroked his hair and spoke calm words and watched until he drifted back to a more peaceful sleep.

Annie followed her around in the day, full of questions that had no answers. It was odd, Lily thought, how for each of them worry took a different face. Many-Doves worked from dawn and well into the night, until she fell into an exhausted sleep. Elizabeth knitted stocking after stocking and wrote letters to every cousin and friend; Nathaniel walked.

Up before first light, he would take his rifle down from the rack over the door and slip out. Lily imagined him on the mountain, his back to the sunrise as he studied the horizon to the north. In his mind's eye he would travel the great lake, winding through islands to where Champlain narrowed into the Sorel, all the way to Nut Island and the stockade.

Every morning she lay awake and hoped that her father would come and ask her to walk with him, and every morning he went alone.

When she had been home a week, Lily began to believe that her father was never going to raise the subject of Simon Ballentyne or Nicholas Wilde with her. At first it was a relief and then, quite quickly, a burden. The surprise was this: his anger would have been easier to bear than the terrible weight of his thoughtful silence.

Then one day she came home and found her father sitting in front of the hearth across from Nicholas Wilde.

She stood in the doorway, her heart beating so hard in her throat that she couldn't make a sound. Instead she closed the door and took off her mantle and hung it on its hook, and then she came into the room in her stocking feet and waited.

"It's time we talked," said her father. "There's business we need to settle."

Lily had seen Nicholas three times since she came home: that night in Curiosity's kitchen, and twice from afar when she was on her way home from the village. She had yet to see Jemima at all. This was the first time she could really look at Nicholas, and what she saw was more painful than any stories told in malice.

He's reaping a fool's bounty, Curiosity had said. At the time it hadn't meant very much to Lily, but now she saw what the last months had cost this man.

Nicholas stared at his hands while he spoke. He said, "I just want to say once more in front of Lily what I said to you before, Nathaniel. I'm sorry for the hurt I've caused. I should have known better than to let you get attached to me, no matter how innocent it was. It was wrong, and I apologize."

There was a stone in her throat, one that would choke her if she did not spit it out or swallow it. But if she said those things that were in her mind, if she put those words out into the world, then they could never be taken back again: they would live in her father's mind and heart for as long as he drew breath. And she could not bear how he would look at her then, if he understood what kind of person she was, really, down deep.

Lily closed her eyes. Nicholas took that for agreement, or at least surrender to the inevitable. "You know I'm married again. It don't matter how I came to make such a mess of things, at least it don't matter to you. I take the blame for it." His voice went hoarse. "I apologize to you. And I wish you well, Lily Bonner. I truly do. Will you shake my hand?"

His hand, long and fine fingered, an artist's hand, she had once told him, that could coax gold-red fruit from the earth. What a child she had been. Lily took his hand and felt how cold it was, and limp, and tentative.

She stood up and left the room, and not until she closed her chamber door behind herself did she realize that she had not spoken a single word to Nicholas Wilde, a man she had loved with all her heart, and now must love and hate in equal measure. For his cowardice, and for his betrayal.

Her father said, "What would you have had the man say to you?"

She had been asleep when he came in, her face damp on a pillow slip wet with her weeping. Now Lily righted herself in the dim of the late afternoon and blinked. For a moment she thought it was her twin sitting on the chair beside the bed. She would have given anything just now to have Daniel beside her; she would have gladly taken whatever hard words he had and asked for more, just for the pleasure of sitting with him. But instead here was her father, her beloved father, looking at her with an expression she could hardly stand to see. Not exactly angry, but worried and disappointed and frustrated too, and struggling with all of that.

She let herself bend over, pressed her forehead to her knees and rocked herself.

"Come, girl," he said, low and soft; her father's calm voice in the night. "Breathe deep. You're safe, now. You're home."

She stayed like that for a while, weeping without sound, her father's hand light on her back. Then she straightened and wiped her face with her hands. "I don't know. I don't know what I wanted him to say. Something else."

Something impossible. Something foolish.

After a moment he said, "I've got two things I need to make clear. First is, no matter what nonsense you've got in your head, I'm not mad at you. Not over something like this. You'll pick up and move on and make more mistakes, and I won't be mad at you about those either, unless you set out to hurt somebody on purpose. The second thing is, I'm glad you're home, daughter. I missed you, but I'm wondering why you came."

Lily raised her head and blinked at him, confused now and so tired that she could have slept for hours. "I came home to hear him say what he said."

He rubbed a thumb across the line of his jaw. "I suppose I can understand that. Will you go back now, to Montreal?"

There was something in her father's expression that she couldn't quite read, some fear, or, Lily corrected herself, hope. Then she heard what she had missed before: the sound of voices downstairs. Gabriel and Annie chattering like squirrels, and a deeper voice in answer.

She said, "Simon's come."

"Aye. He brought word of your brother." And before she could launch herself from the bed he held up a hand. "Daniel's on the mend."

Lily pressed a fist to her throat. "Thank God. Blue-Jay?"

"In good health, or close to it."

She was weeping again, this time in relief. Her father put a hand on the back of her head and rocked her toward him, to kiss her on the forehead.

"Tell me," she said.

It took him a while to gather his thoughts, but Lily could wait, now.

He said, "Your sister took a bullet out of Daniel's side and there's some worry about his arm, but she thinks he'll survive. When he's well enough he'll come home, him and Blue-Jay both."

She blinked hard to clear her eyes of tears. "Come home? How will they do that?"

"Runs-from-Bears and Luke have a plan," her father said. "Simon will tell you the little he knows."

She sat back against the wall. "Simon came back. He said he would."

"Aye. He keeps his word."

Praise indeed, from Nathaniel Bonner. And: "Before we go down, I want you to tell me how you feel about the man, daughter."

Her first impulse was to lie, or to pretend that she didn't know what he was talking about. But Simon was downstairs waiting to give her news. In his calm way he would lay it all out, and it would make sense, and she would be able to sleep again at night. Because Simon was here, with good news.

Her father said, "Do you love the man, Lily?"

She pressed the heels of her palms to her eyes and drew in a breath, and then another. Finally she said, "I don't know."

"Ah," said her father. There was a smile in his voice. "So it's that way, then."

"What?" She took away her hands. "What way?"

"If you said no, I'd have some trouble believing you. I saw how you looked at him when he drove off. If you said yes, I'd have trouble believing that too, after the business with Wilde. But 'maybe,' that's an answer I can live with."

"I doubt that Simon can live with it," Lily said.

"Oh, he'll manage." Her father held out his hand and she took it, and let herself be drawn to her feet. "He's no fool, is your Simon Ballentyne."

Elizabeth sat by the hearth with her stepdaughter's letter in her lap and a hundred questions unanswered in her head. Most of them had to do with her son, and the things that Hannah hadn't said. Because she had written in haste, or perhaps—Elizabeth couldn't free herself of the idea—because she didn't want to worry them any more than she needed to.

The worst possibilities had been faced, now, and put aside. There was still the matter of getting the boys home, but somehow Elizabeth couldn't find it in herself to worry about that or even think about it just yet.

It was time now to think of Lily, and the man who sat on a stool on the other side of the hearth.

Simon Ballentyne, once of Carryck. Ten years Lily's senior, a solemn man with a head for business, well established, respected. A man who loved Lily—that much he had already made clear—and wanted to take her away from here, for good. Forever. To live in another country. And not just any other country, but the one place Elizabeth did not want to go, and would not permit her husband to go.

She had extracted that promise from Nathaniel almost twenty years ago, when the pain of what they had suffered in Québec had been fresh. And here was Simon Ballentyne, of Montreal.

He was studying the cap he held in his hands. Strong, capable hands. Long of finger and broad of palm. Hands that had touched her daughter, Elizabeth was somehow sure, in the most intimate ways a man could touch a woman. Luke had written to them of the growing connection between his business partner and his sister, but Elizabeth had not understood the nature of it until she saw them together, on the morning he had left to take Hannah and Jennet north.

Simon had been a gentleman in every way; he hadn't touched Lily or said anything to her that he could not have said to a stranger, but the look they exchanged had been full of promises and a subdued longing.

Then Curiosity had come to call, thumping the truth down plain on the table for the two of them to look at together.

"In case you ain't took note, our Lily's been with that Simon."

Elizabeth had been dozing with a book in her lap, but Curiosity showed no concern or pity, and her tone did its work. For the first time since the news came that Daniel and Blue-Jay had been taken prisoner, she was truly awake. At that moment she understood—as Curiosity meant her to understand—that she had let her worry for one child blind her to the needs of another.

"Yes," Elizabeth said. "I think you are right."

"And?"

She rocked for a moment. "I don't know," Elizabeth said. "I don't know if I should speak to her about him, or wait for her to come to me." And then, seeing the look on Curiosity's face, a new thought came to her. "Unless you think there's real cause to worry—"

"Now you waking up," Curiosity said.

A new set of images presented themselves, images too disturbing to contemplate.

"Is she? Do you think—"

"No," Curiosity said. "She ain't, I'm pretty sure. She'd come to you or me if she was in a family way."

"Well, then." Elizabeth settled back into her rocker.

"Is that all you got to say?" Curiosity began to ruffle like a hen.

"Of course not. Of course I must speak to her. But—"

"But you ain't even mentioned Nicholas Wilde to her, and now there's Simon Ballentyne to add to the mix."

"You're right," Elizabeth said. "I must speak to her, and soon. But it's such a delicate business. The wrong word might do more damage than no word at all. Perhaps . . . perhaps she needs time to think."

The fire hissed at her, and Curiosity's expression was a study in disgust.

"I am a coward," Elizabeth said finally. "I admit it freely."

Curiosity grunted softly, but didn't disagree.

And still Elizabeth had not found a way to talk to Lily about this situation of hers. They spoke of other things: of her art teachers in Montreal, of Luke's household, and most often of Daniel and Blue-Jay. There was a new calm between them, one that Elizabeth had been loath to upset.

But today Nicholas Wilde had been here, and now Simon Ballentyne sat just a few feet away from her. The men who loved her daughter.

Elizabeth thought for the first time of the cousins she had grown up with, prettier girls with substantial fortunes of their own, who had played suitors one against the other. She had been contemptuous of the whole business, the formal language and stiff postures and tender expectations. Her aunt Merriweather's careful planning, the strategies laid out over tea: as a poor cousin more interested in books than suitors, Elizabeth had observed it all from afar.

Aunt Merriweather had been gone more than five years, but Elizabeth knew exactly what she would have had to say to this state of affairs: a daughter in love with a married man, and sleeping with someone else.

Of course she wouldn't have phrased it like that. Lady Crofton wouldn't have come within a hundred words of such a formulation, or anything that made such a picture in the mind.

About one thing, though, she would have been very clear: Elizabeth had failed in her duties as a mother. The proof was upstairs, her daughter weeping for the man she could not have, while another man waited for her. How it had all come to pass, Elizabeth could hardly explain to herself. Not when her head ached so.

Then Lily was at the bottom of the stair, with Nathaniel just behind her. Elizabeth was relieved to see him.

"Boots," he said. "Let's you and me go have a little discussion and leave Simon and Lily to do the same."

The look on his face was reassuring. There was no outrage there, no disappointment, nothing but calm and even some amusement.

More assuring still was the fact that Lily was looking at Simon straight on, without apology, or embarrassment, or unease. As Simon was looking at her. With friendship, certainly, and affection, and other things that were not for Elizabeth to see, or contemplate.

"Did you come by sleigh?" Lily asked politely, as distant and cool in tone as she might have spoken to a traveling preacher or a distant cousin.

"Aye. I left the horses with the blacksmith and walked up."

"You took a chance," Lily said. "This late in the winter. You may not be able to drive the sleigh back until next season."

He gave her a small smile. "I'm in no hurry to be away."

"I'm glad you're back," Lily said suddenly, her color rising as the words spilled out.

At that Simon Ballentyne produced a smile that made Elizabeth look away, so clearly personal was the message it sent.

Gabriel and Annie were sent away against their wishes and protests, and then Lily read her sister's letter for herself and asked Simon all the questions she could think to ask about Nut Island. Finally they fell into an awkward silence that lasted a full minute.

"I've changed my mind," Simon said finally. "I release you from your promise."

There were many things Lily had imagined him saying, but never this. Simon was looking at her with an expression she couldn't read: composed, calm, a wall that she could not breach.

"You don't want to marry me," Lily said.

"Of course I want to marry you." A flush appeared high on his cheeks. "But I won't hold you to a promise you made under duress."

"So you are proposing?" Lily asked, and blushed herself to hear those words come out of her own mouth.

"No."

"You are not proposing. Forgive me for being dense—"

"I'm not proposing yet."

"Aha. And if I might ask, when exactly do you plan to propose?"

"That depends."

He was looking at her intently, his mouth pressed hard together, a fluttering muscle in his cheek the only indication of what this conversation was costing him.

"Well, then," Lily said, standing suddenly and turning away. She was free of him, and of Nicholas, and could do as she pleased; and she was ridiculously close to tears. "I wish you a good journey back to Montreal. Please do write—"

She let out a very unladylike squeak at the feel of his hands on her waist.

"Lily," he said, so close behind her that his breath was warm on her ear. "Have mercy."

She tried to pull away, and found she could not. "What do you want from me?"

"Patience. It's no easy, what I have to say. Will you sit, please. And listen."

Outside the wind picked up and just that suddenly all the afternoon light was gone, leaving them with the glow of the hearth in the fire, and nothing else. Another winter storm, so close on the heels of the last one at a time when the season should be lessening its grip. Lily could have screamed with frustration.

She said, "Go on, then. I'll stay, for a while at least."

When he was sitting again, she went back to her stool. His face, cast in shadow, was solemn.

"All the way to Montreal and back again I did naught but think of you, and the things I made you do—"

At least this time, they blushed together.

"I made my own decisions."

He said, "Aye. I said it wrong. What I'm trying to say is this. I want you to wife, but I won't push you. I'm prepared to stay in Paradise for six months. After that I must go back to Montreal, for Luke canna manage longer without me. But I hope you'll be ready to go with me then, as my wife."

He pushed out an unsteady breath. Then he got up and began to put more wood on the fire.

"Is that all?" she asked, oddly unsteady in voice, her heartbeat thundering in her ears.

Kneeling in front of the hearth, he shook his head. "No quite."

He went back to his stool and sat. Lily had never seen him so ill at ease; it made her uncomfortable, and she liked it too: Simon Ballentyne at a loss for words.

"Two more things. The first is, I've had one conversation with your father, but I must have another, and today, if you'll permit me. To tell him about my . . . connections."

"Yes," Lily said. "That you must. And the second thing?"

He cleared his throat. Then he leaned forward, his arms crossed on his knees, and looked her in the eye.

"If we go on the way we started, we'll make a child. I won't have the matter settled that way either."

Lily was a little light-headed, but she forced herself to focus on his face. She said, "I see. Well, I have a solution. I'll marry you. Now. As soon as it can be arranged."

His expression went blank and still and utterly devoid of pleasure or thankfulness or relief; none of the things she hoped to see.

"Such a spontaneous demonstration of joy," she said. "I'm over-whelmed."

At least he had the good grace to be annoyed at that, but she cut off his protest.

She said, "I thought you wanted to marry me."

"I do want to marry you. But not yet."

Lily was on her feet, vaguely aware that her temper had slipped away from her and was not to be called back, just now. "Not yet? Why not?"

He stood up to meet her. "I've been trying to tell ye, if ye'll hark—"

Lily made an impatient gesture. "My mother will be very pleased to learn how honorable and noble you mean to be, but what I want—in case you care to know—is to be married as soon as possible."

"Well, I don't," he said. "And I'll tell ye why, if ye care to listen."

Lily's fingers and hands jerked with the need to throw something, something hard, at his head.

"I won't have ye marry me to spite your apple-tree man. I won't do it," he said, his voice rising. "I won't have you like that."

"You've already had me," Lily said, poking him so hard with one finger that he took a step backward. "In case you need reminding. You've had me, and now you're refusing to marry me."

"Damn it, woman, I'm not refusing."

"You are. You promised to marry me and you bedded me and now you're making excuses, you, you cheat! We had a bargain!"

"Why, ye wee—" He broke off, so outraged that nothing came out of his mouth.

They were both breathing hard. For a moment Lily stood outside herself and saw how they must look, how absolutely nonsensical this must sound to anyone who might be listening.

And there it was, what she had noticed in the back of her mind: a creak on the stair.

"Gabriel! Annie!" she shouted. "I'll box your ears if you don't disappear!"

There was a scramble and then, a moment later, the slam of a door.

"Now," she said to Simon. "We'll leave Nicholas out of this. I insist."

"Oh, will we?" Simon said. "And why are ye here at all? Ye badgered me intae bringin ye hame so ye could see him, woman. And ye've seen him, have ye no? And talked to him? That's what aa this is about, admit it."

Lily tried to turn away, but he caught her by the waist.

"You talked to Wilde, and whatever it was he said, he made you angry. That's why you're in a hurry to marry. To teach him a lesson. To teach everybody a lesson. You'll marry me to spite them all."

She howled in frustration. "You ass," she hissed. "If that's what you think of me—"

"Deny it," Simon said. "Tell me it's no true."

"I deny it!" she yelled in his face.

"You're lying," he said dully, and let her go.

She stumbled a little, and then drew herself up, shaking so that she must wind her hands in her skirt to quiet them.

"Listen to me," Simon said. "I love you now as I loved you when we struck that bargain. More, God help me. But until I can be sure of why you want me, we'll wait."

"And what if I love you?" She forced her tone down and down, to a whisper. To a plea.

"Do you love me, Lily?"

Oh, the way he looked at her. Hope and love and wanting all wound together in the tilt of his mouth and the set of his jaw, and his mouth, his beautiful mouth. If he would only smile.

She said, "I want to love you. I mean to love you."

It was the sharpest truth; she saw what it did to him and something inside her clenched. So she went to him and stood on tiptoe, for he wouldn't come down to meet her, and she kissed his mouth. "I will, I will love you."

His arms came around her, trembling a little, unsure, and so warm and familiar and welcome. Lily kissed him again, and this time his head dipped and his arms brought her up and he kissed her back, a tentative kiss, a question. She sighed into his mouth and he slanted his head to kiss her openmouthed and deep and passionate, the kind of kisses she had dreamed of every night while he was away. His mouth, his smell, his hands on her body.

Then he pulled away and looked at her so fiercely that Lily trembled.

He said, "Three months, then. In three months' time, I'll ask you proper and you'll answer and then we'll be married. Am I worth three months' wait, lass?"

She pressed her forehead to his shoulder, breathing in the smell of him. Counted to three and then to ten, tried to organize her thoughts.

Three months. Three months of Missy Parker's questions and Nicholas Wilde's forlorn looks and gossip and jokes about the wedding lace her brother had sent. Three months of waiting and . . . wanting.

She said, "All's fair in love and war, do you remember?"

He laughed gruffly against her hair. "Aye."

"Well, then," Lily said, her hands sliding up his chest to lock around his neck. "As long as we're clear on that."

He frowned down at her, one corner of his mouth twitching in an alarming way. For a moment Lily thought he was going to laugh at her, and then instead he gave her a dry smile.

"You're up to no good," he said, running a hand down her back.

"Oh, aye, you can wager on it," Lily said. She gave him her brightest smile and pulled away. "But first you'd best talk to my father."

In the privacy of their chamber Elizabeth moved into her husband's arms and shuddered once, and then again.

"Do you think Hannah told the whole truth? Do you think he's out of danger?"

Nathaniel's hands made circular motions over her back. "She wouldn't lie about something like that, to save our feelings."

"No," Elizabeth agreed. "She wouldn't. Thank God. And Runs-from-Bears is there."

They stood like that for a long time, and then Elizabeth said, "Do you think we can trust Lily and Simon alone?"

He gave a short and very surprised laugh. "That depends on what you mean."

She pulled away a little to look up into his face. "You don't sound especially worried. It's your daughter's reputation we're talking about."

"Is it? I thought that was pretty much shot. Don't make faces at me, Boots. I could remind you of some things that happened back before we ever got married . . ."

She pulled away and went to the window, where she wrapped her arms around herself and rocked back on her heels. "That was different. I wasn't in love with someone else when I . . . when I came to you."

He was silent for so long that in the end she turned to face him.

Nathaniel said, "She's got a temper, and she's headstrong, I'll give you those things. But don't forget she's your daughter and mine too, and a better judge of character than both of us put together. She always has been."

"That is true," Elizabeth said. "Remember how she made a friend of Dutch Ton."

"And Gabriel Oak."

"And Gabriel Oak," Elizabeth said softly. "But she misjudged Nicholas Wilde."

"No, I don't think she did," Nathaniel said. "The man is good at heart. You would have been satisfied, had you heard the things he said to her. An honorable man, in the end."

"But a weak one."

"You're a hard judge, Boots, but then so is your daughter. I don't think she'd have him now, even if he was free."

She pulled away from him a little. "You want to believe that, Nathaniel, but is it true? She was so long attached to him."

Nathaniel's mouth quirked at the corner. "Not that attached, or she'd never have got to this point with Ballentyne."

"Ah," she said. "Then you see it too."

"Hard to miss, the way they look at each other."

After a moment's thought Elizabeth drew in a deep breath. "And if she falls pregnant, and must marry Simon? Will you be so philosophical then? Ah. I see by your expression that you would not."

"I don't like the idea, I'll admit that. But she's a woman grown, Elizabeth, and we have to let her make her own mind up. Have a little faith in her."

"I do have faith in her," Elizabeth said. "I truly do, but her temperament sometimes does get the best of her." And then: "How long do you think we need leave them?"

That got her the kind of grin that he saved for times like this, when they were alone.

"Oh, no," she said. "Don't look at me that way."

He had already come around the bed to catch her by the elbows and pull her up close. "Don't look at you how, Boots?"

"Like that," she said, when he had finished kissing her. "Like you want to swallow me whole."

"I suppose I could stop looking," Nathaniel said, backing toward the bed with her firmly in tow. "But I got a better idea. Close your eyes and I'll whisper it to you."

At that moment, Gabriel flung open the door with all of his usual energy. Then he and Annie came to a stop just where they were, mouths hanging open.

"Oh," Gabriel said, blushing furiously.

"Just a little kissing, son," said Nathaniel. "No cause for alarm. Come on in, and tell us what it is you want."

"They're yelling at each other, Simon and Lily." Annie said this breathlessly, her hands clasped in front of herself. "She called him a cheat."

"Annie," Elizabeth said, holding out a hand to the girl and motioning her closer. "Were you two listening where you weren't supposed to be?"

Gabriel's face clenched. "I don't like him," he said. "And neither does Lily, by the way she's talking to him. She said—"

"Never mind what she said." Elizabeth stopped him firmly. "We do not eavesdrop."

Nathaniel laughed. "What your mother means, son, is that she certainly would like to hear what they're saying to each other, but it ain't polite, so she's not going to ask."

"Well, then, can we tell you, Da?" Gabriel asked.

"Not me either," said Nathaniel. "But you can come up here and set with us while we wait until they're done."

"Wait until Lily gets done arguing," Gabriel said with a huffing breath. "We'll all starve to death."

"I've made your daughter a promise," Simon Ballentyne began, late that evening.

They had eaten a simple supper together, talking quietly of nothing of real importance, while Gabriel scowled at Simon and Lily avoided his gaze. When the dishes were wiped and put up and Gabriel was in bed, they came together again in front of the hearth.

Now he sat with his hands on his knees, looking at Nathaniel and Elizabeth evenly. The lower half of his face was still paler than his cheeks and forehead; it gave him an oddly lopsided appearance, but all in all, Elizabeth liked him without his beard. She wondered if Lily had asked him to shave it, and then decided she would rather not know the answer to that question.

"More than one promise, I'm guessing," Nathaniel said.

"More than one, aye," Simon agreed. He used a handkerchief to wipe perspiration from his brow.

"Come now," Elizabeth said. "How bad can it be? Just go on and tell us what it is you have to say."

Simon's dark eyes met hers for three long heartbeats, and then he nodded.

"My mother's name before she married was Fiona Moncrieff. She had two brothers, both of whom you've had the misfortune to meet. Angus and John Moncrieff."

Nathaniel saw Elizabeth's color rising, in surprise and something else that he couldn't put a name to straight off. All these years later

Elizabeth was still unable to talk about Angus Moncrieff with anything approaching the logic and reasoning she otherwise held so dear and took such pride in.

He put a hand on Elizabeth's arm and pressed. He said, "Go on."

"There's naught to say except this: I hardly knew my uncle Angus, for my mother distrusted him and would no have him in her house. What he did, the harm he caused you, it all brought shame on the family name that canna be denied. As far as my uncle John is concerned—you knew him as Father Contrecoeur—I couldn't tell ye where he is in the world, or if he's even alive. No more do I care. The last time I saw him was almost twenty years ago, when I was a lad in Carryckton."

The fire ticked in the hearth like a clock. Nathaniel counted Elizabeth's breaths, and watched Simon Ballentyne, who withstood this particular test: he waited, poised, expectant, and said nothing at all.

"Is there more?" Nathaniel said.

"Aye. I love your daughter, and should she decide to take me as husband, I'll spend my life taking care of her." He was watching Elizabeth's face when he said it.

"Does my stepson know about your connection to Moncrieff?" Elizabeth asked. Her tone was sharp, but Ballentyne didn't flinch from the question.

"Aye," said Simon. "Luke's known from the first."

"So he went into partnership with you knowing, and he allowed you to court his sister while she was in Montreal—"

"I would not use the word 'allowed,' Mrs. Bonner—"

Elizabeth's head snapped up sharply. "If you'll permit me to continue."

She was trying, Nathaniel realized now, not to smile. He settled back, curious as to exactly where she was going with her inquiry. Elizabeth had a plan, and Elizabeth with a plan was a formidable force, one not to be tampered with.

She said, "Luke was responsible for his sister's welfare in Montreal, but he permitted"—she paused, her expression daring him to interrupt again—"you to call upon her, alone, I am presuming."

"Aye." He was looking at her without shame or apology, or even, Nathaniel was pleased to see, real fear. A man who couldn't stand up to Elizabeth would have no chance at all with Lily.

A movement on the stair caught Nathaniel's attention: his daughter, who had not wanted to be here for this interview, but who could not quite stay away either.

"Come on down here, Lily," Nathaniel said, waving broadly. "Your ma's about to toss this suitor of yours out into the cold; you might want to watch how she does it."

"She isn't," Lily said, moving down the stairs. "She wouldn't."

"Nathaniel," Elizabeth warned.

He lifted his shoulders at her, palms up. "If you're trying to scare the man away, Boots, why then you're on the right road. Though he's not the kind to scare easy, it looks like."

"I was asking questions, that is all," Elizabeth said. "Have you no questions of your own for this man who wants to marry your daughter?"

"Well, sure I do," he said. "Ballentyne, I recall your father pretty well. Thomas, was his name, is that right?"

"It is."

"And he's still living, and in good health?"

"Aye."

"He's a carpenter, as I remember. You learned that trade from him?"

The question took Ballentyne by surprise, but he answered it willingly. "Aye. But I've been a merchant since I came to Canada."

"Good, then." Nathaniel smiled at his wife. "That's all I want to know. Go on, Boots."

She gaped at him. "Very well. As I'm the only one taking this seriously." A pulse was beating frantically in her throat, but she managed to subdue her tone. "I have some things to say."

Lily had crept closer, and now she stood, arms wrapped around herself, just behind Simon.

Elizabeth said, "Simon, I do not like the fact that you are connected to Angus Moncrieff, I won't pretend that I do. But you've proven yourself to be honest and trustworthy and hardworking, and from what I've seen of you, you're a bright young man. You have my permission to call on my daughter."

Lily's head tilted to one side, as if she couldn't make sense of what she had just heard.

"With a few provisos," Elizabeth finished.

From the top of the stairs, Gabriel's voice came high and thin: "What's a proviso?"

"Gabriel!" shouted Nathaniel. "Back to bed!"

"My conditions," Elizabeth continued, spreading her skirt smooth with her hands, "are these. First, that you will make arrangements to stay in Paradise for a minimum of five months—"

"Ma!" cried Lily.

Elizabeth held up a hand to stop her daughter. "In that time you will lodge with Mrs. Freeman in the village; I will speak to her about it immediately. While you are here, you will work for me. I need someone to oversee the building of the new schoolhouse, as it is clear that Peter Dubonnet cannot handle it on his own. At a reasonable wage, of course. While you are in Paradise, you will call on Lily here, in her home, at reasonable times. On occasion you will be allowed to accompany her to a party or dance, as long as my husband or I or someone we trust is in attendance. You will always be chaperoned."

Lily stamped her foot. "*Chaperoned?* And I have nothing to say about this?"

"Don't interrupt your ma just now, Lily," Nathaniel said, trying not to smile.

"Very good advice," Elizabeth said, without looking at her daughter. "Now, Mr. Ballentyne. You have done us some services, some very kind services, which I have not forgotten. And my stepson trusts you, which is worth a great deal. But it is not everything, I hope you'll understand. In the next months you will have to win my trust, and my husband's."

"And mine, or doesn't that count for anything?"

Elizabeth raised her head very slowly, and looked directly at her daughter. For a moment she held the gaze, and then Lily blushed, and looked away. Simon saw this, and ducked his head, but not without first sending a look Nathaniel's way that told him everything he needed to know about the connection between the two of them.

Lily's voice came hoarse. "We could just elope and get married. You did."

As if she hadn't spoken at all, Simon said, "Mrs. Bonner, I agree to all your conditions."

At that Lily let out a muffled scream and ran back up the stairs. Her chamber door slammed with such force that the braids of corn hung to dry overhead swayed gently back and forth.

"Things are getting back to normal around here," Nathaniel said, not trying to hide his satisfaction. "I haven't seen Lily in such a temper in a long time. The spring and summer promise to be right lively."

That earned him one of his wife's sharpest looks. She got up to go to Lily, leaving the two men in front of the fire.

"I know my uncle caused you a great deal of pain and trouble," Simon said to Nathaniel. "And I understand that you need time."

Nathaniel laughed. "You got a lot to learn about the Bonner women, Simon. It wasn't Angus Moncrieff that brought all this about, though it gave us a shock, I'll admit that."

"It wasn't?" Simon glanced up the stairs.

"Hell, no," Nathaniel said. "Elizabeth just wants to keep Lily close as long as she can. Maybe you can understand that, given the situation with our Daniel. And you being connected to Moncrieff gives her an excuse to make all kinds of demands she wouldn't make otherwise. You played right into her hands, son."

"She's not angry?" Simon sat back, looking not so much confused as intrigued.

"Oh, no," Nathaniel said. "You'll know when she's got a temper on her, there's no mistaking it."

Simon ran a hand over his eyes. "And you, you aren't concerned about my connections to the Moncrieffs, then?"

"Oh, I'm concerned." Nathaniel yawned. "I'll be keeping watch, Simon. You can bet on it."

Chapter 29

That very evening Nathaniel went down to the village with Simon to see to his lodging, and it was five full days before Lily saw him again. Five days in which she barely knew what to do with her frustration and anger, all made worse by the fact that no one seemed to see her side of things. Her first hope had been her father, but he had only laughed at the suggestion that she was being ill used.

"You can always send the man back to Montreal," he had told her after listening to Lily explain just how wrong this whole situation really was, how unfair, how demeaning. "Just tell him there's no hope, you've made up your mind. Then you'll be shut of the whole mess."

Curiosity was no better. "Didn't I tell you your ma would wake up and take note? That Elizabeth, I got to hand it to her. She got you trussed neat as a Christmas turkey. Now this is what I'm wondering: if your Simon don't seem to mind, why are you struggling so hard?"

It was a question Lily did not like to contemplate, because there was no clear answer except the obvious: her mother had joined forces with Simon, and she could not prevail against the two of them. It was childish and petty of her to resent that, but she did. While she was trying to think of a way to admit that to Curiosity that didn't sound quite so terrible, the old woman was watching her with the expression that meant she pretty much understood what was going on without being told.

Without any warning she put a thin arm around Lily's shoulder and hugged her, hard. "What is it exactly that you want that they ain't giving you? When you got an answer to that question, child, then you halfway home."

Twice Lily sat down to write a letter to her cousin Jennet, who must understand what no one else seemed to want to see, and twice she gave it up as a bad job. She threw the paper in the fire, and took some small satisfaction in its burning. Her mother, who used every scrap until it could be used no more, would be outraged.

Except it seemed that Lily had lost the talent of rousing her mother's anger. Elizabeth, relieved now of her worry for her son and nephew, was infused with an almost otherworldly energy and unshakable goodwill. When she was not teaching or doing housework, she was down in the village, consulting with one person or another about the new schoolhouse or writing to everyone who might have an opinion on the undertaking. Her letters to Ethan and her cousin Will alone made the post rider's stops in Paradise worthwhile.

"I thought she didn't like the idea of a new schoolhouse," Lily said to her father, who had looked surprised at the idea.

"What she didn't like was Richard Todd's part in it. But she got over that and I'm glad to see it. She needs the distraction. Your brother's on her mind a lot, and you are too."

No doubt that was true, but Lily, feeling contrary, decided that she would not take part in the schoolhouse plans; she had her own work, after all, and must get back to it. She made this announcement over supper and got only agreement: more frustration, and guilt too; she knew how childish she was being, but not how to stop.

She would not ask questions about Simon or the schoolhouse project, but then she didn't have to. Gabriel and Annie took great pleasure in bringing her a daily report on the particulars: what Curiosity had fed Simon for dinner, how long he had sat with their mother and Peter Dubonnet over plans, how he had come to an agreement with the Camerons about the hauling of timber, how he had helped old Missus Hindle with her lambing, what each and every resident of the village thought of him. All of which, it seemed, was positive, something that annoyed Gabriel so much that Lily was a little discomfited.

"Because I'm put out with him doesn't mean you have to be," she told her little brother. "You might like him, if you gave him the chance."

"Do you want me to like him?" Gabriel had demanded, and Lily was honest enough to admit that she did. "At least be fair," she said. "Give him a chance."

"Even Missy Parker likes him," Annie told her.

"Missy Parker likes anybody in britches," Gabriel said, in the worst of moods. Their mother would have scolded him, but Lily could not.

She took more comfort from her aunt, who seemed to be the only person in the world with nothing to say about Simon, good or bad.

Many-Doves said, "You must make up your own mind what it is you want." And: "Help me with this doeskin."

For Many-Doves it was that simple. Curiosity had said the same thing, of course, but once Many-Doves had spoken she rarely repeated herself.

In the end Lily couldn't stay out of the village, and so she went. Not to see Simon or hear about him—she stayed away from Curiosity's kitchen and the trading post, the two places she was most likely to find him—but to sit in the old meetinghouse with her breath billowing cold around her and look at her own work covering the walls. All the years of her girlhood up in plain sight for anyone to examine. The world looked very different to her now.

The next day she got her father's help to haul what she would need to the meetinghouse: firewood and kindling, buckets and tools, and all the materials she had brought back with her from Canada. She spent a satisfying morning arranging it and then stood back to consider the neat row of pigment pots, the crocks filled with the things that she would need to mix her paints.

What she wanted to do next was to bring her mother here to see it all. Her mother would ask sensible questions, thoughtful questions that made her think, and they might spend the whole day talking about color and shadow and shape.

Instead, Lily loosened the ties on the book she had carried around with her since Gabriel Oak had given it to her just before he died, and sat in a pool of cold sunshine while she studied the work he had done so long ago, before she was born; before her mother had been born. Gabriel had given her this record of his life for safekeeping, and more than that: he had put a pencil in her hand, and shown her the magic of it.

Standing between the stove and a single glass window, Lily began by sketching the things she saw: the Ratz boys dragging a sledge piled high with firewood, a tabby cat perched at the very top. Hardwork Greber trudging along, bent almost double with the weight of filled buckets. Goody Cunningham with her new grand-daughter strapped to her chest, squinting into the sun. A wolf at the edge of the clearing, watching the hens that pecked and strutted around the Hindles' well.

And then, when Lily was just starting to lose herself in the work, Jemima Wilde walked past the window, her head wrapped in a bright blue shawl, her cheeks chapped apple red with the cold. There was a bruise on her jaw, faded to yellow.

She walked straight-backed, head held high, baskets over both arms. The mud was ankle deep and treacherous, and Jemima's mouth was clamped tight in concentration.

Even wrapped against the cold her thickening waist was plain to see, and more than that: how it suited her, to be with child. Ripening fruit, heavy and full of promise. The pencil in Lily's fingers trembled and she put it down, but she could not look away.

Jemima was too concerned with getting where she needed to be to have looked in Lily's direction.

You must make up your own mind what it is you want.

Lily drew in a sharp breath, the small sound filling the empty meetinghouse.

As a younger girl she had sat here with her mother and listened to sermons, first from timid Mr. Gathercole and then from a long line of visiting preachers, none of whom stayed in Paradise very long. Some of them were good men and dull preachers, others made a great lot of noise but no sense at all, but none of them had suspected their sermons had been carried up the mountain to Lake in the Clouds, where Elizabeth Bonner had engaged her children in their dissection, as a person would take apart a gun to examine its parts and find out how it worked. Rarely had any of those preachers been lucky enough to have his sermon survive Elizabeth Bonner's close scrutiny.

Strive to favor the rational over the subjective as you select one course of action among those available to you.

Jemima was almost to the trading post now, balancing baskets as she lifted a foot high and set it down again. From here she could have been anyone, any woman on her way to buy pins or cornmeal.

With a sigh, Lily let her breath go and with it went, quietly, quickly, all the anger she had been holding in reserve for somebody truly deserving. For Jemima, who had finally appeared and presented herself as nothing but another woman who had done her best to pick wisely from among those few poor choices available to her.

Even after Jemima was gone, Lily stayed just where she was for many long minutes.

One of the surest signs of spring in the village of Paradise was the arrival of Black Abe, the hole digger. He came to dig any kind of hole people might need: privies and wells and sawyer's trenches. One of the most important services he performed in Paradise was to dig the long, deep trenches for charcoal burning, which was his primary occupation.

But most of all, when Black Abe came to Paradise it meant that it was time to put all those who had died in the coldest months to rest. He would dig as many graves as they needed, each of them a perfect hole six feet deep with straight sides that looked to have been plastered in place. The digging of a proper grave was an art, and one that Black Abe had mastered. The men of Paradise were satisfied to leave the spring digging to the strange old man.

Black Abe had come over from Africa on a slave ship when he was a young man. How and when he had won his freedom was a story he told willingly in a hoarse, high singsong, but never in the same way twice. Sometimes the ship was called the *Santa Maria* and sometimes the *Cornwall;* sometimes he had been bought by a Dutch farmer from Long Island and other times he had gone to a one-eyed silversmith in Philadelphia. The number of his wives and children shifted like the clouds overhead, and the number of his own years with them. But he could tell anybody who wanted to know the names of every person who had been buried in one of his graves, and the day it was dug.

He was a small man, a wiry twisting of muscle, black as the coal he burned, with great wide hands and feet that had never, as far as the people of Paradise could tell, known shoes. He always arrived in Paradise on foot, leading his mule; he would leave that way too, but nobody had ever been able to figure out just where he went. Even Curiosity, who was the oldest woman in the village now and whose memory was as sharp as flint, knew very little about Black Abe. Or at least there was not too much she was willing to share.

His first stop was always Curiosity's kitchen door, where he was received with her warmest welcome, a substantial meal, the winter's news, and the promise of work. The kilns and ovens in the doctor's laboratory consumed more charcoal than all the other families of Paradise put together and only slightly less than Joshua Hench's forge. When he was done at the doctor's, he would move on to the blacksmithy, where Curiosity's daughter Daisy would take over feeding him.

In the chamber they shared on the second floor of the doctor's house, Callie and Martha watched the weather and calculated when Black Abe might appear. They wondered if he would stay, once the graves were dug, or if he would be sent away: Doctor Todd was dead, after all, and Hannah was gone away to Canada and Jennet with her. Even Ethan, who had never really liked working in the laboratory, was living in Manhattan with his uncle and aunt Spencer while he studied at the college. They took the question to Curiosity, who fixed her gaze on them and laughed out loud.

"As if I could send that old African away before I got him fed up good and proper," she said. "He'll come, don't you worry, and he'll stay until the buttons on his breeches pop."

Then one wet, warm morning the girls came down to the kitchen and found Black Abe at the table, bent over a plate of eggs and ham and cornmeal mush, deep in conversation with Curiosity and Lucy and Simon Ballentyne too. Curiosity hummed as she poured out coffee.

To the girls Black Abe said, "Don't count on spring just yet, children. The winter still setting in my bones."

Looking hard into her porridge Callie said, "Then is it too early for you to dig—" And her voice faltered.

"Oh, Lord," Curiosity said. She came over to put a hand on Callie's shoulder. "Of course not. Why, me and Abe was just talking about it. He'll get started this very day on those graves, won't you, Abe?"

The old man said that he had been planning on exactly that, and wouldn't it be a help if Callie showed him just where her mama was meant to rest, and Cookie Fiddler too, and wasn't that a shame about losing two such good women. He offered the same kindness to Martha, whose grandmother Kuick must also be laid to rest, and found that the girl was too frightened of her mother to make any such suggestions.

Callie looked at Martha's flushed face and tear-bright eyes and wondered if she looked like that: frightened and relieved; eager to get it done, and wanting to run away at the same time.

Curiosity squeezed her shoulder. She said, "You girls got to get on to school, now."

On the way they stopped at the blacksmithy to tell Daisy about Black Abe, and then they did the same thing at the trading post. At school the other children asked questions until Miz Elizabeth got their attention by putting a whole twenty lines from the Constitution on the board for them to learn by heart.

On the way home at dinnertime the girls saw that the meeting-house windows had been propped open and so they stopped there too. Mostly they were shy of bothering Lily Bonner while she worked, but the news that Black Abe had come was enough reason.

Unlike the rest of Paradise, Lily seemed to have no questions to ask about Martha's mother or Callie's father, which meant that the three of them got along just fine. If Lily held any grudges about the way things had turned out she kept them to herself, and more than that: she seemed happy to see them. She showed them her work and sometimes found scraps of paper for them to draw on, and told stories about anything they could think to ask her. They were kindhearted girls and they liked Lily and appreciated her attention, so they never compared her storytelling to Jennet's.

Today they found her wrapped in a leather apron frowning at a line of glass beakers. This was such an interesting sight that Black Abe was forgotten for the moment.

"What are you making?" Martha was especially timid with Lily, but for once her curiosity got the better of her, and she came right up to the table. In the slanting light from the window her hair was as red as fire.

"Watercolor paint," Lily said with a quick, sharp smile. "To see if I can get the color of your pretty hair down on paper. Or I would be, but I'm missing something."

Some of the best stories about Lily had to do with when she was a reluctant schoolgirl in her mother's classroom. To this day the children spoke with respect about the schemes Lily had come up with to get out in the fresh air when she was supposed to be parsing French verbs or writing out arithmetic problems on her slate. And now here she was, always eager to be teaching the things she had learned in Canada to whoever might stand still long enough to listen.

She showed them how she meant to mix the oddest things together—gum arabic, strained honey, glycerin—to make the binder that was the basis of her watercolor cakes.

"But I've misplaced my crock of benzoate of soda," she finished, looking around herself as if it might appear magically. "Or I left it behind in Montreal. In either case I can't finish without it."

She saw the girls exchange meaningful looks.

Callie said, "There must be a hundred filled crocks in Dr. Todd's laboratory. Would you find some there?"

"Oh and," said Martha breathlessly, as if to keep Lily from objecting, "we stopped to tell you that Black Abe is come."

Lily might be distracted, but she knew what that meant. She said, "Well, then. When's the burying?"

"Tomorrow, I think," said Martha, tugging on her plait so hard that the tender skin at her temple reddened.

Callie said, "Won't you come back to the house with us?"

For a few days now, it seemed to Lily, the two girls had been conspiring to get her to Curiosity's kitchen. She didn't know if this was because they had decided they liked Simon and wanted her to spend more time with him, or because they were bored since Hannah and Jennet and Ethan had all gone away, and wanted some excitement. Or maybe, it occurred to Lily, maybe they didn't like the idea that Lily was at odds with her mother, and had taken it upon themselves to draw them back together. Right now it could be all those things, and the arrival of Black Abe on top.

"Did Curiosity send you?" The question didn't come out the way she meant it to.

"We thought you'd want to know." Callie looked indignant and Martha injured. Taken together that was strong medicine indeed.

Lily said, "Very well. Let's go see if there's any soda to be had."

"Then you can get back to your work," offered Callie.

"Yes," said Lily. "Then I can get right back."

Lily spent the walk from the meetinghouse to the doctor's place working out just the right thing to say when she came face to face with her mother or Simon. It was delicate business. She must find the words that would make them understand that she had neither forgotten nor forgiven, nor was she resigned to the situation as they had worked it out between them. Just the right words would make all that clear, and would make them understand even more: that she was not a child, and would not be treated like one.

But neither her mother nor Simon was in the kitchen, as she had thought they must be. Instead there was Sally, spinning directly from a fleece that lay on the floor beside her, while Lucy was busy with dinner. She was moving back and forth between setting the table and stirring the pot that hung from the trivet over the hearth.

"You looking for your ma?" Sally asked. "She supposed to be here for dinner, any minute now."

"I'm not here to see my mother," Lily said. All her good intentions went up in flame, just like that, and in their place she felt herself flush with irritation. "Why would you think I'm looking for my mother?" And she marched back out again, leaving the door open behind her.

"I suppose it was Simon she was hoping to run into," said Lucy, and then she caught her sister's eye and they both giggled.

Callie said, "You shouldn't tease her so," trying to look concerned and understanding and serious. And then all four of them broke down into laughter that drifted out the open door and followed Lily a good ways down the path to the laboratory.

Dr. Todd's laboratory, closed up for long weeks, was damp and dusty and it stank of sulfur and cloves, vinegar and herbs and chemicals. It took a quarter hour of looking to find what Lily needed and another quarter hour before she had found an empty jar, a cork that fit it, and a rag to wipe it out. She worked at the big table, in a spot she made for herself among the pots and bottles.

By the time she had found a funnel, the racing of her heart had slowed and she had a hold of her temper. Or enough of a hold to be honest with herself about a few things. First, that she must learn not to react to teasing. Second, more happily, that Simon had not been there to see her fluster. Third, she was hungry, and that everyone would be sitting down now in Curiosity's kitchen to a dinner of stew and new bread and dried peach compote. Fourth, that her own cold packed dinner was back in the meetinghouse, and finally: that they expected her to stay away, out of obstinacy, and hurt pride.

Lily did not like being predictable, but even worse was the idea that people found her amusing, a little girl to be chucked under the chin. Lily confounded by love. Lily out of sorts, because she couldn't control a man.

The logical thing to do, then, was to show them they were wrong. She would sit across the table from her mother and Simon Ballentyne and pay neither of them any particular attention; she would be polite but disinterested. All her attention would be paid to Black Abe, who must have a year's worth of news to share. Black

Abe was why she had come, after all, and it made no sense to deprive herself of the pleasure of his storytelling.

Lily had just worked this out to her own satisfaction when a shadow fell across the door. A man-sized shadow.

Simon Ballentyne said, "They've sent me to fetch you to dinner."

Lily took a very deep breath and counted to three. Then she gave him her most polite, most distant smile. "That's kind of you," she said. "I'll be along shortly, as soon as I've finished here."

She couldn't make out his expression in the shadows but he shifted a little where he stood: a man who had gone into the bush loaded for bear and found a fawn instead. She had hoped to put him off balance and understood now that she had disappointed him: he got pleasure out of putting her in a temper.

Lily smiled again, and perhaps that was the mistake.

"I'll wait," Simon said easily. He leaned against the door frame and crossed his arms.

"You must do as you please." And then, her voice shaking with the effort: "If you will wait, come in. You're in my light." Then she looked up at him and saw the hesitation on his face.

"Unless my mother forbids it," Lily added, and cursed herself for it.

Simon was working hard at keeping his temper too; she could feel him struggling with it. He cleared his throat. "You spilled some . . . what is that?"

She put down the crock. "It's benzoate of soda," said Lily. "And if I've spilled some it's because you're in my light. As I've already pointed out."

"Aye. Or perhaps it's just that you're nervous to be alone with me and your hands are trembling."

She had picked up the bottle closest to hand and thrown it before the last word was even out of his mouth. It was heavy and rounded and it flew like a fat bird to hit Simon Ballentyne with a thump, right between the eyes. Then it broke neatly in half. The room filled immediately with the scent of rose oil, thick and sweet.

"Uffff," he said, and took a step backward, his heel catching on the door swell. His arms pinwheeled once and then he sat, heavily, his feet inside and the rest of him in the mud.

"Oh," said Lily, a hand pressed to her mouth. The sun was at his back but she could see a trickle of blood on his brow, and oil dripping down his face. His eyes were squinted shut, and his eyelashes were sticky.

Lily laughed. It was a mistake, she knew it, but she could not help herself.

Simon got up gracefully—some part of her noticed that, even now—and he used both hands to wipe his face, advancing on her as he did.

She stepped backward until she came up against the big work-table. To her right was another table, and to her left the reverberating furnace, like a great squat toad.

"You will tease me," she said, and heard her own tone, half petulant, half laughing. "You know I have a temper." And, pleading: "It's only rose oil, and the bottle was almost empty."

"Only rose oil, is it?" He was close enough now for her to see the small crescent-shaped cut between his brows, and the smear of blood.

"Rose oil is good for the skin," Lily said, leaning back.

"Well, then," Simon said. "Let me share it with you."

She flailed at him but he caught up both her wrists in one hand. The reek of the rose oil filled her nose and she coughed.

"Simon," she said. "Simon, wait. Wait, I have to say something."

"Go on, then." He pressed a palm to her cheek and then began to rub the oil in with three fingertips. "What is it you wanted to say? I don't suppose you were about to apologize."

She tried to lean away from the oily hand, coughing out a sound that was meant to be a "no" but sounded more like a laugh.

"Or maybe you just wanted to point out that you've got the better of me. Come in, you said, and in I came. So go on, then, say it. You got the best of me, Lily, and you always will. What else do you want? A kiss, is it?"

She might have denied it, or tried to. She might have, but Simon had already grabbed her up against him and given her what she hadn't asked for. A kiss saturated in rose oil and a flare of temper that came from them both and ignited where their mouths touched.

"What would my mother say?" Lily said.

He bit her lower lip and kissed her again.

She said, "You're to call on me on Sundays. We're to have a chaperone."

Between kisses she said, "She might come up the path and see us, just like this. You with your hands on my—"

He groaned against her mouth, wrapped an arm around her waist. Then he stepped backward pulling her with him, kissing her as he went, until he was at the door. With a kick of his heel it slammed shut, and then he leaned back against it with her pressed all along the length of him, in a fog of rose oil and frustration.

"Lily Bonner," he said, leaning down to look her directly in the eye. "I made a promise and I'll keep it."

"Which promise are you talking about? The one you made to me, or the one you made to my mother?"

He shut his eyes. "Be sensible."

She did the only thing she could think of doing: Lily grabbed Simon by the ears and pulled his mouth to hers and kissed him. She kissed him until he began to give in and then she kissed him some more. Then with a great groan he took her shoulders and held her away from him. Breathing as if he had just run a mile uphill, and how that pleased her.

"Come to dinner now," he said. "And Sunday I'll call on you."

Then he opened the door and went out, and left Lily in the dim, dusty laboratory.

Noses twitched and brows were raised, but nobody said a word about the fact that Lily came to the dinner table smelling just like Simon did: as if they had been rolling around in Missy Parker's rose garden in the full of the summer.

It was not like Curiosity to let such an opportunity go, but the subject was a somber one: tomorrow was the day that the bodies that had been waiting over the winter would finally be set to proper rest. In the ice shed behind the barn there were three coffins and in the village there were more.

"You going to start today?" Curiosity asked Black Abe.

"I don't know," he said. "I smell a change in the weather."

Curiosity looked up at him, her brows pulled down into a sharp vee of disapproval. "Why, Abe, I'm surprised at you. Wouldn't get much done at all if we let a little rain stop us, this time of year. Why, I seen Simon there hauling logs in rain so thick the oxen was almost swimming."

"I'm a Scot, aye." Simon grinned at her. "Bred to the rain."

Lily made a neat pile of her pickled cabbage and then moved it to the other side of her plate, to keep herself from looking up.

Curiosity said, "I'd surely appreciate it if you got started today, Abe. We need to tend to our folks." She was looking at the girls.

"Why, then," Abe said. "I'll do just that."

Suddenly everybody seemed to have something worth saying. They talked among themselves about the weather and graveyards and wasn't this stew tasty, Lucy's dumplings had turned out just right and pass them down, please, there was a little hole in Abe's belly that still needed filling.

Then Callie found her voice all at once. "But what about my pa?" she said. "My pa has to be there too."

There was a small, shocked silence.

"But of course," Elizabeth said. "Of course he must. We wouldn't go ahead without him, Callie."

Tears were streaking over the girl's face. She sobbed, just once, but it was a sound so riddled with pain that Lily's own throat closed in sympathy. Martha looked just as stricken, and for a moment they looked to her like two little glass dolls ready to shatter.

"Callie," Curiosity said. "I'ma go speak to your pa just as soon as I get up from dinner. You can come with me, if you like."

"No." The girl shook her head so hard that her plaits jumped. Next to her Martha had begun to weep too, but silently.

"Well, then I'll go on my own," Curiosity said in her gentlest voice. "Don't matter none, child. Not a bit."

"I'll go with you," Elizabeth said quickly. "Would that be a comfort to you, Callie, if I went to see your father too?"

The girl drew in a long, shaky breath and closed her eyes. By the time she opened them again her expression had calmed, and she nodded.

Then Simon reached over and put a hand on the back of the girl's head. She started at first and then leaned into his cupped palm.

Simon said, "It's right tae weep for her, lass. You must never be ashamed tae weep for your mither. I still weep for mine, betimes."

"Now that's a pure truth," said Black Abe, smiling kindly.

Lily was close to tears too and so she closed her eyes, just for the moment, and still she saw the two girls.

Callie was just now realizing that tomorrow she would have to stand next to her father while the coffins were lowered into a muddy hole: her mother, and Cookie Fiddler, a woman she had known and loved all her life. Tomorrow she would go to those new graves and her father would be there, most likely with his new wife, or maybe she would come uninvited and there would be hard words said. It was months since Dolly Wilde had died, but to these young girls it must seem fresh every day.

As young as they were they had borne up under sorrow and loss and all the meanness of spirit the village could think to dole out, and they had done that without complaint for these many weeks. While Lily was worrying about getting the best of Simon Ballentyne, they were watching the weather and counting the days until graves must be dug.

Lily said, "Martha, Callie, if you girls don't have any other chores this afternoon, I could use your help at the meetinghouse, mixing up pigments."

Callie blinked at her, blinked hard to see through tears.

Martha cleared her throat to say, "May we, Curiosity?"

The old woman picked up a bowl that needed filling and got up from the bench. On her way past Lily she paused and, leaning down, put a noisy kiss on the top of her head.

"Of course you may," she said to Martha. "Cain't think of a blessed thing to keep you busy otherwise. Unless you can, Sally? Lucy?"

"No, ma'am," said Sally solemnly. "Nothing I can think of."

"I was planning on going over to see my ma," Lucy said. "I promised to warp the loom for her."

"Elizabeth? These girls got studying to do that can't wait?"

Lily's mother had a smile she didn't use very much, a smile that started with her mouth but shone out of her eyes too; a smile that said words couldn't describe just how pleased she was. Over the years Lily had tried to draw her mother when she smiled like that, but she had never quite been able to catch it on paper. Right now she thought she might be able to, if she were to get up from the table while it was fresh in her mind.

But that would mean walking away, and she couldn't do that, just now. Somehow she had managed to do just the right thing; she had pleased her mother and Curiosity and all the people who had had cause to be disappointed in her. She wanted to hold on to that for the time being.

Black Abe said, "You look like your ma just now, Miz Elizabeth. I never knowed anybody who could smile quite like her, but she passed it on to you."

"Lily smiles like that too, sometimes," said Simon. His voice was a little hoarse, but his gaze was even and kind and filled with understanding and something else, something like pride. "I've seen it."

"You a fortunate man, Mr. Ballentyne," said Black Abe with a wink to Lily. "Fortunate indeed."

• • •

Later, on their way to the orchard house, Curiosity stopped in the middle of the path and bent over, her arms crossed against her belly. At first Elizabeth thought she was weeping, overcome by the sad scene at the dinner table; Elizabeth might have started too, but then she caught sight of Curiosity's face: she was laughing so hard that she was convulsed with it.

"What?" Elizabeth said, alarmed and irritated too. "What is it?"

Curiosity pulled a kerchief from her sleeve to wipe the tears from her face and chuckled. "I was just remembering that rose stink, and the look on Simon's face when he come to table. I thought I'd just about bust, keeping a straight face."

Elizabeth heard herself giggle. "And then *Lily*. Do you think she threw the pot at him?"

"Oh, ayuh," Curiosity said, her mouth twitching. Then she started to laugh again. "The man got a great bruise coming up between the eyes."

"She always had good aim," Elizabeth offered, and then they were both laughing so that their shoulders shook.

"But they made up," Curiosity said finally, hiccupping softly. "Somehow or another. He got her to come to table. I never thought I'd see the man who could deal with our Lily when she got to feeling stubborn, but it look like Simon got the knack. He can talk to her."

"If he said anything at all," Elizabeth said.

Curiosity straightened suddenly and shot her an amused glance. "You sounding more like Missy Parker every day, girl. I'm surprised at you."

Elizabeth put her knuckles on her hips and shook her head. "Oh, no. Not you too. Nathaniel said the same thing to me, this morning. But I don't understand, I really don't. They are two responsible adults, and I asked them to act accordingly. How is that unreasonable?"

Curiosity linked her arm through Elizabeth's and pulled her along. "Listen now, ain't that thrush got a pretty song?" And then: "Sometimes you get all wound up in that rational thinking you like so much, and you forget what it was like to be young. You got to let those two make they own mistakes."

Overhead the trees were stirring in a rising wind, branches clicking together like bones. Elizabeth saw a flash of red, and then another: the birds were coming back and bringing the spring with them.

"I don't know what else to do," she said. "Should I send Simon away? That would be another kind of injustice, and I think it would do more harm in the long run. She cares for him, and he for her."

Curiosity shrugged her agreement. After a moment Elizabeth went on.

"All I want—all I'm asking for—is that they don't rush into anything. And I have to point out that Simon seems to actually like the arrangement, let's not forget that."

"I ain't telling you what to do," Curiosity said. "But I got to remind you, since you seem to have put it out of your mind, stolen honey tastes twice as sweet."

Elizabeth huffed a small laugh. "You're saying that I've set them a challenge—"

"Not both of them. Just Lily."

"Just Lily, then. I've set Lily a challenge that she must rise to. Which means . . ." Her voice trailed off. "What, exactly?"

"What it mean is, Simon got himself between a rock and a hard place. Lily going to be working hard to make him forget what he promised you. Now he a good man, and I like him. But he ain't nothing more than that and I don't know how long any man could stand up to Lily when she's in a mood to ask, pretty like, for what she want."

Elizabeth sniffed. "You make her sound like . . . like some kind of seductress. As if she had no self-control, or common sense."

Curiosity stopped and turned to face Elizabeth. She peered at her, squinting so that her brows drew together. "I'm thinking just now of another time you and me went walking in these woods, all the way up to Lake in the Clouds. About twenty year ago it was, I know you recall."

For all of her life, Elizabeth had cursed her inability to hide her thoughts. At moments like this she had no chance at all of dissembling, not with anyone who knew her as well as Curiosity.

A carpet of anemone under the sugar maples, white birch not yet in leaf, beech and maple and wild cherry. Yellow-flowered trout lily with its spotted purple leaves. The mountains and their spotty canopy of evergreens, and thousands upon thousands of trees touched with the first tender green. And Nathaniel,

angry at her and wanting her too. In her anxiety and confusion she had chal-
lenged his lack of reasoning.

"Maybe I ain't rational," Nathaniel had said. "But maybe rational ain't
what's called for right now."

And he had been right. They had done the irrational, they had acted
out of love and wanting and the need to be together when everything in Elizabeth argued against it. And it had been the right thing,
in the end. "Yes," she said quietly. "I do recall."

"Good," said Curiosity. "Now maybe you should have a talk
with the girl, and own up to some things. It might get you where
you want to go. You do know where you want to go?"

"Why, yes," Elizabeth said. "I want her to make a good choice. I
want her to be happy. I would like it—" She hesitated.

Curiosity smiled at her. "Go on."

"I would like it if she didn't go so far away as Montreal, but if it
is what she must do . . ." Her voice wobbled and then faded into
nothing.

"They'll make pretty babies, the two of them," Curiosity said.
"Pretty babies with a stubborn streak wide as the sky." She laughed
at that idea, and Elizabeth found herself laughing too.

They came to the edge of the orchard and paused. The sky had begun to darken, filled now with scudding clouds like churning fists.
Elizabeth pulled her shawl closer and straightened her shoulders.

"This might be messy," said Curiosity.

"No doubt," said Elizabeth. "But I have an idea."

Curiosity sent her a startled look.

"Don't worry," Elizabeth said. "Just follow my lead."

In Elizabeth's experience, good manners and forbearance were far
more effective tools in dealing with difficult people than slaps and
hard words. In her life she had had ample opportunity to test this
theory, and rarely had she been disappointed. Drunken trappers,
rude clerks, and condescending patroons were most manageable
when they were slightly off balance, and the easiest way to bring
that about was with a smile and a truly kind word.

She reminded herself of this when the door opened to their knock. Jemima's expression was thunderous, but Elizabeth put a hand on Curiosity's arm to calm and quiet her and met thunder with light.

"Hello, Jemima," she said. "You are looking very well. Do you have a moment for us?"

Some uncertainty flickered across the girl's face, and then was replaced by a reluctant shrug.

"I'm as well as can be expected. What do you want?"

"Just a word with you and Nicholas."

With her mouth pulled into a tight circle and her eyes narrowed, Jemima looked so much like her father that Elizabeth was always taken aback. She felt her own smile falter, but managed to rescue it.

"Come in then," Jemima said, stepping away from the door. She had yet to say a word to Curiosity, but neither did she object when the older woman followed Elizabeth into the dim cabin. "He's in the barn. I'll fetch him."

They were left alone in the main room of the cabin, dim and cool. There was no fire laid, but the ashes were swept and the pots polished and hung neatly. There was something oddly empty about the place, perhaps, Elizabeth told herself, because there was so little furniture. A table, a few chairs, a rug on the rough floor, a sewing basket. There were two dented pewter plates in the dish rack on the wall, but there was no pottery anywhere that Elizabeth could see. She had thought the rumors circulating in the village about Jemima's tempers were exaggerated, but now she must wonder if all the missing things had been sacrificed to a fit of anger.

"Feels deserted," Curiosity said.

And that was it exactly. The cabin was clean and ordered and empty of all sense that people lived here.

Nicholas came in, his cap held in front of him as he ducked his head.

"Is it Callie?" he asked. "Is Callie all right?"

Behind him Jemima snorted softly, her mouth turned down hard at the corners. She had crossed her arms and rested them on the swell of her stomach.

"Callie just fine," said Curiosity. "Healthy as a colt and just as frisky. Martha too."

Jemima might have never known anyone named Martha, for all the expression she showed. She had put her daughter away from her, and that was far more shocking than the sad state of the cabin.

Elizabeth steadied her voice. "We are here on a different matter," she said. "Black Abe is come. You will want to talk to him about your mother-in-law's grave, Jemima, will you not? And I was wondering if you would consider singing tomorrow when we bury Dr. Todd. He specifically requested it."

Next to Elizabeth Curiosity was tense with surprise, though a smile jerked at the corner of her mouth.

Jemima said, "What?"

"Dr. Todd asked that you sing a hymn when he is buried. Are you free tomorrow morning?"

Jemima frowned. "Richard Todd asked for me."

"Yes."

"I don't believe you," she said shortly. "Is it writ down in his will?"

Curiosity snorted softly. "A will ain't for writing down something like that. Listen here, Jemima. Either you care to come sing, or you don't."

Elizabeth could have kissed Curiosity, but she didn't dare even look at her.

Jemima's mouth worked. "All right then."

"Good," said Elizabeth. "At ten, at the family plot." She smiled then, a woman who had accomplished a difficult task and had one more before her.

"What else?" Jemima said. "There's something else you want."

Nicholas had watched all this silently, his gaze moving back and forth from Curiosity to Elizabeth. He said, "You haven't said anything about Dolly or Cookie. They need burying too."

Jemima let out a sound, soft disapproval and resignation all wrapped up together. She turned her face away.

"That's right," said Curiosity to Nicholas. "Black Abe is digging the graves this afternoon."

"I should do that." Nicholas touched his brow with the heel of his hand, as if to keep whatever thoughts he was plagued with to himself.

"Let the African do it," Jemima said, without looking at him.

There was a moment's strained silence, and Elizabeth wondered if she was about to witness one of the fights the village loved to talk about. Then Nicholas made a sound that came up from deep in his gut, and turned his face away.

Jemima turned to Elizabeth, her eyes narrowed.

"You think you're clever," she said, rocking herself gently back and forth. "You think you got the best of me."

Elizabeth started to say something but Jemima held up a hand to stop her. There was no threat in the way she held herself, nor was there anything to read in her expression.

"The day will come," Jemima said. "My day will come, you wait and see."

Curiosity said, "Don't talk foolish."

Then Jemima smiled. It was a smile that would stay with Elizabeth for the rest of the day and into the night; for its cold honesty, and the weight of its promise.

Chapter 30

Dear family,

It is two weeks since I removed the bullet from my brother's side, and so I write to tell you that the wound is healing and there is no sign of infection. He is stronger every day. The rest of the news is not as good. The damage to the nerves in his shoulder must be considerable, for the pain is constant. For the most part he refuses laudanum because, he claims, it clouds his mind, and there are others more in need than he.

The truth is, he has no use of the arm and will not, I fear, for a long time to come. Still he exercises it to keep the muscles from wasting, which Curiosity and my aunt Many-Doves will approve.

He sends the following messages: to his mother, that he is well tended and fed; to his father, he is sorry to have lost the good rifle he was given when he turned twelve; to Gabriel, that maple sugar is worth the work; to his cousin Annie, that he is trusting her to keep an eye on Gabriel lest he drink all the sap before it can be boiled into syrup; to Curiosity, that he is glad of the warm socks she knit for him from the wool of her own good sheep; to his twin Lily, that he has a painting she did of a sleigh moving over a snowy field, sent to him by our brother Luke, and how proud he is of her. And more, that he has learned to approve of Simon Ballentyne, and hopes that she does the same.

Blue-Jay is in good health. He is sent out into the garrison with the other able-bodied men to work, every day. Thus it has been possible for him to see my uncle Runs-from-Bears and they have talked. Because we are only allowed to be with the prisoners from sunrise to sunset, the same hours that he must work, I do not often have the chance to talk to him, but I make sure that he receives his share of the extra food that my brother Luke sends now twice a week.

The spring takes a hard toll on the prisoners. This week three men died of smallpox, two of brain fever, two of pneumonia, another three of their wounds, one when he was crushed by logs while on work detail, and one drowned while trying to escape. In the garrison hospital they have had more deaths still, most from smallpox and typhoid.

Of these twelve prisoners who died, the men have been most affected by the death of a young soldier. In all his time here he never roused himself to tell his name, and so he goes to an unmarked grave. I think of his poor family, and mourn for them.

Jennet writes her own letters, but I will say here what a good help she is to me, both as a surgeon's assistant and as a friend. I do not know how I should manage without her. The prisoners and the soldiers all love her for her kindness, for her good humor, and most of all, I think, for her stories. Luke is less pleased with her for she still refuses to travel on to Montreal. I understand his concern but I would be loath to lose her companionship.

From Luke you will have the rest of the news you must be waiting for.

Your loving daughter
Hannah, also called Walks-Ahead by the Kahnyen'kehàka, her mother's people, and Walking-Woman by her husband's. Written in her own hand the fifteenth day of March 1813.

Dear Father and Stepmother,
I would like to write to you that my brother and cousin will be home in a few weeks' time, but in good conscience I cannot give you false hope. Hannah and Runs-from-Bears agree that he is not strong enough to travel, and may not be for another month or more. You will see that it would be foolish to try anything before he has regained his health. I wish I had better news to share, but I will remind you that Daniel is improving, and for the moment at least is out of harm's way.

There is another matter I need to bring to your attention. I hope that my father might have some knowledge of a man who is now resident at the Nut Island garrison, and is in daily contact with Jennet. I have some suspicions about this person that I have not yet been able to either prove or dismiss on the basis of information available to me. My grandmother has suggested that my father may know more—though she will not say exactly why she believes this—and so I will describe the man here.

He calls himself Father O'Neill, a Catholic priest, and he calls himself an Irishman though he does not speak with the accent. He is a man close to fifty years old, strongly built, six and a half feet tall, graying black hair, blue eyes. His reputation is as a fighting priest. He roams from company to company hearing confessions, saying mass, and joining in skirmishes with great relish. Somehow Jennet gave this priest the idea that she was a Protestant, but open to conversion. She claims in her letters to me that while she is listening to his sermons she is also convincing him to see that the prisoners get the things they need. There is no harm in it, she says, and I am not to worry.

Except for this: my grandmother, who knows of every priest who has ever set foot in Canada, knows nothing of this man. In fact no one had ever heard of him before the start of this newest war, nor is there any record of his arrival. He appeared out of thin air, and I suspect he is up to no good.

I asked Runs-from-Bears to watch this man as well as he might from the followers' camp, and from him I have a little more information. The priest is missing the lobe of his left ear, a fact that is usually hidden by his hair, which he wears loose. He walks like a woodsman, and when Runs-from-Bears gave an owl's hunting cry in the middle of the day, he looked up suddenly and with suspicion, as would any man who had lived for a longer time in the great forests.

For obvious reasons, I cannot go to Nut Island. Neither can Hannah leave, and Jennet will not. I am uneasy at the bone about this man's real intentions; I pursue this matter in whatever way I can. Of course should there be any trouble Runs-from-Bears will see to it that Hannah and Jennet are brought to safety, and that fact alone allows me to pursue this matter less aggressively than I might otherwise.

If indeed you know anything of this man, the courier will wait for an answer from you before he leaves Paradise.

Your loving son
Luke

Chapter 31

"Now I seen some mighty messes in my time," said Curiosity, shutting the kitchen door behind her with a thump. "But I don't think I ever seen the likes of us."

The dozen people who had braved the storm for Richard Todd's burial—the last of three—stood in their best clothes, dripping icy water and mud onto Curiosity's scrubbed floor.

Elizabeth's plans for Dolly Wilde and Cookie Freeman had fallen nicely into place, but on the way from the meetinghouse graveyard to the Todds', the storm had come down on them. *The best laid plans,* Abe had observed, and Nathaniel finished the verse for him in the Scots he had learned from his mother: *must gae agley.*

All Elizabeth's careful plans had to be abandoned. Instead of readings and speeches and the singing of hymns, there had been a rushed prayer before they broke and ran for cover.

Only Black Abe, Nathaniel, and Simon had stayed behind to fill in the grave. Nicholas Wilde, who had come to all three gravesides alone—to Elizabeth's relief and disquiet both—had disappeared as quietly as he had come.

There was a strange humming energy in the room. It was the storm, Elizabeth told herself, and the morning's work, and the fact that everyone had been watching to see if Jemima would come to make trouble. Callie and Martha stood trembling and stunned, but Annie and Gabriel were barely able to sit still.

"You look like you jumped into the rain barrel," Annie said to Gabriel, almost in admiration. "And then rolled around in the dirt."

"Mama, Abe told you the weather was turning," said Daisy Hench to Curiosity. She was already busy at the hearth with kettles and pans, and Lily went to help her. There was a great ham stewing in pot liquor, and from the oven built into the hearth wall came the reviving smell of fresh bread.

Curiosity only sniffed. "You Callie, you Martha," she said in her gentlest voice. "Fetch the good sugar crock, would you please? A day like today call for as much hot sweet tea as a body can hold."

Soon the whole kitchen was in movement: a stack of toweling appeared, clothes were hung up, heads were rubbed dry, and cups of tea were passed from hand to hand.

Elizabeth watched Curiosity set Callie and Martha one task after another, and she saw, too, how some color came into Martha's pale cheeks, and the vacant look left Callie's eyes.

She was standing with Daisy at the big cutting board, wound in fragrant steam from the ham on its platter. "Your mother is a wise woman," she said.

Daisy ran the carving knife over the whetstone. "Sly too." She grinned. "You watch, she'll coax smiles out of those two poor lambs before dinner is done."

Though she didn't like the dining room and rarely used it, Curiosity had decided that the mourners would get their dinner there today. There were fifteen of them gathered around: five Henches, Curiosity, Callie and Martha, Simon, Abe, and four of the Bonners, along with Annie.

Curiosity said, "Ain't this a sight. I wonder what Richard thinking just now, looking down at us."

Next to Elizabeth Nathaniel made a humming sound. She put a hand on his leg to quiet him, and he took her hand in both his own.

"Now I'ma talk a bit, words I was going to say over his grave." Curiosity grinned. "Before the weather made us all cut tail and run." Her glance ran around the table as if she expected an objection and knew just what to do with it should she find any. After a moment she cleared her throat.

"Richard was a troubled man," Curiosity started slowly. "But he did some good. In the end I think he did more good than bad, and may the good Lord give him the credit he got coming. Cain't nobody deny but he had his share of sorrow and more. Times I thought it would get the best of him. He struggled, he surely did, and sometimes he misstepped, but there ain't nobody—not at this table nor who ever walked this earth—but can say the same."

"Amen," murmured Black Abe.

"So I'll ask the Lord to be merciful, and grant the man some rest."

She sat down abruptly, and there was a small silence. Then Elizabeth stood. She said, "I am glad to have known Richard Todd, in spite of all our early difficulties. He took on our Hannah as his student and taught her well. She would be here if she could, to pay her respects.

"Ethan should be here too, and so should Richard's uncle Bump. But even in death Richard had a—I suppose I must call it a compulsion—to hold the people who care most about him at a distance."

Her voice began to waver. Nathaniel squeezed her hand and picked up where she had left off.

"There's something we ain't said, but need to. Most men wouldn't have left an old shoe to a black woman or a Mohawk girl, but Richard Todd left this house to Curiosity and his medical practice to our Hannah. He never did care what other people thought, and I appreciate that about the man. Whatever history there was between us, he wiped the slate clean."

From the far end of the table where Gabriel sat next to Abe came a sharp double rumble. Gabriel clapped both hands over his belly and sent his mother a sheepish look.

"Sorry, Mama," he said.

Abe ducked his head. "It do smell awful good, Miz Elizabeth."

The laughter came and went easily while dishes were passed and passed again. Rain rattled the windows in their frames and the wind made the trees that ringed the house creak and scream, but the food was hot and plentiful and there was an endless supply of hot tea laced with milk and sugar. Elizabeth felt suddenly very sleepy, but then Curiosity raised her voice again.

"I got a letter," she said. "Abe brought it with him when he come from Johnstown. I was waiting for the right time to read it aloud to everybody at once. From Bump."

"Your Bump?" Simon Ballentyne asked Lily, who sat across from him.

"Why, he ain't *her* Bump," said Gabriel, his brow drawn down in outraged disapproval, as if Lily had tried to claim the pies sitting on the sideboard for herself alone.

"That's not what he meant," Lily said to her brother. "And you know it. Simon, if you mean Mr. Bump who called on me in Montreal, yes."

Elizabeth caught Simon's eye, and smiled. It seemed that for today, at least, Lily had decided that she could afford to put aside her irritation with them both.

Gabriel was of a different mind. He studied Simon for a moment and then said, "How'd you get that bruise between your eyes?"

"I was wondering about that myself," said Nathaniel. There was a telltale quivering in the muscles of his jaw, and Elizabeth pinched him under the table.

"Did you fall?" Gabriel asked. "Did you run into a tree?"

"You're mean," Annie said to Gabriel.

"I should rather say he is being rude," Elizabeth corrected Annie. And then: "My, listen to that rain. And it feels to me as though the temperature must be dropping."

"Dropping fast," Nathaniel agreed.

Black Abe glanced up from the pile of ham and potatoes on his plate and nodded. "A hard freeze coming."

"Mrs. Bonner," Simon said. "I don't mind answering the boy's question."

Elizabeth closed her eyes and groaned inwardly, but still she could almost feel the triumphant look that her youngest child shot at her.

Gabriel said, "Well, then, how did you get it?"

Lily's gaze was fixed on her fork, but her color had risen a few shades at least. Simon started to speak and she raised her face and shook her head at him sharply.

She said, "Gabriel. He did not fall, or run into a door or a tree or a fist. That's all you need to know."

There was a moment's strained silence and then Curiosity said, "There's this letter, still, if you done poking at the man, Gabriel."

That got the boy's attention as nothing else had. He ducked his head and allowed that he would like to hear it, pardon him please, and could somebody pass the ham, he was still some hungry.

When the bowls and platters had made another journey around the table Curiosity took the letter out of her bodice and unfolded it. From her apron pocket she took a pair of spectacles and put them on carefully, wiggling her nose like a rabbit until she was satisfied with the way they sat.

Elizabeth, who knew Curiosity as well as anyone, saw the slight tremble in her hands and sat up, interest giving way to fresh anxiety.

She had put the letter down on the table and stood over it, her head at an angle, her whole posture putting Elizabeth in mind of a bird eyeing a worm whole, alert and alive and eager.

" 'Dear Curiosity,' " she began to read.

I find myself on the far side of the great lakes. As of yet I have still not found my nephew Samuel, who is called Throws-Hard by the Kahnyen'kehàka, or any of his children. However, I have spoken to an elderly sachem by the name of Elk-in-the-Snow, who has given me some reason to believe that I must continue this journey farther into Canada. It seems these old bones are not done yet with adventuring, but I do not complain. Indeed, I believe I owe my nephew Richard thanks for making me stretch both my legs and my mind.

Now for the rest of my news, of a surprising nature but a joyful one. In this place I have come across an old acquaintance of mine and someone much closer to you. After many days and nights of conversation I have permission to tell you that your son Almanzo is here, that he is well, and that he regrets to the bottom of his soul the pain he has caused you by his long silence.

He had cause. Not sufficient cause, he now has come to see, but to him it seemed so at the time. It has to do with the death of Hannah's husband, Strikes-the-Sky. More than that I cannot write down here. It is Almanzo's place to tell that story, for Hannah's sake, and for his own, and for yours.

I have told him of his father's death, and he is much shaken but now more determined to come home to you.

Thus this news: your son should be with you in Paradise a week or ten days after you receive this letter. It is time to butcher the fatted calf, Curiosity my dear.

Your true friend,
Cornelius Bump

"My God," Daisy said, and she pressed her hands to her mouth. A great sob escaped anyway, and then a laugh, and then half the room was crying and laughing together. Chairs were pushed out of the way as people made their way to Curiosity, who had read the last part of the letter with tears streaming down her face.

"I'ma feed that boy up good," she said between sobs. "And then I'ma beat him black and blue. Or maybe the other way around."

Lily wrapped her arms around herself and rocked back and forth.

She caught her father's eye and saw many things there: happiness for Curiosity, whose son had been restored to her. Resignation and some relief at the news that confirmed, finally, that Strikes-the-Sky was dead. Confusion and worry and doubt too, all those things wound together.

Simon just looked somber, and a little confused. "It's a long story," she told him. "I'll tell you sometime."

"You can tell him this afternoon, daughter," Nathaniel said. "If he's still planning to call on you." It was more a question than a statement.

Simon said, "Aye, I am."

It was the look the men exchanged that caused Lily to flush with embarrassment and irritation. She said, "I am going to the meeting-house," she said. "There is some work I must finish."

"I'll call for you there at four," Simon said. "And see you home."

"Cobbler for supper," Nathaniel said. "From the last of the dried apples."

Elizabeth, who had been listening but staying out of the conversation, drew in a sharp breath and then turned away.

"Another long story," Nathaniel told Simon. "But not one you'll ever hear." He was grinning in the way that men sometimes grinned at each other, when there was a woman at the heart of the matter.

Lily bit her lip. She had promised herself that she would cause no trouble today, for Callie's sake and Martha's. But there was a limit to even the best of intentions, and she slipped out of the room before she found herself standing on the other side of it.

Inside the meetinghouse, with the woodstove stoked and her wet boots set in front of it and her hooded mantle draped over a chair to dry, Lily sat down to lose herself in work. The storm robbed most of the light out of the afternoon and so she soon had to stop and light the candles. Any other time she would have simply given up for the day and gone home, but she did not like the idea of climbing the mountain in the driving rain. She might have gone to see Joshua Hench at the smithy and borrow a horse, but with her poor luck she would most likely find herself mired before she got very far.

Lily blew out all but one of the candles and found an old blanket that she had wrapped her canvases with. It smelled of dust and camphor and cloves, but it was warm around her shoulders. She settled on the floor near the little stove, and fell to sleep without thinking much about it at all.

• • •

When she woke, sometime later, many things occurred to her at once: there was a cramp in her neck; the fire still burned in the oven, but the room was much colder; and the storm had stopped. In its place was a strange twilight glow that filled the room.

The mantle she had spread out to dry felt good when she wrapped it around herself, so good that she might have gone right back to sleep. But the golden-red twilight would not be ignored, and so she padded over to the window in her stocking feet. At first she did not quite understand what she was seeing.

One of the things Lily remembered most clearly from the little time she had spent with her uncle and aunt Spencer in Manhattan was the chandelier that hung in their front hall. As a child she had been so enchanted by the way it caught light and spun it into colors that she sat under it for long periods of time, just watching. Aunt Spencer had taken note, and when they left for home she pressed a small package into Lily's hand: hard and uneven in shape, wrapped in a piece of silk and tied with a ribbon.

Inside there was a note: "To hang in your chamber window." The crystal was one of Lily's most precious possessions.

Now she saw a world that looked as if it had been carved from the same clear, many-faceted substance. One part of her mind told her very primly that what she was seeing was nothing more than the results of a sudden freeze on the heels of a hard rain. The other part, the part that was an artist, was not satisfied with such a simplistic answer.

Every twig on every branch, every pine needle, every nail head stood out from the next, ablaze in the twilight. It was dazzlingly bright, so bright that Lily's eyes began to water and still she couldn't look away.

As she watched she realized that there was a sound just as odd as the sight of the icy world before her: a low groaning, like a hundred women in travail. It waxed and waned with the wind, and rose and fell and then rose to a scream. With a sound like bone breaking a great branch cracked and crashed to the ground, shedding great sheets of ice that cut through the clear crust that had been laid over the snow.

Another branch fell, out of sight, and then another. Lily watched, fascinated and horrified as the world began to shatter. The wind lifted its voice, a wayward child with a hammer in a house with a thousand windows.

The clamor climbed to a roar that went on and on. With a report as loud and sharp as a rifle shot a birch that stood by the porch of the trading post broke in half.

"Have you ever seen the like?" Simon Ballentyne said behind her, and Lily's heart leapt so that she must put a fist to her breast to quiet it. She struggled to compose her face before she turned.

He said, "I fell a dozen times on my way here from the doctor's place." There was a bloody gash on his forehead, and a tear in his breeches.

"I see that," Lily said.

"Curiosity said to bring you back to her, there'll be nobody going up the mountain this night."

There was no sense in arguing with something so obvious, and so Lily nodded. Then she noticed that Simon had tucked something under his arm.

"What's that?"

"A courier came a few hours ago, from your brother. I stopped in the trading post and he gave me letters to take to Lake in the Clouds." He held them up to show her.

"He's put off by the ice," Lily said.

"Aye," said Simon. "A sensible man. Anna and Jed are making up a cot for him."

From outside there was a series of loud cracks that made Lily jump.

"I just have to put on my boots," she said.

He waited patiently and did not bother her with talk, for which Lily was thankful. She yawned widely and then, too late, covered her mouth.

"It's been a long day," Simon said, and opened the door for her.

It was no more than a hundred feet from the meetinghouse door to the foundation of the new school, and another hundred feet to the trading-post porch. Lily had walked the path a thousand times or more, but she had never seen it looking as it did now, like polished window glass.

Simon took her elbow, or tried to. "I'll manage," she said, and fell, hard, to land on her bum. A branch broke off the oak that stood in the graveyard at exactly the same moment, as if to scold her.

Lily shot Simon a warning look and helped herself up, only to fall again. He shrugged when he saw her accusatory glance. "Hobnailed boots," he explained. "But even so I had a hard time of it. Come, lass, take my arm."

Lily pushed out a great breath and then, finally, nodded. Simon pulled her to her feet without any effort at all and they stood there, face to face, breathing hard.

"You're laughing." Lily frowned at him.

"It's laugh or weep, lass. Now hold on."

They took five small steps without mishap, and then another five. Lily glanced up at him, pleased, and put her foot down wrong.

Later, she wondered what it must have looked like to a casual observer. Two people fighting for purchase, feet flying, clinging to each other and laughing like loons.

Even after they landed, she on her stomach and he on his back, they laughed for a long minute, and then Lily was overcome with hiccups, which set her back to laughing.

"Ach," Simon wheezed finally, wiping tears from his face with a gloved fist. "I fear we'll not get very far. Shall we go back?"

With her nose pressed to the cold ice, Lily considered. There was enough firewood in the meetinghouse to keep them comfortable for a good while, even overnight if need be. She had a small store of food; there were two chairs. She lifted her head to look at the trading post, which seemed ten miles away.

As if she had been called, Anna McGarrity appeared on the porch wrapped in shawls, her hand shading her eyes as she looked in their direction. Then her voice boomed out over the distance.

"It's no use!" she shouted. "Back to where you came from!"

That was enough for Lily. She scooted all the way back, refusing to let Simon help her to her feet.

"My mother will accuse me of planning this whole thing, ice storm and all," Lily said later. They had eaten the little bit of dried venison and cornbread she had stored away, and now they sat in front of the stove in the light of the candles. Very comfortable, and at ease. Lily realized that she was tired of arguing, and content to sit with him like this, talking as they used to.

"Your mother means well," Simon said.

"I am just starting to feel a bit more generous toward you," Lily said. "But that could change quickly."

He smiled into his cup of tea, this time without milk or sugar. "Very well. I'll not mention your mother—"

"Or my father."

"Or your father, if you won't."

"Agreed."

They were quiet for a moment, listening to the wind. In a conversational tone he might use with a stranger on the street Simon said, "The weather's shifting again."

"Hmmmm."

And then, when she felt she could keep her eyes open no longer, Simon said, "You haven't asked about the letters."

She sat up straight. "Is there one for me?"

He pulled them out of his coat and squinted to read in the dim light.

"One in your brother's hand addressed to your father. One in your sister's addressed to the family, and a thin one from Jennet. 'To my cousins,' she's written."

"I'm her cousin," said Lily. She felt Simon's gaze on her. "I'm sure they wouldn't mind if we read it."

Simon made a sound that might have been disapproval, or complicity. He grinned.

"Gabriel will be aye furious if you read it first."

"Reason enough," Lily said, holding out her hand. "The little monster has been far too cheeky of late."

The seal on the letter broke with a soft crack. It was a single sheet, closely written. Lily handed it back to Simon.

"You read it."

He cocked his head at her.

"Go on," she said. "I've never heard your reading voice."

"A test, then."

"One test, yes."

He grunted softly and took the letter, his eyes running down it. Then he hitched his chair closer to the table where the candles stood.

" 'Dear Cousins,' " he read in a clear, clipped voice. " 'Today a dozen fat pigs broke through their pen beside the cookhouse to escape the butcher's knife. It was my good fortune to be close by, for I'll never see the like again: a herd of swine leading His Majesty's finest men-at-arms on a mad chase while the colonel's cook watched from the ramparts, waving his arms in the air and shouting in a lovely broad Scots.

" 'Now, the spring mud is very deep and slippery, which pleased the pigs far better than the men. Mud showers drenched each and every one of them from hat to toe. Oh, and the cursing and the shouting. I was put in mind of the Pirate Stoker.' "

"She does love that pirate," Lily said, delighted. "She never misses a chance to tell a story about him."

"Fabricated out of thin air, no doubt," said Simon with a frown. "It's been twenty years since she saw the man."

He went on: " 'Now, just when it seemed the men had lost all patience and would soon end the fun by means of their muskets, the porkers seem to realize that the river was their only chance of escape. All at once they turned and stampeded for the shore and launched themselves, every one, onto the bit of ice that still remains. Of course it could not hold their weight and they all fell through. The last we saw of them were rosy pink rumps bobbing their way toward Halifax.' "

Lily was laughing with great appreciation, but Simon only stared at the letter in his hand.

"What is it?" Lily said. "Go on."

He cleared his throat. " 'And all the while the cook shouted crossly for his porkers, as if they were naught but playful children sure to come home for tea once they had had their fun.

" 'The best part is this: the prisoners had been set to wood-chopping nearby and thus saw it all, from muddy beginning to watery end. It was aye good to see them laugh. Yours aye, Cousin Jennet.' "

Lily laughed until tears ran down her face but all Simon could produce was a weak smile.

She said, "You're not feeling sorry for the redcoats?"

"Ach, ne," Simon said, and gave a chuckle that convinced Lily only that something wasn't quite right.

She watched him for a moment and then, leaning over quickly, snatched the letter from his hand. He made a grab for her wrist, but Lily was already up and away.

"Give it back," he said, advancing on her with a thunderous expression.

"Not quite yet." When she glanced at it he took the opportunity to leap at her, but Lily wiggled away neatly and ran to the other side of the room, trying to scan the page as she went.

She whirled around to meet him, holding the letter between her back and the wall.

"Simon Ballentyne," she said severely. "Why is it you don't want me to read this letter for myself? Did you leave something out?"

That stopped him. A thoughtful look came over his face, and then resignation.

"Suit yourself, then," he said, holding up both hands as he backed away.

Lily narrowed her eyes at him. "This isn't a trick? You'll let me read it."

"I see no help for it," Simon said. "If not now, you'll read it later when you're home."

Lily considered him for a moment, consumed by curiosity and vaguely concerned too. What could Jennet have written to put him in this state? She thought of her brother, and tried to remember when she had last seen him look as Simon was looking now.

"Is it some story from home?" she said. "Something you did as a boy she's teasing you about?"

His mouth contorted. "Just read the letter, Lily, and have done with it."

"I'll burn it, if you like. Just ask me and I'll put it in the oven. If it's that important to you."

That took him by surprise. He started to say something and stopped himself. Then he ran both hands through his hair and shook his head.

"Read it."

The paper was crumpled from mistreatment and the ink had run a little, but Lily's eyes ran down the page quickly.

"Today a dozen fat pigs . . . soldiers-at-arms . . . lovely broad Scots . . . drenched each and every one of them . . . Stoker . . . muskets . . . stampeded . . . rosy pink rumps bobbing their way toward Halifax."

She glanced at Simon, who was looking at her evenly, as a soldier might look at an officer who was considering an appropriate punishment for some foolish prank.

"Finish it," he said.

Aloud Lily read, " 'And all the while the cook shouted crossly for his grumfies, as if they were naught but playful children sure to come home for tea once they had had their fun.

" 'The best part is this: the prisoners had been set to wood-chopping nearby and thus saw it all, from muddy beginning to watery end. It was aye good to see them laugh. Yours aye, Cousin Jennet.' "

Lily paused, and read it again. She glanced at Simon and at the letter and then into the shadows at the far end of the room.

Simon blinked at her, his expression wary. Lily read the last two paragraphs once more, and then she saw it.

"Ah," she said. "The grumfies. That's it, isn't it. You never did tell me what the word meant."

She gave him a small smile, a bit brittle.

"So you called me a pig, is that it? And you were hoping I wouldn't find out, or I'd forget."

A small explosion of air came from his mouth. "I did no such thing. I said—"

"You said I squealed like a grumfie."

He shoulders slumped. "Aye. It was an unfortunate turn of phrase."

"Unfortunate." Lily turned her back on him, not out of anger, but because she did not want to laugh, just yet. His expression was a odd mixture of regret and irritation and disgust; she could not look at him for long and keep a straight face.

"Unfortunate indeed," she echoed, trying for her mother's most disapproving tone.

Behind her he was silent. "I've apologized, and I'll do it as many times as you like."

"For calling me a pig."

She heard him shift, and when he spoke again, there was some new tension in his voice. "I didnae call ye a pig."

Lily went to the window. The last of the light was gone, but the moon was rising bright enough to throw a shadow.

"Lily," he said, closer now. "Be fair."

"Fair," she said. "What would you consider fair?"

Another longer silence, and she turned.

"Clearly you knew I must be offended, or you would have told me then what it meant."

His mouth worked, the muscles in his jaws knotting and popping. "Aye."

"Let me ask you a question, Simon, and I want an honest answer."

He glanced down at her along the slope of his nose, and nodded.

"What kind of silly, childish, nonsensical person do you take me for?"

His brow creased. She poked him hard with one finger and he took a step backward.

"Did you think that I was wrapped in silk as a girl, here on the frontier?" She poked him again, harder, and followed him as he stepped backward.

"I—"

"You thought I'd faint away."

This time he stepped before she could poke.

"I thought you'd take offense."

She snorted at him. "Because you called me a pig?"

Now he flushed, and his voice rose. "I didnae call ye a pig!"

"A grumfie then."

He grabbed her by the arms and lowered his face so that they were nose to nose. "I didna call ye a grumfie. I said ye squealed like a grumfie. Which ye did."

All Lily's self-control left her then, and she laughed. Right in his flushed face, she laughed, and then when his lips began to jerk, she laughed louder, and finally he laughed too, and then he kissed her.

With a great sigh of satisfaction Lily wrapped her arms around him and kissed him back for a good long time.

Finally he said, "I give in."

Lily smiled against his mouth. "What ever do you mean?"

He pulled her tight against him so that she could not miss his intention. "I give in."

"You mean to make me squeal like a grumfie?"

He pressed his mouth to her forehead and his shoulders shook a little, with wanting and laughter and surrender too, and Lily felt dizzy with the power of it.

"If there's a blanket, aye," he said.

"In front of the stove," Lily said. "Hurry."

Chapter 32

Dear Luke,

For your letter with news of your brother and cousin our thanks. Your stepmother tries to hide her disappointment, and almost succeeds. Of course she would have them home now, but not at the risk of Daniel's health, and so she daily lectures herself and everyone else on the virtues of patience. While I write she is busy with a letter to Hannah and Jennet, which we trust you will see delivered safely into their hands.

I don't know anything of this priest you describe, nor of any man who fits that description of the right age. I have been long out of the north woods and my connections are poor. Now while it is true that many priests are rascals, most are harmless enough. If he is the kind who preys on the weak of mind, then he has met his match in Jennet. If he has some other plan you are right to remember that Runs-from-Bears is close by, and there is yet to be born a priest who could get the better of Bears. I'll remind you that your grandmother's distrust of the church goes deep, and that you were raised on it.

And having said all that, I believe that if in your gut you know he is a danger to your sister and bride, then you must do what must be done to see that no harm comes to them. Consult with Bears, and take action as you see fit.

As far as Jennet is concerned, my advice to you is this: this is not the last time you will be at odds. You are both stubborn and single-minded, and you must learn to pick your battles or resign yourself to losing the war.

Your father,
Nathaniel Bonner

Daughter,
With this post the courier brings you a number of things from your aunt Many-Doves and Curiosity, foremost a crock that they worked all day to fill with unguent. They say you will recognize it for what it is, and to rub it daily into Daniel's shoulder and arm and then to wrap it in the flannel. Many-Doves begs you tell Daniel that without sleep he will not heal, and that he should take the tea she is sending without complaint. Curiosity adds that he must take the laudanum you prescribe for him along with the tea. And if he will not, you are (in her words) to pour it down his gullet and hold his nose until he swallows.

Gabriel sends two carvings, one of a horse and one of a bear, for his brother and cousin to share between them, he says. The carving of the squirrel is for you, and the one of the beaver is, of course, for Jennet. Gabriel and Annie send her word that they are watching her favorite dam closely and will give her a full reporting when she comes home again.

I am sending a large cake of the new maple sugar and a jug of syrup, as well as a cask of cornmeal and a sack of beans. With these things I send my loving concern and faith in you, that you will do everything in your power to see that your brother and cousin regain their health.

We would send more, but the courier balks at boxes of candles and bundles of blankets, and he is eager to be away. Yesterday when he arrived there was an ice storm of such strange intensity that I can hardly describe it. He seems to fear that it might happen again, though the weather has turned warm and the sky is clear.

May this letter reach you quickly, and find you all well.

Your loving stepmother
Elizabeth Middleton Bonner

Postscript: I have written nothing of your sister Lily, not because there is no news, but because there is too much to say in too short a time. She is in love, I think, but struggles with it, as of course she must.

Chapter 33

When the courier had ridden off, Elizabeth stood in the muddy path outside the trading post with her arms wrapped about herself and gave in to tears. They came in a great warm wave and without sound: his Elizabeth, stoical and impatient with sorrow, no matter how honestly she came by it.

Nathaniel put an arm around her shoulders and said nothing; his own throat was swollen almost shut with the things he wanted his daughter to know, but must keep to himself.

"It would be too much, just now," Elizabeth said. "It would be unfair to burden her any more." And then, on an indrawn breath: "Oh, Nathaniel, perhaps we should have."

There was a warm breeze today, one that smelled of sap rising and the ice water that rushed downmountain to swell the Sacandaga to its banks. He could smell Elizabeth's tears too, salty, with a bitter edge.

He said, "And what if Manny doesn't come, after all?"

Under his arm he felt Elizabeth's shoulders tense and then roll forward in surrender. To give Hannah hope that she might finally know what had happened to her husband and then take it away—neither of them wanted to risk that.

Elizabeth wiped her face hastily with her handkerchief and pulled in a shuddering breath just as Simon Ballentyne appeared on the path that came from the doctor's place, bareheaded in the weak spring sun. At this distance the difference in color between his fore-head and the new-shaved cheeks was still clear, and it always made Nathaniel uncomfortable to see, for reasons he didn't ask himself about very closely.

He was coming straight for them, head high, straight of shoulder: a man ready to take the harsh words he knew he had earned. Something else Nathaniel didn't much want to think about, but Elizabeth was of a different mind altogether.

She said, "I think I must own that my arrangements have failed. They must work out this business between them without any inter-ference from us."

He made a sound that meant neither that he agreed nor that he disagreed, but only that he was listening. He was hoping that would satisfy her, but from the sharp look Elizabeth threw his way Nathaniel knew she would not let him off so easy.

Sunday night they had known the ice storm would keep Lily in the village. Simon, who was supposed to bring her home to Lake in the Clouds, would see her safely to Curiosity, where she would spend the night.

Lying in the dark in their bed and listening to the trees groan un-der the sudden burden of ice, they had lain awake thinking of Lily in one room and Simon in the next.

"Curiosity is there," Nathaniel had said. "And the little girls." And still Elizabeth had been awake for a long time, and Nathaniel with her.

Finally he turned to her and said, "And if they are together, Boots, well then. We've got to let her go."

"I know," she said. "I know that. Curiosity made me see that."

"What then?" he asked, smoothing a stray hair away from her face.

"She's so *young*," Elizabeth said.

"Something she'll outgrow," Nathaniel had said, hoping to catch at least a glimmer of her smile in the dark.

"Too soon," Elizabeth said. "And far away from us."

There it was, the worst of it. They might keep Simon Ballentyne here for the summer, but in the fall he would take their daughter away.

"You'll have to give in on Canada," Nathaniel said.

Elizabeth pushed out a laugh. "I suppose I will. It's that or never see our Lily's children." And then, in a more serious tone she said, "I must make the most of these months. At least I have the summer."

She said: "I think she has a better chance of being happy with him than she would with most men. He is not put off by her talent."

"And you ain't worried about the connection to Moncrieff," Nathaniel said. It was a question, and it wasn't. She turned to him in the dark, suddenly.

"Are you?"

Nathaniel let his mind travel back over the years to the idea of Angus Moncrieff. No matter how he concentrated, he couldn't call up the man's face.

"I don't see anything of his uncles in him," Nathaniel said.

Elizabeth bedded her cheek on his shoulder, glad of his warmth and his calm and the fact that when her own hard-won rationalism threatened to desert her, she could count on Nathaniel's.

"Nor do I," she said. And hoped it was the truth.

Monday morning, the worst of the ice already gone, they had picked their way down the mountain over fallen branches and trees snapped in half by the ice to find that Lily had not gone to Curiosity, but had slept in the meetinghouse.

She did not look at either of them directly when she said this, and Nathaniel had an idea of why not. So did Elizabeth, from the color that came into her cheeks and the way her forehead drew down to build a crease between her brows.

"There was no walking anywhere," Lily had explained, her face turned away from them. "And there was enough firewood."

Nathaniel could almost see Elizabeth's mind working, the way she weighed words and phrases and rearranged them until they suited her perfectly. If he had his way, Nathaniel would have left the question unasked, but Elizabeth could not. Last night she had re-solved to let Lily and Simon work things out between themselves, but her curiosity was ungovernable at this moment.

Lily saw it coming too; in any other circumstances it might have made Nathaniel laugh, the silent battle between mother and daugh-ter. *I am going to ask,* Elizabeth's expression said, and Lily's: *Not if I can think of a way to distract you.*

And she had just the ammunition she needed. Lily told them about the courier waiting in the trading post and handed over the letters, and that was the end of uncomfortable questions about ex-actly who had spent the night in the meetinghouse.

But now the courier was off, and Lily was home at Lake in the Clouds, and here was Simon Ballentyne, coming straight at them.

Nathaniel said, "Ice storm kept you off the mountain Sunday, I suppose."

Beside him Elizabeth let out a little sigh. She might confront Lily, but she would leave Simon to Nathaniel.

"Aye," Simon began.

Elizabeth, flustered, did the unthinkable: she interrupted him.

"What good fortune to see you just now," she said, too brightly. "Nathaniel, Simon wants to talk to you about the foundation of the new school. Why don't you two go on, I have some errands to do and then I'll be along."

Simon hid his surprise long enough to agree that, yes, he had a few questions if Nathaniel had the time.

Nathaniel, who knew that Elizabeth had no errands, made a face at his wife when Simon turned his back.

"Coward," he mouthed at her. She blushed prettily and wrinkled her nose at him, but she went off anyway, leaving him alone with the man who had got into the habit of ravishing their daughter.

Simon looked both confused and guilty, but he nodded. "Weel, then," he said. "It won't take long."

Elizabeth went into the trading post, where the usual group of men were lounging around the stove, caught up in an argument about ice storms. Even for the trading post it was a particularly loud argument, but Elizabeth was glad to be overlooked. She went to Anna, who stood behind the counter, and asked to see buttons. It was the first thing that came to mind.

Anna leaned across, her comfortable bosom pressed into the worn wood of the countertop, and whispered.

"Don't worry, I ain't about to say a word to nobody about who slept where after the ice storm."

Startled, Elizabeth felt her jaw drop. She shut it with an audible click; opened it again to say something, anything. A dozen things occurred to her all at once, denials and protestations. Then she heard herself say, "Thank you."

Anna nodded. She had a habit of closing her eyes for a few seconds at a time and then opening them suddenly, like an owl.

She said, "Too much gossip in this place as it is." And then:

"Here's the post rider. This place is going to fill up right quick, Elizabeth. You might want to be on your way if you ain't in a talkative mood. I swear there ain't nothing like a war to set people to writing letters. Even Jemima is in here twice a week sending something off or looking for a letter." She dropped her voice another notch and leaned forward again.

"Don't suppose you knew she's got kin in Boston?"

Elizabeth was torn between reminding Anna that there was already too much gossiping going on, and interest in this rather odd offering. She settled for composing her face in an expression that she hoped conveyed interest without commitment.

Anna said, "A cousin, she says. Writing back and forth regular, the two of them. You wait and see, she'll be in that door in the next five minutes."

Charlie LeBlanc had come up behind Elizabeth so quietly that she hadn't noticed, and she jumped in place when he spoke.

"My thought," he said in his most ponderous tones, "is that our Jemima is looking for somebody to take her in. She's had enough of Paradise, and Paradise of her."

Elizabeth wanted very much to walk away, but Martha came to mind. For Martha Kuick she must speak up, as no one else seemed to remember that Jemima had a daughter.

"Whatever trouble there might be at the Wildes' place, I trust no one is taking joy in it."

Charlie began to worry his thumbnail with his teeth, but Anna had the good manners to at least look abashed.

"Well said. Well reminded." She pushed out a sigh between her teeth.

Elizabeth said, "And if Jemima does have a cousin or friend in Boston, why, I hope it is some comfort to her. Whatever her wrongdoings, even Jemima is made of flesh and blood."

"No need to bash me over the head with my wickedness," Anna said. At that moment the door opened, and a man stepped inside. Not the post rider, as Anna had predicted, but a stranger.

Anna straightened and put on the smile she reserved for well-dressed travelers who might have real coin to spend.

"Good day, sir," she said. "Can I help you?"

A well-formed skull covered with a pelt of white hair swung ponderously in the direction of the counter. All through the trading post voices quieted and eyes turned to the stranger.

Elizabeth had read about albinos, but she had never seen one before. The stranger had skin the blue-white of skimmed milk, and eyes that were almost pink even in the deep shadow provided by the brim of his hat. For all their strange color the expression in his eyes was quick and clear. He had a strong nose, slightly upturned, with prominent flared nostrils. His mouth, small and the color of bruised strawberries, was his oddest feature. When he spoke a row of strong teeth flashed, too perfect to be anything but man's invention.

"I take it you are Mrs. McGarrity." He spoke in an accent Elizabeth could not place right away: clipped, with a singsong quality. "Mrs. Wilde suggested that you might be able to direct me. I am the Reverend Stiles. That boy out there in the wagon—" He jerked a thumb over his shoulder. "That's my nephew Justus Rising."

He said his name as if he expected it to be familiar to her, and then he looked around the crowded trading post in the same way.

"Well, now," Anna said, casting a surprised look at Elizabeth, who was no less at a loss. "If I can help, certainly. Were you wanting directions to find Jemima?"

Charlie LeBlanc found his tongue, as he usually did, to ask just that question that everyone was thinking but would not voice. He said, "Are you some kin of Jemima's then? Come from Boston?"

Elizabeth had a sudden sense of falling, a dizziness that would have got the better of her had she not been close enough to the counter to grab it with one hand. Some part of her understood already what this stranger would say before he opened his mouth, his expression shifting from polite to puzzled. Jemima's face came to mind, the deep-set eyes hooded and knowing. *My day will come, you wait and see.*

"Why, no," said the Reverend Stiles. "I'm no kin of Mrs. Wilde's. Yesterday was the first time I ever met the good lady." He rocked back on his heels and lowered his chin to his chest, the posture of a man about to launch into a sermon. Luckily Charlie caught that too, and asked another question quick.

"You saw Jemima yesterday? But where?"

"Why, in Johnstown," said the Reverend Stiles. "At her attorney's office, where we signed the purchase agreement." He caught the look on Elizabeth's face.

"Madam, are you unwell?"

"I am well enough, sir," Elizabeth said. "Tell me, do I understand you correctly? You have bought the Wildes' property?"

All the men around the stove came closer to stand behind her in a loose half-circle.

"I assumed you would know, Mrs.—"

"Mrs. Bonner," Elizabeth supplied. "And this is Mrs. McGarrity, and Mr. LeBlanc."

For once in her life, Anna was speechless; she made some small sound that was meant to be a greeting.

The Reverend Stiles nodded solemnly. "I have bought the Wildes' place, and I'm here to take possession. Of the orchards and the meetinghouse as well. I've agreed to take up your empty pulpit. Mrs. Wilde impressed upon me how in need this place is of the Lord's word."

"Christ on the bloody Cross," said Charlie, scratching the crown of his head with the stem of his pipe. "Jemima's gone and sold the place out from under Nicholas. I'll bet he doesn't have a clue."

Tuesday morning, Lily woke in her own bed at Lake in the Clouds and listened. The house was empty. Her parents had gone down to the village to give the courier their letters and packages, and left her to sleep, something she might have done for a longer time if not for the noise that she could not identify.

Then it came again: a crashing like dishes breaking, but from outside. More awake now, Lily recognized it for what it was: the great icicles that hung from the eaves, many as tall as her father, were falling. As children she and Daniel had made it their special chore to help the process, taking up fallen branches and leaning out the windows to swipe at the ice.

Those days were gone now, and wouldn't come again. Daniel was in Canada, and when he was well enough he would escape and make his way home, but even then things wouldn't ever be the same again.

She tried to imagine her brother without the use of his arm, but it would have been easier to give him wings and watch him fly away. In her mind she always saw her twin busy with something. That was Daniel, the very essence of him: movement and work and getting things done.

Lily turned her face into her pillow and willed away the tears that wanted to come. Her mother did not weep when she read the letter aloud, though she had gone very pale. Instead she had set herself to work. They all had. Yesterday Lily had spent the day helping Many-Doves and Curiosity, sorting and washing and grinding the herbs and roots they needed. All day she had worked, and into the night.

She hadn't seen Simon Ballentyne, though he had never been out of her thoughts.

When she allowed herself to dwell on Simon, and on herself as she had been with him on the night of the ice storm, she was overwhelmed by so many feelings that she despaired of ever making sense of them. Embarrassment was foremost among them, and not far behind, a kind of stunned astonishment, that her body was capable of feeling such things, and that her heart and mind could survive them.

As soon as her parents went to bed the night before, Lily had dragged out the washtub and started to heat water. Alone in front of the hearth she had climbed into water as hot as she could stand and scrubbed with the fine soap that her aunt Spencer sent from the city. It came all the way from Bruges, a city that Uncle Spencer spoke of often and visited whenever he was in Europe. It smelled of lavender and roses but it could not scrub Simon's smell away, and nothing could. He was in her pores now, and would not be banished.

To herself Lily must admit that what she wanted, what she really wanted right now, at this early hour of the morning, was to go find Simon and have it all happen again. There was a new hunger in her, one that grew steadily and fed on the memories that she couldn't—didn't want to—keep at bay.

She had the idea that if she were free to go seek out Simon she would be able to put Daniel out of her mind, for a short time, at least. He would do that for her, and when they were sated she could talk to him and tell him this latest news, and he would listen.

But they had made an agreement, in the last hour of that long night of the ice storm: they would stay apart during the week, as Simon had promised Lily's mother. He would go about his work and she would go about hers; they would cross paths, certainly—the schoolhouse he was building was next to the old meetinghouse where she did her work. When that happened they might exchange a few words but then they would part, and on Sunday he would call on her as planned. And they would be together, somehow: neither of them had the heart to pretend otherwise. Worn down by passion, satisfied with this compromise, Lily had agreed that she could be patient until Sunday. Now she wondered if that had been foolish; if she could wait so long, or if she would have to go looking for Simon before too many days had passed. She had no pride left where he was concerned, but neither, she was surprised to realize, did she miss it very much.

Her brother was lying in a prison camp in mortal pain and here she lay in the full light of day, thinking of the things she might do with Simon Ballentyne before the sun set, if she happened to come across him alone.

Disgusted with herself, Lily got out of bed and dressed. Gabriel and Annie were playing cards in the workroom, their voices rising and falling as they argued good-naturedly. She slipped out without stopping to eat, and headed for the village.

She was so lost in her own thoughts that Lily didn't notice anything amiss until she was over the bridge. Then it took the Ratz boys to get her attention.

"You're late," Harry shouted as he ran by. "It's already started!"

"What's started?" Lily called back, picking up her pace.

But she got no answer. The boys flew up the trading-post steps and disappeared inside, the door open long enough for Lily to see the crowd of people.

For a moment she paused, and considered. It could be nothing more than Missy Parker and old Mrs. Hindle in the middle of a particularly colorful argument, or Jed McGarrity's latest experiment with distilling schnapps, or one of the trappers who came into Paradise for supplies with a tall tale. She could just go to her work and get it all from Martha and Callie later, but there was something in the way the boys had been running, some energy that filled her with curiosity and dread in equal measures.

She slipped into the crowd and found herself confronted by nothing more than the backs of her neighbors. The only person who took note of her was Simon Ballentyne, who stood in the corner, arms folded. He smiled, a little shyly, she thought, the way she herself must be smiling, and gestured her closer with a small movement of his head.

From the front she heard Jed McGarrity say, "It looks to be in order, signed and sealed and all."

The crowd shifted and muttered as Lily inched her way toward Simon. Then she was close enough to smell him, and the skin rose all along her back and the nape of her neck, and she cursed herself for a foolish twit and turned her back to him to try to see what was happening.

"What is it?" she asked.

Simon leaned forward to talk into her ear, raising his voice a little to be heard, as the talk in the room was growing louder.

"It looks as if Jemima Wilde sold the orchard and farm out from under Nicholas and ran off," he said.

Lily was sure, at first, that she had misunderstood—then she turned her head and saw pity in Simon's expression, and knew she had not.

He told her the rest of it in a few words: Jemima had found a buyer for the orchards through the newspapers, arranged it all by mail, stolen the deed to the land and signed her husband's name. To the buyer—a milk-white man with a great heavy head and a somber expression—Jemima had spun a story that sounded believable: her husband was a sailor who had been called back to his ship, and had signed the papers before he left.

Jemima was gone and wouldn't be back in Paradise ever again.

That was the hardest thing to imagine. As long as Lily had been alive, she had known Jemima Wilde; she could imagine her nowhere else in the world but here.

Those ideas were still ordering themselves in Lily's mind when she heard Nicholas's voice. She went up on tiptoe and still could see nothing, and then Simon simply picked her up and set her on top a pile of crates that gave her better advantage over the room.

Nicholas stood, head bent over the papers in his hands. His hair fell forward so that she couldn't make out his eyes or his expression, but the set of his shoulders made him look as old as the stranger who stood between him and Jed McGarrity.

"His name is Stiles," Simon said, his tone pitched so low that only she could hear him. "From Boston by way of Maine, he says." Seated as she was, Lily could look directly into Simon's eyes, if she only had the courage.

She whispered back, "But it can't be lawful, can it?"

"It's not my signature," said Nicholas just then, as if he had heard her question.

"But the money was paid in good faith," said Stiles in a deep, steady voice. "I'm here with all my worldly possessions, and a nephew to raise. Still, if you could refund the money . . ." His voice trailed off.

Lily caught sight of her mother and father, standing to one side. She had rarely seen her mother look so somber, though her father's expression was, as ever, impossible to read. Because he wished it so.

"No," said Nicholas. "She took the little bit of money I had put by when she went yesterday. To buy linen, she said." His voice sounded high and soft and far away, like that of a man speaking in his sleep.

Jed McGarrity looked as uncomfortable as Lily had ever seen him. He said, "This ain't a matter a constable can settle." He spoke directly to Nicholas, and his tone was full of regret. "But he's got the deed, Nicholas."

"And a signed receipt," said the stranger. "Signed and witnessed."

"And a signed receipt," Jed echoed reluctantly. "It don't look good, but you can go to the courts with it, see what they say."

"What nonsense," said Anna, pushing out of the crowd. "He could go to the *courts*. And feed himself how in the meantime?" With her fists on her ample hips, she waggled her head at Nicholas. "Wake up, man. You go get back what was took from you. Ride after Jemima—she can't have gone far in her condition."

"Do you know where she was going, Mr. Stiles?" Jed asked the question reluctantly, his gaze skittering back and forth between Nicholas and his wife. Anna in a temper was best avoided, and he was looking for a way out of the conversation, anyone could see that.

"I don't," said the reverend. "I'm sorry to say."

Nicholas said, "It's not my signature." He said it like a boy who knew he would be beaten for something he had not done, a boy who had been beaten before without cause and had no hope of any other kind of treatment.

Lily's heart twisted with sorrow and anger and a deep, abiding disgust.

"I'll ride after her for you, Wilde," shouted Praise-Be Cunningham. "I'll drag her back here by her hair, by God, and show her what's what."

At that Nicholas seemed to wake up, finally, and Lily looked away from the sight of his face. Only twice in her life had she seen a person struck so hard. One was her own mother when she lost a child, and the other was Mr. Hindle's mother, who had lived through a Mohawk raid as a child and had never quite been right afterward.

He held out the papers to the man beside him without looking. "Take your deed, Mr. Stiles. I'll be cleared out by the end of the day."

The older man's jowls worked busily, but then he nodded. "Thank you, Mr. Wilde. May the Almighty bless and keep you in your adversity."

There was a moment's stunned silence, and then angry voices rose up again, a wasp's nest poked once too often. Martin Ratz pushed his way to the door but he turned back, his face contorted with outrage.

"Wilde, you're an idiot and a coward if you let that woman get away with stealing you blind. I'd feel sorry for you if you weren't such a pitiful excuse for a man."

Missy Parker was pushing through the crowd too, but in the other direction, toward the front. When she got where she wanted to be she was breathing hard, her ample bosom heaving and flushed. She took a moment to put her cap to rights and pat the kerchief around her neck.

"Watch out, Reverend," Charlie LeBlanc said in a low voice that would not be heard beyond the circle of men at the very back of the room. "You're square in her sights, now."

Behind Lily, Simon grunted softly. Then his hand was on her shoulder, and his breath stirred the hair at her ear.

She leaned toward him, just a little, thinking that he had something to say, and then stayed like that, shoulder to shoulder.

"Reverend Stiles," Missy Parker was saying. "Maybe it's a little unusual how you've come to us, but I for one am glad to have you. We've been too long without a shepherd."

All around the room people began to shift uncomfortably. Lily saw suspicion and disquiet on the faces of most of the women, but the men were amused or annoyed or a little of both. Stiles wasn't the first preacher to think he could bring some order to this particular flock. No doubt the wagering would start as soon as Stiles was out of earshot: how many days it would be before he gave up and sold out. Tonight when the regulars sat down in the tavern they would talk themselves hoarse, cursing Missy Parker and Jemima Wilde both, and the Reverend Mr. Stiles most of all.

Lily could almost feel sorry for the Yankee preacher who had been enticed into this nest of no-nonsense Yorkers. It was a fine joke Jemima had played on them all, and Lily had the uncomfortable idea that it wouldn't be the last one. But Stiles didn't seem to have any sense of that.

The severe old man was looking at Missy Parker from under a tangled mass of white eyebrows, his small mouth pursed tight, out of place in the fleshy face. "The good Lord giveth and he taketh away." His voice boomed out, filling the room. He raised both hands, palm outward, squeezed his eyes shut, and tilted his head back. "Let us pray."

"But not here," Anna McGarrity said, clapping her hands. "And not now. I got a business to run, Reverend Stiles."

The heavy head dropped forward. When he opened his eyes Lily saw a burning anger there, the first sign of the real man, she thought: she would draw him this way, when she had the chance.

"We'll adjourn to the meetinghouse, then," he announced. And seeing the surprise in the faces around him said, "There *is* a meetinghouse, Mrs. Wilde assured me."

Missy Parker cleared her throat importantly and flashed a triumphant look in Elizabeth's direction. "Well, sure we had a meetinghouse, Mr. Stiles. But it was give over to less godly pursuits."

Lily might have spoken up then, but Simon's hand slipped to her waist and tightened. "Wait," he said. "Let your father handle it. Stiles isn't the kind of man who'll pay attention to anything a woman has to say."

It was true and it was infuriating too. Lily caught her father's eye and the shrug that said he was more aggravated than worried and would make short work of the trouble at hand.

"Let's leave it to him," Simon said so softly that no one else could hear. "Come, lass, come away."

Lily swallowed down all the protests that rose up so readily, and let him help her down from the crate. She was at the door when she realized that Nicholas Wilde was standing there too, his hand on the latch, watching her.

She wanted to say something to him, something kind and helpful, something that would make the terrible lost look in his eyes go away. But there were no words that could accomplish that, and Lily felt that lack as surely as she felt Simon's hand on her waist.

Nicholas looked at her for a long moment and then turned his head away. He closed the door behind him.

When Lily found the nerve to follow him, seconds or minutes or hours later, the only sign that he had ever existed were fresh heel marks in the road, already filling with water.

"Will you walk with me for a bit?" she asked Simon, and set off, not waiting for his answer. She turned onto a trail that led up through the woods, a trail she could walk in full dark and never take a misstep, and she walked as hard and fast as the mud and the boggy patches would let her.

Simon stayed close behind. For a white man he walked well, without a lot of extra movement or noise. Her uncle Runs-from-Bears liked Simon, and no doubt this was part of the reason; he had little patience with any man who lumbered through the forests like a cow. Except for Gabriel all her people liked him, though they tried to keep it to themselves.

And I like him too, Lily admitted to herself. She liked his dry humor and calm good sense and the way he talked to his elders, respectful but not fearful; she liked what he had made of himself. She liked the smell of him and the dimples he had hidden for so many years, and the strength in his arms and hands and the way he couldn't hide what he was feeling when he held her. She was aware of him just behind her, down to the shape of the shadow he threw when they passed through a patch of sunlight.

Her father had asked her, as no one else had dared, if she loved Simon Ballentyne, and she had told him the truth: she didn't know. She still didn't know, not really. For a long time she had believed herself in love with Nicholas Wilde, but now that felt to her like a dream only partly recalled.

He'll ask now where we're going, Lily told herself, and determined that she would turn around and go home when he did. But Simon kept his questions to himself and followed her, and she pushed on until every breath burned and she cursed the awkwardness of her skirts.

Birds called in the trees and a squirrel screamed a warning at them; there were tracks in the mud that she might have pointed out: a deer with a fawn, bobcat, quail, bear. Lily took her hairpins down as she walked and put them in the pocket she wore around her waist, shook her head so her hair flew free. Because she felt like it; because she knew that he liked her hair.

They crossed a corner of the Todd pasture that fell away in a slope from the woods. Off in the distance they could see Black Abe tending his charcoal pits, a small figure moving in and out of the smoke. The path went back into the woods, darker here on the east side of the hill that separated this property from Old Judge Middleton's. Lily admitted to herself that she had a destination: her grandfather's abandoned house and farm, on a low hillside that backed onto the endless forests. Whether or not Simon would realize where they were going, that she didn't know and didn't really care, as long as he kept following her.

The house and land belonged to Ethan now, part of his inheritance from his stepfather, but no one in Paradise would ever think of this place as anything but Judge Middleton's homestead.

She said as much to Simon when they had reached the porch. "I hardly remember him," she said. "But the few memories I do have are all to do with this house."

"It's been empty a very long time," Simon said. He was looking at it with his carpenter's critical eye.

"Uncle Todd always saw to it that his property was well looked after," Lily said. "I don't know what will happen to it now that he's gone. I don't think Ethan thinks much about it."

She saw Simon's mouth twitched at the corner. "Maybe he can rent it to Stiles for his meetinghouse."

Lily gave him a hard look and then she went to the door and let herself in without giving him the satisfaction of rising to his bait.

Simon stood on the porch as if he could not quite make up his mind where he wanted to be. Lily said, "He wasn't really my grandfather, you know. Judge Middleton, I mean."

And she walked away, farther into the house. She had been raised by storytellers, and she knew some tricks when it came to drawing her audience along, oh, yes. As she disappeared through the door at the end of hall she heard Simon's step behind her.

The kitchen was dim and cold: the hearth hadn't seen a fire all winter, and the flagstones felt damp even through Lily's winter moccasins. There were mouse droppings in the corner and cobwebs in the great cavity where the fire should have burned.

"Isn't it sad?" she asked Simon as he came through the swinging door. She pointed with her chin at the empty hooks and trivets in the hearth, the bare dish cupboard, the dust on the mantel.

"No one wanted the table," Simon said.

"Too big to get out the door. It was built right here, by Curiosity's husband, you see. So she wouldn't let them break it up for firewood either."

She ran her hand over the oak planking, traced a gouge with her finger.

Simon said, "Are you going to tell me the rest of it, or will you play at games for a while longer?"

Lily pushed out a breath and turned to him. He stood across the table from her, looking at her in his disapproving way down the slope of his nose. No sign of his dimples at this moment. She wasn't in much of a smiling mood herself, she realized.

She said, "It's only my theory, of course. I have no proof. But I think Gabriel Oak is my grandfather."

Doubt and curiosity flickered across Simon's face. "The man who taught you how to draw?"

"Yes," Lily said. "There are a lot of small . . . facts, I suppose you'd call them. If you look at the drawings in the book he left me, you'll see the resemblances. When you put it all together, it seems obvious."

If Simon was shocked, he didn't let it show. "And what does your mother think of this theory of yours?"

Lily shrugged. "I've never had the courage to ask her about it. Maybe she suspects, I'm not sure. There's not much that my mother misses. Curiosity knows, of that much I'm pretty sure. Someday I'll ask her."

Simon frowned at her. "You brought me here to tell me about your grandfather?"

She hesitated. "I wanted you to know that you aren't the only one with family stories that are best left untold. But mostly I brought you here because I could not stand to be in the village even one moment longer."

There was a moment's strained silence between them, and Lily realized Simon was thinking of Nicholas.

She said, "I brought you here because I didn't want to listen to talk about the meetinghouse."

"You know your father won't let Stiles have it," Simon said. "And he can't just take it. It belongs to your cousin Ethan, after all."

Lily blinked at him. "But there will be a lot of arguing. No doubt the Reverend Stiles will get into a philosophical discussion with my mother. He will quote the Bible to her and she will quote it back and throw in Thomas Paine and others he won't know, and he'll be affronted and she'll dig her heels in, and my father will have to intercede. I couldn't bear the idea, not just now." She leaned forward and stemmed her hands on the table.

"Simon."

"Aye?"

"Did I understand what happened back there? Did Jemima really do what they say she did?"

He had been very tense, but his shoulders sagged a bit now. "Aye, I fear so."

She turned suddenly and went to the oak mantel that spanned the hearth. The oven built into the bricks stood open, filled not with bread but an abandoned nest.

"Nicholas will have to leave here," Lily said. "Or hire himself out. Or starve."

To her back Simon said, "Aye. Are you sorry?"

The word took her by surprise, and she laughed. A harsh laugh, a small explosion of displeasure and unhappiness wound into a knot.

"I suppose I'm sorry for what he's lost. He had such dreams for the orchard, and it's been stolen away from him."

To that Simon wisely said nothing at all. After a moment Lily said, "And I'm angry. At Jemima, and at him."

"He'll get his divorce now, if he goes back to the courts."

Lily turned and saw that Simon had not moved at all. He stood just where he had been on the other side of the table, his hands at his sides, his expression carefully, purposefully blank.

"You hadn't thought of that?"

"No," Lily said, flushing. She hadn't thought of it, but Simon doubted that: she saw it in the way his eyes met hers and then lowered. She said. "It doesn't matter, anyway."

"You could have him then, if you still want him. No doubt your cousin would give you this house to live in. He could start over."

Surprise left Lily wordless, just for a moment. There were many things she might have said, all rushing through her head at once, but only one thing that she must say, just now. That Simon was waiting for her to say: that she had no more interest in Nicholas Wilde, and were he free to marry. It was what she should say, what she wanted to say, but somehow it wouldn't ring completely true. Nicholas had been too long a part of her life to dispose of him so easily.

"Ah," Simon said. A small sound, no more than a sigh. He turned then, and started toward the door.

"No," Lily said. "Don't go."

He was angry, she saw it in the set of his shoulders.

"And why should I stay? I don't care to hear your apologies, Lily, or your explanations. You want your apple man, then have him."

He was through the swinging door before she could stop him, but Lily flew after Simon and caught up to him in the hall.

"Simon," she said. "Don't be foolish."

That stopped him in mid-stride, though he didn't turn to her.

She said, "I can't love somebody I don't respect." Her voice came out much softer than she intended, with a crackling quality.

Suddenly Lily felt a little dizzy, and she reached out for the wall, pressed her fingers to it to find her balance.

"What is it you're saying?"

Irritation flooded through her. "You know what I'm saying. After the ice storm, you know exactly what I'm saying."

He turned abruptly and advanced on her with such contained fury that she backed up in alarm until she bumped into the wall.

"Don't play with me, lass. Tell me now, do you still love Wilde?"

He was glowering down at her, his dark eyes narrowed in anger or pain or some strange combination of both. Something small and warm blossomed in Lily to see those things: clear evidence of how important she was to him, that he wanted her. And she was ashamed to have pushed him so far.

She said, "I will always be fond of him. But no, I can't say that I love him. Not anymore."

Simon bowed his head over her and put a hand on the wall near her head. He leaned into her then, the great width and fact of him blocking out what little light there was in the cool dark of the hall.

"And?" he said, his gaze hard and unflinching.

What she wanted to do was grab him by the ears and kiss him, but he was so close that she would have to struggle to raise her arms.

"And what? You want me to say that I love you. I could say it, Simon, but I don't know what it means. I like you, I respect you. I think about you all the time—"

"That's lust," he said sharply.

"Yes," she said, her voice creaking a little with the effort to maintain her composure. "Lust enough to burn down the world. Will you kiss me now, or must I beg?"

A sound escaped him as he bent to her, a gasp that a man might make as he died, full of desperation and hope. The last thing she saw before his mouth touched hers was a flash of his dimples, and then there was nothing in the world but the taste of him, his textures and smells and the fierce wanting that rose up between them.

"You do love me," he said, pressing himself to her. "Even if you're afraid to own it."

"Have it your way," Lily said.

"I'll have you any way I can get you." He laughed against her mouth and held her pinned to the wall, kissed her into senselessness and she kissed him back, deep kisses and passionate, the kind of kisses that she dreamed about and that woke her, trembling and covered with sweat. His kisses, and no one else's.

When he pulled away she let out a sorrowful sound.

"Shall I carry you up the stairs?" he said. "Or will you walk?"

"Up the stairs?" Lily echoed stupidly, her gaze fixed on his mouth.

"Aye, up the stairs. There must be a bed in the house someplace."

"No," Lily said, her hands wiggling their way beneath his mantle, pulling at his clothes impatiently. "All the chambers are empty."

He must have lost track of the conversation then, for he lifted her up to kiss her again and they went on like that for a long time, and then Lily was being danced down the hall between kisses, trailing bits of clothing. The kitchen door swung to let them through and swung shut again and then Simon lifted her and she found herself on the table with him standing between her knees, her skirts already half raised.

"Just the right height," he said, fumbling with his own clothes.

For what? Lily might have asked, out of an odd and truly perverse modesty, but he was showing her that, pulling at her clothing and his own and then sinking into her, hard and impatient, moving into the very heart and core of her in the middle of the deserted kitchen. On a table.

"Oh, Christ," he whispered, pausing for a moment, his breath coming harsh. He held her down with his weight and the thrust of his hips, the absolute fact of him inside her, joined to her, his mouth on hers, wet and warm, the touch of his tongue. He pulled her hips forward and seated himself in her more firmly and Lily could have drifted away into death just then and gone gladly, as long as he went with her, just like this.

"Holy God," he muttered, his face buried in the crook of her shoulder.

She gasped. "And you call me a heathen."

"My grumfie, my love," he whispered against her mouth. "We'll be heathens tegither, the twa of us."

Much later, on their way back to the village, Lily dragged her feet a little, in no hurry to be among people again. She asked herself how she could ever pretend to be her mother's rational daughter, how she had ever thought herself to be that person. She was learning astonishing things about herself that she could hardly share with anyone except Simon.

"I am a little ashamed," Lily said to him. And then: "You have a wicked grin, Simon Ballentyne. Don't let my mother see it on your face or she'll know what you've—" She paused, and cleared her throat. "What we've been doing."

That made him laugh. "As if we could hide it."

"Well, we should hide it," Lily said, a little irritated with him but most of all with herself: she wanted him to kiss her again, but she didn't want to ask for it, and what a wanton thing she was. "It's unseemly, with all that's happened."

Simon shot her a narrow look. "Wilde will survive."

Lily snapped at him. "I was thinking of my brother." And it was true, in part.

At that he fell silent for a while. Then he said: "Do you want me to go back to Nut Island, to see if I can be of any help?"

Since Luke's letter had come, that thought had occurred to Lily more than once.

"My mother would like it," she admitted. "If you went, she'd feel better about Daniel. And it would mean she could stop worrying about me. About us."

Simon said, "And you, Lily? Would you like it?"

She stopped then, and wrapped her arms around herself. "If I thought it would help my brother, I would let you go and not say a word. But no, I wouldn't like having to worry about both of you."

He raised a hand to run a callused thumb along the line of her jaw, and then he leaned down and kissed her. A simple kiss, soft and sweet. Nothing of lust in it, but a strong, simple affection that made her sway toward him.

He said, "You only have to ask, Lily. You know that."

They had stopped where the woods gave way to the Todds' pasture, at the very spot where shadows gave way to light. Lily pressed her forehead to Simon's chest and nodded, glad of the bulk of him and the warmth and his smells. Pressed against him like that she felt the moment his attention shifted, felt the tension that ran through him.

"What?" she said, not looking; not wanting to let the moment go.

"Wilde. There."

She made herself look, then. A horse stood at the fence that surrounded the kitchen garden, an animal she knew: the old gelding that Joshua Hench kept at the smithy and rented out now and then.

And Nicholas Wilde, taking a sapling from the pannier, its root ball wrapped in burlap and twine.

"Paradise Found," Lily whispered, and felt Simon jerk in surprise.

"The tree," she said. "He named the apple Paradise Found. He has—" She swallowed hard. "He had great hopes for it."

Callie had appeared in the open kitchen door, and even at this distance some things were clear: the fists wound in her apron, the pale oval of her face, the slope of her shoulders.

"He's come to tell her goodbye," Simon said. "You should take your leave of him too."

It cost him a great deal to say that, and Lily was thankful. She squeezed his hand, and smiled at him.

"I won't be long," she said. "I promise."

It was no more than five minutes' walk to the kitchen, but by the time she got there Nicholas was already leaving, his expression as still as stone.

He stopped on the step, and would not meet her eye.

"You're going away." It wasn't a question, and he made no move to answer her. The other things she might have asked, about his plans, about Jemima, those questions filled her mouth like bitter vetch, but she swallowed them.

Nicholas studied the hat in his hands for so long that she thought, just for a moment, that he might have changed his mind. Then he walked away without another word, lifted himself into the saddle, and rode away.

The kitchen door still stood open. Lily heard the sound of weeping, and in counterpoint, Curiosity's voice, the low crooning tone she used with hurt things.

What Lily wanted to do was to turn around and run away, but she forced herself up the stairs and through the door, and when she had closed it behind herself and turned, Callie flung herself into her arms so violently that she lost her balance and slid to the floor.

Callie's thin shoulders trembled. "I'll never see him again." Her face, pressed hard against Lily's shoulder, was hot with tears and wet, but Lily heard every word clearly. "I'll never see my father again."

Curiosity stood just a few feet away, holding Martha to her, rocking the child silently.

"You don't know that," Lily said, and heard the tremor in her own voice and, worse, the lie threaded through the words. But when she opened her mouth nothing else would come out. "You can't know that."

"But I do," Callie moaned. "I do."

• • •

Elizabeth had always thought that she would one day make a sharp old woman, quick of wit and tongue, unflinching; silly young women would fear her, and with cause. She would model herself on her aunt Merriweather, she had always told Nathaniel. He had smiled at that and never corrected her, no matter what doubts he had. Now she wondered if she could live up to her aunt's stern example; it seemed to her that with every year she was a little more scattered, softer, unable to strike out, even when it was necessary.

To her daughter she said, "Tell me again what Nicholas said." Supper had come and gone and they sat together around the hearth. Many-Doves was sewing moccasins to send to Nut Island for her son; she never spoke of Blue-Jay, but she never stopped working either, and Elizabeth had the sense that soon she would just leave the mountain and walk north, until she found him.

Something Elizabeth thought of doing, now and then, without any real hope that such a thing might be possible.

Lily took a deep breath and rubbed her forehead with three fingers stained indigo blue. "I wasn't there," she said again. "But what Curiosity told me was, Nicholas is going to find Jemima. Because of the child. Otherwise he would just let her go, that's what he said."

"But Curiosity didn't believe him," Nathaniel said, to no one in particular. "I sure don't."

"No," Lily agreed. "Curiosity didn't believe him and neither did Callie nor Martha."

Gabriel sat at Nathaniel's feet, uncharacteristically quiet, turning a bit of wood in his hands one way and then the other. Elizabeth saw Nathaniel taking the boy's measure and coming up short.

He said, "You've been sitting on something all day, son. You might as well spit it out."

Elizabeth knew her youngest child's expressions as well as she knew the shape and texture of her own hands, and she did not like what she saw in his face. Nor did she like the uneasy looks Annie was sending his way.

He said, "Didn't Jemima go south?"

Elizabeth caught Nathaniel's eye and saw that he knew where this was going, though she herself only suspected.

"She did," he said. "Mr. Stiles saw her in Johnstown."

Gabriel raised his head and looked at his father. "Nicholas went west," he said. "I saw his tracks all the way over past the Big Slough.

Fresh too. Maybe a couple hours old." And then, in an afterthought he turned to Many-Doves. "I was by myself," he said. "All day."

If not for the seriousness of the situation, Elizabeth might have been charmed out of her worry by her son's courtly manners: he meant to absolve Annie, and spare her the trouble he was calling down on himself. Annie's tense expression was replaced by something new: satisfaction, thankfulness, affection.

It was an old problem: Gabriel roamed far beyond the boundaries that had been set for him. He was not a rebellious child by nature, but there was something in him that just could not comply with restrictions on the way he moved through the world. Many-Doves looked up from her sewing, looked directly at Elizabeth, and inclined her head.

If she were to speak now, Elizabeth knew what she would say: *You can no more fence this child in than you could a young wolf. It is in his blood.*

It was true that more than any of the other children, Gabriel had his grandfather Hawkeye's wandering ways. It would take strong rope to keep him on the mountain, and knots as yet unknown to man. Nathaniel was thinking the same thing; she could see the resignation and a little pride, too, in his face.

Lily just looked confused, and very tired. There were circles under her eyes, and a trembling in her hands when she reached for her teacup. Elizabeth saw those things and understood them, or thought she did. She reminded herself of her resolution to stay out of Lily's affairs of the heart.

Nathaniel said, "Headed west, was he?"

Gabriel pushed out a relieved sigh, and he nodded. Now that he had confessed to his wandering without causing an outcry, he perked up. He said, "I followed him a few miles, and he never turned south. He was headed into the bush. Why did he lie about where he was going?"

This question he directed to his mother, but she had no answer for him, or none that she would speak out loud. Elizabeth leaned over and brushed a pine needle from Gabriel's hair.

"I'm not sure," she said. "But tomorrow your father will see what he can find out."

Lily jerked out of her daydream at that, hearing the things Elizabeth had not said, had scrupled to say out loud.

"Da," Lily said, but he only shook his head at her, gently.

"We'll see what we see," he said quietly. "It's time you were off to your bed, Lily, and sleep. And correct me if I got this wrong, but ain't tomorrow the last day of school?"

It was almost comical, the way Gabriel and Annie tried to hide their pleasure as they assured him that he was right, school was about to go into recess as it always did at planting time. If not for fear of hurting their teache. ᵣ feelings, she knew they would be dancing around the room.

What they didn't realize, what she wouldn't tell them, was that she was looking forward to the end of the school term as much as they were, maybe more.

Many-Doves was studying Elizabeth thoughtfully, something that did not escape Lily's attention. She turned to her mother, her brow drawn down to put a crease between her eyes.

"Don't worry about me, daughter," Elizabeth said, answering the question before it was asked. "I'm just a little tired. It has been a difficult spring."

But some suspicion had been aroused in Lily; Elizabeth smelled it rising off her skin like sweat. She got up from her chair and leaned over to kiss her daughter, pressing her nose into the hair at the crown of her head. She smelled of herself, of the little girl she had once been and would always be; of the pigments she ground for her paints, of charcoal, of lavender water. Of Simon Ballentyne.

"My sweet girl," Elizabeth said. "You need your sleep. Go now."

Over the years Elizabeth had never had a student, no matter how disciplined or eager to please, who was able to concentrate on work on the last day of school. Long ago she had given up trying to instill some order into those few hours. Instead she let them bring treats— dried apple rings, fried bread dough dusted with maple sugar—and was satisfied if the day ended without blood loss or broken bones.

They were full of the spring, like sap that must run and run. While the children made piles of books and slates and wiped tables and swept the floor, they talked and sang and told stories and argued. In Elizabeth's hearing they did not talk about the latest scandal in the village, or at least not about Nicholas and Jemima Wilde; they knew how far her goodwill went, and when it was dangerous to test it.

They did tell her, she let them tell her, about Mr. Stiles and his nephew, a thirteen-year-old boy called Justus Rising. Justus had already won many admirers among the children, who were eager to share their enthusiasm with Elizabeth: Justus could touch the tip of his nose with his tongue, his hands were so flexible that he could bend them in half across the palm, he knew the whole Bible by heart, backward and forward, begats and all. He was strong enough to have wrestled all three of the Ratz boys to the ground at once, and he had lost his parents when they got on a ship that was over-run—by pirates—between Brunswick and Boston.

Elizabeth, who had personal experience of pirates and privateers and the gradations between, kept her doubts and her smiles to herself.

"An orphan. He's got something in common with Callie and Martha, then," said Henry Ratz, and a hush came over the room. Not out of respect for the girls—Elizabeth was too familiar with the ways of children to tell herself that—but because they knew she would not approve of the topic of discussion.

She straightened from the pile of primers she was counting and looked around at them.

"An orphan is most usually understood to be a young person who has lost both parents. Callie is not an orphan, nor is Martha," she said. "And I will remind you that you may someday need good-will and generosity of spirit as much as they do now."

And yet she was relieved that the girls had stayed away from school today. She was relieved and the Ratz boys were disappointed, no doubt: she kept an especially sharp eye on them, and reminded herself of the cheerful thought that Jem would not be coming back to her classroom in the fall.

None of them would, not to this classroom. When school started after the harvest, this little cabin would be empty again, and the children would be sitting on new benches in the schoolhouse in the village. Whether or not she would be standing at the front of the room was a question she couldn't answer, just yet, though they asked her more than once.

When she had sent Gabriel and Annie ahead to Lake in the Clouds, Elizabeth went out and sat on the porch step, exhausted, relieved, and anxious all at once.

She had taught in this cabin for almost twenty years, and now that time was over. It was a strange idea, but right, too, somehow. And yet she was close to tears, and her hands trembled so that she wound them together in her lap.

Elizabeth was sitting just like that, her face turned up to the bit of sky the canopy of trees overhead revealed, when she heard someone coming up the path from the village. Nathaniel, she told herself, and even before the thought had passed she knew it was an idle wish. Nathaniel had left at first light to track Nicholas Wilde and might not be back for days. The man coming up the trail had a heavy tread, and he breathed as if he were not accustomed to the climb.

Before he came within sight she knew who it would be, and then he was there: Mr. Stiles, his black preacher's hat pulled down tight over his brow, his face bright red with exertion. There was a Bible tucked under his arm.

She should rise, of course, and greet him as he expected to be greeted, but Elizabeth felt a flush of anger: that he should interrupt these few moments of quiet and contemplation on her last day as the teacher of this school.

He stopped before her, and she saw his throat work as he swallowed once and then again. Then he dragged his hat from his head, leaving spikes of fine white hair that stood up like feathers on a fledgling.

"Goodwife Bonner," he said, inclining his head. "I've come to speak to you about your school. I've heard some disturbing rumors—rumors I might not have believed, had I not seen the evidence myself, on the way up here."

Elizabeth drew in a deep breath, but he pushed on without waiting for her.

"Madam, I understand that you are a rationalist. That much was clear from our discussion yesterday. But I would never imagine that you would go so far as to endanger the souls of children with your foreign notions." The Bible opened across a spread palm, and he began to riffle through pages.

"In Paul's letter to—"

"Mr. Stiles," Elizabeth said curtly, and he frowned at her interruption.

"You are here to tell me that girls need no schooling at all, and that it does the lesser races only harm to be taught above their stations. In any case, you are quite sure that white children should not be taught in the same classroom with black children or Indians. Now if I have anticipated your concerns, I'll bid you good day."

All the color had drained out of his face while she spoke. His skin was like window glass, a book for the study of blood flow. He could not keep his temper to himself, and in this odd fact Elizabeth found some kinship with him. She had never learned the trick of making her face go blank, of hiding what she was feeling.

"You mock me." His voice trembled slightly, and he blinked repeatedly.

"No, sir. I just have no interest in listening to your thoughts on education, on the mixing of races, or on the place of women. I know everything you are going to say. Permit me to spare you and myself the time and effort. I will teach my school as I see fit, and I will take no direction from you, sir. When I hire a new teacher, as I plan to do this summer, I will make sure that that person is of a like mind with me, and willing to suffer your disapprobation. And one more thing, before I take my leave from you and go home to my dinner. You are a Calvinist, Mr. Stiles, and as such you will find yourself very much alone here on the frontier."

His mouth, which had been hanging open, snapped shut like a turtle's. Elizabeth watched that happen again while she got up from her spot on the porch and brushed her skirts into order.

"I see I have my work cut out for me," he said. "The devil has put down roots here." He clutched his Bible to his chest and rocked it like an infant.

Elizabeth didn't like the way he was looking at her, as if her complexion were as transparent as his own; as if he could see through skin and bone to the thoughts in her head. Uncharitable, most of them, bordering on the irrational.

"I've been called far worse in my time, sir, and with less effect."

She had turned and started up the path when he found his voice.

To her retreating back he called, "There's something else I know, Mrs. Bonner, something you may not realize just yet."

Against her better judgment, Elizabeth turned.

Mr. Stiles studied her for another moment, and to Elizabeth it looked as if his nostrils, fine curved and overlarge, were twitching.

He said, "Pardon me for such a personal observation, madam, but you are with child. Two months, or so. A daughter."

Elizabeth could count on one hand the number of times she had swooned in her life, but she knew herself to be dangerously close to that just now. There was a buzzing in her head, anger hot and bright, but stronger still, fear. She closed her eyes and opened them again, and saw that Mr. Stiles was watching her closely, with great interest. As a boy might study a bug caught under a piece of glass.

He touched his nose with one finger. "It's a gift, or a curse, depending on your point of view."

Very softly Elizabeth said, "You're saying you can smell whether or not a woman is with child?"

"I smell many things," said Mr. Stiles. He turned his head south, toward the village, a full two miles straight downhill. "Someone is making lye soap," he said. "A plough is breaking ground. A fawn dropped this morning, about a quarter mile that way." He pointed with his chin, and then sniffed again, the nostrils trembling. "The smelt are running."

His gaze shifted back to her. "I can smell a quickening child. I smell disease in the bone, in the blood. There's a woman in the village, I don't know her name, she has a growth in her breast, no bigger than a beechnut, but growing." He touched a spot on his own chest as if the disease were his own. "Most of all I smell sin. It stinks like lye, Mrs. Bonner. I was put on this earth to rout it out."

Elizabeth's heart was thundering hard, but she forced herself to breathe in and out evenly, once, twice, three times. The expression she presented to Mr. Stiles was distant, superior, disapproving; Aunt Merriweather, dealing with a dinner guest who could not hold his wine, a vaporous woman, her nephew's latest gambling debt.

"How very inconvenient for you, sir. And if you pardon me, I wish you good day."

He made no move to stop her; he didn't call out after her with more predictions or Bible verses. Elizabeth walked steadily and without pausing until she came to the strawberry fields, and then she stopped, and sat down.

When the idea of another child had presented itself a few weeks ago, she had rejected it out of hand. Her courses were not as regular as they had once been, after all: she was forty-nine years old this month. If things went on as she thought they would, she would most likely be a grandmother sometime in the next winter.

And she was with child. With the warm sun on her back, Elizabeth bowed forward to press her forehead to her raised knees, bit her lip until she drew blood and had forced her mind to clear.

A rabbit crouched in the grass a few feet away, twitching, its soft gray-brown pelt trembling. She had lined the cradle her children slept in as babies with rabbit skins.

"I can't," she whispered, and the rabbit blinked at her, another frightened creature, sympathetic and powerless. "I can't, but I must."

The evidence was all there, if only she looked at it calmly. Her weariness, the soreness in her breasts, the lack of appetite. Nausea in the evenings, like a knotted fist in the belly, a little more yesterday than the day before; more to come.

In the almost twenty years of her marriage she had conceived six times. Twice she had miscarried in the first months, but she had borne five healthy children: the twins, Robbie, Gabriel, Emmanuel. Robbie had been stolen away by typhoid at three, and then Emmanuel, last born, had come too early and never caught on to the habit of living, slipping away from them before he had learned to hold his head upright. Nathaniel had carved their graves out of shallow soil and rock.

Not again, she had promised herself then. Never again a small grave. She would put all of her energy into raising the three who were left to her, giving them the best of herself, making them strong. From Many-Doves she had got tea and advice, and from Curiosity, more of the same. What they had not given her, could not give her, were promises. *Nature finds a way when she got a mind to,* Curiosity had warned her.

What Elizabeth wanted now was to have Nathaniel with her. She would say the things out loud that she could not keep to herself: *I am too old for childbirth; I am too old to raise another child; I cannot bear another loss.*

He would look at her and hold her and stroke her hair but he would not make her promises either, even out of pity. *We've managed worse, Boots, you and me.*

But Nathaniel was gone today, and so Elizabeth got up and brushed off her skirts, and straightened her shoulders, and turned back downmountain. If she could not have Nathaniel, she could go to Curiosity.

A daughter. One part of her laughed at the whole idea that Mr. Stiles should be able to smell the child growing in her womb and know it for a daughter. Most likely, she told herself, he suspected that she wanted another daughter. And there was an appealing symmetry in the idea that her last child should be a daughter, as her first had been. Mr. Stiles might be a divining Calvinist, a marble prophet, or he might be nothing more than an observant man, and a devious one.

But he had known a truth that she had not quite admitted to herself. No matter how little she liked the idea, he had been given a formidable gift and tremendous burden.

Elizabeth thought of Jemima Wilde, who had gone away and conjured Mr. Stiles to take her place. A Calvinist among lapsed papists and godless Yorkers, rationalists and Kahnyen'kehàka women doctors, freed black women who owned property and made their own decisions. A fine joke indeed.

Crows called from the jack pines on the ridge. In their raw voices Elizabeth heard Jemima's satisfied laughter.

Curiosity said, "A late child ain't the worst thing, Elizabeth. My Jason didn't come along until I was fifty, and he was the sweetest thing that ever happened to me. I wouldn't give up those few years we had him, not for anything."

Elizabeth studied the pattern of roses on her teacup and said nothing at all, because she did not trust her voice, or the things that might come out of her mouth.

"A girl." Curiosity laughed softly to herself. "Just when you about to get Lily settled. The Lord got a sense a humor, that cain't be denied."

"If Mr. Stiles is right," Elizabeth snapped suddenly. "I don't see why he should be. More likely he is a charlatan with a sharp eye and a knack for saying the right thing."

She might forbid herself the luxury of tears, but her voice trembled, and Curiosity heard that.

"I heard stranger things than a man born with a nose like a bloodhound," Curiosity said, pulling out a stool to sit beside Elizabeth. "And I ain't heard you tell me he wrong about you being with child. I see it in your face, anyway, Elizabeth."

With one long, bony finger she traced the skin under Elizabeth's eyes. "You always do show the mask earlier than any other woman I ever knowed. You sick in the evenings like usual?"

Elizabeth nodded.

"The child settling in good and solid." Her eyes narrowed a little, in concern and understanding. "It wear you down, I know it."

They were silent together for a long moment while Elizabeth thought of the months to come, of discomfort and weariness and of childbed, and the chances that she might not survive it. But if she could get through all that, if she could hold on, there would be another young voice in the house, a new light in the world, Nathaniel's child and her own. If she lived long enough to raise it up.

"I'll be right there with you." Curiosity was reading her mind, in the same way Elizabeth could sometimes read Lily's mind, or Hannah's. There was no need to list her fears; Curiosity knew them, every one.

She said, "I got something I want you to think about."

Elizabeth raised her head. Curiosity would be eighty years old in the fall. Every year was carved into her face but her eyes were bright and full of life. *Manny is coming home,* Elizabeth remembered. *Her son is coming home.* That was right and good, and the tears that Elizabeth had been holding back began to leak over her face.

Curiosity wiped her cheek with one thumb. "You worried about Daniel," she said. "But listen to me now, Elizabeth. Right this minute you got to be thinking about you, what you need here and now. I'm thinking it would be good to have you living nearby, at least until this little girl you carrying come along. And I'm getting too old to be rushing up that mountain when I get the idea I want to see your pretty face."

"This house is filled to bursting," Elizabeth said, surprised out of her melancholy.

"Well, I wouldn't want you *that* close," Curiosity said.

Elizabeth hiccupped a laugh, and then another, and then they were laughing hard.

Curiosity said, "I was thinking of the judge's place, standing there empty so long." She looked at the kitchen door, propped open to let in the spring breeze. "If you and Nathaniel are of a mind to humor an old woman, I'm hoping you'll move into the village for a while at least."

Elizabeth couldn't remember the last time Curiosity had asked for any kind of favor, and this odd request, so unexpected, put her off balance for a moment. It made perfect sense in many ways, but even had it not, Curiosity had asked it of her and that alone meant that she must give it serious thought.

"Many-Doves wants to go to Good Pasture," Elizabeth said. "So she can be closer to Blue-Jay and Daniel. She hasn't said it in so many words, but I think she's only staying at Lake in the Clouds for me."

"Well, then." Curiosity smiled and folded her hands on the table in front of her.

"I don't know what Nathaniel will say."

Curiosity gave her a half-smile. "I do. You ask him right and that husband of yours would haul the moon out of the sky for you, and you know it. Especially in your condition."

"It would mean letting the fields lie fallow this year," Elizabeth said, mostly to herself. "But there is enough money in the bank to buy what we need, certainly." And in that moment she realized that she had already made the decision to leave Hidden Wolf.

•   •   •

Deep in the night, the moon already set, Nathaniel let himself in and stood in the middle of the common room, and listened.

He had built this house with his own hands, and he knew every board and joint. The sounds it made in the wind were as familiar to him as his wife's voice, and its smells as comforting. Wood smoke and beans simmering, wet wool drying, cornbread, lye soap. He breathed in deep and caught, just barely, the scent of his youngest son, though he could not say how he knew it for what it was.

At the bottom of the stairs he paused, thought of going up to check on Gabriel and Lily and then stopped, feeling Elizabeth before he turned to see her, standing at the open door of their chamber. With her hair loose around her shoulders and her shawl gleaming in the night shadows she might have been one of Jennet's witchy women, or the spirit of some well-meaning woman, long gone.

But it was Elizabeth's face and no one else's: heart shaped, with wide-set eyes. If he told her now how fine she looked to him she would blush and turn away, pleased and disbelieving still, after all these years.

Nathaniel went to her, quietly, and touched skin, pale and soft and chill in the night air.

"I've been waiting for you." She was whispering, not because she needed to, but to draw him closer. He bent his head to her.

"Come," she said. "Come to bed."

"As soon as I wash." He put his hands out like one of their boys, being inspected before he was allowed to sit down to supper.

Elizabeth didn't even look. She put her hands on his, lightly, her thumbs stroking the tattoos that circled his wrists.

"Never mind washing," she said. "Come to bed, I have to talk to you."

All day long, on his way home, Nathaniel had been thinking of this moment, of the questions she would ask and the answers he must give her. What he wanted to do—the urge was strong in him—was to lie. It was not something he did often or lightly, keeping the truth from Elizabeth. And now she had things to say to him. She had waited up all night. He clasped her hands hard, harder than he meant to, and she drew in her breath.

He said, "Is there bad news from Canada?"

"No," she said firmly. She shook her head so that her hair tumbled over her shoulders, black and silver. "No word from Canada, no bad news of Daniel. Come, come now, let me talk to you."

He stripped down while she climbed into bed and under the

covers. When he joined her she put her hands on his cheeks and studied his face. Her breath was milky sweet and soft on his skin.

"I guess you missed me," he said, turning his head to kiss her palm.

"I did. I always do. Nathaniel."

"Hmmmm?"

She told him then in the way she had always shared this kind of news: took his hand and put it low on her belly, held it cupped there as if by touch alone he must understand what they had created, the two of them. Forehead to forehead they lay just like that, quietly, breathing each other in and out.

"Are you unhappy?" It wasn't the first question that came to mind, but it was the most important one.

"No," she said. "Never that."

"Scared."

"To the quick."

"Aye," he said. "It scares me too, but mostly it makes me happy, Elizabeth. You and me, we'll manage this. We've managed every-thing else."

"Yes," she said, and drew a deep breath. By the time she had let it out, she was asleep.

He should have followed her into sleep, weary as any man who had walked hard for a day. But his body hummed with movement still, and his mind with answers to the questions she hadn't thought to ask.

In the morning she would remember. Sitting across from him at the table, she would ask while she ladled porridge. Lily would want to know, but she would wait for her mother to ask the question: *What of Nicholas Wilde?*

He could put it out, plain and simple: he had tracked the man west and north, and at the end of the first day had found his horse, or the little that was left of it after the scavengers had finished. On the second day the trail had veered due north and he had followed it until he found what remained of the man.

He could tell them all of the truth, or part of it, or none at all. What happened to Nicholas Wilde.

Nathaniel could say: *Jemima happened to him.* Or: *I lost his trail; I gave up.* Or: *he stumbled across a bear, over a cliff, into quicksand.*

He might say: *I buried him proper and marked the grave,* and that was true. But it would not satisfy Elizabeth, whose curiosity was endless, or Lily. Wilde had been her first love, after all, and a girl like Lily—

he paused and corrected himself—a woman like Lily would hold on to that, for the rest of her life. No matter how Nicholas Wilde had disappointed her.

The fact was, he had to keep the truth from them; but there was another, harder truth that went right along with it: Nathaniel wanted nothing more in the world than to tell Elizabeth the whole of it, to pour out the words and free himself of the pictures they built in his head. But he could not, would not, unburden himself like that. Not tomorrow, or the day after, or when she was safely delivered of this new child, or on his deathbed. It was his burden to bear, as the child was hers.

Chapter 34

Dearest Hannah and Jennet,

For your latest letter, arrived just yesterday, we thank you. Any report is preferable to the work of the imagination. Of course we are glad to know that Daniel is able to leave his bed for short periods of time. We trust that your next letter will bring more such news. I enclose a short letter for him.

I expect that this letter will not reach you until well into the month of May and the beginning of warmer weather. We are sending a bundle of clothing I hope will suit you both, along with some fine-milled soap that cousin Ethan sent.

You both know me well enough to realize that if I dwell on trivialities there must be some matter of importance to share that makes me anxious. Let me give you our news, in the manner of a journalist; that is to say, without embellishment.

First, I am expecting a child, sometime in November. Your surprise can be no greater than was my own, but I trust you will take as much joy in this news as we do. I am easily tired but Many-Doves and Curiosity are well satisfied with my health.

Second, Nathaniel and I have decided, after long deliberation and discussion, that we will live in the village until this child is come. We have already taken up residence at my father's house. It is a drafty place and the hearth smokes when the wind comes from the west, but Nathaniel and Simon have undertaken repairs and improvements and

I believe we shall be very comfortable here. Certainly it is convenient to be so close to the work at the new schoolhouse, and a great comfort to be only a short walk from Curiosity. Her Lucy is come to cook and look after the house, and Callie and Martha are here most days too, all of them carrying out Curiosity's injunction—with surprising tenacity—that I am not to take up anything heavier than a quill.

Lily, too, has been excessively considerate and kind, and much more even tempered, but whether my condition or Simon Ballentyne deserve the credit for that transformation is unclear to me. Or perhaps it is simply the move into the village, as Lily is very pleased to be closer to the old meetinghouse. When she has finished with her share of the housework she goes there, every day, to draw and paint.

Third, and this is a circumstance that will be clear to you already, as your aunt brings you this letter: Many-Doves has decided to remove to Canada until her son and my own are free and on their way home. Annie is gone with her. All this has put Gabriel in a very poor mood indeed. The solitary comfort in all this is the fact that there will be no corn to weed this summer.

And now. How I hate the need to write down the details of the tragedy in the village.

Jemima Wilde is run away and her husband disappeared into the bush. Nathaniel tracked him for two days and then came home none the wiser. Before he went away Nicholas brought Curiosity an apple sapling and a letter writ in his own hand and witnessed by Mr. McGarrity, giving her care of his Callie until he comes home.

I do not think we will ever see him again. Such a terrible waste, it hardly bears contemplation.

As far as Jemima is concerned, I confess that I had not realized the depth of her anger, nor how far it would drive her. By the time she had finished with Nicholas, he lost his daughter, his unborn child, his livelihood, the orchards he worked with such dedication and passion, his reputation, and his self-respect.

> *Because this beast, at which thou criest out,*
> *Suffers not any one to pass her way,*
> *But so doth harass him, that she destroys him;*
> *And has a nature so malign and ruthless,*
> *That never doth she glut her greedy will,*
> *And after food is hungrier than before.*

The orchard and farm have been sold to a Mr. Stiles, originally of Maine, who is a part-time farmer but a full-time missionary, and came to us determined that our souls must be saved. If he were simply a dull man, I could wait for him to tire of the recalcitrant Yorker temperament, but every day I see new evidence of a devious and supple mind. Because he has no meetinghouse he has taken to preaching in the middle of the village, where it is difficult to avoid him. If there were not other things of greater importance to occupy me, he would be a worthy opponent.

This letter is already two and one-half sheets, close-written, and Gabriel asks for a little space, thus I leave you, Your loving E.M.B.

Dear Sister and Cousin. Annie is gone to Canada to help rescue our Daniel and Blue-Jay and here am I, feeding bad-tempered hens. There may be no corn to weed this year but there is cabbage and pompkin and beans in the kitchen garden and when they sprout weeds who will be sent to pull them? Lily paints and draws and makes eyes at Simon, who teases her and calls her Grumpy when he thinks no one will hear him, and she frowns at him and smiles, all at once, though I should get my ears boxed if I called her such a name. If that's what love is about, then it's a silly business, say I, and one I want no part of.

All in all things are in a sorry state here and I hope you come home soon and bring Daniel and Blue-Jay and Annie too. And if there are more stories like the runaway porkers for Jennet to send, it would be a comfort to me in my misery.

Your brother and cousin, Gabriel Bonner

Chapter 35

Of the many adjustments that moving into the village required of them, the one that was hardest for Elizabeth was something that not even Nathaniel, with all his reservations, had thought to warn her about.

Not many rumors were robust enough to survive the hard walk up Hidden Wolf. At Lake in the Clouds they had been sheltered from the gossip and quarrels that circled the village like a fever passed hand to hand.

But now they had moved into the house where Judge Middleton had held court. The villagers, many of whom had come to Paradise as his tenants, were in the habit of bringing the judge all their disagreements. His word was final in matters as diverse as property boundaries, the digging of wells, naming dogs, and marital squabbles.

His death had left a great gap in the village, one that was filled inadequately and reluctantly by Jed McGarrity. Jed had never wanted to be constable and was always looking for a replacement. Elizabeth had done him a great favor, unawares, by presenting herself as another ready source of wisdom.

"Ben Cameron was here today," she told Nathaniel on their third evening. They were having a supper of milk and bread and berries in the kitchen, which seemed empty after a day of visitors.

"Let me guess," Nathaniel said. "The fence."

"Indeed. He wanted to talk to you, but settled in the end for telling me the whole story. As if I had never heard it before."

"And you said?"

"I gave him tea and gingerbread and told him he'd need to consult a lawyer. He went away with a full stomach, but unsatisfied."

"I hope you've got more gingerbread," Nathaniel said. "Tomorrow Ignaz Hindle will be here to tell his side of the story." He worked his shoulders to loosen the muscles. "Who else was here?"

"Anna, complaining about Mr. Stiles. Missy Parker, complaining about Anna and making not quite veiled remarks about Lily and Simon. Mr. Stiles, wanting to read the Bible to me. Horace Greber, asking me to write to Mariah and ask her to come back home. Half my students, it seemed to me, at one point or another. It was looking a bit like a meetinghouse until Gabriel chased them all away."

Nathaniel laughed out loud at that. "That's my boy."

"I think I shall have to post visiting hours," Elizabeth said, a little ashamed of the whining tone in her voice. "Or perhaps just station Gabriel at the door with a musket."

"That would suit him," Nathaniel said. And: "Where is he?"

Elizabeth poured more milk into her tea. "Curiosity is giving him his supper. I even sent Lucy to help Daisy set out her seedlings, I was that eager for some quiet."

"Missing the mountain," Nathaniel said.

Elizabeth nodded. "More than I imagined."

"We can move back."

Curiosity had brought one of her cats as a welcoming gift, a huge tabby with tufted ears who had promptly given birth to ten kittens in a basket of Elizabeth's good linen. For a long moment she watched as the mother tended her newborns, one eye on the spot where Nathaniel's hunters sprawled senseless in front of the hearth. Then she shook her head. "It's for Curiosity's peace of mind as much as my own, Nathaniel."

He nodded at that, resigned. "And where's Lily?"

"I suppose she's walking with Simon."

Nathaniel grunted into his cup. "That's one word for it."

Elizabeth gave him a severe look. "Nathaniel Bonner," she said. "If you are unhappy with this state of affairs, then I suggest you talk to your daughter and her young man. Perhaps you will have more success than I."

Her short temper wasn't a surprise—Nathaniel recalled the early months of her other pregnancies too well to expect anything else—

but he knew from hard experience that it would do no good to try to mollify her when she was sick to her stomach. The evenings were the worst. Other women were uneasy in the morning and got it over with; Elizabeth carried it with her all day and into the twilight. Now she was pale, her upper lip beaded with sweat. Soon she would bring everything up that was on her stomach—which wasn't much, by the look of the plate in front of her—and then fall into an exhausted sleep.

Nathaniel wiped berry juice from his chin. "No need to bite my head off. I ain't criticizing."

"No, but you aren't helping either."

"Maybe so. But I have given the whole business some considerable thought." He leaned across the table to put a hand on her wrist. "I got an idea that may settle your worries without stepping too hard on the girl's pride."

"Does it involve bloodshed?"

He laughed at that. "No more than it did when you and me were getting around to tying the knot."

A horrified look crossed her face. "Nathaniel, you won't encourage them to elope. You wouldn't."

"Hell, no," Nathaniel said. "What I got in mind has to do with giving Lily the chance to change her mind, if that's what she needs to do."

"Well, come along then," she said, tapping the table with a finger. "Spit it out."

"It's got to do with your aunt Merriweather," Nathaniel said.

Her mouth had begun to soften into a smile when the dogs righted themselves suddenly, the fur bristling down their spines—a signal louder than any knock.

Elizabeth's hands flew up and then settled like restless birds.

He said, "Easy, Boots. I'll send them away, whoever it is."

But then he hadn't been expecting to open the door to Almanzo Freeman, given up for dead long ago and now returned to the land of the living.

It was more than ten years since they had last seen Manny, and to Nathaniel it looked as though he had spent every day of it in battle. He had gone away a young man and come back a soldier, of a particular kind. It was in the way he stood, his hand curled around the barrel of his rifle; it was in the set of his shoulders, the expression that gave away nothing: not pain or joy or hope.

As a boy he had resembled his father, but Manny had grown into a copy of Galileo Freeman: compactly built but broad in the shoulder, hard muscled, with the gleam of steel in his eye. His skin glowed deep brown in the evening light from the open door, and Nathaniel saw that there were lines of raised tattoos on his forehead and neck and at his wrists.

English came hard to him, all his sentences laced with Kahnyen'kehàka rhythms, softened sounds, long pauses.

To Elizabeth, who understood what it was to worry for a son, none of that was of importance.

"You haven't been to see your mother," she said for the third time. She was sitting at her place at the table, too angry to get up and greet Manny properly.

Nathaniel stood behind her, his hand on her shoulder.

"Give the man some room to breathe, Boots." He squeezed lightly. "It ain't exactly easy."

It was the wrong thing to say, he felt that from the way her muscles tensed beneath his hand. But Manny saw that too, and jumped in before Elizabeth could take the opportunity.

"I don't suppose I got anything easy coming to me," he said in his deep, quiet voice. "I don't even know why I stopped here, except I saw the smoke coming from the chimney and I thought maybe there'd be some familiar faces."

Elizabeth's expression softened, and she closed her eyes. When she opened them they were damp with tears.

"I'll go with you."

Nathaniel said, "We'll all go."

In Curiosity's kitchen garden they stopped, all three of them, in shadows that smelled of new turned earth. In the dark Elizabeth's face floated like a heart carved from bone. She gripped Nathaniel's arm so hard that he felt the bruises rising under the skin.

"Go ahead," he said to Manny. "We'll be in directly."

Then he walked her over to the deeper shadows and held her head while she was sick, each spasm rocking her like a fist to the gut. He spoke calm words, nothing that made any sense, nothing that she would remember later; it was the sound that mattered, she had told him once. Something to hold on to.

When she had finished he held her, trembling, against his chest and stroked her hair. Her breaths came deep, with a hiccup at the end like a child who has cried itself into exhaustion. What he wanted to do, just now, was to pick her up and carry her home, but already he could feel her gathering her strength.

"I must go in to Curiosity," she said. "She will need me."

Nathaniel pressed his mouth to the top of her head. "I'd say Manny is the one needing help. I wouldn't want to be in his shoes just now."

That got him a weak smile. Elizabeth said, "I shall have to write to Hannah, now. It can't be put off any longer. She will need to hear what Manny has to tell, after all."

They thought of that, each of them. The things Manny hadn't told them he would tell—must tell her. They each imagined Hannah with that letter in her hands, reading. Her husband's name on the page, followed by a line of words like crows on a fence, like footprints. She would have to follow them wherever they might lead.

"Maybe she'll be glad," Nathaniel said. "It might be a relief, to know something for sure after all this time. You wrote just that in the last letter, if I recall right. 'Any report is preferable to the work of the imagination.'"

"Yes," Elizabeth said softly. "I said that, and it is true, I think. But I do not like to be the one making the report."

"You won't be," Nathaniel said. "Whatever happened, it's for Manny to tell the story."

Within just a few days it became clear that Manny had few details he was willing to share with anyone at all, even his mother. To those who deserved an explanation—his sister, his brother-in-law and nieces and nephew, the Bonners—he said the same things: he was sorry to have worried them, he was glad to be home.

"He don't even ask many questions, not even about his boy," Curiosity told Lily when Manny had been back three days. Lily had stopped by on her way to the village to say hello, though she couldn't keep from blushing at such a transparent half-truth.

But Curiosity was too distracted to tease her about Simon; her only son showed no interest in news of his only child, and for all her wisdom of the world, that was one thing she had trouble digesting.

Mostly to herself Curiosity said, "No doubt he was counting

on Hannah being here. Got things to say to her before he can move on."

At times like this Lily tried to think like her mother, who had the knack of saying just the right thing, or of knowing when silence would serve better than any words. Then she said what came to mind, before she could stop herself.

"He knows Hannah will be back," Lily said. "But I think it will be a while before he understands that the others are really gone. He spends a lot of time at the graves."

Lily knew this because both the graveyards—the one for the slaves and the other one—were between the meetinghouse where she did her work and the woods that went down to the lake. Now that she kept the door and shutters open for light and air she saw everyone who came and went on that path. There were people who visited their dead every day. Anna McGarrity spent a few minutes in the early morning talking to her father as if he were lying abed, too lazy to get up; Callie and Martha tended the little flower bed they had planted at Dolly's feet.

Manny went by the meetinghouse windows every day and stayed in the graveyard for long hours. Just yesterday Lily had followed him, out of equal parts curiosity and worry, and found that he did nothing more than stand and study the crosses that marked the graves. Galileo Freeman, Polly Freeman, Margaret. Father, sister, niece, all out of his reach, unable to hear his apologies and explanations.

It was the loss of his father that seemed to settle on Manny hardest. Like a man caught in an unexpected hailstorm; he must take what the heavens served him.

She said, "He has an awful lot of grieving to catch up on."

Somehow that turned out to be the right thing to say. Curiosity's expression cleared, her distraction giving way to thoughtfulness and, then, resignation. She took Lily by the shoulders and kissed her on the cheek.

"You got a lot of your mama in you, Lily. I know you don't like to hear such a thing, no girl your age do. But you got the best of her."

"But I don't mind," Lily said, embarrassed and pleased. "Just lately I've been wishing I could be more like her. More rational."

That made Curiosity really laugh, a deep, heartfelt laugh, and she wrapped her arms around Lily and rocked her.

"Feel a little crazy, don't it? Sometimes I wonder what the good

Lord thinking arranging things the way he do. Falling in love ain't no better than losing your mind, seem like."

Lily nodded, too embarrassed to respond.

"Let me tell you something I told my girls when they fell. There ain't no shame in it, what you feeling. And the truth is, it don't last, child. No fire could burn that hot and bright without letting up. The whole world would burn down. So you be thankful for it while you got it. What comes after has got its own charms."

"How long will that take?" Lily asked.

Curiosity hummed a little, thoughtfully. "For some the burning part don't last no time at all. For most I suppose it take a year or so before they slow down a bit. And then there's folks like your daddy and ma—"

"Oh, no," Lily said, pulling away. "I don't want to hear this."

"—who never do lose that feeling, not entirely. Not many women your mama's age got to worry about increasing, after all. Look at you blushing, child. You make me laugh."

"Jokes this early in the morning?" Simon said at the door. He was rubbing the sleep from his eyes, and a deep beard shadowed his cheeks.

Lily opened her mouth to say something and then shut it again, shook her head and turned away.

"I have work to do," she said. "Goodbye."

"Wait!" Simon called after her. "I'll walk down to the village with you."

Lily fluttered her fingers at him without turning around. "You haven't had your breakfast. Goodbye."

Curiosity's laughter stayed with her all the way down the garden path.

A difficult morning was made worse by Mr. Stiles, who was waiting, Bible tucked under his arm, at the door of the meetinghouse. Lily was still fascinated by his person, the contrast of his dusty black clothing and white hair and pinkish eyes, the way the blood moved beneath skin the color of January ice. Those things intrigued her, but not enough to make her want to listen to the man preach. That she would hear no matter what her feelings when he took up his spot just outside the trading post and launched into his daily sermon.

Mr. Stiles was particularly fond of St. Paul's gospel and his wisdom on the place of women, and returned to the topic—it seemed to Lily at least—every other sermon. Now he had decided he must bring the word to her directly, and there was nothing she could do, really, to evade him. Her mother, who was both frustrated by the man and vaguely interested in him, had made it clear that they were all to be polite.

Which would not include turning around and running away, Lily reminded herself, though the thought had a certain appeal. She could spend some time with her mother, just the two of them. It was something Lily hadn't done since they moved into the village. *Because I've been busy,* she told herself. *No other reason.* And: *What an awful liar you are. You can't even fool yourself.*

"Miss Bonner," Mr. Stiles began, bowing stiffly from the shoulders. "Can you spare me a little of your time?"

Lily managed a tight smile and a nod, and then she went through the door he held open for her.

He was patient, Lily had to give him that much. While she arranged her worktable and sorted through brushes and looked at great length for a drawing that didn't exist, he stood quietly, hat in hand, and waited.

It was no use, of course. Lily pushed out a sigh. "How can I help you, sir?"

"I would like you to take my likeness," said Mr. Stiles. "And one of my nephew as well. To send to my brother and his family in Maine."

She had been expecting something very different, and for a moment Lily could hardly think what to say.

"You do take commissions?" Mr. Stiles cocked his head, lifted a shoulder.

"I suppose I do," Lily said. "The question has never come up before. Did you want a painting? Oil? Watercolor?"

"Oh, nothing as fancy as that." His gaze skimmed over the work pinned to the walls. "A good likeness in pencil will serve very well. I can pay any reasonable price."

Lily stood with her hands pressed to the tabletop, leaning forward a little. "Mr. Stiles, I have the impression you do not approve of the work I do here. From your sermons . . ." Her voice trailed away. She had not meant to give him that, the acknowledgment that she must listen to his preaching.

It pleased him, as she knew it must. His expression was eager. "Yes?"

"You do not hold a very high opinion of independent women."

And then something occurred to her, something that struck her as almost funny. She said, "You will preach to me while I work, is that it?"

"I will read my Bible," said Mr. Stiles.

"Aloud."

"It has a fine sound to it, read in a sure voice. I assure you."

Lily had to bite back a smile. "Sir, no matter what you may have heard about my family, I am not unfamiliar with the Bible."

Mr. Stiles had a disquieting smile; it drew his lower lip down into a corner and made a bow out of the small red mouth. "You will take the commission?"

She let out a laugh, short and sharp. "You are persistent, Mr. Stiles."

"I am much blessed," he agreed.

"You don't really want your likeness taken, do you? This is just a way to get me to listen to your preaching."

The older man leaned forward so far that Lily caught sight of a perfect pink circle at the crown of his head, the first clear sign that he was struggling with his temper. When he straightened again he said, "You are refusing my custom?"

Lily thought in silence for a moment. She said, "I propose a compromise. I will take your nephew's likeness first. If you are satisfied with my work, and we can come to agreement on how to proceed, I will take yours when his is finished."

It was a fine piece of reasoning, Lily thought, as she watched him think it through. A wily old man, her mother called him, not without some measure of appreciation.

He bowed again. "Very well. I will send Justus to you."

Lily watched Mr. Stiles walk away through the village, his pace deliberate. He left her with the uneasy feeling that she had somehow managed to give him what he wanted without ever revealing to her what that might be, exactly.

In spite of the visitors who came by at the oddest times, Lily liked her spot in the middle of the village; she liked the movement and noise and most of all she liked sitting on a stool in the doorway and putting what she saw down on paper. This morning it was old Mr. Hindle, Jock's father, who sat on a stump plying the blade of his scythe with a whetstone. A dry stump of an old man, with a face carved out of leather under a straw hat. He had tucked a bunch of heartsease into the wide leather belt that held the whetstone pouch, wilting now but the colors still bright: yellow and a deep purple just the color of the old man's eyes. What delighted Lily most was the fact that he had the biggest ears she had ever seen on a human being, great boats stuck to his head with lobes like limp griddle cakes.

She was still occupied with those ears when a shadow fell across her lap and she started out of that place where she went while she worked.

The morning was half gone, and the world was full of noise: from the sawyer's pit by the new school building came the rough voice of metal cutting into wood; a child was weeping piteously—one of the Ratz girls, she saw now, who had spilled an apron full of eggs into the rutted lane and flapped her hands at a riot of puppies who were determined to take advantage of her poor fortune. Mr. Stiles in loud voice, reading from Corinthians from an upended box in the lane in front of the trading post. From the mountain came the echoing bellow of a moose in rut.

Manny Freeman was standing beside her.

"Didn't mean to startle you."

The first needlelike pain of a headache darted behind Lily's eyes, but she smiled. "I need to get out of the sun anyway."

He followed her into the shade of the meetinghouse, where a botfly bounced and buzzed against the walls.

"Blackfly coming on now," Manny said in a conversational tone. "Won't be no peace until frost."

That was a fact of the north woods, one so obvious to anyone who had grown up here—as both of them had—that Lily found it odd to have it raised as a topic of discussion. For the rest of the season she would start her day by rubbing Curiosity's pennyroyal ointment into her skin and looking at the world through a beating, shimmering haze of gnats and no-see-ums and blackflies. Horses and mules and oxen would have the worst of it, twitching and switching and some-times running mad when the flies got the better of them.

"Oh," Lily said. "You've been thinking about Polly."

Manny stood at the window, looking down the lane to the point where it disappeared into the woods. "The team run away with them, did I understand that right?"

"Yes." Lily came up beside him. "Just there. It happened very fast, I think. The team took off and the wagon turned over. They didn't suffer, either of them."

"Good," Manny said. He glanced at her, and Lily saw the sweat beading on his upper lip. He said, "Might I have a look at your drawings?"

Lily hardly remembered Manny, who had already moved away to Manhattan when she was a little girl. Maybe, she reasoned to herself, that was why he seemed comfortable with her.

"Of course," she said, taking care to keep her voice even. There were tears on his face now, but she turned away as if that were as commonplace as the buzz of flies. She went to her worktable and let him be, and in a quarter hour he cleared his throat, as if to tell her that he had got hold of himself.

"It's like walking back in time," he said. He had switched to Kahnyen'kehàka, but Lily had the sense that he didn't even realize it. Kahnyen'kehàka was her second language and she answered him in kind.

She said, "If you would like to take some you're welcome to them. There are quite a few of your father and your sister. And here."

She walked to the far wall and searched for a moment. "Here's one of your son. He was just walking when I drew this. When he was little Polly sent him here to spend the summer with your folks."

A laughing child, bright-eyed and keen, with full round cheeks. Lily held out the drawing to Manny and he took it without looking.

"Here's another one, the last time he was here. Two years ago, I think, just before he started as a cooper's apprentice."

Manny looked at the drawings, his face set and blank.

"A cooper's apprentice, you say."

"In Albany. He's got a real talent for the work, I've heard. And he writes to your mother faithfully, every month."

In a voice small and far away Manny said, "He looks like his mama. Like my Selah."

"Does he?" Lily leaned over to look at the drawing. "I never did get to take her likeness, I'm sorry to say. She was here for such a short time with us."

"It was a short time," Manny said. "Too short." Then he raised his head and looked at her. "I think of her every day."

"Of course you do," Lily said. "How could you not?"

Without warning Manny leaned toward her, and Lily had the odd and disquieting idea that he was going to whisper a secret in her ear. But he had nothing to say, not in words. Manny simply put his forehead against her brow, gently, lightly. She felt him tremble and then stop trembling.

"Thank you," he said quietly.

"Why, you're welcome." Lily brought up a hand and patted him on the shoulder, as a mother pats a child who needs comfort but believes himself too grown-up to ask for it and would be mortified to know how very clearly he wore his need on his face.

For that moment they stood just so, forehead to brow, her small hands patting. Lily made soft sounds, humming sounds in her throat; she had no singing voice but wished just now that she had, so that she might sing to him as Curiosity would.

Then another sound, an indrawn breath, and Lily jumped in surprise.

Justus Rising was standing in the open door, his mouth a perfect O of surprise and astonishment and delight. Lily saw that much before he dashed away, his heels kicking up dirt. And she saw something else, something more disturbing: a look flashed across Manny's face. She could not call it anger, no more than she could compare the weak flame of a tallow candle to a lightning strike.

Most days she would wait for Simon to break at noon and they would walk together to their dinners: he ate at Curiosity's table and Lily went home to her mother's. But the morning's work had unsettled her and she started off with Manny. No sign of Mr. Stiles or Justus, and Lily was relieved and then angry at herself, to be so easily unsettled by the disapproval of a slow-witted boy.

It might have been awkward walking together; most men could not suffer to be near a woman who had seen them in a moment of weakness as she had seen Manny, weeping for his father and sister. But Manny seemed to have forgotten the whole episode, or at least to have put it away for now.

Lily's own mind was not so obedient; she could hardly walk this path without thinking of Simon. First she had run away from him in Curiosity's kitchen and now she had gone ahead without him to dinner. He would think her angry, or playing at games, when in reality she was disappointed to have missed him.

And what a surprise that was. After Nicholas she had believed herself unreceptive to such things, but Simon had sneaked up on her, wooed her so efficiently that she had little way to defend herself. She had gone from liking him to falling in love with him in a long, slippery sliding motion, her heart and her body wound up in it so tightly that she couldn't say what part of the things she felt were love and what was lust.

And here was the stand of birch trees where they often stopped, without discussion. Simon would catch her wrist and pull her to him and they would kiss until they were both breathless, with the birds flitting around them, buntings and cedarwings and sparrows. They would press together and move together until he broke away, flushed and at the point of no return. It was always Simon who stopped, and every time Lily was surprised and unsettled and frustrated by his self-control. Later, her irritation was replaced by other worries: that he would think her wanton. A strange word she had never really understood until now, the power and heft of it.

When Lily got up the courage to ask him, to use that word, he had looked at her with such honest surprise that she had the first vague understanding that he was as lost as she was, as given up to it.

Sometimes, when she was feeling the weather and the rush of her own blood with more intensity than usual, Lily would touch him in ways that she knew he could not ignore, and with those touches she would draw him deeper into the shadowy woods and they would make a place in a bed of new ferns, and come to dinner late, each making excuses to the faces around the table that no one believed.

But now there was Manny, walking not with her but a little ahead, his eyes moving constantly as any good woodsman's must. It was his walk that made it clear how long he had lived among Indians, and how deeply he had gone into that way of life. Lily thought of Hannah when she first came home after such a long time away.

She said, "You could write to Hannah, you know. My parents send letters and packets through my brother Luke, every few weeks."

"I haven't writ a word in more than ten years," Manny said. Not an outright rejection of the idea, and that meant something.

"It's not something you forget. If you've got a mind to write, that is."

He pushed a thoughtful breath out and pulled another in, and then he smiled a little. "Don't know that I've got much of a mind for anything at all these days."

"I've seen you helping Abe with the charcoal."

Manny shrugged. "He's got a restful way about him."

They were quiet the rest of the way until the fork in the path that would take Lily back home.

He said, "I'll have to go see the boy."

Lily waited, watching his face for some sign of what he was asking. Then she saw that he hadn't really been talking to her, but to himself.

Manny touched a finger to his brow and left her, and for a moment Lily watched him walking away.

•   •   •

The Bonners ate their dinner in the kitchen as there was still no table in the dining room, Lily and her family and the women who came to help in the house and garden all crowded together. Gabriel entertained them all with his stories, and sometimes Lily's mother would read something aloud from the latest newspaper and there would be a discussion.

Lily wanted to draw the scene: Lizzie Cameron listening so hard that all the muscles in her face drew into a knot of concentration as she tried to follow what Elizabeth meant her to understand. Jane Cunningham's little bow mouth with its pale chapped lips pursed in disapproval: she liked the Bonners well enough and was glad of the work, but could not countenance women discussing politics at the dinner table. Lily's father watching all this, amused with it, prone to tease a little. Gabriel sincere and playful at the same time. Lily's mother, pale of complexion, circles under her eyes, worn thin by weariness and the demands the child was making on her, but happy.

Lily liked the noise and laughter and scolding for a number of reasons, but most of all she liked being able to disappear into the crowd and hide in plain sight. If they asked her she gave them some detail of her morning, but mostly the others were happy to carry on without her. Today Lily would have had a good story to tell, about Mr. Stiles and his plan to preach to her while she drew, but she came into the kitchen to find it almost empty, and only two places set at the table.

Her mother said, "I wanted to have a little time with you, daughter, so I sent them all away."

Just that easily she forgot about Mr. Stiles and Justus Rising and even Manny with tears on his face; she forgot about everything but Simon and the last time he had put his hands on her—yesterday, in the cool of the forests. She could see him still if she closed her eyes, a halo of gnats circling his dark head and his expression so very severe with wanting.

"No need for alarm," said her mother. "I've no complaints to make."

Now Lily was very confused, but she forced her face into a calm questioning and took up the loaf of bread to cut slices.

"What did you want to talk about then?" Focusing on the gleam of the knife, the feel of the handle in her hand.

"Money."

Lily sat down and folded her hands in her lap.

Her mother said, "You know that my aunt Merriweather left me a bequest when she died."

Lily could not say where this conversation might be going, but there was some small alarm bell ringing in her head. She nodded, because her mother was waiting for a response of some kind.

"It is quite a lot of money, actually. An annuity of two hundred fifty pounds a year. It has been sitting in the bank in England and gathering interest these eight years."

Lily said, "But you can't get to it just now, then. With the war."

"Not just now, no." Her mother sat across the table, her calm eyes seeing far too much, understanding things Lily could not put down even if she had all the paper and paint in the world. "But the war will not last forever. And then I would like you to have it all. I shall have the bequest transferred to your name."

A soft sound came from her own mouth. Lily pressed her fingers to her lips. "I don't understand."

"Then let me explain."

When she had something important to say, Lily's mother was in the habit of turning her head and lowering it until her chin almost rested on her chest. When she was a little girl it had seemed to Lily that her mother was listening to someone only she could hear, and that only if she paid very close attention.

She spread her hands flat on the table and took in a deep breath. "Just before I was to marry your father, my aunt Merriweather gave me the same gift I am giving you now. She offered me money and the opportunity to use it to my own ends, without interference."

She paused a moment. "What she really gave me, of course, was a choice. Between the opportunity I had always wanted—the one I came here to realize—and life with your father."

"Did you choose well?" Lily asked, her voice sticking a little in her throat.

"Yes. I chose well. I would change nothing, even if I could. So now I am giving to you what my aunt gave to me, something very simple: the opportunity to choose. You may wait until the war is over and claim the income. With it you could live very comfortably in Manhattan, or in England or even on the Continent. Many painters spend time in Rome, and you could do that too, if you are careful with your expenditures."

Lily met her mother's eye. There was nothing unusual in her expression; she might have been explaining a difficult passage out of some scientist's treatise on fossils. No anger, no malice, no joy. A waiting, as if she were a vessel waiting to be filled: with cool water or vinegar, that much was up to Lily.

"You don't want me to marry Simon," Lily said. "Is that it?"

"That is not it, absolutely not." The first color rose in her mother's face. "Understand me now, daughter. If you choose to marry Simon and go to live with him in Montreal, you will have my blessing. How could I do any less, given my own history?"

"But you are hoping that I'll go off to Europe."

"Some part of me hopes for that, yes. But another part hopes just as sincerely that you will not. I do like Simon, and I respect him. I think he would be a good husband to you."

"If I marry, what happens to the money?"

A smile flickered in the gray of her mother's eyes, touched the corner of her mouth. "It is yours, whatever you decide. It will give you some measure of security. A married woman should have that, though the law doesn't see it thus."

"And my father agrees with this?"

"Haven't you guessed?" Lily's mother asked. "It was your father's idea to start with."

Such a clever husband, Elizabeth thought, who could find a way to put a wife's worries to rest and secure their daughter's future in such a simple, elegant way.

Now, sitting at the table while Lily wiped the few dishes, Elizabeth found herself smiling, pleased with him and herself too, and most of all with Lily, who had taken this offer in the spirit it was meant. No doubt there would be many more days of uncertainty in which she would question herself closely, but for the moment Elizabeth felt truly peaceful.

Of course, it remained to be seen how Simon would react. She had set him many small tests in the weeks since he came to Paradise, all of which he had met with a curious combination of intelligence and thoughtfulness and something she could only call native intuition. This newest test would tell most about him.

Most men would take offense; certainly men raised as he had been. In that world, the laird's word was law and women made a place for themselves in the shadows. Simon might be outraged at the idea that Lily would want to make her way in the world without his protection or the protection of any man at all.

Over the years Elizabeth had come to the conclusion that even reasonable men had a good dose of the apostle Paul brewing in their bellies, and needed very little provocation to spew him forth.

Her own husband, her calm and reasonable and unflappable Nathaniel, confronted with a similar charge so many years ago, had balked like a mule. Offended, yes, and threatened, and those two things together had loosened the tight control he kept on his temper. In the hours before they were wed they had argued so intensely that she remembered much of it word for word all these years later. *Damn your father and damn your aunt Merriweather and most of all goddamn to everlasting hell your know-it-all Mrs. Wollstonecraft.*

She had wondered many times if her aunt Merriweather had ever known the chaos that had been wrought with her gift of independence. Most probably not; she had been far away in England, with no real understanding of the place where Elizabeth had chosen to make a life for herself or the challenges she faced.

Now, watching her own daughter, Elizabeth knew exactly what she had started. Lily must go to Simon with this newest challenge, and they would work it out between them. Or they would not. She had a sense that Simon would see this newest and most serious challenge to his courtship as a puzzle to be solved, and if he trod lightly—if Lily understood well enough how to let him do that— they would come to an agreement.

"He's the kind of man who won't swaddle her," Nathaniel had said, when they were talking this whole delicate business through. "He'll make sure she has what she needs and then he'll stand back and wait his turn."

Elizabeth trusted her husband's intuitions, but more than that, she knew he was talking about more than food and clothing and a sound roof over Lily's head.

There was a knock at the kitchen door. Elizabeth got up from the table.

She said, "I'm away to take my nap, now, Lily. Please make my excuses to your Simon."

Chapter 36

With the arrival of the warmer weather the war woke like a bad-tempered bear, and with that, Hannah began to dream more and more of Strikes-the-Sky. Quiet dreams that left more questions than they raised, and stayed with her and followed her through the day as she went about her work.

Her husband never said very much to her, or if he did the memory of the words themselves faded in the morning light. It was a mystery and frustrating; if he had things to tell her she wished he would do it. She had questions she wanted to ask him; mostly, she wondered about the boy, who never showed himself.

When she mentioned the dreams to Jennet, she got a thoughtful silence in response.

"I never dream of Ewan," her cousin said finally, a little wistfully. "The truth be told, I can hardly remember his face. It was all so long ago, a hundred years at least, in a faraway place where fairies romp in the wood."

"That's a fine state of affairs," Hannah said. "Your husband has disappeared altogether and mine is around every corner."

"If I were still at Carryckcastle no doubt it would be the same for me," Jennet said. "I ran away from everything familiar, but you're back in the middle of it all."

That was a fine bit of reasoning, and Hannah had to agree that it made sense. She hadn't ever thought to find herself anywhere near any war, ever again, but now they often woke to the distant stuttering of artillery fire. Traffic on the river grew more frantic day by day: boats and ships, canoes and barges and bateaux of every size, all bearing supplies or troops or munitions, soldiers and sailors swarming like ants before a storm. Wounded men were brought to the garrison over land and water both, though most of these Hannah never saw. To her the garrison hospital was as big a mystery as ever; she had never been invited inside, and what she knew of the doctors who worked there she had second- and thirdhand from guards and the other women in the followers' camp.

Not that she had any real interest to be included in that brotherhood, she told herself. She saw the results of their work in the number of graves that were dug, and that was more information than she cared for already.

The prisoners were almost more than Hannah could handle, even with Jennet's good help and Mr. Whistler there to handle the heavy work. There had been no deaths in the stockade for two weeks, which must of course please her, but every day brought two or three new men, mostly militia, mostly young, all hungry and worn down to cartilage and bitterness.

It was true that Hannah could count on basic provisions now: the men were not well fed, but neither did they lie awake at night with cramps in their empty bellies. There was a steady flow of the essential medicines and other supplies that Luke sent around various corners. The worst of it now was the heat, the flies, and the crowding. For the first there was no cure at all; for the second, a limited amount of relief in bear grease and ointment; and for the last nothing except the hope of escape or, for some, death.

In the evenings, after a long day in the stockade, Hannah and Jennet sat down to eat a simple meal with Runs-from-Bears and Sawatis. Every day she felt them watching her closely, waiting for her to say the words they needed to hear: Daniel was well enough now to travel. Except she couldn't say that, and could not say when that day might come with any certainty.

It was not her uncle's way to worry about what could not be changed; instead he went off in his canoe and came back with bundles of herbs and roots and tobacco, all put together by Many-Doves who was in a well-hidden camp two miles downriver.

The truth was, Blue-Jay was strong enough to travel, and if not for Daniel, they would have spirited him away weeks ago. When she was very tired, the part of Hannah that was more Bonner than Kahnyen'kehàka worried about that, about the sacrifice her Mohawk family was making for her white half brother. The other, stronger part of her always stopped her before she suggested to Runs-from-Bears that he should take his son and leave this place.

It was her job to heal Daniel, and she must put all her powers of concentration in that alone; there was no time for guilt, Hannah reminded herself, and even less for self-doubt.

On a morning so damp and warm that it made her think of steaming bread, Hannah went to the stockade before first light, leaving Jennet asleep on her pallet. Over the weeks they had worked out which of the men were willing to let her in before the rest of the camp followers, in exchange for a few coins—another one of Luke's many contributions. When she was too tired to stop herself, Hannah wondered what would become of her brother if it ever became public knowledge that the grandson of the erstwhile lieutenant governor of Lower Canada was pouring so much money and effort into the care of the American invaders.

Hannah rose from her pallet and walked to the fort in quiet desperation, as a sister but mostly as a doctor, perplexed and undone by her own failure. She went to sit next to Daniel in the crowded pungent dark of the stockade and listen to his breathing, in the hope that somehow he would reveal to her the one thing she wanted most to know: how to save his life.

For all her life, Jennet had been a sound sleeper and possessive of that state. She could not be depended on to rouse herself; that Hannah did, most mornings, by shaking her or, when that failed, by flicking cold water on her face.

Now that Hannah had got in the habit of rising before first light to go to the stockade, Runs-from-Bears had taken over the job of waking Jennet, which he did by the simple expedient of sticking his head into the shack and letting out a shriek that made her jump to her feet.

In some part of her sleeping mind Jennet, struggling reluctantly toward a waking state, realized that Runs-from-Bears had forgotten about her. The piece of stretched doeskin that covered the single small window was glowing with sunlight, which meant that she had opened her eyes and was lying on her side; which meant that she was awake, and without prodding.

Hannah's pallet was empty, and more than that: someone was crouched behind her. Jennet held herself very still and closed her eyes.

It was not Runs-from-Bears or his son or any other Indian; the bear grease that they used to protect themselves from the flies was far too distinctive to miss. Jennet's heart kicked into a rapid gallop while her mind raced. A dry clicking in her throat she swallowed down only with great difficulty, and her ears ringing in alarm. She opened her eyes because she could not bear the dark.

A man's shadow passed the window and then another, and with them voices. Runs-from-Bears and Sawatis, talking easily together. She wondered if she could call an alarm quickly enough to save herself from whatever or whoever it was—a man, she told herself, no wolf, no dog—who had found his way here. A soldier, most likely; for weeks Hannah had been warning her that she flirted too much with them all, made light of the moon eyes they threw her way. A soldier would have a weapon. And if he did, why was he waiting?

Runs-from-Bears was talking again, something about the river and the wind. Mohawk was a fearfully difficult language but Jennet recognized some words, now, and was trying to learn more. *Andiatarocté,* she heard: tail of the lake, their name for Lake George. They had no idea that she was here, or that she was not alone.

She forced herself to breathe normally and, in one quick movement, made ready to roll away from the pallet.

A hand stopped her, clamped firmly on her waist; before she could scream another hand covered her mouth and without thinking she put her teeth to work even as she opened her eyes and saw Luke's face.

"Christ Almighty!" he hissed, and jerked his hand away. "That's a fine welcome, girl."

Jennet pushed herself back and away, pulled her knees to her chest and blinked at him. "Luke."

"What's left of me. You've got teeth like a beaver."

"Well, why didn't you announce yourself?" Jennet asked, and then, to her horror, she heard herself giggle. The shock, she told herself, and the relief.

"That's it, laugh." He was trying to look angry, and failing. "First you attack me and then you laugh at me. Call me a fool but I was hoping for a different kind of welcome."

"I thought you were here to ravish me." The words were said before she could stop them, and then she really did laugh. "I mean, I thought you were a stranger here to do me harm."

Luke was busy wrapping his hand with a handkerchief—she had managed to draw blood, it seemed—and Jennet reached out and took it away from him. "Let me do that. And now tell me what you mean by sneaking in here and disturbing my sleep, Luke Bonner."

"It's good to see you too, girl."

He grinned this time, his familiar and beloved smile spreading across his face. The cool gray of his eyes grew warmer as they moved down her length. Her breasts pressed against the chemise that was her only nightdress, and he liked that; she watched his eyes go drowsy with arousal. Jennet made herself concentrate on his hand, the three small teeth marks oozing blood.

"Of course I'm glad to see you," she said, almost prissily.

"How glad?" His free hand was on her arm, pulling her closer.

"As glad as I was to see you the last time you came," Jennet said. "Until you started in being bothersome."

"Bothersome, is it?" Luke leaned forward and put his mouth to her ear. "That's a new word for an old business. Come, hen, have you no better way to welcome me after a month of keeping to your lonely bed?"

Jennet let herself go to him then, moving into his arms and against him, her heart racing again but now for a good reason.

She said, "Hannah will be waiting for me in the stockade."

Luke bore her back down to the pallet, laughing quietly against her mouth. "So she will," he said. "And all for naught. There's some ravishment needs to be taken care of, first."

They had such a noble and reasonable agreement: Luke would stay away from Nut Island for everyone's safety, and as soon as Hannah had settled in, Jennet would come to him in Montreal. Except that Hannah's work had never lessened and Jennet could not leave her, and so one day they had come back to the followers' camp in the evening to find him waiting there with Runs-from-Bears, deep in a discussion about how to get the prisoners out of the stockade, off the island, and over the border.

He had looked up at them as they came in and smiled as if it were nothing unusual that he would come to take his tea in this tiny shack. Jennet had been shocked and angry and pleased beyond measure to see him, and that night Hannah had taken her pallet to sleep somewhere else, anywhere else; Jennet had never thought to ask, later, where she had gone. Nor could she find it in herself to be discomfited by that. If anyone understood it must be Hannah.

Luke had come to try to get her to leave, of course. He had some ideas about Father O'Neill that first made Jennet laugh out loud and then made her angry. And wasn't it just like Wee Iona's grandson to see a great conspiracy behind every Roman collar, she asked, and did he hear himself, how he sounded more jealous than worried for her welfare?

But he hadn't risen to her goading. Instead Luke insisted that she write him a report every day on what the priest had said and done and who he had spoken to, and Jennet had asked him if he wanted her to spend more time with the good father, or less?

In the end it turned out that he had risked coming to Nut Island not only because he was worried about the priest, or even because he had letters and medicine and soap and lovely white-flour rolls with fresh butter, but because of a passion he could no longer control. And how could she stay angry at that? He had kept her flat on her back for most of the night, alternately arguing with her and making love to her, sometimes both at once.

In the morning he had slipped away again, never discovered by the guards or anyone else, as he had promised. And left her behind, because she insisted, and when he was gone how she had struggled to hide her disappointment. In him, in herself.

And here he was again, so beautiful that he took her breath away. Already the spring sun had begun to turn his hair lighter and his skin—covered now with a keen, sweet sweat—was darkening.

When she could breathe again, Jennet became aware of the sounds of the camp all around them: women's voices and children, the business of cooking and eating and getting ready for the day. No doubt they had made themselves heard, which should embarrass her unto death but Jennet could find no energy for that particular exercise. Later, of course, the women would want to know which of the men from the fort she had finally let into her bed; that would take a bit of handling, of course.

Luke turned on his side, his great strong hand on her shoulder, dark against light, his thumb stroking. Then he said, "Come with me to Montreal. We'll spend a month in bed. I want to see if I can make you screech like that again."

She smacked him smartly and then rubbed her cheek against his hand. "You shouldn't ask, and you know it. I canna leave your sister."

He nodded, as if she had given him the answer he expected and not a word more.

"And I don't screech."

"Like a panther in the night."

"Tell me this," Jennet said. "First I was a beaver and now a panther. Why is it you must always think of me as some four-legged beast?"

"Now there's an idea," he said, and flipped her over neatly. Jennet scrambled away from him, laughing and kicking and tumbling, until her back was against the wall and he held up his hands in surrender.

She could not keep the question to herself any longer, and so out it came in a hiccup: "How long can you stay?"

He leaned forward and kissed her cheek, as sweetly as a boy. "I'm already gone, girl."

Her face twitched with disappointment, but she managed a small smile and saw the same things in his face that he must see in hers.

"Tell me about Daniel first," he said.

Jennet thought about what to say while she pulled her chemise to rights. "He's in terrible pain. The damage to the nerves in his arm and shoulder, says your sister. Not that you would ever hear it from him, understand. There's never a word of complaint from him, but you can see it on his face, what it's doing to him. As if somebody had used a knife to carve it into him."

Luke was silent for a moment. "And he still can't use the arm." Asking her to say the words that he didn't want to hear.

"He can move it, but the pain is enough to make him swoon, if you can imagine that of Daniel Bonner. Hannah won't even let him walk about, she's that worried about keeping the arm still. Though he does, of course, when she's gone."

"And the wound?"

"Healing," Jennet said, and then: "More slowly than Hannah hoped it would."

"It's the pain distracting him," said Luke.

"The worst of it is, he's lost all hope," Jennet said. "He barely talks to anyone except to Blue-Jay and Hannah, and there's a bitterness in him that breaks my heart, Luke. He's convinced himself he's going to lose the arm, though Hannah tells him that it's no the case."

She watched Luke thinking, his expression blank but his eyes bright and a thousand thoughts moving behind them, weighing and calculating and weighing again. He wouldn't let himself feel his brother's pain because he couldn't afford that distraction. It was what she expected of him, but she admired it nonetheless.

He said, "We can wait another four or five weeks at the most. Jennet, listen." He leaned closer. "My leaning is to tell you as little as possible of our plans, so you'll be as surprised as the next person when the time comes—"

"You'll get no argument from me on that count," Jennet said.

"—but there is something I need to ask you. If things go wrong, it could be that I'll have to stay out of Canada."

She looked at him then and saw no real worry in his face. "For how long?"

Luke shrugged, the muscles in his shoulder rolling. "For good, most likely. If things go wrong."

"But what of the business? What of Forbes and Sons and the rest of it?"

"I've already hired another manager, and I can sell out my shares on short notice—"

"If things go wrong," she finished for him. "You're willing to risk everything you've built up for yourself in Montreal?"

The corner of his mouth twitched, some of the old humor there in him, the fearlessness of the younger man she had known in Scotland. "For my brother? Of course. The question I'm putting to you is, whether you're willing to settle down someplace else. Boston or Manhattan or Albany."

He was watching her closely, as if he weren't quite sure of what she would say but meant to hide his worry.

"Madame del Giglio said I would be traveling farther than Montreal," Jennet said, suddenly remembering.

"Well, then," Luke said with a sour grin. "That settles it. We might as well pack up right now and get ourselves on the road."

"Tease me if you must," Jennet said, fighting back the irritation that pushed its way up. "But here's your answer: I came this far for you, Luke Bonner, and I'm not about to give up now. I'll follow you to the ends of the earth if I must."

"Let's hope that won't be necessary," he said, reaching for her with a tender expression. She caught his hand in her own and held it, feeling the energy there and the heat of him, the nature of his purpose.

"There's something else," Jennet said, and she wondered at herself that her body should be roused by nothing more than the way he was looking at her. Such sad, terrible, important things still needed to be said and here she was, covered with gooseflesh at the touch of him.

She said, "I fear Hannah won't leave when the time comes."

Luke raised an eyebrow and tilted his head, and Jennet went on.

"You may spirit Blue-Jay and Daniel away without a peep, but in the end I think she'll stay for the sake of the others. She won't be able to turn her back on them."

Luke raised a hand to push a curl out of Jennet's face and then his fingers moved down and flicked open the buttons on her chemise she had finally managed to do up. "Of course she wouldn't leave the prisoners," he said. "We knew that all along."

Jennet caught his wrist and held it. "Oh, you did. Then pray tell me, how did you plan to get her away from here? Are you going to knock her senseless and carry her off in a sack?"

"Don't be silly." He pressed a knuckle to her breastbone and then ran it down to her belly so that she gasped and tried to turn away.

"What then?" Jennet said, fumbling to contain his hands; too late.

"We'll take them all," Luke said. "So there's no one for her to stay behind for."

"Wait." Jennet twisted with all her strength to stop him, pushed with both hands against his shoulders. "You intend to empty the whole stockade? A hundred prisoners or more, they'll just walk away with the blessing of the commander?"

"More or less," Luke said, taking her hands and pinning them to the pallet to either side of her head. "Any more questions?"

"Not just now," Jennet said, and pulled him to her.

Chapter 37

Daniel, long and lean and hard muscled like his father and grandfather and all the Scotts of Carryck before him, had always been—in Curiosity Freeman's words—a good eater. His twin, Lily, Daniel's opposite in this as in so many things, liked to tease him that he would eat anything that didn't crawl away from his plate, and some things that would have, if he weren't so fast with a fork and knife.

Now Daniel was so painfully thin that Hannah sometimes felt herself halt with panic at the sight of him. She made sure that he got half her own ration of food as well as his own, and still he was starving.

It had been a very long time since she had kept a daybook and even longer since she had thought of ones she had lost in the wars, but now, unexpectedly, the impulse to write down what she was observing had risen strong in her. Maybe that way some truth would reveal itself. She bartered tobacco and tea from her small store for paper; Runs-from-Bears brought her quills; and one of the women in the camp made her ink out of gall and dried blueberries.

On the rough paper Hannah drew diagrams of the musculature of the arm, the pathways of nerves and blood vessels. She asked herself questions and fought for answers, and in the end she always came to the same frustrating end: Daniel's pain was mechanical, and she could not fix it; his anger was monumental, and there was nowhere for it to go but deeper into the very marrow of his bones.

That was the nature of prisons, after all. To let men cook in their own juices, without any means of relief. Her brother was like a woman in travail whose legs have been bound together, torn in two by an ungovernable force.

This night at least Daniel had slept, but with help. Hannah knew that if she leaned forward she would be able to smell the laudanum on his breath, sickly sweet. She should have been satisfied that he was getting the rest he needed so desperately. Instead Hannah was deeply uneasy. She feared that Daniel was close to surrender, as even the strongest fish must finally give up when it has fought the line to the end of its endurance.

With that thought foremost in her mind, Hannah sat and waited for the light, and when it had come, thin and gray and sodden, she roused herself and went about her work.

His name is Samuel Cade. He is a Burlington boy, born on the shore of the great lake. Its water runs in his veins. He has taken up the patriots' cause by putting his mark on a piece of paper and following his four elder brothers into the navy.

Well fed and strong, with square hands and a resolute set to his chin; a bright boy, nimble and biddable. Within a week he is brought to the attention of Lieutenant Markham, sailing master of the sloop Ferret. Catcher Markham, the men call him behind his back, for he is like a great wolfhound when he's got the Tory stink in his nose: he will run himself to ground to catch his prey.

For a month Samuel has been a powder boy on Catcher Markham's twelve-gun sloop. Day by day they prowl the northern waters of Champlain, watching for Tories sly or stupid enough to venture into American waters. In preparation for that day, they drill.

The first mate prowls the deck, surly, his quirt doing his talking for him. Sam, quick and able as he is, has a half-dozen of Mr. Tate's quirt marks on his shoulders and back. Some of the newer crew, the landsmen most especially, wear as many stripes as a tomcat.

To Sam, Mr. Tate and his quirt are just a distraction; the man he must please, more than the sailing master or his own father or the Lord God himself, is Mr. Kirby, his gun captain.

In the dark of night, swinging in their hammocks, the sailors tell stories of Mr. Kirby. They know the ships he has served on, the merchantmen and privateers that made his fortune—for he is rumored to be a wealthy man—before he signed onto the Ferret. In the year four he made a name for himself fighting the Mussulmen off the shore of Tripoli. Three times he has turned down promotion. Mr. Kirby prefers guns to men.

The gun captain speaks to the officers when they address him; his tone is respectful but distant. To his gun crew Mr. Kirby has more to say: his tone hard or encouraging or sharp, as needed. He has only three mates among the crew, men like himself: war hardened and somber. Sam cannot say he has ever seen Mr. Kirby smile.

Sam is the youngest and least experienced of Mr. Kirby's four-man crew, and he knows what it will take to win the respect he wants. He works hard, he pays attention; he learns everyone's job in addition to his own. In battle, gun crews are first in the line of fire, and it might fall on him to manage the rammer or even the powder horn.

The drills go on and on. Marines take up train tackle to haul in the guns and then the crew takes over, loading and firing. Then it all starts again. In. Load. Out. Fire. Again. Again. Sam moves back and forth from the main hatch to his gun port, hoisting powder and shot, filling the rack, watching. Always watching how the others handle their tools: rammer, pick, sponger, budge barrel.

On the first day of drilling Sam's mouth and nose are gritty with gunpowder within a half hour. His hands, hard as leather, throw new blisters anyway. He has been warned that the blisters will break and close and ooze and break again. When they close for good the gunpowder will have tattooed itself into his palms.

Another powder boy, one Sam knows only as a farmer's son out of New-York State, slips and falls just as the number two carronade is being hauled in. The gun crushes the bones in the boy's arm with a crack like a spar breaking. Sam, brought up on the water, is torn between pity and disdain; the boy's screams are ample proof that a landsman has no place on board a sloop of war. When he is put off at Burlington Sam wonders if he will ever see the boy again on this side of the grave.

Belowdecks while he waits for sleep, breathing in the familiar stench of pitch and bilgewater, Samuel dreams of being a gun captain. He loves the lake in the same heedless, instinctive way he loves his mother, but what he wants, what he dreams of, is serving on one of the great warships on the open sea. Thirty-eight guns or more, twenty-pounders, swivel cannons, and a bright copper gun captain's knife tucked in his belt. Now he is called boy, or powder boy, or monkey, but then they will call him Mr. Cade.

When the crew of the Ferret has been drilling for two weeks, Sam begins to wonder if the war is a true thing, or only a story made up to sell newspapers, a dream told by a conspiracy of men desperate for bloodshed.

The gun crews continue to drill, though they can fire and reload in a minute's time. But every ship they see, every canoe and raft, is American, though not all are friendly. There are smugglers enough—Sam recognizes them all, knows them by name, as he knows where they live and the names of their children. There are revenue boats on the lake, but never enough to keep up with the smugglers, who are a cunning lot.

On a cool summer morning Sam gets what he has been wishing for when two British gunboats venture onto the lake. Forty-eight-feet long, twenty-six sweeps, and sloop rigged, they dart as sleek and quick as wasps.

He would like to be among the men working the sails—the better to see their prey—but Sam Cade must be satisfied with listening to the drums and the shouted orders and reports. The Ferret flies north under a press of canvas, but the captain is not satisfied; he sends the topmen scurrying up the lines and soon Sam feels the ship respond like a horse to the lash: she heels and charges.

This is everything he had hoped for and waited for and still there is something not quite right; he hears it in the voices of the men, and worse, he sees it in the expression on his gun captain's face. When he can bear it no longer he dares to ask Mr. Ogilvy, who is scratching his jaw with the touch-hole pick.

"The captain's taking us over the border into Canada," says the older man, his eyes darting quick under a beetling brow. "He wants those gunnys."

They are sailing into enemy waters, then. Against orders; against common sense. Sam is trying to understand it, to sort it out for himself, what it might mean, when the order comes: gun crews to the ready. Sam Cady, ten years old, looks to his gun captain for direction, and follows his lead.

Just a few hours later, in the heat of battle, the rush and roar and stink of billowing gun smoke, Sam does not have to be told the plain truth: they are lost. The wind has turned against them; they have come this far into Canada and are stuck like a cork in a bottle. On one side is Nut Island, its fortifications studded with gun ports, every one of them open and belching fire. Oarsmen maneuver gunboats: a pack of wolves playing with its kill. If not for the smoke, Sam would be able to see the opposite shore and its legion of lobsterbacks, more Tory soldiers and sailors and militia than he has ever seen before, or imagined.

They are listing hard to starboard, the deck as steep as a roof, slick with water and blood. Dead men slide away like rag dolls tossed thoughtlessly down a hillside, faces streaked with sweat and gunpowder.

They have fought hard. They have done damage: two gunboats sunk, another capsized. Sam Cade, numb with noise and fear and a holy anger, has done his part and more; he says this to himself aloud.

The sleeve of his shirt flaps in bloody tatters; his arm is full of splinters from shoulder to wrist. It must hurt, he knows that by looking at himself, but at this moment he doesn't feel it at all. It is much harder to look at what is left of Mr. Ogilvy, and so he simply does not. Mr. Jamison, the third of their gun crew, is long gone.

Somewhere in the heavy haze of gun smoke is an officer who is shouting orders, but at this moment it is only Mr. Kirby who interests Sam. Great fists of noise pummel the listing ship; Sam is still upright only because he is holding on to the tackle line, his gaze fixed on his gun captain.

Mr. Kirby crooks a finger at him and Sam leans forward, curls himself forward to hear, his head canted up at an angle. The gun captain's expression shifts, just then, and Sam sees something he cannot first credit: Mr. Kirby is smiling.

"What?" Sam shouts at him. "What?"

Mr. Kirby turns suddenly and just that simply Sam understands. Looking at the gun captain's back, he understands that the man has taken death's measure and found some satisfaction in it.

In the stockade, there was complete and watchful silence. The dozen men who hadn't been sent out with the work parties stood or sat facing the single high barred window that looked over the river, flinching in harmony with every new explosion. The walls shook, the ground beneath their feet shook, the men shook too. In fear, in excitement.

Hannah held her brother's hand, watching his face, because she could not quite credit what she saw there: a wakefulness absent these many weeks. A new interest, a sparking of his native curiosity. Pearls of sweat on his upper lip, and yet his skin was cool to the touch. No fever; or at least, no fever of the body, Hannah corrected herself.

Her own pulse was quick. She tried not to think of Jennet, who had still not appeared when the first cannon fire was heard. No doubt she was still in the followers' camp, staying put under Runs-from-Bears' watchful eye.

It was harder not to think of the other prisoners—Blue-Jay among them—who had been sent out today to dig trenches. She had asked the guard, and got no answer at all. Which could mean that he didn't know, or that he didn't care to risk her reaction when he gave her the news.

There was nothing she could do for them, just now; what she must do instead was to prepare for whatever was left of the ship's crew. They would come to her door—to this door—before the day was done.

And yet Hannah couldn't make herself move away from Daniel's side, or take her eyes off the men who were keeping watch at the window.

They perched on a wobbly stack of boxes and blankets, their faces pressed to the bars. One of them was a newer prisoner, a boy from Maine called Locke, sturdy as a young oak and strong but with a wound to his hand that was still suppurating. The other was Matthews, Hannah remembered, called Long John for some reason she hadn't figured out, or maybe didn't really want to know. He had lost an eye in a skirmish on the border, but he was the most experienced sailor among them and the best man to make sense of what was happening on the river.

For two hours Locke and Matthews had been standing in just that posture, putting the battle into words. As if we were all blind, Hannah thought. As if these were all young boys eager for a game that had been forbidden to them. Every maneuver, every volley, was taken up with great interest and discussed in low tones. Through it all the same chorus, the same question without an answer: what in the name of the Almighty had possessed the captain to sail his sloop into a nest of Tories? He was outgunned, outmanned, outthought.

They might have turned and run, but then the wind left them stranded.

"That's it, then," Daniel said quietly. "It's over."

But it took another hour, while the men seethed like a pot brought to the boil. Mr. Whistler wailed, grasping his beard with both hands and waggling his head. Wordless, for once, and without a quip to make the men laugh.

The others were more able to say what they thought. Bile and bitterness poured out of them, not for the Tories, but for the ship's captain.

"Running a good sloop like that to rack and ruin," Matthews said. And: "The beating he's taking from the Royal Artillery won't seem much if he shows his face in here, by God."

Daniel said, "Not much chance of that. They'll send the officers to Montreal, or Québec."

"If they live," Hannah said.

"Oh, Christmas Christ Jesus," called Locke. "She's going down."

Matthews turned his long, thin face away from the window and looked down at the others. "Better make room, boys, we're about to get some fresh blood."

Fresh blood. The stink of it, the way it shone, slippery and hot. They were awash in it, wading in it; Hannah was vaguely aware of blood spatter tacky on her face and arms, as some part of her mind noted the flies in a feeding frenzy.

Jennet was there, suddenly, struggling to hold down a sailor with a face full of splinters and shrapnel, bones poking out of a thigh like ragged white teeth. Under Hannah's own hands blood pulsed from a chest wound. The sailor had been dragged out of the water and he shook uncontrollably; the cold was the only reason he was still alive, but it had only put off the inevitable by a few minutes.

"I don't want to die," he told her. All of his lower teeth were broken off at the gum and an apron of blood spilled down his chin. "I don't want to die." And then he did, the life running out of him just that simply.

She went from body to body. Most dead, or too near to it to be saved. Mr. Whistler and the others well enough to lend a hand dragged the bodies to the far wall. A dozen, two dozen. A twelve-gun sloop would have a crew of about seventy-five men, she had been told, and at one point Hannah had the odd idea that she would be forced to watch every one of them die.

Crushed limbs, burns, wounds of every kind. Splinters the length of a finger, an arm, a cannon, as deadly as any bullet. Injuries such as she had never seen before, tending to men fallen on battlefields to the west, far from water and ships.

In the mass of men shoved into the stockade there were a half dozen or so who seemed to be uninjured. They worked along with the rest, and while they worked they told the story.

"Ah, Christ," she heard one of them say. "What a damn waste."

"Markham?" came the question, and the answer: "Fell with the first volley, damn his eyes."

Jennet came up and whispered in Hannah's ear. "The captain of the guard wants a word. Ask him for blankets." And then she was gone.

• • •

The captain of the guard was a small, dapper man with a neat mustache, cool brown eyes, and no use for Indians. He said, "How many of them will live?"

Hannah wiped hands on her overdress, leaving streaks of blood and grit. "I don't know. Thirty, perhaps. I haven't had a chance to examine them all yet."

A muscle in his cheek twitched. "The commander wants you in the hospital. There are too many wounded for the doctors."

That, finally, cut through Hannah's preoccupation. She thought at first that she must have misunderstood, and found by his expression that she had not. He was as displeased with this idea as she was, and as surprised by it.

"I am needed here," Hannah said. "When these men are seen to, I will come."

He wanted to object, she could see that. But his dislike of her was stronger, and so he simply turned and walked away.

On the other side of the stockade a man was screaming, a rhythmic, high-pitched wailing. It stopped suddenly: he was dead, or he had fainted.

"Hannah!" Jennet called.

She was halfway across the room, winding around men unconscious and dead and writhing in pain, when she remembered about the blankets.

It was near dark before she came across Liam Kirby. They brought him in with the last batch. Among them were five men and a boy near death, his skull crushed so that his eyes bulged. She was dealing with the boy when Mr. Whistler came to her.

"There's a gunny here with a back wound you ought to look at," he said. He rubbed a thumb over his pendulous lower lip. "He came in walking but he won't be walking much longer, from the look of him. Unless you can dig out the lead without bleeding him to death in the process."

"Ask Mrs. Huntar to have a look," Hannah said. "I can't leave this boy."

"Mrs. Huntar went to find her priest," Mr. Whistler said. "She's after blankets and tea and the like."

Hannah was holding the boy with his head bedded on her shoulder. He was clammy and cold with river water. Under what was left of his shirt his abdomen was a mass of bruises, a sack filling with blood. His breath hitched once and then again. He drew in a long whistling breath and never let it out again.

Mr. Whistler leaned down and took the dead boy, picked him up like an infant in spite of the long dangling legs. "I'll look to this one," he said gruffly. "If you'll have a look at the gunny."

It was his back she saw first, the long arch of spine bracketed by a scattering of neat holes. Grapeshot, meant to take apart rigging and shatter spars, had found an easier target. Mr. Whistler had cleaned the wounds and dressed them and the man would die anyway.

Because, Hannah reckoned to herself, some ten pounds of cast iron was buried in the broad, sun-darkened back. She could almost see it, nestled among ribs and along blood vessels. Shivering with every heave of the lungs.

He would die as surely as the boy Mr. Whistler had just taken away, but it would take him longer. No doubt by the end of it he would think the shipmates who were being piled up beside a hastily dug trench grave luckier than he himself.

In the failing light Hannah crouched down next to the gunner and touched his shoulder. She knew him then, before he turned his face to her. She saw the knowing come to him just a second later. He had opened his mouth to ask for water—the word was forming on his lips—when he recognized her. It touched his eyes and then moved across his face.

"Hannah," he said hoarsely. His breath was heavy with laudanum. Mr. Whistler had done the right thing in dosing him, but just at this moment Hannah wished that he had waited.

"Rest easy, Liam," she said, forcing her voice into line. Her tone calm, gentle, reassuring. "Let me look after you now."

His eyelids flickered once, twice.

"You must sleep," she said. "Don't fight it."

Liam said, "I'm afraid to close my eyes."

His blue eyes, so very familiar to her and yet completely wrong, in this place, at this time. "You're safe here."

He smiled at that, a little twist of the mouth that meant he doubted but would not challenge her.

"You are safe," she said again.

"Women's promises," he muttered. And slid away into sleep.

· · ·

Her hands shook for an hour. Jennet, back from her errand with blankets and other good things, forced Hannah to take a cup of tea and a piece of bread, and watched until she had finished both.

"Tell me," Hannah said.

"Sixty-seven men on the sloop," Jennet recited. "Thirty-eight still alive, all of them"—she gestured with her hands—"right here."

"Four or five of these will be dead by morning," Hannah said. *Another one by week's end.* This last thought she kept to herself, fighting the urge to turn around. He must still be there; she had not conjured Liam Kirby up out of the water like a creature in an old story, like one of Jennet's selkies. She said, "We'll need more of everything."

"Aye, weel." Jennet's mouth contorted. "Don't worry overmuch about that, just now. You need your own rest, Hannah, or you'll fall over on your face." She leaned forward, put a hand to her cousin's cheek.

She whispered, "We had a visitor this morning, from Montreal."

Hannah forced herself to focus, and now she took note of Jennet's color, higher than it should have been, even in the heat and distress of this day.

"That's why you were so long. Letters?"

Jennet nodded. "Letters, aye, and news. But naught that canna wait. For a bit, at least, while you take your rest."

Hannah opened her mouth to tell Jennet that she could not turn away, not just now: there was a man with a broken arm that must be set, and others, too, who needed her attention. She meant to explain all that, calmly, clearly, but instead something very different came out of her mouth.

"Liam Kirby is here," she said.

Jennet's jaw dropped. She shut it with a click. "You don't mean—"

"I do." She was looking for the words that might make sense of what she was thinking when she saw her brother Daniel moving across the room, weaving in and out among the wounded. He was carrying a basin of water in the crook of his good arm, and while he was very pale, he looked more composed, more sure of himself, than he had in weeks.

And he was headed straight for Liam Kirby. Hannah watched him come closer and then pause, his expression shifting only a little from concentration to puzzlement and then surprise.

"Is there bad blood between them, then?" Jennet asked, following Hannah's gaze.

"No. Or at least, I don't think there is, not anymore."

Not since Liam spoke up for me and saved my life, she might have added. *On the day I took Strikes-the-Sky as my husband.*

One of the wounded was keening, behind her somewhere. The double doors had opened and the work party was coming into the already overcrowded stockade, hurried along by the guards. Mr. Whistler called a question and a hand covered with dried blood reached up from the floor and caught the fabric of her overdress.

Daniel looked up and met her gaze, and then he turned his attention back to Liam Kirby.

Runs-from-Bears was waiting for Jennet when she came through the gates. She could not remember ever being so tired before, worn down to the bone; her feet would not obey her. Runs-from-Bears took her arm and steered her and she had a strange but very appealing idea: he might carry her, like an infant.

Instead she drew in a deep breath and held it until her vision cleared a little.

It had taken more than a few days for Jennet to be really comfortable with Bears. As girls Hannah had told her the story of how Runs-from-Bears earned his name, but in person he was something very different than she had imagined. He was neither the kindly uncle Hannah described nor one of the savages she had seen so often rendered in blurry ink in one of her father's newspapers.

The problem was that his face showed so little emotion. His eyes were very black and very alert, but she could find nothing in them that was familiar to her.

At first. Then Elizabeth had said something odd: the problem was not in how Runs-from-Bears looked, but in what Jennet insisted on seeing. At first she had been confused by this, then a little affronted, and finally Jennet had been embarrassed by the plain truth of it. And so she had watched Runs-from-Bears and now she could hardly remember why he had frightened her so.

Right at this moment she was glad of the hand that supported her arm, and most of all she was thankful that he hadn't greeted her with a hundred questions. It only took a moment for her to remember the question she had for him.

"Is he safe away?"

Bears made a sound, a low hum in his throat, that satisfied her.

She volunteered information of her own. "Hannah will stay with the wounded tonight."

A fine tension rose, quite suddenly, in Runs-from-Bears; she felt it move from his hand into her arm just as the familiar voice made itself heard.

"Mrs. Huntar."

She pivoted. The pale oval of Father O'Neill's face seemed to float in the dark. Jennet blinked hard. She felt Runs-from-Bears moving away from her, five steps, ten, far enough away to watch but not to be watched.

"Father. What are you doing here?"

How rude, her mother would have said. But she was itchy with dried blood and she smelled, and right now Jennet had no strength left; certainly she was nowhere near sharp enough to parry with Father O'Neill, who never seemed to tire of finding ways to test her.

"Last rites," he said. "One of Maggie's girls got too close to the battle and caught a three-pounder for her curiosity."

His tone was almost cheerful, a man well pleased with his day's work. Jennet was glad of the dark, which would hide her distaste. It was the only word she could find for how she felt about Father O'Neill: a deep and abiding aversion, a growing thing with roots.

"I will stop by tomorrow and see what I can do for the family," Jennet said. She felt Runs-from-Bears watching, and was glad of him there.

"Your prisoners have all the blankets they require?"

She nodded. "Yes. Thank you for your help."

"I'll be by tomorrow, then."

Jennet made a humming sound. "Things are very crowded in the stockades now, as you can imagine—"

"Come now, Mrs. Huntar," said the priest. "There's always room for the word of God. You wouldn't have me turn my back on those who need it most?"

"Of course not," Jennet said.

She was so relieved to be away from the priest that she forgot her weariness and picked up her pace for the rest of the walk back to the camp. When Runs-from-Bears appeared out of the dark to take his spot beside her, she stopped.

"What is it?"

He said, "That girl he went to pray over? She died at midday."

A simple sentence. Jennet turned it around in her mind one way and the other, and then she saw what Bears meant her to see: the priest had been outside the garrison for some six hours since he gave last rites. He had lied to them, just now. But why?

It might be possible, Jennet reasoned to herself, to draw Runs-from-Bears into a discussion about the priest. She could not talk to Hannah about her suspicions and certainly not to Luke; Hannah would ask her to leave this place and Luke would insist on it, and Jennet had no intention of going anywhere just at the moment. Runs-from-Bears would listen first, and if there was real cause to worry, he would tell her that without making demands of her.

But she was so very tired, and the words she would need to make herself clear would not present themselves. It was all so insignificant, really: the odd word here and there, his expression when he did not know she was observing him. She could hardly say what she was thinking: Father O'Neill is up to something. She must laugh herself at the sound of it. It was the nature of priests, after all, even the best of them. Always angling after souls. Ghouls, every one.

Hannah put down a pallet next to her brother's cot. Sleep came to her quickly and, on its heels, her husband.

He was waiting for her in the middle of the strawberry fields on Hidden Wolf. Strikes-the-Sky as she had first seen him all those years ago, his head shaved for battle and a hawk feather in his scalp-lock. He watched her walking toward him and then he smiled and held out his hand and she sat with him there in the sun.

After a while she said, "Why does the boy never come to see me? Is he still angry?"

He studied the clouds and asked a question to match her own.

"Are you still angry with him?"

What an odd question, she thought of saying. As if she could stay angry at the child she had borne out of her own body. He had gone from this life and left her emptied of everything but longing.

She said, "Give me another child, then."

"Can you bear the pain of it?" her husband asked.

Hannah started awake. In the first gray light she saw that Daniel was sitting on the edge of his cot, his body bowed forward so that his forehead almost touched his knees, his injured arm cradled against his stomach. He rocked himself, humming. Moaning. Her little brother who did not cry out when a broken wrist was set, that man was choking on his own moans.

She shook her head to clear it of the dream, rubbed her eyes until they obeyed her and adjusted to the low light. Then she sat up.

"Leave me," he whispered before she could reach out. "Leave me be."

"It's always worst this time of night," said Blue-Jay from her other side, his voice pitched low. "In an hour the worst will be over."

"No," Hannah said. "It won't take that long."

She would go to the table where all the medicines were kept and get the laudanum he needed; there was not much of it left, and others with an equal claim on it, but just at this moment Hannah cared for nothing but chasing the sound of her brother's pain away.

When she stood, Blue-Jay reached out and grabbed her hand. "Elder Sister," he said to her in Kahnyen'kehàka. "Do not take his pride away from him along with everything else. If he can bear the pain, then so must you."

She hesitated for a moment, and then sat down again. Hannah forced herself to listen to the others, to turn her mind away from Daniel.

All around her men were sleeping. They filled the air with mutterings and wheezing and the occasional sharp cry. If she lifted her head she would see the corner where the worst of the wounded had been put. A crushed hand, broken ribs, flesh torn open by iron and wood, lungs still seeping river water. Liam Kirby.

Mr. Whistler had arranged him sitting up, with a thick wad of blanket on his lap that he could lean into. Full of laudanum, Liam would sleep for an hour more at least, and then he would wake and they would talk. There were things he might want to say, and other things that she must say to him, before it was too late.

The hand had to come off. It was Mr. Whistler who explained it to the marine, his tone not cruel, but gruff enough to make it clear there was no room for argument. All the bones were crushed, he explained, and the blood vessels with them.

"If she don't take it off, it will putrefy and get into your blood and that will be the end of you," said Mr. Whistler in his strange way, both curt and clear.

The marine was a man close to forty, with a bristling pate of gray hair and red-rimmed eyes glazed over with pain and laudanum.

"I don't care to have no Indian squaw cutting on me," he said finally.

"Then you'll die," Mr. Whistler said plainly. "It's up to you."

"What about that Mrs. Huntar, or one of the Tory surgeons?"

Mr. Whistler grunted. "Mrs. Huntar is no doctor, man, and the Tory surgeons got no time or interest in your sorry hide. No more do I, if you're going to be such a stubborn ass and turn away the help of a good surgeon because you don't like the look of her."

In the end the marine thought better of his decision and by noon Hannah had finished. Mr. Whistler took the hand away wrapped in a bit of rag while she finished dressing the wound. The marine had fainted dead away, a small mercy. There would be few others.

Sitting on the next cot, Daniel watched her work. "It's important to make sure the stump is wrapped just tight enough. Too little and it will bleed. Too much and it will putrefy."

She had got into the habit of talking to Daniel about the things she did, what went into a fever tea or a lung poultice, why she was lancing an infected heel, what a granulating wound looked like and when to leave it be. He never said very much or even asked a question, but he watched closely, and Hannah was glad to have found some small way to distract him from the agony in his shoulder and arm.

He said, "Liam Kirby is watching you."

Hannah was not so easily distracted. She kept her eyes on the task before her. "When I am finished here I will dress his wounds."

"That's not what he wants. He wants to talk."

She forced herself to meet her brother's gaze. "I hadn't planned on taking a vow of silence. I can do both things at once."

Daniel blinked at her. "Are you going to ask him?"

She might have pretended not to understand, but this was Daniel, after all, and he would not be so easily put off. Ten years ago Liam Kirby had disappeared from Paradise. Hannah would like to have claimed that she never thought of that summer, that she had moved on and had no interest in raising the dead.

What a bloody summer it had been. Young Reuben, Eulalie Wilde, Molly LeBlanc, Gabriel Oak. Kitty Todd and her infant daughter. Selah Voyager. Ambrose Dye.

Of course she needed to talk to Liam, but her plan was to focus on the one thing that would be a comfort to him now, in the last hours of his life. He did not know about his daughter, or he would have asked about her. It was the one thing she had to offer him, and she wanted no answers in return.

Suddenly Hannah felt herself flush with anger and weariness. "If you really want to know, Daniel, then ask him yourself."

"I did," said her brother. "But it's you he wants to talk to."

Even with the able-bodied out on work parties, the stockade was crowded almost past bearing. The guards had allowed them smudge pots, which helped a little with the flies but added to the stink and heat. Jennet, her hair plastered to her forehead by sweat, was flush with color and seemed unsteady on her feet as she moved through the room offering water and bread and gruel.

Every one of the men brightened and even the most morose of them managed a few words for her. Jennet had that gift. She could draw a man out of himself and back into the world. Maybe, Hannah thought, because Jennet reminded them of their sisters and mothers and wives. Whether it was her face or the way she spoke to them or the stories she told, the men loved her, and Hannah was thankful. Jennet gave the things she could not, would not give.

Few of the men spoke to Hannah; fewer still called her by name. Mr. Whistler called her Doctor, Daniel and Blue-Jay called her by her Mohawk name, Walks-Ahead. When they were alone Jennet called her Hannah.

The others called her you or you there or Mohawk. They most probably would have called her worse, if not for Blue-Jay and Daniel, who had the knack of a hard look.

Most of the prisoners averted their eyes when she went by, and if there was something they wanted to ask her or to say, they used Mr. Whistler to pass those words back and forth, though Hannah stood there in front of them. She had never expected anything else, never known any other treatment from white men.

Hannah was satisfied to let her cousin tend to their hearts and minds while she looked after their health and did what she could to see that their bodies recovered. Or in the cases where she had nothing to offer, she did all she could to see that they left this world with as little pain as possible.

As Liam Kirby must leave, and soon. As a boy he had seemed almost indestructible; now he was a strong man in his prime, but it would be only a matter of days before his wounds brought him low. Looking at his back, Hannah knew her limits as a healer. She could not reach inside him to set right what was wrong. No one could, no doctor or surgeon in this world. Listening with her ear to his side she heard his lungs laboring, and the first faint crackling that meant they were already overburdened. There was bleeding she could not see, and could not stop.

When she raised her head, Daniel was there, watching her over the curve of Liam's back. Daniel was too young to remember Liam Kirby as a boy, in the days he had lived among the Bonners at Lake in the Clouds. All Daniel knew were stories of the man Liam had become—not all of them good.

"I want to sit up," Liam said, his voice hoarse with effort. "Help me sit up."

Together they righted him, using folded blankets to prop him into place. His breath came fast and hard and smelled of hot salt and copper.

He had eyes of a faded blue, like an indigo-dyed shirt left too long in the sun. In the early light Hannah saw the evidence of these past ten years and what they had wrought: deep creases at the corners of his eyes and mouth, and early white among the deep red of his hair.

He was looking at her, too, and taking her measure.

Liam said, "How long?"

Hannah felt rather than saw Daniel tense, but at this moment she could not spare him anything at all.

"A day. Maybe two."

Liam nodded. A muscle twitched in his cheek. He asked none of the questions she might have expected, most probably, Hannah knew, because he had seen other men die of such wounds and needed no reminding.

"I never thought to see you again," he said. "Never wanted to."

And what was there to say to that? Hannah kept quiet.

"Your husband?"

She lifted a shoulder and inclined her head toward it. "The wars in the west."

Liam's expression did not change, though there was a hitch in his breathing. After a long moment he said, "I thought I knew where to start, and now nothing comes to mind."

"Start with Micah Cobb," said Daniel. "Start with Selah Voyager, and why she had to die."

Hannah shot her brother a hard look. "It is his story, brother. Let him tell it."

"Don't scold the boy," Liam said. "He has a right."

It stung Daniel hard, to have Liam Kirby take his side; to be called a boy. Hannah put a hand on her brother's good arm and pressed.

"Micah Cobb," Liam said. "He is in hell, where he belongs. Right alongside Ambrose Dye. Where I will join them, no doubt, in short order." He rocked forward and caught his breath.

"You must sleep," Hannah said. "We can finish this conversation later."

"No," said Liam. "I will finish it now, while I have the strength."

Hannah thought of telling him the truth: she had no interest in this story, and in fact she wished it were possible to simply close her ears as she closed her eyes when the light was too bright to bear.

"Why did you kill Cobb?" Daniel asked. "Did it have to do with Selah?"

Liam answered Daniel's questions, but it was Hannah he was looking at. He said, "I would have saved Selah if I could, but it would have given the others away. Your mother and father, and the other runaways."

Daniel's mouth twitched to show his dissatisfaction with Liam's version of events. He would not call Kirby a liar, but he came as close as he dared.

"So you killed Cobb in revenge for Selah?"

"I never said I killed Cobb. I just helped Manny Freeman find him and then stood back and let it happen."

A soft sound escaped Daniel's throat, doubt giving way to sudden understanding. But Liam wasn't finished.

"Later I was sorry I didn't do the job myself. Manny got revenge for his Selah, but I never got that satisfaction." He shot Hannah a sidelong glance. "You know about Jenny. Mrs. Kerr told you the story."

"Yes," Hannah said. "She told me. I'm sorry for your loss."

At that Liam looked almost amused. "Oh, she's not dead. At least she wasn't when I last had word of her. Jenny's up at Grand Banks, her and her sister both. Cobb sold them to a voyageur who set them both to whoring. They took to the work and wanted no other."

There was a long silence while Hannah contemplated the heart of a woman who would leave Liam Kirby to lead such a life. Daniel was flushing, with embarrassment and irritation, Hannah thought; he wanted the talk to go in a different direction, and had little interest in runaway wives.

"That's when you signed on to the navy," Daniel said.

"Aye. And here I am, at the end of a piss pot of a life with nothing to show." He coughed out a rough laugh. "That's my confession, Daniel Bonner. Take it home to Paradise and parcel it out as you please. It'll make some folks happy at least."

Daniel had the good grace to look abashed, but Hannah's attention was on one thing alone.

She said, "But you do have something to show for yourself. You have a daughter by Jemima Kuick. She is a good girl, quick-witted and clever and kind, and she has your coloring and I think she'll have your height as well, when she is finished growing."

Liam was looking at Hannah as if she were speaking a language he did not know. The fever had put high color in his face, and for a moment it seemed to Hannah that she could make out his younger self shimmering just beneath the surface. Liam Kirby as a boy, always laughing, full of mischief, unable to hold a grudge.

He said, "I always wondered. What is she called?"

"Martha."

He made a small sound, opened his mouth to speak and then closed it.

Hannah saw the question he was afraid to ask.

"She knows that you are her father."

He managed a small nod and his gaze shifted from Hannah to Daniel. "You watched her grow up. What can you tell me about her?"

Daniel's jaw flexed, and Hannah knew exactly what he was thinking. Her brother did not wish to like Liam Kirby or to help him, but in the end, Hannah knew, there were things to admire in the man. Daniel would be drawn in. Liam was dying, and it was in her brother's power to give him the only story that could truly comfort him. Daniel was Elizabeth's son, after all, and he would not turn away.

"You there, Walking-Woman." The sergeant-at-arms called to her from across the room, sharp in tone and impatient. "The colonel is asking for you."

"I am coming," Hannah called back. And to her brother: "Don't tire him out with too much talk. You both need your rest."

When she rose she saw that Jennet was waiting at the door, trying to hide her worry, and failing completely.

•   •   •

On the way to the blockhouse, Jennet took Hannah's arm at the elbow and held her back until they were five good steps behind the
sergeant-at-arms. Then she whispered.

"Let me talk," she said. "I have a better chance of getting the best
of the colonel."

That was certainly true, Hannah might have pointed out, as she
had only met the man one time when she first came to the garrison.
Since then all negotiations with him had been handled by Jennet,
who was clearly worried about this unusual summons in the middle
of the day.

Soldiers were drilling on the parade ground, the shouts of ser-
geants and corporals moving them like so many puppets from one
place to the next. Infantry with their muskets, most of them, but
there were other units as well, Hannah could not help but notice:
artillery and even a squad of riflemen in their green coats, Baker rifles slung at precise angles.

An invasion force; the thought stung Hannah suddenly, and she
remembered where she was. Sooner or later these men would
march over the border, and the detritus would find its way back
here.

And still she was glad to be out in the air. The heat felt good on
Hannah's hair and she thought how pleasant it would be to find a
shady spot beneath a tree where she could sleep for a few hours,
away from the stench of blood and sour wounds. She was imagining
this when the guard stopped them at the blockhouse door.

"Mrs. Huntar," he said in a low voice. "Come to join the celebrations?"

"Och, I see. Have the officers been drinking, then, Andy?"

The man winked at her. "Without pause," said the old Scot. "It's
no every day they sink an American ship, ye ken."

On the narrow stair Hannah asked, "Why would they send for
me?"

"I'm not sure," Jennet said, taking her cousin's elbow once more.
"But stay close."

The room stank like a tavern. Tobacco and spilled liquor and vomit.
Except Hannah could not imagine any alehouse as finely furnished
as this one: heavy wooden chairs and tables, silver, crystal, all polished to a gleaming radiance. Paintings on the walls, all religious or

military in their subject matter. A stone carving of the Madonna in one corner.

And three officers sitting around the table in the middle of the room, with Colonel Caudebec at their head. Hannah did not recognize any of them, though Jennet would know them. The table, covered by a stained velvet cloth, was crowded with cups and bottles and a great platter of meat and bread. Hannah's stomach rumbled gently and she tried to remember the last time she had taken any food.

"Here you are!" called the colonel. "Here you are! Come in then, come in. Reed, what are you waiting for, man, the lady needs a chair!"

A servant came toward them and greeted Jennet with a bow. For Hannah there was nothing but a flick of the eyes.

Jennet's hand tightened on Hannah's arm.

"Thank you kindly," she said. "But we canna stay, Colonel. There's a great deal of work waiting for us in the stockade."

Such a simple statement, and yet the officers found it amusing. They laughed in the way of men deep in their cups, loudly and without reserve.

"Never mind about them," said the colonel, a hint of irritation in his voice. "They won't be your concern much longer."

"I'm afraid we must away, sir," Jennet said, in her best, most polite voice, the one that meant she had a tenuous hold on her temper. Two things occurred to Hannah: from the look on the colonel's face he did not suffer refusals with good grace, and more important, he had just let something slip she could not ignore.

"What do you mean, they won't be our concern?" Hannah heard herself ask the question and saw the effect it had, all good humor leaving the faces around the table, draining away to be replaced by surprise and disapproval.

"You speak English," said Caudebec.

Hannah calmed her expression. "Why, yes, sir."

"So you understood the orders brought to you yesterday, but chose to ignore them in your wisdom."

"Colonel—" began Jennet, but he shot her such a stern look that Jennet's voice died away.

He leaned forward. "Madam Indian, did I not send orders for you to report to the surgeons in the hospital? Did I not send those orders yesterday *evening*?"

Hannah folded her hands in front of herself. "You did, sir."

"And did you ignore those orders?"

"No, sir."

His shoulders rolled forward. "You did report to the hospital?"

"No, sir."

"Then you disobeyed my orders!"

"No, sir. I told the sergeant I would go to the hospital as soon as the wounded prisoners were tended to."

"Aha! And did you do that?"

"When I am finished with the wounded prisoners, I shall. Of course. But your men did their job very well, sir, and the Americans suffered for it."

It was a fine bit of footwork that Hannah had learned over the years: a weak man is easily distracted by a compliment, and a drunk man was a weak man.

"To victory!" proposed a young lieutenant, his cup raised up.

The colonel ignored him, and the cup wobbled its way back to the table.

"You are insolent as well as disobedient," said the colonel, and Hannah saw that he was not quite so drunk as she had supposed at first.

"If I may ask," Jennet began gently. "You said something about the prisoners?"

The colonel held his hand out and snapped his fingers. His secretary looked down at a bit of paper peeking out from his jacket, fixing on it owlishly as if it were some odd new appendage, and then he began to tug at it. When he finally had freed it, he put it into the colonel's waiting hand.

"For my own part, I'd just as soon drown every one of the damn traitors like puppies," he said. "But Montgomery has other ideas." His eyes moved down the paper and he began to read.

A rushing began in Hannah's ears, so loud that she wondered at first if she might faint. It was only Jennet's firm grip on her arm that kept her knees from buckling. She pressed a nail into the thin flesh between thumb and first finger until her vision and her hearing both cleared.

". . . surely not the wounded," her cousin was saying.

"Every one of them," said the colonel. "In a few days they'll be on their way to Halifax and out of my sight. And you, Mrs. Huntar—" He managed a small jerk of a smile. "Father O'Neill has arranged a place for you among the Grey Nuns in Montreal, as you

asked him to. A widow without resources who refuses to re-
marry"—he cleared his throat roughly—"can hope for no better."

For once Jennet seemed to be speechless, though her fingers
tightened on Hannah's arm convulsively. The colonel didn't seem
to notice her distress, and turned his attention to Hannah.

"As for you," he said. "You'll stay here and report to the bloody
hospital. To scrub floors, if that's what the surgeons want of you.
Do you hear?"

Hannah managed a nod, though her mind was racing, moving
from question to question, all of them crucially important, none of
them she could put into words. Underneath all that a sentence was
repeating itself: *Away from here, away, away from here. You must get them
away from here.*

"You are dismissed," said the colonel. "Mrs. Huntar, remove
your pet Indian from my sight."

There was, indeed, a great deal of work to be done among the
wounded in the stockade, but without discussion Jennet and
Hannah walked back to the followers' camp. Once out of the garrison gates and out of the guards' earshot, Hannah paused.

"What was all that about marriage? Caudebec asked you to
marry him?"

"No!" Jennet said. "Don't be ridiculous. Colonel Caudebec
never said a word to me of marriage. Unless—" She paused, her
mouth pressed hard together. "Unless he sent the offer through the
priest."

"Who never related it."

Jennet shook her head. "Nor did we ever speak of the Grey
Nuns."

"Luke was right about O'Neill then," Hannah said. "But what is
he up to?"

Jennet let out a strangled giggle. "Perhaps the Grey Nuns pay
him a bounty for every novitiate he delivers."

"You make jokes even now," Hannah said, with more affection
than frustration.

The guards were watching them, and so they moved on, more
slowly.

Hannah said, "We must get word to Luke." It was what they
were both thinking, but it was good to hear the words.

"He has a plan," Jennet said. "I was supposed to talk to you about it, but the battle—" She broke off and drew in a hitching breath. "And there is other news, I was waiting for the right moment."

"Not now," said Hannah. "Now we have to find my uncle. He will have to leave for Montreal straightaway."

But there was no sign of Runs-from-Bears or Sawatis when they reached the cluster of shacks that had been their home for the summer. Deflated, the two women sank down on their straw-filled pallets and looked at the cold fire pit. One of them would have to go looking for Bears, but for the moment they could do nothing but catch their breath and try to order their thoughts.

Finally Hannah looked up. "Is there bad news from Paradise?"

"Oh, no," said Jennet with a half-smile. "Just the opposite. Your sister and Simon Ballentyne are married. Or they must be, by now. I thought Daniel should have the news from you, you understand."

She reached under her blanket and took out the letters Luke had brought less than a full day ago.

"I haven't read it," Jennet added. "What I know I have from Luke."

Hannah took the letter written in her stepmother's hand and broke the seal. Her voice cracked a little as she began to read aloud.

Dear Children, dear Niece,
Hannah and the twins must recall how every January while they were young we spent a week or so reading *Hamlet* in front of the hearth after supper. Dear Curiosity would join us, because no matter how many times she heard the play read aloud she was always finding something new in it to mystify or delight her.

The raising of children is a little like reading the same play or book over and over again. If it is a well-written work, it may seem very familiar but still every turn of the page brings surprises with it.

Our Lily is to marry Simon Ballentyne next Sunday. When they return to Montreal in the late summer or fall, they will be married again in the Catholic church, to fulfill Simon's obligation to his own upbringing and family. When the war is finished, and as soon as Simon's business obligations permit, they will travel to Europe for six months or a year, so that Lily can study for a short while at least. Then they will return to Montreal where they will make their home.

They arrived at this compromise after much discussion and consultation, and I am satisfied that it is sensible and solid. They have our blessing, your father's and mine, and Curiosity's as well, and the approval of the village. The one unfortunate and notable exception is Reverend Stiles, who daily preaches in the open air on the sins of the flesh. He stops just short of accusing your sister directly, but not much short. Your father holds his temper admirably, but how long Simon may do the same, I cannot say.

Because so many of our family are gone, Lily does not want a wedding party. More than that, a wedding party without cousin Jennet seems to her unjust, for it was Jennet who first brought Simon Ballentyne to her attention. Gabriel, who is sullen and unhappy at the need for any wedding at all, for once does not seem to mind the lack of a party. And yet, in the end I think we will convince them both that you who cannot be here would not deny her the pleasure of such a celebration.

To this happiest of news I add more: Almanzo Freeman is returned home to his mother and family. We know little as yet of what kept him away so long or the troubles he must have endured. In time, perhaps, he will be more able to talk of those lost years, but for now we are satisfied to see him every day in improving health and spirits.

I write this news of Manny knowing that it will be of particular import to our Hannah and must even cause her some pain. Thus, with this letter I enclose another, written by Manny for Hannah's eyes alone. No one knows what it contains except Manny himself, and thus it shall remain, forever, unless Hannah should decide one day to share the story he has to tell.

For our Daniel there is also a letter from his beloved sister. Even in his current extremity we believe there will be some small measure of relief and joy in the words she writes to him alone, and more, that he will find it in himself to welcome Simon into our family with all the generosity of spirit that we know he has in his power to bestow.

With all our love and good wishes for improved health and a quick and safe homecoming, I remain your devoted mother, stepmother, and aunt

Elizabeth Middleton Bonner

There was a long moment's silence when the last words had faded away. Jennet watched her cousin closely, examining her expression for some sign of what she was feeling and thinking.

In her lap was the second letter, written in an unpracticed but strong hand. Hannah touched it with one finger, traced the letters of her own name once and then again. There was a fierceness about her now, the same concentration that came over her when she picked up a scalpel and made ready to cut into living flesh.

Then she rose from her pallet with the letter in her hand. With a flick of the wrist she sent it flying so that it landed among the ashes in the cold fire, and then she turned toward the door.

"I'm going to find my uncle," she said. "Are you coming along?"

Chapter 38

Up to her elbows in soapy water, sweat-soaked in the heat, Lily looked up from the floor she was scrubbing to Curiosity, who stood on a stool, her arms full of curtains.

"Hope you got some sweet talk ready," Curiosity mumbled around the pins in her mouth. "Here come Simon, and he don't look pleased."

Lily sat back on her heels and wiped the hair out of her face. There was a slight breeze coming up from the lake, and the idea came to her, odd but very appealing, of simply dashing down the path and jumping into the water. Along the way she could shed her clothes and loosen her hair, she thought. After all, if the villagers got such pleasure out of gossiping about her, she might as well give them something at least halfway true to talk about.

Then Simon was at the open door, blocking the light and the breeze.

"Is it so?" he asked shortly. "Have you put off the wedding again?"

"Just a week," Lily said, gathering her skirts and hoisting herself up. He stepped forward to take her by the elbow and lifted her effortlessly.

"So that the cabin will be ready," she finished, and found herself almost nose to nose with the man she was supposed to have married ten days ago.

"The cabin," he said.

She pulled her arm away and blew a hair out of her eyes. "Yes, Simon, the cabin. This cabin. Our home. You don't want to move into a pigsty, do you?"

His mouth twitched, whether in preparation for laughter or shouting, Lily wasn't quite sure. He was frustrated, that much she could see.

At the window Curiosity said, "You two got a lifetime ahead of you for arguing and making up too. Right now I need help. Come on over here, Simon, and give me a hand with these ornery curtains."

The cabin was two small rooms in a clearing, no space even for a decent kitchen garden, which was why nobody had showed any interest in it in the years since Jack MacGregor had died. But Lily liked the way it sat on a little hill looking over the lake. She liked the fact that the sun filled the larger room for most of the morning. And most of all she liked that it was only ten minutes' walk to the village and the meetinghouse; that was worth a great deal.

Simon had agreed that the cabin was well situated and would suit, and he helped cheerfully enough, cleaning out the well and carrying water and digging a trench for the necessary. With a little wheedling Lily had even got him to make her new shelves and a number of other small things that tried his patience but pleased her mightily.

Curiosity ordered him about too, but he didn't seem to mind. He did his best for her, but he talked while he worked and asked the questions Lily had answered before and must answer again: did it really take so long to get the bed linens in order, and why it was that pewter had to come from Johnstown, and was it sensible for Lily to be asking for a new stove when she didn't much like cooking, after all, and more than that, why were they going to so much trouble to furnish a cabin where they would live for less than a year?

Another woman might have been frustrated, but Simon's questions pleased Lily, just as it pleased her to look at him. There was sawdust in his hair and eyebrows and his beard shadow was dark though it was hardly midday, and when he looked at her there was a burning in his eyes, an impatience barely held in check. Once she had thought him rather plain, something that confused her and amused her, too, that she had been so willfully blind.

"What you really asking," Curiosity said when Simon had run out of questions. "Is whether our Lily got cold feet. You worried about her running out on you." Curiosity shook her head at both of them as though they were unruly children. Before Lily could say anything, Curiosity waved a hand to stop her.

"I'ma go home and see if those girls got dinner on the table yet. You stay here and tell the man what he want to hear, child. I don't know about young people these days, I truly do not."

There was a short silence between them after Curiosity had disappeared down the steps with her basket over her arm, and then Simon cleared his throat.

"Well?"

Lily crossed the room to him in five quick steps. "Of course I'm not going to change my mind. Would I be spending all my time making this cabin into a home for us if I planned to run off?"

She put a hand on his arm and felt the pulse jumping there. It was a shameful thing, but she took considerable pleasure in the discomfort he didn't quite manage to hide.

"You're stuck with me now, Simon Ballentyne," she said. "Like it or not."

That earned her the smile she wanted, the one that flashed his dimples and made his face come alive. She pushed the dark hair away from his face and he caught her hand, turned its palm to his mouth and kissed it. They might have done more—a shiver ran up Lily's back at the things he suggested, his mouth against her ear—but it was dinnertime, and her stomach rumbled loud enough for him to hear it.

On the way home for dinner Simon had his own news to share: Anna McGarrity had promised them a rooster and three hens as a wedding present, and he had come to an agreement with the Cunninghams: Simon would build them a new shed in return for his second-best milch cow.

"Your friends are doing their level best to keep us here," he said finally. "Though I can't understand why."

She poked him then, hard, in the ribs, and he yelped and jumped out of her reach.

"You ungrateful wretch," he said in a conversational tone. "And here was I, planning to put in your new stove tomorrow."

"How peculiar, that the idea of a new stove should give me gooseflesh," Lily said. "Who would have thought I'd take to housekeeping?"

He came closer and nudged her with his hip. "If that's all it takes to give you goose bumps, girl—"

"Stop," she said, swerving away. "Not ten minutes ago we agreed that we can't be late for dinner again. My mother's patience is not endless. Keep your hands to yourself, and tell me about the schoolhouse."

She saw straightaway that it was the wrong subject to raise. It made Simon think of less pleasant things, and now that he had turned his mind in that direction she would have the devil's own time turning it back again.

"He was at it again today," Simon said.

Lily needn't ask for details. The Reverend Stiles continued to preach every day in the very middle of the village, sometimes for more than an hour, and, it seemed to Lily, always on the same topic. Since she had stopped working at the meetinghouse in the mornings while she was busy at the cabin, she had only heard about these sermons.

"If it does not bother me, Simon . . ." she began, and then her voice trailed away at the look he shot her.

They walked in silence for a while through grass ripe for haying, alive with grasshoppers and small darting animals desperate to find new cover.

Finally Lily said, "I have lived all my life in this village. People here know me, Simon. He can say what he likes, they won't believe him."

"He's calling you a whore." Simon's voice went hoarse and broke.

At that Lily must pause. "By name? He called me a whore by name?"

"All but," Simon muttered. "It's aye clear who he's talking about."

"Promise me something," Lily said suddenly, stopping to turn to him and put her hands on his upper arms. "Promise me you won't let Stiles get the best of you. Don't raise a hand to him, Simon. Promise me."

His mouth was set hard, and lines appeared at the corners of his eyes, as if he were looking at something that did not please him. This was one of the times when Lily saw how much like her father Simon Ballentyne really was: he would not be led, not even by her, when what she wanted went against his best judgment.

"I could promise you the moon and stars if you ask me, Lily Bonner, and what would that mean? What's in my power to give, that you'll have."

For the rest of the walk they said nothing at all. Now and then Lily sent him a sidelong glance and saw how lost he was in his thoughts. Just before they reached home, he turned to her.

He said, "The very least I must do is discuss it with your father."

"Get on with it then," Lily said. "He's standing at the door there waiting for you."

Nathaniel saw straight off that Simon had things to talk about, but he knew that Elizabeth would not allow such a discussion at her dinner table.

He had been watching his wife closely for the last weeks and had finally convinced himself that Curiosity was right: she was healthier than any woman her age carrying for the seventh time had any right to be. So he settled in for the stormy months, battened down and rode out her moods.

Now they ate cold chicken and new beans and lettuce from the kitchen garden while they spoke of the things she approved, and nothing else. She asked some questions about Lily's morning and what there was left to do at the old MacGregor cabin.

"We've got to stop calling it that," Lily said.

"What would you call it, then?" Simon asked her, one brow arching, which meant he was in a teasing mood and would wind her up if given half a chance.

Elizabeth put a stop to that, though a little reluctantly. She said, "In the village they call it the Ballentyne place."

"Already?" Lily asked.

"You sound displeased, daughter," Nathaniel observed. "Did you want it to be known by your name?"

"Well, no," Lily said. "I suppose not."

"It takes some getting used to, I suppose," Nathaniel said. "Giving up one name for another."

Simon was watching Lily closely, not with worry or displeasure, but as he might watch a deer he was tracking to learn more about her habits. Elizabeth saw this with some satisfaction. She had the idea that he was the kind of man who knew better than to try to herd Lily where she wasn't yet ready to go.

Then talk turned to the schoolhouse, which was pretty much done; Nathaniel had to give Ballentyne credit for good work done fast and clean. There was some back-and-forth about the fieldstone for the chimneys and going to Johnstown for the window glass. For

all her early misgivings, Elizabeth was pleased with the new building, and to Nathaniel's satisfaction, she had even regained some of
her old spark when she talked about the next school year, and the
hiring of a teacher.

The Wednesday post had brought three more application letters
in response to the advertisement she had sent to the Albany and
Manhattan papers.

"The long and short of it is," Nathaniel finished up for her, "not
one of the three suits your mother." He gave Lily a little jab with his
elbow, and winked at her. It was an old family joke, her mother's
dissatisfaction with other teachers.

Elizabeth flushed a little but held up her chin. "Would you have
less than the best possible teacher for the children of Paradise?"

"You know I wouldn't, Boots," Nathaniel said. "But I got this
feeling you're talking yourself clean out of hiring anybody at all."

Elizabeth's mouth twitched, but she wouldn't rise to the teasing,
not just now.

"That is not true. I will write again to Will and ask about gradu-
ates from the African Free School."

"Cousin Will Spencer," Lily said to Simon. "He's a trustee at the
school, in Manhattan."

Lily was in the habit of helping Simon through family discussions by
throwing him bits of information. That more than anything else made
it clear to Nathaniel that she meant to go ahead and marry the man.

Ballentyne knew how to listen and keep his thoughts to himself,
but this time something passed over his face, a question that was easy
enough to read. Elizabeth caught it as neatly as a tossed apple.

"You disapprove, Simon?"

Ballentyne met her gaze directly. "No," he said shortly. "I don't
disapprove. But I imagine it won't be easy, bringing in a black
schoolteacher."

Nathaniel watched his wife with equal parts wariness and curiosity. Elizabeth was studying Ballentyne from across the table, the
small vertical line between her brows very pronounced. He knew
what that meant, but Ballentyne might not understand, just yet,
what he had let himself in for.

"Simon," Elizabeth said on an indrawn breath. "I hope you are
not the kind of man to run from a challenge."

He gave her an easy grin. "I'm to marry your daughter, am I no?"

Nathaniel had to bite back a smile, and even Elizabeth could not
help but nod in concession.

"You think the people of Paradise will not like such a person as a teacher?" Her tone had shifted a little.

"Of course they won't, Ma," Lily said. "Why pretend otherwise? If you want to hire somebody from the Free School, you're going to have a fight on your hands. Why not just hire Manny, at least he'll have a chance."

At the look on Elizabeth's face—surprise, revelation, and a good dose of irritation at her own witlessness—Nathaniel had to laugh. "There you go, Boots," he said. "Problem solved, and cleverly."

Elizabeth's mouth shut with a click. "I must admit, it certainly should have occurred to me. Manny graduated from the Free School, after all. I wonder that Curiosity never raised the topic."

"Maybe Curiosity is more worried about the trouble it will cause than you are," Lily suggested.

But Elizabeth either did not hear this very reasonable suggestion, or discounted it out of hand. She put fork down and rose from the table with a distracted air.

"Sit down, Boots," Nathaniel said. "You can go talk to Curiosity and Manny after dinner. Another hour ain't going to make any difference, and there's another problem we got to put our minds to. With any luck we can solve it just as quick."

Nathaniel saw Lily's back go very straight; she knew what it was, then, and so did Ballentyne, by the look on his face.

"What is it, Nathaniel?" Elizabeth asked, one hand on the swelling at her waist.

"It's the Reverend Stiles," Ballentyne answered for him. "Isn't that so?"

"It is," Nathaniel said. "Jed came to talk to me about it today. Stiles has got a nasty way with words, and he gets worse every day."

"The Bill of Rights is very clear about free speech, Nathaniel," Elizabeth said primly. It was her schoolmistress voice, and Nathaniel knew what was coming.

"The more attention you pay to the man, the happier he will be. Ignore him, and he will tire of his campaign soon enough."

"Have you heard his preaching lately?" Ballentyne asked, his tone sharp enough to earn him one of Elizabeth's severest looks.

"I would not give him the pleasure," she said coldly.

"I am glad to know it," Ballentyne said. "For it would pain you to hear the things he's saying about Lily."

Elizabeth's mouth twitched, but before she could speak, Nathaniel cut in. "Don't ask him to repeat it, Boots. I wouldn't let him even if he cared to say the words out loud."

Lily put down her cup with a sharp sound. "And do I have anything to say about this?"

Elizabeth's expression cleared. "Of course you do. Would you like your father and your bridegroom to avenge your good name, Lily? Would tar and feathers be a suitable punishment, or do you have something else in mind?"

"For Christ's sake, Boots," Nathaniel said, pushing out a sigh. "All I'm going to do is talk to the man. Weren't you just telling us about free speech being protected by the Constitution?"

She closed her eyes briefly and then opened them again, and managed a small smile. "I was. Very well, if Lily agrees I shan't object. The two of you go off to see what sense you can talk to the Reverend Stiles. I wish you an entertaining afternoon of it."

"Lily?"

His daughter looked at him as if he were a child asking for another piece of pie he didn't need and shouldn't have. A strange thing, to have the girl grow up on him while his back was turned, but there it was.

Finally she nodded. "You won't be happy until you do, so go talk to him. Do try to come up with something less extreme than relieving him of his offending tongue."

Nathaniel caught Ballentyne's gaze and wondered if Lily realized that he was capable of that, and more.

He said, "Between us I'll wager we can come up with something a sight less messy."

They found Stiles finishing his own dinner of cabbage and bread, alone at the table. No sign of young Justus Rising, and Nathaniel wasn't sure how to feel about that. On the one hand he thought the boy needed to hear what he had to say, and on the other he had the sense it wouldn't do any good. Justus Rising reminded him of a half-witted dog, just sly enough to keep himself fed and quick to use his teeth. The kind that couldn't be taught because he didn't care to learn.

The cabin was dim and smelled strongly of sour clothes and sweat. It struck Nathaniel as odd, given the fact that Stiles was supposed to have such a good sense of smell, but then some men were partial to their own stink.

They went out on the porch to talk, where there was a fine view of the apple orchards. The trees were heavy with green fruit. It was a pretty spot, the orchard, built up out of hard work and dreams: Nicholas Wilde had wanted to come up with the perfect apple, not for pressing, but for eating. The villagers had laughed at him and then learned not to laugh; he had earned their respect over the years. And then Jemima Southern had come along. Nathaniel thought of the day he had gone into the bush to find Nicholas, and then he pushed the pictures away.

On the horizon a good summer storm was working itself up, fists of dark cloud punching closer.

"Thunder before the afternoon is done," said Stiles. "Hail too."

Nathaniel started to have his thoughts read so easily, and then he settled his face; he wouldn't let the man spook him so easy.

"Thunder at twilight," he agreed. "Doesn't bode well."

Stiles made an agreeable sound in his throat. "Did you two gentlemen come to talk to me about the weather?"

"You know why we're here," Ballentyne said, not a man to dance around the matter at hand.

Stiles blinked once and again. "I expect I do."

"Listen then, and listen close," Nathaniel said. He scratched his jaw thoughtfully while he considered his words.

"You're new here, so let me make something clear you most probably don't know. My father and my grandfather and his people before him were hunting these mountains a hundred years ago and more. We've always been here, and we ain't going nowhere. That's the first thing."

He paused. There was no reaction at all from Stiles, so he went on.

"We survived every kind of sickness over the years, more wars than I care to think about, settlers coming and going, fortune hunters of every stripe. They've tried to starve us out and burn us out and frighten us away. We're still here. We're staying right here. That's the second thing."

Ballentyne stood quietly, all his muscles tensed, his eyes alive: ready to move, ready for battle. He had been trained well at Carryck, and Nathaniel was glad to have him along.

"Do go on," Stiles said.

"Last thing. We protect our own, and we don't tolerate anybody coming after our women and children. I'll admit it's been some years since we had cause to remind folks of that fact, but make no mistake, Mr. Stiles. You'll stop bad-mouthing my daughter or I'll show you just what I mean."

Stiles crossed his arms on his chest and rocked forward, his head canted sharp to the right as if he were thinking through a difficult puzzle.

"You object to the truth being spoken plain, then."

Ballentyne moved, just an inch, but Nathaniel held up a hand to stop him.

"Your version of the truth."

Stiles rocked a little more. "My truth comes from the good book. From the word of God. Your daughter is—"

"I'd advise you to stop just there," Ballentyne said, stepping up close. "Keep your version of the truth to yourself. And you'll keep a civil tongue in your head or I'll feed it to the dogs."

Nathaniel had to admire Ballentyne's tone, no bluster in him at all, and no mistaking that he meant every word. Except that Stiles didn't seem overly concerned.

After a moment Stiles said, "Perhaps I did make a mistake. Paradise may not be the God-fearing place I was told it would be."

There were many things Nathaniel might have said to that, but he wasn't about to bring up the topic of Jemima Southern.

"Get out then. Sell the orchard and get out."

And he saw, just then, that he had misjudged the man and mistook his game. Something small and satisfied flickered in Stiles's expression, and then was gone, banished. But Nathaniel knew what he was going to say.

"Very well, I am willing to sell you the farm and orchards for four hundred dollars. In silver."

Ballentyne coughed a laugh, but there was nothing amused about it at all. "Silver," he echoed.

"In time of war." Stiles spread his hands out in front of him. "Paper money is less than dependable."

"You bloody bastard," Ballentyne said. "You thieving, no-good, backhanded—"

Nathaniel held up a finger to stop him. "That's twice what you paid for this place."

"Is it?" Stiles rocked on his heels, his hands clasped behind his back. "Why, yes, now that you mention it. I believe that's true."

At that Nathaniel laughed. "You had just about everybody fooled, I'll give you that."

"Gentlemen," said Stiles slowly, looking hard at Nathaniel and then at Simon. "I see you are not interested in the transaction I propose. If you'll pardon me, I must finish my notes on tomorrow's sermon."

With a little bow he turned away from them and disappeared back into the shadows.

"Well, goddamn the man," said Nathaniel, mostly to himself.

Ballentyne grunted. "That's a job we'll have to handle on our own."

While she did her chores and did them well and without complaint, Lily had always disliked housework. To her surprise she found that it wasn't quite so boring now that it was her own place she was looking after. There was a certain satisfaction in the progress she made, day by day.

My own home, she said sometimes when something particularly nasty had to be scraped off the floor. *Mine and Simon's.* All the things she had been sure she did not want: a husband, a cabin in Paradise, and now she could hardly keep from smiling.

And as soon as the war was over, they would go away. She would hold him to that promise, and herself too. But for now there were two rooms she would set to rights, and when they were weary of traveling, weary of Canada, they would have this place to come back to.

The first task Simon had taken on was the repair of the roof, and then he had cleaned the chimney and hearth, so that the storm that had come on so quick and fierce did not stop Lily from her afternoon's task, scrubbing down the cupboards that stood to either side of the hearth. Which meant she must first empty them out, no small thing at all, for it seemed that Jack MacGregor had been the kind of man who was loath to throw away even the smallest, most inconsequential bit of string.

Lily found muslin bags full of curled bits of stiffened fur and scraps of deer hide, a great tin of arrowheads that would please Gabriel, dusty piles of newspaper clippings that crumbled at a touch, a bundle of letters tied with string that she put aside to ask her mother about, bits of crockery, and tucked behind a bundle of rags, three perfect teacups and saucers of such translucent delicacy that she was almost afraid to touch them.

For a good while Lily studied a cup, holding it in her hands as she would an egg. The firelight played on the rich glazing and made the pattern of flowers and vines seem to glow, and for the life of her she could not imagine why Jack MacGregor, who had been a dour old trapper with no family and no friends, had kept such a treasure for himself. There was a story here, certainly. Curiosity was coming by this afternoon with linen, maybe she would know what to make of it.

Behind Lily the door opened with a squeak—the hinges still needed oiling, she kept forgetting to mention it to Simon—and she turned to show Curiosity the cup she held in her hands.

Justus Rising closed the door behind himself before Lily could quite collect her thoughts. He was dripping wet and his face was charged with high color. His eyes shone in the light of the candles she had lit against the darkening of the storm. They were red rimmed and Lily was reminded of a possum, a slow animal that could lash out quite unexpectedly when cornered.

She said, "Go away, Justus," but the sound of her voice was lost in a lazy roll of thunder. Lily stood and put the cup down carefully on the table on its saucer. When the thunder had stopped she cleared her throat.

"Justus, leave here immediately. You are not welcome."

The boy said nothing at all; he was all burning blue eyes and a gaping mouth. He came forward slowly then he held out a fist and uncurled his fingers. A half-dozen small coins rattled onto the table.

"Is that enough?"

Lily stepped backward and bumped into the cupboard. She might have asked him, *Enough for what,* or *What do you mean,* but she saw exactly what he wanted.

It was odd, how her mind could do so many things at once. One part of her was so shocked that she might have just let her knees fold beneath her. To be propositioned thus by a boy, by the preacher's nephew, it was beyond her mind's ability to cope. She wasn't angry, not quite yet, but it sat there like a stone in her belly, ready to be vomited up.

He's calling you a whore. Simon's voice came to her then, and she realized that she should have taken what he had to say more seriously. And where was Simon? She glanced at the window and saw only rain.

"He won't bother us just now," said Justus Rising. "He's at the trading post talking to Jed McGarrity."

"Go away," Lily said mechanically. Her voice cracked, and she cleared her throat again. "Go away immediately."

"My money ain't good enough for you?" His high color had begun to fade but it came back in a rush. "How much did the nigger give you?"

No weapons within reach, none except her own mind. Lily

forced her thoughts to order themselves, composed her face, and summoned up her mother's spirit.

"Justus Rising," she said. "You have insulted me in the worst way possible. Take your money and leave here, and I will not tell my father about this."

"Oh, like it's any surprise to him, that you spread your legs for coin." The boy wiped his dripping nose with the back of his hand and spat into the corner. "I expect he was your first customer. Wouldn't that be the way, him half savage like he is? Don't play innocent with me, not with me, missy. I seen you in the woods, with that great Scot. He had you pinned to a tree with your legs wrapped around him, and he was riding you right rough, though I'll admit you looked to be enjoying it."

And then the boy simply launched himself across the table, as if he were some kind of great cat dropping out of a tree. Lily moved fast, but not quite fast enough; he got her by the hair and yanked so hard that roaring pain wiped out everything else in the world.

The candles went out in the tumble and for a moment there was only the roiling dark of the storm. Then a flash of lightning filled the room in a tripling pulse, and in that bone-white light the boy's face looked like a skull.

He was grinning, a wide, panting grin, and he wrapped his hand and arm more firmly in her hair, pulled her head up to him and tried to press a wet kiss to her mouth. Still stunned, Lily managed to turn her head only a little, and felt his lips on her jaw like leeches.

He grunted at that, dissatisfied, and grunted again when she managed to use her elbow on him. While he wrapped her hair around his arm more firmly he used his free hand to sweep the table clear.

That sound roused her from her stupor. Lily used her arms and her legs as best she could; she twisted and bucked and screamed, once and then again, while he pinned her to the table with his body.

The lightning showed her his expression, resolute. Nothing much there, no anger, no lust: a workman thinking through a problem. That scared her most of all, and Lily screamed again.

Justus Rising made a shushing sound, as if she were a troublesome child and not a grown woman, about to be married. With a yank he pulled her down the table so that her legs hung off the far edge.

"I'll get a better hold on you like this," he said. "Ride some of the rough off you."

"Simon Ballentyne will kill you." Her voice came in a harsh whisper.

He hummed agreement. "If he can catch me." Then he hooked a dirty rag from the mess on the floor and stuffed it into her mouth.

"Rutting and talking don't go together," he said. "Though I wouldn't mind a little moaning now and then, you want to urge me on."

I am fighting for my life. The thought came to her, quick and clean, and with it anger roared up out of her and Lily rose up against him with every bit of strength she had.

The boy grunted once and then again and then frowned at her in the flickering lightning, pressed his arm across her throat.

"Stop," he said. His tone a little breathless but utterly reasonable. "Stop fighting and maybe you'll like it. I'm not as big as your Scot but I'm no mean portion either."

She coughed around the dirty rag and began to choke, the taste of lye soap making her gorge rise. He watched her choking and then seemed to come to a decision. With his free hand he pulled out the rag.

"You see," he said. "I'm no monster."

She spat in his face and saw all the good humor run out of his expression. Had time to think, *Oh, no,* and then his fist had buried itself in her gut and the pain took her down. He lifted her head and slammed it down against the table so hard that she almost lost consciousness.

Don't let him get the best of you. She heard Daniel's voice now, and closed her eyes and wished for him, for her father, for anyone at all, but she was alone and so she did what she could; she arched her back and hoped to push the boy off her long enough to catch her breath.

But Justus Rising was well grown and strong and he shook her like a puppy.

Don't let him. Sister, don't.

Her brother's voice did something for Lily, spurred her flagging strength and she arched up and managed to dislodge the boy—he was distracted by his fumbling at his breech buttons—long enough to slam her fist into his ear.

The boy grunted. "If that's the way you want it." He was reaching under her skirts, and Lily lifted her head to snap at him, her teeth grazing the skin of his cheek, and saw what he looked like when a real anger came over him: like the devil himself.

"No!" she screamed into his face, her own anger roiling up out of her to match his. "No!"

Another crash of thunder, this one loud enough to wake the

dead. The boy blinked, his expression shifting suddenly from determination to surprise, and then he collapsed forward, his whole weight on Lily until she bucked once more and he rolled off to crash to the floor.

Martha Kuick stood there, both hands wrapped around a length of firewood, her eyes wide and wild with fright and anger and a deep, abiding satisfaction. Behind her was Callie Wilde, a shovel in her hands, and then Curiosity appeared in the door. She pushed her way into the room, stepped over a broken chair, and put her arms around Lily, who had rolled herself from the table to stand, retching, at the hearth.

Over her shoulder she said, "Did you kill him, child?"

Martha was crouched on the floor next to the still form of the boy.

"No, ma'am, he's still breathing."

"Too bad," Curiosity said. She patted Lily's back while she retched.

"Callie, see if you can find the candles and get 'em lit. A fire would be a good thing just now too. And some water for Lily. I wish I had some of Axel's schnapps left over, I surely do."

Lily wanted to talk, but breathing was taking all of her concentration and energy. Under Curiosity's stroking hands she felt her body begin to quiet, the rushing of her blood ebbing slowly. She began to shake.

"That's right," Curiosity said. "You breathe deep, now. You safe, girl. I got you."

"Should I fetch Jed McGarrity?" Martha asked.

"Simon," Lily managed to say. "My father."

"I know you'd like to have your menfolk just now, and your mama too," Curiosity said evenly. "But let's think this thing through before we go running off half-cocked."

A candle came to life, and then another. At their feet Justus Rising groaned and twitched. Curiosity looked down at him thoughtfully.

"First of all we got to get us some stout rope," she said. "And then I want you girls to go fetch the Reverend Mr. Stiles. Invite him over here to do some preaching. I'm in the mood for a little fire and brimstone, myself."

An hour later Callie and Martha, carefully instructed on exactly what to say, left the cabin. The storm had passed and the late summer afternoon was all shining green and damp gold, but even sitting in the sun Lily could not stop shaking.

She listened to Curiosity talking. Curiosity had an especially deep voice for a woman, and old age had added an edge to it, a crackling like walking through leaves in the fall. Everything about her voice was a comfort, but the words themselves made little sense to Lily. Something about Mr. Stiles and money and the orchard, and the things he had said when he had been confronted by Simon and Lily's father.

There was a cup of tea in her hands, sweetened with honey and milk. Lily took another sip and felt it settle in her belly, closed her eyes in the sunlight and saw Justus Rising's smile. She started and the cup sloshed in her hands, but Curiosity was there and she reached in quickly.

"No harm done," she said firmly. Her hand settled on Lily's arm and pressed. "You listen to me, Lily. No harm done. He shook you up bad, but we got there in time."

"Just in time," Lily said.

"Listen to me," Curiosity said, more firmly. "You got a choice now. You can let yourself get caught up in what might have happened or you can use this. You got the power now. If you get it in your head to waste the opportunity, why, you can say the word and your menfolk will teach that boy a lesson he won't never forget. But then he'll be here still, every day, for you to see. No, Lily, you got to pull yourself together and think. The boy was trying to take something from you, but what he did was, he gave you the power. You going to throw that away?"

Don't let him.

What? she wanted to ask her brother. More than anyone else, she wanted her brother just now. *Don't let him do what? Control me? Hurt me? Take something away?*

She lifted her face to the sunshine and listened. After a while she said, "Tell me then. Tell me what it is we have to do."

They left the room as it was, though it bothered Lily greatly. While they waited, she looked for the shards of the china cups and saucers, putting every little bit she found into a careful pile. In a bucket full of water she found one of the cups, whole and unharmed. It seemed to her a miracle, and it loosed the tears that had been hovering just out of reach. Curiosity handed her a handkerchief and let her get on with it.

"Now look at this," Curiosity said, turning the china cup in her long fingers. "I don't think I ever seen anything so pretty in my life. Look at the way it takes up the light. Do you suppose someplace there's folks who drink out of cups like this one, regular like?"

"I think there must be," Lily agreed, her voice still shaking. "Though it's hard to imagine."

Curiosity made a humming sound deep in her throat. "I expect you'll see all kind of strange things when you go traveling the world. And you'll put it all down on paper, won't you, and we'll sit here looking at your drawings and wonder at it all."

Lily was shaking so that she could hardly speak. What she wanted to say was, *No, no, no, I'm never going away from here, from you, from any of my people, from home.* But some part of her mind knew that this was Justus Rising's poison still inside of her, trying to put down taproots.

It would please him to know that he could put such fear into her that she would simply roll herself into a ball and go to sleep for the rest of her life. And she would not allow him to have any such power over her.

She said, "Yes. I will, I promise."

"I know you will," Curiosity said softly. "You are the brightest light, Lily Bonner. You do shine on."

Her long hand cupped the back of Lily's head and rocked it gently, and then Curiosity got up and went back to watching at the window.

Lily dried her face and was doing the same for the cup when she heard Callie's voice on the porch, and Mr. Stiles.

Curiosity straightened her back and gave her headwrap a tug to set it to rights. Then she looked hard at Lily and seemed to be satisfied with what she saw. She opened the door.

All Lily could see was Curiosity's long form, outlined by sunshine.

"Mr. Stiles," she said. "Ain't it good of you to come so quick like. We got something of yours around back. And then Callie here got a business proposition for you. But first say hello to our Lily, would you?"

She stepped aside and the sunlight filled the cabin. Lily felt it on her swollen mouth and the bruise on her jaw; she saw it on Mr. Stiles's shoulders and the slope of his hat.

He stood there for a very long moment. She could make out nothing of his face or his expression, but his whole being seemed to shiver, just slightly.

Finally he cleared his throat. He said, "Where is my nephew?"

"Tied up out back, like I said," said Curiosity. "Now let's us have a word about Miss Callie's proposition."

It was a delicate business Curiosity had proposed, but Lily had no doubt that the old woman would manage it, and so it was. When the talking was done, Lily let herself be shuffled off and hid away, first with Curiosity's daughter Daisy and then in Uncle Todd's laboratory. She was vaguely aware that her father and Simon must be looking for her, that her mother would be worried, but she knew, too, that Curiosity would handle all that.

It was Callie and Martha who brought her word that she could come out. Callie put a piece of paper in Lily's hands—steady now, or steadier, at least—and waited for her to read it.

"This is a bill of sale," Lily said. "You've bought the orchard and the farm . . . for forty dollars?"

Callie nodded. She was flushed with pleasure and trying not to show it. Thinking still of what had happened at the cabin, and what might have happened.

Martha said, "Curiosity lent her the money. She said Callie can pay it off after the harvest and first pressing."

"I'm pleased for you, Callie."

Callie sat down with all the thoughtless grace of a young girl. "Manny is going to run the farm. He says he didn't really want to teach school anyway. Your mama didn't seem to mind too much."

Lily kept her thoughts to herself, but the girls were too excited to notice.

"Do you think maybe Levi will come back to work the orchards? Manny can't do it all on his own, and Curiosity says we have to keep going to school." Callie said this with such seriousness that Lily found herself smiling for the first time in a long afternoon.

"I would guess he'd be pleased to come back to Paradise," she said. "He and Manny together will make sure the orchards flourish." *As your father would have wished.* This last she kept to herself, and neither did Callie raise the subject of Nicholas Wilde. Out of superstition or resignation, Lily wasn't sure. They had had no word from or of Nicholas since the day he handed over everything he owned to Stiles.

They were quiet for a moment, and then Martha seemed to remember something. She said, "They left an hour ago. Mr. Stiles and

Justus. Curiosity says you should come now, before Simon decides to ride after them."

"Simon knows?" Lily asked, alarmed.

"No!" Callie said, almost too quickly.

Martha gave her friend a stern look. "But they all suspect something must have happened."

Callie nodded. "That's why Curiosity wants you to come now, so that your menfolk can see that you're all right and stop them from doing anything foolish."

"Curiosity thinks I can stop Simon, does she?" Lily said with another, smaller smile. "I hope she's right."

"I don't," Callie said, turning her face away. "I hope Simon rides after them and hangs Justus Rising from the first tree he sees."

Lily put an arm around the girl and hugged her tight. There was little to say that wouldn't have sounded false, and so she summoned up an old song out of her childhood memories, a song whose words she couldn't recall, but with a melody so sweet that it could not be forgotten. It was all the best she had to give.

Chapter 39

"Was he a good husband to you?"

Liam Kirby's voice came hushed and raw in the gathering darkness and touched Hannah's face like a hand.

All around them the men, wounded and whole, lay awake and listening. There was no such thing as privacy in this stockade; in that way it put Hannah in mind of a Kahnyen'kehàka longhouse.

She said, "Yes. He was a good husband."

"You bore him children."

"A son," Hannah said, and before the question could be asked: "He is dead."

"Ah." There was a long pause filled by Liam's hitching breaths. In and in and out. A faint rattling sound from his lungs, or maybe she was just imagining that.

"It is not my past that is important just now."

A flicker of a smile moved across his face, rough with beard, his lips fever-blistered. He said, "You want to sing my death song, Walks-Ahead?"

Blue-Jay moved fitfully on his cot just behind Hannah, and she put out a hand to quiet him.

"For that you would have to tell me the rest of your story."

Liam grimaced and managed a small shake of the head. He was in considerable pain, but he would expend what little energy he had hiding it.

Hannah said, "You would have liked Strikes-the-Sky, and he would have liked you."

"That doesn't sound like a compliment, the way you say it."

She drew a breath and held it for a moment. "It is, and it is not."

"Will you marry again?"

Hannah made a sound in her throat. "I cannot imagine it."

He turned his head away. "You will marry again."

She said nothing, and after a while Liam seemed to understand that she would not be drawn into this particular conversation.

"Your father. He is well?"

"Yes, all my family are well." She looked into the dark where Daniel lay listening, but could make out nothing.

Hannah said, "You gave up bounty-hunting."

"You know that I did. You shamed me out of it."

She made a sound deep in her throat, one that said she doubted such a simple explanation but would not challenge him.

"We used to have such good arguments," Liam said. "Why do you hold back?"

"I have no energy for such things," Hannah said. "And neither should you waste yours."

"Will you tell me how to die as you told me how to live?"

She drew up in surprise, and shock, and shame. When she could make herself speak she said, "Ask what you like."

"Tell me about my daughter."

In the next cot a sailor with a fever in his lungs coughed explosively. Hannah went to give him water, and when she came back she settled down again and tried to order her thoughts.

"What has Daniel told you?"

"That she looks like me," Liam said. "That she is nothing like her mother. That Jemima has run off and left the girl an orphan."

"He read you the letters from home," Hannah said.

Liam closed his eyes. "I can almost hear Elizabeth's voice in the written words. She tries hard not to judge, but she cain't hide it."

"Where Jemima is concerned, she fails, yes." Hannah had thought herself to be empty of curiosity after so many years, but a question came to her and in her weariness she put it to words.

"Why Jemima?" she asked. "Why ever did you take up with Jemima that summer?"

He said, "You know the answer to that."

A flush of anger drove the weariness from Hannah. "Do not lay the blame on me, Liam Kirby."

His head turned toward her, his face a pale oval in the darkness. "The blame is mine," he said. "Mine alone. I was lonely and angry and I let myself be brought low. What will you tell her about me?"

For a moment Hannah was confused. She saw herself and Jemima, tried to imagine that conversation.

He touched her hand. "Will you tell my daughter about me?"

"Yes," Hannah said.

"Tell her all of it," Liam said. "The bad and the good both. So she doesn't make more of me than she should. Tell her, I'm sorry I never got to see her."

Hannah nodded in the dark. "Yes. I will do that."

He cleared his throat, and when he spoke next he brought forth the language they had spoken as children, the language of her mother's people. The words came rough and poorly formed from his mouth, but he was offering her something and Hannah could not refuse it.

He said, "I should have waited that summer, when you were in Scotland. I shouldn't have run off. Things would be different now, if I hadn't been so impatient."

"Tell me," Hannah said, though she didn't want to hear any of it. "Tell me how."

And she sat while he spoke, haltingly, slowly, reaching for words, to draw her the picture of a Paradise that might have been.

When he slept, finally, she leaned over and pressed her mouth to his brow, and then Hannah went to her own cot and waited for sleep.

Rumors were as unavoidable as lice in the crowded, overheated stockade, and sometimes almost as irritating. The soldiers brought all news to Jennet, as they might bring a coin to a banker to find out what it was made of. Jennet was not generally easily persuaded and sometimes laughed out loud at a particularly outrageous claim, though never in such a way as to insult a man's dignity.

Since the sinking of the *Ferret,* soldiers had been pouring into the garrison by the dozens, militia and regulars both. When the work parties returned in the evenings with details, the debates began.

"They've got the blood lust now," an old sergeant told Jennet. "They liked the taste of the *Ferret* just fine and now they'll go hunting."

Long John took offense at such pessimism. "Let the bloody lobsterbacks show their face on American waters," he grumbled. "And the Vermont boys will make short work of them."

The other kind of rumor was even more disturbing. Mr. Whistler brought it to Jennet and presented it like a particularly disgusting piece of offal.

"They say we're to be moved to Halifax, Miss Jennet. To a prison ship."

Jennet, who liked Mr. Whistler for his careful ways, his odd humor, and his unwavering loyalty to Hannah, paused from her work to smile at him. "Who exactly has been saying such a thing?"

Mr. Whistler pursed his lips and dug into the thicket of beard on his neck. "Word came in with the work party. Sometimes the guards talk free around them."

The man Jennet was tending let out a long groan that ended in a soft whimper of pain. Some men needed comforting in their extremity and others chafed under it. This one, a sailor with three teeth and a stunning collection of scars on his back, was the latter type.

She said, "Pull yourself together, Mr. Mason. You still have your leg, after all. Is that not worth some pain?"

The muscles in the broad throat flexed as he swallowed, but the sailor managed a nod.

Mr. Whistler handed her a piece of toweling that once she would not have used to wipe down a dog, but now Jennet took it gladly. To him she said, "I doubt it will come to that."

He had bright brown eyes under a single long, bristling white eyebrow, and now they were fixed on her as if they could dig right into her mind to whatever thoughts she was hiding away. But Jennet had been raised to keep secrets carefully and close, and finally Mr. Whistler heaved a shoulder in grim resignation and went off with the basin of bloody water.

"Heard about them Tory prison ships," said the sailor. He had a high, broken voice, ruined by shouting or drink or both. "Don't much care for the idea of dying in one of them."

"Nor shall you," Jennet said.

She meant to sound sure of herself but in fact it was all a ruse; she was sure of nothing at all. Two days since Runs-from-Bears had left for Montreal, and still there was no word, from him or from Luke. During the day she could keep her worry to herself, but alone with Hannah it spilled out of her.

"Has Luke ever given you cause to doubt him?" was Hannah's only response to Jennet's long recitation of worries.

Which was true, of course, but hard to remember in the heat of the day, when the flies covered the faces of the wounded and the stench of sweat and blood and excrement was thick enough to spoon.

They had lost another four of the survivors from the American ship, and soon they would lose Liam Kirby, who was waning visibly, almost from hour to hour. For a while Jennet had wondered if he would prove Hannah wrong and rally, somehow expel the foreign metal out of his chest cavity by pure force of will.

The oddest thing, the most unexpected thing, was the way Daniel had come to life as Liam Kirby slipped away. It was not something to be thankful for, certainly. She told herself that as she caught sight of Daniel. His injured arm was strapped firmly to his side, but with his free hand he was holding a cup to Kirby's mouth.

Behind Jennet a man's low moan rose suddenly into a wail, and she went to see to it.

The thing Hannah feared most of all, more than the idea of a prison ship, was fever, and fever had come to the stockades, as she had known it must. She could smell it in the sweat of the man who tossed in his sleep. Whether it was typhoid or some other prison fever she could not yet tell, but that would show itself by the time the day was out.

Now she stood looking at her medicine stores, or the little that was left of them. There was some laudanum, enough fever tea to get them through today, and nothing beyond tepid water and a quart of vinegar to treat everything else.

Mr. Whistler stood beside her at the little worktable and hummed to himself, something he did when he was uneasy. He had been humming all morning.

"Will you go, then?" He asked the question without looking at her.

"I suppose I must." It was the last thing she wanted to do, but it seemed as though she could no longer find excuses to avoid visiting the garrison hospital. She would scrub their floors, if it meant the medicines the men must have.

"No hope of a shipment from our friend?" Mr. Whistler asked.

Hannah said, "There is always hope, Mr. Whistler. While I am gone, would you see to it that the fever tea is divided evenly where it is most needed?"

He nodded. "And the laudanum?"

"Mrs. Huntar will see to the laudanum."

Jennet would try to see to the laudanum, that was true. Daniel would refuse it, insisting that his portion go to Liam Kirby. Unless he died while Hannah was gone.

"Very well." He paused, and in a lowered voice he said, "You won't let them keep you too long?"

"No," Hannah said. "I will not."

She went to Daniel first, to tell him what she was planning. Liam had fallen into a restless sleep, curled on his side. The dressings on his back, changed just hours ago, were already crusted over with blood and discharge.

"His mind is wandering," Daniel told her. "It's the pain that does it. He thinks I'm Rudy McGarrity."

Jed McGarrity's son Rudy had died of the scarlet fever long ago.

"He's in the shadow lands," Hannah said.

If Many-Doves were here she would sing the songs that would help Liam make his way, but right now Hannah could think only of O'seronni medicine, of the laudanum which would make his passing easier.

She crouched down next to them and put a finger to the pulse in Liam's throat. Fast and uneven, it told the rest of the story.

"He told me something this morning. A long time ago, when his brother wouldn't let him go to school, he would look in the window, until our father caught him at it one day. There was something about Ephraim Hauptmann getting himself stuck in an ink bottle."

Hannah found herself smiling. "I haven't thought of that in years." Hot tears prickled behind her eyes.

"Go on," Daniel said. "I'll sit with him. Don't let the French doctors get the best of you."

"And how do you suppose I should manage that?"

Her brother had eyes the green of a spring forest, and he blinked at her now in the way that said she was being dense.

"Why, speak to them as Curiosity would."

That made her laugh aloud. "I'll try that," Hannah promised.

For all the weeks she had spent here, Hannah had managed to avoid the army surgeons who ran the hospital on the far side of the parade grounds. She knew what she would find there, the kind of welcome she could expect, the questions they would ask. Ten years ago she had spent a summer at the Kine-Pox Institution in Manhattan, learning as much about white doctors as she had about vaccinations and anatomy and surgery.

She might help herself by listing her teachers, or at least the teachers these men might have heard about and respect. Some of them had reputations that reached as far as Québec and Halifax and London: Hakim Ibrahim Dehlavi ibn Abdul Rahman Balkhi. Dr. Valentine Simon, Dr. John Ellingham, Dr. Karl Scofield, Dr. Paul Savard. Dr. Richard Todd. Those names might make them listen, at least, to what she had to say; they might win her some of the medicines she must have.

Or they might look at her: muddy hem and bloodstained apron, weary eyed and stinking of the men she cared for, and laugh in her face.

That she would suffer, too, if it resulted in the things she needed, the medicines she must have.

I am Walks-Ahead, she reminded herself. *I am the daughter of Sings-from-Books of the Kahnyen'kehàka people. I am the granddaughter of Falling-Day who was a great healer, great-granddaughter of Made-of-Bones who was clan mother of the Wolf for forty years, I am the great-great-granddaughter of Hawk-Woman, who killed an O'seronni chief with her own hands and fed his heart to her sons. I am the stepdaughter of Bone-in-Her-Back.*

They might laugh, yes, but they could take nothing away from her. Nothing of importance.

This thought came to her in her stepmother's voice, steady and calm and true, and Hannah stopped where she was and straightened her shoulders.

And heard another voice, just as familiar.

She stopped and looked around herself, for the first time. The parade ground was teeming with troops at drill and there was a new ship at the docks, flying Royal Navy colors. That in itself was nothing unusual; ships came and went so often with men and supplies that Hannah had long ago stopped paying attention.

But this particular ship had brought out Colonel Caudebec, pale of complexion and red eyed, to greet its passengers, his junior officers in tow.

At first her mind would make no sense of what she was seeing. The midday sun danced on polished swords, gold buttons, buckles and chains; she narrowed her eyes and forced herself to look, and still there they were, walking toward her.

Three of the visitors were in uniform, but it was the last man who had all of Hannah's—and Colonel Caudebec's attention.

Luke had his head inclined slightly toward Father O'Neill, who was speaking to him with great seriousness. The two men, almost of equal height, were an oddly impressive sight, one sun-blond, the other black haired, both long of bone and strongly built, one in his prime and the other, the priest, still vital in the way of hardworking men who strode into their fifties without slowing.

". . . the quartermaster next week," the priest finished, just as the men passed Hannah, who stood, unable to move, unable to look away, as she should. As she must.

"Yes, well, current events dictated otherwise," Luke said in a voice and tone that Hannah had never heard from him before. More English than Canadian or Scots, all authority. A man who expected deference from army officers and got it without question. If he saw Hannah he gave no indication, nor did any of the others.

"That's so," said another officer. He was a soft man with a puddinglike gut that strained his uniform jacket. A paymaster or quartermaster, one of the men who feed paper into the maw of war.

Then they were gone.

"Major Watson of the Forty-ninth Fencibles," said a voice behind her, in the singsong accents of the French Canadians. "And Captain Le Couteur of the Chasseurs."

Hannah put a hand to her throat as if she could quiet the mad flutter of her pulse. With some effort she composed her face before she turned.

One of the voltigeurs who were such friends of Jennet's stood there, his gaze still fixed on the retreating backs of the officers.

"Don't know the others by name," he said in an apologetic tone. "I hope they've brought the coin with them. It's two months we've been without pay."

"The man out of uniform?" Hannah asked. "What is he doing here?"

The voltigeur worked his shoulders. "A merchant by the name Luke Bonner, head of Forbes and Sons. Surely you've heard of them, they own half Montreal. Met his sister a few months back, a pretty little thing."

If he knew more, he was hiding it well. Nor did he take any real note of Hannah's lack of reply; his tongue was loosed and he seemed eager to talk.

"No doubt he's bringing the colonel some more pretties. A man overfond of paintings and fine dishes and such is the colonel. It's bred into them, you know."

His mouth twisted and twitched as if the idea caused him physical pain.

"Bred into who?" Hannah asked, distracted.

"Why, the Papists. French or Irish or Roman, they've all got a weakness for glittery things. Like crows." He looked more closely at her. "You aren't one of them, are you? Has Caudebec's fighting priest won you over?"

"No," Hannah said. "I've never even had a conversation with him." That was true. She always managed to be busy elsewhere when he came into the stockade to say mass for the Catholic French Vermonters.

"He thinks he's got Mrs. Huntar in his net, he does. A sly one, is Father O'Neill." A muscle in his cheek twitched. "And a wild man on a battlefield."

Hannah was having some trouble paying attention, but the next turn in the conversation brought her back quickly.

"That ship is crawling with marines," the voltigeur said thoughtfully. He squinted, his eyes moving over masts and deck. "It must be true that they'll be taking the prisoners with them when they go. Will Mrs. Huntar be going with them?"

There it was, then, the reason he had stopped her. She met his gaze and he lowered his eyes, a flush crawling up from the linen at his throat.

"You will have to ask her that, Mr.—"

"MacLeod," he said, bowing from the shoulders. "Lieutenant Kester MacLeod. Will you give her my regards?"

Hannah said, "Yes, I will do that." She turned in the direction she had come.

"I thought you were on your way to the hospital?" he called after her.

Hannah pretended she didn't hear the question, and broke into a trot.

Jennet had always liked to think of herself as a woman who rose to the occasion, one who would have fought alongside her forefathers at Stirling and Bannockburn, Falkirk and Holyrood. But here was a simple and unpleasant truth that she must confront: she was as nervous as a cat in this stockade of angry and agitated men. The prisoners needed calm and fortitude, but what Jennet most wanted and needed to do was scream and run away.

Luke was with the colonel, and what did that mean? The same

question she had asked herself a hundred times and still no answer came to her.

"Will you go with us, Mrs. Huntar?" asked one of the younger boys. His splinted leg was the only thing that kept him from following her around the stockade like a puppy, even on the best of days. Today, after the guards had herded all the prisoners into the exercise yard to hear Colonel Caudebec tell them that they were to be transported, she could not turn around without bumping into him.

"Why, Jamie," Jennet said, forcing her voice into playfulness. "Did ye think I'd leave the lads go off without me?"

The work parties had been brought back early, which was both a fortunate thing—the women had set them to hauling water so that all the men could wash—and an unfortunate one. Tempers were frayed and the heat was intense, and more than once it had fallen to Jennet to stop hard words from escalating into something far more dangerous.

The only men who had taken the news calmly were the worst off, those few who would not survive the journey.

Jennet turned now to look at the far spot the men called the hospital corner, where the unfortunates had been segregated away. Hannah was there, as she had been most of the afternoon, and so were Daniel and Blue-Jay. They were arguing, Jennet saw that by the tense line of Hannah's back and the way Daniel held his head.

"At least that lot have a choice," said one of the men in a low, dissatisfied tone. "They don't have to go if they don't care to go."

"Aye, they can die here or die there. Is that a choice you'd care to make, Harry Flynn?" Jennet spoke more harshly than she meant to, and saw that she had succeeded only in angering the old militiaman.

"We'll die there anyway, won't we? How many men ever leave one of them prison ships whole? Might as well put a bullet in my head now."

"At least that would shut you up," said another man. "Would I had the bullet to give you."

There was uneasy laughter, and Jennet took that opportunity to pick her way across the room.

Hannah arguing with her brother was nothing unusual, but just now Jennet didn't like what she heard as she came closer. Daniel, flushed the color of ripe plums with sweat on his brow, as angry as she had ever seen him.

In a hoarse whisper he said, "You'll leave it to us, sister, and see to your patients."

Blue-Jay looked unconcerned, which was a small comfort. He sent Jennet one of his cheerfully enigmatic half-nods, and then he said something in Kahnyen'kehàka, his voice pitched so low that no one else could hear them. Daniel flinched, and Hannah looked away, her irritation plain to read.

"What is it?" Jennet asked.

"I intend to stay behind with the men who are too sick to travel," Hannah said.

"Well, that's no surprise," Jennet said. "Did you think she'd run off from her patients?"

"She wants me to stay behind too," Daniel said, batting furiously at the flies that circled his head. "But I'll carry her out of here on my back if I have to, hogtied and gagged."

"Ah." Jennet saw Hannah's closed expression, and Blue-Jay's watchful one. She leaned in very close so that their four heads made an uneven circle.

"Don't you think we should wait to see what Luke and Runs-from-Bears have planned before we go rushing off on our own?"

That earned her a rare full grin from Blue-Jay. "That's just what I told them, but you know it's impossible to talk sense to the Bonners when they've got their blood up."

Jennet did not often have the chance to spend time with Blue-Jay, something she regretted. If she were ten years younger, she would have fallen in love with him with no encouragement at all, for his clear, clever way of looking at things, his generosity of spirit, and not least, she admitted to herself, for his striking looks. He had his father's height and build and his mother's beauty.

"We can't just bloody sit here and wait for Luke to rescue us," Daniel hissed. "How do we get word to him? Do you intend to march over there and demand an explanation?" He rocked on his heels and Jennet realized that he had not had any laudanum for hours, and must be in terrible pain.

She forced herself to concentrate on his face. "As a matter of fact, cousin, that's just what I plan. The colonel sent word that I'm to dine with him and his visitors, don't you know."

"Would you have time to stop by the hospital and ask for laudanum?" Hannah asked.

"I'll make time," Jennet said. She paused, feeling their eyes on her. "I'll go right now."

•   •   •

Outside the stockade it seemed that there was no trouble in the world at all: no war at the doorstep, no trouble ahead; not even the blackfly or the heat could dampen the grim good spirits of every soldier she saw. They were looking forward to spilling more blood, and on top of that, the paymasters had come.

When Jennet came back from the followers' camp, scrubbed and combed and made as presentable as she could be in this place, she heard the details from the guards: in the morning the paymasters would set up their tables in the shadow of the colonel's blockhouse and the soldiers would line up to get their due.

"Before we—" Uz Brodie began and then stopped himself.

"Before you sail south," Jennet finished the thought.

He ducked his head. "You'll be safe away. Nothing to concern you, Mrs. Huntar."

Blood and money, yes. The whole garrison hummed with it. Even the small, plump French doctor who greeted her in the hospital was in a generous mood. He gave her the medicines she wanted to help the prisoners on their way to Halifax, like an indulgent uncle who could refuse a favorite niece nothing at all. Jennet watched the cadet make his way toward the stockade with the box and then she took a deep breath, once and twice and three times, before she went to join the colonel's supper party.

In the cooling evening breeze she paused to look at the garrison that had been her home these many months. Gulls wheeled and screeched overhead against a cloudless high-summer sky. Troops drilled on the parade ground, coatees of scarlet, buff, green, navy, aglitter with brass and pewter and silver, gleaming badges on tall felt shakos. Somewhere a sergeant was screaming at some unfortunate soldier who had proved his unworthiness yet again. One of the washerwomen went by, her back bowed over the basket she carried, her dark face blank.

Jennet would not be unhappy to leave this place, she told herself, if only she knew where she was going. Tomorrow night she might be sleeping on the transport ship, or in a feather bed in Montreal, or someplace else that she could not imagine just now.

She smoothed her skirt, touched her hair, and turned toward the colonel's quarters.

Chapter 40

Though Jennet had been called to the colonel's quarters many times, those few minutes that it took to move from the heat and misery of the stockades to the blockhouse were never enough to prepare her for the transition. The perfumed and glittering plenty should have angered her, but first and foremost, they gave her a headache.

Now and then the colonel had requested that she sup with the officers, but this evening was out of the ordinary, even for Colonel Caudebec. The cook had been hard at work for a whole day at least: there was lamb, roast beef, a haunch of venison, river trout fried in butter, fresh oysters, great bowls of peppered and mashed turnips, carrots baked in brown sugar and wine, new peas and beans glistening with pork fat, and a tureen of ragout big enough to wash in. Jennet's empty stomach churned in appreciation, while her mind was busy with other things.

To her left was a major who had been introduced to her as Jacques-René Boucher de la Bruére, of the Second Battalion of the Lower Canada Select Embodied Militia. In spite of his very long name and title de la Bruére was an unleven loaf of a man, short and squat, radiating a damp warmth. He wore a carefully molded and waxed mustache that curled at the ends, and a scar that ran from his left ear to the corner of his mouth. At first, at least, he showed far more interest in the food than he did in Jennet, which suited her very well.

To her right sat Luke Bonner, of Forbes and Sons, a cousin of the Earl of Carryck. Surely, the colonel prompted, Jennet must know of the Carrycks of Annandale? Jennet did, of course; she told the officers so without flinching, though her heart was hammering so loudly that she could barely hear herself speak.

As far as Mr. Bonner himself was concerned, she had no idea if he had scars on his face or even if he still had two eyes; Jennet steadfastly refused to look him in the face for fear of what her own expression might give away.

For an hour she concentrated on her plate, glad of the conversation that went on without her, listening to Luke's part of it for some hint of what was to come tomorrow and of course finding nothing. Luke barely looked at her, spoke to her only when it was necessary, and then with courtesy that bordered on the cold. He might be a stranger, a man she had never seen before and would never see again.

To amuse herself, Jennet tried to imagine that, to see him as another woman might. Tall and broad in the shoulder, firm of jaw, his blue eyes missing little, giving away nothing. Intriguing, foreboding, mysterious. Looking at him as he was this night, no one would ever imagine the man he could be, the way he could laugh himself into a helpless quivering mass, his fine singing voice, the wild streak in him that showed up when he was on horseback, or held her in his arms. The tenderness he was capable of, his sweet teasing when the need was on him.

"More wine?" asked one of the cadets who served, and Jennet, deep in her thoughts, started.

"Go on, go on," bellowed the colonel. "Don't deny yourself tonight, Mrs. Huntar. I doubt you'll get any Paxareti equal to that in your convent, or any wine at all, eh?"

"Convent?" asked a young lieutenant, his head inclined politely but the distaste obvious in the set of his mouth. "You are to enter a convent, Mrs. Huntar?"

"The Grey Nuns of the Hôpital Général," answered Colonel Caudebec for her. "Father O'Neill there has arranged it all. You must know of the charitable works of the sisters, Lieutenant Hughes?"

"That must be why her hair is cropped," said the long, consumptively thin man called Lieutenant Hughes. He was wearing the scarlet jacket of the Thirty-ninth Foot, which was unfortunate, given his pale red hair and sunburned face. He studied Jennet with an uneasy fascination, as if she were a talking dog or a horse with two heads. Which she supposed she must be, to him. Englishmen had the oddest ideas about Catholics: tails and horns and midnight masses where the blood of infants was spilled.

"My hair is short because of the heat," Jennet said. "I prefer comfort to fashion." She wished immediately that she had not let her irritation get the better of her. The men's attention was focused on her now, something she had been trying to avoid.

"She's a Scot," said Major Wyndham of the King's Rangers, his surprise breaking through what had seemed a permanent expression of boredom. "A Scot and a Catholic. No wonder she's so far from home."

"I am a Scot, sir," Jennet said, giving him her most withering look, the one she had learned from her mother. "But I do speak English. There is no need to talk about me in the third person, as if I were a dumb animal."

That got her a sharp and contemplative look, but no apology.

"It is true what you say," said another major, this one with heavily French accented English. His tone was friendlier, at least, and he looked at Jennet when he spoke to her. "Life is not easy for us Catholics in Scotland, is it, madame?"

"Mrs. Huntar is a new convert. She never suffered under those unfortunate and unfair restrictions while she was in Scotland," said the colonel, saving Jennet the trouble of lying. He raised a glass in the priest's direction. "But Mr. Bonner can tell you something of Catholics in Scotland, I think. He lived at Carryck for some years."

Luke would not rise to such bait, but the priest was another matter. Until this moment he had added nothing to the conversation, but now he said, "It is true that the faithful suffer great deprivations in Scotland. But in this country Mrs. Huntar need never worry about such things."

"Either you are exceedingly positive in your outlook," Major Wyndham said shortly, "or exceedingly naïve. There is no love lost between the two faiths in Canada."

It was something Luke might have said, had he not been keeping his own counsel. Jennet could feel his attention focusing on the priest who had concerned him for so many weeks, and she might have screamed in frustration: men would play their silly games when there were more important things to be said and done.

"What do you think of the Paxareti?" She turned to Lieutenant Hughes, who started at the abrupt and unexpected address from the solitary lady at the table.

"Damned fine," said the younger man, who had taken so much of the wine that his words slurred and his language suffered. "Now that they've shipped Boney off to Elba it should be easier to get more of it, I hope."

Wyndham snorted. "Hughes, you talk about the Peninsular War as if it were all a plot to deprive your table and inconvenience you. Let me remind you that good men died by the thousands while you sat in Québec with a lady on each knee."

Lieutenant Hughes let out a barking laugh and made no effort to defend himself against these charges.

"You were there, I take it, Major Wyndham?" asked Major de la Bruére.

"From Talavera to Salamanca," interjected Colonel Caudebec. "Ask him anything except how he ended up over here, eh, Kit?"

Jennet breathed a sigh of relief as the discussion turned to Bonaparte's war, a topic that had the military men's full attention, and Luke's too, if his expression was to be believed. She settled more comfortably into her chair and was wondering how she was ever to have a private word with him when Major de la Bruére leaned toward her.

He whispered, "Are you as bored as I am with the endless stories of Bonaparte?"

His hand crept into her lap, warmly pulsing, slightly damp; pelted like a rat. Jennet caught her breath, closed her eyes, picked up the unwelcome hand as gingerly as she would a soiled handkerchief, and moved it away.

The hand came creeping back, as Jennet had feared that it would.

"Perhaps you might be willing to show me around the garrison after supper?" crooned the little major. "Your lodgings are in the followers' camp, is that correct?"

For all of her girlhood, Jennet had listened to her mother's warnings about her temper. *Remember Isabel.* Those words came to her now, and with it the memory of her beloved half sister, who had struck out in anger and paid for it with her life.

The major's thick fingers wrapped themselves in the thin fabric of Jennet's skirt, and try as she might she could not call Isabel's face into her memory. She picked up her knife and sliced neatly into the soft web of flesh between thumb and first finger.

The major pulled away from the table, his chair catching on the Turkey rug and tipping suddenly back, wobbling for a moment before it deposited him with a thump on the floor. His bellow,

Jennet noted with grim satisfaction, was like that of a calf being castrated.

"Oh, dear," Jennet said in her most refined tone. "What a great deal of blood."

There was a stunned silence that erupted into movement. Half the officers were hiding smiles, or trying to, while the others scrambled to help the man to his feet. A tray of glasses was dropped and a cadet tripped and fell into the jumble of men. When he was finally pulled to his feet, de la Bruére stood, pale and trembling, a napkin clutched in his bleeding hand.

"Mrs. Huntar!"

"Yes?" she asked, working very hard to put just the right confusion into her tone. And then: "Did you want me to look at it, sir? I think perhaps you should call one of the surgeons, Colonel, it looks as though the major might require stitches."

De la Bruére's mouth twitched, and for a moment Jennet thought that he would accuse her openly. What would happen then, if the colonel would be amused or affronted, that she could not predict. Nor did she particularly care, at this moment. Suddenly she was weary beyond memory, and simply uncaring of what was to come next.

Then Luke's hand settled on hers under the table. The long fingers wound into hers and squeezed, gently. Jennet drew in a deep breath and held it while Luke pressed something small and hard into the palm of her hand.

"A surgeon, by all means," said the colonel. "But do come back when your hand is bound. The cook has prepared a special treat. But only if you are feeling up to it, of course."

Beside her Luke grunted softly, and Jennet looked up to see something truly surprising. Colonel Caudebec: he was staring at de la Bruére with a cool, knowing, and dismissive smile.

Jennet excused herself as soon as it was viable, babbling thanks, unable to concentrate on anything beyond the small rectangle of paper she had tucked into her bodice. At the bottom of the stair she paused in the smoky light of a lantern and listened, but all she heard was the murmuring of the guards who stood in front of the blockhouse, the wind, and the rocking of the boats crowding the river. Her fingers trembled so that she lost her grasp on the paper.

Even as she snatched at it, the breeze sent it tumbling into the darkness.

She swore to herself and followed, her gaze fixed on the small rumpled square of light in the shadows. She had just managed to put her foot down on it when she heard steps behind her.

"Mrs. Huntar."

Jennet scooped up the paper and pressed it to her breast. "Yes, Father O'Neill?"

"What have you got there?"

She came forward. "My handkerchief. The breeze took it from me."

"Yes, the weather is turning." He stood, his form straight and steady, watching the western sky where ships' masts would be visible in the daylight. "They will have the wind they need tomorrow for their attack."

She made a sound that was meant to be agreeable but came out more like a squeak of distress.

"Your concern for your charges is admirable, Mrs. Huntar, but sure and you must not credit the horror stories you hear of the prison ships at Halifax. They will be adequately looked after."

Jennet hummed again, thankful to have been so misunderstood. While the priest talked on in his soothing voice about the prisoners and their transport and trust in God, Jennet's mind was working madly. She had no idea what was in the note, whether she was meant to meet Luke somewhere in the next few minutes or take word to Hannah, but there was nothing for her to do but to wait until the priest had talked himself out.

"Let me tell you something more about the Grey Nuns," he said.

Jennet's palm cramped around the rumpled paper with its precious, invisible words. She would be able to read them in the light of the lanterns at the main gate, she reasoned to herself. Unless the priest decided to walk her to the followers' camp, which would be a disaster. That unpleasant thought had just presented itself when Jennet realized that he was waiting for some word from her.

"Until tomorrow, then," he said. In the faint light from the lantern she saw that he seemed not so much affronted by her lack of attention as vaguely amused.

"Yes, of course. Good night," Jennet said, and turned toward the gates.

"Mrs. Huntar?"

She paused. "Father?"

"Your confessor will need to hear about what happened here this evening. Your temper must be brought under control."

Jennet had the almost ungovernable urge to laugh aloud. She bit her lip. "Of course," she said, and then disappeared thankfully into the dark.

"Where is Hannah?" It was the first thing out of Luke's mouth once he found her in the copse of pines at the far northern end of the island, just beyond the followers' camp. The air was cool here, ripe with river water and gathering dew.

"In the stockade, of course," Jennet said. She pulled her shawl more tightly around herself. "There is one patient in very poor condition." As of yet there had been no chance to tell Luke about Liam Kirby, but now was not the time, Jennet reasoned.

She said, "We've been frantic with worry."

His tone gave away his smile. "Not frantic, surely." His hand settled on the nape of her neck and his head bent forward so that she felt his breath there. "I've seen you frantic, girl, don't forget."

"You are shameless," Jennet said, but she could not bring herself to step away from him, not even when he put his mouth to the curve of her neck and used his teeth.

"What of tomorrow?" she said, leaning back against him. "What of the plans? You have plans, don't you?"

"Plans." He pressed the corner of her mouth with his thumb and she half turned into his kiss, helpless as ever. "I have plans for you, little nun."

When she could speak she said, "But what—"

He kissed her again, his hands moving fitfully over her back, up from her waist to the curve of her breasts. Jennet heard herself whimper into his mouth.

"Luke," she said as firmly as she could.

He said, "There's nothing to do until tomorrow. Let them march the prisoners onto the ship, and things will follow from there."

Jennet hiccupped a laugh and caught his hands, held them still against her. "Wait. Do I understand? You plan to hijack the ship?"

Luke pushed out a sigh and put his mouth to her ear. "Don't be ridiculous. I am a merchant of high standing and impeccable reputation. I don't play at pirates." Then he grinned at her like a boy.

"Oh, dear," Jennet said. "This will be messy, I fear."

"Not if you do as I ask," he said in a more serious tone. "The important thing is that you should all get on the ship without fuss. Make sure the men aren't planning any revolt. It would only work against them."

"We should tell them what is to come, then?"

"Tell them to go peacefully, and to be ready."

Jennet's heart was beating very fast, with excitement and dread both. She said, "There are some patients who are in very poor condition."

"Have the others carry them," Luke said. "No matter what, they must all be on the ship. All of you must be on the ship. All of you." His hands tightened on her, and his breath moved her hair so that gooseflesh rose all along Jennet's back.

"I can't be with them. I'm supposed to be going to Montreal with Father O'Neill; you heard them at supper. I thought I could simply walk away from the convent—"

"No." His hands tightened on her. "You'll tell him you've had a change of heart. Tell him Hannah needs you. Tell him you can't leave the sick men."

"It would be un-Christian of me," Jennet said, canting her head up for his kiss.

Luke smoothed her hair away from her face. "Unless you would rather go for a nun."

Jennet made a face at him. "Where will you sleep tonight?"

That made him laugh. "Missed me, did you?"

Irritated, Jennet ran a hand up his breeches. "Look who's talking," she said. "You could hammer nails with that."

He hitched a breath and pressed her hips to his so that she felt every inch of him. "Sounds painful."

She turned her face to give him the line of her jaw. "Then come back to the camp with me and we'll find something better to do with it."

"No," Luke said, letting her slide down to the ground. "I mustn't be seen anywhere near the camp, and I've got work to do yet tonight. It's less than two hours till first light."

He turned his face up to the sky and his eyes moved across the sweep of stars. "I will see you on the ship tomorrow, and then tomorrow night I'll have you in my bed."

"If all goes well," Jennet added softly.

He caught her up against him tightly, kissed her hard. "Never doubt it," he whispered against her mouth. "I wouldn't have it any other way."

• • •

In the blessed and unexpected cool of the night, the men had found some relief in sleep. Hannah sat awake beside Liam Kirby listening to the uneasy sounds of their dreams. She was fuzzy-headed with weariness, but she would find no rest tonight.

Liam slept on his side, curled toward her, his breathing shallow and quick. Sitting beside his cot, she could feel the fever radiating off him, as if his belly were filled with live coals. In the light of a single tallow candle she examined his face and saw no surprises there, no miracles waiting. His eyes had already begun to sink into his skull, and his breath smelled of corruption.

She took a rag from the bowl beside him and wiped his face and neck, singing under her breath in a melody that she hoped would bring him some comfort. She sang the story of his life, as she knew it, in the language of her mother's people. It was a service she had never been able to offer her husband, and so she sang for him too. It brought her some measure of peace, though she was not sure she had earned it.

Manny Freeman's face came to her in the darkness, but it was Strikes-the-Sky whose voice she heard.

Why do you turn away from the truth?

She said, *Haven't I had enough of death? Do I need to see it written out in words?*

Liam stirred and coughed, convulsed with the pain and coughed again. Hannah dribbled liquid from a spoon into his mouth and he swallowed and groaned and swallowed again.

"Don't waste laudanum on me," he said.

"Will you argue with me even now?" She made a soft ticking sound and managed a half-smile. In the candlelight his eyes were dull, streaked with red, his lashes matted. She wiped them gently.

"Dying shouldn't be so hard," he said. "It shouldn't be harder than living."

It was an odd piece of wisdom and it made Hannah smile. "How would you choose to die, then, Liam?"

"In my bed of old age," he said. "With you beside me."

"I am beside you now," Hannah said.

He made a sound. She thought he would slip away again into sleep but instead his hand came out of the shadows and settled on her knee.

With an unsteady voice she said, "I have been wanting to ask you about Treenie."

His mouth jerked at one corner, in surprise or displeasure, she wasn't sure. "Your mother never got my note? I wrote to her when Treenie ran off, it must be five years ago."

Elizabeth would have shared that news, if it had been in her power, and Hannah said so.

"I thought she might head back for Paradise," Liam said. "Women and red dogs do seem to run back there."

"Ah," Hannah said. "You think I should not go home?"

Liam coughed, lost the rhythm of his breathing and coughed again. It was some time before he had the power of speech again.

He said, "This is what you were born to do."

"Pick lice?"

His face contorted. "You were born to be a doctor. There's a peacefulness about you when you are working among the men, I've seen it come over you like a veil."

"I do what I have been trained to do," Hannah said. "And when my work is done here I'll go home to Lake in the Clouds."

"To set broken bones and lance boils." Liam grunted. "To deliver babies. Will that be enough for you?"

"More than enough," Hannah said, and unexpected irritation flooded up from her gut. "I'll be content."

"You'll be bored."

She said, "What is it you would have me do? Stay here for the rest of the war, watching men die because I don't have the medicines I need to help them?"

No answer came, because Liam had drifted away into the delirium that boiled up out of his fever, his face twitching with it.

Behind her came Jennet's low whisper. "Hannah."

Jennet was usually so careful not to call her by that name while they were in the stockade, Hannah jerked with surprise. But when she turned she saw that her cousin brought news that must be good: her expression was alive with it.

She said, "We must wake Daniel and Blue-Jay."

"Now?" Hannah said.

"Immediately." Jennet leaned forward and pressed Hannah's shoulder with her hand. "They will be glad of what I have to tell them." She gave it to Hannah in the words she had rehearsed on her way here, quick and neat, but she could do nothing about the tremor in her voice or the way her hands shook.

Hannah was quiet for a moment, her expression calm. Once she glanced at Liam Kirby, and then away.

"All the men?"

"Aye, all of them."

Hannah nodded. "I will be glad to leave this place."

Jennet said, "I'll go now and gather our things."

"Then I'll speak to Daniel." Hannah's gaze shifted back to Liam Kirby.

"We will move him," Jennet said. She leaned forward to take her cousin's hand, squeezed it hard. "We won't leave him here to die alone."

"It won't come to that," Hannah said. "Go now, and be quick."

Daniel, roused from his poor sleep, was fully awake by the time Hannah had finished telling him what he must know. The muscles of his jaw were tight with pain, but there was something new in his expression as well, hope or satisfaction or both. He went off to wake Blue-Jay and begin the spreading of the news.

Hannah forced herself to breathe deeply, once and then again. Tonight they would be free, or dead; in either case she would be able to put down the responsibility for these men, most of whom had accepted her help only grudgingly, and who would not look her in the face if they passed her on the street.

Liam jerked, and she started so that the bowl of water in her lap sloshed. "You're awake."

He said, "He's a fool, your half brother. But a brave one." Hannah wondered again that he was still alive, clinging to this minute and the next, though they brought him only pain.

"You think we will fail?" Hannah asked.

Liam grimaced. "He'll get away with it, and more. The luck of the Bonners."

Hannah's fingers picked at her wet skirts. Liam was thinking of his brother Billy, who had died on Hidden Wolf, a bloody death and one he deserved. At her father's hands.

"You still want revenge?"

His lips were split and caked with fever, his smile a fearful thing. "No," he said. "I'm long past that. Curiosity told me once that Nathaniel did me a favor the day my brother died, and I've come to see the truth of it." He huffed a weak cough and spat blood, swore under his breath. "It's not revenge I want."

Hannah leaned over him and put her hand to his cheek, rough with beard, and found that his skin was dry and warm; the fever had left him. It had boiled all the wet out of him and it was ebbing away, a fire without fuel.

She said, "Do you want me to send word to Jenny?"

He grunted, displeased. "You are a strange woman, Hannah Bonner. I'm talking love to you here and you bring up my wife."

There were tears on her face, but Hannah didn't wipe them away. He should know that she would mourn him.

"What is it you want, Liam? I'll give it to you if I can."

This time his smile was softer, boylike, almost innocent but for the fresh blood on his teeth. "All I want now is death. Can you give me that, Walks-Ahead? Will you help me with that?"

A whispering had come up all around them like the wind rising in trees, cooling and welcome. Men's voices stripped of anger and ripe with hope, passing news back and forth as they would share an unexpected gift of food.

Hannah said, "I can. I will."

In the hour before dawn the garrison was already alive with movement. Jennet skirted the parade grounds where the troops were assembling, turned her face away; she wanted to know nothing of the battle they were going to fight, would not think about the friends she had made here, the men who would go off in the first light of day to kill and be killed.

There was a little path, one she was not supposed to know about, that ran behind the armory to a gap in the garrison fortifications. The soldiers used it to slip in and out to see the women in the followers' camp, risking floggings and worse for a few moments' pleasure. Jennet took it now so as not to be seen coming and going by the sentries. Later, when the prisoners had escaped, there would be an investigation, and she would not give the guards anything to report if she could help it.

If all went well.

Jennet's blood raced so that it hummed in the tips of her fingers and made them jerk.

Once away from the garrison she ran, light-footed in the dark. She stumbled once and then again and forced herself to slow down. Thought of Luke, and wondered where he was just now, whether he had gone off to meet with Runs-from-Bears and Sawatis. This very night she would be in his bed, but it made her tremble to think of that, like a girl who planned to sneak out after dark to meet a lover her father disapproved.

Instead she thought of the things she must secure, the things she dare not leave behind.

As she came into the camp a soldier shot past her, no more than a boy, really, tousle-headed and frantically buttoning his breeks. He had fallen asleep. After the battle was done, while the others stood in line to get their pay, he would be strung up for a flogging. And still Jennet did not doubt that he would be back here before the stripes had healed on his back, unless he died today on Lake Champlain. He barely looked at Jennet, who was the least of his problems.

She was thinking of the nature of men while she slipped from shadow to shadow, thinking of the things they risked for the people they loved, of Luke, who had put everything on the line for his brother, and for her. The certain awareness of her good fortune made her pause in the dark and offer a small prayer of thankfulness.

The dark had given way enough to show her the outline of shacks, which meant, hopefully, that she would not need to waste precious moments with candle and flint box to find what she wanted. That thought had just formed itself in her mind when she saw that there was a light already, flickering weakly around the bearskin that served as a door.

Luke, and Runs-from-Bears. She heard herself breathe a great sigh of relief as she pulled back the door skin.

Father O'Neill stood in the middle of the shack, the candle on the low table throwing his shadow up to the roof: a long black ghost jittering there.

Jennet's voice caught in her throat but all that came from her mouth was a soft sound, a quick sigh.

"Lady Jennet of Carryck," said the priest with a small, satisfied smile. "And here I thought you'd be asleep in your lover's arms until dawn. I suppose you've come to get these?"

The letters she had hidden away. The ones she had promised Hannah to burn. Letters from Lake in the Clouds, from Luke, from her mother in Scotland. She had wrapped them in oilskin and put them in a hollow scraped out of the hard ground beneath her pallet. Because she could not bear to part with them; because she was a fool.

In the same moment something came to her with the force of a hammer blow: Father O'Neill was wearing rough breeches and a worn leather jerkin over a muslin shirt, and he looked nothing like a priest out of his soutane. Because, she understood now, he was no priest. Because Luke had been right to warn her about this man.

"Give me those," she said, her voice creaking. And then, more firmly: "They don't belong to you."

He raised his eyebrows, all dark good humor, and ignored her outstretched hand. "I'll admit, you had me fooled for a good long while. I never would have taken you for an earl's daughter, much less an American spy. If you hadn't given yourself away last night I would be much the poorer." He looked with some satisfaction at the letters in his hand.

"You followed me."

He made a clicking sound with his tongue. "I was seeing to my own business, and there you were, the two of you."

"So you took the opportunity to come back here and steal."

O'Neill scratched his jaw with one thumbnail. "Curiosity has ever been my downfall. But these letters cleared up my confusion, and quite nicely too. Won't the colonel be surprised to know he invited a pair of spies to his supper table."

"We are not spies." Jennet's voice came clear, and she was thankful for that much.

"And do you doubt the colonel will see it that way, once he's read these? The Earl of Carryck a secret Catholic and his sister working against the Crown in Canada, now won't that be news from Aberdeen to London? I wonder if they'll build a scaffold big enough to hang all of you at once, or if you'll have to wait your turn. Perhaps," he said, with a broad smile, "they'll string you up next to your sweetheart, if you ask nicely."

Jennet was in danger of fainting, for the first time in her life. She balled her fists in her skirts to keep them from shaking and bit her lip hard enough to draw blood. With every bit of strength she could summon, she steadied her voice. "You'll be there with us, I'm sure. To turn me in you must turn in yourself."

"That would be sloppy of me, would it not? But I've got another idea, one that will please me, at the least."

The question escaped her before she could stop it. "Who are you?"

He bowed from the shoulders. "Anselme Dégre of Barataria, by way of Acadia, at your service. Now why don't you sit down here and listen to my proposition. If it's to your liking, why, your friends will go off to their fate with no interference from me. Or we could go straightaway and pay a visit to the colonel. Which will it be?"

Her gaze skittered through the tiny shack, moving over pallets and bowls and the few skirts and bodices hung from nails in the rough walls. Nothing that would serve as a weapon. She thought of running; no doubt she could disappear quick enough, but she would not, could not leave the letters in his hands. It seemed that there was hardly enough air to breathe, and what was there reeked with rancid tallow and sweat and her own bitter foolishness.

"What do you mean to do with me?"

He laughed out loud, a pleased laugh, full of pride, not only at his own clever plan but that she had caught on to it. "Let me put your mind to rest, cher. I've got no interest in bedding you."

That idea hadn't presented itself just yet, and still Jennet felt herself relax. "Then what?"

He turned his head sharply to listen as women walked through the camp, arguing softly. When he looked at her again some of the playfulness had left his expression. "Sad to say, there's no time for more talk just now."

"Don't let me keep you," Jennet said. "I'll take my letters and you can be off, I'll say nothing to the colonel."

He took the letters and tucked them into his shirt, patted them fondly. "It won't be that easy, I fear. You've got two choices. I can tie you up neatly with the letters tucked into the ropes, and send a sentry along—" He held up a hand to stop her protest. "In which case you'll hang and your lover with you, and the prisoners will rot in a prison ship. Or you can come along with me now and give them the chance to get away."

Jennet caught the edge of the table to keep herself from swaying. "You want me to come with you?"

"We're off for warmer waters, Lady Jennet, far south of here. Out of reach, so to speak."

"Luke will follow us," Jennet said. "He will come after me. He'll never give up."

"No doubt he would try," said Anselme Dégre. "Were it not for the letter you're about to write."

Daniel Bonner, eighteen years old, born and raised on the frontier in New-York State, having served for a few short months as a rifleman in the American cause, rose on a bright summer morning that would be his last as a prisoner, and knew that he was done with war.

In a line with the rest of the prisoners he shuffled out of the deserted garrison toward the transport ship *Fair Winds*. There were many sailors among the prisoners, and they spoke among themselves about the ship in no complimentary terms. Even from this good distance they diagnosed rot and weakened timbers and poor knees. Not that it mattered, they said in lower voices, and elbowed each other knowingly.

If not for the fact that Daniel stood in line waiting to be shackled, he might have found something to laugh at in the rumors that the men passed back and forth. In the few hours since Jennet brought her news the story had grown to astonishing proportions. The entire American navy waited just around the next bend in the river, it seemed, and was poised to deliver swift justice and freedom.

Daniel wondered what they would say if he told them that it wasn't a navy who would rescue them, but his own brother and uncle and cousin. He had unlimited faith in his own people, but even so, he could hardly imagine how they would manage what they had promised. They could not turn the ship for American waters without sailing directly into the British force that had left at dawn to provoke a battle; to sail north was only to go deeper into Canada.

He turned his head away while the blacksmith worked, and reminded himself that the manacles would be struck off before the sun had set.

And still their weight dragged on his left arm, freed of its sling. The part of his mind that could still think about these things with some degree of detachment noted that the pain had a particular quality today, as though a hot wire had been stuck into his shoulder joint. A pain that moved like a live thing with a mind of its own, burrowing into bone like a worm into sand.

There had been no more laudanum this morning. In the night his sister had given the last of it to Liam Kirby, and then waited with him until he was gone. Unable to sleep, Daniel had watched. Hannah's expression had never changed all through that terrible hour. She was as steady as the stars and as fragile as crystal, not thirty years old but when she finally rose up and let his body be taken away, she moved like a woman at the end of a long life.

The war had taken the use of his arm from Daniel, but his sister had not got away so easy.

Daniel would have refused the laudanum if there had been any for the taking. Not because he welcomed the pain or wanted to punish himself, but because the stuff made him stupid, and today he must have his wits about him. He was going home, finally, and for good. The idea filled him with relief and terror both.

He wanted his people the way he wanted to breathe; he could

not close his eyes without seeing them, or dream without hearing their voices. But on the mountain where he had been born and raised there would be no avoiding the question that he pushed away every waking minute of the day. He would see it in his mother's face and hear it in every word his sister spoke. They would do everything in their power to help him heal, but every day it would be asked in a hundred different ways: what would he do with his life if he never regained the use of his arm? If he couldn't handle a rifle, if he couldn't set a trap, or skin a deer, or wield an axe. Who would that man be; what would he see when he looked into the glass?

"Three ships and two dozen gunboats gone south," Daniel heard one man say to another as the line of prisoners shambled through the garrison past the deserted parade ground. "And what fine weather it is for a bloodbath. May every one of the bastards find a grave at the bottom of the lake."

A year ago Daniel would have despaired to think that he would have no part in the battle that must be taking place right now. He had left home eager for war and the chance to prove himself, as his father had done and his grandfathers before him. The lessons he had learned on Nut Island were not the ones he had hoped for, and they left a bitter taste in his mouth.

"Move along there," shouted the guards to the clashing rhythm of men in chains. "Step lively!"

On the other side of the parade ground there was a sudden shouting, men running back and forth in high agitation, the flash of sunlight on muzzles. An officer came toward the docks in a dead run, waving his arms frantically.

"Hold! Hold there! Stop!"

Before he went to war, Daniel had tried to imagine the kind of fear that lived on battlefields and fed on gunfire; he had asked his father and uncle and his grandfather about it, and they had all told him the same thing: the fear could be, must be banished. It was the first, the unavoidable enemy; a man who couldn't outrun fear for his own life would never be a warrior.

That was one kind of fear, Daniel learned now, and here was another. As officers and marines ran toward the ship, guns at the ready, he felt the weight of the chains that bound him and thought of his sister and cousin, and knew himself to be powerless. The agony of his shoulder was nothing to this new pain.

The captain had come off the ship to meet the officers just where the line of prisoners had stopped. He was a great plug of a man with an outsized face flushed a peculiar shade of plum.

"Colonel Caudebec," panted the officer who had come from the blockhouse. "Colonel Caudebec is murdered and the paymasters with him. Throats cut." He put back his head and shouted to the sky. "Christ Almighty!" Then he threw his body forward and vomited onto his boots.

"When?" asked the captain, turning to another officer. "How?"

The men, officers and guards alike, began talking all at once, their voices raised and clashing. It seemed that nothing of any sense would ever be said, until another officer appeared approaching from the direction of the followers' camp. He was moving at a lope, fast and easy, and Daniel had the idea that of all the military men he had seen thus far on this island, this unnamed major—by his uniform one of the infamous King's Rangers—would be the most serious threat on a battlefield.

A short officer, a barrel-shaped captain, began shouting orders in a combination of English and French: the prisoners were to be returned to the stockade, the ship searched for the missing pay chests, the garrison surrounded. Then he saw the captain from the King's Rangers approaching and he seemed to collect himself. He pulled at his coat, straightened his hat, and made an attempt to calm his expression.

"Major Wyndham," he said. "Everything is under control. We will have the rascals within the half hour."

"The rascals are long gone," said the major. "Keep everyone where they are for the moment." Then he turned, his gaze scanning the men and sailors who stood along the dock.

"Mr. Bonner," he called. "A word, please, and right away."

Daniel closed his eyes and concentrated on breathing, in and out, as he tried, without success, to gather his thoughts. When he looked again, his brother was standing beside Major Wyndham, their heads bent together.

Blue-Jay was standing just behind Daniel, and so he took a step in that direction. He spoke Mohawk, and kept his voice low. "Where are my sister and my cousin?"

The answer came back in the same language. "The guard says that Walks-Ahead is already on the ship. She went on board with the injured men an hour ago, while we were in the exercise yard."

"And Jennet?"

There was a pause while Blue-Jay looked through the crowd. "No sign of her." And then, "Have a look there, the ship's captain."

Except the man who came down the gangplank wasn't any captain. He was wearing the uniform of a Royal Navy officer, that much was true, but he had never worn one before this day and, Daniel would wage his other good arm on it, would never wear one again after.

Jim Booke was directing the guards to carry on with the boarding of the prisoners, never raising his voice and staying well clear of the officers who stood on the shore.

The other men would all know of Jim Booke by his reputation, but none of them had ever seen the man, which was a good thing. Some one of them would give the game away, otherwise. Instead it looked, just for the moment, as if they might rebel.

A few minutes ago they had been glad to see the ship and eager to board, thinking themselves close to freedom; now they balked, some of them looking to Daniel for assurances he could not give them. In the end muskets were argument enough, and the slow shuffle toward the gangplank began again.

At dawn Mr. Whistler had come to wake Hannah with the news that the guards were come with the litters, and the sickest men were to board the transport ship first, and right away. She rubbed her eyes while he talked, and slowly two things came to her. Liam was dead, and Jennet had yet to come back from the followers' camp.

Daniel and Blue-Jay had already been marched out into the exercise yard to be manacled, but she was not so worried about them. It was Jennet's absence that disturbed her. But there was no time to do anything about that. She turned her mind to tending to the sick.

And still when the opportunity came, she could not keep herself from asking questions of the guards. None of them had seen Jennet. Even the friendliest of them had nothing to add that was any comfort.

Uz Brodie said, "She's supposed to be going to Montreal with the priest, is what I heard, and he left hours ago."

"Unless she changed her mind?" asked one of the younger guards with a hopeful expression. "I can't see Mrs. Huntar as a nun, not for the life of me."

Hannah's uneasiness grew all through the next hour of moving men who should have been left in peace. While she adjusted splinted legs and put rolled blankets under strained backs she tried to keep her mind off Jennet, and failed completely.

Perhaps she had gone with the priest, and would let herself be taken to the convent in Montreal. From there she could easily leave, and make her way to Luke's place. Perhaps she had already gone on board the ship with Luke, and was waiting there impatiently.

That must be it, of course. And still Hannah fumbled with the simplest tasks, and could not gather her thoughts.

By the time her patients were on board the *Fair Wind,* Hannah had the first evidence that Luke's plan was in place. She had never before been on board a Royal Navy transport ship, but she knew by looking at them that the sailors were her countrymen, regardless of the uniforms they wore. They were met by an officer who dismissed the garrison guards with a few curt words and then waited until those men were gone before he spoke to her.

"You're wanted in the captain's quarters, ma'am. I'm to tell you the prisoners will be well looked after there."

Mr. Whistler looked the man up and down. "Tell me, son," he said with a wink. "Where is it in England that you got that New-York accent?"

"A piece west of London," came the gruff answer. "Newburgh on the Hudson."

In the captain's cabin there were hastily put together berths for the sick men, and waiting among them, Many-Doves. Hannah looked at her aunt and cousin for a long moment before she could make her legs move her forward, and then she walked into her, where she stood, shaking, and without words.

When she could control her voice she said, "Daniel and Blue-Jay will be coming on board with the other prisoners."

"They'll be brought straight here," Luke said. He had come into the cabin behind her. His color was high, and his eyes bright with excitement or worry or both, Hannah could not say.

Hannah said, "I don't know where Jennet is. Do you?"

If he had an answer it was lost in the shouting that rose suddenly from the shore.

"What's that?" Mr. Whistler went to the porthole and squinted out. "Holy Mother, what's happened?"

Hannah heard it then, the sound of men shouting, loud enough to be heard over the creaking of the ship and the wind. The sound of plans gone awry, of disaster.

Luke went to look, and then he came back to Hannah. He put a hand on her shoulder and squeezed. "Listen to me now, sister. Are you listening?"

Hannah nodded.

"When I give the signal, this ship will sail immediately, with or without me. In that case Jim Booke will have command until Runs-from-Bears comes on board. If you must sail without me, then do not look back. Do you understand?"

There were many questions she wanted to ask, but only one thing she could think to say.

"We will not leave you behind."

"You will, if I say so," said her brother, his gaze hard and his grip on her shoulder unrelenting. "I promise you I will do everything in my power to stay alive. Will you be satisfied with that?"

"What choice do I have?"

"None," said Luke. "None at all."

From the portholes they could see everything that was happening on the dock: the officers swarming, the shouting, the guards running back and forth. Blue-Jay and Daniel stood near each other in the line of prisoners, their faces turned toward the gates.

"Did he say Jim Booke?" asked Mr. Whistler of Tim Munro, a fisherman out of Burlington who wore the uniform of a first lieutenant. "Did I hear him right, Jim Booke?"

"You did."

"Damn me," murmured Mr. Whistler in reverential tones. "But that Bonner has got balls the size of muskmelons. To dress Jim Booke up like a redcoat and parade him in front of the whole garrison."

"And money like Croesus, to outfit us all and the ship, and pay us, every man jack of us, a whole month's pay for a few days' work. To tell you the truth, I would have done it for nothing, if he asked me. Anything to bloody the nose of a lobsterback."

With one part of her mind Hannah heard all this, but the rest of her, the biggest part of her, could not look away from the scene in front of the garrison. She should turn away now and see to her patients, talk to her aunt, make sure that all was ready for the men. But she could not make herself move, and thought she never could, until she knew Jennet to be safe. If she looked hard enough, she told herself, if she concentrated, she could make Jennet appear.

"What the hell is going on down there?" asked Mr. Whistler. "Looks like trouble."

It was trouble, of the worst kind. Another one of Luke's men came in to share the news, a sailmaker out of Plattsburgh who could hardly speak for agitation.

"Slow down, Hitchens," said Munro. "Are you telling us the commander's murdered and all the paymasters with him?"

"One of the paymasters ain't dead yet, but aye, that's the gist of it. And somebody's took two months' pay for a thousand men, sailors and shipbuilders and common soldiers—"

"Did you hear anything about Jennet Huntar? Did you hear that name at all?"

Hitchens sucked in his lower lip and pushed it out again. "Never heard that name mentioned, no."

"And the priest?" Hannah asked, insistent. "Have you heard them talk about the priest?"

He was not a quick-witted man, this Hitchens, but he was pleased to be able to give a better answer. "Aye, there was talk of a priest, he's gone missing, too, and feared murdered."

Hannah lost her balance and reached out to catch herself, stumbled and almost fell but for Mr. Whistler, who caught her arm.

"Steady now," he said. "Steady. Look, they're sending the boys on board. It's got nothing to do with us, whatever happened to their blood money, and you can't regret the loss of that damn Caudebec, can you? We'll be off, wait and see, every last one of us, before the hour is out. Mrs. Huntar will be hiding nearby, never fear."

Hannah turned her head and saw that Many-Doves, who said nothing, who saw everything, understood what Hannah had not—could not—put into words.

The priest was gone, and Jennet with him.

Luke's plan was an elegant one, so simple that it could follow its course without him. The ship would weigh anchor some miles downriver, where two dozen Kahnyen'kehàka waited with canoes and rafts to ferry the prisoners to shore. The same men would serve as guides, and with their help the prisoners would disappear into the woods and eventually over the border. The men too sick to travel would be taken to a hunting camp a few miles inland where they would be hidden and looked after until they were well.

Many-Doves named the women who would be there to look after the injured men. They were all known to Hannah, women she could trust with the men she had fought to save. After so many weeks of worry for strangers, she was free of them.

Hannah's brother and cousin would be back in New-York before midnight, and home again in a few days' time. The ship would not be missed, because it had never belonged to the Royal Navy to begin with. Stripped of its purloined colors and standards it would be scuttled. The truth wouldn't be known until the real transport came in a week's time, and by then there would be no trace of the *Fair Winds,* the men who had sailed her, or the prisoners.

All of whom were belowdecks. Their manacles had been struck off before the garrison was out of sight, and by the time they left this ship they would be new men, well clothed, with weapons and ammunition, food and water, everything they needed to make their way back home. She need not worry for them anymore.

Daniel sat next to Hannah while Booke and Munro explained all of this, a dozen times and a dozen more, and still she found it hard to make sense of anything.

Blue-Jay was on the other side of the small cabin, a prisoner again, this time to his mother's ministrations. He endured the lecture she poured over his head like water from a breached dam while he ate the things she pressed on him, but there was no joy in him at this reunion.

They should be rejoicing, all of them, but they could not.

"You must have faith in Luke," Daniel said to himself as much as to her.

"Read it to me again," she said.

Daniel wiped the sweat from his brow. His hand trembled, and Hannah noted with a strange and almost cold detachment that he was in terrible pain, in spite of the fact that his arm was back in its sling. On the table before them was a dose of laudanum, as yet untouched.

"Please," she said.

He looked at the letter in his lap. It had been written on a cover torn from a Bible, written in haste with a piece of charcoal, many of the words smeared beyond recognition. Delivered to them by a breathless boy just moments before the ship weighed anchor, Hannah had read it a hundred times already but must hear it again.

Daniel's voice came rough as he did what his sister asked of him.

My beloved,

The man you know as Father O'Neill has proof in his possession that would, first, cause my brother the Earl to forfeit all he is and owns to the King, and second, send us all to the gallows as American spies. If you follow me or have

me followed, if you make any attempt to interfere or rescue me, O'Neill will
pass the letters he has to those who can do my family and yours the most harm.

Jennet Scott Huntar of Carryck
Signed by my own hand the month of July in the year of our Lord 1813.
Mon cher, forgive me my foolishness.

Below those lines, Luke had written:

I will bring her home to Lake in the Clouds before the summer is
done.

"But why the cards?" Daniel asked aloud, as he had asked before. He bent his head over the table to study them.

The seven of swords. The queen of swords.

"Why these cards?" he murmured again. "Why did she leave these particular cards?"

His eyes were clouded with worry, and his hands shook. But for once Hannah had no comfort to offer this younger brother, no wise or hopeful words, nothing but her own despair.

Chapter 41
Early August 1813, Paradise

"I still don't understand it," Annie said to Gabriel. "I wasn't gone all that long. How come you let so much happen without me?"

When Elizabeth came out of the trading post she found the children sitting on the steps. They had been in the lake, as had every child in the village; it was so hot that they would live in the water, every one of them, if it weren't for the fact that they got hungry now and then. Elizabeth resolved, right then, to go up to Lake in the Clouds at the first opportunity, so she could do the same in privacy.

Gabriel was scuffing the dirt with his bare heel, scowling so hard that his lower lip turned inside out. "I told them not to do it. I told them not to get married until you all got back, but Lily wouldn't listen to me."

"Maybe they could get married again," Annie suggested. "Don't you think that would be nice? Now that Daniel and Blue-Jay are back, and Hannah, and my folks? They could pretend it was the first time, and have the party all over again. And Blue-Jay and Teres could get married again too, and wouldn't that be a fine party?"

"I think that's the stupidest idea I ever heard," Gabriel said, disgusted. "It wasn't no fun the first time, except for maybe the cake Curiosity made. It had two dozen eggs in it, and two pounds of butter, and a whole cone of sugar. But it sure wasn't good enough to go through that all over again. All that kissing and crying." He gave a mock shiver that sent the water flying from his hair.

"Well, I'm sorry I missed it," Annie said stubbornly. "I'm sorry I wasn't here to see Curiosity run that preacher off too."

That was enough of eavesdropping; Elizabeth had no wish to hear any story that involved the Reverend Stiles, not ever again. She coughed to alert them to her presence, which made Gabriel jump into the air. He scrambled away from the steps, his face contorted with surprise and guilt.

"Sorry, Ma," he said. "Sorry. I didn't mean it, truly I didn't. It was an awful nice wedding, really it was." He straightened his back like the soldier he wanted to be and almost barked the next sentence, one he had learned by rote. "I'm mighty happy for Lily and Simon, I sure am."

"There is no need to tell falsehoods," Elizabeth said as she came down the stairs. "You are entitled to your opinion, though I do wish you really were happy for your sister. She is very content, you know."

Elizabeth stopped in front of the children as Gabriel ducked his head in sorrow and—Elizabeth had no delusions about it—disagreement. Time and Simon would have to win the boy over, because she was certainly having no success with him. He was in mourning for the sister who was lost to him, and he could see it no other way.

She said, "There are parcels to carry home. I'm going to make a cake."

Gabriel's expression was so comic that Elizabeth could hardly be offended.

"You needn't look so alarmed. It might not be as good as the one Curiosity made for the wedding party, but I trust it will be edible."

"Why would you want to make a cake in this heat?" Annie asked, as ever the politic one of the two.

"Why, for your brother and his new wife," Elizabeth said. "We couldn't be there when Blue-Jay married, but we can certainly do our best to welcome his bride to Paradise."

Annie looked away quickly, too polite and kind to say what she was thinking, though Elizabeth could read it very clearly from the way her mouth jerked.

"There is no need to worry," Elizabeth said with all the dignity she could muster. "I have studied the recipe very closely, and this time I believe I will be successful."

"I better come along and help," Gabriel said solemnly. "There might be some mistakes and you'll need help cleaning up."

"You know, you could just give up on baking, Auntie." Annie's expression was all solicitous concern. "You don't have to be good at everything."

Did the child realize that she was mimicking Elizabeth herself? She swallowed her smile and allowed that it was true that her cakes often went wrong, but she wasn't ready to concede defeat quite yet. Baking was far more challenging than chemistry, where measurements could be depended upon and any result, no matter how unexpected, was interesting and worthwhile.

"I heard that you shouldn't be out walking in the sun," Gabriel said, when they had come about half the way. "Da said so."

Elizabeth pulled up short in surprise. It was true that Nathaniel's hovering over her had increased in proportion to the expansion of her waist. At times he was so excessively considerate that she could hardly contain her irritation. Beyond that, he wasn't above issuing commands, something he would never dare to do in other circumstances. An unborn child was a tyrant, and it made Nathaniel into one too.

All that had eased a little since the homecoming. They were all of them so preoccupied with Daniel's health that her own was forgotten, at least temporarily.

She was just about to ask Gabriel who exactly had decided that moderate exercise and sunlight were detrimental when she realized that they stood at that spot on the path where the doctor's place was visible between the trees.

Annie, who could be more direct than Gabriel when she really wanted something, did not bother with diversions. "Can we stop and see Curiosity? I'll bet she's got something cool to drink."

"You just want to see Martha and Callie," Gabriel said, grumbling a little that his cousin had not gone along with what he had counted as a very fine distraction.

"Never mind, I see your plan," Elizabeth said. "You two are hoping that Curiosity will talk me out of baking this cake. Oh, ye of little faith."

"No," Annie said. "Or not just that." She blushed her apology. "I'm sure you'll make a very good cake, Auntie. It's just that there's a post rider come and he's standing right there talking to Curiosity—and maybe there's a letter for us."

Elizabeth's heart lurched into a faster rhythm, and for a moment she lost the ability to put a sentence together out of simple fear.

"Maybe there's word of Jennet and Luke," Gabriel said, hopping in place.

"Perhaps," Elizabeth said, trying to control the tremble in her own voice. And then she gave in to the inevitable. "Go and see, then."

Gabriel dashed off before the words had completely left her mouth, but Annie, sweet Annie, came closer and touched Elizabeth's hand.

"Are you coming, Aunt?"

"No," Elizabeth said. "You go ahead. I'll continue on my way home, or your uncle will come looking for me."

In the shade of a stand of beech trees Elizabeth stopped and lowered herself onto a stump. To catch her breath. To order her thoughts.

More than Daniel's health, more than Hannah's state of mind, Elizabeth was worried about Jennet and Luke, and so was Nathaniel. They often talked half the night, trying to work out from the little bit of information they had what might have happened. Nathaniel found the letter Luke had written so many months ago, and read the parts about the priest aloud.

"I should have paid more attention," he said, mostly to himself.

Elizabeth didn't correct him, because it would do no good. And because he was right. They should have paid more attention, and insisted that Jennet put herself out of harm's way. But they had been thinking of Daniel's welfare, of Hannah and Blue-Jay, and they had been selfish.

Just a few days after the wanderers had returned home, a special messenger had arrived, one of the men whom Luke depended on to move back and forth across the border without detection. He brought a single item: a broadsheet folded into quarters. Elizabeth had read it so many times that she could almost recite it word for word, but in the course of the day she felt the need to see the ink on the page, as she did now. She took it out of her basket and read it again.

Substantial Reward!!!

For information leading to the apprehension of the liar, murderer, thief, and abductor of women calling himself Father Adam O'Neill.

This man has impersonated a Roman Catholic priest for more than a year, insinuating himself into military camps and garrisons from the Great Lakes to the Sorel. Once he had gained the confidence of the officers, it was his habit to rob the paymasters and disappear.

On June 25 the imposter Father O'Neill murdered Colonel Marcel Caudebec and three other officers in the garrison at Île aux Noix before disappearing with almost five thousand pounds. At the same time he abducted a young widow as a hostage.

The lady is by name Mrs. Jennet Huntar, originally of Scotland. She is twenty-nine years old, short of stature and slender, with blond hair in curls, cropped short. Her eyes are blue, and she has a small red scar in the shape of a star on her left palm. Her life is in danger while she is in this man's power.

The criminal known as O'Neill is a man a full six feet tall, strong of build, about fifty years old. He wears his black hair long to cover the fact that his right earlobe has been severed. Nothing is known as yet of his real name, his place of origin, or his destination, except that he meant to go south when he left Canada, probably by ship.

For any reliable information on this criminal the subscriber will pay generously, in proportion to the usefulness of the report.

Luke Scott, Forbes & Son,
Rue Bonsecours, Montreal

The text was repeated in French, and in the margin Luke had written a few short sentences. He was putting an advertisement with similar wording in every newspaper from Halifax to Saint Domingue. What he didn't write, what he didn't need to say, was that his search had been less than fruitful in its first days.

"Ma," came Daniel's voice from just behind her. Elizabeth, lost in her thoughts of Luke and Jennet and the man called O'Neill, jumped a foot into the air. She hid the broadsheet in the folds of her skirt even as she scolded herself for such foolishness.

Daniel put his hand on her shoulder and held it there for a moment.

"I've been calling your name, didn't you hear me?" He settled down next to her on the log and stretched out his legs, strong and lean and burned brown by the sun.

"Lost in my thoughts," Elizabeth said, patting him on the knee. He was wearing a hunting shirt, breechclout, and summer moccasins and he carried only a knife on his belt and no other weapon, not even a rifle. Because he could make no use of one, though he spent hours every day trying to relearn the things he had been doing without reflection since he was a boy.

In spite of all that, and even with an arm in a sling, her firstborn son looked to her to be a perfectly made human being. He was too thin, but that would soon be remedied. His color was much better already.

Elizabeth touched the eagle feather that hung from the cord that bound his hair. He caught her hand and held it away from himself.

"Ma."

"Yes, I'm sorry."

Something else that had changed: the son who had once loved to have his scalp rubbed, who had climbed into his mother's lap when he was far too big for such things, all traces of that boy were gone. Daniel disliked being touched, as he disliked being indoors or in any confined space, as he disliked sleeping in a bed. He slept outdoors, on a pallet he put down in a different place every night.

They were silent for a moment.

Finally he said, "There's a few trees down in the wind just beyond Eagle Rock."

"Ah," Elizabeth said. "You've been far today."

"My legs still work just fine."

She caught her breath and let it go. It would do no good to lecture him about hope and perseverance, and even less to humor his mood. But there was something that must be said, and so she did.

"You know," Elizabeth said slowly. "If I were to find myself in your position—" He stiffened, but she carried on. "For example, if I were to suddenly lose my sight and be unable to read, I know that I would be less than stoic about it."

But eventually I would move on.

That sentence hung unsaid between them, words dancing like dust motes in the shafts of light that slanted through the branches.

"Ma," he said. "I need time to think things through."

"There are many options open to you." She said it with more certainty than she felt.

"I know that." He stood abruptly, and held out his good hand to help her to her feet. "I know that, I do." And then: "I know you want me to take the school, and I'm thinking about it."

"I never was very good at hiding my thoughts," Elizabeth said. "Though for years I've been trying to learn that trick." She forced herself to stop talking, though it cost her a great deal.

They stood side by side in the silent woods where dragonflies shimmered in the heat. Elizabeth had the sudden sense that something unexpected, unwanted, was coming. She raised a hand to stop him even before he had begun, but there was no force in nature that could silence him once he had decided to speak up.

"I'm moving back to Lake in the Clouds. I know you and Da have to stay here in the village, but I . . ." His words trailed away.

"You what?" Elizabeth said, as calmly as she could manage.

"I need to be on the mountain," he said.

She said nothing, because she could not trust her voice.

He said, "I was hoping you'd understand."

The things she understood were many. Her son was a grown man who wanted, who needed, to be out on his own. Lily had left them and now Daniel must too. He would never come back again, not in the way she wanted him to.

"Have you spoken to your father?"

He nodded.

"And he gave you permission."

"Unhappily."

"Well, then, I can do no less."

She pressed her handkerchief to her forehead. "You will come to supper this evening?"

His hesitation was so very slight that Elizabeth could almost overlook it.

"Of course," he said. "Of course I'll be there."

She said, "You must still live in the world, Daniel. You understand that?"

He managed a grin for her, and in it she saw something of his old self. "You'll see me pretty much every day," he said. An answer to the question she had asked, and one she hadn't.

"The sad truth is, we can't laze around here all afternoon." Lily made this announcement around a great yawn, as she stared up through the trees to the sky. "There is work to be done yet today."

She and Simon had come deep into the forest to bathe in a little pond that Lily had always favored. It was cool here in the grove of beeches and white pine, as cool a place as there was to be found on an August afternoon, outside the caves at Lake in the Clouds.

Thinking of the mountain generally produced a wave of homesickness in Lily, but today the heat took even that out of her. This pond—as children they had called it the frog pond—was only a quarter hour's walk from their cabin. She could come here as often as she pleased, with or without Simon.

Her husband. Sometimes she said that word to herself, just to hear it. She had a husband; she was a married woman. An idea so very odd that it made her turn and hide her face in the blanket.

Not that she had any regrets, Lily told herself firmly. She had married a good man, a reliable man, a man worth loving. A man who made her breath catch in her throat and her heart gallop, who made her laugh. And if there *was* something missing, maybe it was something she didn't really need anyway.

Lily had been thinking about it for a long time now, and she had come to the conclusion that the tenderness she had felt toward Nicholas Wilde—something that was absent when she looked at Simon—had less to do with love than it did with pity. If Nicholas ever came back to Paradise, something Lily tried to imagine now and then, she had the idea that it would be far harder for him than it would be for her.

Simon worried about Nicholas, she could almost smell it at times when she caught him looking at her in a certain way. But he would not raise the subject, out of pride and most certainly out of fear at what she might say. And because he was wise enough to let sleeping dogs lie.

Lily raised her head from the blanket and watched Simon floating on his back like a log. A strangely dappled log, Lily observed. Stripped down, Simon presented an odd picture. He was darkly tanned on face and neck and arms, and since he had been working without his shirt—something he had hesitated to do at first—his back and chest were now almost as dark.

But from the waist down he was milk white, because he had re- fused to give up his breeks for a breechclout, even in the unbearable August heat. Lily teased him about this unmercifully, but he never wavered.

"I've shaved my beard for you," he would say. "But I will keep the other bits I hold dear out of the public eye. I don't like the way Missy Parker looks at me as it is."

His modesty surprised her and at the same time it was endearing. And it was true that women watched him. Lydia Ratz had stopped Lily in the village shortly before the wedding, not to ask about Stiles, as Lily had been dreading, but to voice an opinion.

"You never were mean, Lily Bonner, not like some. I hope you won't be the kind who won't let her husband dance with other women. He's a good dancer, is your Simon."

"As long as it's only dancing you're talking about," Lily had an- swered with her sweetest smile. "And dancing where I can see you, forbye."

She used some of Simon's expressions, now and then, because they amused her and it irritated him, though he tried to hide it. They spoke quite a lot about his past in Scotland.

"Did you never wear a kilt, then?" she asked him, and realized too late that she had invited a history lecture. If she protested he would remind her that she was half Scots herself, and plough ahead with his story.

There were benefits to be had to letting Simon go on with these occasional lessons. While he talked of the indignities visited upon the Scots by vengeful England, including the banning of the kilt, she could watch him walking back and forth, the play of muscles in his throat, the broad turn of his wrist when he raised a hand to make a point.

Sometimes she wondered if being married had damaged her ability to reason. Certainly she found herself contemplating things so strange that she had no words to describe them. And neither was it necessary, she told herself firmly. There were other things in the world beyond the physical fact of her husband's presence, the mechanics of the male body, and the things they did together.

Important, interesting, engaging things. Except it was hard to keep her mind on any of them just now, in the first weeks of her marriage.

Watching Simon float, Lily wondered if she could make sense of her thoughts if she picked up paper and pencil and let herself draw what she was seeing. It was an idea that came to her quite often, and every time she was startled, as she was now, to feel herself blushing so fiercely that she felt it deep in her belly.

Lily sat up suddenly and pulled her chemise about herself. "It's getting late!"

Simon opened one eye and peered at her without changing his position. "Late for what? Are you lonely over there, Lily my love?"

"Late in the afternoon," Lily said. "Late in the day. Late for tea, late for supper. Late because in case you didn't realize, my mother's threatening to make a cake."

"I like cake," Simon said, his arms moving through the water in long sweeps as he propelled his way to the bank.

"Not my mother's cakes," Lily said. "Even the pigs have a hard time working up enthusiasm for my mother's cakes. The only person who ever choked down a whole piece—" She stopped herself.

Simon came to stand next to the blanket, shaking himself like a dog so that the cold water rained over her. She should scold him, but now that she had raised the topic of her brother all the playfulness in her had drained away.

"Your brother," Simon said, falling down beside her. "Shall we talk of Daniel now?"

Lily grimaced. How many times had he asked the question in the last days?

"No," she said briefly, turning away. "I can't talk about him without getting angry, and I don't want to be angry just now."

Simon made a satisfied sound deep in his throat and knelt down beside her, leaning over to press a kiss to her cheek.

"Oh, look," he said in his most innocent voice. "Your linen is wet through. Shall we hang it up to dry?"

Lily laughed and batted his hands away from her buttons. "You are insatiable."

"And you," he said, running a hand down her hip. "You are a liar if you're claiming you don't want me again. The proof is right here, if you'll just open—"

"Simon," Lily said, slapping his hands away yet again. "Anyone could come by here, you know. This spot is known to the whole village."

"In all the times we've been here nobody has ever come by," he said. "Or maybe we were just too busy to notice if they did."

That made her sit up again and clutch her gown to her breast. Lily's hair, half-wet still, clung to her face and shoulders and to the outline of her breasts, but it was her eyes that caught Simon's attention, filled to brimming with reluctant tears.

"Come now," he said softly, pulling her down again to hold her. "He'll talk to you when he's able. You know he will."

"He talks to me now," Lily mumbled against his neck. "Except he doesn't say anything of importance."

They were quiet for a moment in the cool of the forest shade, listening to the birds overhead.

"Why won't he talk to me?" Lily said.

Simon stroked her head and tried to think of something to say that would be both truthful and comforting. He had been looking for those words since the day Daniel had come home from the war, and he would continue looking, without success.

Because he hadn't come home, not really, not the way his sister expected of him. He had lost the use of his arm, maybe forever. He had left other things behind too, things that were harder to put into words but that sat plain enough for any man to see on his face.

"I'm his twin," Lily said. "Who else understands him as I do?" Then she stiffened slightly and raised her face to look at Simon directly.

"We should have waited," she said. "With the wedding, we should have waited."

"Perhaps," Simon said, thinking to himself that it would have made no difference at all; it wasn't his sister's wedding that weighed Daniel down, nor was it his mother's rounded belly or the fact that his family had moved off the mountain.

It did have something to do with Jennet, who had sacrificed a great deal—maybe everything—to win him his freedom. That weighed heavy on him and Blue-Jay both. If it weren't for their mothers, Simon had the idea, the two young men would have gone off already to join in Luke's search for Jennet. Simon felt the same way himself; she was the laird's sister, after all.

But Luke had promised to bring her home by the end of this very month, and they must be satisfied with that, though the days ticked on without word. In another week it would be September, and if they had no message by then, it would be next to impossible to keep the Bonner men in Paradise. The women would fight them, but nothing short of the end of the world would keep them from going after Jennet.

He said part of what he was thinking aloud. "Pray God Luke has found their trail."

Lily gave him a sharp look. "Pray God he is on his way here with Jennet even as we speak."

"Aye." Simon rubbed his eyes. "But I fear it won't be as easy as that."

"You blame yourself," Lily said, with sudden understanding, and she saw Simon duck his head like a schoolboy. "But why? From everything I've heard—"

"He had everyone fooled. Aye."

"The colonel and the garrison—"

"And Jennet herself and Hannah. Aye," he repeated.

"But then how—"

"Because," he said, forcefully, angrily. "Because I saw the man the last time I was on the island and I never looked at him hard enough. I took him to be the priest he claimed to be."

This had never occurred to Lily. In all the talk about what had happened on Nut Island, he had been quiet, adding very little to the conversation.

"There's no cause for despair," Lily said, wanting to comfort herself as much as Simon. "You've said yourself that there's no one in all of French Canada with better connections than Luke."

To that he had nothing to say, and with good reason; it was a poor excuse for optimism, and they both knew it. On the way home it occurred to Lily that all three of her brothers were unhappy: Gabriel because he had not yet accepted the fact of Simon in his sister's life, Luke because his bride had been stolen away from him by a man who had posed a threat he had not been able to forestall, and Daniel, for reasons she did not like to list for herself.

"And my mother is making a cake."

Simon seemed to have followed the tortuous path of her thoughts; he put an arm around her shoulder and pulled her close as they walked. "A diversion that will lift her spirits, no doubt."

"Even if it does mean sour stomachs all around."

Simon slapped his stomach twice. "There was never a Ballentyne born who couldn't stand up to a wee piece of cake."

"Good," Lily said. "Then you can eat my portion as well as your own."

"Blue-Jay looks contented," Hannah said. "I think Teres will make him a good wife."

"She'll make a better wife than a daughter-in-law, at least at first," said Nathaniel.

They were sitting at Lake in the Clouds, close enough to the water to catch the cooling breeze from the waterfalls, but just out of the spray. Blue-Jay and Runs-from-Bears were in the water, and Many-Doves sat on a flat rock on the far side of the lake. Beside her was the young woman who had come with them from Canada, Blue-Jay's new wife, called Teres.

In many ways she was a younger version of Many-Doves; she had the same still beauty and serious way of looking at the world, but the similarities ended there. Teres was not so attached to the old ways as her mother-in-law, which delighted Annie and worried Runs-from-Bears.

"Ayuh," said Nathaniel. "It will be a long winter up here on the mountain." But there was more amusement in his expression than worry. Hannah supposed he was thinking of his own new son-in-law, and about Lily. Both families had adjustments to make.

"Everything's changing." Hannah said it mostly to herself, but her father seemed to understand what she was unable to say more directly.

"That's the way of it," he said. "You thinking of your little sister?"

"Of Lily, yes, and Blue-Jay, and the new baby coming, and Daniel."

"Daniel will find his way, though it don't feel that way just now. And what of you?" Nathaniel asked, getting to the heart of it.

"I don't know." She paused. "I don't know where I belong. How I fit in. It feels as though I've caught some kind of fever in the blood."

"That's the war," Nathaniel said. "Being caught up in it like you were. And it's Jennet."

Jennet. Hannah drew in a hard breath and held it. Jennet, who was never very far from her thoughts, but whose name she could not say out of fear.

But there were other things that must be said, and if those words were to come to her, it could only be here, on this mountain where she was born and raised. They wouldn't be hurried, but that didn't matter: her father was a patient man and he would let his children lead their own lives.

His eyes were following an eagle circling overhead, but he was waiting for her, ready to listen, willing to understand.

She said, "I never read the letter that Manny wrote to me."

He was waiting for the rest of it, and in the meantime there was nothing to read in the way he was looking at her. No disappointment, no expectations.

"Not so long ago it was all I could think about, but now—I don't want to know how he died."

He rubbed a thumb along his jaw and then looked over his shoulder, toward the little graveyard where their people were buried.

"I always thought your grandfather would come back here to die," he said. "To be buried next to her." He looked into the shadows for a long moment, thinking of his mother, of the grandmother Hannah had loved so dearly and lost so young.

"But he never came. I expect he's gone now, but I don't know that for a fact. Sometimes I wake up at night wondering, and you know, daughter, I think maybe that's just what he wanted. He wanted me to think of him out there in the world someplace. It's a comfort to me, that much I got to admit. To think he might walk up the mountain some morning and be standing there when I wake up—if I live another fifty years, I'll still be wondering if maybe—" He paused. "If that's what he wanted, then it's the kind of gift a father can give to a son."

"But not a husband to a wife," Hannah completed for him. "I *know* Strikes-the-Sky is dead."

"Do you?"

She flushed with sudden and unexpected agitation, feeling the color rising in her face. The things she wanted to say would sound childish and petulant, and so she made herself breathe in and out before she spoke.

"Yes. I know it in my heart. In my bones."

"And if you're wrong?"

Hannah's head jerked up. "I'm not. I'm not wrong."

"Late at night, you don't sit up sometimes, thinking maybe you heard his voice?"

She stiffened.

"I thought so."

After a long time her father said, "Manny's been waiting for you to come find him, you know. He needs to tell you as much as you need to hear it."

He started to get up, but Hannah held out a hand to stop him. She said, "Before he died, Liam said that Paradise would be too small for me. That I couldn't be content here, after . . . everything. I thought at first it was just his bitterness talking. He was bitter, Da, and with cause. But I can't forget what he said either."

Her father was looking at her, hard. It was his turn to be unsettled, and Hannah felt some satisfaction and some embarrassment.

"Where is it you're thinking of going?" Nathaniel asked, his voice even and steady. As if they were talking about what to have for supper.

"Nowhere," she said, more sharply than she intended. "There is nowhere I want to go." What she meant to say, what she could not bring herself to say, was more complicated: she belonged nowhere else. There was no place for her to go.

"And you can't quite sit still either."

"Yes," she said on a sigh. "That's it."

Her father said, "There was a letter from Ethan, come just before you got home."

"I'm not interested in Manhattan—" She began, and stopped herself when she saw by his expression that she had jumped to the wrong conclusion.

"He's got four new families willing to settle here, take up the empty farmsteads, and maybe more. All of them got some kind of trade. All of them got children. I suppose he was thinking he needed to fill up the new schoolhouse."

"Is he sending along a teacher too?" Hannah asked, a little unnerved by this unexpected turn in the conversation.

"Not yet, though he's looking. I got the idea he could scare up old Queen Bess if we asked him to, or that Mr. Kant your mother likes so much."

"Ah." Hannah wrapped her arms around her knees and put down her head. "And what about a doctor? Is that what you're thinking, you should ask Ethan to find a doctor for Paradise?"

Nathaniel Bonner was not easily flustered. He looked her straight in the eye. "That's a question for you to answer, daughter. I've been wondering, to tell the truth—"

She interrupted him again. "If I still wanted to give up medicine."

"Pretty much." And then, after a longer pause. "You needn't worry about leaving people here without a doctor, is what I'm saying. If that's on your mind."

Hannah gave a sharp laugh. "What I need are answers, not more questions."

Nathaniel pushed himself up, his long legs unfolding. "I know what you need," he said, looking down at her. The sun was at his back and she could not see his face, but Hannah had the idea that he was smiling at her. "It just ain't in my power to give it to you. But I'll say this. Moving on ain't a cure either. There's something your ma said to me a long time ago, I never have forgot it. She said, every one of us has got a few demons that we carry with us wherever we go, whether we want to or not. They can't be shook off or run away from."

"You want me to stay in Paradise," Hannah said.

"I'm asking you not to run off for the wrong reasons," he said, holding out a hand to help her to her feet. Then he smiled at her, and cupped her face with his hand. "And I'm hoping you'll stay around too. Right now, though, we got to get down to the village. Your stepmother has got this supper party planned, and she'll need some help."

Hannah walked out on a rock that leaned over the lake, balancing there as she had done so many hundreds of times, as a girl and young woman, poised for the fall.

"Will you stop by and see Manny?"

Her father's question came to her above the roar of the falls and it followed her down into the water, cold and clear and absolute.

From the door Curiosity said, "Elizabeth Middleton Bonner, you promised."

Elizabeth started and dropped the spoon in her hand so that it clattered on the table.

"You promised that you'd come to me next time you got it in your head to bake a cake. And now look at you. You ain't got the sense God gave a gnat, I swear. Stoking the oven in this heat."

"But this time I think I have figured it out," Elizabeth said, too pleased with herself to take Curiosity's grumbling seriously. "I went very slowly, really I did."

"Hmmm." Curiosity came closer and sniffed at the batter in the bowl. "Well, I suppose we got a miracle or two due we could call in." And she laughed her deep, rough laugh when Elizabeth smacked her on the shoulder.

"Who tattled on me?" Elizabeth asked. "I suppose it must have been Gabriel and Annie."

Curiosity raised her eyebrows so high that they disappeared beneath her headcloth. "Ain't nobody said a word to me about you and a cake. I would have been over here long ago if they had. I come to bring a letter."

"Let me guess, Ethan has found another ten families to settle here."

"Not yet, though I wouldn't put it past the boy. No, this letter here, this one for Nathaniel. Address was writ in a fancy hand and that's all I know." Curiosity studied the writing as if there were something hidden in the curlicues that would reveal itself with enough contemplation. "I ain't sunk so low as to open a letter don't got my name on it, no matter how curious I might be." She pushed up her sleeves.

"Hand me that pan, I'ma grease it for you." And then, in a tone that was too carefully modulated: "Daniel come talk to you yet?" Curiosity said.

Elizabeth sent her a sharp look. "I suppose I was the last to hear about this newest plan of his, as usual. He gets permission from everybody else and then comes to me."

"I think it will do the boy some good, Elizabeth," Curiosity said. "He's got some demons to tussle with, and it's best he do it up there on that mountain where he come into the world. Many-Doves right there to make sure he don't starve, and Bears will see to it he too busy to feel sorry for himself."

Elizabeth stopped and pressed a hand to her eyes.

Curiosity's tone softened. "I know it hard, with him just home and all."

The tears she had been holding back for so many days loosed

themselves without warning. They rolled down Elizabeth's face in great heavy drops that spilled into the batter before she could catch them.

"Never mind," Curiosity said. "A little salt won't hurt it none. Might just do the trick too."

"It's from a lawyer," Nathaniel said, looking at the letter on the kitchen table with something less than enthusiasm. He had no love of lawyers, nor of anyone associated with the legal profession, a prejudice Elizabeth had never been able to cure him of.

"It won't bite." She meant her tone to be playful, but feared it was more impatient. Not that it would worry Nathaniel; he wasn't a man to be hurried.

Elizabeth was sitting with her feet up, directing Sally in the setting of the table while she fanned herself with a folded newspaper. There were just the three of them in the kitchen for the moment.

Nathaniel met her gaze and she gestured with her chin at the unopened letter. It was written on heavy paper, and the seal cracked open with a pop.

"Well?" Elizabeth said. "Is it from a lawyer?"

"Aye. A Mr. Prime, of Manhattan." His eyes ran down the page in a skittering movement, his mouth pursing harder with each line scanned.

"Liam Kirby's lawyer," he said.

"Liam Kirby?" Elizabeth echoed. Sally heard the name too, and turned toward them.

"Read it for yourself, if you don't believe me." He held the letter out to her, and Elizabeth shook her newspaper at him.

"No need to be so cross. What does he want?"

"Well," Nathaniel said, turning the page over and reading on. "First off, it looks like Liam claimed Martha as his natural daughter and heir just before he died—"

Elizabeth started to interrupt, but Nathaniel's sharp look stopped her.

"Says here somebody sent him a letter writ by Liam, witnessed and all."

"Why, that must have been Hannah," Elizabeth said. "And she said nothing at all."

Nathaniel hummed his agreement. "Second, it seems Liam asked that Will Spencer and I be appointed her guardians. And—"

His eyes ran more quickly over the third page of the letter. "There's an accounting of what Martha's got coming to her."

Sally put a bowl of cucumbers down on the table with a thump. "Go on, then, before I die of wondering. What did he leave little Martha?"

"Everything he owned," Nathaniel said, putting the letter down. "Which makes Martha a very wealthy young girl. If this Mr. Prime is to be believed."

Over supper it was all they could talk about. Nathaniel read part of the letter aloud while the faces around the table gave him their perfect attention.

Some of Daniel's old humor came back to him for the moment. He said, "Maybe I should have joined the navy after all, if there was that kind of prize money to be got."

"It's not all prize money," Nathaniel said. "Mr. Prime writes that Liam inherited most of it himself. From a widow by the name of Mrs. Nora Kerr of Park Street."

His head swung around to Hannah, who had started visibly. "Do you know that name?"

"Yes. I knew Mrs. Kerr when I was in Manhattan. She was a friend of Uncle and Aunt Spencer's. Kitty and I dined with her while we were there."

It seemed a lifetime ago, those days in Manhattan. Hannah was struggling with the memories, though she tried not to show it. "Mr. and Mrs. Kerr took Liam in when he was first in the city."

"Well." Elizabeth was clearly relieved to hear such a reasonable explanation. She leaned back in her chair and crossed her hands over her belly.

"What were you worried about, Ma?" Daniel asked with a half-grin. "Did you think this Mrs. Kerr was some loose woman who left him all her money out of gratitude for his attentions?"

"You are crude, Daniel," she said in a conversational tone. Nathaniel saw that she wanted to correct her son's poor manners, but was too pleased to see some of his old spirit to discourage him. If he wanted to get up on the table and dance a jig she would have said nothing at all to ruin the moment. The old Daniel, the one they were still waiting for, had been joyful in spirit and able to share that with everyone around him.

"Have you spoken to Martha yet?" Lily asked.

"After supper," Nathaniel said.

"I wonder what the girl will think, to hear such news." Simon asked the question of no one in particular. "To know herself wealthy in one stroke."

"Relieved," said Lily. "Thankful."

"Frightened," said Daniel. He looked at the faces around him. "My guess is, she'll be worried about Jemima coming back to lay a claim."

Elizabeth's face flooded with color and then drained again.

Daniel said, "I'm sorry, Ma, but you know it's true. If Jemima got wind of this—" He looked toward the letter. "All that money and land, she'd be back here in a blink."

"But would she have a claim on it?" Elizabeth looked at the letter as if it might answer her question. And then: "I fear she might. Martha is her daughter, and she is not yet of a legal age." She put both hands on her belly, as she always did when something frightened her, as if to give the child growing there comfort she could not spare herself.

Daniel was too wound up in the idea of Jemima to notice the distress he was causing his mother, but Lily was not. She jumped in before Nathaniel could.

"I don't think we need worry about that," she said firmly, sending her brother a hard look. "I would wager that Jemima is as far away from here as the money she took from—from that preacher will allow her to go. How she could possibly hear about what happened to Liam, or this bequest—I can't imagine it."

Nathaniel put down his fork. "I expect you're right, Lily. But it's probably best if we don't advertise the news anyway. It's enough for Martha to know, and Curiosity."

"And the lawyers in Manhattan," said Daniel.

"Aye, well," Nathaniel said. "I suppose I'll have to deal with them, like it or not. I'm just thankful Will Spencer is in the city so I won't have to go down there myself."

Simon had been quiet through this exchange, but there was something bothering him. Elizabeth saw it too. She said, "Simon, tell me what you are thinking."

Nathaniel had a good deal of respect for Simon Ballentyne, and he had come to like him. There were times, though, when he was too quick to speak his mind. In that way he and Lily were alike, and Nathaniel worried occasionally that she had chosen the man because he challenged her in ways few men could. A marriage based on that particular kind of spark alone could go cold, and it worried him.

Lily put her hand on Simon's arm and made a low, warning sound, but he only covered it with his own and went on to answer the question put to him.

"Perhaps the girl would want her mother to come back if she had the choice. Jemima may be mean tempered and cruel hearted, but it would take more than that to cut the tie that binds mother to daughter. And I'm wondering if she'd hesitate to say what she truly wants for fear of offending the people who have been kind to her."

For one strange moment, Nathaniel had the odd idea that his former mother-in-law's spirit was in the room, and that she had used Simon's mouth to speak her mind from the grave. Falling-Day would have said exactly the same thing, and she would have been just as right.

Elizabeth was looking as surprised as Nathaniel felt, but there was no displeasure in her expression. She said, "Why, Simon, what a philosopher you promise to be."

"I suppose that's why you married him, sister," Daniel said dryly. "His debating skills."

Lily was still enough of a newlywed to blush, but she lifted her chin and looked her brother directly in the eye. "That's part of it, aye. I hope one day you'll do as well for yourself when you go looking for a bride."

Daniel's jaw clenched so hard that the muscles there rolled and twitched. His eyes were tear bright and hard, and in them Nathaniel saw that the boy had given up on any kind of normal future for himself.

Across the table he met Elizabeth's eye.

You see? Her expression spoke to him clearly. *You see now how it is with him?*

He was starting to see it, yes. Nathaniel looked at his middle son, and understood that he had come home from one war to fight another.

Chapter 42

It seemed to Lily that the earth had slipped out of its orbit and was moving, day by day, closer to the sun. It was the only possible explanation for temperatures beyond measuring, the kind of still heat that drained the very color from the world and turned it into a dusty, shimmering, pallid image of itself.

She gave up cooking—no sane person, she claimed, could think of lighting the stove in such heat—and so they ate cold meat and cheese and stale bread, or Simon ate them: Lily found the heat had robbed her of her appetite for most things, food first among them.

There were other things she gave up, things she missed more. Once a day she went to see her mother—who was not supposed to move about in the heat but would, if it was the only way to see her children. After this visit to her mother, which she paid in the earliest, coolest part of the day, Lily moved lethargically from home to frog pond to meetinghouse.

"You needn't look at me like that," she told Curiosity on the third day of the heat wave. They had crossed paths in the center of the village, Lily on her way home and Curiosity about to pay a call on Goody Cunningham, who had the shingles. "I'm not with child. My courses just started."

"Hmmm." Curiosity's lips pursed themselves and only then did Lily realize that she had given something away.

Not that she wanted to fall pregnant, not so soon, but she had half expected her courses to stay away and had been surprised when they did not. And neither could she keep herself from wondering at the workings of her own contrary body.

In the village folks spoke of rain as they might speak of the Second Coming: as something they were supposed to believe in, no matter how unlikely it seemed. The men sitting on the porch at the trading post spoke of little else but the weather, watching the sky and talking of other heat waves, most especially the one in the summer of '72 or maybe it was '79—the argument raged on—when the corn died on the stalk for lack of rain.

Another week of such temperatures without rainfall would bring them to that point, but such things were not said aloud. The heat stripped them of everything but their superstitions. If someone came up with the courage to suggest some kind of heathen sacrifice or a rain dance, even Missy Parker would have hesitated before condemning such godlessness.

Only a few seemed not to mind the heat so very much. Lily's own father and brother and male cousins suffered less in their breechclouts. Simon had yet to give up his breeks for Mohawk dress, but the heat would not slow him down. Day by day he went about building benches and bookcases and whatever else his mother-in-law wanted for the new schoolhouse, without pause or complaint.

Lily could not help but hold his equilibrium against him, though she spoke of it only to her brother on one of his rare visits.

"He grew up in rainy Scotland," she pointed out. "It's quite unreasonable of him to manage so well."

At least she could still make Daniel laugh. It was a small thing but she cherished it, and when he came to sit with her she worked at winning his smile, desperate to make him comfortable enough to confide in her. He was affectionate and attentive and every day a little more distracted, and it broke her heart as much as the heat wrung her dry.

He had come to accept Simon as her husband, and if he had doubts he kept them to himself, along with so many other things.

It was Simon who kept Lily afloat in the rising August heat. On the days she forced herself to go down to the meetinghouse to work a little, he would bring an offering: an early apple, a sunflower from Anna's garden, a piece of maple sugar.

"You are very good to me when I am such a cranky old thing,"

Lily said on the seventh day of the heat wave. He had come late in the afternoon, carrying an earthenware jug of cool water laced with ginger and mint, collected from Curiosity's kitchen.

Lily swallowed half the water in three long gulps and offered him the rest after she wet her handkerchief with it.

"And how am I to respond to that?" Simon said. "No matter what I say it is bound to get me in trouble."

On reflection it was clear to Lily that Simon was right, though she would not say so aloud. Instead she wiped her face and neck with the dampened handkerchief and looked down at the picture she had been working over—beech trees stirring in a fictional breeze—and she scowled at it. From the corner of her eye she saw the way Simon was watching her, as a bird might watch a snake.

"What?" she asked. "What? Have I grown horns?" She patted her forehead.

He leaned across the table and kissed her right there where a horn should have been. "You're a wicked-tongued creature betimes, Lily, but I'll no be put off by a few sharp words." He was grinning.

Fighting back a smile she said, "You are a thief, sir. Leave me my mood, no matter how poor it may be."

"There's a better way to shift your mood," he said, catching her arm and pulling her around the table.

"Not now, Simon, really—"

But he had something very different in mind. He placed her in front of the window and tilted her head up.

"Relief in sight," he said.

The sky had been like a glazed blue bowl for so many days, but now on the horizon clouds were gathering and the eternal blue was giving way, darkening like a bruise to a tarnished copper streaked with pinks and purples.

"I could never put those colors down on canvas," she said. "They defy capture."

Simon hummed into her ear. "A storm at twilight, and a long cool night to follow."

"The wind is coming up. A proper storm. I do love a summer storm."

"Aye, and one to raise the roof by the look of it."

For a moment they stood quietly and watched the sky churning in the distance, clouds tumbling upon themselves like wrestling boys determined to draw blood. The wind came in short gusts at first, stirring the dust in the road and the limp leaves in the trees. It touched Lily's damp hair and made her tremble.

The storm was stirring more than the clouds in the sky. In the village people had begun to move about. Women took washing down, boys chased chickens and pigs to get them under cover. Children ran from the trading post to the well and back again, their bare heels kicking up dust. Martha Kuick and Callie Wilde came up from the lake, running so that their wet hair streamed behind them. Martha put back her head and let out a long, undulating cry that bounced back from the heavens. Her life had taken a turn for the better, and while she was not directly cheerful since the news came from Manhattan, she seemed far more settled and sure of herself.

Simon folded his arms around Lily and she leaned back, her head bedded in the hollow of his shoulder, and shivered in delight.

She said, "Best of all I like a storm when I'm snug in bed and can hide under the covers when the thunder crashes. If we start home now we'll be wet through by the time we get there. We'll have to take off our clothes to dry." She laughed out loud in delight.

Against her hair Simon said, "What a wanton you are, Lily Ballentyne." He worked up a dramatic sigh and rocked her against him. "But if nothing else will do—"

"Simon," Lily said suddenly. "A rider, look."

"It will be McGarrity," Simon said, nipping at the soft skin behind her ear. "Anna's expecting him this evening from Johnstown."

"Maybe she is," Lily said, pulling away. "But that is not Jed. It's Luke. Luke's come home, and all he's brought with him is the storm."

Outside the first fat drops of rain struck the ground like small fists. In the time it took Luke to walk into the meetinghouse the sprinkling had turned into a downpour that filled the world with cold sweet air. The first thunder rolled toward them from a great distance, and the chill that ran up Lily's spine robbed her of the ability to speak.

"I saw you at the window," Luke said by way of greeting. There were dark circles under his eyes, and a few days' growth of beard on his face. "Are the folks up on the mountain, or down here?"

"Hello to you too, brother," Lily said. She could not quite manage a smile, though she was so relieved to see him finally after so many days of waiting that she felt a little faint.

"Here in the village," Simon said, too eager for news to worry about manners. "They're here. What news, then, man? Don't keep us waiting. What of Jennet?"

Luke wiped his face on his sleeve, all his attention on his little sister.

Lily was overcome with sudden dread. His news would be bad, and it would devastate Daniel and Blue-Jay and Hannah, who had left Jennet behind and would never be able to forgive themselves for that. Her own grief could be nothing to that burden.

"What of Jennet?" Simon said again, his voice hoarse. "Have you no word of her?"

Luke blinked at them. "No," he said. "I've found no trace of her or of O'Neill."

"But what of the advertisement?" Lily asked. "In all those newspapers—"

Luke shrugged impatiently. "I've had twenty some letters."

"And?" Simon prompted.

"All of them worthless," Luke said. "Except maybe this one."

From his shirt he took a piece of paper, folded in half. There were only two words written on it, in an unschooled and awkward hand.

Anselme Dégre

"This is O'Neill's real name? How do you know that this is reliable?" Lily asked.

"Because that's all there is, Lily," Simon said, turning the ragged piece of paper over. "Whoever wrote this didn't ask for money, you see."

"Or it's someone trying to throw me off the track. As if I had one."

Luke sat down on one of the two chairs, leaned back and pressed his palms to his forehead. "I've followed his footsteps all over Canada and all I've got to show is a name and the Queen of Swords." He gave a sharp laugh. "Isn't that just like Jennet?"

Simon nudged Lily. "Show him, lass."

Luke's head came up sharply. "Show me what?"

"It's not much," Lily said. "But it might be a help. Simon was looking through the drawings I sent from Montreal in December and he found it."

She took what she was looking for from a pile of papers on the worktable, and held it out to her brother.

A simple drawing of a man standing in front of a tinker's stall at the market, his head turned to show his profile. He wore a countryman's rough clothing and his hair hung free from under a fur cap. A good-looking man, smiling openly at a girl who was walking by.

"Where . . ." Luke cleared his throat. "How in hell's name—"

"I was sketching everything I saw when I first came to Montreal, you remember. Simon picked it out of the pile. And I've got a dozen drawings of Jennet too—I thought maybe it would help you to have their likenesses."

What she never expected to see, what rocked her harder than the idea that Jennet was still lost to them, were the tears in her brother's eyes. She went to Luke and put her arms around his neck and her cheek to his.

"Thank you," he said hoarsely.

Simon put his hand on Luke's shoulder and met Lily's eye and she understood that she had somehow done the right thing. She had given Luke what he needed above all else: proof that the man he was chasing was not made of smoke, but of flesh and blood, and as such, could be run to ground.

Along the horizon where the mountains lined the sky, fledgling storms made nests of flickering color against the bowl of the heavens. In the pause between the first, short storm and the coming of the second, Hannah paused in her walk down the mountain, crouched under the fragrant dripping boughs of a fir. She had stayed later than she meant to at Lake in the Clouds; she might have stayed all night, but for Simon, who had ridden up the mountain with the report that Luke was come, and without Jennet.

In the distance the sky sparked and caught on fire, glowing green and gold and purple. Over the village of Paradise lightning jumped from cloud to cloud and then it put down long legs and walked the earth. The thunder came with a great rip of sound. Hannah closed her eyes and saw the light still, throbbing bloodred.

She went on. They would be gathering in the kitchen to hear what Luke had to report, and she must be there, no matter how painful it might prove to be.

By the time she came to the strawberry fields the storm was directly overhead and howling like a demon. A triple pulse of lightning crossed the sky and twinned itself, one arm reaching out to bat at a tree that stood at the far edge of the fields. Hannah had climbed that pine as a child and knew every branch of it, and now in a single careless touch it split in two. The noise echoed in her head.

She ran for the old schoolhouse, and found Daniel already there hunched on the porch to watch the storm.

Hannah knew many things about this younger brother that neither of them had put into words. That he was in more pain than ever, because he pushed himself to do things he could not. That he was consumed by anger and guilt. That he was both truly pleased for his sister and for Blue-Jay, who had found mates, and consumed by desires he feared could never be realized. That he sometimes thought of dying with a lover's yearning. That he would not indulge those thoughts because when they came to him he saw his mother's face. That he spent a great deal of time here at the old schoolhouse, where he had learned to read and write, to do sums and name the continents.

He went inside with her, not to be out of the rain, but as a begrudging courtesy.

After a long pause he said, "I'm glad they left the benches." And: "Look, the mark where Jemima Southern pinned Dolly Smythe's plait to the table with a knife. Even back then—" He stopped, out of weariness and sadness and other things writ plain on his face.

He said, "The girl has taken to following me around like a shadow."

"Do you mind?"

Daniel shrugged his good shoulder. "She's got all these questions about Liam that I can't answer. But I suppose it don't matter much. She just needs to talk about him."

Martha did, indeed, need to talk about the father she had never even seen, so much so that her natural shyness couldn't stop her from asking everyone for stories of Liam Kirby. The facts of her conception and birth meant far less than the idea that her father had been a brave man and one well liked. Those things were far more important to her than the money and land he had left her.

Mostly to himself Daniel said, "Martha reminds me of Lily, a little. She's single-minded like Lily was at that age."

The lightning was coming so fast now that Hannah could count the cracks in the floor. Much of what Daniel was saying was lost in the thunder, but she followed him anyway.

"—geography. She wouldn't learn the names of the rivers in Africa for love or money, do you remember? Until Da told her that somewhere in Africa a schoolgirl was refusing to remember words like 'Hudson' and 'Mohawk' and 'Canajoharee.'"

Hannah said, "You talk about Lily as if she were a thousand miles away."

Daniel had his back to her, but she saw the muscles along his spine tense.

"She feels that far away to me," he said finally. "She feels as far away from me as Jennet does."

He had had the news, then. That explained some of his mood.

"You saw Simon on his way back to the village."

"I did."

"They will be waiting for us," she said. "We can't get much wetter than we are already."

"I'm not going. I don't need to hear what Luke has to say."

Hannah felt anger prickling on the back of her neck, in the palms of her hands.

She said, "What a horse's arse you can be at times, Daniel Bonner."

He grunted at that. A double bolt of lightning filled the room and he turned his face away from it.

When the thunder had rolled away Hannah was standing in front of him. "You'll turn as mean and spiteful as Richard Todd if you carry on like this. Do you see how you're dragging everyone down into your sorry state? Do you see how Lily watches you, the pain she's in? You're not the only one hurting, you know."

"You've no cause to talk to me like that," Daniel said, his complexion blotched with pale color in the bluish haze of lightning.

"Oh, don't I?" The urge to slap him was so strong that Hannah backed away, her arms firmly crossed to keep her hands pinned against her sides. "I suppose you think not. Who could know how hard a time you've had, after all."

At least he had the good grace to duck his head at that, an acknowledgment of sorts.

"It's Jennet we should be thinking about now," Daniel said.

"A convenient excuse," Hannah said. "But not a very good one. There is nothing you can do for Jennet at this moment, but a great deal you could do for Lily."

"I could go with Luke to find Jennet." He shouted it, his voice crackling like shattered glass. "I could do that, but he won't let me. None of you will let me do anything. You want me to be the good-natured cripple, the long-suffering, the philosophical. I can't do that. I can't do that."

"Don't be ridiculous," Hannah said sharply. "That's not what I want at all. Not what anyone wants for you, and it needn't be your lot."

He had turned his back to her, his shoulders so tense that she had the idea he might shatter if she dared to touch him.

"You are being unfair," Daniel said, his voice heavy with tears.

"I am being fair beyond measure," Hannah said. "I am telling you the things you need to hear. I am not indulging your self-pity, that is true. And I never will."

The darkness came again, and when it passed in a weak pulse of lightning, Daniel was gone into the storm.

They were waiting in her mother's kitchen, all of them gathered around the table. Hannah's father and stepmother, Lily and Simon, Curiosity, and Luke, who got up to greet her. His lips were cold against her cheek, and he smelled of Curiosity's chamomile tea and long hours in the saddle.

Curiosity muttered harsh words about lung fevers and foolish behaviors while she folded a shawl around Hannah's shoulders and rubbed her head with a piece of toweling.

Simon said, "Daniel should be here by now."

"He will come," Hannah said. "But we shouldn't wait for him."

Curiosity was looking at her sharply, but Hannah refused to meet the old woman's eye.

Luke's story was not long in the telling. A name, a face, a direction for him to take: south.

"The *Isis* is on her way upriver from Halifax," Luke said. "I have some people to talk to in Montreal—" He touched Lily's drawing, which lay on the table in front of him. "And then I'll join her."

The *Isis*. Spoken out loud, the name touched each of them like a hand. The merchantman the Bonners had sailed on to Scotland, against their will, when the twins were still infants. It was right, somehow, that Luke should sail off on the *Isis* to find Jennet and bring her home.

"And then what?" Lily asked.

"Depends on what there is to learn in Montreal. But I expect we'll sail straight for Kingston. I'm hoping Giselle will have some connections that will work to my favor."

Nathaniel saw a quiver, very faint, pass over Elizabeth's face. It bothered her to hear Luke call his mother by her Christian name, but in some small way that she would be ashamed to admit, it also satisfied her.

"The *Isis* is often in those waters, I suppose." Elizabeth worked through the strategy for herself, moving from one point to the next, looking for flaws. "It's just another buying expedition, one you have chosen to join."

"That's my reasoning, yes."

Simon made a soft sound. "There's no suspicion in Montreal, then, about what happened on the island?"

"No. That part of the plan worked out well enough." He was looking at the letter Jennet had scribbled on that day, the words *priest* and *mon cher* and *forgive me.*

From the parlor came the sound of children playing at cards, their voices raised in argument. Gabriel was trying to bully Annie and Callie and Martha into his view of things, and not making much progress.

Elizabeth's hands fluttered on the tabletop until Nathaniel covered them with one of his own.

She said, "Luke, you could have just sent a letter with this information, but you chose to travel all this way. Tell us why."

"You want me to come with you," Simon said.

All eyes turned to him, all except Lily's, which remained fixed on Luke, who was shaking his head.

"I need you here, close enough to Montreal to get there in a few days, if Mason should get himself into trouble."

"Should we go back to Montreal?" Lily asked, although she could hardly disguise her distress at the idea.

"No," Luke said firmly. "Absolutely not. Not until the danger is past."

He meant to kill the priest, they understood that without being told. The man held Jennet's life in his hands, and the lives of everyone at Carryck.

"It's me you want on the *Isis,*" Hannah said. "Isn't that right?"

The whole plan fell into place that easily, though Nathaniel hadn't seen it coming. He understood at that moment that Luke would have never asked outright; he needed Hannah to step forward, and she had done that.

Curiosity was not so pleased with what seemed to Nathaniel to be inevitable. She said, "You still got that Musselman doctor on board the *Isis,* don't you?"

"Yes," Luke said. "It's not for her skills as a doctor I want Hannah. I need her help. I don't think—" He cleared his throat. "I can't do this by myself."

There it was, the one thing he must say to win them over. Curiosity's expression softened and Elizabeth closed her eyes in an attempt to ban her tears.

"That's a step in the right direction," Nathaniel said. He would have said more, he would have offered his own services and companionship, anything and everything, to keep Hannah nearby and safe. She had already suffered so much. But to help one child he must let the other go.

Hannah said, "Da, it's all right. I'll go with him. I want to."

It was the truth. She did want to go, though Nathaniel had the idea she wouldn't be able to put her reason into words.

They could stop her, of course. Elizabeth could ask her to stay and help her deliver this last precious child. Curiosity could speak of brittle bones and weariness and how hard it was to get up in the cold and go out to look after the sick. They could bind her to them, all of them, with need and love and worry. But they would not. They knew her as well as she knew them, and they would not ask her to stay.

She said, "When do we leave here?"

"Tomorrow, if you can be ready."

Hannah studied her own hands, lying flat on the table. She felt her father's gaze resting on her, the question he would not put into words, the worries he would hold close.

"I can." She raised her head and looked at each of them in turn. "I'll get started packing just as soon as I've had a chance to talk to Manny."

Curiosity put her hands on the table and pushed herself up to lean across the table toward Hannah. There were tears in her eyes, and resignation, and something of her old fiery anger.

"Girl, you think you just going to walk on, you got to think again. Your stepmama made a fine cake, and you will eat your fair share before you leave this kitchen."

Simon gave the first hiccup of surprised laughter, and they all followed. Curiosity sat down again, satisfied. She couldn't change Hannah's fate or keep her safe, but she had made her laugh, and that was enough, for this moment.

Outside the storm had picked up again, and rain lashed at the windows.

Dawn came, as it must, and Nathaniel Bonner was awake to see it.

The world outside the window was a strange one: dripping wet, wrapped in a cocoon of mist and rain. Light crept into this world on soft padding feet, as stealthily as a thief.

He threw his senses out around him, a swirling of a cloak that dropped down to touch his children, all of them close by. Daniel had come in late and sat for a long time with Luke, talking through the plans he could take no part in. He had gone to sleep on the cot in the room off the kitchen, and so for this night at least all three boys were under this one roof.

Hannah was just over the hill in her chamber at the doctor's place, Lily a little farther away through the woods, sleeping with her good husband beside her. Tomorrow they would be scattered again. Only Gabriel would be left to them, but for this moment, at least, he knew where they were and that they were safe, and he would hold on to that for as long as he could.

Nathaniel felt the need to say those words out loud to Elizabeth, but she had left their bed a half hour ago to wrap a cloak around herself and go out into the rain. So many years on the edge of the wilderness and she still sought out the privacy of the necessary, no matter the weather, no matter the hour.

And no matter how he listened, he could hear only the sound of the rain: on the roof, falling through the trees, drumming against the skin of the world.

She had hung the lantern by the kitchen door to light her way. It cast a great golden web of light, an empty crystal orb floating in the mist.

The first glimmerings of real fear had begun their climb up from his belly when he saw her.

She came into the lantern light on a twirl, arms extended, palms open. Somewhere along the path she had lost her shawl and given herself up to the rain. Her white nightdress, wet through, clung to her shoulders and breasts and the high round curve of her belly. She put back her head to let her hair fall behind her to the ground, her heart-shaped face held up to the rain, her mouth opened in a soundless, breathless laugh.

She turned her face and saw him at the window. She might have shrieked in surprise and dashed into the house, or flushed with color and stalked off with the remnants of her dignity pulled around her. She might have scolded him for watching without making himself known.

Instead she smiled, and held out her hand.

Come.

Nathaniel ran silently through the hall, barefoot on the cool wooden stairs, his skin rough with gooseflesh.

She met him at the door. Hand in hand they ran away from the house and the lantern light, past the barn and into the high grass of the pasture where the mist was alive with first light. It shimmered on her wet skin and in the curls that fell down over her shoulders to her breasts, it tasted of high summer on her mouth.

They ran like children through the milky warm rain, laughing like loons into the echoing mist.

Nathaniel knew that he would remember it for the rest of his life.

In their chamber, toweling themselves dry, they listened to the house come awake. Gabriel's quick step on the stair, on his way down to the kitchen where Sally would have started breakfast. Daniel's voice, deep and rough with sleeplessness in response to Luke's question.

Elizabeth paused, her head canted hard to one side, the hairbrush caught in mid-pull, the girlishness draining out of her face as she listened. Nathaniel could follow her thoughts without any trouble at all.

The day could not be held back. It would bring another parting from Hannah, who must go back out in the world to heal herself. From Luke, who drifted back and forth between his many lives, who must find the woman he had vowed to keep and protect. Daniel would leave this house to go back to Hidden Wolf, where he would make a life, solitary, sufficient unto himself, determined to mend. Sometime soon, too soon, Lily would be leaving too, to places they could not yet name or imagine.

"Lily," Elizabeth said, plucking his thought out of the air. "Lily will be coming to help."

She leaned back and kissed her husband, her lips cool and damp still with the rain, and went down to her children.

Author's Note

One of the things I like best about this kind of storytelling is the opportunity to lure unsuspecting readers into historical waters, most especially when the times and places in question are little known. American history, as it is taught in the schools today, pays scant attention to the War of 1812. Most students are shepherded from the Revolution directly to the Civil War, and more's the pity, to have such important and exciting stories fade away into nothingness.

All that is an introduction to a confession: in pursuit of a good story, I have fiddled with the facts. The war, as it happened in the summer of 1813 in French Canada and New York State, looked a lot like the story you'll read here, but not exactly like it. As the narrative required, I nudged dates (but just a little); I took the two major events of the summer of 1813 in the region in question and played havoc. Among other things I changed the names of the ships, regiments, and persons involved. Sometimes I created battalions out of whole cloth. I did this to free myself from the need to be fair to individuals and the historical record. So, there's no need to contact me to tell me what I got wrong; I know (for example) that the King's Rangers never existed in this time and place, because they are my invention.

Occasionally you will find real historical personages popping in and out of the story. Who is real and who isn't is a question I'm not going to answer here. If I've done my job well and you're curious enough, you will pursue that question on your own. There are a multitude of excellent military historians who have written about the period.

As ever, I am thankful to the many people who answered my innumerable questions on matters from gunpowder to the rigging of sails. I am especially thankful to Wendy McCurdy, Nita Taublib, and Irwyn Applebaum at Bantam; to my friend and agent Jill Grinberg; to my always and forevers, Bill and Beth.

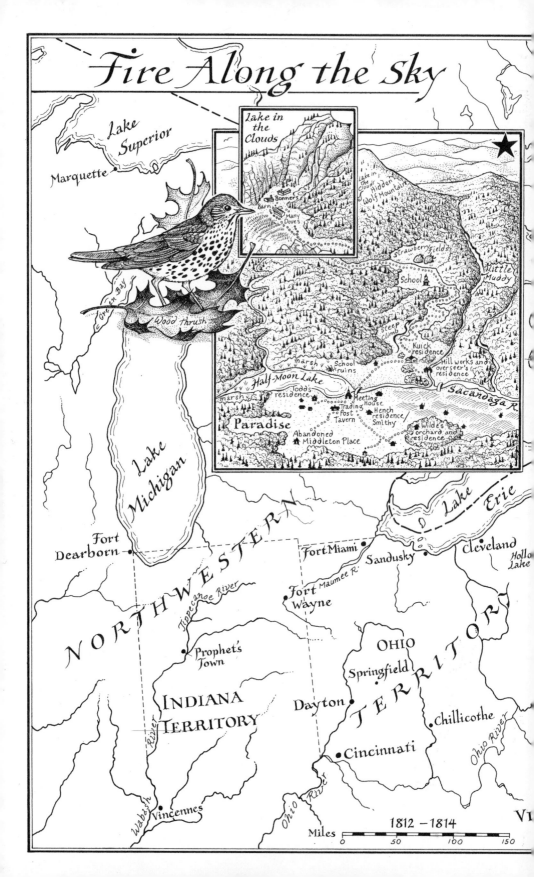

Fire Along the Sky

Lake Superior

Marquette

Lake in the Clouds

Bonner's

Barn

Many Doves

Lake in the Clouds

Hidden Wolf Mountain

Strawberry Fields

School

Little Muddy

Wood Thrush

Green Bay

Steep Climb

Kuick residence

Hill works and overseer's residence

marsh

School ruins

Meeting House

Sacandaga R.

Half-Moon Lake

Todd's residence

Trading Post Tavern

Hench residence/ Smithy

marsh

Lake Michigan

Paradise

Abandoned Middleton Place

Wilde's orchard and residence

Lake Erie

Fort Dearborn

Fort Miami

Sandusky

Cleveland

Hollo Lake

NORTHWESTERN

Tippecanoe River

Fort Wayne

Maumee R.

Prophet's Town

OHIO

Springfield

Wabash River

INDIANA TERRITORY

Dayton

TERRITORY

Chillicothe

Ohio River

Cincinnati

Vincennes

Ohio River

1812 – 1814

Miles

0   50   100   150

VI